STEPHEN JONES lives in London. He is the winner of two World Fantasy Awards, three Horror Writers Association Bram Stoker Awards and two International Horror Guild Awards as well as being a twelve-time recipient of the British Fantasy Award and a Hugo Award nominee. A full-time columnist, television producer/director, and genre movie publicist and consultant (the first three *Hellraiser* movies, *Night Life*, *Nightbreed*, *Split Second*, *Mind Ripper*, *Last Gasp* etc.), he is the co-editor of *Horror: 100 Best Books*, *The Best Horror from Fantasy Tales*, *Gaslight & Ghosts*, *Now We Are Sick*, *H.P. Lovecraft's Book of Horror*, *The Anthology of Fantasy & the Supernatural*, *Secret City: Strange Tales of London* and *The Mammoth Book of Best New Horror*, *Dark Terrors*, *Dark Voices* and *Fantasy Tales* series. He has written *The Essential Monster Movie Guide*, *The Illustrated Vampire Movie Guide*, *The Illustrated Dinosaur Movie Guide*, *The Illustrated Frankenstein Movie Guide* and *The Illustrated Werewolf Movie Guide*, and compiled *The Mammoth Book of Terror*, *The Mammoth Book of Vampires*, *The Mammoth Book of Zombies*, *The Mammoth Book of Werewolves*, *The Mammoth Book of Frankenstein*, *The Mammoth Book of Dracula*, *Shadows Over Innsmouth*, *Dancing With the Dark*, *Dark of the Night*, *Dark Detectives*, *White of the Moon*, *Exorcisms and Ecstasies* by Karl Edward Wagner, *The Vampire Stories of R. Chetwynd-Hayes* and *Phantoms and Fiends* by R. Chetwynd-Hayes, *James Herbert: By Horror Haunted*, two volumes of *The Conan Chronicles* by Robert E. Howard, *Clive Barker's A-Z of Horror*, *Clive Barker's Shadows in Eden*, *Clive Barker's The Nightbreed Chronicles* and the *Hellraiser Chronicles*. You can visit Stephen Jones' web site at http://www.herebedragons.co.uk/jones

Also available

The Mammoth Book of Ancient Wisdom
The Mammoth Book of Armchair Detectives & Screen Crimes
The Mammoth Book of Arthurian Legends
The Mammoth Book of Battles
The Mammoth Book of Best New Horror 99
The Mammoth Book of Best New Science Fiction 12
The Mammoth Book of Bridge
The Mammoth Book of British Kings & Queens
The Mammoth Book of Cats
The Mammoth Book of Chess
The Mammoth Book of Comic Fantasy
The Mammoth Book of Dogs
The Mammoth Book of Erotica
The Mammoth Book of Gay Erotica
The Mammoth Book of Heroic and Outrageous Women
The Mammoth Book of Historical Detectives
The Mammoth Book of Historical Erotica
The Mammoth Book of Historical Whodunnits
The Mammoth Book of How It Happened
The Mammoth Book of International Erotica
The Mammoth Book of Jack the Ripper
The Mammoth Book of Lesbian Erotica
The Mammoth Book of Lesbian Short Stories
The Mammoth Book of Men O'War
The Mammoth Book of Mindbending Puzzles
The Mammoth Book of Murder
The Mammoth Book of New Erotica
The Mammoth Book of New Sherlock Holmes Adventures
The Mammoth Book of Nostradamus and Other Prophets
The Mammoth Book of Oddballs and Eccentrics
The Mammoth Book of Private Lives
The Mammoth Book of Seriously Comic Fantasy
The Mammoth Book of Short Erotic Novels
The Mammoth Book of Sports & Games
The Mammoth Book of Sword & Honour
The Mammoth Book of Tasteless Lists
The Mammoth Book of the Third Reich at War
The Mammoth Book of True War Stories
The Mammoth Book of 20th Century Ghost Stories
The Mammoth Book of Unsolved Crimes
The Mammoth Book of War Diaries and Letters
The Mammoth Book of the Western
The Mammoth Book of the World's Greatest Chess Games

THE
MAMMOTH BOOK OF
BEST NEW
HORROR

VOLUME ELEVEN

Edited and with an Introduction by
STEPHEN JONES

Robinson
LONDON

Constable & Robinson Ltd
3 The Lanchesters
162 Fulham Palace Road
London W6 9ER

First published in the UK by Robinson,
an imprint of Constable & Robinson Ltd 2000

A copy of the British Library Cataloguing in
Publication Data is available from the British Library.

ISBN 1–84119–167–1

Printed and bound in the EU

CONTENTS

ACKNOWLEDGMENTS

I would like to thank Douglas E. Winter, Sara Broecker, David Barraclough, Mandy Slater, Andrew I. Porter, Jo Fletcher, Bill Congreve, Gordon Van Gelder, William K. Schafer, Robert Morgan, Peter Crowther, David Pringle, Frederick S. Clarke, Andy Cox, Peter Atkins, Nancy Kilpatrick and Don Hutchison for their help and support. Special thanks are due to *Locus*, *Interzone*, *Science Fiction Chronicle*, *Variety* and all the other sources that were used for reference in the Introduction and the Necrology.

INTRODUCTION: HORROR IN 1999 copyright © Stephen Jones 2000.

HALLOWEEN STREET copyright © Steve Rasnic Tem 1999. Originally published in *The Magazine of Fantasy & Science Fiction*, Number 575, July 1999. Reprinted by permission of the author.

OTHERS copyright © James Herbert 1999. Originally published in *Others*. Reprinted by permission of the author.

GROWING THINGS copyright © T.E.D. Klein 1999. Originally published in *999: New Stories of Horror and Suspense*. Reprinted by permission of the author.

UNHASPED copyright © David J. Schow 1999. Originally published in *White of the Moon: New Tales of Madness and Dread*. Reprinted by permission of the author.

THE EMPEROR'S OLD BONES copyright © Gemma Files 1999. Originally published in *Northern Frights 5*. Reprinted by permission of the author.

THE ENTERTAINMENT copyright © Ramsey Campbell 1999. Originally published in 999: *New Stories of Horror and Suspense*. Reprinted by permission of the author.

HARLEQUIN VALENTINE copyright © Neil Gaiman 1999. Originally published in *World Horror Convention 1999 Program Book*. Reprinted by permission of the author.

THE STUNTED HOUSE copyright © Terry Lamsley 1999. Originally published in *Subterranean Gallery*. Reprinted by permission of the author.

JUST LIKE EDDY copyright © Kim Newman 1999. Originally published in *Interzone*, Number 148, October 1999. Reprinted by permission of the author.

THE LONG HALL ON THE TOP FLOOR copyright © Caitlín R. Kiernan 1999. Originally published in *Carpe Noctem*, Number 16. Reprinted by permission of the author.

LULU copyright © Thomas Tessier 1999. Originally published in *Lulu and One Other*. Reprinted by permission of the author.

THE BALLYHOOLY BOY copyright © Graham Masterton 1999. Originally published in *Encre Noire*, December 1999. Reprinted by permission of the author.

WELCOME copyright © Michael Marshall Smith 1999. Originally published in *White of the Moon: New Tales of Madness and Dread*. Reprinted by permission of the author.

BURDEN copyright © Michael Marano 1999. Originally published on *Gothic.Net*, March 1999. Reprinted by permission of the author.

NAMING THE DEAD copyright © Paul J. McAuley 1999. Originally published in *Interzone*, Number 149, November 1999. Reprinted by permission of the author.

AFTERSHOCK copyright © F. Paul Wilson 1999. Originally published in *Realms of Fantasy*, December 1999. Reprinted by permission of the author.

A FISH STORY copyright © Gene Wolfe 1999. Originally published in *The Magazine of Fantasy & Science Fiction*, Number 578, October/November 1999. Reprinted by permission of the author and the author's agent, the Virginia Kidd Agency, Inc.

JIMMY copyright © David Case 1999. Originally published in *Brotherly Love and Other Tales of Trust and Knowledge*. Reprinted by permission of the author.

In memory of
FRANCES GARFIELD
(1908–2000)
last of the Southern belles.

INTRODUCTION

Horror in 1999

IN BOTH BRITAIN AND NORTH AMERICA MASS-MARKET HORROR PUBLISHING slipped slightly in 1999, despite an upturn in the number of science fiction and fantasy titles released. The young adult horror market also continued to decline (more so in the US), although vampire books were still popular – particularly the numerous *Buffy*-related tie-ins.

Barnes & Noble Inc., and Ingram Book Group called off their proposed merger when reports leaked out that the US Federal Trade Commission would recommend opposing the book retailer's $600-million bid to acquire the major wholesaler. Both companies announced that protracted litigation would not be in their best interests, and that they planned to work closely together as they moved forward with alternative plans, including the building of new distribution centres. The merger had been opposed by many independent booksellers since it was announced in November 1998.

When Bertelsmann AG bought Random House in 1998, merging it with Bantam Doubleday Dell to create America's biggest publishing house, the company promised that the move would enhance the "effectiveness and independence" of the various imprints and divisions. However, that promise was apparently forgotten when Bertelsmann announced it would be merging eight of its publishing units into four new groups. These included the amalgamation of Bantam and Dell, and the merging of Anchor Books and Vintage Books into a division of the Knopf Publishing Group. Meanwhile a number of SF editors at Del Rey were let go or else moved to other departments. Bertelsmann also bought an 80 per cent share in German publisher Springer Verlag for an estimated $600 million, and agreed to merge its book club activities in Italy with Mondadori.

In spring the HarperPrism imprint reduced its annual number of titles by almost half, and just a couple of months later cut them back again. Then in a surprise move in mid-June, Rupert Murdoch's News Corp., owner of HarperCollins, announced its purchase of The Hearst Corporation's book division, which included the Avon and Morrow imprints, for an estimated $180 million. Three months later more than seventy people were made redundant, including the former head of HarperPrism, John Silbersack; executive editor of HarperPrism, John Douglas; publisher of Avon, Lou Aronica and Clive Barker's editor Paul McCarthy. A third of the adult imprints and almost half of the young adult lines also disappeared.

Formed in 1982 when Herman Graf and Kent Carroll left Grove Press, New York publishing house Carroll & Graf was purchased by independent distributor Publishers Group West through its Avalon Publishing Group subsidiary. However, the company was soon hit with a class action suit, originally filed by attorneys in 1998 on behalf of five Carroll & Graf authors, claiming the under-reporting of royalty payments and the holding of unreasonable reserves against returns. C&G president Herman Graf told the trade that he thought the ruling was an error and had "no merit whatsoever".

Following the purchase of UK publisher Cassell by Anthony Cheetham's Orion Group, the Gollancz (hardcover) and Millennium (paperback) genre lists were merged under the control of Orion Managing Director Malcolm Edwards.

Meanwhile, in late May, British bookseller WHSmith bought Hodder Headline for £185 million cash, a reported 43 per cent above the market value of shares at the time. The sale included all the company's publishing divisions, including Hodder & Stoughton, Headline, New English Library and others. As an immediate result, shares in the publisher jumped 40 per cent while WHSmith's shares fell 28 pence.

Nick Robinson and Ben Glazebrook announced in November that they had agreed terms to transfer their shareholdings in Robinson Publishing Ltd. and Constable & Co. Ltd into a single publishing company, Constable & Robinson Ltd. Robinson staff moved into Constable's London offices the following month, with the production, sales and marketing and accounts departments merged at a cost of only two redundancies. For the next year, Robinson & Constable would continue to publish under their respective imprints.

California's General Publishing Group, which published *Forrest J Ackerman's World of Science Fiction* amongst other titles, went bankrupt and had its assets sold at auction in mid-June.

Carol Publishing, whose imprints included Citadel Press, Lyle Stuart and Birch Lane Press, ceased business in August after its proposed sale to distributor LPS fell through. Carol had liabilities of $12.3 million against a backlist of 1,300 titles, valued at $25.6 million, which included trade paperback editions of all Philip K. Dick's short stories, a controversial exposé of L. Ron Hubbard, and various "unauthorized" media tie-ins.

Despite winning a runner-up award of £750.00 in the Shell LiveWIRE Young Business Start Up Awards, Matt Weyland's Pulp Publications, which reprinted classic adventure stories under the Pulp Fictions imprint by Jules Verne, H. Rider Haggard, Edgar Wallace and others, filed for bankruptcy in October with debts of £56,800 owed to its Finnish printers and British artist Bob Covington, amongst others.

In November, the commissioning editor of Virgin Books' new SF imprint Virgin Worlds announced that the publisher would not be buying any more titles in the foreseeable future because sales reaction to the three launch titles in March had been less enthusiastic than hoped. Of course the lack of big name authors, dull cover art and negligible sales and marketing promotion had nothing to do with the book trade's reaction.

Packager Byron Preiss announced the formation of iBooks, a new trade paperback imprint to be distributed by Pocket Books in America, which would be heavily promoted on the Internet. And agent Richard Curtis launched E-Rights™, which would distribute electronic editions of books whose rights had reverted back to the authors. A 5,000-title list was expected within a year.

An article in the 8 February edition of the *New York Times* revealed that Amazon.com had been charging publishers for advantageous placement and recommendation features. The criticism this provoked resulted in the online bookseller offering refunds to customers who had ordered the recommended books. Meanwhile, despite a huge rise in Amazon.com sales and customers, the company continued to make a dramatic loss, much of it due to acquisitions of other online companies.

In a blow to both publishers and authors, Australia's upper chamber of Parliament agreed to apply a 10 per cent Goods and Services Tax on books, to be introduced in 2000. Higher GST on materials may also increase costs to publishers, prompting fears of higher cover prices. However, the tax would not apply to overseas books ordered through e-mail retailers outside the country.

Following a ludicrous attempt by parents in South Carolina to ban her popular *Harry Potter* books for children because they were "dark and evil", author J.K. Rowling responded by stating, "I have yet to meet a single child who has said they want to be a Satanist, or is interested in the occult because of the books."

However, in a move reminiscent of the infamous 1925 "Monkey Trial" in Dayton, Tennessee (in which the teaching of Charles Darwin's theory of evolution was banned in schools), when a school superintendent in Zeeland, Michigan, decided that the *Potter* titles were only suitable for older readers, teachers were prevented from reading the books in class, and children required parental permission before they could borrow them from school libraries or use them for book reports. Incredibly, the *Potter* books were then banned in schools in a dozen other American states and the titles were named by the American Library Association as the "most challenged" books of 1999.

Yet despite the negative reaction of some narrow-minded Americans, Rowling was the biggest-selling author of 1999. Her début fantasy novel *Harry Potter and the Philosopher's Stone* (retitled *Harry Potter and the Sorcerer's Stone* for its US publication) sold almost 500,000 copies in Britain alone, closely followed by the sequel, *Harry Potter and the Chamber of Secrets*. The third book in the series, *Harry Potter and the Prisoner of Azkaban*, was published in July. In a poll of the UK's highest-paid women, 35-year-old Rowling ranked third with an estimated income of £14.5 million, after worldwide sales of the books she started writing in an Edinburgh cafe while an unemployed single parent reached a reported 30 million. Warner Bros. bought the film and merchandising rights for an estimated £1 million.

According to a Top 100 list submitted by book publishers to *Publisher's Weekly,* John Grisham was the bestselling author of the 1990s with combined sales of more than sixty million copies. Stephen King narrowly beat out Danielle Steel for second place with cumulative sales of 38.3 million, with his six-part series *The Green Mile* being the author's top selling title during the decade. In 1999, King's fantastical prison drama was reissued in a single "soon to be a major movie" volume.

To tie-in with the ABC-TV mini-series shown during the February "sweeps" period, King's original 300-page screenplay for *Storm of the Century* was published as a trade paperback, which also included an introduction by the author in which he discussed the filming.

King also surprised his fans with a previously unannounced new novel, *The Girl Who Loved Tom Gordon,* which appeared in April. About a young girl lost in the woods who created an imaginary friendship with her hero, the real-life Red Sox baseball relief pitcher of the title, the book had a 1.25 million-copy first hardcover printing in America but was actually published in Britain first.

Following the Columbine High School shootings in April, when two students killed twelve classmates and a teacher before shooting themselves, King asked Penguin to withdraw from publication his novel *Rage,* originally issued under his "Richard Bachman" byline, with the next printing.

The same month, King celebrated his 25th anniversary as an author with a dinner party for around ninety guests at Tavern on the Green in New York City. Amongst those invited were Salman Rushdie, Peter Straub, Richard Chizmar, George Romero and Warren Zevon. Stanley Wiater provided the questions for a King trivia quiz, which was won by the author's biographer, Douglas E. Winter.

Then on 19 June, Stephen King was seriously injured while walking along a rural highway when he was hit by a Dodge Caravan after 41-year-old driver Bryan E. Smith lost control. The author was thrown fourteen feet and suffered multiple fractures to his right leg and hip, a collapsed lung, a lacerated scalp and various facial injuries. He was taken to the Central Maine Medical Center in Lewiston where, after surgery, he was described as being in a serious, but stable condition. He was released on 9 July after four more operations on his injuries and faced several months of physical therapy.

While the driver faced charges of aggravated assault and driving to endanger (his driver's license had already been suspended four times previously), King bought the van which hit him for $1,500 and revealed to a local newspaper that he was "Going to take a sledgehammer and beat it." To avoid jail, Smith later pleaded guilty to driving to endanger after a charge of aggravated assault was dropped, and he was suspended from driving for six months.

According to one tabloid newspaper, the widow of "renowned" psychic Peter Hurkos claimed that her husband, who had been dead eleven years, was responsible for the accident because King had "stolen" Hurkos' life story for his novel *The Dead Zone*. The same source also revealed that King's 29-year-old lesbian daughter, Naomi, was planning a same-sex "ceremony of union" with her 53-year-old graduate school professor.

In Britain, a special paperback edition of the 1998 collection *Bag of Bones*, only available through WHSmith bookstores, included the additional sixty-page story "Blind Willie"; this was one of five interconnected, sequential stories which formed the basis of King's collection *Hearts in Atlantis*, published in September. Ranging over the last three decades of the twentieth century, each story contained a hint of the supernatural and all were influenced by the 1960s and the Vietnam War. However, because of his injuries from the accident, publicity appearances by the author were cancelled.

King also released a three-story collection (two original) in November entitled *Blood and Smoke*, but only as a three-and-a-half hour audiobook. Read by the author himself, each of the stories dealt with cigarette smoking. In the UK, Hodder Headline Audio Books also issued *Stephen King Live!*, a recording of the author's Royal Festival Hall appearance in August 1998 when he read the unpublished short story "LT's Theory of Pets" and answered questions from novelist and broadcaster Muriel Gray.

Meanwhile, a San Francisco doctor discussed a new medical condition known as "Stephen King wrist" in the *Western Journal of Medicine.* Its symptoms of pain in the wrist and weakness in the hand's grip were apparently caused by reading King's books in bed and holding the hefty tomes with just one hand!

Hannibal, Thomas Harris's much-anticipated sequel to *The Silence of the Lambs,* was rushed into print less than three months after it was delivered to the publisher, with a one-day laydown of around 500,000 hardcover copies. Once again FBI agent Clarice Starling was forced to confront the evil Dr Lecter, whose whereabouts had been discovered by one of his surviving victims looking for revenge.

With a first printing of 500,000 copies, Anne Rice continued her "New Tales of the Vampires" series with *Vittorio, the Vampire,* set in historical Florence and the seventh volume overall in her "Vampire Chronicles". The trade paperback of Rice's 1998 novel *The Vampire Armand* added a five-page "conversation" with the author.

With a move to British publisher Macmillan (who paid a reported £2 million for two books) James Herbert's latest novel, *Others,* featured private investigator Nicholas Dismas, who was hired to find a missing baby and uncovered the dark secrets of a mysterious nursing home and his own existence. The novel was also released as a Macmillan Audio Book, read by actor Robert Powell. At the same time, Herbert's backlist was reissued in paperback editions under the Pan imprint.

Peter Straub's contemporary horror novel *Mr. X* was set in the southern Illinois town of Edgerton and involved family secrets, *doppelgängers,* a psychic serial killer, Lovecraft's Cthulhu Mythos and jazz music. The latter also featured predominantly in Straub's superb 1994 novella *Pork Pie Hat,* about a legendary New York jazz musician and the extraordinary story he tells set on Halloween. It was published in Britain as a slim hardcover in the "Criminal Records" series edited by Otto Penzler.

Dean Koontz's *False Memory* was about mind control and had a first hardcover printing in America of more than 400,000 copies. Robin Cook's latest medical thriller, *Vector,* involved the effects of bioterrorism, John Saul's *The Right Hand of Evil* was a Southern Gothic about a Louisiana family's dark history, and Thomas M. Disch's blackly comic *The Sub: A Study in Witchcraft* concerned a substitute teacher who was haunted by the ghost of her apparently abusive father and discovered that she had the power to transform humans into beasts.

Olivia was the fifth and final volume in the pseudonymous "Logan Family" series of Gothic horror novels credited to the late V.C. Andrews® (probably Andrew Neiderman). From (presumably) the same author came *Misty*, *Star*, *Jade*, *Cat* and *Into the Garden*, which formed "The Wildflowers" series about a group of girls undergoing therapy. Under his own name, Neiderman published *Neighborhood Watch*, about a Stepford-like community.

According to his official website, author Robert R. McCammon decided to retire from the publishing business.

Jeff Long's *The Descent* was an ambitious lost world horror novel in which mankind discovered a labyrinth of demon-haunted caverns beneath the Earth's surface.

Following the death of Harry Keogh, E-Branch's new Necroscope was already under the influence of a vampire in Brian Lumley's *E-Branch: Invaders*, the tenth volume in the long-running series and the first in a new trilogy. Tor Books also published the second volume in Lumley's *Titus Crow* omnibus series, containing the early novels *The Clock of Dreams* and *Spawn of the Winds*.

Richard Laymon's *Come Out Tonight* was a kidnapping thriller, while the author's *Among the Missing* involved adultery and a California serial killer. *The Return* by Andrea Hart was another serial killer novel.

Charles Grant completed his "Millennium Quartet" series with *Riders in the Sky*, in which mankind battled the Four Horsemen of the Apocalypse. *The Hush of Dark Wings* and *Winter Knight* were the second and third volumes, respectively, in Grant's *Black Oak* series, in which the members of the eponymous security firm investigated flying shapeshifters in Kansas and a centuries-old ghost in an English village.

Another English ghost was the titular heroine of Peter S. Beagle's *Tamsin*, while *Aunt Dimity's Christmas* was the fifth volume in Nancy Atherto's supernatural mystery series.

Set in the contemporary New York art scene and the upstate community of Kamensic Village, Elizabeth Hand's *Black Light* involved a secret society's age-old battle with witchcraft and the attempted resurrection of old gods. While a nature photographer discovered a pool used more than a century before by a spiritualist cult for weird rites in James P. Blaylock's latest slice of West Coast weirdness, *The Rainy Season*.

Twin teenage sisters discovered they had *The Heart of a Witch* when they joined a coven in Judith Hawkes' novel, and Chet Williamson continued his paranormal series *The Searchers* with the third volume, *Siege of Stone*.

Frank M. Robinson belatedly revisited the theme of his 1956 novel *The Power* as a race of mutant telepaths forced their victims to kill themselves in *Waiting*. *Thunderhead* was Douglas Preston and Lincoln Child's follow-up to their previous bestsellers *Relic* and *Reliquary* and involved Native American witchcraft and a legendary lost city of gold.

Kim Newman's *Life's Lottery: A Choose-Your-Own-Adventure Book* was an interactive novel which allowed the reader to become the central character and make his choices for him.

Graham Masterton's *Snowman* was the fourth in the series about psychic school teacher Jim Rook. From Piatkus Books, Mark Morris's *Genesis* was about a journalist who began experiencing strange hallucinations and unspeakable nightmares.

Graham Joyce's *Indigo* involved a mysterious manuscript which revealed how to achieve invisibility and took its English protagonist on a quest to Chicago and Rome. A woman found herself drawn to the mysterious Greek island of Voros in Simon Clark's *Judas Tree*, which was compared by its publisher to both *Rebecca* and *The Shining*.

In Bentley Little's *The House*, five strangers discovered they shared a dark childhood memory as they returned to the identical homes in which they were born. The family in Elizabeth Massie's *Welcome Back the Night* experienced psychic visions as they attempted to change the future.

Charles Wilson's hi-tech thriller *Embryo* involved unethical medical experiments with an artificial womb, while *The Reckoning* by Thomas Monteleone was a Millennial horror novel about a new pope created from DNA taken from the Shroud of Turin.

Phil Rickman's *Midwinter of the Spirit* was a sequel to *Wine of Angels* and the second in his series of mysteries featuring exorcist

Merrily Watkins. *The Haunt* by J.N. Williamson featured a family menaced by an over-protective ghost.

Although better known for his *Buffy the Vampire Slayer* novelizations, Christopher Golden's *Strangewood* turned out to be an atmospheric horror novel in which the son of author Thomas Randall was held hostage in the fantasy world his father created. In Lisa Goldstein's *Dark Cities Underground* a man discovered that he could re-enter a dark fantasy world chronicled by his author mother.

Musician Greg Kihn's fourth novel, *Mojo Hand*, involved murder by voodoo and the return of Blues legend Robert Johnson. Andrew Vachss' anti-hero Burke returned in *Choice of Evil*, in which the vigilante teamed up with a witch-woman and others to track down a serial killer who had apparently returned from the dead. The novel was optioned by New Line Cinema.

Sean Hutson moved to publisher Macmillan with his latest novel, *Warhol's Prophecy*, and in Windsor Chorlton's *Cold Fusion* a man emerged from a coma into a twenty-first century in the grip of a cosmic winter, where his memory held the key to both the past and the future. *Dead Cold* was a novel from celebrity spoon-bender Uri Geller and featured a psychic who shared a link with a murderer.

A serial killer was hunted by a reluctant psychic and others in *The Visionary* by Don Passman. Written by pseudonymous author Michael Bishop (*not* the well-established genre writer), *Seven Deadly Sins* was about a serial killer who had sold his soul.

Tom Piccirilli published two new novels, *Hexes* and *Sorrow's Crown*, the latter a sequel to the author's *The Dead Past*. Owl Goingback's *Darker Than Night* featured a house which was a gateway to another world, and a woman developed a psychic link with the dead in Elizabeth McGregor's *Second Sight*.

Martha C. Lawrence's *Aquarius Descending* was the third novel in the series about psychic detective/parapsychologist Elizabeth Chase, and a young woman discovered her telekinetic powers in *Teek* by "Steve Krane" (aka Steven Swiniarski/S. Andrew Swan). New York City detective Charlie Parker used an old psychic and necromantic visions to track a serial killer in John Connolly's *Every Dead Thing*.

Graveyard Dust by Barbara Hambly was the third in the author's historical mystery series featuring free Creole Benjamin

January, who was threatened by a voodoo curse while investigating a murder. *The Visitant* was the first in Kathleen O'Neal Gear and W. Michael Gear's "Anasazi Mysteries" series.

A horror novelist moved into one of those pesky haunted houses in Barbara Rogan's *Suspicion*, while scientifically-created ghosts were conjured up in *Skeptic* by Holden Scott.

Richard Bowes' *Minions of the Moon* was an urban supernatural novel based on a series of stories, one of which won the 1998 World Fantasy Award for Best Novella. Noel Hynd's *The Lost Boy* was another ghost novel, and Nina Kiriki Hoffman's *A Red Heart of Memories* also involved magic and ghosts.

Authors Arthur Conan Doyle and Charles Dodgson (aka "Lewis Carroll") teamed up to investigate a murder during a seance in Roberta Rogow's *The Problem of the Spiteful Spiritualist*. Barbara Michael's *Other Worlds* collected two stories set in a gentleman's club, where Conan Doyle and Harry Houdini were amongst those who debated the tales involving a poltergeist and a possibly haunted house.

In Brian Stableford's futuristic bio-tech thriller *Architects of Emortality*, policemen Watson and Holmes and an amateur detective named Oscar Wilde investigated a series of killings apparently committed by man-eating plants. *Hunter* by Byron Huggins was a techno-thriller featuring the world's greatest hunter on the trail of a genetically-created monster, while a small town was invaded by the eponymous *Incubus* by Ann Arensberg.

Originally published by Arrow Australia, Aurealis Award-winning author Kim Wilkins' *Grimoire* involved a group of power-hungry academics trying to reassemble a Victorian volume to summon up Satan in present-day Melbourne. There was more magic in Traci Harding's *Alchemist's Key*, set in an English village, while Victor Kelleher's *Into the Dark* was about the real Count Dracula and the young boy he took into his service. *Underground* by Mudrooroo was the third in the Australian author's "Masters of the Ghost Dreaming" sequence, revolving around a clash of mythologies.

The spirit of a nineteenth century suffragette appeared to her modern descendent in Kate Muir's *Suffragette City*, and Jilly Cooper's mainstream novel *Score* also featured ghosts.

Available as an attractively-packaged CD from Savoy Records, 1960s pop singer P.J. Proby read three extracts from David

Britton's infamously suppressed novel *Lord Horror*, accompanied by the BBC Philharmonic Orchestra.

Communion Blood was the twelfth volume in Chelsea Quinn Yarbro's series featuring vampire Comte de Saint-Germain, while *The Soul of an Angel* was the second volume in Yarbro's *Sisters of the Night*, a packaged series about Dracula's trio of undead brides, illustrated by Christopher H. Bing.

P.N. Elrod's *The Dark Sleep*, the eighth in "The Vampire Files" featuring undead detective Jack Fleming, was set in the world of showbusiness, and published in hardcover. *Lords of Light* was the third volume in the vampire series by Steven Spruill, which began with *Rulers of Darkness* and *Daughter of Darkness*.

Meanwhile the Science Fiction Book Club collected two of Laurell K. Hamilton's "Anita Blake" novels from 1998, *Burnt Offerings* and *Blue Moon*, in the omnibus *Black Moon Inn*. The hardcover came with a shrinkwrapped poster of Luis Royo's cover art.

The Hunt was the first volume in Susan Sizemore's series *Laws of the Blood*, about a group of vampire Enforcers. Sherry Gottlieb's *Worse Than Death* was a sequel to her humorous mystery *Love Bite*, as an undead LA cop in the early 1990s discovered that his conversion to vampirism resulted in sexual impotence. Mary Ann Mitchell's *Sips of Blood* featured an undead Marquis de Sade living in the twenty-first century.

Published by Hot Biscuit Productions, *The Guardian* was a first novel by Beecher Smith, in which a centuries-old member of the undead returned to protect the world from evil.

The Cowboy and the Vampire was an offbeat Gothic Western by Clark Hays and Kathleen McFall, in which a New York reporter was rescued from the undead by a Wyoming rancher. The third volume in Mark Sumner's comedy-mystery series, *News from the Edge: Vampires of Vermont*, involved tabloid reporter Savvy McKinnon investigating the existence of Count Yorga in the eponymous state and encountering some men in black along the way.

The Fifth Elephant, the 24th volume in Terry Pratchett's never-ending humorous "Discworld" series, involved officers from the Ankh-Morpork City Watch who found themselves in the land of vampires, werewolves and big lumps of mythical elephant fat.

Anne Rice's sister Alice Borchardt was back with *Night of the Wolf*, a sequel to her 1998 historical werewolf novel *The Silver Wolf*. Donna Boyd's *The Promise* was a sequel to the author's romantic werewolf novel *The Passion*. It was about a woman in Alaska who discovered an injured wolf and a mysterious diary.

Lycanthropic detective Ty Merrick investigated the murder of sailors by mutant monsters in *The Red Sky File* and the death of an opera singer in *The Radon File*, the fourth and fifth volumes respectively in Denise Vitola's series.

A prehistoric Native American shapeshifter was released in Western writer Robert J. Conley's *Brass*, while a female shape-changer was betrayed in Holly Lisle's *Vengeance of Dragons*, the second book of "The Secret Texts" and a sequel to the author's *Diplomacy of Wolves*.

Film director Wes Craven's disappointing first novel, *Fountain Society*, involved a top-secret brain operation.

Helena Dela's début, *The Count*, was a humorous Gothic ghost story, while in Patrick Redmond's *Something Dangerous*, a group of English schoolboys became involved with the occult.

Alanna Morland's first novel, *Leopard Lord*, involved a noble-man who inherited the power to transform into a bestial big cat, and a witches' coven was revived in modern Massachusetts in J.G. Passarella's début, *Wither*.

Mystery writer Max Allan Collins novelized Universal Studio's new version of *The Mummy*, Frank Lauria novelized *End of Days*, Robert Tine novelized *The Astronaut's Wife*, and Bruce Bethke novelized the misguided *Wild Wild West* movie, which included eight pages of black and white stills.

David Cronenberg's *eXistenZ* was novelized by "John Luther Novak" in Britain, although the American edition revealed that its true author was Christopher Priest. As a nice added bonus, Peter Lerangis's novelization of *Sleepy Hollow* also included Washington Irving's original story.

Richard Matheson's *A Stir of Echoes* and Shirley Jackson's *The Haunting of Hill House* were two classic ghost novels from the 1950s reissued to tie-in with film adaptations.

S.P. Somtow's *Temple of Night* was the latest original novel in *The Crow* series. *Predator: Big Game* was an original novelization based on the movies and Dark Horse Comics' series by "Sandy Schofield" (aka Dean Wesley Smith and Kristine Kathryn Rusch), and *War* was the latest in the *Aliens vs. Predator* series by S.D. Perry.

In 1999, Pocket Books' *Buffy the Vampire Slayer* series firmly established itself as the *Star Trek* of horror tie-ins with *Obsidian Fate* by Diana G. Gallagher, *Power of Persuasion* by Elizabeth Massie, *Resurrecting Ravana* by Ray Garton, *Sins of the Father* by Christopher Golden, and *Immortal* by Golden and Nancy Holder.

Golden and Holder also collaborated on another original *Buffy* series, *The Gatekeeper Trilogy*, with *Out of the Madhouse*, *Ghost Roads* and *Sons of Entropy*. All three novels were included in an omnibus book club edition. Holder also published the third volume in *The Angel Chronicles* and a novelization of the first episode of that spin-off show.

Keith R.A. DeCandido kicked off the *Buffy* series *The Xander Years* with a novelization of three episodes from the popular show, and Yvonne Navarro's first volume of the young adult series *The Willow Files* was also based on three episodes from the TV series. The young adult series of *Buffy* novelizations continued with *Visitors* by Laura Anne Gilman and Josepha Sherman, and *Unnatural Selection* by Mel Odom.

A skin graft from a car crash victim resulted in FBI agents Mulder and Scully travelling to Thailand and uncovering a decades-old plot from the Vietnam War in the adult novel *The X Files: Skin* by Ben Mezrich. The *X Files* young adult series continued with *Dark Matter* by Easton Royce, *Howlers* by Everett Owens, *Grotesque* by Ellen Steiber and *Regeneration* by Everett Owens.

The Legacy: The Hidden Saint by Rick Hautala was based on the Canadian TV series and involved the secret society investigating an apparent ghost of a child killed in a terrorist attack. *Dreams of the Dark* by Stephen M. Rainey and Elizabeth Massie was a novelization of the old *Dark Shadows* series, with an introduction by actress and author Lara Parker. Publishing editor Ginjer Buchanan was the author of the *Highlander* novelization *White Silence*, and Eliza Willard's *Charmed: The Power of Three* was a young adult novelization of the TV show about a trio of witchy sisters.

The young adult series of *Sabrina, the Teenage Witch* novelizations continued with *18: I'll Zap Manhattan* by Mel Odom, *19: Shamrock Shenanigans* by Diana G. Gallagher, *20: Age of Aquariums* and *21: Prom Time* both by David Cody Weiss and Bobbi J.G. Weiss, *22: Witchopoly* by John Vornhold, *23: Bridal Bedlam* by Diana G. Gallagher, *24: Scarabian Nights* by Nancy Holder, *25: While the Cat's Away* by Margot Batrae, *26: Fortune Cookie Fox* by Cathy East Dubowski, *27: Haunts in the House* by John Vornholt, and *28: Up, Up and Away* by the prolific Nancy Holder. *29: Millennium Madness* was an anthology of twelve stories based on the TV series and Archie comic book, while *Sabrina Down Under* was an anonymous novel based on the TV movie of the same title.

Based on the Hallmark Entertainment mini-series, James Mallory's *Merlin: The Old Magic* and *Merlin: The King's Wizard* were the first two volumes in a trilogy. *Indiana Jones and the Secret of the Sphinx* by Max McCoy was the 12th volume in the Lucasfilm series of original novelizations, and Mark Morris's *Doctor Who: Deep Blue* was the 19th volume in the BBC Books series of "Missing Adventures".

Small press publisher DreamHaven Books published Neil Gaiman's annotated script for his ghostly *Babylon 5* episode *Day of the Dead* as a trade paperback.

In September one of the world's largest toy companies, Hasbro, Inc., agreed to buy games company Wizards of the Coast for an estimated $325 million. In addition to *Magic: The Gathering*, Hasbro also acquired the *Pokémon* (an abbreviation of "Pocket Monster") Collectable Card Game, TSR's *Dungeons & Dragons* and more than seventy American retail outlets as part of the acquisition. The company announced that it planned to add to its publishing programme with a series of children's novels based on properties it owned.

White Wolf's *World of Darkness* series continued with *Toreador* by Stewart Wieck, *Tzimisce* by Eric Griffin, *Gangrel* by Gherbod Fleming, *Setite* by Kathleen Ryan, *Lasombra* by Richard E. Dansky, and *Ventrue* and *Assamite* both by Fleming again, all based on the *Clan* role-playing game. Also published by White Wolf, Lucy Taylor's *Eternal Hearts* was an erotic vampire novel set in modern-day Washington and based on the *Vampire: The Masquerade* role-playing game. It was stylishly illustrated by John Bolton.

Ravenloft: Spectre of the Black Rose by James Lowder and Veronica Whitney-Robinson was a sequel to the same authors' *Knight of the Black Rose*, also based on the TSR role-playing game and probably one of the last titles to be published under that imprint, following the Hasbro acquisition.

Resident Evil 3: City of the Dead and *4: Underworld*, both by S.D. Perry, were based on the zombie video game, while Greg Rucka's *Batman: No Man's Land* was set in a post-holocaust Gotham City destroyed by earthquakes.

Meanwhile, Berkley Books' series of Marvel Comics tie-ins was suspended when Marvel Entertainment claimed that its contract with Bryon Preiss's various packaging companies had been breached because of non-payment of royalties and other considerations. Copies of titles already printed were not distributed until an agreement was eventually reached amongst all the parties involved.

Jonathan Carroll's mainstream novel *The Marriage of Sticks* concerned a New York rare book dealer who was haunted by tangential ghosts from her past and present and had the power to change her own fate. The first printing was actually published in Poland in a 25,000-copy edition which quickly became a bestseller there.

Salman Rushdie used the myth of Orpheus as the basis of his contemporary novel of magical-realism, *The Ground Beneath Her Feet*, about a singer lost in an earthquake. Robert Irwin's novel *Satan Wants Me* dealt with sex and Santanism in the 1960s.

Brian Hodge moved into the crime and suspense genre with *Wild Horses*, a tale of dark secrets and retribution, while Don Webb's dark crime novel *Essential Saltes: An Experiment* involved the theft of a murder victim's ashes.

Barry Yourgrau's *Haunted Traveller* charted the strange journeys of its eponymous character, and Stewart O'Nan's *A Prayer for the Dying* was a thin novel set in the last half of the nineteenth century, when a deadly plague infected the inhabitants of a rural Wisconsin town.

A psychiatrist, a spiritualist and a ghost confronted each other over a girl apparently possessed by a spirit from Atlantis in Brooks Hansen's *Perlman's Ordeal*.

*   *   *

As part of its World's Classic series, the Oxford University Press (OUP) reissued Oscar Wilde's short 1891 novel *The Picture of Dorian Gray* in hardcover with a new introduction by Edmund White, while a new edition of the book from Tor included a foreword and afterword by Nancy Springer.

Also from OUP, *Miss or Mrs?*, *The Haunted Hotel*, *The Guilty River* was a collection of three novellas by Wilkie Collins, the middle tale being a ghost story, edited and with an introduction by Norman Page and Toru Sasaki.

Thorne Smith's humorous fantasies *Topper Takes a Trip* and *The Night Life of the Gods* were reprinted as trade paperbacks with new introductions by Carolyn See.

Dark Ladies was a welcome omnibus reprint of Fritz Leiber's classic novels *Conjure Wife* and *Our Lady of Darkness* in trade paperback. Jack Williamson's classic 1948 werewolf thriller *Darker Than You Think* was also reissued in trade paperback, with a new introduction by Douglas E. Winter and evocative illustrations by David G. Klein taken from a 1984 edition.

The Pit and the Pendulum and Other Stories by Edgar Allan Poe was a young adult collection of seven stories illustrated by James Prunier with notes by Henri Justin, while *The Pit and the Pendulum and Other Stories* collected seventeen tales by Poe with an introduction by Christopher Bigsby. Mary Shelley's *Frankenstein* was published as an illustrated hardcover by Doubleday in a New York Public Library Collector's Edition.

Penguin published H.P. Lovecraft's *The Call of Cthulhu and Other Weird Stories* in their Twentieth-Century Classics series. With an introduction and notes by S.T. Joshi, it collected eighteen classic tales. *More Annotated H.P. Lovecraft* edited by John Gregory Betancourt and Leigh Grossman was an illustrated trade paperback collection of ten Lovecraft stories annotated by Joshi and Peter H. Cannon.

Dennis Etchison's 1982 collection *The Dark Country* (with an introduction by Ramsey Campbell) and David J. Schow's 1990 collection *Seeing Red* (with an introduction by T.E.D. Klein) were both reissued by California's Alexander Publishing.

Great Weird Tales: 14 Stories by Lovecraft, Blackwood, Machen & Others also included fiction by Frank Belknap Long and F. Marion Crawford and was edited by S.T. Joshi.

* * *

Following reports that R.L. Stine, whose combined sales are more than 300 million, would be ending his popular *Goosebumps* volumes because of lawsuits and in-fighting with Scholastic Press, his packager Parachute Press announced that the author would be moving to HarperCollins with a new series, *The Nightmare Room* (based on his book *The Nightmare Hour*), and a twelve-book limited *Goosebumps* series.

The Nightmare Hour, Stine's first original hardcover for children, included ten stories each illustrated by a different artist (including Bernie Wrightson and John Collier) and was supported by a signing tour and a nationwide contest. Meanwhile, the author continued his *Fear Street: Seniors* series with *Last Chance*, *The Gift*, *Fight*, *Team*, *Sweetheart*, *Spring Break*, *Wicked*, and *Graduation*, the final book in a twelve volume series about a cursed class of students at the Shadyside High School.

Marking the character's 20th anniversary, *Bunnicula Strikes Again!* was James Howe's sixth novel about the vampire rabbit who drained the juice from vegetables. A group of teenagers were trapped in a netherworld in Christopher Pike's *The Grave*, and Brad Stickland continued John Bellairs' *Johnny Dixon* series with *The Wrath of the Grinning Ghost*, with a cover illustration by Edward Gorey, as usual.

Nancy Springer's *Sky Rider* was about a teenager's dying horse and a ghost, while Helen V. Griffith's novella *Cougar* featured a boy at a new school who faced up to bullies with the help of a ghostly horse. In Louise Hawes' *Rosey in the Present Tense* the ghost of a teenager's dead girlfriend could only be seen by him and his dying grandmother; a boy was haunted by a girl from the First World War in *The Rinaldi Ring* by Jenny Nimmo; a young man killed in an accident was given the opportunity to live his life over and over again in William Sleator's *Rewind*, and a family had more than just ghosts to contend with in *Paulina* by Lesley Howarth.

Susan Price's *The Ghost Wife* was possessed by a murderous spirit in the Point Horror Unleashed title. The series also included *Facetaker* by Philip Gross, about a photobooth which captured souls, and *Skinners* by John Gordon, in which a horror writer began to believe his own stories.

In the tradition of James Herbert, Paul Zindel's *Rats* involved mutant rodents from a New York City dump, and there were more killer rats in *The Boy Who Kicked Pigs* by *Doctor Who* actor Tom Baker, illustrated by David Roberts.

Vivian Vande Velde's *There's a Dead Person Following My Sister Around* was a comedy in which eleven-year-old Ted's little sister had a ghostly imaginary friend, and a young man accused of murder teamed up with a witch and a dead man to prove his innocence in *Never Trust a Dead Man* from the same author.

In *The Apprentice* by Gordon Houghton, Death picked a zombie to become his new assistant. Neal Shusterman's *Downsiders* involved the discovery of a lost civilization living in forgotten tunnels beneath New York City, and a young girl was afraid that the eponymous character would punish her in Pete Johnson's *The Creeper*.

The first in *The Secret Circle* series by L.J. Smith, *The Initiation* was about a High-School coven of witches. *Blood Stone* and *Dark Paths* were the sixth and seventh volumes, respectively, in Alan Frewin Jones's *Dark Paths* series involving ancient sacrifices on a Greek island.

A vampire's past came back to haunt her in Amelia Atwater-Rhodes' début novel, *In the Forests of the Night*, and the omnibus *Vampire Heart* by J.B. Calchman collected two previously-published novellas, "Kiss of the Vampire" and "Dance of the Vampire", along with a new one, "Touched by the Vampire".

Thomas McKean's *Into the Candlelit Room* was a collection of five original young adult stories. *Odder Than Ever* collected nine stories about unusual creatures by Bruce Coville, while *Bruce Coville's Shapeshifters* was an anthology of fourteen stories (eleven new) by such writers as Jane Yolen, Jack Dann, Lawrence Watt-Evans and Jessica Amanada Salmonson.

The Essential Clive Barker was a mixed bag sampler of four stories, fifty-three novel and playscript excerpts and a pretentious foreword by Armistead Maupin, with each section introduced by the author.

Michael Marshall Smith celebrated his first decade as a writer with *What You Make It*, a hardcover collection of seventeen superior short stories (including the previously unpublished title story) and a poem.

Uncut was a retrospective trade paperback collection of twenty-one short stories (two original) by Christopher Fowler, with an introduction by the author about his experience at a particularly bad signing in Rochester. Douglas Clegg's _The Nightmare Chronicles_ was another paperback original, collecting thirteen linked short stories, based around a family of serial killers and their not-quite-what-he-appears-to-be child victim.

Peter Crowther had two collections of stories published in 1999. _The Longest Single Note and Other Strange Compositions_ from Cemetery Dance Publications was an impressive volume containing twenty-six stories and poems (three original plus a novel extract) covering the past seven years, with an introduction by Michael Marshall Smith. It was available in a signed edition of 500 copies and a lettered edition. Crowther's _Lonesome Roads_ from Welsh publisher RazorBlade Press shared one story with his other collection and contained three novellas (one original) plus an introduction by Graham Joyce.

Just in time for the Australian World Science Fiction convention, Australia's MP Books released _Antique Futures: The Best of Terry Dowling_, which collected thirteen tales with an introduction by Jack Dann. From Hodder Headline Australia, Gary Crew's _Force of Evil_ was a collection of crime and horror police procedurals, illustrated by Shaun Tan.

Tanya Huff's collection _What Ho, Magic!_ included fifteen stories, four featuring vampire-hunter Vicki Nelson, while Edgar Allan Poe's _Dead Brides_ from Creation Books was billed as a collection of five classic vampire stories, with a foreword by James Havoc and an introduction by Jeremy Reed.

Wolves of Darkness was the second volume in _The Collected Stories of Jack Williamson_, published in hardcover by Haffner Press and containing ten stories plus essays and letters from 1931–33. Harlan Ellison contributed the introduction, and there was an afterword by the author. A signed and slipcased edition limited to 100 copies was also available.

Amongst much publicity fanfare and rumours of a $300,000 advance, the anthology _999: New Stories of Horror and Suspense_ was launched with a series of online discussions and readings in September. Intended to represent the state of the horror field at the end of the Millennium, its neat 666 pages featured twenty-nine "never-before-published" stories and novellas by William Peter Blatty, Joe R. Lansdale, David Morrell, Ramsey Campbell,

Stephen King, Thomas Ligotti, Kim Newman, F. Paul Wilson, Gene Wolfe, Neil Gaiman, T.E.D. Klein, Tim Powers and Michael Marshall Smith, amongst others. Editor Al Sarrantonio not only included one of his own stories, but in his introduction claimed that there are "literally no professional markets for good horror fiction". Although many of the stories were very good, few were exceptional; at least one was an uncredited reprint and a couple of others were obviously rescued from bottom drawers.

Subterranean Gallery was a much more accurate representation of the current state of modern horror fiction, ably edited by Richard T. Chizmar and Subterranean Press publisher William K. Schafer. Containing twenty stories of horror and crime (four reprints) and published in signed editions of 500 numbered and 26 lettered copies, its list of contributors included Jack Ketchum, David J. Schow, Graham Joyce, Joe R. Lansdale, Terry Lamsley, Christa Faust, Richard Laymon, Chaz Brenchley and Norman Patridge.

Canada's Aurora Award-winning anthology series *Northern Frights* reached its fifth volume with eighteen stories and a poem under the editorship of Don Hutchison. Although it included new fiction by Hugh B. Cave, Nalo Hopkinson, Gemma Files, Nancy Kilpatrick and Robert Charles Wilson, amongst others, one of the best stories in the book was an atmospheric reprint from Rebecca Bradley about an ancient Irish mud monster.

The latest in the Horror Writers Association series of original anthologies was *Whitley Strieber's Aliens*, featuring twenty-one close encounters by P.D. Cacek, Nina Kiriki Hoffman, Esther Friesner and others, plus an introduction by Strieber. *Isaac Asimov's Werewolves* edited by Gardner Dozois and Sheila Williams collected six stories from the eponymous magazine, by such authors as S.P. Somtow, Suzy McKee Charnas and Pat Murphy.

In *The Best from Fantasy & Science Fiction: The Fiftieth Anniversary Anthology*, editors Edward L. Ferman and Gordon Van Gelder reprinted twenty-one stories published in the magazine between 1994–98.

Master's Choice edited by Lawrence Block collected eighteen reprint mystery stories with introductions by the authors, including Stephen King and Harlan Ellison. Edited by James Frenkel, *Technohorror: Inventions in Terror* contained sixteen reprints

involving machines by King, Ellison, Robert Bloch, Ray Bradbury, Ramsey Campbell and others.

Night Shade: Gothic Tales by Women was edited by Victoria
Brownworth and Judith M. Redding and featured seventeen
feminist stories (two reprints) from Seattle's Seal Press. *Night-
shade: 20th Century Ghost Stories* edited by Robert Philips
collected twenty-seven "literary" ghost stories by Shirley Jackson,
Joan Aiken, Gabriel Garcia Marquez and F. Marion Crawford,
amongst others. *The Open Door and Other Ghost Stories* contained fourteen stories chosen by editor Philip Gooden.

With Elizabeth Ann Scarborough, the ubiquitous Martin H.
Greenberg edited *Vampire Slayers: Stories of Those Who Dare to
Take Back the Night*, which included eleven tales of the undead by
Hugh B. Cave, Manly Wade Wellman and others. Greenberg was
also the uncredited co-editor with Denise Little of *A Dangerous
Magic*, which collected fifteen stories of supernatural lovers by
Peter Crowther, Andre Norton, actor John DeChancie and others.

Along with Stefan Dziemianowicz and Robert Weinberg,
Greenberg edited the Barnes & Noble anthology *100 Hilarious
Little Howlers* which included amusing stories (three original) by
Howard Wandrei, Peter Cannon, Joe R. Lansdale, Gahan Wil-
son, Tim Lebbon, Edgar Allan Poe, Hugh B. Cave, Karl Edward
Wagner, Donald A. Wollheim, Les Daniels, Gordon Van Gelder,
Saki, Irvin S. Cobb, Ramsey Campbell and numerous other –
mostly horror – writers.

Neonlit: Time Out Book of New Writing Volume 2 was again
edited by Nicholas Royle and included twenty-five new stories by
such authors as Margaret Drabble, Joel Lane, Ramsey Campbell,
Jonathan Coe and the editor himself. Michael Moorcock, who
contributed the introduction, chose Rhonda Carrier's story from
the book as the winner of his Jack Trevor Story Memorial Cup
prize of £500. Royle also edited *The Time Out Book of Paris
Short Stories* and included Kim Newman and Christopher Kenworthy amongst its seventeen authors.

Edited by Maxim Jakubowski, *Chronicles of Crime: The
Second Ellis Peters Memorial Anthology of Historical Crime*
included a surprising new variation on the Jekyll and Hyde
narrative from Kim Newman and a burial alive story by Basil
Copper, along with contributions from Ian Rankin, Ed Gorman
and Peter Tremayne, amongst others.

The Year's Best Fantasy and Horror: Twelfth Annual Collection edited by Ellen Datlow and Terri Windling contained thirty-eight stories and eight poems, with many of the shorter stories falling into Windling's fantasy category and the longer tales reflecting Datlow's horror choices. Edited by Stephen Jones, *The Mammoth Book of Best New Horror* celebrated its tenth anniversary with nineteen stories and novellas, along with the usual overview of the previous year, necrology, list of useful addresses and short testimonials by numerous well-known authors and editors. Only three stories (by Dennis Etchison, Peter Straub and Kelly Link) appeared in both "Year's Best" volumes.

The progenitor of genre small press publishers, Arkham House, marked a return to form with *New Horizons: Yesterday's Portraits of Tomorrow*, the final science fiction anthology edited by the late August Derleth, which was published in an edition of 3,000 copies. The volume, which collected thirteen stories from the 1920s and '30s, included fiction by H.G. Wells, Frank Belknap Long and Murray Leinster, plus two previously unpublished tales by David H. Keller (completed by Paul Spencer), and Derleth and Mark Shorer.

Also from Arkham, *Dragonfly* by Frederic S. Durbin was a Halloween tale told from a ten-year-old girl's point-of-view, while *Sixty Years of Arkham House* was compiled by S.T. Joshi and listed all the imprint's (more than 230) books to-date, along with a brief history of the company by August Derleth and Joshi, plus various indexes.

Minneapolis imprint Fedogan & Bremer finally published Basil Copper's new collection *Whispers in the Night: Stories of the Mysterious and Macabre*, containing eleven stories and novellas (three reprints), an introduction by Stephen Jones, and some excellent illustrations by Stephen Fabian. Jones was also the editor of *Dark Detectives: Adventures of the Supernatural Sleuths*, published under the F&B Mystery imprint. Illustrated by Randy Broecker, it contained ten stories (six reprints) featuring psychic detectives by Peter Tremayne, William Hope Hodgson, Basil Copper, Manly Wade Wellman, Brian Lumley, R. Chetwynd-Hayes, Brian Mooney, Clive Barker, Jay Russell and Neil Gaiman, along with an original eight-part novel by Kim Newman and an extensive historical introduction by the editor. As usual, both books were also published in signed and numbered 100-copy slipcased editions.

Fedogan & Bremer also reissued its first book, the 1989 collection *Colossus: The Collected Science Fiction of Donald Wandrei* in a revised and expanded 10th anniversary edition of 1,000 copies, edited by Philip J. Rahman and Dennis Weiler, with an introduction by Richard L. Tierney.

Subterranean Press announced that it had signed a long-term contract with author Joe R. Lansdale for a mid-five-figure advance. Lansdale's *Something Lumber This Way Comes* was a short children's story about a vampiric house, illustrated by Doug Potter and available in a signed edition of 500 copies. There was more twisted Texas weirdness in *Waltz of Shadows*, the first in Subterranean's *Lost Lansdale* series, and originally intended for the Mysterious Press until the author discarded it. It was published in a signed edition of 1,000 copies and a $195.00 lettered edition.

Subterranean's regular edition of the late Charles Beaumont's collection *A Touch of The Creature* was limited to 1,000 copies, signed by the author's son, Christopher Beaumont, and priced at $40.00. Meanwhile, a thirteen-copy signed and lettered edition was bound in cloth and leather and contained two previously unpublished stories ("The Blind Lady" and "The Child"), plus an original sketch by Beaumont. This extremely limited traycased edition was also signed by Richard Matheson, who contributed the afterword, and was priced at $650.00.

Lovingly edited and introduced by David J. Schow, *The Devil With You! The Lost Bloch, Volume I* was the first in a proposed series from Subterranean Press reprinting some of the late Robert Bloch's less accessible fiction. It contained four novellas from the 1940s and '50s, a foreword by Stefan Dziemianowicz, and an interview with Bloch by the editor. *All of Us Are Dying and Other Stories* was a long-overdue collection of twenty-three new and reprint stories, plus teleplays and non-fiction by *Twilight Zone* author George Clayton Johnson. Published as a 600-copy signed and numbered hardcover and a 26-copy signed and lettered edition, the book also included an introduction/interview by Christopher Conlon and an afterword by Dennis Etchison.

Kafka Americana was an attractive, slim hardcover that collected five bizarre short stories by Jonathan Lethem and Carter

Scholz, signed by the authors and limited to 600 numbered and 26 lettered copies. Subterranean also reissued Ray Garton's first novel, the 1984 *Seductions*, in a new 500-copy hardcover edition with a foreword by the author, an afterword by Richard Laymon and illustrations by Earl Geier.

British independent publisher Pumpkin Books marked its third year with well-deserved World Fantasy and British Fantasy Award nominations, and added to its impressive raft of titles with Hugh B. Cave's new novel *Isle of the Whisperers*, in which an archaeologist accidently opened a doorway to another dimension and released an evil which preyed upon an island community during darkness. It was illustrated by John Coulthart. *Brotherly Love and Other Tales of Faith and Knowledge* was an extremely welcome and long-overdue collection of six new novellas and stories by David Case, with an introduction by Ramsey Campbell and an impressive cover by Les Edwards. Both books were published in 750-copy hardcover editions.

Edited by Stephen Jones and illustrated by Randy Broecker, *White of the Moon: New Tales of Madness and Dread* was limited to 1,000 copies and contained 20 original stories and a poem by Christopher Fowler, David J. Schow, Caitlín R. Kiernan, Ramsey Campbell, Graham Masterton, Terry Lamsley, Paul J. McAuley, Kim Newman, Michael Marshall Smith, Jeff VanderMeer, Jo Fletcher and others.

Waltzes and Whispers collected fifteen savage and satirical stories by Jay Russell, seven of them original, along with an introduction by Michael Marshall Smith, an afterword by Kim Newman, and some stylish illustrations from John Coulthart. *Wishmaster and Other Stories* (erroneously titled *The Wishmaster* on the dustjacket) collected ten horror stories (three original), one poem and the title screenplay by Peter Atkins, along with an introduction by Ramsey Campbell and illustrations by Randy Broecker. Both books were limited to 750 hardcover copies and were also available in variant library editions.

Edited by Jo Fletcher and created by Stephen Jones, *Horror at Halloween* was a trade paperback from Pumpkin Books aimed at older teenagers. It contained a "mosaic novel" of five original interlinked novellas set in Charles Grant's haunted town of Oxrun Station, by Stephen Bowkett, Diane Duane, Craig Shaw Gardner, John Gordon and Grant himself.

From Gauntlet Publications came a signed hardcover edition of Poppy Z. Brite's 1998 paperback original novelization *The Crow: The Lazarus Heart*. It was limited to 1,000 hardcover copies featuring a new introduction by the author, an afterword by John Shirley, and illustrations by J.K. Potter. Also from Gauntlet, F. Paul Wilson's second "Repairman Jack" novel *Conspiracies* was published in an edition of 450 copies signed by the author and Ed Gorman, who supplied the afterword, with illustrations by Harry O. Morris. This time Jack encountered all kinds of weirdness while his dreams were disturbed by the demon Rakoshi.

Cemetery Dance Publications kicked off a busy year with the hardcover novellas *411* by Ray Garton and *Right to Life* by Jack Ketchum (aka Dallas Mayr), both of which involved heroic felines. They were followed by Garton's dark suspense novel *Biofire* and *Lynch: A Gothik Western*, a hardcover novella by Nancy A. Collins about a gunslinger brought back from the dead. Returning from the grave was also the theme of the aptly-titled *Rot*, Gary Brandner's riff on "The Monkey's Paw", published as a slim but expensive signed limited hardcover of 1,000 copies.

Other signed CD editions included *The Poker Club* by Ed Gorman, limited to 750 copies: *Come Out Tonight* by Richard Laymon, limited to 1,250 copies, and Laymon's *Cuts*, limited to 1,500 copies. *California Sorcery* edited by William F. Nolan and William K. Schafer collected twelve stories (nine original) by such West Coast writers as Ray Bradbury, Richard Matheson and Charles Beaumont. It was issued in a limited edition of 1,500 copies signed by both editors.

From Overlook Connection Press came a 1,000-copy signed and leatherbound edition of Stephen J. Spignesi's *The Lost Work of Stephen King: A Guide to Unpublished Manuscripts, Story Fragments, Alternative Versions and Oddities*. It included numerous photographs and an essay on humour by King which were not in the 1998 trade edition from Birch Lane Press. Also from Overlook, the long-awaited *Spares: The Special Edition* reprinted the preferred text of Michael Marshall Smith's 1996 novel about cloning, along with a "lost" chapter, three connected short stories (one original), a brief introduction by Neil Gaiman and an afterword by the author. This was available in a 500-copy signed limited edition ($45.00), a 100-copy slipcased "Sterling" edition ($85.00), and a signed lettered edition of 52 copies published in a deluxe wooden slipcase with glass ($400.00). Overlook's edition of *Off Season: The Unexpurgated Edition* by Jack Ketchum included restored text and a new introduction by Douglas E. Winter.

After a delay, Seattle's Silver Salamander Press published Simon Clark's short story collection *Salt Snake & Other Bloody Cuts* in a 500-copy trade paperback edition, a 100-copy numbered hardcover edition and a 50-copy lettered edition bound in leather. The book collected twenty-five stories (two original) by the British author.

Crossroads Press issued Joe R. Lansdale's hardboiled novel *Freezer Burn*, about a petty crook who encountered a travelling carnival and freak show in the East Texas swamps. Illustrated by George Pratt, it was available in a signed edition of 400 copies and a leather-bound, lettered edition.

Published by Bereshith/ShadowLands and edited by John Pelan, *The Last Continent: New Tales of Zothique* was an original hardcover anthology of nineteen stories inspired by the dying fantasy world created by Clark Ashton Smith. With an introduction by Donald Sidney-Fryer and illustrated by Allen Koszowski and Fredrik King, contributors included Gene Wolfe, Brian Stableford, Mark Chadbourn, Lucy Taylor, Don Webb, Jessica Amanda Salmonson, Charlee Jacob, Mark McLauglin and Rhys Hughes. It was available in a signed edition of 500 copies, and a slipcased deluxe edition of 50 copies which included a limited edition art print.

From artist Alan M. Clark's new IFD Publishing came *Bedtime Stories to Darken Your Dreams* edited by Bruce Holland Rogers and designed and illustrated by the publisher. It featured twenty-three short horror stories and poems (eleven original) from Jane Yolen, Steve Rasnic Tem, Melanie Tem, Elizabeth Massie and others.

My Own Private Spectres was a welcome English-language collection of sixteen stories by Belgian author Jean Ray, edited and translated by Hubert Van Callenbergh for publisher Midnight House. Available in an edition of 350 numbered copies, the book also included a useful bibliography plus artwork by Allen Koszowski.

From Meisha Merlin, Adam Niswander's novel *The Repository* involved the late Ambrose Bierce, Satan and a war between the Fellowship of Magic and a witch. *Deep Into the Darkness Peering* was a massive retrospective of Tom Piccirilli's fiction from Terminal Fright Press, containing forty stories (six original), an introduction by Poppy Z. Brite and an interview with the author by Richard Laymon.

Britain's new Birmingham-based publishing imprint Toxic launched in August with crime author Mark Timlin's post-apocalyptic novel *I Spied a Pale Horse*, set in the near-future where a modern Black Death had decimated the world population.

Edited by Christopher C. Teague, *Nasty Snips* was a paperback anthology of thirty-five "short, sharp shocks" (five reprints) and four poems by D.F. Lewis, Steve Lockley, Tim Lebbon, Simon Clark, Edo van Belkom, Amy Grech, James S. Dorr, Mark McLaughlin and others. It was the first publication from MT Enterprises of Wales. *The House Spider & Other Strange Visitors* contained ten stories (three original) by Kurt Newton. It was published by Delirium Books in a signed and numbered hardcover edition of just fifty copies, with an introduction by Charlee Jacob and artwork by Roddy Williams.

A detective was on the trail of a Cthulhu-worshipping serial killer in *Nightmare's Disciple* by Joseph S. Pulver, Sr, published by Chaosium. From the same publisher, *The Ithaqua Cycle* edited by Robert M. Price collected fourteen tales of the Cthulhu Mythos' legendary Wind-Walker from such authors as August Derleth, Brian Lumley and Algernon Blackwood. Price also edited *The Antarktos Cycle*, an anthology of ten pseudo-Lovecraftian stories and a poem, which included short novels by Edgar Allan Poe and John Taine, and *Tales Out of Innsmouth: New Stories of the Children of Cthulhu*, featuring thirteen stories from Gary Myers, Brian McNaughton, Peter H. Cannon and others, along with interior illustrations by Dave Carson.

Specialist Lovecraftian bookstore Mythos Books published two HPL-inspired trade paperback collections. *Ancient Exhumations* by Stanley C. Sargent contained seven stories (two original) with a preface by Robert M. Price and illustrations by various artists, while *Dreams of Lovecraftian Horror* collected fourteen stories by W.H. Pugmire, introduced, illustrated and co-edited by the above-mentioned Sargent.

Edited by James Van Hise in a 2,000-copy edition, *The*

Fantastic Worlds of H.P. Lovecraft was an oversize paperback containing twenty-seven reprint articles by August Derleth, Will Murray (who revealed a previously unknown 1932 collaboration between E. Hoffman Price and HPL), S.T. Joshi, Peter Cannon, Robert Weinberg and others. It was profusely illustrated by Dave Carson, Allen Koszowski, Stephen E. Fabian and even Lovecraft himself.

From London's Citron Press "New Authors Co-Operative" came the self-published collection *The Other Side of the Mirror* by Alan David Price, with an introduction by Ramsey Campbell. BuzzCity Press published Michael Cisco's début novel, *The Divinity Student*, illustrated by Harry O. Morris.

As always, it was a busy year for Canada's Ash-Tree Press. *Six Ghost Stories* reprinted the 1919 collection by architect T.G. Jackson in a 500-copy edition, with an extensive introduction by Richard Dalby. Also limited to 500 copies, *Ghost Gleams* was the first-ever reprint of the 1921 young adult collection by the obscure W.J. Wintle. It contained fifteen stories, a lengthy introduction and bibliography by Dalby, a 1903 article by the author, and an afterword by Peter J. Wire. Originally published in a 250-copy edition by the Ghost Story Press under the title *Fear Walks the Night*, *The Night Wind Howls: Complete Supernatural Stories* was a bumper collection of sixty-one stories and one account of a "real" haunting by Frederick Cowles, limited to 600 copies. The book included a foreword by the author's son, Michael Cowles, an introduction by Hugh Lamb and an afterword by Neil Bell.

More Binscombe Tales: Sinister Sutangli Stories collected twelve stories (five original) by John Whitbourn in an edition of 500 copies, along with an introduction and lengthy afterword by the author in which he discussed the series and several unwritten Binscombe tales. The second volume in Ash-Tree's *Occult Detectives Library* was *Norton Vyse: Psychic*, containing six stories originally published by Rose Champion de Crespigny in *The Premier Magazine* in 1919. It was edited by Jack Adrian and also limited to 500 copies.

Out of the Dark Volume Two: Diversions by Robert W. Chambers was the second Ash-Tree collection of the author's fiction to be edited and introduced by Hugh Lamb. Containing thirteen stories dating from after 1900, and a bibliography, it was limited to 500 copies. With an introduction by Richard Dalby and limited to 600 copies, *The Terraces of Night* contained twelve stories by Margery Lawrence and was the second of the author's *Club of the Round Table* collections, originally published in 1932.

H.R. Wakefield's *Strayers from Sheol* reprinted the fifteen stories from the 1961 Arkham House edition along with four previously uncollected stories in a 500-copy edition with an introduction by editor Barbara Roden. *The Wind at Midnight* by Georgia Wood Pangborn contained sixteen stories and nine poems by the American author along with an introduction by editor Jessica Amanda Salmonson and a preface by Patricia A. McKillip in an edition of 500 copies.

Published in a 600-copy edition, *The Passenger* by E.F. Benson was the second in a proposed five-volume set of *Collected Spook Stories* edited and introduced by Jack Adrian and containing fourteen stories dating from 1912–21. Richard Dalby edited and introduced Amelia B. Edwards' *The Phantom Coach: Collected Ghost Stories*, which contained sixteen stories and three pieces of non-fiction in an edition of 500 copies.

In *The Ash-Tree Press Annual Macabre 1999*, editor Jack Adrian reprinted six stories dealing with the concept of "time" by Tom Gallon, Neil Gow, Eric Ambrose, W.J. Makin, Donald Shoubridge and Laurence Meynell. It was limited to 500 copies. *The Talisman* was a new novel about the influence of an evil Babylonian statue by Jonathan Aycliffe, published in an edition of 600 copies.

Warning Whispers by A.M. Burrage was the penultimate volume in Ash-Tree's extended five-volume set of the author's ghost stories. Edited and with an introduction by Jack Adrian, it contained twenty-five stories and was limited to 500 copies. First reprinted by Ash-Tree in 1994, A.N.L. Munby's *The Alabaster Hand* was reissued in a newly re-set 350-copy edition with an introduction by Michael Cox.

From Tartarus Press and limited to just 200 signed and numbered copies, *In Violet Veils and Other Tales of The Connoisseur* was a collection of nine stories (six original) by Mark Valentine about the eponymous occult detective. *Forever Azathoth and Other Horrors* was a collection of seventeen Lovecraftian pastiches and parodies (three featuring Jeeves and Wooster) by Peter H. Cannon, published in a signed hardcover edition of 250 copies.

The Doll Maker and Other Tales of the Uncanny collected the 1953 title story along with "The Trespassers" and "A House of Call" by Sarban (aka John William Well) in an edition of 200 copies, along with a new afterword by Mark Valentine and a bibliography. Limited to 500 numbered copies, Sarban's *The Sound of His Horn and The King of the Lake* reprinted the short 1952 alternate-world novel along with a newly discovered novella set in a magical Morocco.

The Collected Strange Stories of Robert Aickman was a massive two-volume collection of forty-nine stories by the late British author, published by Tartarus in association with Durtro Press. With an appreciation by David Tibet and a memoir by Ramsey Campbell, the £70.00 set was limited to 500 hardcover copies.

Welsh small press imprint Sarob Press was founded in 1998 by Robert Morgan to publish limited hardcover editions of rare, classic and modern supernatural novellas, novels and short story collections. *Margery of Quether and Other Weird Tales* by S. Baring-Gould appeared in a 200-copy edition which was edited and introduced by Richard Dalby and contained seven classic ghost stories. *The Blue Room and Other Ghost Stories* was the first volume in Dalby's *Mistresses of the Macabre* series from Sarob. Collecting seven neglected stories from the 1890s by Lettice Galbraith, it was followed by *In the Dark and Other Ghost Stories* by Mary E. Penn, which contained eight obscure stories from the late 1880s. Both titles included fascinating introductions by the editor and were published in editions of 250 numbered copies.

Also from Sarob came a welcome 200-copy reissue of L.H. Maynard and M.P.N. Sim's 1979 collection *Shadows at Midnight*, illustrated by Douglas Walters. The authors significantly revised all ten stories for the new edition, as well as adding two new tales of ghostly manifestations. First published in book form in 1875, *Vampire City* by French author Paul Féval was a forgotten Gothic parody translated and edited (with an introduction, afterword and notes) by Brian Stableford in an edition of 250 numbered copies. It was illustrated by Tim Denton.

Sixteen "hardcore horror" stories (six original) by Charlee Jacob were collected in *Dread in the Beast* from Florida's Necro Publications, available in signed editions of 300 numbered trade paperbacks and 52 lettered hardcovers. From the same publisher came Gerard Houarner's novel *Road to Hell*, with an introduction by Brian Hodge. It was available in a signed trade paperback edition of 300 copies, and a 52-copy hardcover which sold out prior to publication.

Guy N. Smith's Black Hill Books published the first volumes of the author's *Horror Shorts* and *Mystery & Horror Shorts* under its Bulldog Books imprint. Each title appeared in a magazine format and contained, respectively, eleven and fifteen (eleven original) stories. Other titles from Black Hill included Smith's latest horror novel *The Busker* and Gavin Newman's Elizabethan whodunit, *An Unholy Way to Die*, which tied in with a short story competition judged by the author.

Available in trade paperback and a limited hardcover edition, *Really, Really, Really, Really, Weird Stories* from California's Night Shade Books collected thirty-seven stories (nine original) by John Shirley, arranged in order of increasing weirdness.

Canadian publisher Quarry Press collected twenty horror and dark fantasy stories (two original) by Edo van Belkom in *Death Drives a Semi*, along with an introduction by Robert J. Sawyer. From W. Paul Ganley's Weirdbook Press came Darrell Schweitzer's *Refugees from an Imaginary Country*, a collection of nineteen old-fashioned horror and mystery stories, illustrated by Stephen E. Fabian.

Edited by June Hubbard, *Dead Promises* from Michigan's Chameleon Publishing contained eighteen Civil War ghost stories (two reprints) from such authors as Scott Nicholson, Jan Stirling, Owl Goingback, Wendy Webb and Stephen Gresham. The eighth and final volume of Wayne Edwards' *Palace Corbie* appeared from Merrimack Books as a hefty paperback anthology of twenty-seven stories and poems by Douglas Clegg, Caitlín R. Kiernan, Mark McLaughlin, Charlee Jacob, Tom Piccirilli, D.F. Lewis, Jeff VanderMeer, Yvonne Navarro, John Pelan, Wayne Allen Sallee and others.

Australia's Ticonderoga Publications issued Stephen Dedman's first collection *The Lady of Situations*, containing thirteen stories (one original).

Author and editor Peter Crowther launched PS Publishing with four original novellas all published in 500-copy signed trade paperback editions. The first titles were Graham Joyce's atmospheric tale of *doppelgängers* and cannibalism, *Leningrad Nights*, with an introduction by Peter Straub, and *How the Other Half Lives*, a dark fantasy by James Lovegrove, introduced by Colin Greenland. Both were also available in lettered hardcover editions of fifty-two copies with colour dustjackets. The latest instalment in Kim Newman's *Anno Dracula* sequence, *Andy Warhol's Dracula* (published simultaneously with the online magazine *Event Horizon*) included an introduction by F. Paul Wilson and was available as a 125-copy hardcover. Michael Marshall Smith's offbeat SF novella *The Vaccinator*, which involved alien sightings in Florida's Key West and contained an introduction by M. John Harrison, was also released in a 150-copy hardcover edition.

As an author, Peter Crowther teamed up with James Lovegrove for the chapbook novella *The Hand That Feeds*, published by Maynard Sims Productions. In fact, along with their magazine *Enigmatic Tales*, Mick Sims and Len Maynard dominated the UK market with their series of Enigmatic Novellas chapbooks, which included *The Dark Fantastic* by Paul Finch, *Candlelight Ghost Stories* by Anthony Morris, *In the Mirror* by Sarah Singleton and *Alternate Lives* by Paul Bradshaw. Except for the Singleton title, each booklet contained two stories, with Iain Maynard illustrating the Morris title and the others featuring artwork by Gerald Gaubert. *Icarus Descending* by Steve Savile had an introduction by John Pelan and was the second in the series of Enigmatic Variations chapbooks. And as if all that wasn't enough, the pair also launched the *Haunted Dreams* series of booklets with *Silent Turmoil*, containing two of their own stories, again with illustrations by Iain Maynard.

Along with its publishing programme of limited edition hardcovers, Subterranean Press also issued a series of signed and numbered chapbooks. Thomas Tessier's *Lulu and One Other* contained both the atmospheric title story and "Nightsuite" in a 250-copy edition plus 26 lettered copies. *Peter and PTR* was an odd item which contained two deleted prefaces and an introduction by Peter Straub for his novel *Mr. X*, published in an edition of 250 copies and a 52-copy lettered state. Along the same lines, Poppy Z. Brite's draft story for her first novel appeared as *The Seed of Lost Souls*, along with an interview with the author, in a printing of 500 copies and 52 lettered editions. Also from Subterranean, *Triple Feature* included three stories by Joe R. Lansdale, one co-written with Bill Pronzini and Jeff Wellman.

Published in an edition of just 320 copies by Masters of Terror Press, Tim Lebbon's novella *White* was a *tour de force* chiller from one of Britain's most promising new horror writers. From Florida's Buzzcity Press, *The Divinity Student* by Michael Cisco involved the eponymous character searching the brains of corpses for forbidden words, illustrated by Harry O. Morris.

Following its 1998 chapbook of S.P. Somtow's *A Lap Dance With the Lobster Lady*, Bereshith/ShadowLands Press published *Of Pigs and Spiders* in a signed and numbered edition of 333 copies. It contained two grisly horror collaborations by Edward Lee and John Pelan, and David Niall Wilson and Brett Savory.

Jeff VanderMeer continued to chronicle the alternate world he created in *The Hoegbotton Guide to The Early History of Ambergris by Duncan Shriek*, a novella in the form a guide book, published by Necropolitan Press. Winner of the 1999 Blood & Guts Horror Story Competition, Steve Vernon's *A Fine Sacrifice* was published by Canada's Bad Moon Books.

Edited by Tina L. Jens and published in editions of 250 copies by Chicago's Twilight Tales/11th Hour Productions, *Animals Don't Knock! Tails from the Pet Shop* featured fiction from, amongst others, Jody Lynne Nye, Nancy Kilpatrick and the editor; *When the Bough Breaks* included stories of children in peril and perilous children by Algis Budrys, Robert Weinberg, Yvonne Navarro and Bruce Holland Rogers, and *Play It Again, Sam* contained six stories about music by Lawrence Schimel, Michael Marano, Mort Castle and others.

Much more substantial was *Book of Dead Things*, also edited by Jens, in an edition of 500 copies. It featured twenty-three stories and poems (ten original) by Scott A. Cupp, Jo Fletcher, Karen E. Taylor, Robert Weinberg, Bruce Holland Rogers, Lawrence Schimel, Sephera Giron, Yvonne Navarro, Edo van Belkom, Brian Hodge and others, plus a cover illustration by Alan M. Clark. Also from Twilight Tales, *The Crawling Abattoir* was a collection of nine stories by Martin Mundt with an introduction by Jay Bonansinga. It appeared in an edition of 200 signed copies.

From Britain's B.J.M. Press, *Nightscapes* featured ten stories by Michael Pendragon, illustrated by Gerald Gaubert and others, along with a hyperbolic introduction by publisher/editor John B. Ford and an afterword by Paul Bradshaw.

Published by Nashville House, Gary William Crawford's chapbook *In Shadow Lands* collected nineteen poems with illustrations by Margaret Ballif Simon. *Shadows Before the Maining* from Gothic Press contained thirty-six poems by Scott C. Holstad.

Dell Magazines signed a deal with e-book publisher Peanut Press to offer electronic editions of its magazines *Analog*, *Asimov's*, *Alfred Hitchcock* and *Ellery Queen* at the same price as the print versions. Meanwhile, the online magazine *Event Horizon* edited by Ellen Datlow went on "indefinite hiatus" in December while it tried to find new investors and sponsorship.

Under new publisher DNA Publications, George Scithers and Darrell Schweitzer's oversized *Weird Tales* returned to a regular schedule with four quarterly issues featuring stories by Tanith Lee, Ian MacLeod, Thomas Ligotti, Ramsey Campbell, Lawrence Watt-Evans, Lord Dunsany, Ian Watson, Hugh B. Cave (a voodoo/Cthulhu tale), Andy Duncan, James Van Pelt, Brian Stableford and Schweitzer himself, plus artwork from the always-excellent Stephen E. Fabian, George Barr, Russell Morgan, Allen Koszowski, Rodger Gerberding, Denis Tiani and others. John Gregory Betancourt edited the first issue of the *Weird Tales Library* in a trial magazine-format, reprinting novels by Darrell Schweitzer and Alan Rodgers along with one of his own short stories.

With a handy new format and a stylishly re-designed logo, David Pringle's *Interzone* published its usual twelve issues of SF and fantasy with darker stories by Brian Stableford, Tanith Lee, Garry Kilworth, Christopher Kenworthy, Kim Newman, Paul J. McAuley, Richard Calder and Ian Watson, interviews with Tom Holland, Chaz Brenchley, Don Webb, Terry Dowling and James Herbert, plus the usual review columns and features. There were special issues celebrating the Australian WorldCon and Michael Moorcock, plus the magazine's 150th edition.

Under editor Gordon Van Gelder, *The Magazine of Fantasy & Science Fiction* celebrated fifty years of publication and produced its usual eleven issues (including a 350-page double volume), which featured the usual intelligent mix of science fiction, whimsical fantasy and horror, including stories by Ian Watson, Lisa Tuttle, Joel Lane and Chris Morgan, Gary A. Braunbeck, Nancy Etchemendy, Steve Rasnic Tem, M. John Harrison, Lucy Sussex, Mary A. Turzillo, Harlan Ellison, Jonathan Carroll, Gene Wolfe and Scott Bradfield; non-fiction from Elizabeth Hand, Douglas E. Winter, David J. Schow, Neil Gaiman, David Langford, Judith Merril and Ray Bradbury, plus a Gahan Wilson cartoon.

Richard T. Chizmar's *Cemetery Dance* celebrated its tenth anniversary issue with fiction by Dennis Etchison, Poppy Z. Brite, Joe R. Lansdale, Douglas Clegg, Norman Patridge and Ed Gorman, plus an interview with Ramsey Campbell. However, the magazine never quite made its new bi-monthly schedule, and other issues included stories from Richard Matheson, William F. Nolan, George Clayton Johnson, Michael Marshall Smith, F. Paul Wilson and Chaz Brenchley, novel excerpts by Peter Straub and Joe R. Lansdale, plus interviews with Wilson, Peter Crowther and the late Robert Bloch.

From Andy Cox's TTA Press came four classy-looking issues of the magazine of "slipstream" fiction, *The Third Alternative*. It included stories by Michael Marshall Smith, Ian Watson, James Van Pelt, Jason Gould, Matt Coward, Mike O'Driscoll and Yvonne Navarro, interviews with Smith, Michael Moorcock and Jonathan Carroll, and the usual features and reviews by Tony Lee, Peter Crowther and Allen Ashley.

The same publisher also launched a new twice-yearly title, *Crimewave*, edited by Mat Coward and Andy Cox and devoted to crime fiction. Each perfect-bound edition included fiction from unknown writers and such well-known names as Ian Rankin, Molly Brown, Peter Crowther, Mike O'Driscoll, Steve Rasnic Tem and Tom Piccirilli.

TTA Press also published two issues of *Zene*, the writers' guide to the world's independent press. It featured guidelines for markets in Britain, Ireland, Canada, America and Australia, plus news about conventions, meetings, workshops, organizations and competitions. Writers supplied a guide to current publishers, Rhys Hughes debunked another horror cliché and also looked at zombies, Antony Mann discussed submission protocol and Paul Williams investigated the importance of research.

TTA also set up an e-mail discussion group called *Storyville1*, where anyone involved in fiction (writing, reading or publishing) and other creative media were able to get together and chat about anything that interested them. Those curious could contact tta-press@aol.com and ask to be added to the list.

The British SF fiction magazine *Odyssey*, which was launched in 1997 and edited by Liz Holliday, folded after eight issues. A failure to attract enough advertising was blamed. Canada's glossy bi-monthly *Rue Morgue Magazine*, edited by Rod Gudino, celebrated its second year of publication around Halloween. With a reported circulation of 50,000, it included a mix of news, reviews and articles about books, films and music, along with an interview with Neil Gaiman.

Patrick and Honna Swenson's quarterly digest magazine of science fiction and dark fantasy, *Talebones*, published four attractive-looking issues containing fiction and poetry from, amongst others, Larry Tritten, Hugh Cook, Mary Soon Lee, Bruce Boston and Bruce Holland Rogers; interviews with Connie Willis, Jonathan Lethem and Ed Bryant, plus review columns by Bryant, Janna Silverstein and others. Following its launch in 1998, Sherry Decker and Evelyn Gratrix's *Indigenous Fiction* released two digest-sized issues with fiction and poetry by Mike O'Driscoll, Stepan Chapman, Paul Lewis and others.

In France, the 50th issue of Marc Bailly's *Phenix: La Revue de L'Imaginaire* appeared as a special 500-plus page paperback with stories by Graham Masterton, Robert McCammon and others. Meanwhile, Daniel Conrad and Benoît Domis' *Ténèbres* reached its sixth issue with fiction from, amongst others, Ian Watson, Ramsey Campbell and Daniel Perlman, along with interviews, news and reviews.

"Black River", a novelette by Dean Koontz, appeared in Issue 63 of *Mystery Scene*. Barry Hoffman's *Gauntlet: Exploring the Limits of Free Expression* included fiction by F. Paul Wilson, along with interviews with Wilson and Neil Gaiman, plus various articles about strip clubs and exotic dancers.

The February issue of *Book and Magazine Collector* contained Richard Dalby's in-depth profile of author Basil Copper, along with a bibliography of his first editions. Matt Leyshon's *Blood from 'Stones*, published by Manchester's Waterstones bookstore, featured a number of book reviews, fiction by Simon Bestwick, Don Webb, D.F. Lewis and Tim Lebbon, articles by D.M.

Mitchell and Damon Jarry Butterworth, and interviews with Michael Marshall Smith and Stephen Jones.

The Summer issue of Florida's *Journal of the Fantastic in the Arts*, edited by W.A. Senior, included academic articles on *Dracula* and other Bram Stoker titles, plus the vampire books of Stephen King, Dan Simmons and others. *Bite Me* was a new glossy magazine aimed at vampire fans, edited by Arlene Russo and published quarterly from Scotland.

The second issue of the glossy *Bloodstone: The Magazine for Vampires* featured the bizarre world of Anne Rice, a reappraisal of the 1994 movie *Interview With the Vampire*, a six-page review of the Vampyria II convention, and an astonishing personal attack on critic and novelist Kim Newman.

As usual, the October issue of *AB Bookman's Weekly* was a tie-in with the World Fantasy Convention and included an article on James Blish by Henry Wessells.

Despite its title, Shawna McCarthy's *Realms of Fantasy* from Sovereign Media included a regular book review column by Gahan Wilson, fiction by Andy Duncan and F. Paul Wilson, articles on the new *Mummy* film and *Sleepy Hollow*, and a profile of artist Rowena Morrill. From the same publisher, Scott Edelman's *Sci-Fi Entertainment*, the official magazine of the Sci-Fi Channel, featured articles on *Virus*, *The Matrix*, *Deep Blue Sea*, *Wild Wild West*, *Stigmata*, the *Alien* series and of course *The Phantom Menace*, along with the usual *Star Trek*, *Babylon 5* and *X Files* coverage.

Frederick S. Clarke's *Cinefantastique* reverted to its bi-monthly schedule half-way through the year. Issues focused on the career of Ray Harryhausen, *Buffy the Vampire Slayer*, George Lucas, *Xena Warrior Princess*, *The Mummy*, Disney's animated *Tarzan*, *The X Files* and the latest James Bond film, *The World is Not Enough*.

Tim and Donna Lucas's bi-monthly *Video Watchdog* passed its 50th issue with all the usual fascinating reviews plus features on *The Horrible Dr. Hichcock* and the Esperanto *Incubus*, tributes to Stanley Kubrick and Oliver Reed, and a remarkable three-part examination of the life and work of low budget film-maker Andy Milligan.

Future Publishing's *SFX* passed its 50th monthly issue under editor Dave Golder with plenty of *Buffy* features, articles about tie-in novels, interviews with James Herbert, Ben Bova, Peter F. Hamilton, Angus Scrimm, Robert Rodriguez, Chris Carter, David Cronenberg and Brian Clemens, plus regular columns by David Langford and John Brosnan.

Edited by David Richardson, Visual Imagination's *Starburst* passed its 250th monthly edition along with three specials containing interviews with Dean Koontz, Iain Banks, Jonathan Carroll, Ben Bova and Brian Clemens, more features on *Buffy*, plus the inevitable articles about *Star Wars*, *Star Trek* and *The Blair Witch Project*. Meanwhile, its sister title *Shivers* also looked at *Buffy* and *Blair Witch*, along with *The Sixth Sense*, the *Psycho* and *The Mummy* remakes, plus an interview with Graham Masterton and features on modern vampires and The Boys and Girls of Horror.

The 75th edition of Michael Stein and James J.J. Wilson's always-fascinating *Filmfax: The Magazine of Unusual Film & Television* was a giant-sized issue that included a major 40th anniversary celebration of Rod Serling's *The Twilight Zone* with an article by the late Charles Beaumont and interviews with writers Richard Matheson, George Clayton Johnson and Jerry Sohl.

Jay Russell's commentary about the collapse of the market for horror fiction, "Dead and Buried", appeared in the March issue of Charles N. Brown's *Locus*, along with a welcome interview with writer and illustrator Gahan Wilson. Other interviewees in the monthly news and reviews magazine included Neil Gaiman, Jack Dann and Janeen Webb, and Frank M. Robinson. Andrew I. Porter's chatty *Science Fiction Chronicle* began the year with its 200th issue, and went on to publish another four. It included interviews with the ubiquitous Gaiman and British editor/author Jane Johnson, along with the usual news, reviews, columns and convention reports.

Necronomicon Press began the year with new issues of Robert M. Price's Lovecraftian fanzines *Crypt of Cthulhu*, *Cthulhu Codex*, *Midnight Shambler*, *Tales of Lovecraftian Horror* and *Parts* (featuring an interview with artist Richard Corben), plus S.T. Joshi's *Lovecraft Studies*. However, no new publications appeared after the summer because of the terminal illness of proprietor Marc Michaud's father.

Necrofile: The Review of Horror Fiction published only two issues edited by Stefan Dziemianowicz, Joshi and Michael A. Morrison, while *Ghoul Warnings and Other Omens . . . and Other Omens* was a revised and expanded edition of Brian Lumley's 1982 poetry collection, with new illustrations and an introduction by Donald W. Schank and a new afterword by the author. It was available in a trade paperback edition of 800 copies, a signed hardcover edition of 250 copies, and a lettered edition of 26 copies.

In the autumn Michaud announced that he was dropping the imprint's magazines in order to concentrate on books. *Lovecraft Studies* would continue as a perfect-bound annual, while David Wynn of Mythos Books was set to take over *Crypt of Cthulhu*. Despite announcing that *Necrofile* would survive as an online magazine, no further editions appeared during the year.

The prolific editorial team of Mick Sims and Len Maynard added to their publishing empire with four perfect-bound issues of *Enigmatic Tales*, featuring traditional-style ghost stories by Andrew Vachss (a reprint), Tina Rath, D.F. Lewis and Gordon Lewis, Mark McLaughlin, Rick Kennett and A.F. Kidd, Paul Finch, Ian Hunter, Peter Tennant, Steve Savile, Steven Lockley, Rhys Hughes and others (including A.M. Burrage and Jules Verne!). Along with some fine artwork by Alan Hunter and Gerald Gaubert, the best part of each issue was "Hugh Lamb's Tales from the Grave", in which the renowned British editor resurrected several forgotten stories and contributed typically knowledgeable and entertaining introductions to each of them.

Subtitled "A Magazine of Disturbing Fiction", Paul J. Lockey's quarterly *Unhinged* included stories by the ubiquitous L.H. Maynard and M.P.N. Sims, along with Peter Tennant, D.F. Lewis and others. The duo also had a story in Sue Phillips and Anna Franklin's quarterly *Strix*, along with Paul Finch, Simon Bestwick and others. However, the magazine folded with its 17th issue in November.

With stories in three out of the four issues published, the Maynard and Sims team were also regulars in Sian Ross's *Sci-Fright*, which also featured fiction and poetry by Rhys Hughes, D.F. Lewis, Paul Finch, Simon Bestwick, Peter Tennant, Steve Sneyd and Mark McLaughlin.

The first issue of Cullen Bunn's *Whispers from the Shattered*

Forum, published by Undaunted Press, contained stories and poetry by McLaughlin and others, as did the fourth issue of Jack Fisher and Matt Doeden's *Flesh & Blood*, which also featured Charlee Jacob, Mary Soon Lee, Todd French, Wendy Rathbone and others, along with an interview with Poppy Z. Brite.

The ever-busy McLaughlin also turned up in Tracy Martin's quarterly *MindMares* with an interview and story, along with Scott H. Urban, Todd French and the equally productive Charlee Jacob, who also appeared in the 11th issue of McLaughlin's own annual magazine, *The Urbanite*, which was devoted to "Strange Nourishment". Jeffrey Osier was the Featured Writer and Artist, and there was also fiction and poetry by Marni Scofidio Griffin, John Pelan, Jo Fletcher and others.

Under the editorship of David Bell, *Peeping Tom* only managed two issues in 1999. These included contributions from Ian Watson, Mark Chadbourn, Peter Tennant and Keith Brooke, Allen Ashley, and Tim Lebbon and D.F. Lewis.

Lewis also had a story in the second issue of John M. Navroth's *Midnight Carnival*, which featured a cover illustration by Pablo Picasso! From the same publisher, Pentagram Publications, came the *Masters of the Macabre 1999 Calendar*, with each month dedicated to an individual author, including Edgar A. Poe, H.P. Lovecraft, Robert Bloch, Clark Ashton Smith, August Derleth, M.R. James, Arthur Machen and Ray Bradbury.

As usual, Graeme Hurry published two perfect-bound issues of *Kimota*, which featured stories by Joel Lane, Paul Finch, Jason Gould, Steven Lockley, Peter Tennant and David J. Howe, as well as some unexpected artwork by Stephen Gallagher. Kimota Publishing also produced *Mason's Rats*, a little booklet containing three linked stories by Neal L. Asher.

California's Dark Delicacies bookstore published *Conjuring Dark Delicacies*, a ring-bound cookbook in aid of a charity caring for abused and abandoned dogs. Among those who contributed recipes were Stephen King, Richard Laymon, Tim Curry, F. Paul Wilson, Brian Hodge, Nancy Holder, Ed Bryant, Peter Atkins, Stephen Jones, Jo Fletcher, Kathy Ptacek, Jack Ketchum, Christa Faust, Simon Clark, P.D. Cacek and Lawrence Schimel. It also featured artwork from Clive Barker, Bernie Wrightson and others.

Gordon Linzner's *Space and Time* published two large-size

issues and reached its 90th edition with fiction and poetry by Charlee Jacob, Denise Dumars, Trey R. Baker, Stephen Antczak and others, along with some fine illustrations from Andrew Chase Murphy, Barb Armata, Ron Wilber, Allen Koszowski and Bruce Conklin.

One of *Space and Time*'s associate editors, Michael Laimo, was the featured author in the third issue of Shane Ryan Staley's *The Twilight Garden* with five stories, an interview and bibliography. Peggy Nadramia's *Grue Magazine* returned after a hiatus of two years with its 19th issue, featuring fiction and poetry by Wayne Allen Sallee and others.

Dale L. Sproule stepped down as editor with the 11th issue of the Canadian magazine *TransVersions*, which included fiction and poetry by Steve Sneyd, Gemma Files, James Van Pelt and others, plus an interview with James Morrow. The book review section only featured Canadian titles and authors. Darrell Schweitzer was amongst those who contributed poetry to David C. Kopaska-Merkel's *Dreams and Nightmares*.

The irregular double-magazine *Dark Regions/Horror Magazine* included fiction by Peter Crowther, P.D. Cacek, Michael Bishop and others in the *Dark Regions* portion, and interviews with Cacek and Edward Bryant in the *Horror Magazine* section, which also featured reviews.

The three latest issues of Michael Malefica Pendragon's *Penny Dreadful* (one of which was a tribute to Edgar A. Poe) contained fiction and poetry by Charles A. Gramlich, John B. Ford, D.F. Lewis, Charlee Jacob, James S. Dorr, Bruce Boston and numerous others, including the editor himself. "The White Issue" of *Vampire Dan's Story Emporium* included an interview with publisher Jim Baen, plus stories and poetry by Ken Wisman and others.

Following the collapse of Britain's Vampyre Society in 1998, Thee Vampire Guild (founded in 1990) and its magazine *Crimson* closed down in 1999. The two issues of Angela Kessler's vampire magazine *Dreams of Decadence* featured fiction and poetry by Tanith Lee and others.

From Rosemary Pardoe's Haunted Library Publications, the M.R. James-inspired *Ghosts & Scholars* featured stories and articles by Tina Rath, Steve Duffy and others, along with the excellent artwork of Douglas Walters and Paul Lowe. Pardoe also edited *The Fenstanton Witch and Others*, containing seven ghost story drafts by James (four previously published in *Ghosts & Scholars*).

The Ghost Story Society's *All Hallows*, edited by Barbara and Christopher Roden, continued to set the standard by which all society publications should be judged. The three perfect-bound issues included a Robert Aickman special, supernatural fiction by Paul Finch, Stephen Volk and others, plus the usual fascinating articles and in-depth book reviews. Unfortunately, so far as an understanding or appreciation of modern horror went, many of its contributors appeared to be trapped in a nineteenth century time-warp.

Vincent M. Harper became the latest editor of the *Horror Writers Association Newsletter*, which suffered from an irregular schedule and unattractive design.

Although Jane Prior took over the editorship from Debbie Bennett half-way through the year, the British Fantasy Society's newsletter *Prism UK* maintained it's bi-monthly schedule and published six issues filled with news and reviews, along with Chaz Brenchley's regular column, profiles of Bernard Herrmann and Jonathan Carroll, and interviews with Glenda Noramly, Stephen Laws, Nicholas Royle, Peter James, Gary Gianni, Tim Lebbon and the ever-popular Neil Gaiman. Issue 38 of the BFS' *Dark Horizons* finally appeared as a perfect-bound magazine, edited by Peter Coleborn and Mike Chinn and featuring fiction, poetry and articles by Rudy Kremberg, Anne Gay, Allen Ashley and others.

The British Fantasy Society also published *Miscellany Macabre: Tales of the Unknown* which collected ten stories (three original) and an article by bookseller Ken Cowley, nicely illustrated by David Bezzina and with an introduction by Ramsey Campbell. It was also available in a signed and numbered edition of 150 copies.

After publishing for almost a quarter of a century, academic small press imprint Borgo Press ceased operations at the end of June. In a statement, owners Robert Reginald (aka Michael Roy Burgess) and his wife Mary A. Burgess revealed that they had become "virtual slaves to the business". Borgo published 300 books since it was founded in 1974.

From Greenwood Press, *Imagining the Worst: Stephen King and the Representation of Women* was edited by Kathleen

Margaret Lant and Theresa Thompson and collected eleven critical essays about the author's treatment of women in his work. George Beahm's *Stephen King Country: The Illustrated Guide to the Sites and Sights That Inspired the Modern Master of Horror* from Running Press was exactly what the title claimed, while *Stephen King: A Reader's Checklist and Reference Guide* appeared from Checkerbee.

Children of the Night: Of Vampires and Vampirism was a study of modern-day vampires and new theories about the origin of the undead by British academic Tony Thorne. Edited by Leonard G. Heldreth and Mary Pharr, *The Blood is the Life: Vampire in Literature* from Bowling Green State University Popular Press contained eighteen critical essays about vampire fiction, including the works of Stephen King, Anne Rice, Chelsea Quinn Yarbro, S.P. Somtow and Nancy A. Collins.

Weighing in at nearly 1,000 pages, the second edition of J. Gordon Melton's *The Vampire Book* was an impressive A-Z encyclopedia of the undead, completely "revamped" by Visible Ink Press.

In *American Nightmares: The Haunted House Formula in American Popular Fiction*, also published by Bowling Green State University Popular Press, Dale Bailey took a critical look at haunted house motifs in works by Stephen King, Shirley Jackson, Edgar Allan Poe and Nathaniel Hawthorne, amongst others.

From Cornell University Press, Dan McCall's *Citizens of Somewhere Else: Nathaniel Hawthorne and Henry James* compared the work of the two authors. The University of Georgia Press's *Nursery Realms: Children in the Worlds of Science Fiction, Fantasy, and Horror* was a collection of critical essays edited by Gary Westfahl and George Slusser.

Chris Jarocha-Ernst's *A Cthulhu Mythos: Bibliography & Concordance* from Armitage House described itself as an "idiosyncratic" listing of Cthulhu Mythos fiction and poetry, which also included various letters from Lovecraft.

From Scarecrow Press, *The Haunted Mind: The Supernatural in Victorian Literature* edited by Elton E. Smith and Robert Haas was a collection of nine critical essays covering the works of Dickens, Kipling, Le Fanu, Stevenson, Wilde, Henry James, Mary Shelley and others. Also published by Scarecrow, editor Neil

Barron's *Fantasy and Horror: A Critical and Historical Guide to Literature, Illustration, Film, TV, Radio, and the Internet* ran to more than 800 pages and listed over 2,300 titles and nearly 1,000 authors. Contributors included Stefan R. Dziemianowicz, Mike Ashley, Steve Eng, Bob Morrish, Brian Stableford and Michael A. Morrison.

In Germany, Hans Joachim Alpers, Werner Fuchs and Ronald M. Hahn edited *Lexicon der Horrorliteratur* for Fantasy Publications. The 400-page encyclopedia included entries on international horror writers, the Bram Stoker Awards and German-edition series.

Published by Florida's MicroMags as a pocket-sized paperback, Cliff Linedecker's aptly-titled *Awful Horror Stories* contained thirteen purported true tales of witches, ghouls, cannibals, crazed killers, vampires and other creatures of the night – all in just seventy-two pages.

From Titan Books, Stephen Jones's *The Essential Monster Movie Guide* contained reviews of nearly 4,000 films, TV shows and videos based around ten classic monster characters, along with hundreds of mini-biographies of key actors and technicians and an extensive introduction by the legendary Forrest J Ackerman.

Also from Titan, Ken Mogg's *The Alfred Hitchcock Story* was a beautifully-designed centenary tribute to the Master of Suspense, packed with rare stills and posters (many in colour) and with an introduction by Janet Leigh. As part of the centenary celebrations, on 13 August Pat Hitchcock-O'Connell unveiled an English Heritage Blue Plaque in Cromwell Road, West London, to honour her father. Alfred Hitchcock lived in the road at No. 153 from 1926 until 1939, when he left London for America.

Kim Newman's fascinating look at Jacques Tourneur's 1943 film *Cat People* was published as part of the BFI's Film Classics series of illustrated trade paperbacks. Cynthia A. Freeland's *The Naked and the Undead: Evil and the Appeal of Horror* was a critical examination of horror movies.

From McFarland, *Women in Horror Films, 1930s* and *1940s* was a two-volume set by the knowledgeable William Gregory Mank which looked at the careers of such past scream queens as Mae Clarke, Miriam Hopkins, Gloria Stuart, Fay Wray, Elsa Lanchester, Valerie Hobson, Evelyn Ankers, Simone Simon,

Acquanetta and Gale Sondergaard. *John Carradine: The Films* was a long-overdue book-length study of the actor's sixty year career, expertly detailed by Tom Weaver.

In *Jack the Ripper: His Life and Crimes in Popular Entertainment*, Gary Coville and Patrick Luciano investigated the representations of the real-life serial killer in fiction, films and TV. *Count Dracula Goes to the Movies: Stoker's Novel Adapted, 1922–1995* by Lyndon W. Joslin was a critical study of the celluloid Count, while Lee Kovacs looked in depth at nine supernatural movies, including *Wuthering Heights*, *The Uninvited*, *Liliom* and *Ghost*, in *The Haunted Screen: Ghosts in Literature and Film*, also from McFarland.

The Buffy Chronicles was an unofficial companion to the TV series by Canadian writer N.E. Genge. Andy Meisler's *Resist or Serve: The Official Guide to the X Files* was the fourth volume in the series and a guide to the fifth season episodes.

Written by Peter Haining and profusely illustrated, *The Nine Lives of Doctor Who* was the first biography of the nine actors who played the television time-traveller.

In April, Jerry Siegel's widow Joanne Siegel and his daughter Laura Siegel filed documents with the Copyright Office in Washington which could result in DC Comics losing half the rights to the Superman character within two years.

Due to a loophole in the copyright law, Siegel's family reclaimed certain rights five months later, resulting in them sharing in 50 per cent of the revenue from products featuring Superman and related characters produced after the date of the claim. In 1938 Siegel and Joe Shuster sold DC the rights to Superman for $130.00, and it was not until 1978 that the company agreed to pay the co-creators $20,000 per year until their deaths. DC still retained half the rights held by Shuster, who left no direct heirs.

Batman: The Complete History was a follow-up to Les Daniels's equally impressive 1998 volume on Superman. The stunning full-colour tribute to the life and times of The Dark Knight was beautifully designed by Chip Kidd.

Neil Gaiman returned to *The Sandman* mythos he created with the text and graphic novel *The Dream Hunters*, based on an ancient fairy tale and illustrated by the highly stylized brushstrokes of famous Japanese artist and film animator Yoshitaka Amano. Meanwhile, Hy Bender's *The Sandman Companion* was an illustrated hardcover "Dreamer's Guide" to the award-winning comics series from DC/Vertigo. It included extensive interviews with Gaiman and asked such questions as "Why Should I Read a Comic Book?" and "Why is the Series So Long?"

Writer Joe R. Lansdale and comics artist Sam Glanzman collaborated on *Red Range*, a graphic novel series for Mojo Press, in which nineteenth century Texas avenger the Red Mask battled both the Klan and dinosaurs.

Published by Oneiros Books in trade paperback, H.P. Lovecraft's *The Haunter of the Dark and Other Grotesque Visions* collected numerous black and white illustrations and three comic-strip adaptations of Lovecraft's stories by British artist John Coulthart, with an introduction by Alan Moore.

Spectrum 6: The Best in Contemporary Fantastic Art from Underwood Books contained exactly what its title said – more than 200 pieces of full colour art chosen by a jury and edited by Cathy Fenner and Arnie Fenner. From the same imprint, *Legacy: Selected Paintings & Drawings by the Grand Master of Fantastic Art* was the second superlative selection of art by Frank Frazetta with a foreword by Danton Burroughs (the grandson of Edgar Rice), which was also published in a limited edition of 2,500 copies containing a extra 16 pages of illustrations.

For fans of Universal Studios' classic screen monsters, California's Sideshow Toy released two series of superbly detailed action figures of the Frankenstein Monster, The Mummy, The Wolf Man, The Bride of Frankenstein, The Phantom of the Opera and The Creature from the Black Lagoon, based on the likenesses of the actors who played them.

Sideshow's series of Little Big Heads also featured eight of the classic Universal monsters, along with four caricature figures from *The Munsters* and two from *Bride of Chucky*. The company's Monster Shredders featured Dracula, The Mummy, The Creature from the Black Lagoon, The Invisible Man and the Frankenstein Monster with skateboards, and there were also bobbing head versions as well.

From the Cartoon Network and Equity Marketing came a set of *Scooby-Doo!* bendable figures featuring Scooby, Shaggy,

Velma, Daphne and Fred, while the collectible action figures included two Scoobys, Shaggy and Velma.

Apparently, you *can* fool most of the people most of the time. The premise of *The Blair Witch Project*, described as "the scariest horror film ever made", was that in 1994 three documentary film-makers set out to investigate the eponymous legend and found themselves lost in the Maryland woods and possibly menaced by unseen forces (evidenced by bundles of sticks and small piles of stones). Shot on Hi-8 video and 16 mm for just $40,000, and improvised by the three actors/cinematographers based on instructions left for them by student film-makers Daniel Race Myrick and Eduardo Sanchez, the film quickly passed the $130 million mark at the American box office. In Britain it took $1.2 million during its opening weekend on just thirty-six screens, resulting in the highest ever per screen average for a nationwide release in the UK.

Despite the "lost film" conceit (previously utilized in such movies as *Cannibal Holocaust* [1979] and *The Last Broadcast* [1997]), some very clever marketing on the Internet, and the relentless hype generated by its premier at the 1999 Sundance Film Festival, *The Blair Witch Project* was neither very scary nor very interesting. Nothing much happened, even less was explained, and the viewer was left with a trio of whining protagonists who simply were not worth caring about. However, due to its phenomenal success, anyone with a camcorder who had read M.R. James or H.P. Lovecraft were soon out there shooting for their chance to become a millionaire, while Hollywood announced a sequel, a prequel and a possible big-budget remake. Emperor's new clothes anyone?

Amongst the spoofs and pastiches which followed the surprise success of *The Blair Witch Project* were the softcore video release *The Erotic Witch Project* and a short entitled *The Blair Fish Project*. Meanwhile, an independent Florida producer named Sam Barber claimed that he was cheated out of an executive producer's credit on *Blair Witch* but failed in his attempt to get an injunction against the film's distributor, Artisan Entertainment, who purchased the worldwide rights for just $1 million.

The other most overrated film of 1999 was *The Matrix*. In this admittedly flashy but conceptually empty sci-fi thriller, written and directed by the Wachowski brothers, Keanu Reeves was even more wooden than usual as a new Messiah plugged into the eponymous alternate reality where he ended up battling sinister men in sunglasses in beautifully choreographed fight sequences. At least Josef Rusnak's *The 13th Floor* had a plot, as Vincent D'Onofrio investigated a murder mystery in a 1937 virtual reality world.

Renny Harlin's *Deep Blue Sea* was much more fun, as three giant genetically-mutated intelligent sharks menaced survivors of a storm-wrecked ocean laboratory and gobbled up Samuel L. Jackson. Scientist Bridget Fonda discovered that a giant crocodile was chewing up the locals in Steve Miner's *Lake Placid*, knowingly scripted by TV's David E. Kelley.

In Japan, four years after Toho announced that it was retiring its biggest star, Takao Okawara's *Godzilla 2000: Millennium* revived the fortunes of the original Godzilla and wiped away the memory of Roland Emmerich's 1998 pretender.

Writer/director Stephen Sommers' $80,000,000 "re-imagining" of *The Mummy* had Brendan Fraser's likeable mercenary hired to lead an expedition to a lost city, where he unwittingly released Imhotep (Arnold Vosloo), a vengeful 3,000 year-old Egyptian high priest who planned to unleash ten plagues upon the world. The action-packed adventure easily passed $250 million in worldwide box office takings.

Loosely based on the story by Washington Irving, *Sleepy Hollow* starred Johnny Depp as timid New York constable Ichabod Crane who used eighteenth century science and reason to investigate a series of beheadings by a supernatural headless horseman. Beautifully designed and directed, Tim Burton's homage to Hammer horror (and the late Mario Bava) included cameos by Christopher Lee, Michael Gough and an uncredited Martin Landau.

Tom Hanks headed an impressive ensemble cast in Frank Darabont's three-hour adaptation of *The Green Mile*, based on Stephen King's six-part novel. Set in a Louisiana prison during the Depression, convicted child-killer John Coffey (Oscar-nominated Michael Clarke Duncan) brought magic into the lives of everyone on death row, including a mouse. Amy Irving recreated her supporting role for Katt Shea's *The Rage: Carrie 2*, a belated and unnecessary sequel to the 1976 original, starring Emily

Bergl as the new telekinetic terror, based on characters created by King.

Peter Hyams' *End of Days* was a silly Millennial horror movie in which Arnold Schwarzenegger's washed-up New York cop attempted to stop Gabriel Byrne's smoothly villainous Devil from impregnating a woman before the new century and fulfilling a prophecy which would trigger the Apocalypse. Byrne was also playing on the other team when, much to the church's consternation, Patricia Arquette's Pittsburgh hairdresser began displaying mysterious wounds in Rupert Wainwright's flashy *Stigmata*.

However, His Satanic Majesty's lowest point probably came in his scene with Saddam Hussein in the animated *South Park: Bigger, Longer & Uncut*, based on the popular TV series.

Director Joel Schumacher introduced Nicholas Cage's investigator to the world of snuff movies and hardcore porn in the ludicrous *8 mm*, scripted by Andrew Kevin Walker of *Se7en* fame. Russell Mulcahy's grim serial killer thriller *Resurrection* starred co-producer Christopher Lambert as a Chicago detective hunting for a crazed murderer who amputated a limb from each victim as he attempted to recreate the figure of Christ on the cross. David Cronenberg had a cameo as a sympathetic priest.

Cronenberg's own *eXistenZ* was nowhere near as clever as it thought it was. Set in the near future, Jude Law's naïve young marketing executive found himself protecting unlikely games creator Jennifer Jason Leigh in the bio-mechanical reality she created. Unfortunately, the game-within-a-game scenario was obvious from early on, and the director clumsily telegraphed most of the plot "surprises".

The same could not be said of M. Night Shyamalan, whose low-key supernatural mystery *The Sixth Sense* not only managed to make audiences jump, but also boasted the most unexpected twist ending of the year. Despite taking nearly $300 million at the US box office and featuring terrific performances from Haley Joel Osment as the eight-year-old who could see ghosts and Bruce Willis as a strangely subdued child psychologist, it was still a surprise when the film was nominated for six Academy Awards.

Based on the short novel by Richard Matheson, David Koepp's atmospheric low-key thriller *Stir of Echoes* featured Kevin Bacon as a Chicago telephone lineman who started seeing the spirit of a murdered girl after he was hypnotized. Despite a low budget, it was certainly better than Jan De Bont's remake of *The Haunting*, based on the classic book by Shirley Jackson, which replaced the scares with computer-generated effects and wasted an interesting cast that included Liam Neeson, Catherine Zeta-Jones and Lili Taylor.

House on Haunted Hill was a fun remake of William Castle's 1959 "B" movie, in which Geoffrey Rush's amusement park mogul Stephen Price invited five strangers to an old insane asylum with the promise of $1 million each if they survived the night. Jeffrey Combs turned up as the evil spirit of a demented doctor.

Devon Sawa played a slacker teen possessed by a homicidal hand in Rodman Flender's *Idle Hands*, yet another variation on *The Beast With Five Fingers*. Meanwhile, the man who started the teen slasher revival, Kevin Williamson, decided to turn down scripting the second *Scream* sequel to make his directing début on the dark thriller *Teaching Mrs. Tingle*, which quickly disappeared from theatres. The title had been pointlessly changed from *Killing Mrs. Tingle* in the wake of the Columbine High School shootings.

Antonio Banderas's 10th century Arab nobleman found himself teamed with a group of Norse warriors and Omar Sharif to battle cannibals in John McTiernan's *The 13th Warrior*, based on the 1976 novel *Eaters of the Dead* by Michael Crichton. Robert Carlyle arrived at a remote nineteenth century military base in the Sierra Nevada and began eating the inhabitants in the aptly-titled *Ravenous*.

A number of people, including John Cusack and Cameron Diaz, found themselves in the eponymous actor's head in Spike Jonze's surreal *Being John Malkovich*.

French actor Patrick Timsit co-scripted and directed *Quasimodo d'el Paris*, a contemporary comedy inspired by Victor Hugo's novel, about a serial killer and a plot to turn kidnapped women into gargoyles.

Writer/director Rand Ravich's *The Astronaut's Wife* was a silly riff on both *I Married a Monster from Outer Space* and *Rosemary's Baby* as Johnny Depp's NASA astronaut returned from a mission changed, and his pregnant wife (Charlize Theron) discovered that she was carrying telepathic alien twins who were preparing for an insidious invasion of the Earth.

Based on the Dark Horse comic book series, *Virus* was a fun SF/horror thriller that had its release delayed and quickly disappeared at the box office. When the crew of a cargo tug took refuge on an apparently abandoned Soviet military ship, they discovered an alien lifeform creating a deadly army of cyborgs with which to wipe out humanity.

Ignoring two cable TV movie spin-offs, Jean-Claude Van Damme returned as zombie soldier Luc Devreux in *Universal Soldier The Return*, a belated theatrical sequel to the 1992 original.

Supposedly based on the 1960s sci-spy TV series, Barry Sonnenfield's bloated comedy Western *Wild Wild West* was all special effects and no story. The family of TV scriptwriter Gilbert Ralston, who died in the spring, claimed that he had created all the elements of the series and filed a law suit against CBS and Warner Bros.

Once again proving that putting the author's name into the title is the kiss of death, writer/director Michael Hoffman couldn't resist tinkering with *William Shakespeare's A Midsummer Night's Dream*, moving the action to nineteenth century Tuscany and having his entire star cast perform as if they were in a children's pantomime.

Despite all the anticipation surrounding George Lucas's long-awaited $116 million prequel to his 1977–83 trilogy, it could never live up to the hype and audience expectation. However, *Star Wars Episode 1 The Phantom Menace* was neither as good as it should have been nor as bad as had been expected. In fact, it turned out to be a lively space opera in which Liam Neeson's Jedi master and his apprentice Ewan McGregor helped Natalie Portman's young queen save her planet from Ray Park's evil Darth Maul.

The animated *Pokémon The First Movie* was impossible for anyone over the age of twelve to understand.

The year's five top-grossing films at the US box office were all genre titles: *Star Wars Episode 1 The Phantom Menance*, *The Sixth Sense*, *Austin Powers The Spy Who Shagged Me*, *The Matrix* and Disney's animated *Tarzan*.

At the Oscars in March, Bill Condon won the Best Adapted Screenplay for *Gods and Monsters*. While in October, 2,000 readers of Britain's *Total Film* magazine voted for their 25 Scariest Movies Ever. *The Exorcist* came top, followed by *Halloween*, *The Shining*, *A Nightmare on Elm Street* and *Scream*. Other notable entries were the 1963 *The Haunting* (7th), the

1960 *Psycho* (8th), *Hellraiser* (16th) and the 1968 *Night of the Living Dead* (23rd).

According to composer Lord Andrew Lloyd-Webber, his 1986 musical of *The Phantom of the Opera* became the most commercially successful entertainment of the twentieth century when worldwide ticket sales passed $3 billion. The album of the stage show had already sold 25 million copies.

Dario Argento's disappointing version of *The Phantom of the Opera*, starring an unscarred Julian Sands, was finally released on video and DVD in America.

Talos the Mummy was a $10 million "B" movie directed by Russell Mulcahy as a tribute to Hammer and the work of Ray Harryhausen. The impressive supporting cast included Honor Blackman, Shelley Duvall and Christopher Lee.

In Michael Almereyda's *The Eternal*, Christopher Walken played a mad Irishman trying to revive a 2,000-year-old shape-shifting Druid witch. John Franklin reprised his role as Isaac from the 1984 original in Kari Skogland's *Children of the Corn 666*, starring Nancy Allen and Stacy Keach, and a government team investigated a slaughter at a scientific outpost in *Lycanthrope – Pray for Sunrise*, starring co-producer Robert Carradine.

Carnival of Souls was a creepy, atmospheric reworking of the 1962 original in which the line between reality and nightmare blurred for Bobbie Phillips's bar owner as she was menaced by a demonic clown (comedian Larry Miller). Wes Craven and Anthony Hickox were among the executive producers.

Filmed in South Africa, *From Dusk Till Dawn 2: Texas Blood Money* was a direct-to-video follow-up to the 1996 original, in which a band of robbers planning a bank heist didn't know that their leader had been bitten by one of the undead. Bruce Campbell and Tiffany Amber-Thiesen turned up in a fun opening sequence which had nothing to do with the rest of the movie, which was executive produced by Quentin Tarantino and Robert Rodriguez, amongst others.

Modern Vampires (aka *Revenant*) was yet another failed attempt by director/co-producer Richard Elfman to make a coherent movie. Featuring Casper Van Dien, Natasha Gregson Wagner, Kim Cattrall, Robert Pastorelli, Udo Kier, and Rod

Steiger as an obsessed Van Helsing, rarely had such an impressive cast given such uniformly terrible performances.

Laughing Dead was an impressive-looking independent feature, written and directed by Patrick Gleason and set in a diseased post-apocalyptic Los Angeles populated by cannibalistic mutants and controlled by an ages-old vampire who had transformed the city into a human slaughterhouse.

Filmed in Britain by director Elisar Cabrera, *Witchcraft Mistress of the Craft* was the tenth episode in the low budget, softcore video franchise and the first to be shot outside America. The awful Eileen Daly played a vampire who teamed up with a Satanic serial killer to bring a demon to Earth. *Titanic 2000 Vampire of the Titanic* was an erotic horror video set aboard the new cruise ship, where Tammy Parks' undead lesbian attempted to seduce Tina Krause into becoming her eternal soulmate. The untalented Krause also read two stories from a cursed book in the independent release, *The Vampire's Curse*, the second of which involved a search for the tomb of Vlad the Impaler.

Independent erotic video *Vampire Carmilla* was an updated version of J. Sheridan Le Fanu's novella, while *Caress of the Vampire 3 Lust of the Night Stalker* was a softcore sequel to the 1997 original, in which an undercover Florida police officer hunted for a 200 year-old alien vampire serial killer.

Universal's cartoon feature *Alvin and the Chipmunks Meet Frankenstein* involved Alvin, Simon and Theodore encountering the real Dr Frankenstein and his Monster in a movie studio attraction.

Over 23–24 October at London's Royal Festival Hall, the Kronos Quartet performed Philip Glass's new music score for the 1931 film version of *Dracula*, which appeared on new prints of the film released on both video and DVD.

Writer/director David J. Skal created a number of documentary supplements to accompany the reissue on DVD of such classic Universal movies as *Frankenstein*, *Bride of Frankenstein*, *Dracula*, *The Wolf Man* and *The Mummy*. These fascinating extras included contributions from Donald F. Glut, Rick Baker, Sara Karloff, Christopher Bram, Bill Condon, Clive Barker, the late Ivan Butler, John Landis, Curt Siodmak and many others. Skal and Sam Irvin also produced a half-hour supplement for the DVD of *Gods and Monsters*, featuring interviews with Ian

McKellen, Brendan Fraser, Lynn Redgrave, Gloria Stewart, Curtis Harrington, Bill Condon, Clive Barker and Christopher Bram.

The appointment of a new film and video censor in Britain resulted is *The Texas Chainsaw Massacre* being passed uncut after twenty-five years and released nationwide, while the film which started the so-called "Video Nasty" purge in the UK, Abel Ferrara's 1979 production *The Driller Killer*, was finally re-released on video.

The first in producer Val Lewton's series of stylish low budget "B" movies for RKO, *Cat People* (1942), and its marvellously poetic sequel-of-sorts, *The Curse of the Cat People* (1944), were reissued on a welcome double-bill in British cinemas.

In a totally different class, Quentin Tarantino's Rolling Thunder Pictures re-released an uncut version of the 1977 opus *Mighty Peking Man* (aka *Goliathon*) for midnight screenings across America.

Shown in three two-hour segments, Stephen King's latest TV mini-series *Storm of the Century* was billed as an "original novel for television". Colm Feore played the demonic stranger who arrived on a remote island off the New England coast during a massive snow storm and started killing the locals until they gave him what he wanted.

The Turn of the Screw was director Ben Bolt's heavy-handed TV movie based on the often-filmed story by Henry James, in which an impressionable young governess (Jodhi May) believed that her two secretive charges were under the corrupting influence of the ghosts of a pair of dead lovers.

Tony Marchant's *Bad Blood* was an overwrought mini-series directed by Tim Fywell and shown in three one-hour episodes on British TV. Desperate to adopt a child, infertile British heart surgeon Joe Harker (Alex Jennings) and his wife travelled to Romania, where their adoption of three year-old Valentin resulted in Joe apparently being possessed by evil.

Based on the novel *Alchemist* by Peter James, *The Alchemists* was a dull two-part genetic engineering thriller involving a drug which created cyclopic new-born babies. Much more engrossing was *Doomwatch: Winter Angel*, a TV movie based on the 1970s sci-fact series created by Kit Pedler and Gerry Davies. Trevor Eve played a scientist who discovered that an energy corporation would not stop at murder to protect the first man-made black hole.

Despite an all-star voice cast that included Kelsey Grammer, Ian Holm, Patrick Stewart and Peter Ustinov, it was the animatronic effects created by Jim Henson's Creature Shop which were the real stars of John Stephenson's new version of George Orwell's nightmarish *Animal Farm*.

Filmed in Australia, *Sabrina Down Under* was the third in an "alternative" series of TV movies in which the teenage witch (again played by producer Melissa Joan Hart) discovered a colony of merfolk living in a remote lagoon.

Although star David Duchovny threatened to sue Twentieth Century Fox and creator Chris Carter for what he claimed were millions of dollars in unpaid royalties, *The X Files* kicked off its seventh season with a story involving an alien spacecraft discovered on the West African coast which could create blank-eyed zombies. More traditional members of the walking dead were featured in a scary episode set on the eve of the new Millennium, in which FBI agents Mulder (Duchovny) and Scully (Gillian Anderson) consulted with former profiler Frank Black (played by Lance Henrikson, who reprised his role from Carter's cancelled *Millennium* series). In another episode, the duo encountered Andrew J. Robinson's cryptozoologist who had been bitten by an apparently extinct Chinese dog and turned into a murderous shapeshifter. Carter's new SF series *Harsh Realm* was cancelled by the Fox Network after just three episodes, leaving a further five episodes completed but unaired.

Following April's Littleton High School massacre in Colorado, the second part of the season finale of *Buffy the Vampire Slayer* was pulled from TV screens in America, along with Nancy Holder's novelization, *The Evil That Men Do*. The episode was eventually screened in July. During the show's third season, Buffy (Sarah Michelle Gellar) and Willow (Alyson Hannigan) went to college, where the teenage vampire-hunter fell in love with a soldier (Marc Blucas) from a covert organization of demon-hunters, werewolf Oz (Seth Green) betrayed Willow with another lycanthrope, a scientist created a patchwork monster from human and demon parts, and James Marsters's sardonic vampire Spike became a series regular.

Creator Joss Whedon's spin-off series *Angel* had the tortured vampire (David Boreanaz) move to Los Angeles, where he teamed up with Cordelia (Charisma Carpenter) and demonic guardian angel Doyle (Glenn Quinn) to save the souls of others. Other *Buffy* regulars guest-starred in various episodes.

During the truncated final season of *Hercules the Legendary Journeys*, Kevin Sorbo's Greek muscleman discovered that his old comrade Prince Vlad was actually the king of the vampires and wanted Hercules's blood to make himself more powerful.

Created by brothers Jonas and Josh Pate, *GvsE* was a quirky comedy series in which Clayton Rohner's murdered journalist returned to Earth to battle human-looking demons known as "Morlocks" and save lost souls in Hollywood.

An investigation into a series of apparent vampire slayings around St Valentine's Day lead Nancy Anne Sakovich into the clutches of husband-and-wife bloodsuckers in an episode of the Canadian series *PSI Factor Chronicles of the Paranormal*. In the Canadian teen series *Big Wolf on Campus*, Brandon Quinn's high school senior was bitten by a wolf and transformed into a pointy-eared lycanthrope during extreme situations. Anybody remember *Teen Wolf* (1985)?

The three magical Halliwell sisters, Prue (Shannen Doherty), Piper (Holly Marie Combs) and Phoebe (Alyssa Milano), en-countered a cursed Egyptian urn, a lycanthropic shapeshifter, the ghost of a murder victim, a photographer who remained youthful by draining the life-force from young women, and various evil warlocks and demons in the always charming *Charmed*.

The Christmas episode of the British police procedural series *The Bill* involved an all-night stakeout in a reputedly haunted pumping station and an encounter with a murder victim from the 1950s. In the UK police series *Taggart*, a Scottish spiritualist contacted the spirit world and apparently received helpful advice from the long-dead Taggart, much to the surprise of his colleagues.

The wonderful Diana Rigg starred in *The Mrs Bradley Mysteries*, a short-lived BBC series based on the detective/mystery novels by Gladys Mitchell. As high society sleuth Adela Bradley, she investigated sightings of a ghostly soldier and unmasked a killer who was the disciple of a Satanic cult leader.

In the two-part *Star Trek Voyager* episode "Dark Frontier", Captain Janeway (Kate Mulgrew) and her crew were caught in a trap set by the creepy Borg Queen to assimilate Seven of Nine (Jeri Ryan). *Total Recall 2070* was a futuristic detective series that owed more of its setting, characters and plot to *Blade Runner* than it did to the 1990 film it was named after. Even worse, Philip K. Dick wasn't even credited!

Based on a series of young adult books, *Roswell* (aka *Roswell High*) concerned the adventures of three alien teenagers and their friends living in the desert town of the title. William Sadler played the suspicious local sheriff and guest stars included executive producer Jonathan Frakes and Carroll Baker.

In Disney's *So Weird*, Cara DeLizia played fourteen-year-old computer whiz Fiona Phillips, who travelled across America on board a tour bus with her rock star mother and used her web page to investigate paranormal and supernatural encounters. These included a young girl who turned out to be a red-eyed werewolf. Henry Winkler made an appearance as a ghost and was also one of several co-executive producers.

In the third season of the Canadian/German series *Lexx*, the motley crew of the intelligent insectoid spaceship travelled around the universe and ended up on a planet of the walking dead. More blank-eyed zombies turned up in the British comedy sitcom *Spaced*, about a pair of mismatched flatmates.

Based on the novel by Robert Heinlein and the 1997 movie, *Roughnecks: Starship Troopers Chronicles* was a stunning-looking computer-animated series aimed at children. Paul Verhoeven was co-executive producer on some episodes. *Roswell Conspiracies Aliens, Myths & Legends* was a confusing cartoon series with the premise that aliens had been on Earth for centuries and were the basis for such myths and legends as vampires, lycanthropes and zombies.

Mona the Vampire was a cartoon series based on the series of children's books by Sonia Holleyman, about an imaginative ten year-old schoolgirl who liked to dress up as one of the undead. *Sabrina, the Animated Series* was another cartoon series for young children, in which Melissa Joan Hart voiced Aunt Hilda and Aunt Zelda, and her sister Emily played Sabrina.

In the animated *Sherlock Holmes in the 22nd Century*, the consulting detective was brought back to life in New London in 2103. Episodes were based on "The Valley of Fear" and *The Hound of the Baskervilles* by Sir Arthur Conan Doyle.

The Simpsons episode "Thirty Minutes Over Tokyo" featured the dysfunctional family being attacked by giant Japanese monsters Godzilla, Mothra, Gamera and Rodan, while Bart dressed up as a vampire. *Star Trek*'s George Takei was the special guest voice. In "The Simpsons Halloween Special X", Marge accidently ran over Ned Flanders, who turned out to be a werewolf; Bart and Lisa were exposed to X-rays and became superheroes, and Homer's failure to fix the Y2K bug resulted in the end of the world. The guest voice was *Xena* star Lucy Lawless.

The irreverent *South Park* included a boxing match between Jesus and Satan, and a Halloween episode involving ghostly pirates. The Halloween episode of MTV's clay animation comedy show *Celebrity Deathmatch* featured a wrestling match between Frankenstein's Monster and the Wolfman.

The Sci-Fi Channel's *Curse of the Blair Witch* was an hour-long spoof documentary from the writers/directors of *The Blair Witch Project* which purported to investigate the "true" Maryland legend through fake interviews, TV reports and newsreel footage. Presented and scripted by deadpan radio dj Mark Kermode from a dark wood, *The Blair Witch Phenomenon* was a Channel 4 documentary which looked at the hype surrounding the film when it was released in the UK in October.

"Escape from Witch Island" was a *Blair Witch*-inspired episode of the teenage soap opera *Dawson's Creek*, created by Kevin Williamson.

The busy Mark Kermode also interviewed a surprisingly candid John Carpenter for the BBC documentary *The Night He Came Home: John Carpenter's Halloween*, which celebrated the film's 30th anniversary.

Andy Starke and Pete Tombs created a series of fascinating documentaries which were shown as part of Channel 4's low budget *Eurotika!* season of exploitation films. With each half-hour show devoted to such subjects as British director Michael Reeves; Spanish film-makers Jess Franco, José Ramòn Larraz and Paul Naschy; French director Jean Rollin; Italian film-makers such as Mario Bava, Renato Polselli, Dario Argento and Lucio Fulci; and mad doctors in European horror films; amongst those interviewed were Franco, Larraz, Naschy, Rollin, Polselli, Ian Ogilvy, Ian Sinclair, Tony Tenser, Michel Lemoine, Peter Blumenstock, Monica Swinn, Brigitte Lahaie, Kim Newman, Erika

Blanc, Luigi Cozzi, Amando de Ossorio, Jorge Grau, Caroline Munro and many others.

Ray Harryhausen created his first new stop-motion sequence in twenty years for the Channel 4 documentary *Working With Dinosaurs: The Stop-Motion World of Ray Harryhausen*, in which the master animator discussed his career along with tributes from many of his contemporaries, friends and fans, including James Cameron, Dennis Muren, Stan Winston, Forrest Ackerman, Joe Dante, Prof. Christopher Frayling, Charles H. Schneer and John Phillip Law. It was narrated by Tom Baker.

Over five days in October, Universal Studios' New Media Department presented *Stage Fright: The Haunting of Stage 13* on the Internet. In *Blair Witch* style, it presented footage, photos and documents recently discovered by a pair of independent film historians which detailed the troubled production of a silent version of *Carmilla* and the legendary ghost of its female star. There was even a live webcast from the site of the actress's supposed death.

Ramsey Campbell received the Grand Master Award at the World Horror Convention 1999, held over 4–7 March in Atlanta, Georgia. The convention, whose other Guests of Honour included authors John Shirley and Michael Bishop, artist Lisa Snellings and Toastmaster Neil Gaiman, attracted more registrations than any previous WHC.

The fifth annual International Horror Guild Awards were also presented by Gaiman at the WHC convention on 6 March. The winners were *Fog Heart* by Thomas Tessier in the Novel category; a tie between Michael Marano's *Dawn Song* and Caitlín R. Kiernan's *Silk* for First Novel; John Shirley's *Black Butterflies* for Collection, and *Dark Terrors 4* edited by Stephen Jones and David Sutton for outstanding achievement in the Anthology category. Peter Straub's "Mr. Club and Mr. Cuff" (from *Murder for Revenge*) won for Long Form; Lucy Taylor's "Dead Blue" (from *Imagination Fully Dilated*) won for Short Form, and the Nonfiction award went to *The St. James Guide to Horror, Ghosts & Gothic Writers* edited by David Pringle. DC/Vertigo Comics' *Transmetropolitan: Back on the Street* by Warren Ellis and Darick Robertson won in the Graphic Story/Stories category; David B. Silva and Paul F. Olson's weekly e-zine *Hellnotes* won for Publication, and the Artist award went to Edward Gorey. Bill Condon's *Gods and Monsters* was voted top in the Movie category and *Buffy the Vampire Slayer* beat out the competition for Television. IHG judge Hank Wagner announced Ray Bradbury's Living Legend Award.

(Bradbury himself suffered a mild stroke in November, but after experiencing temporary paralysis on his right side was expected to make a full recovery.)

The 1999 Bram Stoker Awards honouring Superior Achievement in Horror During 1998 were announced on 5 June by the Horror Writers Association in Hollywood, California. Bill Condon's *Gods and Monsters* and Alex Proyas' *Dark City* tied for Screenplay; Nancy Etchemendy's story "Bigger Than Death" (from *Cricket*) won Work for Young Readers, and the Nonfiction award went to Paula Guran's e-zine, *DarkEcho*. The Anthology award was presented to *Horrors! 365 Scary Stories* edited by Stefan Dziemianowicz, Martin H. Greenberg and Robert Weinberg; John Shirley's *Black Butterflies* picked up Collection and Bruce Holland Rogers' "The Dead Boy at Your Window" (from *The North American Review*) was honoured in Short Fiction. Peter Straub's "Mr. Clubb and Mr. Cuff" won again in the Long Fiction category, Michael Marano's *Dawn Song* collected First Novel, and the Novel winner was *Bag of Bones* by Stephen King. Bram Stoker Awards for Life Achievement went to Roger Corman (who sent a video-taped acceptance) and Ramsey Campbell, and the HWA trustees also honoured Barry Hoffman of Gauntlet Press with the Specialty Press Award. No Awards were presented in the Illustrated Narrative and Other Media categories.

Edgar Allan Poe: Illustrations of a Tormented Mind was an international festival commemorating the 150th anniversary of the author's death, held in the Czech city of Prague from 3 August until 30 October. Organized by The Edgar Allan Poe Society of Prague, the ambitious event included paintings and illustrations; many rare books, manuscripts and signed editions; exhibits, theatre, opera and films.

The fourth NecronomiCon returned to Providence, Rhode Island, over 20–22 August with author Fred Chappell, publisher W. Paul Ganley and artist Jason Eckhardt as Guests of Honour. Despite some problems with the organization, this Lovecraft-inspired gathering included the usual talks, panels and readings, along with a Lovecraft exhibit at the John Hay Library, a walking tour of College Hill, and former Baptist minister Robert M. Price's Sunday Cthulhu prayer breakfast.

The 1998 British Fantasy Awards were presented at Fantasy-Con XXIII in Birmingham over 17–19 September. Guests of Honour were Louise Cooper, Raymond E. Feist, Graham Masterton, Robert Rankin and Mike Tucker. Stephen King's *Bag of Bones* won The August Derleth Award for Best Novel, Best Anthology was *Dark Terrors 4* edited by Stephen Jones and David Sutton, and Ramsey Campbell's *Ghosts and Grisly Things* was voted Best Collection. Stephen Laws's "The Song My Sister Sang" (from *Scaremongers 2: Redbrick Eden*) collected Best Short Fiction, Bob Covington was voted Best Artist and Andy Cox's *The Third Alternative* picked up the Best Small Press award. The Karl Edward Wagner special award went to Diana Wynne Jones.

To mark the 20th anniversary of Rosemary Pardoe's *Ghosts & Scholars* magazine, a M.R. James Weekend was held in Rochester, Kent, over 30–31 October. Prof. Christopher Frayling was the Guest of Honour, and the event included talks, a quiz and a mini-auction.

Although The 25th World Fantasy Convention returned to its spiritual home of Providence, Rhode Island, over 4–7 November, there was a distinct lack of things Lovecraftian. This was reflected in the choice of Robert Silverberg, Patricia A. McKillip, artists Leo and Diane Dillon, and Charles De Lint as Guests of Honour; Samuel R. Delany as Special Guest, and John M. Ford as Toastmaster. In the World Fantasy Awards, the Best Novel award went to *The Antelope Wife* by Louise Erdrich, Best Novella was Ian R. MacLeod's "The Summer Isles" (from *Asimov's*), and the Best Short Story was "The Specialist's Hat" by Kelly Link (from *Event Horizon*). Karen Joy Fowler's *Black Glass* was voted Best Collection, the Best Anthology award went to *Dreaming Down Under* edited by Jack Dann and Janeen Webb, and Charles Vests was voted Best Artist. The late Jim Turner was given the Special Award – Professional for Golden Gryphon Press, and Richard Chizmar received the Special Award – Non-Professional for Cemetery Dance Publications. The Life Achievement award went to Hugh B. Cave.

California book dealer Barry R. Levin announced his 12th Annual Collectors Awards, with Neal Stephenson and Avon Books winning the Collectors Award for 1999 as Most Collectable Author of the Year and Most Collectable Book of the Year (for the limited edition of Stephenson's *Cryptonomicon*), respectively. Mathew D. Hargreaves was presented with the special Lifetime Collectors Award for His Outstanding Bibliographic Contributions to the Study of the Works of Anne McCaffrey.

According to a panel at the 1999 Frankfurt Book Fair, there are only five years left for traditional publishing and bookselling. After that, the process of producing physical books will have to radically change or else become extinct. Meanwhile, Microsoft optimistically predicts that by the year 2020, 90 per cent of all books will be sold in electronic format. Of course, Microsoft would say that, wouldn't they?

But as the world enters a new Millennium, there is no question that publishing is changing. During the final decades of the 1990s, cheaper printing costs and the growth in home technology resulted in a proliferation of so-called small press publishers.

Of course, that was nothing new in the genre of fantastic literature. Ever since the early days of science fiction fandom there had been mimeographed magazines and booklets produced on stencils. Arkham House was one of the first specialist hardcover publishers, created by August Derleth and Donald Wandrei in 1939 to keep the work of H.P. Lovecraft in print. Their first book, the Lovecraft collection *The Outsider and Others*, was published in a hardcover edition of 1,200 copies and at $5.00 it took many years to sell out. However, that did not dissuade other specialist imprints such as Fantasy Press, Gnome Press and Shasta from springing up, and by the 1970s and '80s there were a multitude of small publishers (albeit mostly American) producing some very handsome volumes, often in signed, numbered and limited editions.

Unfortunately the propagation of these limited volumes, coupled with the increased cost of many so-called "collectible" editions being bought up by speculators (who justifiably found themselves stuck with titles which were not increasing in value and which they could no longer sell), resulted in a collapse of the market at the end of the 1980s. It is probably just a coincidence that this depreciation also mirrored the boom and bust which the commercial horror field was going through at the same time.

Yet, ironically, it was the small press which came to the rescue of the moribund horror genre. At a time when mass-market publishers on both sides of the Atlantic were frantically culling their horror lines and thus neatly supporting their own self-created collapse of the field, small press imprints such as Cemetery Dance Publications, Subterranean Press, Fedogan & Bremer, Gauntlet Press, Mark V. Ziesing, Tanjen, Pumpkin Books, Overlook Connection Press, Terminal Fright Press, Silver Salamander Press and myriad others, including the venerable Arkham House, stepped in to publish many of those horror authors who suddenly found themselves orphaned by their editors, and allowed some of the new and upcoming writers an opportunity to appear in book-form for the first time.

Because of their relatively low overheads and a desire to issue the type of books which they wanted to see published, these smaller imprints were also willing to take risks – to produce anthologies and single author collections, which the big publishers had mostly ignored, along with shorter chapbooks and novellas.

It is arguable whether all the books produced by these new imprints deserved publication, and far too often such basic considerations as editing and design were overlooked in favour of Big Names and a bewildering selection of different limited formats. Yet despite the emergence of an apparent small press horror mafia (you publish my book and I'll publish yours; you blurb my book and I'll blurb yours; you vote for me and I'll vote for you . . .), many of these volumes were handsome productions and there were numerous worthy works which only saw publication in these limited editions.

The other trend to emerge from the independent imprints in the 1990s was the reissuing of "classic" collections of supernatural fiction from the nineteenth and early-twentieth century. Ash-Tree Press, Tartarus Press, Sarob Press and others began rediscovering out-of-print authors and bringing their long-forgotten or barely anthologised stories back into print. Despite the dedicated work of such editors as Hugh Lamb, Richard Dalby, Jack Adrian and Mark Valentine, to name only a few, it was often obvious why some of this fiction had stayed out of circulation for so long. Much of it had little affiliation to modern horror fiction, nor could it all be considered worth preserving between expensive hardcovers. Also, while these books flooded the limited edition horror market, they were also effectively squeezing out new and original titles by contemporary authors. Any market – even the small press market – can only support so much until it collapses under its own weight. After all, that is exactly what had happened to mass-market horror back in the 1980s.

The problem was that with the proliferation of home computers and cheap printing anybody could set themselves up as a publisher, whether they had any skill or not. Soon writers who had never bothered to hone their craft through training and experience were churning out their own novels, collections, chapbooks and anthologies in often cheap and nasty-looking editions. Many of these cottage entrepreneurs were also apparently unable to differentiate between their home-produced products and the world of professional publishing. Suddenly anybody and everybody could call themselves a "published" author – no matter how few copies they produced or whether these were mostly distributed amongst family and friends. These publications might have a patina of professionalism, but in reality they were not much better than vanity publications.

Now, with the explosion of the Internet and the exponential advances in new technology, things are about to get much worse.

The current buzz-word in publishing is "e-books", or "print-on-demand". Just about anyone can set up a trade publishing house and have access to an online distribution system these days. Significantly, Microsoft and barnesandnoble.com have already teamed up to create systems which offer free downloads of e-titles. Meanwhile, Florida-based distributor BookWorld announced that it would offer more than 500 e-books on its site.

As we all know, traditional bookshops no longer have the shelf-space to keep a copy of every volume on display or the discount incentive to stock mid-list titles. On-demand books will ensure that titles no longer go out of print. California's Babbage Press is already reissuing worthwhile books by David J. Schow, Dennis Etchison, S.P. Somtow, John Shirley and others, and electronic book publisher E-Rights has over 300 titles by such authors as Harlan Ellison, Fritz Leiber and Melanie Tem available. Pulpless.com is being distributed by Ingram Books and offers a wide range of volumes, from such well-known names as Piers Anthony, Robert Silverberg and Norman Spinrad to lesser-know authors, and DarkTales Publications recently released the first volume of *The Asylum*, an original anthology of fifteen horror stories by Douglas Clegg and others, as an on-demand title.

But the question we have to ask ourselves is, if enough readers actually wanted to buy these titles in the first place, wouldn't a commercial imprint be only too delighted to publish them? You only need to look at Tor Books' quality Orb imprint or Gollancz's successful SF Masterworks and Fantasy Masterworks series to see that publishers are more than willing to reprint titles which they believe can sell enough copies to make them viable. It is also worth noting that most on-demand books are more expensive, and thus less competitive, than similar volumes in the bookstores.

The other way to get your work out there is through online publishing. There are already companies who will manage every stage of cyberpublishing, from design and editorial to logging the number of (paying) visitors to the site. However, in a reverse of the traditional process, authors must pay these publishers an "advance" for their packaging services.

So in what way, if any, does this new form of distribution differ from so-called "vanity publishing"? The blunt answer is, it doesn't. However, there is no longer any way in which we can define what constitutes a vanity publisher. The majority of self-published work, whether it is electronic or between covers, is usually pretty poor and, let's be honest, if it was any good in the first place chances are it would have found a commercial or small press publisher willing to support it.

Of course, there are notable exceptions to any rule. Recently Stephen King released his latest novella, "Riding the Bullet", exclusively on the Internet. The initial demand was phenomenal, with 400,000 downloads in the first twenty-four hours. The author estimated that he would make as much as $450,000 for the story (he would have received around $10,000 if he had sold it to *The New Yorker* or a similar magazine). Sure, someone like King can put a new 16,000-word novella up on the web at $2.50 a hit and it will be a big success, but how many people will pay – or even bother to read – e-serials by lesser-known or unknown authors? Horror writer Douglas Clegg was one of those who pioneered e-serials with his novel "Naomi" (subsequently published in book form by Subterranean Press and Leisure Books), and several other horror authors have jumped on the bandwagon since, but to less effect. It is already questionable whether this kind of publishing poses any threat to traditional print publishers, but it will be interesting to see how successful they are in a marketplace which is already becoming over-crowded.

One of the areas where electronic publishing has already established itself is in magazine (or, if you prefer, "fanzine") publishing. The horror genre already has established online news magazines such as *DarkEcho* and *Hellnotes*, and even *Locus* runs its own, separate, web version. Even such esteemed SF titles as *Galaxy* and *Omni* have attempted to make the move to online editions, with variable results. It has yet to be proved that any of these online magazines are making any profit, as the failure of Ellen Datlow's critically-acclaimed *Event Horizon* proved when it was put "on indefinite hiatus" in December while a wealthy investor was sought.

So what will happen to books such as the one you are now holding? Does the success of King's novella sound a death knoll for the printed and bound book?

I for one certainly hope not. If people want to read books in electronic format, then let them do so. But I still want to experience the feel and smell of a nicely bound volume which I can dip into on a train or bus, in the garden, on the beach, or in bed. And, perhaps most importantly of all, as a collector I want a book which is actually designed and edited and will look good on my shelf.

Although this new technology is still in its infancy, there is little doubt that electronic publication is here to stay and that electro-nic books are set to play an important role in the future of the publishing industry. However, I would like to believe that no matter what advances we see over the coming years, no e-book is ever going to replace the purely tactile pleasure of holding a handsomely-crafted volume; and if a title is truly worth preser-ving, then it will make it back into print somehow.

All publishing is dictated by market forces, and in the end it will be you, the reader, who will make that final choice . . .

The Editor
May, 2000

STEVE RASNIC TEM

Halloween Street

STEVE RASNIC TEM HAS HAD more than 250 short stories published in such magazines and anthologies as *Fantasy Tales*, *Weirdbook*, *Whispers*, *Twilight Zone*, *Crimewave*, *The Magazine of Fantasy & Science Fiction*, *The Third Alternative*, *New Terrors 1*, *Shadows*, *Cutting Edge*, *Dark at Heart*, *Forbidden Acts*, *MetaHorror*, *Dark Terrors 3*, *Horrors! 365 Scary Stories*, *White of the Moon*, *The Year's Best Fantasy and Horror* and previous volumes of the *Best New Horror*. A collection entitled *Ombres sur la Route* appeared in France several years ago, and he won the 1988 British Fantasy Award for his story "Leaks". He lives in Denver, Colorado, with his wife, horror author Melanie Tem. They have four children and three grandchildren.

About the following story (which will serve as the title tale in a new German-language collection), the author reveals: "I've always had a thing for Halloween stories – having published over a half dozen of them so far. Perhaps because it is the one time of the year that even conservative, repressed types celebrate the dark side. Certainly it's become commercialized, and kids and adults running around in scary masks no doubt have little or no understanding of the deeper meanings of the figures they are emulating, but to my mind that only heightens the *frisson*. We wear masks of monsters and the dying while hiding from ourselves that we are, indeed, monsters and dying. We're a funny old race."

H ALLOWEEN STREET. No one could remember who had first given it that name. It had no other. There was no street sign, had never been a street sign.

Halloween Street bordered the creek, and there was only one way to get there – over a rickety bridge of rotting wood. Grey timbers had worn partway through the vague red stain. The city had declared it safe only for foot or bike traffic.

The street had only eight houses, and no one could remember more than three of those being occupied at any one time. Renters never lasted long.

It was a perfect place to take other kids – the smaller ones, or the ones a little more nervous than yourself – on Halloween night. Just to give them a little scare. Just to get them to wet their pants.

Most of the time all the houses stayed empty. An old lady had supposedly lived in one of the houses for years, but no one knew anything more about her, except that they thought she'd died there several years before. Elderly twin brothers had once owned the two centre houses, each with twin high-peaked gables on the second storey like skeptical eyebrows, narrow front doors, and small windows that froze over every winter. The brothers had lived there only six months, fighting loudly with each other the entire time.

The houses at the ends of the street were in the worst shape, missing most of their roof shingles and sloughing off paint chips the way a tree sheds leaves. Both houses leaned toward the centre of the block, as if two great hands had attempted to squeeze the block from either side. Another three houses had suffered outside fire damage. The blackened boards looked like permanent, arbitrary shadows.

But it was the eighth house that bothered the kids the most. There was nothing wrong with it.

It was the kind of house any of them would have liked to live in. Painted bright white like a dairy so that it glowed even at night, with wide friendly windows and a bright blue roof.

And flowers that grew naturally and a lawn seemingly immune to weeds.

Who took care of it? It just didn't make any sense. Even when the kids guided newcomers over to Halloween Street they stayed away from the white house.

*   *   *

The little girl's name was Laura, and she lived across the creek from Halloween Street. From her bedroom window she could see all the houses. She could see who went there and she could see everything they did. She didn't stop to analyze, or pass judgments. She merely witnessed, and now and then spoke an almost inaudible "Hi" to her window and to those visiting on the other side. An occasional "Hi" to the houses of Halloween Street.

Laura should have been pretty. She had wispy blonde hair so pale it appeared white in most light, worn long down her back. She had small lips and hands that were like gauges to her health: soft and pink when she was feeling good, pale and dry when she was doing poorly.

But Laura was not pretty. There was nothing really wrong about her face: it was just vague. A cruel aunt with a drinking problem used to say that "it lacked character." Her mother once took her to a lady who cut silhouette portraits out of crisp black paper at a shopping mall. Her mother paid the lady five dollars to do one of Laura. The lady had finally given up in exasperation, exclaiming "The child has no profile!"

Laura overheard her mother and father talking about it one time. "I see things in her face," her mother had said.

"What do you mean?" Her father always sounded impatient with her mother.

"I don't *know* what I mean! I see things in her face and I can never remember exactly what I saw! Shadows and . . . white, something so white I feel like she's going to disappear into it. Like clouds . . . or a snowbank."

Her father had laughed in astonishment. "You're crazy!"

"You know what I mean!" her mother shouted back. "You don't even look at her directly anymore because you *know* what I mean! It's not exactly sadness in her face, not exactly. Just something born with her, something out of place. She was born out of place. My God! She's eleven years old! She's been like this since she was a baby!"

"She's a pretty little girl." Laura could tell her father didn't really mean that.

"What about her eyes? Tell me about her eyes, Dick!"

"What *about* her eyes? She has nice eyes . . ."

"*Describe* them for me, then! Can you *describe* them? What color are they? What shape?"

Her father didn't say anything. Soon after the argument he'd stomped out of the house. Laura knew he couldn't describe her eyes. Nobody could.

Laura didn't make judgments when other people talked about her. She just listened. And watched with eyes no one could describe. Eyes no one could remember.

No, it wasn't that she was sad, Laura thought. It wasn't that her parents were mean to her or that she had a terrible life. Her parents weren't ever mean to her and although she didn't know exactly what kind of life she had, she knew it wasn't terrible.

She didn't enjoy things like other kids did. She didn't enjoy playing or watching television or talking to the other kids. She didn't *enjoy*, really. She had quiet thoughts, instead. She had quiet thoughts when she pretended to be asleep but was really listening to all her parents' conversations, all their arguments. She had quiet thoughts when she watched people. She had quiet thoughts when people could not describe her eyes. She had quiet thoughts while gazing at Halloween Street, the glowing white house, and all the things that happened there.

She had quiet thoughts pretending that she hadn't been born out of place, that she hadn't been born anyplace at all.

Laura could have been popular, living so close to Halloween Street, seeing it out of her bedroom window. No other kid lived so close or had such a good view. But of course she wasn't popular. She didn't share Halloween Street. She sat at her desk at school all day and didn't talk about Halloween Street at all.

That last Halloween Laura got dressed to go out. That made her mother happy – Laura had never gone trick-or-treating before. Her mother had always encouraged her to go, had made or bought her costumes, taken her to parties at church or school, parties the other kids dressed up for: ghosts and vampires and princesses, giggling and running around with their masks like grotesquely swollen heads. But Laura wouldn't wear a costume. She'd sit solemn-faced, unmoving, until her mother finally gave up and took her home. And she'd never go trick-or-treating, never wear a costume.

After she'd told her mother that she wanted to go out that night her mother had driven her around town desperately trying to find a costume for her. Laura sat impassively on the passenger side, dutifully got out at each store her mother took her to, and each time shook her head when asked if she liked each of the few remaining costumes.

"I don't know where else we can try, Laura," her mother said, sorting through a pile of mismatched costume pieces at a drugstore in a mall. "It'll be dark in a couple of hours, and so far you haven't liked a *thing* I've shown you."

Laura reached into the pile and pulled out a cheap face mask. The face was that of a middle-aged woman, or a young man, cheeks and lips rouged a bright red, eye shadow dark as a bruise, eyebrows a heavy and coarse dark line.

"But, honey. Isn't that a little . . ." Laura shoved the mask into her mother's hand. "Well, all right." She picked up a bundle of bright blue cloth from the table. "How about this pretty robe to go with it?" Laura didn't look at the robe. She just nodded and headed for the door, her face already a mask itself.

Laura left the house that night after most of the other trick-or-treaters had come and gone. Her interest in Halloween actually seemed less than ever this year; she stayed in her bedroom as goblins and witches and all manner of stunted, warped creatures came to the front door singly and in groups, giggling and dancing and playing tricks on each other. She could see a few of them over on Halloween Street, not going up to any of the houses but rather running up and down the short street close to the houses in I-dare-you races. But not near as many as in years past.

Now and then her mother would come up and open her door. "Honey, don't you want to leave yet? I swear everybody'll be all out of the goodies if you don't go soon." And each time Laura shook her head, still staring out the window, still watching Halloween Street.

Finally, after most of the other kids had returned to their homes, Laura came down the stairs wearing her best dress and the cheap mask her mother had bought for her.

Her father and mother were in the living room, her mother having retrieved the blue robe from the hall closet.

"She's wearing her best dress, Ann. Besides, it's damned late for her to be going out now."

Her mother eyed her nervously. "I could drive you, honey."

Laura shook her head.

"Well OK, just let me cover your nice dress with the robe. Don't want to get it dirty."

"She's just a *kid*, for chrissake! We can't let her decide!" Her father had dropped his newspaper on the floor. He turned his back on Laura so she wouldn't see his face, wouldn't know how angry he was with both of them. But Laura *knew*. "And that *mask*! Looks like a *whore's* face! Hell, how can she even see? Can't even see her eyes under that." But Laura could see his. All red and sad-looking.

"She's doing something normal for a change," her mother whispered harshly. "Can't you see that? That's more important."

Without a word Laura walked over and pulled the robe out of her mother's arms. After some hesitation, after Laura's father had stomped out of the room, her mother helped her get it on. It was much too large, but her mother gasped "How beautiful!" in exaggerated fashion. Laura walked toward the door. Her mother ran to the door and opened it ahead of her. "Have a good time!" she said in a mock cheery voice. Laura could see the near-panic in the eyes above the distorted grin, and she left without saying goodbye.

A few houses down the sidewalk she pulled the robe off and threw it behind a hedge. She walked on, her head held stiff and erect, the mask's rouge shining bright red in the streetlights, her best dress a soft cream color in the dimness, stirred lightly by the breeze. She walked on to Halloween Street.

She stopped on the bridge and looked down into the creek. A young man's face, a middle-aged woman's face gazed back at her out of dark water and yellow reflections. The mouth seemed to be bleeding.

She walked on to Halloween Street. She was the only one there. The only one to see.

She walked on in her best dress and her shiny mask with eyes no one could see.

The houses on Halloween Street looked the way they always did, empty and dark. Except for the one that glowed the color of clouds, or snow.

The houses on Halloween Street looked their own way, sounded their own way, moved their own way. Lost in their own quiet thoughts. Born out of place.

You could not see their eyes.

Laura went up to the white house with the neatly trimmed yard and the flowers that grew without care. Its colour like blowing snow. Its colour like heaven. She went inside.

The old woman gazed out her window as goblins and spooks, pirates and ballerinas crossed the bridge to enter Halloween Street. She bit her lip to make it redder. She rubbed at her ancient, blind eyes, rubbing the dark eyeshadow up into the coarse line of brow. She was not beautiful, but she was not hideous either. Not yet. In any case no one ever remembered her face.

Her fine, snow-white hair was beautiful, and long down her back.

She had the most wonderful house on the street, the only one with flowers, the only one that glowed. It was her home, the place where she belonged. All the children, all the children who dared, came to her house every Halloween for treats.

"Come along," she said to the window, staring out at Halloween Street. "Come along," she said, as the treat bags rustled and shifted around her. "You don't remember, do you?" as the first of the giggling goblins knocked at her door. "You've quite forgotten," as the door began to shake from eager goblin fists, eager goblin laughs. "Now scratch your swollen little head, scratch your head. You forgot that first and last, Halloween is for the dead."

JAMES HERBERT

Others

JAMES HERBERT IS NOT JUST Britain's number one bestselling
writer of horror/thriller fiction – a position he has held ever since
the publication of his first novel, *The Rats*, in 1974 – but he is also
one of our greatest popular novelists, whose books are sold in
thirty-three other languages, including Russian and Chinese.
Widely imitated and hugely influential, his eighteen novels (which
include *Fluke*, *Shrine*, *The Magic Cottage*, *Haunted*, *Creed*,
Portent, *The Ghosts of Sleath* and *'48*) have sold more than
42 million copies worldwide.

The following story is extracted from his latest novel, *Others*,
in which private investigator Nicholas Dismas is hired to find a
missing baby, apparently taken away at birth. The trail leads to a
mysterious nursing home called Perfect Rest, where Dismas not
only discovers the dark secret of the Others, but also the enigma
of his own existence . . .

"This story stands on its own," explains the author, "and is
certainly a good indication of where I stand now as a writer. It
also has a lot to say about prejudice in society, particularly from
the victim's point of view. In fact, it has a whole lot of things to
say. The twist, of course, is who the attackers turn out to be . . ."

IT WAS AROUND 10:30 THAT NIGHT that I stepped outside the
pub in a side street near the seafront, the steady drizzle that
had marred the day over with for the moment, but the streets still

shiny damp. The noise from the saloon bar behind me died with the closing of the door and I took in great lungfuls of almost pure sea air, exhaling long and hard to rid my lungs of the residue cigarette fumes they'd been collecting over the past couple of hours. I felt only a little better now, the irritating sense of dissatisfaction that had been dogging me for most of the day dulled by booze and company. A burst of laughter behind me was raucous enough to pass through the thick wood and glass of the pub door and I was pretty sure it wasn't at my expense: I knew nearly all the regulars, who were mainly of the – how shall I put it? – of the "exotic" variety; young and not so young gay men, pensioned-off chorus boys of untold age but with fabulous stories to tell, cultured antique dealers who'd had other careers in their prime, but who now saw this last profession as a means of genteel employment for themselves and their (invariably younger) part-ners. There were shammers and schemers, duckers and divers, women who love women, the lonely and the disparate. A good bunch. And whenever I entered that bar I was greeted with friendly calls rather than odd stares.

The air may have been moist, but it was warm; warm and scented with the aroma of sea and salt. As I began to walk towards the front, depression settled over me like a well-worn cloak, and even the bright promenade lights at the end of the long, narrow street failed to offer any cheer. Moving along the glisten-ing pavement I wondered why this mood of – what? I couldn't focus on it. Inadequacy, perhaps? – had pursued me all day. Since I'd first opened my eye that morning, in fact. Since my conclusion that there really was nothing more I could do for Shelly Ripstone.

When I'd rung her earlier, she'd pleaded with me to stay on the case, even phoned me back seconds after I'd broken off the call. She'd offered to double my fee if only I would agree to continue the search for her lost son, and nothing I said would convince her that it would be pointless, that the child – and now I was beginning to doubt there ever was a child – had died only minutes or seconds after being born. Doctors didn't lie. The authorities might, but then why should they in such a case?

Shelly had become more distressed. Didn't I understand that a mother intuitively, *instinctively*, knew these things? And besides, the clairvoyant, Louise Broomfield, also had no doubts that her son was still alive. The evidence – or lack of it – said otherwise, I told her, but that had made her more aggressive. Pleadings became insults. But fine, I'd had plenty of those in my time. Firmly, and quite politely, I said my goodbyes and replaced the receiver.

This time she didn't ring back.

I could, of course, have mentioned the fact that she had not been entirely open with me, that maybe – well, quite likely – her motivation had more to do with her late husband's money than maternal love. But that would have been rude of me. And unnecessary.

Even so, this night I reviewed the case in my mind as I shuffled on towards the sea, yet still I could make no sense of her claim. Even if Shelly Ripstone *née* Teasdale had given birth eighteen years ago and the hospital had been razed to the ground some time afterwards, the baby's short existence would still have been noted by the General Registrar Office. But it seemed nothing at all had been documented, neither at the London office nor the one at Southport, where all such records were kept after the closedown of Somerset House in the capital. Also, in adult tracing the method is relatively simple, even if the disappearance is intentional (I rule out murder and dismemberment here); credit card purchases, the electoral roll, National Insurance number, bank statements, car registration, friends and associates – all conspire to track down an absconder; but when there is no life history, when there isn't even any evidence that the subject of the trace was even born in the first place except for the word of a bereaved widow of dubious (although understandable) motivation and possibly of distracted mind, then finding that person is next to impossible.

There was *nothing* I could do. I'd only waste time and the client's money, and I'd never been into that kind of scam. No, I'd made the right decision. The assignment was a dodo, a dead duck. The agency had done all it could. So what was nagging at me? Why couldn't I let it go?

"Spare some change, chief?"

I'd almost passed by the figure huddled in a doorway before his voice, both plaintive and cheerful at the same time, brought me to a halt. I peered closer, searching for a face among the darkness and rags, but only when the headlights of a car crawling down the narrow street lit us both up did I find one. Wide, friendly eyes looked up at me and I realized the beggar was a kid, somewhere between seventeen and twenty, with spiky hair and a ring through his nose and grime on his skin that looked more than a week old. The sleeves of his ragged jumper were pulled over his hands, even though there was no coolness to the night, and his well-worn boots were metal-tipped and too hardy for the season.

"Just for a bit of food, like," he said, working for whatever I was prepared to give him. He seemed uncomfortable under my scrutiny, perhaps with my features. What he couldn't appreciate, though, was that I was only doing my job. Even half-drunk, I did what I always did when I came upon vagrants or beggars (not necessarily the same thing): I gave them the once-over – all of us at the agency did – trying to catch any resemblance to photographs on our files, old images of persons gone astray, missing youths, absent husbands, absconded wives, even mothers or fathers who'd decided normal society wasn't all it was cracked up to be. You never knew when you might strike it lucky.

He became uncertain, having had a good look at me as the glare from the headlights had peaked before moving on. He appeared very uncomfortable now that we were in the shadows again. He drew up his boots and curled up in the doorway, his body seeming to shrink.

"It's okay," I said quietly – soothingly, I hoped. "When did you last eat?" It was important for me to know.

He didn't answer straight away. His neck craned from the untidy bundle of clothes, and he looked around the doorway's corners, up and down the street, as if searching out other company. This was a lonely little side road though.

"This morning," he answered at last, his face featureless in the gloom. He cleared his throat, a nervous rasp.

I sighed and rummaged through my pockets, finding only a pound coin and a few odd pence. "Fuckit," I grumbled to myself and reached inside my jacket for my wallet. Pulling out a ten-pound note, I sensed a fresh, a more trusting, alertness about the boy.

"Promise me you'll get yourself something to eat, okay?" I thrust the note towards him and he accepted it with both hands.

"Bloodyell," he said in a low breath. "Thanks, man. I mean, really – thanks."

"Sure." I stepped away from him. "Remember: food. Right?"

I could just make out the nodding of his head before I turned away, already wondering if he'd stick to the handout's condition, or if he'd head straight for his regular supplier. A tenner wouldn't buy him much, so maybe he'd just drink it away. I let it go: I could only make the offer – the rest was up to him. I'd learned a long time ago it was all you could do.

As I neared the seafront there was more activity. Tourists strolled arm in arm along the broad pavements that edged the wide King's Road, many of them still in shorts and T-shirts, despite the earlier drizzle and the lateness of the hour, all of this – the people, the coast road, the edge of the beach below the promenade railings – lit up by street lamps and festive lights, lights from hotels, restaurants, the big cinema and theatre complex, lights from traffic rushing by as if late for curfew. And noise came from all directions, the jabber of crowds and their laughter, and muted music from bars and clubs, the conversations of diners drifting from open doorways.

I stepped over a puddled gutter that rainbowed oil or spilt petrol in its waters, and waited anxiously for a break in the traffic, a chance to cross the broad expanse of road at my own lively but slow speed. The gay lights of the Palace Pier stretched out into the blackness, their mirror image on the sea below dancing with every wave that rushed to shore. The pier resembled an ocean liner in celebratory mood.

Taking my chance, I made it to the centre of the road, then waited for a gap in the opposite lane's flow. Faces stared out at me from passing cars, one or two vehicles even slowing down so that their occupants could take a more leisurely look, and I saw myself with their eyes, a ridiculous stunted shape, bent as if cowering in the roadway, a clown of a figure whose mask was not funny in transient headlights, its shadows too severe, mien too crooked, the body too unseemly. Laughter passed me by as I waited; someone even took the trouble to wind down a passenger window and call out to me, call out something I didn't quite hear and did not want to hear. I seized the moment to hobble the rest of the way, my bad leg dragging across tarmac as it does when I'm tired or inebriated, my left arm waving in the air ahead for balance. I arrived safely but a little dead in heart.

A group, a horde, of language students – Brighton is always full of language students – paused to allow me through, the hush in their voices as I avoided touching any of them making their alien whispers easy to comprehend. I lowered my head even more, ashamed, vulnerable – naked under their gaze – not even my alcohol haze dimming the ocular assault, and I kept moving until I reached the ornate rail overlooking the lower promenade and beach. There I leaned, my chest pressed against hard metal, my only eye watching the blackness of the sea's horizon, a barely visible dark against dark, and I concentrated on that alone so that self-pity would not overwhelm me. My breath came in short heaves and my hands clenched the rail tightly until my thoughts, my feelings, began to settle; not calm – I didn't feel calm at all – but to quieten down, become absorbed into me so that my hands on that rail no longer trembled, so that my gasps steadied, my breathing became deeper, more even. With the quietening, there soon came the question: why had I panicked so quickly, so easily? Ridicule was something I'd borne for as long as I could remember and pity for the same length of time, but I'd learned to cope; hadn't accepted, could never accept either insult, but I'd learned to endure. So why this abrupt overpowering fright? Why had my mental equilibrium, that hard-earned stability gained only after a lifetime of abuse and sniggers and curious glances if not downright ogling and well-meaning but so often *de*meaning patronization, why had it so swiftly deserted me? Had I only kidded myself that I'd adapted to all those jibes and kindnesses? Well no, because I knew I'd only ever placed a barrier between myself and the prejudices and good intentions of others. I suppose my surprise tonight was that the shield was gossamer-thin instead of cast-iron thick. Even the whisky and beer I'd consumed that night had failed to dull the senses, to thicken that self-preserving defence even more.

An urge to be nearer the sea overcame me (because the sea was clean and as far away from people as I could get?) and I lurched from the railings, heading towards the ramp that led to the boulevard below. I was aware that my shambling walk was exaggerated by weariness – and yes, no excuses, by alcohol too – the limp now a parody of my normal gait, my hump even more rounded. Crouched and shuffling, I hastened down towards the beach, momentum increased by the slope's angle.

The ramp was wide enough for wheelchairs and delivery vans

alike, but not user-friendly for hunchbacks of awkward stride, and I steered myself to one side so that I could slide my hand along its rail, steadying myself, occasionally gripping to control the descent. Near the bottom, customers were overflowing from the Zap club, milling around its door, spilling out on to the level boulevard. Getting in my way.

Now I deliberately kept my head bowed, my one eye watching other people's feet as the noise from the club's open door became horrendous, the chatter of voices around me intimidating. I could tell by the shifting of legs that some of the crowd were anxious not to become an obstacle in my way; others failed to notice me though, only becoming aware when I tried desperately, solicitously, to nudge by without giving offence. A girl's shriek was followed by laughter, a male's derision followed by embarrassed shushes.

At last I was through, but as I raised my head to see the way ahead I was confronted by the customers of the Cuba Bar, a large section of its patronage seated at tables arranged in an open area outside the bar itself. I slunk around them, regretting my impulse to reach the seashore, aware that not only did people *en masse* stare harder but that they felt anonymous enough to voice their humour or shock. Several of them pointed me out, and one or two shouted comments, and only when my feet crunched pebbles did I stop running.

I sneaked away from the bright lights towards sweet covering darkness, away from mocking sounds and cries of pity, making my way diagonally across the beach so that I'd also be moving closer to home in my sea quest. Noise behind me became a general hum of voices and music, the stony shore grew dimmer with every shuffling pace, and I'd almost reached my tidal sanctuary when I heard the insult that was the worst of all, the one I dreaded because it was never the end of it, it was always the precursor to further torment.

"Oi, fuckin Quasimodo!"

They were sitting around in a circle on the stones, unnoticed in my rush, difficult to see in their mainly dark attire. They drank from cans of beer but the smell that drifted across our neutral ground was pure weed; their spliffs glowed in the gloom, bright one moment, a dull amber the next, each burning dot thick with Jamaican promise. I ignored the call, hurrying on, my feet sliding

on the little pebble hills that spoiled any rhythm I could build, but
something large and hard struck the hump of my back. The stone
clunked on to the beach and I went on.

"*The bells, the bells!*" someone behind me wailed to much
snickering.

I stopped, hung my head, closed my eye for a moment, then
turned to face them.

I was between the group and the boulevard, between it and the
broad stretch of light from the roadway above, so that as they
collectively stood, some moving sluggishly as though heavy with
dope and booze, one, the nearest to me, rising almost sprightly,
fired by youth's arrogance, I could see their shapes in the muted
illumination, could take in their leathers and amulets, their spiked
collars, their freaked hair and high, laced boots. They were an
unlovely bunch.

I could just make out the peppy one's leering grin, no mercy in
that expression.

"Going swimming, Quozzie? Only swim at night, do yer?"

The others enjoyed the taunt, adding their own drolleries.
"Didn't know the freak show was in town." "What yer do for
sex, date a spazzie?" "Didn't know abortions could walk about."
You know, remarks of that ilk, and others that were plain
degenerate. Every one seemed to inspire the next, and the gang
had great fun.

"Oh shit," I said quietly to myself, then turned away and began
moving again, not rushing, just taking it steady, not wanting them
to see how much I was shaking. Shaking with rage, with fear, with
impotence.

A beer can hit me this time, half full so that liquid spilt into my
hair, ran down the back of my neck.

"Hey, we're talkin to you, 'umpback!"

I didn't reply. I kept going.

Footsteps crunching after me.

Knowing I couldn't outrun them, I whirled around and it must
have been my expression that stopped them dead, shadows
formed by the dim light probably deepening my scowl, maybe
even making me look fearsome.

"Listen to me," I said, allowing anger to override my nervousness. "I'm not bothering you, so just leave me alone. Okay?"

But the sprightly one, the arrogant one, the one I assumed was the leader, swaggered towards me, features screwed up into a grimace that was as ugly as mine.

"You got it wrong, Quozzie. You are botherin us."

Another step closer allowed me to see a face so full of loathing and bigotry that it surely must have poisoned this one's soul; it came in waves, a silent rant against everything this zealot thought of as abnormal and not up to the perceived order of things. Although my gaze never left those venomous eyes, I was aware that the others were outflanking me so that soon I was surrounded. I took a step back; my main tormentor took a step forward.

I sensed no euphoria among them, no laid-back pleasantry that the fat Jamaicans and drink should have induced, and I began to suspect they had all been on something harder earlier that evening, maybe Ice, which was the drug of the moment in Brighton around that time, a street methamphetamine, pure crystal shit that gave a big rush that ultimately and invariably fucked up the brain with its worsening withdrawals. Sometimes the tweakers freaked out with meth psychosis and hallucinations, and that was never a time to be around them.

I consoled myself with the thought that this merry little band of junkheads could just as easily be on GHB, or Liquid Ecstasy, both popular drugs around the clubs, whose comedowns sometimes could be scary as well; then again, they could be on the nutter stuff, Special K. Whichever, I figured their smoking mixed with booze was their way of making the descent easy on themselves. Only it didn't seem to be working: aggression was bristling from this mob.

"Look," I said placatingly, hoping the tremble in my voice wasn't too noticeable, "what d'you want from me? D'you want money? I've got money. I can give you some." I reached for my wallet, an action replay of a short time earlier when I'd willingly offered charity to the beggar. I wasn't proud of myself at that moment, but if that was what it took to get me off the hook, then so be it.

"Yeah, we want money."

Eyes looked greedily at the notes in my hand. "But we don't want some, we want all of it."

My wallet, as well as the notes, was snatched away and when I reacted, reflexively reaching out to grab it back (cash was one thing, credit cards and driving licence was another) something whacked against my head. I think it must have been another, even larger, stone from the beach, because I heard it crack as it struck my temple, and it hit me so hard I fell to my knees.

My brain went numb for a second or two and I brought both hands up to the wound, rocking there on the beach on my knees. I remember crying out, pleading with them to stop it there and then, not to let it go further, that I was hurt enough, but then they were on me, kicking, punching, pounding me until everything became a blur – everything except the pain – and I was tumbling, tumbling forward and curling into a foetus position, a frightened, confused, malformed thing scrunched up as small as I could make myself, there to be pummelled and humbled because I was an oddity, because I was an oddity with money, because I was an oddity with money who wouldn't fight back.

I don't know how long it went on for – a thousand years, two minutes? In its way, it was a lifetime – but I heard them calling me names, snarling their hatred, screeching their bile, and I absorbed it, let the pain and the name-calling sink into my system, so that soon my body and my mind had swallowed it whole, and then I allowed it – blows and words – to deaden me. That was the only way I could make it tolerable.

And when it was finally over and the five leather and amulet clad girls had walked off, I cursed them under my breath and prayed that one day the sickness inside each and every one of them would cause them to suffer the way I had suffered that night.

It began to spit with rain again.

T.E.D. KLEIN

Growing Things

T.E.D. KLEIN LIVES MOST OF THE TIME in New York City. In addition to Rod Serling's *The Twilight Zone* Magazine, he also edited a true-crime monthly, *CrimeBeat*. He scripted the Dario Argento movie *Trauma* (which he describes as "unwatchable"); his novel *The Ceremonies*, a *New York Times* bestseller, won a British Fantasy Award for Best Novel, and one of the stories in his collection *Dark Gods* won a World Fantasy Award for Best Novella. He sometimes reviews genre books pseudonymously.

As the author recalls: "In the late 1980s, with time on my hands after leaving *Twilight Zone* magazine, I waited till precisely the height of the real-estate market, and – fuelled by an inheritance and revenue from *The Ceremonies* – I bought myself a country house in upstate New York, just across the dirt road from the cabin where Whitley Strieber claims to have been buggered by aliens. Although the house in "Growing Things" is (thank God) considerably different from my own, the story was inspired by that purchase, and by my life-long addiction to advice columns in *Yankee* and various how-to magazines."

"HEY, HONEY, LISTEN TO THIS ONE. It's downright scary."
The magazine, drawn from near the middle of the pile, was yellowed, musty-smelling. Herb licked his lips with a fat tongue and squinted at the page with the corner turned down. "'Dear Mr. Fixit, Early this spring a peculiar roundish bulge

appeared under the linoleum in my bathroom, and now with the warm weather it's beginning to get larger, as if something is sprouting under there. My husband, who is not well, almost tripped over it yesterday. What is it, some sort of fungus? How can I get rid of it without having to rip up the linoleum? As we cannot afford expensive new flooring, we are relying on you.' Signed, 'Anxious'."

"I shouldn't wonder she was anxious," said Iris, from her cloud of lemon oil and beeswax. She'd been giving the old end-table a vigorous polishing and was slightly out of breath. "Who wants to share their bathroom with a bunch of toadstools?"

"Don't worry, Fixit's got it under control. 'Dear Anxious, Sounds as if you have a pocket of moisture trapped between the floorboards and the linoleum. Often a damp basement is the culprit. Simply drill a hole up from the basement to release the moisture build-up, then seal the area with flash patch or creosote.' " Herb rubbed his chin. "Sounds simple enough to me."

"Not in *this* house."

"What do you mean?"

"We don't have a basement, remember? You'd have to get down on your belly and slither beneath the house, with all that muck down there."

"Hah, you're right! Certainly wouldn't want to do that!" Herb's stomach shook as he laughed. "Thank God the damned bathroom's new."

In fact, the bathroom, clean and professionally tiled, was one of the things that had sold them on the house. Herb liked long showers, and Iris – who, unlike Herb's first wife, had never had to make time for children – was given to leisurely soaks in the tub.

The rest of the place was in, at best, an indifferent state of repair. The rain gutters sagged, the windows needed caulking, and, if the house were to serve as anything more than a summer retreat from the city, the ancient coal-burning furnace in an alcove behind the kitchen would have to be replaced. Eventually, too, they'd have to add more rooms; at present the house was just a bungalow, a single floor of living space crowned by a not-too-well-insulated attic littered with rolls of cotton wadding, damaged furniture, and other bric-a-brac abandoned by the former owners. Who these owners were was uncertain; clearly the place hadn't been lived in for years, and – though the real-estate lady had denied it – it had probably been on the market for most of that time.

The two of them, of course, had hoped for something better; they were, in their way, a pair of midlife romantics. But Herb's alimony payments and an unexpected drubbing from the IRS this April had forced them to be practical. Besides, they had three acres' worth of woods, and stars they could never have seen from the city, and bullfrogs chanting feverishly in the marsh behind the house. They had an old woodshed, a swaybacked garage that had once been a barn, and a sunken area near the forest's edge, overgrown with mushrooms and moss, that the real-estate lady assured them had been a garden. They had each other. Did the house itself need work? As Herb had said airily when a skeptical friend asked if he knew anything about home repair, "Well, I know how to write a cheque."

Secretly he nourished the ambition of doing the work himself. Though he had barely picked up a hammer since he'd knocked together bookends for his parents in a high school shop class, he felt certain that a few carefully selected repair manuals and a short course of *This Old House* would see him through. If fate had steered him and Iris toward that creature of jest, the "handyman special," well, so be it. He would simply learn to be a handyman.

And fate, for once, had seemed to agree; for, among the artifacts left by the previous owners was a bookshelf stacked high with old magazines.

Actually, not all that old – from the late 1970s, in fact – but the humidity had aged them, so that they had taken on the fragile, jaundiced look of magazines from decades earlier. Iris had wanted to throw them away – "Those mouldy old things," she'd said, curling her lip, "they smell of mildew. We'll fill up the shelves with books from local yard sales" – but Herb refused to hear of it. "They're perfect for a country house," he had said. "I mean, just look at this. *Home Handyman. Practical Gardener. Growing Things Organically. Modern Health*. Perfect rainy day reading."

Luckily for Herb, there were lots of rainy days in this part of the world, because after three months of home owning it had become clear that reading do-it-yourself columns such as "Mr Fixit" – a regular feature in *Home Handyman* magazine – was a good deal more fun than actually fixing anything. He'd enjoyed shopping for tools and had turned a corner of the garage into a rudimentary workshop; but now that the tools gleamed from their hooks on the wall and the necessary work space had been cleared, his enthusiasm had waned.

In fact, a certain lassitude had settled upon them both. Maybe it was the dampness. This was, by all accounts, one of the wettest summers on record; each week the local pennysaver sagged in their hands as they pulled it from the mailbox, and a book of stamps that Iris bought had long since stuck together. Dollars had grown limp in Herb's wallet. Today, with the summer sky once more threatening storms, he lay aside the *Handyman* and spent the afternoon with his nose buried in a back issue of *Country Kitchen*, while Iris, unable to transform an end-table from the attic into something that passed for an antique, put away her beeswax and retreated to the bedroom for a nap.

It was growing dark by the time she awoke. Clouds covered the sky, but the rain had not come. Despite the afternoon's inactivity, they were both too tired to cook; instead they had dinner by candlelight at a roadside inn, along a desolate stretch of highway several miles beyond the town. They toasted one another's health and wished that they were just a few years younger.

The house felt chilly when they returned; the air seemed thick with moisture. They'd already had to buy themselves wool mattress pads to keep their sheets from growing clammy. To-night, to take the dampness off, Herb built a fire, carefully examining the logs he carried inside for spiders and insects that could drop off and infest the house. He remembered a line he'd seen in *Practical Gardener*, something about being constantly on watch for "the blight on the peach and the worm in the rosebud."

This evening, though, it was *Home Handyman* that drew him back. He'd started weeks before with the older issues at the bottom of the pile and had steadily been working his way up. While on the couch Iris yawned over a contemporary romance, he engrossed himself in articles on wood-stove safety, building a patio, and – something he was glad he'd never have to worry about – pumping out a flooded basement.

The issue he'd just pulled out, from the top half of the pile, was less yellowed than the ones before. "Here's a letter," he announced, "from a man who's had trouble removing a tree stump next to his house. Mr. Fixit says he'd better get rid of it fast, or it'll attract termites." Herb shook his head. "Christ, you can't let down your guard for a second out here. And here's one from a man who built a chimney but didn't seal it properly." He chuckled. "The damn fool! Filled his attic with smoke." He eyed their fireplace speculatively, but it looked solid and substantial, the flames merry. He turned back to the magazine. The next page had the corner folded down. "Some guy asks about oil stains on a concrete floor. Mr. Fixit recommends a mixture of cream of tartar and something called 'oxalic acid.' How the hell are you supposed to find . . . Hey, listen to this, here's another one from that same woman who wrote in before. 'Dear Mr. Fixit, The advice you gave me previously, on getting rid of bulges under the linoleum in my bathroom by drilling up from the basement, was of little use, as we have no basement, and due to an incapacity my husband and I are unable to make our way beneath the house. The bulges—'"

Iris looked up from her book. "Before it was just *one* bulge."

"Well, hon," he said, thinking of her in the tub, "you know how it is with bulges." He made sure he saw her smile before turning back to the column. "'The bulges have grown larger, and there's a definite odour coming from them. What should we do?' Signed, 'Still Anxious'."

"That poor woman!" said Iris. She stretched and settled back into the cushions. "You don't suppose it could be radon, do you?"

"No, he says they may have something called 'wood bloat.'" Herb shuddered, savouring the phrase. "'Forget about preserving the linoleum,' he says. 'Drill two holes deep into the centre of the bulges and carefully pour in a solution of equal parts baking soda, mineral spirits, and vanilla extract. If that doesn't do the trick, I'd advise you to seek professional help.'"

"She should have done that in the first place," said Iris. "I'd love to know how she made out."

"Me, too," said Herb. "Let's see if the story's continued."

He flipped through the next few months of *Home Handyman*. There were leaky stovepipes, backed-up drains, and decaying roofs, but no mention of the bulges. From the couch came a soft bump as Iris lay back and let the book drop to the rug. Her eyes closed; her mouth went slack. Watching her stomach rise and fall in the firelight, he felt suddenly and peculiarly alone.

From outside came the whisper of rain – normally a peaceful sound, but tonight a troubling one; he could picture the land around the house, and beneath it, becoming a place of marsh and stagnant water, where God knows what might grow. The important thing, he knew, was to keep the bottom of the house raised above the ground, or else dampness would rot the timbers. Surely the crawlspace under his feet was ample protection from the wetness; still, he wished that the house had a basement.

Softly, so as not to wake his wife, he tiptoed into the bathroom – still smelling pleasantly of paint and varnish – and stared pensively at the floor. For a moment, alarmed, he thought he noticed a hairline crack between two of the new tiles, where the floor was slightly uneven between the toilet and the shower stall; but the light was bad in here, and the crack had probably been there all along.

By the time he returned to the front room, the fire was beginning to go out. He'd have liked to add more wood, but he didn't want to risk waking Iris. Seating himself back on the rug with a pile of magazines beside him, he continued his search through the remaining issues of *Home Handyman*, right up till the point, more than three years in the past, when the issues stopped. He found no further updates from "Anxious"; he wasn't sure whether he was disappointed or relieved. The latter, he supposed; things must have come out okay.

The issues of *Handyman* were replaced by a pile, only slightly less yellowed and slightly less substantial, of *Modern Health*, with, predictably, its own advice column, this one conducted by a "Dr Carewell". Shingles on roofs were succeeded by shingles on faces and legs; the cracked plaster and rotting baseboards gave way to hay fever and thinning hair.

"I have an enormous bunion on my right foot," one letter began, with a trace of pride. "I have a hernia that was left untreated," said another. Readers complained of planter's warts, aching backs, and coughs that wouldn't quit. It was like owning a home, Herb thought; you had to be constantly vigilant. Sooner or later, something always gave way and the rot seeped in. "Dear Dr Carewell," one letter began, where the page corner had been turned down, "My husband and I are both increasingly incapacitated by a rash that has left large rose-red blotches all over our bodies. Could it be some sort of fungus? There is no pain or itching, but odd little bumps have begun to appear in the centre." It was signed, "Bedridden".

All this talk of breakdown and disease was depressing, and the mention of bed had made him tired. The fire had almost gone out. Glancing at the doctor's reply – it was cheerily reassuring, something about plenty of exercise and good organic vegetables – he got slowly to his feet. From another room came the creak of wood as the old house settled in for the night.

Iris snored softly on the couch. She looked so peaceful that he hated to wake her, but he knew she'd fall asleep again soon; the two of them always slept well, out here in the country. "Come on, hon," he whispered. "Bedtime." The sound of the rain no longer troubled him as he bent toward her, brushed back her hair, and tenderly planted a kiss on her cheek, rosy in the dying light.

DAVID J. SCHOW

Unhasped

DAVID J. SCHOW WORKS AS A SCREENWRITER AND AUTHOR from his home in the Hollywood hills. Some of his recent book releases include *Wild Hairs*, a collection of his non-fiction columns from *Fangoria* magazine, and a new edition of his 1990 short story collection *Lost Angels*. As an editor, *The Lost Bloch, Volume II: Hell on Earth* is published by Subterranean Press. He also turns up in his namesake David J. Skal's documentary which appears on Universal's DVD release of *Creature from the Black Lagoon*.

"Lists of blown-out, stale, or out-of-date relationships. Everybody has one," reveals the author, "and each list charts the peaks and valleys of a lifetime of looking for love. The trick with 'Unhasped' – figure the title out for yourself – was to structure the telling of the tale as a classic stairway of teases. Writing is sexy when it works correctly. Reading is a matter of seduction."

IT WAS ALL ABOUT CLOSURE, Ethan told himself. The women in the box were past, they were history, the only challenge they represented now being that of their disposition.

Bodies, from the past.

Ethan closed the lid and secured its tiny brass hasp. The box had originally been made to house Torpedo cigars hand-rolled in Honduras and a faint tang of tobacco still clung.

A nonsmoker, he despised cigars above cigarettes, which he disliked more as a matter of social responsibility. The flash fad of cigar-smoking had made life a photo op for feckless humanoids who swathed their fat asses in Docker khaki and helmed the steroidal station wagons recently euphemised into "suburban utility vehicles" to distinguish their priapism from the flaccidity of vans. It was all very American – big butt, big car, big stogie. Drive something you can't control, puff, and grin with the moronic joy of a dog gnawing a cat turd. *Click*. Your life is the perfect consumer snapshot.

It made slow, helpless rage flex inside Ethan, snapping his hands into fists against the ephemeral. He hated being taken for just another whore of fashion. He hated SUVs and trendoids. He hated cigars. But cigar *boxes*, he liked. His grandfather had kept radio serial collector's pins in a cigar box. Just as some wine bottles were far too elegant to contain mere fermented grape juice, the containers for cigars were frequently – no, *always* – cooler than the contents.

At the top of the pile in the cigar box was Valerie. Snugged in with her were Silla, Barbara, Jennifer, Tokay, Wendy, Shari . . . Ethan allowed himself a guilty little grin. A complete inventory would require that he spill out the box again, and take notes. The women in his life numbered too many to permit eidetic recall of them all, or even get them in the right order. The most important ones had left evidence of their passage through his existence – small pockets of happiness in the memory quadrant of his mind; letters and cards and photos, some still aromatic with spicy, private scents, some actually beginning to yellow with age. He recalled his amusement at trying to remember the women in his life who had, by coincidence or a quirk of astrology, used the same fragrance or employed identical brands of stocking.

Valerie was best thumbnailed as ebullient, long of leg and stout of breast and ready to party. She wrote fatuous notes with a lot of exclamation points and deployed the word *love* easily, too easily, with no weight to it, which had always struck Ethan as somehow shallow. Valerie burned fast and climaxed easily; her signature scent like honeydust. She aerobicized, logged wage hours at a savings and loan, and idealized a future in a condo. Once she got married, her life-targets would essentially have been obliterated with sharpshooter precision.

Silla was a college student, a lit major who looked devastating in those little round glasses, who enjoyed arguing poets, drinking

Pinot Grigio, and any movie in which Barbara Stanwyck played hard-bitten. Their first kiss had been the night of a party which Silla's boyfriend had also attended. Everyone shotgunned a lot of alcohol and respirated loads of dope. Ethan crashed on the sofa, half-expecting Silla's roomate, a tawny and flirtatious lass named Iris, to drag him into her waterbed just to drown out the noise of Silla and the boyfriend fucking. Apparently the boyfriend pumped Silla quickly and crudely, executed a half-roll, and lapsed into unconsciousness. Silla emerged an hour later, seeking fruit juice from the fridge during the darkest part of the night. Her conversation with Ethan was whispered, hushed, risky and fun. They were all over each other in no time, there in the complete darkness. It was like fantasy sex with a ghost.

Barbara was a paralegal who smelled like night-blooming jasmine and later admitted that the first thing she looked at was Ethan's butt, in an elevator. She loved to touch you while she talked, pointed things out, or illuminated; her earnestness and need for physical contact radiated off her and convinced you to play, too. She liked to laugh during sex for all the right reasons, and made it a life mission to utterly destroy any bed in which she slept. Her apartment was a disaster, Ethan remembered; it always looked as if it had just been ransacked by burglars.

Tokay was the offspring of Sixties parents whose racial collaboration had gifted her with outstanding bone structure and perfectly leavened, cafe au lait skin, and by the time she met Ethan she had actually broken into modeling. Lanky and girlish, she looked exactly like that phylum of too-young up-and-comers whose film debuts always displayed them as one step shy of jailbait. Even asleep she was photogenic. Even with drool dotting the pillow. She had a bladder the size of a grape and had to dash to the bathroom six times a night; Ethan wondered how anyone could get any useful sleep with so many interruptions. Since she virtually never had to pay for her own clothes, she had skillful tastes in addition to a discerning eye to which Ethan learned to defer. She was so attractive that strangers assumed she was an idiot; Ethan had been privileged to know better.

Wendy was one of Ethan's thunderbolt women, a memory that still had the power to move him. The first time he had ever seen her, he had thought: *This is a woman who is everything you desire, and she will never have anything to do with you.* He first saw her two years before they ever spoke. Their first contact was embarrassingly accidental; Ethan stammered and fumbled and totally blew it; Mister Uncool. Later they fell into the habit of talking on the phone when Ethan *had* no phone; he'd sortie out to a post office in the dead of night and commandeer a payphone for hours. They cultivated a non-physical intimacy that was deeper than her maintenance relationships with a bland menu of hopeful marriage candidates; she joked to Ethan that her "suitables" all looked so alike they had begun to blur in her mind, like microwave entrées. She came to his apartment to celebrate their mutual birthdays (on a date precisely between the two) and played him the way Hendrix played a Strat – and although she did not pour lighter fluid on him, it could be said that she had indeed set him on fire after the solo. It was only then, years after his first lamentable sighting of her, that Wendy admitted her longstanding crush, a thing she had kept secret, and dear to her heart, all that time, hoping for a turn of events like the one that led to them naked and delirious together, and this was the very first time Ethan had thought to himself: *This is a woman I could marry.*

There was no room in this box for Annie, the already-married woman with whom Ethan had conducted a brief and not entirely guilt-free affair, or Marybeth, who had dunned him with phone calls until he had changed his number, or Kristen, the drama psycho, or Marjorie, the medically-certified madwoman.

Sometimes you have to get involved with people to understand that there are some people with whom you should *never* get involved.

There in the box, the corpses of relationships gone by.

Valerie, Barbara and Shari had all gotten married and reproduced, and by doing so, they were no longer attractive to Ethan; he acknowledged that while this view might seem totalitarian, it was at least honest. The photos and memorabilia of them recalled a time when they were unburdened by parenthood and undespoiled by the ravages of birth. They did not "glow." Silla moved away to become a teacher and Ethan had never heard from her again. Tokay had also gotten married. Having broken into modeling, modeling had in turn broken her. The last conversation she'd had with Ethan involved too many details about how her recreational use of chemicals had literally caused her skeleton to start dissolving; her new husband was a producer type who happily paid all her medical bills. She counted herself lucky, like a war vet who'd only lost one leg. The light in her eyes had been cruelly doused, and everyone had hugged everyone else and moved on. Wendy had tired of Ethan and likewise moved on. She tired easily of everything. There was love, and there was security, and she had vanished on a quest for the latter, leaving Ethan with his box of memories.

He remembered Talis, and Joanie, and Celeste, and Stacey, and all the others, and dredged up one-liners to tag and distinguish each of them – Charise's French-model breasts, the dusk violet of Darian's eyes. He found it to be a no-win contest with low aims; a colourless list of statistics concerning whose clitoris was the largest or whose gaze ran the deepest or who was the best kisser; measurements and personal bests; an accountant's view of the erotic that emphasized how fleeting some of these encounters had been. Not Ethan's flavour at all, especially since such a line of thought inevitably led to the one who had been the biggest mistake . . .

. . . still Marjorie, the delusional parasite who had learned the trick of successfully mimicking human behavior, the one who would get away with murder as long as blonde hair and blue eyes were commodities. All's fair, Ethan begrudged, but a city ordinance should disallow cutie-pie names like *Margie* to such creatures.

The cigar box came equipped with a keyed lock on the hasp that was strictly for show. The key matched the hasp and was as tiny as a jeweler's tool. Ethan smiled and placed the key on the topmost photo in the box – Valerie doing a panty-flash in a restaurant; it would have classified as porn in Japan, but it was a keeper for Ethan – and placed the box inside of a fireproof document locker he'd bought at some office megastore. It was warrantied to withstand all manner of life-rending catastrophes and featured a somewhat burlier lock.

Victoria would soon be homeward bound, so it was time for Ethan to wrap his ritualistic stroll through the memory maze. He locked the document box and stashed it among the gone-to-seed jogging shoes and old tax records that inhabited his end of the big walk-in closet. It was like insurance confirming that his marriage to Victoria would prevail. He sustained the irrational fear that to completely erase all evidence of the women of his past would

doom, in some arcane fashion beyond his cognizence, the relationship that had matured into the most important of his life. The
box represented a piece of his past that he felt compelled to keep.

Dark of hair, dark of gaze, Victoria had blindsided his obsessive control over his romantic life. When the powder-burns of
the mad Margie had ceased to bleed on contact, Ethan saw to it
that his next few liaisons were pure matters of technical efficiency,
the no-strings, no promises, I'll-call-you bullshit of the Nineties.
Katherine, Nastasja, Becky and two different Cynthias, one of
them British.

Then came the notorious Barney meeting. Or non-meeting.

It was utterly out of character for Ethan to pit-stop at a
coffeehouse, which he had not liked ever since insectile yupsters
had invented crass compound words like "moccachino". But a
confab with his friend Barney was running an hour late (Barney
had thoughtfully run excuses via cellphone), and Ethan craved an
espresso jolt, so . . .

He immediately regretted walking through the door. He could
smell cigars. The air was fogged. Poseurs pecked away on laptops
in the dark. Idiots with an entirely manufactured nostalgia for the
1970s disported themselves in styles of attire so sickening that
they transcended time – they sucked when they were new, and
they sucked even more now. The place stank of rich brats on the
slum and callow freeloaders wasting time. Before Ethan could
flee, a guy with a lot of facial piercings was asking him about his
"poison".

Which was when he heard Victoria, reading aloud.

There was a postage-stamp-sized stage for struggling artists
and musicians of ill practice; one had to angle sideways past the
stage to get to the bathrooms, and this being a java emporium, the
traffic was a nearly unbroken, antlike flow. The dark-haired,
dark-gazed woman on the platform paid them no notice, directing her occasional glances toward the five people grouped closest
to her in a crescent of rapt attention. She acknowledged them
from time to time during her narrative, as all the best readers do,
with rewarding little glances up from her manuscript pages,
neither breaking the flow of words nor reading her work too
quickly. Ethan noticed that she seemed to miss all the pitfalls that
transformed good writers into bad performers.

Her story had to do with a protagonist mourning a long-dead

love, straight out of Poe except that this main character got what she wanted – the return of the hyper-idealized love – which turned out to be many things she had not wanted, although the fiction was not limited to the hidden baggage of wishmaking. At least, this was as much as Ethan could glean, having walked in on the middle. He joined the semi-circle of listeners, so nothing else would be missed. He sipped his espresso very quietly and forgot about everyone else in the room.

She read with total concentration and complete conviction, threading her tale to its end, whereupon Ethan made sure he was the first to applaud, and the foremost to quiz her on the story.

He amused her by guessing correctly about the section of the story he had missed, and when she asked about his deductions, he told her that given the characters and circumstance, it was the only beginning that fit the rest of the story or made sense.

"It's like the difference between blank verse that flows so well it seems to rhyme—" he began.

She finished for him: "And poetry that rhymes but sounds clunky."

"Exactly."

Years later they still kidded each other about that night, and poor Barney, who had been forgotten entirely, blown off by Ethan, who had fallen in love.

Barney postponed forgiving Ethan until he met Victoria. Then he congratulated him. Past that it was all pretty academic. "So, does this mean, like, Lorissa is available for uh dating?" Barney was a card.

"You can have Margie."

Barney screeched, then made a face-hugger motion, then a vampire cross, with his fingers. "Sooner would I chug a barium martini. A double."

It's a rare value in life, to have that friend who understands without explanation or argument.

Barney and Ethan had once compared high school archetypes; the theory ran that whomever one found attractive, during that pubescent pheromonal waterfall that delineated secondary school, formed the template for one's attractions for the rest of one's earthly life. While Barney, to this day, lamented many of his candidates as lost (which meant he still fantasized about them), Ethan realized that not only had he picked off every archetype that had made his teenage heart flutter, he had actually nailed some of them before graduation. There was no flavour he had not tasted.

Ethan checked the kitchen clock. Victoria was on her way home, and it was time to bury the loves of his past, for reasons that made sense to Ethan and needed to make sense to no one else.

His only remaining problem was where to hide the key.

Most sinks have narrow tuck areas excellent for concealing currency, the odd dope stash, or keys. The problem with sinks – even the areas the most anal retentive never cleaned – was the moisture that could attract bugs, which could eat and thus destroy documents and money and weed. No way to secure a key there. Even wrapped in plastic, it might rust.

Another big black hole where special keys were concerned was that people tended to store them in places they were sure to remember . . . and promptly forgot. Nor was this the sort of key that could be effectively hidden in plain sight.

Ethan decided in favor of the wormwood.

The east wall of the home he shared with Victoria had been an addition to the original house, and was the only section of the whole structure with a fascia of wormwood – an incredibly fragile, earth-toned grain full of natural holes. Ethan guessed it had been stylish sometime around 1961, for dens and such. Behind those boards waited a library of unused, hidden space. Pry marks would show on the delicate wood so he inserted a rubber-coated hook (originally for hanging bicycles) through one of the knotlike holes and loosened the plank by metered jerks. He tapped in a finishing nail so it could hang on the backside of the secret-panel board.

Sneaky guy, so sly, should be a spy.

He thought of wrapping the key in black paper (so it would not reflect errant light through a purely-by-chance knothole at a rare, one-in-a-thousand angle) and was about to hang it and reposition the plank when he looked between the wall joists and found another key. It was dotted with rust, hanging on a twist of old picture frame wire. Otherwise, it looked very much like the newly-wrapped key in his hand.

His mind built a story in the spark of a synapse, sideswiping odd plot bumps and flash-forwarding to the Act Three whammy. His eyes were seeking another document box before his brain caught up.

Fifteen minutes, tops, and Victoria would be barging through the front door, asking if he was home, if he was naked, or decent, and he'd hear the crackle of bags-full of whatever store-bought booty the day had brought. Best to just fix the wall and get on with life.

Sally had been a close-cropped natural redhead with mint green eyes, whose big sexual talent was for arching her spine the way a cat did when grabbing the carpet with splayed claws. It was her brazen choice for optimum penetration. Ethan liked it because there were times you didn't want to look into the eyes of the person with whom you were fucking. Sally was another one that had gotten cornered – marry *now*, reproduce *now*, your life has meaning *now* – and several years afterward, when she recontacted him without warning, Ethan had to explain to her that in seeking him, she was seeking a past that no longer existed. No, he would not have an affair. No, he would not fuck her once "for old times' sake." She tried to restoke the embers of their passion, coming on to him heavily, her breath stinking of loss and bad choices; she told him she understood about his not wanting to have intercourse with her because of the baby – babies – and offered to suck him off. Ethan watched in horror as the woman he thought he once knew seemed to slide from pixieish to pixilated, like a beaver shot clunking down in a slide projector to replace a Monet.

Sally was one of the bad ones who had not made it into the box. A memory too uncomfortable to hold.

The batteries in his metal detector had burst and leaked some months back. Ethan sanded the contacts down with one of Victoria's emery boards and, fortunately, the device still worked when loaded with fresh power cells. It had been bought on a whim from a catalogue, used once on El Capitan beach on a blustery, overcast day, and stashed in the garage forevermore. Victoria and Ethan had raked in eighteen dollars in loose change plus about a quarter-million bottle caps, and actually discovered an ancient Royal typewriter buried in the sand. Ethan remembered joking about pirate treasure when he saw the needle swing over past the noon-spot on the gauge. It was exciting, if only for a moment. It meant the dreaming part of your brain hadn't given up or died when you weren't looking.

Bang, the needle swung over, and that old thrill was back.

Ethan was standing in front of the fireplace. Because of the hearth, the carpet was only loosely anchored on this end of the room by two strips of tack-runner. It peeled up easily. Between floorboards Ethan caught the glint of the metal the scanner had already assured him was there.

The mystery key was a perfect fit.

The house creaked and Ethan's heart seemed to stumble over a hurdle. Victoria. Any minute now. If this was her box of the past, safely interred and *locked*, for god's sake, wasn't that enough reason to leave it alone? He thought of claiming he'd found it by accident, realized how lame *that* was, and blushed. She probably had old love letters in there. What was that old saying about love letters being the only correspondence anyone should keep? Maybe there was something about him. Maybe poetry. The prospects were pretty scary. Maybe photographs. He just wanted to see one secret photo; one glimpse of her when she wasn't looking. Because he loved her.

The topmost items in the box were photographs. But they had nothing to do with Victoria. This was not her box.

It was Ethan's.

Beckah had told Ethan before they ever went to bed together that she had a bifurcated uterus. It seemed an oddly intimate admission; then again, what better way to get to know someone in a hurry? While copulating, Ethan realized this was not a transient matter of tit size or vaginal elasticity; this was a woman who was *built* differently from the other women he'd known. She worked publicity gigs for a small music label; he'd first spotted her sheathed snakeskin-tight into a leather dress at a screening where free copies of the soundtrack CD were handed out as perks. She was confident and imperious; she knew she turned heads. She was another who wore glasses, but wore them well, and knew they were part of her power persona. Another one who, in a cruel world, would never bother with Ethan . . . so he called her up for lunch, and within a week she had told him about her uterus.

Liz was Ethan's first married woman (years prior to the mistake that had been Annie), and the first who had ever told him he was "beautiful" with his clothes off. Wed out of high school, her marriage was like an expired library card, a pointless and outmoded thing. Her husband Richard (Ethan always referred to him as "Dick") was more sanguine with maintaining a "show wife" than actually loving her or taking the time to talk to her. He would have deemed life copacetic if Liz had insisted on having her own room in the house; no prob. What Richard the Dick did *not* like was the concept of divorce in a community property state. Their actual bedroom, which Ethan had seen a grand total of once, contained a canopy bed the size of Ethan's first studio apartment, and when he called it the "tundra," Liz had laughed, then confided that she rarely laughed in this room. Liz and Ethan never fucked on that bed. It was like a rule.

So Ethan fucked Liz in the sink where Richard the Dick prepared his coffee every morning. Hoisted her ass right into the stainless steel and had even used the little rinsing hose to cool off her back.

Now that he was looking at the photographs, Ethan could remember the people in them. But they had not occurred to him, not even in passing, not for years, as though they had been surgically subtracted from his memory center.

Cory, to cite another example. Chinese, her eyes slightly a-knock (which made her unbearably cute), lithe, with a lush furl of the thickest, blackest hair on Earth. A photographer who was rarely photographed herself. Here she was, right in Ethan's grasp, right now, one side of her mouth turned up in an evil smile, her eyes (not crossed) glaring straight at the camera in an under-exposure that blew all the background details to inky darkness. Since she was wearing dark garments she appeared to be a head and hands floating in a void; then of course there was all that luscious hair to account for.

Staring at the picture, Ethan tried to remember making love to Cory and only caught fragments, snap images, single-frame impressions that sped past as though being chased.

Cory was the one who always dug her heels into his ass when she orgasmed. Or – accounting for position – grabbed him so hard when she came that she raised bruises. She had strong hands and a grip like a trash compactor.

Ethan could not recall what had become of Cory. Where the split was. Whether their breakup had been good or bad.

Victoria was half an hour late. Typical. Ethan could not resent his wife's absolute disdain for the clock because it was one of his Top Ten personality traits as well. He sorted through the remaining data in the box. Here a vague impression; there a twinge of remembrance, all of it wispy and insubstantial. Ghosts, playing him for an idiot.

Jacqui, Amanda, Marielle. He tried to boot up their faces from the log of his life. Their faces, scents, and voices, their distinguishing details, their bodies. Emma and Megan and Julia.

At the bottom of the box, Ethan found another key.

The third box was literally entombed in the west wall downstairs, in a room that served multiple duty as a library, a study for Victoria, and guest bedroom. It was full of mismatched furniture; anything that got superceded in the living room wound up in retirement down here. A panel of gypsum board had been cut out of the wall with a keyhole saw, then replaced and repainted. It was not a cache intended for easy access. It was a Tell-Tale Heart abyss of frightening possibilities for Ethan, who had shuffled through the pack of women in the second box again, straining to remember them and dredging up only lees and dust. He recalled childhood meals with more individuality.

The box inside the wall was another cigar box – something familiar, at least. It was caked in lath powder and firmly bound with filament tape that had completely dried out, giving it a mummified aspect, strands of fiber floating away from it like errant eyebrows or threads from ghost shrouds. The smokes, Ethan noted, had been imported Laguna Negra Rectangulares, and he knew them to be vile, dense as plug tobacco formed into a stick. That much, he remembered.

A car passed on the hill outside, and Ethan listened to the motor. Not Victoria's car; some rice-burning SUV piece of junk. The damned sun was going down out there in the world, and she had not thought to call. Ethan usually let the machine grab calls. He would have picked up, right now, for Victoria. He felt himself descending into a sort of Chinese box puzzle in which he might become mentally imprisoned. Deep inside the inmost box within all the larger boxes was a timeless place where he might slowly lose his mind, years thieved in the pursuit of madness while outside, perhaps a minute had elapsed since he'd sealed the first box in the chain.

Enough stalling. Open it, already.

The tape was dry and useless but many of the filaments held

fast, absurdly, and Ethan thought of battling the clutch of a hand in rigor mortis. It shredded, loosing a cloud of sneezy dried adhesive.

More pictures, more women, some naked, some not.

The first one's name was . . . Ashley, that was it. Ashley of the burgundy pubic hair and the Southern accent. She had made up some forgotten nickname for his cock and spoke to it in a little girl voice, which made him feel like a child molester when he was in a bad mood. Ethan had smashed her face with a garden trowel while they were fucking, and he had climaxed while she shuddered gently into death.

He could remember now. The photograph helped because he had snapped it after Ashley's head was all bloody.

And Loreli. Strangled with picture-hanging wire while he pumped her from behind. He'd made a bonfire out of her remaining parts in the desert, the following night. Coyote barbeque.

Here was Loreli, face purpled, eyes white with death; a real Kodak moment.

Trish, he'd shot through the heart. Clean, neat, quick, small-caliber, like a film noir murder, almost bloodless. After taking her picture, he'd dumped her in the bay near Point Pitt.

Bettina and Sara were the Hammer Twins, not because they were actual twins, but because Ethan had killed them with the same hammer, a carpenter's whack with a 14-pound clawed head. They *had* looked pretty much alike when he'd finished swinging. Bettina had been Ethan's first experiment with corrosive acids, the kind you were not supposed to dispense without using eye and breathing protection, because the fumes were murder.

Most of Florice, he'd eaten.

The camera can have a most uncompromising eye, and the photos jogged the appropriate memory: Bridget – drowned and dismembered. Holly – skinned and left for predators. Lorissa, he had not fucked until after he'd killed her; a straight knife gig that definitely made her "no longer available for dating." (Ethan tried never to lie to his friends, and had told his pal Barney the truth about her. Basically.)

That bugged him, Barney's habit of pointedly mentioning that Ethan had always been "surrounded by women" prior to marrying Victoria. Then came new uninvited commentary, along the lines of: "What do you care; *you're* happily married." Barney needed to get out more; specifically, he needed to hang around women more, women who were adults and not relatives, women who could socialize him and terminate his enduring state of girlfriendlessness.

But there was a price, Ethan knew. One could wind up with Kristen the drama psycho or Margie the neural nightmare, and finish life as a drained husk.

Margie, that cunt, had finally gotten what she deserved, payback for every crime against sanity for which her blue eyes or blonde hair had permitted her to skate. He had kneecapped her with a .22 target pistol. She had shrieked for "someone" to rescue her. "Someone" always rescued the Margies of the world, but not today. Ethan put a round into the meat of each of her upper thighs. More screaming, more bullshit pouring from her face in an endless torrent designed to prove her rightness in all things. Ethan saved her face for last. Another soft-nosed slug into each hand. Two more into her tits, puncturing the implants, her blood adulterated by gushing saline. He let her pass out and wake up before he shot her again in the throat. The yammering ceased. He reduced her to a shitbag of animal hate – her true face – before he blew her false skin face clean off her skull, destroying most of the teeth. He extracted the rest with pliers and cut off her fingertips with duck-billed tin snips so no one would ever know who she was. Which had always been a big deal to Margie, so it was particularly apt that no one would ever know what had become of her. They might suspect; but never know.

Doubly ironic, since no one had ever asked.

Ethan remembered something else. It was Margie that had turned him. One bad relationship can do that.

But he remained the master of his destiny, determined that not even a world of Margies could scuttle his happiness with someone as unique as Victoria.

The can of paint he would use to mend the wall was in a storage cabinet in the downstairs bathroom, the big bathroom. So it was settled that he had to go into the bathroom; it was unavoidable.

Whether he'd find the clawfoot tub empty or full, he could not recall.

GEMMA FILES

The Emperor's Old Bones

GEMMA FILES WAS BORN IN LONDON, ENGLAND, and is the daughter of two actors – Gary Files (best known for a continuing role on the Australian TV soap opera *Neighbours*) and Elva Mai Hoover (nominated for a 1984 Best Supporting Actress Genie award for her work as Betty Fox in *The Terry Fox Story*). She has a B.A.A. in Magazine Journalism from Ryerson University, and has spent the last seven years writing freelance film criticism for a popular local news and culture review in Toronto, Canada. She also teaches screenwriting at the Trebas Institute. In 1998, as part of the Third Annual On The Fly Festival of Video Shorts, she wrote and directed her first short film, *Say Thanks*.

Her first professional fiction sale was to *Northern Frights 2*, since when her stories have appeared in such magazines and anthologies as *Grue*, *Transversions*, *Palace Corbie*, *Seductive Spectres* and *Demon Sex*, and since 1993 her work has received an honourable mention in every issue of Ellen Datlow's *The Year's Best Fantasy and Horror* anthology.

In 1997, Files's short stories "Fly-by-Night" and "Hidebound" were optioned by *The Hunger*, a half-hour anthology TV series produced by Telescene for Showtime and TMN, under the aegis of Tony and Ridley Scott's Scott Free production company. More recently, she was contracted to adapt her own stories "Bottle of Smoke" and "The Diarist" for the series' 1999 season. She is now working on a (non-horror) feature film script for Toronto's Hungry Eyes Film Food production company.

"The Emperor's Old Bones" won the International Horror

Writers' Guild Award for Short Fiction and, as the author recalls:
"I first saw the Emperor's Old Bones cooked on a Discovery
Channel special, and immediately thought: 'Say, wait a sec – what
if that carp was a person? Who would *do* that to anybody else . . .
and *why*?' Thus, Tim Darbersmere and Ellis Iseland were born –
yet more proof that I should watch less TV, and possibly get my
head examined (again)."

Oh, buying and selling . . . you know . . . life.
                                    – Tom Stoppard, after J.G. Ballard

ONE DAY IN 1941, NOT LONG AFTER THE FALL OF SHANGHAI,
my amah (our live-in Chinese maid of all work, who often
doubled as my nurse) left me sleeping alone in the abandoned
hulk of what had once been my family's home, went out, and
never came back . . . a turn of events which didn't actually
surprise me all that much, since my parents had done something
rather similar only a few brief weeks before. I woke up without
light or food, surrounded by useless luxury – the discarded
detritus of Empire and family alike. And fifteen more days of
boredom and starvation were to pass before I saw another living
soul.

I was ten years old.

After the war was over, I learned that my parents had managed
to bribe their way as far as the harbour, where they became
separated in the crush while trying to board a ship back "Home".
My mother died of dysentery in a camp outside of Hangkow; the
ship went down halfway to Hong Kong, taking my father with it.
What happened to my amah, I honestly don't know – though I do
feel it only fair to mention that I never really tried to find out,
either.

The house and I, meanwhile, stayed right where we were –
uncared for, unclaimed – until Ellis Iseland broke in, and took
everything she could carry.

Including me.

"So what's your handle, *tai pan*?" She asked, back at the
dockside garage she'd been squatting in, as she went through the
pockets of my school uniform.

(It would be twenty more years before I realized that her own endlessly evocative name was just another bad joke – one some immigration official had played on her family, perhaps.)

"Timothy Darbersmere," I replied, weakly. Over her shoulder, I could see the frying pan still sitting on the table, steaming slightly, clogged with burnt rice. At that moment in time, I would have gladly drunk my own urine in order to be allowed to lick it out, no matter how badly I might hurt my tongue and fingers in doing so.

Her eyes followed mine – a calm flick of a glance, contemptuously knowing, arched eyebrows barely sketched in cinnamon.

"Not yet, kid," she said.

"I'm really very hungry, Ellis."

"I really believe you, Tim. But not yet." She took a pack of cigarettes from her sleeve, tapped one out, lit it. Sat back. Looked a me again, eyes narrowing contemplatively. The plume of smoke she blew was exactly the same non colour as her slant, level, heavy-lidded gaze.

"Just to save time, by the way, here're the house rules," she said. "Long as you're with me, I eat first. Always."

"That's not fair."

"Probably not. But that's the way it's gonna be, 'cause I'm thinking for two, and I can't afford to be listening to my stomach instead of my gut." She took another drag. "Besides which, I'm bigger than you."

"My father says adults who threaten children are bullies."

"Yeah, well, that's some pretty impressive moralizing, coming from a mook who dumped his own kid to get out of Shanghai alive."

I couldn't say she wasn't right, and she knew it, so I just stared at her. She was exoticism personified – the first full-blown Yank I'd ever met, the first adult (Caucasian) woman I'd ever seen wearing trousers. Her flat, Midwestern accent lent a certain fascination to everything she said, however repulsive.

"People will do exactly whatever they think they can get away with, Tim," she told me, "for as long as they think they can get away with it. That's human nature. So don't get all high-hat about it, use it. Everything's got its uses – everything, and everybody."

"Even you, Ellis?"

"Especially me, Tim. As you will see."

*   *   *

It was Ellis, my diffident ally – the only person I have ever met who seemed capable of flourishing in any given situation – who taught me the basic rules of commerce: to always first assess things at their true value, then gauge exactly how much extra a person in desperate circumstances would be willing to pay for them. And her lessons have stood me in good stead, during all these intervening years. At the age of sixty-six, I remain not only still alive, but a rather rich man, to boot – import/export, antiques, some minor drug-smuggling, intermittently punctuated (on the more creative side) by the publication of a string of slim, speculative novels. These last items have apparently garnered me some kind of cult following amongst fans of such fiction, most specifically – ironically enough – in the United States of America.

But time is an onion, as my third wife used to say: the more of it you peel away, searching for the hidden connections between action and reaction, the more it gives you something to cry over.

So now, thanks to the established temporal conventions of literature, we will slip fluidly from 1941 to 1999 – to St Louis, Missouri, and the middle leg of my first-ever Stateside visit, as part of a tour in support of my recently-published childhood memoirs.

The last book signing was at four. Three hours later, I was already firmly ensconced in my comfortable suite at the down-town Four Seasons Hotel. Huang came by around eight, along with my room service trolley. He had a briefcase full of files and a sly, shy grin, which lit up his usually impassive face from some-where deep inside.

"Racked up a lotta time on this one, Mr Darbersmere," he said, in his second-generation Cockney growl. "Spent a lotta your money, too."

"Mmm." I uncapped the tray. "Good thing my publisher gave me that advance, then, isn't it?"

"Yeah, good fing. But it don't matter much now."

He threw the files down on the table between us. I opened the top one and leafed delicately through, between mouthfuls. There were schedules, marriage and citizenship certificates, medical records. Police records, going back to 1953, with charges ranging from fraud to trafficking in stolen goods, and listed under several different aliases. Plus a sheaf of photos, all taken from a safe distance.

I tapped one.

"Is this her?"

Huang shrugged. "You tell me – you're the one 'oo knew 'er."

I took another bite, nodding absently. Thinking: did I? Really? Ever?

As much as anyone, I suppose.

To get us out of Shanghai, Ellis traded a can of petrol for a spot on a farmer's truck coming back from the market – then cut our unlucky saviour's throat with her straight razor outside the city limits, and sold his truck for a load of cigarettes, lipstick and nylons. This got us shelter on a floating whorehouse off the banks of the Yangtze, where she eventually hooked us up with a pirate trawler full of US deserters and other assorted scum, whose captain proved to be some slippery variety of old friend.

The trawler took us up- and down-river, dodging the Japanese and preying on the weak, then trading the resultant loot to anyone else we came in contact with. We sold opium and penicillin to the warlords, maps and passports to the DPs, motor oil and dynamite to the Kuomintang, Allied and Japanese spies to each other. But our most profitable commodity, as ever, remained people – mainly because those we dealt with were always so endlessly eager to help set their own price.

I look at myself in the bathroom mirror now, tall and silver-haired – features still cleanly cut, yet somehow fragile, like Sir Laurence Olivier after the medical bills set in. At this morning's signing, a pale young woman with a bolt through her septum told me: "No offense, Mr Darbersmere, but you're – like – a real babe. For an old guy."

I smiled, gently. And told her: "You should have seen me when I was twelve, my dear."

That was back in 1943, the year that Ellis sold me for the first time – or rented me out, rather, to the mayor of some tiny port village, who threatened to keep us docked until the next Japanese inspection. Ellis had done her best to convince him that we were just another boatload of Brits fleeing internment, even shucking her habitual male drag to reveal a surprisingly lush female figure and donning one of my mother's old dresses instead, much as it obviously disgusted her to do so. But all to no avail.

"You know I'd do it, Tim," she told me, impatiently pacing the trawler's deck, as a passing group of her crewmates whistled appreciatively from shore. "Christ knows I've tried. But the fact is, he doesn't want me. He wants you."

I frowned. "Wants me?"

"To go with him, Tim. You know – grown-up stuff."

"Like you and Ho Tseng, last week, after the dance at Sister Chin's?"

"Yeah, sorta like that."

She plumped herself down on a tarpaulined crate full of dynamite – clearly labelled, in Cantonese, as "dried fruit" – and kicked off one of her borrowed high-heeled shoes, rubbing her foot morosely. Her cinnamon hair hung loose in the stinking wind, back-lit to a fine fever.

I felt her appraising stare play up and down me like a fine grey mist, and shivered.

"If I do this, will you owe me, Ellis?"

"You bet I will, kid."

"Always take me with you?"

There had been some brief talk of replacing me with Brian Thompson-Greenaway, another refugee, after I had mishandled a particularly choice assignment – protecting Ellis's private stash of American currency from fellow scavengers while she recuperated from a beating inflicted by an irate Japanese officer, into whom she'd accidentally bumped while ashore. Though she wisely put up no resistance – one of Ellis's more admirable skills involved her always knowing when it was in her best interest not to defend herself – the damage left her pissing blood for a week, and she had not been happy to discover her money gone once she was recovered enough to look for it.

She lit a new cigarette, shading her eyes against the flame of her Ronson.

"Course," she said, sucking in smoke.

"Never leave me?"

"Sure, kid. Why not?"

I learned to love duplicity from Ellis, to distrust everyone except those who have no loyalty and play no favourites. Lie to me, however badly, and you are virtually guaranteed my fullest attention.

I don' remember if I really believed her promises, even then. But I did what she asked anyway, without qualm or regret. She must have understood that I would do anything for her, no matter how morally suspect, if she only asked me politely enough.

In this one way, at least, I was still definitively British.

Afterward, I was ill for a long time – some sort of psychosomatic reaction to the visceral shock of my deflowering, I suppose. I lay in a bath of sweat on Ellis's hammock, under the trawler's one intact mosquito net. Sometimes I felt her sponge me with a rag dipped in rice wine, while singing to me – softly, along with the radio: A faded postcard from exotic places . . . a cigarette that's marked with lipstick traces . . . oh, how the ghost of you clings . . .

And did I merely dream that once, at the very height of my sickness, she held me on her hip and hugged me close? That she actually slipped her jacket open and offered me her breast, so paradoxically soft and firm, its nipple almost as pale as the rest of her night-dweller's flesh?

That sweet swoon of ecstasy. That first hot stab of infantile desire. That unwitting link between recent childish violation and a desperate longing for adult consummation. I was far too young to know what I was doing, but she did. She had to. And since it served her purposes, she simply chose not to care.

Such complete amorality: it fascinates me. Looking back, I see it always has – like everything else about her, fetishized over the years into an inescapable pattern of hopeless attraction and inevitable abandonment.

My first wife's family fled the former Yugoslavia shortly before the end of the war; she had high cheekbones and pale eyes, set at a Baltic slant. My second wife had a wealth of long, slightly coarse hair, the colour of unground cloves. My third wife told stories – ineptly, compulsively. All of them were, on average, at least five years my elder.

And sooner or later, all of them left me.

Oh, Ellis, I sometimes wonder whether anyone else alive remembers you as I do – or remembers you at all, given your well-cultivated talent for blending in, for getting by, for rendering yourself unremarkable. And I really don't know what I'll do if this woman Huang has found for me turns out not to be you. There's not much time left in which to start over, after all.

For either of us.

*   *   *

Last night, I called the number Huang's father gave me before I left London. The man of the other end of the line identified himself as the master chef of the Precious Dragon Shrine restaurant.

"Oh yes, *tai pan* Darbersmere," he said, when I mentioned my name. "I was indeed informed, that respected personage who we both know, that you might honour my unworthiest of businesses with the request for some small service."

"One such as only your estimable self could provide."

"The *tai pan* flatters, as is his right. Which is the dish he wishes to order?"

"The Emperor's Old Bones."

A pause ensued – fairly long, as such things go. I could hear a Cantopop ballad filtering in, perhaps from somewhere in the kitchen, duelling for precedence with the more classical strains of a wailing erhu. The Precious Dragon Shrine's master chef drew a single long, low breath.

"*Tai pan*," he said, finally, "for such a meal . . . one must provide the meat oneself."

"Believe me, Grandfather, I am well aware of such considerations. You may be assured that the meat will be available, whenever you are ready to begin its cooking."

Another breath – shorter, this time. Calmer.

"Realizing that it has probably been a long time since anyone had requested this dish," I continued, "I am, of course, more than willing to raise the price our mutual friend has already set."

"Oh, no, *tai pan*."

"For your trouble."

"*Tai pan*, please. It is not necessary to insult me."

"I must assure you, Grandfather, that no such insult was intended."

A burst of scolding rose from the kitchen, silencing the ballad in mid-ecstatic lament. The master chef paused again. Then said: "I will need at least three days' notice to prepare my staff."

I smiled. Replying, with a confidence which – I hoped – at least sounded genuine: "Three days should be more than sufficient."

The very old woman (eighty-nine, at least) who may or may not have once called herself Ellis Iseland now lives quietly in a genteelly shabby area of St Louis, officially registered under

the far less interesting name of Mrs Munro. Huang's pictures
show a figure held carefully erect, yet helplessly shrunken in
on itself – its once-straight spine softened by the onslaught of
osteoporosis. Her face has gone loose around the jawline,
skin powdery, hair a short, stiff grey crown of marcelled
waves.

She dresses drably. Shapeless feminine weeds, widow-black.
Her arthritic feet are wedged into Chinese slippers – a small touch
of nostalgic irony? Both her snubbed cat's nose and the half-
sneering set of her wrinkled mouth seem familiar, but her slanted
eyes – the most important giveaway, their original non-colour
perhaps dimmed even further with age, from light smoke-grey to
bone, ecru, white – are kept hidden beneath a thick-lensed pair of
bifocal sunglasses, essential protection for someone whose sight
may not last the rest of the year.

And though her medical files indicate that she is in the pre-
liminary stages of lung and throat cancer, her trip a day to the
local corner store always includes the purchase of at least one
pack of cigarettes, the brand apparently unimportant, as long as it
contains a sufficient portion of nicotine. She lights one right
outside the front door, and has almost finished it by the time
she rounds the corner of her block.

Her neighbours seem to think well of her. Their children wave
as she goes by, cane in one hand, cigarette in the other. She nods
acknowledgement, but does not wave back.

This familiar arrogance, seeping up unchecked through her
last, most perfect disguise; the mask of age, which bestows a kind
of retroactive innocence on even its most experienced victims. I
have recently begun to take advantage of its charms myself,
whenever it suits my fancy to do so.

I look at these pictures, again and again. I study her face,
searching in vain for even the ruin of that cool, smooth, inven-
tively untrustworthy operator who once held both my fortune
and my heart in the palm of her mannishly large hand.

It was Ellis who first told me about The Emperor's Old Bones –
and she is still the only person in the world with whom I would
ever care to share that terrible meal, no matter what by doing so,
it might cost me.

If, indeed, I ever end up eating it at all.

*   *   *

"Yeah, I saw it done down in Hong Kong," Ellis told us, gesturing with her chopsticks. We sat behind a lacquered screen at the back of Sister Chin's, two nights before our scheduled rendezvous with the warlord Wao Ruyen, from whom Ellis had already accepted some mysteriously unspecified commission. I watched her eat – waiting my turn, as ever – while Brian Thompson-Greenaway (also present, much to my annoyance) sat in the corner and watched us both, openly ravenous.

"They take a carp, right – you know, those big fish some rich Chinks keep in fancy pools, out in the garden? Supposed to live hundreds of years, if you believe all that 'Confucius says' hooey. So they take this carp and they fillet it, all over, so the flesh is hanging off it in strips. But they do it so well, so carefully, they keep the carp alive through the whole thing. It's sittin' there on a plate, twitching, eyes rollin' around. Get close enough, you can look right in through the ribcage and see the heart still beating."

She popped another piece of Mu Shu pork in her mouth, and smiled down at Brian, who gulped – apparently suddenly too queasy to either resent or envy her proximity to the food.

"Then they bring out this big pot full of boiling oil," she continued, "and they run hooks through the fish's gills and tail. So they can pick it up at both ends. And while it's floppin' around, tryin' to get free, they dip all those hangin' pieces of flesh in the oil – one side first, then the other, all nice and neat. Fish is probably in so much pain already it doesn't even notice. So it's still alive when they put it back down . . . alive, and cooked, and ready to eat."

"And then – they eat it."

"Sure do, Tim."

"Alive, I mean."

Brian now looked distinctly green. Ellis shot him another glance, openly amused by his lack of stamina, then turned back to me.

"Well yeah, that's kinda the whole point of the exercise. You keep the carp alive until you've eaten it, and all that long life just sorta transfers over to you."

"Like magic," I said.

She nodded. "Exactly. 'Cause that's exactly what it is."

I considered her statement for a moment.

"My father," I commented, at last, "always told us that magic was a load of bunk."

Ellis snorted. "And why does this not surprise me?" She asked, of nobody in particular. Then: "Fine, I'll bite. What do you think?"

"I think . . ." I said, slowly, ". . . that if it works . . . then who cares?"

She looked at me. Snorted again. And then – she actually laughed, an infectious, unmalicious laugh that seemed to belong to someone far younger, far less complicated. It made me gape to hear it. Using her chopsticks, she plucked the last piece of pork deftly from her plate, and popped it into my open mouth.

"Tim," she said, "for a spoiled Limey brat, sometimes you're okay."

I swallowed the pork, without really tasting it. Before I could stop myself, I had already blurted out: "I wish we were the same age, Ellis."

This time she stared. I felt a sudden blush turn my whole face crimson. Now it was Brian's turn to gape, amazed by my idiotic effrontery.

"Yeah, well, not me," she said. "I like it just fine with you bein' the kid, and me not."

"Why?"

She looked at me again. I blushed even more deeply, heat prickling at my hairline. Amazingly, however, no explosion followed. Ellis simply took another sip of her tea, and replied: "'Cause the fact is, Tim, if you were my age – good-lookin' like you are, smart like you're gonna be – I could probably do some pretty stupid things over you."

Magic. Some might say it's become my stock in trade – as a writer, at least. Though the humble craft of buying and selling also involves a kind of legerdemain, as Ellis knew so well; sleight of hand, or price, depending on your product . . . and your clientele.

But true magic? Here, now, at the end of the twentieth century, in this brave new world of 100-slot CD players and incessant afternoon talk shows?

I have seen so many things in my long life, most of which I would have thought impossible, had they not taken place right in front of me. From the bank of the Yangtze River, I saw the bright white smoke of an atomic bomb go up over Nagasaki, like a tear in the fabric of the horizon. In Chungking harbour, I saw two grown men stab each other to death over the corpse of a dog because one wanted to bury it, while the other wanted to eat it. And just beyond the Shanghai city limits, I saw Ellis cut that farmer's throat with one quick twist of her wrist, so close to me that the spurt of his severed jugular misted my cheek with red.

But as I grow ever closer to my own personal twilight, the thing I remember most vividly is watching – through the window of a Franco-Vietnamese arms-dealer's car, on my way to a cool white house in Saigon, where I would wait out the final days of the war in relative comfort and safety – as a pair of barefoot coolies pulled the denuded skeleton of Brian Thompson-Greenaway from a culvert full of malaria-laden water. I knew it was him, because even after Wao Ruyen's court had consumed the rest of his pathetic little body, they had left his face nearly untouched – there not being quite enough flesh on a child's skull, apparently, to be worth the extra effort of filleting . . . let alone of cooking.

And I remember, with almost comparable vividness, when – just a year ago – I saw the former warlord Wao, Huang's most respected father, sitting in a Limehouse nightclub with his Number One and Number Two wife at either elbow. Looking half the age he did when I first met him, in that endless last July of 1945, before black science altered our world forever. Before Ellis sold him Brian instead of me, and then fled for the Manchurian border, leaving me to fend for myself in the wake of her departure.

After all this, should the idea of true magic seem so very difficult to swallow? I think not.

No stranger than the empty shell of Hiroshima, cupped around Ground Zero, its citizenry reduced to shadows in the wake of the blast's last terrible glare. And certainly no stranger than the fact that I should think a woman so palpably incapable of loving anyone might nevertheless be capable of loving me, simply because – at the last moment – she suddenly decided not to let a rich criminal regain his youth and prolong his days by eating me alive, in accordance with the ancient and terrible ritual of the Emperor's Old Bones.

* * *

This morning, I told my publicist that I was far too ill to sign any books today – a particularly swift and virulent touch of the twenty-four-hour flu, no doubt. She said she understood completely. An hour later, I sat in Huang's car across the street from the corner store, watching "Mrs Munro" make her slow way down the street to pick up her daily dose of slow, coughing death.

On her way back, I rolled down the car window and yelled: "*Lai gen wo ma, wai guai!*"

(Come with me, white ghost! An insulting little Mandarin phrase, occasionally used by passing Kuomintang jeep drivers to alert certain long-nosed Barbarian smugglers to the possibility that their dealings might soon be interrupted by an approaching group of Japanese soldiers.)

Huang glanced up from his copy of *Rolling Stone's Hot List*, impressed. "Pretty good accent," he commented.

But my eyes were on "Mrs Munro", who had also heard – and stopped in mid-step, swinging her half-blind grey head toward the sound, more as though scenting than scanning. I saw my own face leering back at me in miniature from the lenses of her prescription sunglasses, doubled and distorted by the distance between us. I saw her raise one palm to shade her eyes even further against the sun, the wrinkles across her nose contracting as she squinted her hidden eyes.

And then I saw her slip her glasses off to reveal those eyes: still slant, still grey. Still empty.

"It's her," I told him.

Huang nodded. "'Fort so. When you want me to do it?"

"Tonight?"

"Whatever you say, Mr D."

Very early on the morning before Ellis left me behind, I woke to find her sitting next to me in the red half-darkness of the ship's hold.

"Kid," she said, "I got a little job lined up for you today."

I felt myself go cold. "What kind of job, Ellis?" I asked, faintly – though I already had a fairly good idea.

Quietly, she replied: "The grown-up kind."

"Who?"

"French guy, up from Saigon, with enough jade and rifles to buy us over the border. He's rich, educated; not bad company, either. For a fruit."

"That's reassuring," I muttered, and turned on my side, study-ing the wall. Behind me, I heard her lighter click open, then catch and spark – felt the faint lick of her breath as she exhaled, transmuting nicotine into smoke and ash. The steady pressure of her attention itched like an insect crawling on my skin: fiercely concentrated, alien almost to the point of vague disgust, infinitely patient.

"War's on its last legs," she told me. "That's what I keep hearing. You got the Communists comin' up on one side, with maybe the Russians slipping in behind 'em, and the good old US of A every-where else. Philippines are already down for the count, now Tokyo's in bombing range. Pretty soon, our little outfit is gonna be so long gone, we won't even remember what it looked like. My educated opinion? It's sink or swim, and we need all the life-jackets that money can buy." She paused. "You listening to me? Kid?"

I shut my eyes again, marshalling my heart-rate.

"Kid?" Ellis repeated.

Still without answering – or opening my eyes – I pulled the mosquito net aside, and let gravity roll me free of the hammock's sweaty clasp. I was fourteen years old now, white-blonde and deeply tanned from the river-reflected sun; almost her height, even in my permanently bare feet. Looking up, I found I could finally meet her grey gaze head-on.

" 'Us'," I said. " 'We'. As in you and I?"

"Yeah, sure. You and me."

I nodded at Brian, who lay nearby, deep asleep and snoring. "And what about him?"

Ellis shrugged.

"I don't know, Tim," she said. "What about him?"

I looked back down at Brian, who hadn't shifted position, not even when my shadow fell over his face. Idly, I inquired: "You'll still be there when I get back, won't you, Ellis?"

Outside, through the porthole, I could see that the rising sun had just cracked the horizon; she turned, haloed against it. Blew some more smoke. Asking: "Why the hell wouldn't I be?"

"I don't know. But you wouldn't use my being away on this job as a good excuse to leave me behind, though – would you?"

She looked at me. Exhaled again. And said, evenly: "You know, Tim, I'm gettin' pretty goddamn sick of you asking me that question. So gimme one good reason not to, or let it lie."

Lightly, quickly – too quickly even for my own well-honed sense of self-preservation to prevent me – I laid my hands on either side of her face and pulled her to me, hard. Our breath met, mingled, in sudden intimacy; hers tasted of equal parts tobacco and surprise. My daring had brought me just close enough to smell her own personal scent, under the shell of everyday decay we all stank of: a cool, intoxicating rush of non-fragrance, firm and acrid as an unearthed tuber. It burned my nose.

"We should always stay together," I said, "because I love you, Ellis."

I crushed my mouth down on hers, forcing it open. I stuck my tongue inside her mouth as far as it would go and ran it around, just like the mayor of that first tiny port village had once done with me. I fastened my teeth deep into the inner flesh of her lower lip, and bit down until I felt her knees give way with the shock of it. Felt myself rear up, hard and jerking, against her soft under-belly. Felt her feel it.

It was the first and only time I ever saw her eyes widen in anything but anger.

With barely a moment's pause, she punched me right in the face, so hard I felt my jaw crack. I fell at her feet, coughing blood.

"Eh—!" I began, amazed. But her eyes froze me in mid-syllable – so grey, so cold.

"Get it straight, *tai pan*," she said, " 'cause I'm only gonna say it once. I don't buy. I sell."

Then she kicked me in the stomach with one steel-toed army boot, and leant over me as I lay there, gasping and hugging myself tight – my chest contracting, eyes dimming. Her eyes pouring over me like liquid ice. Like sleet. Swelling her voice like some great Arctic river, as she spoke the last words I ever heard her say: "So don't you even *try* to play me like a trick, and think I'll let you get away with it."

Was Ellis evil? Am I? I've never thought so, though earlier this week I did give one of those legendary American Welfare mothers $25,000 in cash to sell me her least-loved child. He's in the next room right now, playing Nintendo. Huang is watching him. I think he likes Huang. He probably likes me, for that matter. We are the first English people he has ever met, and our accents fascinate him. Last night, we ordered in pizza; he ate until he was sick, then ate more, and fell asleep in front of an HBO basketball game. If I let him stay with me another week, he might become sated enough to convince himself he loves me.

The master chef at the Precious Dragon Shrine tells me that the Emperor's Old Bones bestows upon its consumer as much life-force as its consumee would have eventually gone through, had he or she been permitted to live out the rest of their days unchecked – and since the child I bought claims to be roughly ten years old (a highly significant age, in retrospect), this translates to perhaps an additional sixty years of life for every person who participates, whether the dish is eaten alone or shared. Which only makes sense, really: it's an act of magic, after all.

And this is good news for me, since the relative experiential gap between a man in his upper twenties and a woman in her upper thirties – especially compared to that between a boy of fourteen and a woman of twenty-eight – is almost insignificant.

Looking back, I don't know if I've ever loved anyone but Ellis – if I'm even capable of loving anyone else. But finally, after all these wasted years, I do know what I want. And who.

And how to get them both.

It's a terrible thing I'm doing, and an even worse thing I'm going to do. But when it's done, I'll have what I want, and everything else – all doubts, all fears, all piddling, queasy little notions of goodness, and decency, and basic human kinship – all that useless lot can just go hang, and twist and rot in the wind while they're at it. I've lived much too long with my own unsatisfied desire to simply hold my aching parts – whatever best applies, be it stomach or otherwise – and congratulate myself on my forbearance anymore. I'm not mad, or sick, or even yearning after a long-lost love that I can never regain, and never really had in the first place. I'm just hungry, and I want to *eat*.

And morality . . . has nothing to do with it.

Because if there's one single thing you taught me, Ellis – one lesson I've retained throughout every twist and turn of this snaky thing I call my life – it's that hunger has no moral structure.

Huang came back late this morning, limping and cursing, after a brief detour to the office of an understanding doctor who his father keeps on international retainer. I am obscurely pleased to discover that Ellis can still defend herself; even after Huang's first

roundhouse put her on the pavement, she still somehow managed
to slip her razor open without him noticing, then slide it shallowly
across the back of his Achilles tendon. More painful than debili-
tating, but rather well done nevertheless, for a woman who can
no longer wear shoes which require her to tie her own laces.

I am almost as pleased, however, to hear that nothing Ellis may
have done actually succeeded in preventing Huang from completing his mission – and beating her, with methodical skill, to
within an inch of her corrupt and dreadful old life.

I have already contacted my publicist, who witnessed the whole
awful scene, and asked her to find out which hospital poor Mrs
Munro has been taken to. I myself, meanwhile, will drive the boy
to the kitchen of the Precious Dragon Shrine restaurant, where I
am sure the master chef and his staff will do their best to keep him
entertained until later tonight. Huang has lent him his pocket
Gameboy, which should help.

Ah. That must be the phone now, ringing.

The woman in bed 37 of the Morleigh Memorial Hospital's
charity wing, one of the few left operating in St Louis – in
America, possibly – opens her swollen left eye a crack, just far
enough to reveal a slit of red-tinged white and a wandering,
dilated pupil, barely rimmed in grey.

"Hello, Ellis," I say.

I sit by her bedside, as I have done for the last six hours. The
screens enshrouding us from the rest of the ward, with its
rustlings and moans, reduce all movement outside this tiny area
to a play of flickering shadows – much like the visions one might
glimpse in passing through a double haze of fever and mosquito
net, after suffering a violent shock to one's fragile sense of
physical and moral integrity.

. . . and oh, how the ghost of you clings . . .

She clears her throat, wetly. Tells me, without even a flicker of
hesitation: "Nuh . . . Ellis. Muh num iss . . . Munro."

But: she peers up at me, straining to lift her bruise-stung lids. I
wait, patiently.

"Tuh—"

"That's a good start."

I see her bare broken teeth at my patronizing tone, perhaps
reflexively. Pause. And then, after a long moment: "Tim."

"Good show, Ellis. Got it in one."

Movement at the bottom of the bed: Huang, stepping through the gap between the screens. Ellis sees him, and stiffens. I nod in his direction, without turning.

"I believe you and Mr Huang have already met," I say. "Mr Wao Huang, that is; you'll remember his father, the former warlord Wao Ruyen. He certainly remembers you – and with some gratitude, or so he told me."

Huang takes his customary place at my elbow. Ellis's eyes move with him, helplessly – and I recall how my own eyes used to follow her about in a similarly fascinated manner, breathless and attentive on her briefest word, her smallest motion.

"I see you can still take quite a beating, Ellis," I observe, lightly. "Unfortunately for you, however, it's not going to be quite so easy to recover from this particular melée as it once was, is it? Old age, and all that." To Huang: "Have the doctors reached any conclusion yet, as regards Mrs Munro's long-term prognosis?"

"Wouldn't say as 'ow there was one, *tai pan*."

"Well, yes. Quite."

I glance back, only to find that Ellis's eyes have turned to me at last. And I can read them so clearly, now – like clean, black text through grey rice-paper, lit from behind by a cold and colourless flame. No distance. No mystery at all.

When her mouth opens again, I know exactly what word she's struggling to shape.

"Duh . . . deal?"

Oh, yes.

I rise, slowly, as Huang pulls the chair back for me. Some statements, I find, need room in which to be delivered properly – or perhaps I'm simply being facetious. My writer's over-developed sense of the dramatic, working double-time.

I wrote this speech out last night, and rehearsed it several times in front of the bathroom mirror. I wonder if it sounds rehearsed? Does calculated artifice fall into the same general category as outright deception? If so, Ellis ought to be able to hear it in my voice. But I don't suppose she's really apt to be listening for such fine distinctions, given the stress of this mutually culminative moment.

"I won't say you've nothing I want, Ellis, even now. But what I really want – what I've always wanted – is to be the seller, for once, and not the sold. To be the only one who has what you want desperately, and to set my price wherever I think it fair." Adding, with the arch of a significant brow: "—or *know* it to be *un*fair."

I study her battered face. The bruises form a new mask, impenetrable as any of the others she's worn. The irony is palpable: just as Ellis's nature abhors emotional accessibility, so nature – seemingly – reshapes itself at will to keep her motivations securely hidden.

"I've arranged for a meal," I tell her. "The menu consists of a single dish, one with which I believe we're both equally familiar. The name of that dish is the Emperor's Old Bones, and my staff will begin to cook it whenever I give the word. Now, you and I may share this meal, or we may not. We may regain our youth, and double our lives, and be together for at least as long as we've been apart – or we may not. But I promise you this, Ellis: no matter what I eventually end up doing, the extent of your participation in the matter will be exactly defined by how much you are willing to pay me for the privilege."

I gesture to Huang, who slips a pack of cigarettes from his coat pocket. I tap one out. I light it, take a drag. Savour the sensation.

Ellis just watches.

"So here's the deal, then: if you promise to be very, very nice to me – and never, ever leave me again – for the rest of our extremely long – partnership—"

I pause. Blow out the smoke. Wait.

And conclude, finally: "—then you can eat first."

I offer Ellis the cigarette, slowly. Slowly, she takes it from me, holding it delicately between two splinted fingers. She raises it to her torn and grimacing mouth. Inhales. Exhales those familiar twin plumes of smoke, expertly, through her crushed and broken nose. Is that a tear at the corner of her eye, or just an upwelling of rheum? Or neither?

"Juss like . . . ahways," she says.

And gives me an awful parody of my own smile. Which I – return. With interest.

Later, as Huang helps Ellis out of bed and into the hospital's service elevator, I sit in the car, waiting. I take out my cellular phone. The master chef of the Precious Dragon Shrine restaurant answers on the first ring.

"How is . . . the boy?" I ask him.

"Fine, *tai pan*."

There is a pause, during which I once more hear music filtering in from the other end of the line – the tinny little song of a video game in progress, intermittently punctuated by the clatter of kitchen implement. Laughter, both adult and child.

"Do you wish to cancel your order, *tai pan* Darbersmere?" The master chef asks me, delicately.

Through the hospital's back doors, I can see the service elevator's lights crawling steadily downward – the floors reeling themselves off, numeral by numeral. Fifth. Fourth. Third.

"*Tai pan?*"

Second. First.

"No. I do not."

The elevator doors are opening. I can see Huang guiding Ellis out, puppeting her deftly along with her own crutches. Those miraculously-trained hands of his, able to open or salve wounds with equal expertise.

"Then I may begin cooking," the master chef says. Not really meaning it as a question.

Huang holds the door open. Ellis steps through. I listen to the Gameboy's idiot song, and know that I have spent every minute of every day of my life preparing to make this decision, ever since that last morning on the Yangtze. That I have made it so many times already, in fact, that nothing I do or say now can ever stop it from being made. Any more than I can bring back the child Brain Thompson-Greenaway was, before he went up the hill to Wao Ruyen's fortress, hand in stupidly trusting hand with Ellis – or the child I was, before Ellis broke into my parents' house and saved me from one particular fate worse than death, only to show me how many, many others there were to choose from.

Or the child that Ellis must have been, once upon a very distant time, before whatever happened to make her as she now is – then set her loose to move at will through an unsuspecting world, preying on other lost children.

. . . these foolish things . . . remind me of you.

"Yes," I say. "You may."

RAMSEY CAMPBELL

The Entertainment

RAMSEY CAMPBELL WAS PRESENTED WITH BOTH the World Horror Convention's Grand Master Award and the Horror Writer Association's Bram Stoker Award for Life Achievement in 1999. His recent novels included *The One Safe Place, The Long Lost, Silent Children, The Pact of the Fathers* and *The Darkest Part of the Woods*. An earlier novel, *The Nameless*, has been filmed as *Los Sin Nombre* by Spanish director Jaume Balaguero.

"Since the anthology 999 was meant to be a statement of the continuing vigour of our field," explains the author, "I thought I'd attempt the kind of nightmare where the supernatural and the psychological meet that I especially enjoy writing. The notion of someone's ending up as a grotesque seaside entertainment had been in my notebooks long before it turned up in Simon Sprackling's really rather splendid film *Funny Man*. While writing the tale I was aware of echoes of 'The Hospice' by my old friend Robert Aickman, and so I tried to make my story not too much like it. I also think the influence of another master, Thomas Ligotti, is discernible."

B Y THE TIME SHONE FOUND HIMSELF BACK IN WESTINGSEA he was able to distinguish only snatches of the road as the wipers strove to fend off the downpour. The promenade where he'd seen pensioners wheeled out for an early dose of sunshine, and backpackers piling into coaches that would take them inland to the Lakes, was waving isolated trees that looked too young to be out by themselves at a grey sea baring hundreds of edges of foam. Through a mixture of static and the hiss on the windscreen a local radio station advised drivers to stay off the roads, and he felt he was being offered a chance. Once he had a room he could phone Ruth. At the end of the promenade he swung the Cavalier around an old stone soldier drenched almost black and coasted alongside the seafront hotels.

There wasn't a welcome in sight. A sign in front of the largest and whitest hotel said NO, apparently having lost the patience to light up its second word. He turned along the first of the narrow streets of boarding houses, in an unidentifiable one of which he'd stayed with his parents nearly fifty years before; but the placards in the windows were just as uninviting. Some of the streets he remembered having been composed of small hotels had fewer buildings now, all of them care homes for the elderly. He had to lower his window to read the signs across the roads, and before he'd finished his right side was soaked. He needed a room for the night – he hadn't the energy to drive back to London. Half an hour would take him to the motorway, near which he was bound to find a hotel. But he had only reached the edge of town, and was braking at a junction, when he saw hands adjusting a notice in the window of a broad three-storey house.

He squinted in the mirror to confirm he wasn't in anyone's way, then inched his window down. The notice had either fallen or been removed, but the parking area at the end of the short drive was unoccupied, and above the high thick streaming wall a signboard that frantic bushes were doing their best to obscure appeared to say most of HOTEL. He veered between the gateposts and came close to touching the right breast of the house.

He couldn't distinguish much through the bay window. At least one layer of net curtains was keeping the room to itself. Beyond heavy purple curtains trapping moisture against the glass, a light was suddenly extinguished. He grabbed his overnight bag from the rear seat and dashed for the open porch.

The rain kept him company as he poked the round brass bellpush next to the tall front door. There was no longer a button, only a socket harbouring a large bedraggled spider that recoiled almost as violently as his finger did. He hadn't laid hold of the rusty knocker above the neutral grimace of the letter-slot when a woman called a warning or a salutation as she hauled the door open. "Here's someone now."

She was in her seventies but wore a dress that failed to cover her mottled toadstools of knees. She stooped as though the weight of her loose throat was bringing her face, which was almost as white as her hair, to meet his. "Are you the entertainment?" she said.

Behind her a hall more than twice his height and darkly papered with a pattern of embossed vines, not unlike arteries, led to a central staircase that vanished under the next floor up. Beside her a long-legged table was strewn with crumpled brochures for local attractions; above it a pay telephone with no number in the middle of its dial clung to the wall. Shone was trying to decide if this was indeed a hotel when the question caught up with him. "Am I . . ."

"Don't worry, there's a room waiting." She scowled past him and shook her head like a wet dog. "And there'd be dinner and a breakfast for anyone who settles them down."

He assumed this referred to the argument that had started or recommenced in the room where the light he'd seen switched off had been relit. Having lost count of the number of arguments he'd dealt with in the Hackney kindergarten where he worked, he didn't see why this should be any different. "I'll have a stab," he said, and marched into the room.

Despite its size, it was full of just two women – of the breasts of one at least as wide as her bright pink dress, who was struggling to lever herself up from an armchair with a knuckly stick and collapsing red-faced, and of the antics of her companion, a lanky woman in the flapping jacket of a dark blue suit and the skirt of a greyer outfit, who'd bustled away from the light-switch to flutter the pages of a television listings magazine before scurrying fast as the cartoon squirrel on the television to twitch the cord of the velvet curtains, an activity Shone took to have dislodged whatever notice had been in the window. Both women were at least as old as the person who'd admitted him, but he didn't let that daunt him. "What seems to be the problem?" he said, and immediately had to say "I can't hear you if you both talk at once."

"The light's in my eyes," the woman in the chair complained, though of the six bulbs in the chandelier one was dead, another missing. "Unity keeps putting it on when she knows I'm watching."

"Amelia's had her cartoons on all afternoon," Unity said, darting at the television, then drumming her knuckles on top of an armchair instead. "I want to see what's happening in the world."

"Shall we let Unity watch the news now, Amelia? If it isn't something you like watching you won't mind if the light's on."

Amelia glowered before delving into her cleavage for an object that she flung at him. Just in time to field it he identified it as the remote control. Unity ran to snatch it from him, and as a newsreader appeared with a war behind him Shone withdrew. He was lingering over closing the door while he attempted to judge whether the mountainous landscapes on the walls were vague with mist or dust when a man at his back murmured "Come out, quick, and shut it."

He was a little too thin for his suit that was grey as his sparse hair. Though his pinkish eyes looked harassed, and he kept shrugging his shoulders as though to displace a shiver, he succeeded in producing enough of a grateful smile to part his teeth. "By gum, Daph said you'd sort them out, and you have. You can stay," he said.

Among the questions Shone was trying to resolve was why the man seemed familiar, but a gust of rain so fierce it strayed under the front door made the offer irresistible. "Overnight, you mean," he thought it best to check.

"That's the least," the manager (presumably) only began, and twisted round to find the stooped woman. "Daph will show you up, Mr . . ."

"Shone."

"Who is he?" Daph said as if preparing to announce him.

"Tom Shone," Shone told her.

"Mr Thomson?"

"Tom Shone. First name Tom."

"Mr Tom Thomson."

He might have suspected a joke if it hadn't been for her earnestness, and so he appealed to the manager. "Do you need my signature?"

"Later, don't you fret," the manager assured him, receding along the hall.

"And as for payment . . ."

"Just room and board. That's always the arrangement."

"You mean you want me to . . ."

"Enjoy yourself," the manager called, and disappeared beyond the stairs into somewhere that smelled of an imminent dinner.

Shone felt his overnight bag leave his shoulder. Daph had relieved him of the burden and was striding upstairs, turning in a crouch to see that he followed. "He's forever off somewhere – Mr Snell," she said, and repeated, "Mr Snell."

Shone wondered if he was being invited to reply with a joke until she added "Don't worry, we know what it's like to forget your name."

She was saying he, not she, had been confused about it. If she hadn't cantered out of sight his response would have been as sharp as the rebukes he gave his pupils when they were too childish. Above the middle floor the staircase bent towards the front of the house, and he saw how unexpectedly far the place went back. Perhaps nobody was staying in that section, since the corridor was dark and smelled old. He grabbed the banister to speed himself up, only to discover it wasn't much less sticky than a sucked lollipop. By the time he arrived at the top of the house he was furious to find himself panting.

Daph had halted at the far end of a passage lit, if that was the word, by infrequent bulbs in glass flowers sprouting from the walls. Around them shadows fattened the veins of the paper. "This'll be you," Daph said, and pushed open a door.

Beside a small window under a yellowing lightbulb the ceiling angled almost to the carpet, brown as mud. A narrow bed stood in the angle, opposite a wardrobe and dressing-table and a sink beneath a dingy mirror. At least there was a phone on a shelf by the sink. Daph passed him his bag as he ventured into the room. "You'll be fetched when it's time," she told him.

"Time? Time . . ."

"For dinner and all the fun, silly," she said, with a laugh so shrill his ears wanted to flinch.

She was halfway to the stairs when he thought to call after her, "Aren't I supposed to have a key?"

"Mr Snell will have it. Mr Snell," she reminded him, and was gone.

He had to phone Ruth as soon as he was dry and changed. There must be a bathroom somewhere near. He hooked his bag over his shoulder with a finger and stepped into the twilight of the corridor. He'd advanced only a few paces when Daph's head poked over the edge of the floor. "You're never leaving us."

He felt absurdly guilty. "Just after the bathroom."

"It's where you're going," she said, firmly enough to be commanding rather than advising him, and vanished down the hole that was the stairs.

She couldn't have meant the room next to his. When he succeeded in coaxing the sticky plastic knob to turn, using the tips of a finger and thumb, he found a room much like his, except that the window was in the angled roof. Seated on the bed in the dimness on its way to dark was a figure in a toddler's blue overall – a Teddy bear with large black ragged eyes or perhaps none. The bed in the adjacent room was strewn with photographs so blurred that he could distinguish only the grin every one of them bore. Someone had been knitting in the next room, but had apparently lost concentration, since one arm of the mauve sweater was at least twice the size of the other. A knitting needle pinned each arm to the bed. Now Shone was at the stairs, beyond which the rear of the house was as dark as that section of the floor below. Surely Daph would have told him if he was on the wrong side of the corridor, and the area past the stairs wasn't as abandoned as it looked: he could hear a high-pitched muttering from the dark, a voice gabbling a plea almost too fast for words, praying with such urgency the speaker seemed to have no time to pause for breath. Shone hurried past the banisters that enclosed three sides of the top of the stairs, and pushed open the door immediately beyond them. There was the bath, and inside the plastic curtains that someone had left closed would be a shower. He elbowed the door wide, and the shower curtains shifted to acknowledge him.

Not only, they had. As he tugged the frayed cord to kindle the bare bulb, he heard a muffled giggle from the region of the bath. He threw his bag onto the hook on the door and yanked the shower curtains apart. A naked woman so scrawny he could see not just her ribs but 'the hollow of her buttocks was crouching on all fours in the bath. She peered wide-eyed at him over one splayed knobbly hand, then dropped the hand to reveal a nose half the width of her face and a gleeful mouth devoid of teeth as she sprang past him. She was out of the room before he could avoid seeing her shrunken disused breasts and pendulous grey-bearded stomach. He heard her run into a room at the dark end of the corridor, calling out "For it now" or perhaps "You're it now." He didn't know if the words were intended for him. He was too busy noticing that the door was boltless.

He wedged his shoes against the corner below the hinges and piled his sodden clothes on top, then padded across the sticky linoleum to the bath. It was cold as stone, and sank at least half an inch with a loud creak as he stepped into it under the blind brass eye of the shower. When he twisted the reluctant squeaky taps it felt at first as though the rain had got in, but swiftly grew so hot he backed into the clammy plastic. He had to press himself against the cold tiled wall to reach the taps, and had just reduced the temperature to bearable when he heard the doorknob rattle. "Taken," he shouted. "Someone's in here."

"My turn."

The voice was so close the speaker's mouth must be pressed against the door. When the rattling increased in vigour Shone yelled "I won't be long. Ten minutes."

"My turn."

It wasn't the same voice. Either the speaker had deepened his pitch in an attempt to daunt Shone or there was more than one person at the door. Shone reached for the sliver of soap in the dish protruding from the tiles, but contented himself with pivoting beneath the shower once he saw the soap was coated with grey hair. "Wait out there," he shouted. "I've nearly finished. No, don't wait. Come back in five minutes."

The rattling ceased, and at least one body dealt the door a large soft thump. Shone wrenched the curtains open in time to see his clothes spill across the linoleum. "Stop that," he roared, and heard someone retreat – either a spectacularly crippled person or two people bumping into the walls as they carried on a struggle down the corridor. A door slammed, then slammed again, unless there were two. By then he was out of the bath and grabbing the solitary bath-towel from the shaky rack. A spider with legs like long grey hairs and a wobbling body as big as Shone's thumbnail scuttled out of the towel and hid under the bath.

He hadn't brought a towel with him. He would have been able to borrow one of Ruth's. He held the towel at arm's length by two corners and shook it over the bath. When nothing else emerged, he rubbed his hair and the rest of him as swiftly as he could. He unzipped his case and donned the clothes he would have sported for dining with Ruth. He hadn't brought a change of shoes, and when he tried on those he'd worn, they squelched. He gathered up his soaked clothes and heaped them with the shoes on his bag, and padded quickly to his room.

As he kneed the door open he heard sounds beyond it: a gasp, another, and then voices spilling into the dark. Before he crossed the room, having dumped his soggy clothes and bag in the wardrobe that, like the rest of the furniture, was secured to a wall and the floor, he heard the voices stream into the house. They must belong to a coach party – brakes and doors had been the sources of the gasps. On the basis of his experiences so far, the influx of residents lacked appeal for him, and made him all the more anxious to speak to Ruth. Propping his shoes against the ribs of the tepid radiator, he sat on the underfed pillow and lifted the sticky receiver.

As soon as he obtained a tone he began to dial. He was more than halfway through Ruth's eleven digits when Snell's voice interrupted. "Who do you want?"

"Long distance."

"You can't get out from the rooms, I'm afraid. There's a phone down here in the hall. Everything else as you want it, Mr Thomson? Only I've got people coming in."

Shone heard some of them outside his room. They were silent except for an unsteady shuffling and the hushed sounds of a number of doors. He could only assume they had been told not to disturb him. "There were people playing games up here," he said.

"They'll be getting ready for tonight. They do work themselves up, some of them. Everything else satisfactory?"

"There's nobody hiding in my room, if that's what you mean."

"Nobody but you."

That struck Shone as well past enough, and he was about to make his feelings clear while asking for his key when the manager said "We'll see you down shortly, then." The line died at once, leaving Shone to attempt an incredulous grin at the events so far. He intended to share it with his reflection above the sink, but hadn't realised until now that the mirror was covered with cracks or a cobweb. The lines appeared to pinch his face thin, to discolour his flesh and add wrinkles. When he leaned closer to persuade himself that was merely an illusion, he saw movement in the sink. An object he'd taken to be a long grey hair was snatched into the plughole, and he glimpsed the body it belonged to squeezing itself out of sight down the pipe. He had to remind himself to transfer his wallet and loose coins and keys from his wet clothes to his current pockets before he hastened out of the room.

The carpet in the passage was damp with footprints, more of which he would have avoided if he hadn't been distracted by sounds in the rooms. Where he'd seen the Teddy bear someone was murmuring "Up you come to mummy. Gummy gum." Next door a voice was crooning "There you all are," presumably to the photographs, and Shone was glad to hear no words from the site of the lopsided knitting, only a clicking so rapid it sounded mechanical. Rather than attempt to interpret any of the muffled noises from the rooms off the darker section of the corridor, he padded downstairs so fast he almost missed his footing twice.

Nothing was moving in the hall except rain under the front door. Several conversations were ignoring one another in the television lounge. He picked up the receiver and thrust coins into the box, and his finger faltered over the zero on the dial. Perhaps because he was distracted by the sudden hush, he couldn't remember Ruth's number.

He dragged the hole of the zero around the dial as far as it would go in case that brought him the rest of the number, and as the hole whirred back to its starting point, it did. Ten more turns of the dial won him a ringing padded with static, and he felt as if the entire house was waiting for Ruth to answer. It took six pairs of rings – longer than she needed to cross her flat – to make her say "Ruth Lawson."

"It's me, Ruth." When there was silence he tried reviving their joke. "Old Ruthless."

"What now, Tom?"

He'd let himself hope for at least a dutiful laugh, but its absence threw him less than the reaction from within the television lounge: a titter, then several. "I just wanted you to know—"

"You're mumbling again. I can't hear you."

He was only seeking to be inaudible to anyone but her. "I say I wanted you to know I really did get the day wrong," he said louder. "I really thought I was supposed to be coming up today."

"Since when has your memory been that bad?"

"Since, I don't know, today, it seems like. No, fair enough, you'll be thinking of your birthday. I know I forgot that too."

A wave of mirth escaped past the door ajar across the hall. Surely however many residents were in there must be laughing at the television with the sound turned down, he told himself as Ruth retorted. "If you can forget that you'll forget anything."

"I'm sorry."

"I'm sorrier."

"I'm sorriest," he risked saying, and immediately wished he hadn't completed their routine, not only since it no longer earned him the least response from her but because of the roars of laughter from the television lounge. "Look, I just wanted to be sure you knew I wasn't trying to catch you out, that's all."

"Tom."

All at once her voice was sympathetic, the way it might have sounded at an aged relative's bedside. "Ruth," he said, and almost as stupidly "What?"

"You might as well have been."

"I might . . . you mean I might . . ."

"I mean you nearly did."

"Oh." After a pause as hollow as he felt he repeated the syllable, this time not with disappointment but with all the surprise he could summon up. He might have uttered yet another version of the sound, despite or even because of the latest outburst of amusement across the hall, if Ruth hadn't spoken. "I'm talking to him now."

"Talking to who?"

Before the words had finished leaving him Shone understood that she hadn't been speaking to him but about him, because he could hear a man's voice in her flat. Its tone was a good deal more than friendly to her, and it was significantly younger than his. "Good luck to you both," he said, less ironically and more maturely than he would have preferred, and snagged the hook with the receiver.

A single coin trickled down the chute and hit the carpet with a plop. Amidst hilarity in the television lounge several women were crying "To who, to who" like a flock of owls. "He's good, isn't he," someone else remarked, and Shone was trying to decide where to take his confusion bordering on panic when a bell began to toll as it advanced out of the dark part of the house.

It was a small but resonant gong wielded by Mr Snell. Shone heard an eager rumble of footsteps in the television lounge, and more of the same overhead. As he hesitated Daph dodged around the manager towards him. "Let's get you sat down before they start their fuss," she said.

"I'll just fetch my shoes from my room."

"You don't want to bump into the old lot up there. They'll be wet, won't they?"

"Who?" Shone demanded, then regained enough sense of himself to answer his own question with a weak laugh. "My shoes, you mean. They're the only ones I've brought with me."

"I'll find you something once you're in your place," she said, opening the door opposite the television lounge, and stooped lower to hurry him. As soon as he trailed after her she bustled the length of the dining-room and patted a small isolated table until he accepted its solitary straight chair. This faced the room and was boxed in by three long tables, each place at which was set like his with a plastic fork and spoon. Beyond the table opposite him velvet curtains shifted impotently as the windows trembled with rain. Signed photographs covered much of the walls – portraits of comedians he couldn't say he recognised, looking jolly or amusingly lugubrious. "We've had them all," Daph said. "They kept us going. It's having fun keeps the old lot alive." Some of this might have been addressed not just to him, because she was on her way out of the room. He barely had time to observe that the plates on the Welsh dresser to his left were painted on the wood, presumably to obviate breakage, before the residents crowded in.

A disagreement over the order of entry ceased at the sight of him. Some of the diners were scarcely able to locate their places for gazing at him rather more intently than he cared to reciprocate. Several of them were so inflated that he was unable to determine their gender except by their clothes, and not even thus in the case of the most generously trousered of them, whose face appeared to be sinking into a nest of flesh. Contrast was provided by a man so emaciated his handless wristwatch kept sliding down to his knuckles. Unity and Amelia sat facing Shone, and then, to his dismay, the last of the eighteen seats was occupied by the woman he'd found in the bath, presently covered from neck to ankles in a black sweater and slacks. When she regarded him with an expression of never having seen him before, and delight at doing so now, he tried to feel some relief, but was mostly experiencing how all the diners seemed to be awaiting some action from him. Their attention had started to paralyse him when Daph and Mr Snell reappeared through a door beside the Welsh dresser that Shone hadn't noticed.

The manager set about serving the left-hand table with bowls of soup while Daph hurried over, brandishing an especially capacious pair of the white cloth slippers Shone saw all the residents were wearing. "We've only these," she said, dropping them at his feet. "They're dry, that's the main thing. See how they feel."

Shone could almost have inserted both feet into either of them. "I'll feel a bit of a clown, to tell you the truth."

"Never mind, you won't be going anywhere."

Shone poked his feet into the slippers and lifted them to discover whether the footwear had any chance of staying on. At once all the residents burst out laughing. Some of them stamped as a form of applause, and even Snell produced a fleeting grateful smile as he and Daph retreated to the kitchen. Shone let his feet drop, which was apparently worth another round of merriment. It faded as Daph and Snell came out with more soup, a bowl of which the manager brought Shone, lowering it over the guest's shoulder before spreading his fingers on either side of him. "Here's Tommy Thomson for you," he announced, and leaned down to murmur in Shone's ear "That'll be all right, won't it? Sounds better."

At that moment Shone's name was among his lesser concerns. Instead he gestured at the plastic cutlery. "Do you think I could—"

Before he had time to ask for metal utensils with a knife among them, Snell moved away as though the applause and the coos of joy his announcement had drawn were propelling him. "Just be yourself," he mouthed at Shone.

The spoon was the size Shone would have used to stir tea if the doctor hadn't recently forbidden him sugar. As he picked it up there was instant silence. He lowered it into the thin broth, where he failed to find anything solid, and raised it to his lips. The brownish liquid tasted of some unidentifiable meat with a rusty undertaste. He was too old to be finicky about food that had been served to everyone. He swallowed, and when his body raised no protest he set about spooning the broth into himself as fast as he could without spilling it, to finish the task.

He'd barely signalled his intentions when the residents began to cheer and stamp. Some of them imitated his style with the broth while others demonstrated how much more theatrically they could drink theirs; those closest to the hall emitted so much noise that he could have thought part of the slurping came from outside the room. When he frowned in that direction, the residents chortled as though he'd made another of the jokes he couldn't avoid making.

He dropped the spoon in the bowl at last, only to have Daph return it to the table with a briskness not far short of a rebuke. While she and Snell were in the kitchen everyone else gazed at Shone, who felt compelled to raise his eyebrows and hold out his hands. One of the expanded people nudged another, and both of them wobbled gleefully, and then all the residents were overcome by laughter that continued during the arrival of the main course, as if this was a joke they were eager for him to see. His plate proved to bear three heaps of mush, white and pale green and a glistening brown. "What is it?" he dared to ask Daph.

"What we always have," she said as if to a child or to someone who'd reverted to that state. "It's what we need to keep us going."

The heaps were of potatoes and vegetables and some kind of mince with an increased flavour of the broth. He did his utmost to eat naturally, despite the round of applause this brought him. Once his innards began to feel heavy he lined up the utensils on his by no means clear plate, attracting Daph to stoop vigorously at him. "I've finished," he said.

"Not yet."

When she stuck out her hands he thought she was going to return the fork and spoon to either side of his plate. Instead she removed it and began to clear the next table. While he'd been concentrating on hiding his reaction to his food the residents had gobbled theirs, he saw. The plates were borne off to the kitchen, leaving an expectant silence broken only by a restless shuffling. Wherever he glanced, he could see nobody's feet moving, and he told himself the sounds had been Daph's as she emerged from the kitchen with a large cake iced white as a memorial. "Daph's done it again," the hugest resident piped.

Shone took that to refer to the portrait in icing of a clown on top of the cake. He couldn't share the general enthusiasm for it; the clown looked undernourished and blotchily red-faced, and not at all certain what shape his wide twisted gaping lips should form. Snell brought in a pile of plates on which Daph placed slices of cake, having cut it in half and removed the clown's head from his shoulders in the process. Though the distribution of slices caused some debate: "Give Tommy Thomson my eye," a man with bleary bloodshot eyeballs said.

"He can have my nose," offered the woman he'd seen in the bath.

"I'm giving him the hat," Daph said, which met with hoots of approval. The piece of cake she gave him followed the outline almost precisely of the clown's sagging pointed cap. At least it would bring dinner to an end, he thought, and nothing much could be wrong with a cake. He didn't expect it to taste faintly of the flavour of the rest of the meal. Perhaps that was why, provoking a tumult of jollity, he began to cough and then choke on a crumb. Far too eventually Daph brought him a glass of water in which he thought he detected the same taste. "Thanks," he gasped anyway, and as his coughs and the applause subsided, managed to say "Thanks. All over now. If you'll excuse me, I think I'll take myself off to bed."

The noise the residents had made so far was nothing to the uproar with which they greeted this. "We haven't had the entertainment yet," Unity protested, jumping to her feet and looking more than ready to dart the length of the room. "Got to sing for your supper, Tommy Thomson."

"We don't want any songs and we don't want any speeches," Amelia declared. "We always have the show."

"The show," all the diners began to chant, and clapped and stamped in time with it, led by the thumping of Amelia's stick. "The show. The show."

The manager leaned across Shone's table. His eyes were pinker than ever, and blinking several times a second. "Better put it on for them or you'll get no rest," he muttered. "You won't need to be anything special."

Perhaps it was the way Snell was leaning down to him that let Shone see why he seemed familiar. Could he really have run the hotel where Shone had stayed with his parents nearly fifty years ago? How old would he have to be? Shone had no chance to wonder while the question was, "What are you asking me to do?"

"Nothing much. Nothing someone of your age can't cope with. Come on and I'll show you before they start wanting to play their games."

It wasn't clear how much of a threat this was meant to be. Just now Shone was mostly grateful to be ushered away from the stamping and the chant. Retreating upstairs had ceased to tempt him, and fleeing to his car made no sense when he could hardly shuffle across the carpet for trying to keep his feet in the slippers. Instead he shambled after the manager to the doorway of the television lounge. "Go in there," Snell urged, and gave him a wincing smile. "Just stand in it. Here they come."

The room had been more than rearranged. The number of seats had been increased to eighteen by the addition of several folding chairs. All the seats faced the television, in front of which a small portable theatre not unlike the site of a Punch and Judy show had been erected. Above the deserted ledge of a stage rose a tall pointed roof that reminded Shone of the clown's hat. Whatever words had been inscribed across the base of the gable were as faded as the many colours of the frontage. He'd managed to decipher only ENTER HERE when he found himself hobbling towards the theatre, driven by the chanting that had emerged into the hall.

The rear of the theatre was a heavy velvet curtain, black where it wasn't greenish. A slit had been cut in it up to a height of about four feet. As he ducked underneath, the mouldy velvet clung to the nape of his neck. A smell of damp and staleness enclosed him when he straightened up. His elbows knocked against the sides of the box, disturbing the two figures that lay on a shelf under the stage, their empty bodies sprawling, their faces nestling together upside down as though they had dragged themselves close for companionship. He turned the faces upwards and saw that the figures, whose fixed grins and eyes were almost too wide for amusement, were supposed to be a man and a woman, although only a few tufts of grey hair clung to each dusty skull. He was nerving himself to insert his hands in the gloves of the bodies when the residents stamped chanting into the room.

Unity ran to a chair and then, restless with excitement, to another. Amelia dumped herself in the middle of a sofa and inched groaning to one end. Several of the jumbo residents lowered themselves onto folding chairs that looked immediately endangered. At least the seating of the audience put paid to the chant, but everyone's gaze fastened on Shone until he seemed to feel it clinging to the nerves of his face. Beyond the residents Snell mouthed "Just slip them on."

Shone pulled the open ends of the puppets towards him and poked them gingerly wider, dreading the emergence of some denizen from inside one or both. They appeared to be uninhabited, however, and so he thrust his hands in, trying to think which of his kindergarten stories he might adapt for the occasion. The brownish material fitted itself easily over his hands, almost as snug as the skin it resembled, and before he was ready each thumb was a puppet's arm, the little fingers too, and three fingers were shakily raising each head as if the performers were being roused from sleep. The spectators were already cheering, a response that seemed to entice the tufted skulls above the stage. Their entrance was welcomed by a clamour in which requests gradually became audible. "Let's see them knock each other about like the young lot do these days."

"Football with the baby."

"Make them go like animals."

"Smash their heads together."

They must be thinking of Punch and Judy, Shone told himself – and then a wish from the floor succeeded in quelling the rest. "Let's have Old Ruthless."

"Old Ruthless" was the chant as the stamping renewed itself – as his hands sprang onto the stage to wag the puppets at each other. All at once everything he'd been through that day seemed to have concentrated itself in his hands, and perhaps that was the only way he could be rid of it. He nodded the man that was his right hand at the balding female and uttered a petulant croak. "What do you mean, it's not my day?"

He shook the woman and gave her a squeaky voice. "What day do you think it is?"

"It's Wednesday, isn't it? Thursday, rather. Hang on, it's Friday, of course. Saturday, I mean."

"It's Sunday. Can't you hear the bells?"

"I thought they were for us to be married. Hey, what are you hiding there? I didn't know you had a baby yet."

"That's no baby, that's my boyfriend."

Shone twisted the figures to face the audience. The puppets might have been waiting for guffaws or even groans at the echo of an old joke: certainly he was. The residents were staring at him with, at best, bemusement. Since he'd begun the performance the only noise had been the sidling of the puppets along the stage and the voices that caught harshly in his throat. The manager and Daph were gazing at him over the heads of the residents; both of them seemed to have forgotten how to blink or grin. Shone turned the puppets away from the spectators as he would have liked to turn himself. "What's up with us?" he squeaked, wagging the woman's head. "We aren't going down very well."

"Never mind, I still love you. Give us a kiss," he croaked, and made the other puppet totter a couple of steps before it fell on its face. The loud crack of the fall took him off guard, as did the way the impact trapped his fingers in the puppet's head. The figure's ungainly attempts to stand up weren't nearly as simulated as he would have preferred. "It's these clown's shoes. You can't expect anyone to walk in them," he grumbled. "Never mind looking as if I'm an embarrassment."

"You're nothing else, are you? You'll be forgetting your own name next."

"Don't be daft," he croaked, no longer understanding why he continued to perform, unless to fend off the silence that was dragging words and antics out of him. "We both know what my name is."

"Not after that crack you fetched your head. You won't be able to keep anything in there now."

"Well, that's where you couldn't be wronger. My name . . ." He meant the puppet's, not his own: that was why he was finding it hard to produce. "It's, you know, you know perfectly well. You know it as well as I do."

"See, it's gone."

"Tell me or I'll thump you till you can't stand up," Shone snarled in a rage that was no longer solely the puppet's, and brought the helplessly grinning heads together with a sound like the snapping of bone. The audience began to cheer at last, but he was scarcely aware of them. The collision had split the faces open, releasing the top joints of his fingers only to trap them in the splintered gaps. The clammy bodies of the puppets clung to him as his hands wrenched at each other. Abruptly something gave, and the female head flew off as the body tore open. His right elbow hit the wall of the theatre, and the structure lurched at him. As he tried to steady it, the head of the puppet rolled under his feet. He tumbled backwards into the mouldy curtains. The theatre reeled with him, and the room tipped up.

He was lying on his back, and his breath was somewhere else. In trying to prevent the front of the theatre from striking him he'd punched himself on the temple with the cracked male head. Through the proscenium he saw the ceiling high above him and heard the appreciation of the audience. More time passed than he thought necessary before several of them approached.

Either the theatre was heavier than he'd realised or his fall had weakened him. Even once he succeeded in peeling Old Ruthless off his hand he was unable to lift the theatre off himself as the puppet lay like a deflated baby on his chest. At last Amelia lowered herself towards him, and he was terrified that she intended to sit on him. Instead she thrust a hand that looked boiled almost into his face to grab the proscenium and haul the theatre off him. As someone else bore it away she seized his lapels and, despite the creaking of her stick, yanked him upright while several hands helped raise him from behind. "Are you fit?" she wheezed.

"I'll be fine," Shone said before he knew. All the chairs had been pushed back against the windows, he saw. "We'll show you one of our games now," Unity said behind him.

"You deserve it after all that," said Amelia, gathering the fragments of the puppets to hug them to her breasts.

"I think I'd like—"

"That's right, you will. We'll show you how we play. Who's got the hood?"

"Me," Unity cried. "Someone do it up for me."

Shone turned to see her flourishing a black cap. As she raised it over her head, he found he was again robbed of breath. When she tugged it down he realised that it was designed to cover the player's eyes, more like a magician's prop than an element of any game. The man with the handless watch dangling from his wrist pulled the cords of the hood tight behind her head and tied them in a bow, then twirled her round several times, each of which drew from her a squeal only just of pleasure. She wobbled around once more as, having released her, he tiptoed to join the other residents against the walls of the room.

She had her back to Shone, who had stayed by the chairs, beyond which the noise of rain had ceased. She darted away from him, her slippered feet patting the carpet, then lurched sideways towards nobody in particular and cocked her head. She was well out of the way of Shone's route to the door, where Daph and the manager looked poised to sneak out. He only had to avoid the blinded woman and he would be straight up to his room, either to barricade himself in or to retrieve his belongings and head for the car. He edged one foot forward into the toe of the slipper, and Unity swung towards him. "Caught you. I know who that is, Mr Tommy Thomson."

"No you don't," Shone protested in a rage at everything that had led to the moment, but Unity swooped at him. She closed her bony hands around his cheeks and held on tight far longer than seemed reasonable before undoing the bow of the hood with her right hand while gripping and stroking his chin with the other. "Now it's your turn to go in the dark."

"I think I've had enough for one day, if you'll excuse—"

This brought a commotion of protests not far short of outrage. "You aren't done yet, a young thing like you." "She's older than you and she didn't make a fuss." "You've been caught, you have to play." "If you don't it won't be fair." The manager had retreated into the doorway and was pushing air at Shone with his outstretched hands as Daph mouthed, "It's supposed to be the old lot's time." Her words and the rising chant of, "Be fair" infected Shone with guilt, aggravated when Unity uncovered her reproachful eyes and held out the hood. He'd disappointed Ruth, he didn't need to let these old folk down too. "Fair enough, I'll play," he said. "Just don't twist me too hard."

He hadn't finished speaking when Unity planted the hood on his scalp and drew the material over his brows. It felt like the clammy bodies of the puppets. Before he had a chance to shudder it was dragging his eyelids down, and he could see nothing but darkness. The hood moulded itself to his cheekbones as rapid fingers tied the cords behind his head. "Not too—" he gasped at whoever started twirling him across the room.

He felt as if he'd been caught by a vortex of cheering and hooting, but it included murmurs too. "He played with me in the bath." "He wouldn't let us in there." "He made me miss my cartoons." "That's right, and he tried to take the control off us." He was being whirled so fast he no longer knew where he was. "Enough," he cried, and was answered by an instant hush. Several hands shoved him staggering forward, and a door closed stealthily behind him.

At first he thought the room had grown colder and damper. Then, as his giddiness steadied, he understood that he was in a different room, further towards the rear of the house. He felt the patchy lack of carpet through his slippers, though that seemed insufficient reason for the faint scraping of feet he could hear surrounding him to sound so harsh. He thought he heard a whisper or the rattling of some object within a hollow container level with his head. Suddenly, in a panic that flared like white blindness inside the hood, he knew Daph's last remark hadn't been addressed to him, nor had it referred to anyone he'd seen so far. His hands flew to untie the hood – not to see where he was and with whom, but to see which way to run.

He was so terrified to find the cord immovably knotted that it took him seconds to locate the loose ends of the bow. A tug at them released it. He was forcing his fingertips under the edge of the hood when he heard light dry footsteps scuttle towards him, and an article that he tried to think of as a hand groped at his face. He staggered backwards, blindly fending off whatever was there. His fingers encountered ribs barer than they ought to be, and poked between them to meet the twitching contents of the bony cage. The whole of him convulsed as he snatched off the hood and flung it away.

The room was either too dark or not quite dark enough. It was at least the size of the one he'd left, and contained half a dozen sagging armchairs that glistened with moisture, and more than twice as many figures. Some were sprawled like loose bundles of sticks topped with grimacing masks on the chairs, but nonetheless doing their feeble best to clap their tattered hands. Even those that were swaying around him appeared to have left portions of themselves elsewhere. All of them were attached to strings or threads that glimmered in the murk and led his reluctant gaze to the darkest corner of the room. A restless mass crouched in it – a body with too many limbs, or a huddle of bodies that had grown inextricably entangled by the process of withering. Some of its movement, though not all, was of shapes that swarmed many-legged out of the midst of it, constructing parts of it or bearing away fragments or extending more threads to the other figures in the room. It took an effort that shrivelled his mind before he was able to distinguish anything else: a thin gap between curtains, a barred window beyond – to his left, the outline of a door to the hall. As the figure nearest to him bowed so close he saw the very little it had in the way of eyes peering through the hair it had stretched coquettishly over its face, Shone bolted for the hall.

The door veered aside as his dizziness swept it away. His slippers snagged a patch of carpet and almost threw him on his face. The doorknob refused to turn in his sweaty grasp, even when he gripped it with both hands. Then it yielded, and as the floor at his back resounded with a mass of uneven yet purposeful shuffling, the door juddered open. He hauled himself around it and fled awkwardly, slippers flapping, out of the dark part of the hall.

Every room was shut. Other than the scratching of nails or of the ends of fingers at the door behind him, there was silence. He dashed along the hall, striving to keep the slippers on, not knowing why, knowing only that he had to reach the front door. He seized the latch and flung the door wide and slammed it as he floundered out of the house.

The rain had ceased except for a dripping of foliage. The gravel glittered like the bottom of a stream. The coach he'd heard arriving – an old private coach spattered with mud – was parked across the rear of his car, so close it practically touched the bumper. He could never manoeuvre out of that trap. He almost knocked on the window of the television lounge, but instead limped over the gravel and into the street, towards the quiet hotels. He had no idea where he was going except away from the house. He'd hobbled just a few paces, his slippers growing more sodden and his feet sorer at each step, when headlamps sped out of the town.

They belonged to a police car. It halted beside him, its hazard lights twitching, and a uniformed policeman was out of the passenger seat before Shone could speak. The man's slightly chubby concerned face was a wholesome pink beneath a streetlamp. "Can you help me?" Shone pleaded. "I—"

"Don't get yourself in a state, old man. We saw where you came from."

"They boxed me in. My car, I mean, look. If you can just tell them to let me out—"

The driver moved to Shone's other side. He might have been trying to outdo his colleague's caring look. "Calm down now. We'll see to everything for you. What have you done to your head?"

"Banged it. Hit it with, you wouldn't believe me, it doesn't matter. I'll be fine. If I can just fetch my stuff—"

"What have you lost? Won't it be in the house?"

"That's right, at the top. My shoes are."

"Feet hurting, are they? No wonder with you wandering around like that on a night like this. Here, get his other arm." The driver had taken Shone's right elbow in a firm grip, and now he and his partner easily lifted Shone and bore him towards the house. "What's your name, sir?" the driver enquired.

"Not Thomson, whatever anyone says. Not Tommy Thomson or Tom either. Or rather, it's Tom all right, but Tom Shone. That doesn't sound like Thomson, does it? Shone as in shine. I used to know someone who said I still shone for her, you still shine for me, she'd say. Been to see her today as a matter of fact." He was aware of talking too much as the policemen kept nodding at him and the house with its two lit windows – the television lounge's and his – reared over him. "Anyway, the point is the name's Shone," he said. "Ess aitch, not haitch as some youngsters won't be told it isn't, oh en ee. Shone."

"We've got you." The driver reached for the empty bellpush, then pounded on the front door. It swung inwards almost at once, revealing the manager. "Is this gentleman a guest of yours, Mr Snell?" the driver's colleague said.

"Mr Thomson. We thought we'd lost you," Snell declared, and pushed the door wide. All the people from the television lounge were lining the hall like spectators at a parade. "Tommy Thomson," they chanted.

"That's not me," Shone protested, pedalling helplessly in the air until his slippers flew into the hall. "I told you—"

"You did, sir," the driver murmured, and his partner said even lower "Where do you want us to take you?"

"To the top, just to—"

"We know," the driver said conspiratorially. The next moment Shone was sailing to the stairs and up them, with the briefest pause as the policemen retrieved a slipper each. The chant from the hall faded, giving way to a silence that seemed most breathlessly expectant in the darkest sections of the house. He had the police with him, Shone reassured himself. "I can walk now," he said, only to be borne faster to the termination of the stairs. "Where the door's open?" the driver suggested. "Where the light is?"

"That's me. Not me really, anything but, I mean—"

They swung him through the doorway by his elbows and deposited him on the carpet. "It couldn't be anybody else's room," the driver said, dropping the slippers in front of Shone. "See, you're already here."

Shone looked where the policemen were gazing with such sympathy it felt like a weight that was pressing him into the room. A photograph of himself and Ruth, arms around each other's shoulders with a distant mountain behind, had been removed from his drenched suit and propped on the shelf in place of the telephone. "I just brought that," he protested, "you can see how wet it was," and limped across the room to don his shoes. He hadn't reached them when he saw himself in the mirror.

He stood swaying a little, unable to retreat from the sight. He heard the policemen murmur together and withdraw, and their descent of the stairs, and eventually the dual slam of car doors and the departure of the vehicle. His reflection still hadn't allowed him to move. It was no use his telling himself that some of the tangle of wrinkles might be cobwebs, not when his hair was no longer greying but white. "All right, I see it," he yelled – he had no idea at whom. "I'm old. I'm old."

"Soon," said a whisper like an escape of gas in the corridor, along which darkness was approaching as the lamps failed one by one. "You'll be plenty of fun yet," the remains of another voice said somewhere in his room. Before he could bring himself to look for its source, an item at the end of most of an arm fumbled around the door and switched out the light. The dark felt as though his vision was abandoning him, but he knew it was the start of another game. Soon he would know if it was worse than hide and seek – worse than the first sticky unseen touch of the web of the house on his face.

NEIL GAIMAN

Harlequin Valentine

NEIL GAIMAN USED TO HAVE A LIFE, with three children, a house, and a pumpkin patch in the garden. Instead of a life, these days he just has a novel – a great big novel called *American Gods*, which just seems to get longer and longer the more he writes it. Nobody has seen him for months. The children are very understanding and he hopes the novel will be done before they graduate, get jobs, and marry.

He has also been keeping himself busy with a bestselling fairy tale for adults, *Stardust*; an acclaimed short story collection, *Smoke and Mirrors*; scripting the English-language version of Hayao Miyazaki's *anime*, *Princess Mononoke*, and completing a scary book for children entitled *Coraline*. He recently won the Bram Stoker Award for his graphic novel *Sandman: The Dream Hunters*, but the door fell off.

Gaiman was Master of Ceremonies at the 1999 World Horror Convention, and here he explains the background to the following story, which was first published in the program book: "'Harlequin Valentine' was inspired by a Lisa Snelling's statue, of a little jester Harlequin, and by drawings I saw as a child of harlequinades. There always seemed to be something sinister about the character of Harlequin – sinister and innocent at the same time, and I've always loved the motifs and repeating conventions of harlequinades."

IT IS FEBRUARY THE 14TH, at that hour of the morning when all the children have been taken to school and all the husbands have driven themselves to work or been dropped, steambreathing and greatcoated at the rail station at the edge of the town for the Great Commute, when I pin my heart to Missy's front door. The heart is a deep dark red that is almost a brown, the colour of liver. Then I knock on the door, sharply, *rat-a-tat-tat!*, and I grasp my wand, my stick, my oh-so-thrustable and beribboned lance and I vanish like cooling steam into the chilly air . . .

Missy opens the door. She looks tired.

"My Columbine," I breathe, but she hears not a word. She turns her head, so she takes in the view from one side of the street to the other, but nothing moves. A truck rumbles in the distance. She walks into the kitchen and I dance, silent as a breeze, as a mouse, as a dream, into the kitchen beside her.

Missy takes a plastic sandwich bag from a paper box in the kitchen drawer, and two sections of kitchen towel, and a bottle of cleaning spray. Then she walks back to the front door. She pulls the pin from the painted wood – it was my hat pin, which I had stumbled across . . . where? I turn the matter over in my head: in Gascony, perhaps? or Twickenham? or Prague?

The face on the end of the hatpin is that of a pale Pierrot.

She pulls the heart from the pin, and puts the heart into the plastic sandwich bag. She wipes the blood from the door with cleaning spray, and she inserts the pin into her lapel, where the little white-faced August face stares out at the cold world with his grave silver lips.

Naples. Now it comes back to me. I purchased the hatpin in Naples, from an old woman with one eye. She smoked a clay pipe. This was a long time ago.

Missy puts the cleaning utensils down on the kitchen table, then she thrusts her arms through the sleeves of her old blue coat, which was once her mother's, does up the buttons, one, two, three, then she places the sandwich bag with the heart in it determinedly into her pocket and sets off down the street.

Secret, secret, quiet as a mouse I follow her, sometimes creeping, sometimes dancing, and she never sees me, not for a moment, just pulls her blue coat more tightly around her, and she walks through the little town, and down the old road that leads past the cemetery.

The wind tugs at my hat, and I regret, for a moment, the loss of my hatpin. But I am in love, and this is Valentine's Day. Sacrifices must be made.

Missy is remembering in her head the times she has walked into the cemetery, through the tall iron cemetery gates: when her father died; and when they came here at All Hallow's, the whole school mob and caboodle of them, partying and scaring each other; and when a secret lover was killed in a three-car pile up on the interstate, and she waited until the end of the funeral, when the day was all over and done with, and she came in the evening, just before sunset, and laid a white lily on the fresh grave.

Oh Missy, shall I sing the body and the blood of you, the lips and the eyes? A thousand hearts I would give you, as your valentine. Proudly I wave my staff in the air and dance, singing silently of the gloriousness of me, as we skip together down Cemetery Road.

A low grey building, and Missy pushes open the door. She says Hi and How's It Going to the girl at the desk who makes no intelligible reply, fresh out of school and filling in a crossword from a periodical filled with nothing but crosswords, page after page of them, and the girl would be making private phone calls on company time if only she had somebody to call, which she doesn't, and, I see, plain as elephants, she never will. Her face is a mass of blotchy acne pustules and acne scars and she thinks it matters, and talks to nobody. I see her life spread out before me: she will die, unmarried and unmolested, of breast cancer in fifteen years' time, and will be planted under a stone with her name on it in the meadow by Cemetery Road, and the first hands to have touched her breasts will have been those of the pathologist as he cuts out the cauliflower-like stinking growth and mutters "Jesus, look at the size of this thing, why didn't she *tell* anyone?" which rather misses the point.

Gently, I kiss her on her spotty cheek, and whisper to her that she is beautiful. Then I tap her once, twice, thrice, on the head with my staff, and wrap her with a ribbon.

She stirs and smiles. Perhaps tonight she will get drunk and dance and offer up her virginity upon Hymen's altar, meet a young man who cares more for her breasts than for her face, and will one day, stroking those breasts and suckling and rubbing them say "Honey, you seen anybody about that lump?" and by then her spots will be long gone, rubbed and kissed and frottaged into oblivion . . .

But now I have mislaid Missy, and I run and caper down a dun-carpeted corridor until I see that blue coat pushing into a room at the end of the hallway and I follow her into an unheated room, tiled in bathroom-green.

The stench is unbelievable, heavy and rancid and wretched on the air. The fat man in the stained lab coat wears disposable rubber gloves and has a thick layer of mentholatum on his upper lip and about his nostrils. A dead man is on the table in front of him. The man is a thin, old black man, with calloused fingertips. He has a thin moustache. The fat man has not noticed Missy yet. He has made an incision, and now he peels back the skin with a wet, sucking sound, and how dark the brown of it is on the outside, and how pink, pretty the pink of it is on the inside.

Classical music plays from a portable radio, very loudly. Missy turns the radio off, then she says "Hello, Vernon."

The fat man says "Hello Missy. You come for your old job back?"

This is The Doctor, I decide, for he is too big, too round, too magnificently well-fed to be Pierrot, too unselfconscious to be Pantaloon. His face creases with delight to see Missy, and she smiles to see him, and I am jealous: I feel a stab of pain shoot through my heart (currently in a plastic sandwich bag in Missy's coat pocket) sharper than I felt when I stabbed it with my hatpin and stuck it to her door.

And speaking of my heart, she has pulled it from her pocket, and is waving it at the pathologist, Vernon. "Do you know what this is?" she says.

"Heart," he says. "Kidneys don't have the ventricles, and brains are bigger and squishier. Where d'you get it?"

"I was hoping that you could tell me," she says. "Doesn't it come from here? Is it your idea of a Valentine's card, Vernon? A human heart stuck to my front door?"

He shakes his head. "Don't come from here," he says. "You want I should call the police?"

She shakes her head. "With my luck," she says, "they'll decide I'm a serial killer and send me to the chair."

The Doctor opens the sandwich bag, and prods at the heart with stubby fingers in latex gloves. "Adult, in pretty good shape, took care of his heart," he said. "Cut out by an expert."

I smile proudly at this, and bend down to talk to the dead black man on the table, with his chest all open and string-bass-picking fingers. "Go way Harlequin," he mutters, quietly, not to offend Missy and his doctor. "Don't you go causing trouble here."

"Hush yourself. I will cause trouble wherever I wish," I tell him. "It is my function." But, for a moment, I feel a void about me: I am wistful, almost pierrotish, which is a poor thing for a harlequin to be.

Oh Missy I saw you yesterday in the street, and followed you into Al's Super-Valu Foods and More, elation and joy rising within me. In you, I recognised someone who could transport me, take me from myself. In you I recognised my Valentine, my Columbine.

I did not sleep last night, and instead I turned the town topsy and turvy, befuddling the unfuddled, causing three sober bankers to make fools of themselves with drag queens from Madame Zora's Revue and Bar, and slipping into the bedrooms of the sleeping, unseen and unimagined, slipping the evidence of mysterious and exotic trysts into pockets and under pillows and into crevices, able only to imagine the fun that would ignite the following day as soiled split-crotch fantasy panties would be found poorly hidden under sofa cushions and in the inner pockets of respectable suits.

But my heart was not in it, and the only face I could see was Missy's.

Oh, Harlequin in love is a sorry creature.

I wonder what she will do with my gift. Some girls spurn my heart; others touch it, kiss it, caress it, punish it with all manner of endearments before they return it to my keeping. Some never even see it.

Missy takes the heart back, puts it in the sandwich bag again, pushes the snap-shut top of it closed.

"Shall I incinerate it?" she asks.

"Might as well. You know where the incinerator is," says the Doctor, returning to the dead musician on the table. "And I meant what I said about your old job. I need a good lab assistant."

I imagine my heart trickling up to the sky as ashes and smoke, covering the world. I do not know what I think of this, but, her jaw set, she shakes her head and she bids goodbye to Vernon the pathologist. She has thrust my heart into her pocket and she is walking out of the building and up Cemetery Road and back into town.

I caper ahead of her. Interaction would be a fine thing, I decide, and fitting word to deed I disguise myself as a bent old woman on her way to the market, covering the red spangles of my costume with a tattered cloak, hiding my masked face with a voluminous hood, and at the top of Cemetery Road I step out and block her way.

Marvellous, marvellous, marvellous me, and I say to her, in the voice of the oldest of women, "Spare a copper coin for a bent old woman dearie and I'll tell you a fortune will make your eyes spin with joy," and she stops. Missy opens her purse and takes out a dollar bill.

"Here," says Missy.

And I have it in my head to tell her all about the mysterious man she will meet, all dressed in red and yellow, with his domino mask, who will thrill her and love her and never, never leave her (for it is not a good thing to tell your Columbine the *entire* truth), but instead I find myself saying, in a cracked old voice, "Have you ever heard of Harlequin?"

Missy looks thoughtful. Then she nods. "Yes," she says. "Character in the Commedia del Arte. Costume covered in little diamond shapes. Wore a mask. I think he was a clown of some sort, wasn't he?"

I shake my head, beneath my hood. "No clown," I tell her. "He was . . ."

And I find that I am about to tell her the truth, so I choke back the words and pretend that I am having the kind of coughing attack to which elderly women are particularly susceptible. I wonder if this could be the power of love. I do not remember it troubling me with other women I thought I had loved, other Columbines I have encountered over centuries now long gone.

I squint through old woman eyes at Missy: she is in her early twenties, and she has lips like a mermaid's, full and well-defined and certain, and grey eyes, and a certain intensity to her gaze.

"Are you all right?" she asks.

I cough and splutter and cough some more, and gasp, "Fine, my dearie-duck, I'm just fine, thank you kindly."

"So," she said, "I thought you were going to tell me my fortune."

"Harlequin has given you his heart," I hear myself saying. "You must discover its beat yourself."

She stares at me, puzzled. I cannot change or vanish while her eyes are upon me, and I feel frozen, angry at my trickster tongue for betraying me. "Look," I tell her, "a rabbit!" and she turns, follows my pointing finger and as she takes her eyes off me I disappear, *pop!*, like a rabbit down a hole, and when she looks back there's not a trace of the old fortune-teller lady, which is to say me.

Missy walks on, and I caper after her, but there is not the spring in my step there was earlier in the morning.

Midday, and Missy has walked to Al's Super-Valu Foods and More, where she buys a small block of cheese, a carton of unconcentrated orange juice, two avocados, and on to the County One Bank where she withdraws two hundred and seventy nine dollars and twenty-two cents, which is the total amount of money in her savings account, and I creep after her sweet as sugar and quiet as the grave.

"Morning Missy," says the owner of the Salt Shaker Café, when Missy enters. He has a trim beard, more pepper than salt, and my heart would have skipped a beat if it were not in the sandwich bag in Missy's pocket, for this man obviously lusts after her and my confidence, which is legendary, droops and wilts. *I am Harlequin, I tell myself, in my diamond-covered garments, and the world is my harlequinade. I am Harlequin, who rose from the dead to play his pranks upon the living. I am Harlequin, in my mask, with my wand. I whistle to myself, and my confidence rises, hard and full once more.*

"Hey, Harve," says Missy. "Give me a plate of hash browns, and a bottle of ketchup."

"That all?" he asks.

"Yes," she says. "That'll be perfect. And a glass of water."

I tell myself that the man Harve is Pantaloon, the foolish merchant that I must bamboozle, baffle, confusticate and confuse. Perhaps there is a string of sausages in the kitchen. I resolve to bring delightful disarray to the world, and to bed luscious Missy before midnight: my Valentine's present to myself. I imagine myself kissing her lips.

There are a handful of other diners. I amuse myself by swapping their plates while they are not looking, but I have trouble finding the fun in it. The waitress is thin, and her hair hangs in sad ringlets about her face. She ignores Missy, who she obviously considers entirely Harve's preserve.

Missy sits at the table, and pulls the sandwich bag from her pocket. She places it on the table in front of her.

Harve-the-pantaloon struts over to Missy's table, gives her a glass of water, and a plate of hash-browned potatoes, and a bottle of Heinz 57 Varieties Tomato Ketchup. "And a steak knife," she tells him.

I trip him up on the way back to the kitchen. He curses, and I feel better, more like the former me, and I goose the waitress as she passes the table of an old man who is reading *USA Today* while toying with his salad. She gives the old man a filthy look. I chuckle, and then I find I am feeling most peculiar. I sit down upon the floor, suddenly.

"What's that, honey?" the waitress asks Missy.

"Health food, Charlene," says Missy. "Builds up iron." I peep over the tabletop. She is slicing up small slices of meat on her plate, liberally doused in tomato sauce, and piling her fork high with hash browns. Then she chews.

I watch my heart disappearing into her rosebud mouth. My valentine's jest somehow seems less funny.

"You anaemic?" asks the waitress, on her way past once more, with a pot of steaming coffee.

"Not any more," says Missy, popping another scrap of raw gristle cut small into her mouth, and chewing it, hard, before swallowing.

And as she finishes eating my heart, Missy looks down and sees me sprawled upon the floor. She nods. "Outside," she says. "Now." Then she gets up, and leaves ten dollars beside her plate.

She is sitting on a bench on the sidewalk. It is cold, and the street is almost deserted. I sit down beside her. I would caper around her, but it feels so foolish now I know someone is watching.

"You ate my heart," I tell her. I can hear the petulance in my voice, and it irritates me.

"Yes," she says. "Is that why I can see you?"

I nod.

"Take off that domino mask," she says. "You look stupid."

I reach up and take off the mask. She looks slightly disappointed. "Not much improvement," she says. "Now, give me the hat. And the stick."

I shake my head. Missy reaches out and plucks my hat from my head, takes my stick from my hand. She toys with the hat, her long fingers brushing and bending it. Her nails are painted crimson. Then she stretches and smiles, expansively. The poetry has gone from my soul, and the cold February wind makes me shiver.

"It's cold," I tell her.

"No," she says, "It's perfect, magnificent, marvellous and magical. It's Valentine's Day, isn't it? Who could be cold upon Valentine's Day? What a fine and fabulous time of the year."

I look down. The diamonds are fading from my suit, which is turning ghost-white, pierrot-white.

"What do I do now?" I ask her.

"I don't know," says Missy. "Fade away, perhaps. Or find another role . . . A lovelorn swain, perhaps, mooning and pining under the pale moon. All you need is a Columbine."

"You," I tell her. "You are my Columbine."

"Not any more," she tells me. "That's the joy of a harlequinade, after all, isn't it? We change our costumes, we change our roles."

She flashes me such a smile, now. Then she puts my hat, my own hat, my harlequin-hat, up onto her head. She chucks me under the chin.

"And you?" I ask.

She tosses the wand into the air: it tumbles and twists in a high arc, red and yellow ribbons twisting and swirling about it, and then it lands neatly, almost silently, back into her hand. She pushes the tip down to the sidewalk, pushes herself up from the bench in one smooth movement.

"I have things to do," she tells me. "Tickets to take. People to dream."

Her blue coat that was once her mother's is no longer blue, but is canary yellow, covered with red diamonds.

Then she leans over, and kisses me, full and hard upon the lips.

Somewhere a car backfired. I turned, startled, and when I looked back I was alone on the street.

I sat there for several moments, on my own.

Charlene opened the door to the Salt Shaker Café. "Hey. Pete. Have you finished out there?"

"Finished?"

"Yeah. C'mon. Harve says your ciggie break is over. And you'll freeze. Back into the kitchen."

I stared at her. She tossed her pretty ringlets, and smiled at me, briefly. I got to my feet, adjusted my white clothes, the uniform of the kitchen help, and followed her inside.

It's Valentine's Day, I thought. Tell her how you feel. Tell her what you think.

But I said nothing. I dared not. I simply followed her inside, a creature of mute longing.

Back in the kitchen a pile of plates was waiting for me: I began to scrape the leftovers into the pig-bin. There was a scrap of dark meat on one of the plates, beside some half-finished ketchup-covered hashbrowns. It looked almost raw, but I dipped it into the congealing ketchup and when Harve's back was turned I picked it off the plate and chewed it down. It tasted metallic and gristly, but I swallowed it anyhow, and could not have told you why.

A blob of red ketchup dripped from the plate onto the sleeve of my white uniform, forming one perfect diamond.

"Hey, Charlene," I called, across the kitchen. "Happy Valentine's day." And then I started to whistle.

TERRY LAMSLEY

The Stunted House

TERRY LAMSLEY WAS BORN IN THE South of England but has lived in the North for most of his life. He likes it there. A winner of both The World Fantasy Award and International Horror Critics Guild Award, the author lives in Buxton, in Derbyshire, a setting he has used in many of his stories.

A hardcover reprint of his first collection, *Under the Crust*, appeared from Canada's Ash-Tree Press in 1997, and it was followed by *Conference With the Dead* and *Dark Matters* from the same publisher. His acclaimed short stories have been included in such anthologies and magazines as the *Best New Horror* and *The Year's Best Fantasy and Horror* series, *Taps and Sighs*, *Dark Terrors 3* and *4*, *Subterranean Gallery*, *White of the Moon*, *Midnight Never Comes*, *The Mammoth Book of Dracula*, *Lethal Kisses*, *100 Fiendish Little Frightmares*, *Ghost & Scholars*, *All Hallows* and *Cemetery Dance*.

"The only thing I can say about 'The Stunted House' is that it was written in the dead of winter," Lamsley reveals. "I wanted to dream up a gloriously sunny day, and did so, but it soon all went wrong, for me as it did for my characters, and I ended up with yet another nightmare on my hands."

> lady will you come with me into
> the extremely little house of
> my mind.
> — E. E. Cummings

T HEY DROVE SLOWLY UP THE HILL for ten minutes until, around a sharp curve, the road abruptly ended. A couple of concrete posts supporting a rusty iron pole had been set up at the termination of the tarmac to prohibit further progress for vehicles, beyond which a grassed-over track meandered away into the steeply sloping field beyond. When they got out of the car Mel stood for some time facing the sea with her hands on her hips, deeply breathing the warm, still air, while Ambrose got the shopping bag containing a blanket and their lunch out of the boot.

"That was a surprise," he said. "It didn't look like a road to nowhere."

"Blame me," Mel said. "I chose the route."

"I assumed it would take us a good way along the coast."

"Never mind. It's brought us to this marvellous place." Mel was in a receptive mood, ready to take whatever the day might bring.

"Suits me too," Ambrose said.

They passed the barrier and picked their way through collapsed coils of old and flaking barbed-wire. Mel snapped off a six inch section of greyish wire, held it in her fingers and pretended to sniff it, as though it were a delicate flower. Smiling at this pantomime, they made their way down to the bottom of the field until they came to a low wall along the edge of a cliff. A long way below, the ocean was nudging the rocks at the tips of a small beach with tiny, lazy waves.

"That's the place to be," Ambrose observed.

"Pity we didn't bring towels and costumes."

"True. But I can't see how we get down there, can you?"

Mel shook her head. "There must be a path somewhere though. Someone's bathing over there. See?"

Ambrose looked where she pointed and was just in time to see a white body slide off the edge of a large rock and sink into the water. It reappeared a good way out and swam swiftly away from them around the edge of the cliff.

"Well, whoever that was isn't inhibited by the lack of a costume," he said.

"Do you think it was a man or a woman?"

"Couldn't tell."

"Didn't look as though they'd been out in the sun much. That very pale skin."

"First day here, perhaps. Like us. That's how we'd look naked in this strong sunlight."

"Good swimmer, anyway," Mel said enviously.

They waited a while, mistakenly expecting the bather to reappear, then ventured along the wall, searching for a way down. The wall curved up ahead of them along the cliff without a break and they had no choice but to follow it until they were up level with the end of the road again, but on the other side of the field. The wall there was too far from the edge of the cliff for them to see down to the beach, and they were becoming somewhat frustrated by this impediment to their progress when Mel stopped and said, "There's some sort of building up ahead. A house, I think."

Part of a green wooden roof had become visible, as though it had risen out of the ground behind the bushes at the top of the field.

"Odd we didn't notice it before," Ambrose said. "What a place to live."

"And what a view it must have."

"There's a good chance we are on private land, Mel. I thought that when I saw the barbed-wire when we came off the road."

"That had been there for ages," she said.

They moved away from the line of the wall to get a better look at the house as they ascended the hill. Mel kept her nose towards the building like a pointer dog on the scent, and had begun to walk more quickly. Ambrose dropped a few yards behind. The prospect that they could soon come across indignant strangers who might order him off their land made him wary. He would rather have skirted around the building somehow, but he knew the strength of Mel's curiosity, and understood that she would have to investigate her "find".

When they got close they could see the place had a ramshackled, weather-worn appearance. It was made almost entirely of wooden boards painted pale green and yellow. Ambrose thought it bore some resemblance to a beached boat, and teased Mel with the thought that it may have been put together from the relics of wrecks, but she took this possibility seriously, and seemed charmed by it.

"I believe it's empty," she said, when they reached the front gate.

Ambrose was somewhat relieved, but he thought he knew what Mel would suggest next, and he was not wrong.

"I wonder if we can get in?" she said.

Ambrose gave her a smile that was not quite good humoured. "We're out picnicking, remember. Not house hunting."

"But it's such an unusual building," Mel protested. "It's worth taking a few shots of it, I think." She hauled her camera out of its case and snapped the building from both sides, then cursed because she only had seven frames left on the reel of film in the camera, and had forgotten to buy a replacement.

"I bet the road we came up reached this far once," Ambrose suggested.

Mel agreed. "I guess some people lived here all their lives and died when they were very old. The place went to pot. It went so far nobody wanted to take it over. No one will ever buy it."

"Not even for the view?"

Mel had forgotten about the view. She turned to look back in the direction from which they had come and said, "Oh my *God*. That is *amazing*."

"It's not bad," Ambrose admitted.

"It's *enchanting*. I bet it's even better from up there," Mel said, turning around and pointing upwards.

The front section of the ground floor had a flat roof that was railed about like a balcony. It was this feature in particular that gave the structure something of a ship-shaped appearance. A nautical-style brass ladder bolted to the wall next to the front door lead up to the balcony. Mel ran up the garden path, ascended the ladder, stepped on to the balcony, waved down to Ambrose, and took a photograph of him.

"There's a little bench up here and a table," she said. "This is the perfect place for it."

"For what?"

"Our picnic. Come on up."

From that high position the silver sunlight, sharply reflected by the glimmering sea, was painful to the eyes. When they had eaten their sandwiches Ambrose moved the bench back into the slender shelter of the shadows from the first floor section of the house at the rear of the balcony and half closed his eyes. It was past mid-day and the sun had begun its slow glide towards the western horizon. The heat and food had oppressed Ambrose but Mel's energetic enthusiasm was unabated. She chattered wildly on about how they should buy, rent or squat in the house, grow their own vegetables, and live off fish from the sea and whatever they could find from beachcombing. They would spend most of their time just watching the view change with the hours and seasons. She was passionately in love with the place. She wanted it. She would have it, by fair means or foul.

Her babble was such innocuous nonsense Ambrose was not moved to make any comment. They had been getting on each other's nerves recently and the holiday was a make or break affair between them, but the first day had started well, and he didn't want to spoil things. He just wished she would shut up. He wanted to bake quietly along with the landscape and let his consciousness drift off and blend with the prevailing atmosphere of drowsy contentment. Maybe Mel sensed this because she fell silent at last, then whispered something he didn't catch, and sneaked off to explore. As he heard her descending the ladder Ambrose grinned with relief, stretched his legs, closed his eyes, and gave himself up completely to the void.

The shadow he was sheltering in had stretched forward almost a yard when he woke up. Seen from that dark place the world spread out before him looked like a fragile, insubstantial display of pure, incandescent light and colour, and he watched it blaze for a while, mesmerised, without thinking. Soon, he became aware that he was thirsty and remembered the bottle of mineral water he had left in the shopping bag, but the bag was not where he had left it. Realising Mel must have taken it with her, he sighed and went to the front of the balcony to look for her. There was no sign of her and he began to wonder if, with her insatiable curiosity, she had forced an entry into the building. She was capable of doing such a thing. He hurried down the ladder to the ground and began to circle the house, peering through grimy windows into vacant rooms for sight of Mel, expecting at any moment to find a broken pane of glass or a splintered door, her point of entry.

When he reached the rear of the building he saw that the back door stood wide open. Closer inspection convinced him it had not been forced, and he stood some time gazing into the pastel gloom of the kitchen beyond. Inside, as out, every surface was painted with the same bleached greens and yellows that reminded Ambrose of the insipid colours of garments worn by very young babies.

He had become increasingly uneasy about the house as he ventured around it, and now he understood why. The doorway was smaller than it should have been; the top about a foot lower then was normal. Everything about the house was slightly stunted. Ambrose, who was below average height, found, when he passed through the narrow entrance, that he had to stoop considerably. Once inside, his head almost touched the ceiling.

The interior of the building smelled much more sharply of the sea than did the air outdoors. In the kitchen, that had a stone sink with no taps, there were cupboards on the walls, a couple of straight-backed chairs and a crude table: all obviously home-made to basic and unimaginative designs that seemed to represent a simpleton's notion of furniture. Everything was a few sizes smaller than would have been comfortable for Ambrose's use. The question of how Mel had managed to get into the house was answered by the presence of a long, heavy key resting on the table. Ambrose could see beside it the marks of the tips of the fingers of the person who had put it there, in the layer of talcum-like dust on the surface of the table. He tried the key in the lock, which turned easily, though with a rusty snap. Presumably, Mel had found the key hidden somewhere outside – above the door, perhaps – and had let herself in. It was not unusual for people to conceal a key like that, as a precaution against the possible loss of another, in such an unfrequented place as this. And it was typical of Mel that she had been able to find it easily. She had an instinct for the discovery of lost, unseen things.

The uncarpeted boards creaked peevishly every time he took a step, but Ambrose could hear no sound of Mel moving about elsewhere in the house. Perhaps she was hiding. If so, he was not amused. He called her name again sharply and got no reply. If she wants to hide I suppose I must seek, he reasoned, but he was in no mood to enter into such a game.

The house had five rooms, two up and three down, plus a tiny, stinking toilet, and it did not take Ambrose long to inspect them all. When, after awkwardly climbing the steep, narrow stairs he entered the totally empty rooms on the first floor he became certain that Mel was not in the building. He looked out of one of the windows behind the balcony in which they had eaten their lunch, half expecting to see Mel lying on the blanket he had left on the flat roof, but there was no sign of her at all. Her absence was beginning to annoy him now. He was hurt that she had deserted him, and he felt foolish creeping about alone in the diminutive house. It occurred to him that if Mel had herself explored the building she would have had no trouble with the height of the doors because because she was so petite – hardly five feet tall.

A single sharp sound from the floor below made Ambrose start, but he immediately felt relief because he was sure Mel had returned from wherever it was she had wandered to, and was probably now looking for *him*.

He stumbled out down the tight tunnel of the staircase, pressing his hands against both walls for support, and returned to the kitchen. Mel was not there, and Ambrose noticed at once that the key was no longer where he had left it, in the lock. He crossed to the door and turned the handle, but the door would not open. He knelt down, peered through the keyhole, and saw the key was in place on the other side of the door.

He was sure Mel would not, knowingly, have shut him in, but he felt a surge of anger towards her anyway. Where was she? What the *hell* did she think she was doing?

It then occurred to Ambrose for the first time that there might be a third party involved in the events of the last ten minutes. The owner of the building, perhaps?

That was one possible explanation, but why hadn't this person shown their face? He, Ambrose, presented, he was well aware, a harmless enough figure, who offered no threat to anyone. Not even to the presumably undersized people the house had been built for.

But there was another possible explanation, even more uncomfortable to contemplate. That someone had managed to separate himself and Mel: had lured her away, tricked him into entering the house, and locked him up there. In which case, Mel could be in danger. In that remote place anything could happen. Anything could be *done*.

The lock kept the heavy door very securely in place when Ambrose pushed against it. He lifted one of the chairs, thinking to batter his way out, then noticed the window over the stone sink was held in place by a simple iron fastener turned against the frame. It opened easily, offering Ambrose a three foot square exit. He clambered onto the sink, wriggled headfirst out and down to freedom, and found himself on his hands and knees on the garden path.

The garden was empty of signs of cultivation, apart from a row of woody gooseberry bushes and a couple of long-unpruned and drooping apple trees. Some way from the house the path wound around to the left, towards the sea. Ambrose, meandering speculatively along it, noticed that a few blades of grass that had grown up between the stone slabs from which it was made looked crushed, but had not yet withered, indicating that someone might have passed that way recently. Ambrose followed the path until he came to a continuation of the wall he and Mel had walked along earlier, and from beside which they had first had sight of the curiously stunted house. At this higher elevation he found a gap in the wall that would have been invisible from below, and through it, he discovered, the path soon led to a flight of descending steps cut in the side of the cliffs, presumably giving access to the beach below. On the top step Ambrose found the fragment of barbed wire Mel had snapped off, lying lengthwise along the path as though it had been put there to point the way.

Sure, now, he was on the right track, Ambrose trotted down the steps as fast as he could. When he had descended about half way down the cliff the steps ran out and he found himself walking along a narrow, apparently natural ledge. Feeling slightly vertiginous, he stopped to rest briefly, and gazed down at the beach for any sign of Mel. Once, in among the big rocks at the head of the beach, he thought he saw a flash of what could have been pale flesh – Mel's bare arms, perhaps? He stared hard at that point for some time, but saw no further movement. Nevertheless, he made sure he could find the spot when he reached the beach.

The water in the bay was smooth and empty but, a little way out, a small boat had drifted into sight – a peculiar, dumpy little vessel with one square sail that gave it an old-fashioned or toy-like look. A couple of brief beams of sharp, fractured light from the boat made Ambrose wonder if someone out there was gazing landward through binoculars. Watching him, perhaps? Or someone else, down on the beach? Mel?

He continued on his way until, to his surprise and irritation, the ledge narrowed down to nothing when he was still a dozen feet above the beach. An almost smooth escarpment partly coated with seaweed fell away to his right without, as far as he could see, offering any cracks or bumps that could act as footholds to assist his descent. Very cautiously, Ambrose, who was unused to such exercise, knelt at the edge of this precipice, with his back to the beach, and tried to lower his legs towards the sands below. He managed with difficulty to get his lower half hanging over the ledge, but he became nervous when he tried to lower himself further. For a while he was stuck in this undignified position, unable to move up or down. Then, almost in panic, he made an uncoordinated grab upwards, at nothing in particular, and his balance altered and he fell. His chin hit the edge of the ledge as he went, causing him to bite his tongue.

Then he was sprawling face-down on the sand, with his mouth full of blood. But he was okay: nothing felt broken. He got to his feet, dusted the sand from his face and hands, and spat blood against the cliff.

The place where he had thought he had seen the flash of what could have been bare flesh was easily identifiable on the far side of the little cove and he jogged across towards it, feeling bruised but triumphant; glad that he had at least managed to reach the beach. The large rocks close to the cliffs, that he had used as a marker, surrounded a couple of small but deep pools and concealed a tiny, quite separated stretch of beach beyond, at the very tip of the bay. Ambrose could see at once that the second beach was deserted, but there were many lines of small footprints and other less easily identifiable indentations crisscrossing the sand. Mel's feet were tiny – the prints could have been hers. Many of the individual foot-marks were wide apart, as though Mel, if it had been she who had made them, had been running. Ambrose noted that the tide seemed to be coming in, so the prints could have been there for some time, depending on how far out the low tide line was.

He turned his attention to the rocks, reasoning that she was probably nearby, sunbathing contentedly and even, perhaps, asleep. He tried a shout to rouse her, but when he opened his mouth he realised his bitten tongue had swollen. The only noise he could make was a dry growl in the back of his throat.

He extended his search along the beach and almost at once found Mel's camera in its canvas case, near the base of the cliffs. Ambrose flicked open the lid of the case, glanced at the frame counter on the top of the camera, and saw there was only one shot left. So – she had taken photos since he had last seen her. Of what? he wondered.

He pulled the instrument out of its case and saw at once that it could take no more pictures. The lens was smashed and part of the casing cracked and battered. The reel of film inside had almost certainly been exposed, but Ambrose carefully repacked the camera and hung it around his neck on the chance that some part of the film might be developable.

Nearby, he found the plastic bag that had contained their lunch. There was no doubt it was the same bag because it was emblazoned with the name of the shop, over a hundred miles away, where he and Mel had obtained it the previous day. Now it contained the empty mineral water bottle, and nothing else. Ambrose kicked it away from him angrily.

The possibility that Mel had taken a swim, gone out of her depth, and drowned now forced itself into his consciousness. He had a vision of her under the sea, possibly quite nearby, still half-conscious perhaps, but drifting down deeper and deeper into death. He yelled her name aloud involuntarily, and the grotesque sound of his voice, along with the pain in his mouth, filled him with a surge of desperate helplessness.

He stared out across the sea. The surface of the water was peculiarly flat and empty, except for the thin white swirl of the wake of the boat he had noticed earlier, weaving aimlessly around just beyond the mouth of the bay. To his annoyance, he saw another glint of reflected sunlight from the craft, and again sensed he was being observed. He shook his arms above his head more as a threat than a greeting, and was surprised when the boat lurched forward, circled sharply around towards him, and began to head inshore. It yawed unsteadily through the water and, as it got nearer, Ambrose could see it had an ungainly, home-made look that reminded him of the house at the top of the cliffs. It was painted similar colours too. A naive, local style of craftsmanship, perhaps? There was a little square cabin at the prow of the vessel and a raised area in front of the single mast that could have been a hatchway. When the boat was about a hundred yards out it cumbrously changed tack, swung around parallel with the line of the beach, and came to a halt. Ambrose wondered how the thing had been able to sail about at all, on such a windless day. He watched the becalmed vessel for a while, quite sure he was being watched back. There was no sign of activity on the deck or in the cabin.

For some minutes the boat exercised such a fascination over him, Ambrose forgot why he had come to the beach in the first place. Then the waves of the swiftly incoming tide rolled over his feet, the spell snapped, and the appalling loss of Mel bit back at him, and got him moving again.

After a further aimless and ultimately fruitless exploration of the beach, Ambrose waded out into the sea until it was up to his waist. Then he turned and stared up at the wooden house in the field at the top of the cliffs. He could see all of one side of the roof, most of one gable end, and the railings along the balcony at the front of the building, where he and Mel had eaten their picnic.

Somebody was standing on the balcony, waving a tattered black flag on a long pole. Because this standard was flapping back and forth in front of the individual holding the pole, it was impossible to see clearly what manner of person was manipulating it, but Ambrose could see it was not Mel. Whoever it was was about her height, but very broad of shoulder, with a large, bearded head topped with dark hair. Ambrose jerked his arm up automatically to make an answering gesture, but he arrested its motion at shoulder height and twisted around to look back at the boat. It had not moved, but the flashing lights he had seen earlier had recommenced. It was possible, he realised, that someone on board might be using the sun's rays to signal to the mainland. But the lights seemed to reflect back out of the empty air just above the craft. There was no sign of life on board: the deck was still unoccupied.

The tide was rising so fast Ambrose could now feel the sea water climbing up his chest. The childish fear of deep water he had never been able to conquer stirred uncomfortably within him, and he started to wade ashore, almost losing his balance when he tried to step out too fast on the insubstantial, shifting sand. Realising, as he got nearer to the beach, that he would soon lose sight of the house above him behind the wall on the cliff-top, he glanced up one last time as he stumbled on, and came to an abrupt halt.

There were now two people standing on the balcony. The sun shone directly into his eyes from its position behind and just above the top of the roof but, when he made a visor of his hand, he could see well enough to make out the individual he had first seen, holding the pole vertically now, with the dark flag hanging limply from its top, and next to that person, standing bolt upright, the figure of a slim, small woman with short blond hair, wearing a familiar yellow dress. As far as Ambrose could tell, Mel was looking down straight at him, but, if she saw him, she did not wave and, for some reason, neither did he. He stared fixedly at her and started to shiver, as though he had belatedly and suddenly become aware how cold the water he was immersed in had become.

Mel adjusted her position and adopted a more casual posture, hugging herself, with her bare arms folded across her breasts. Her head was tilted slightly forwards and sideways, as though she were calmly contemplating some pleasing sight – the beauty of the landscape she had admired so much earlier that day, perhaps. Ambrose remembered how ardently she had wished she could gaze at it forever, through the changing seasons, and said she could do so without ever getting bored. When she had spoken like that, he had been briefly jealous of the house that, to his eyes, had appeared an ugly and thoroughly unworthy rival for his affections and Mel's attention.

Ambrose heard a splash in the water some distance behind him. He guessed someone had dived off the boat, but he did not turn to confirm this surmise. Instead he hurried forward again, starting to run as soon as he was able, making his own wild splashes with his feet as he pelted through the increasingly shallow water.

There was hardly any beach left now. A thin strip of sand remained visible, close to the point where he had first dropped onto the beach, but the teeth of the tiny incoming waves were biting greedily into what little remained to be consumed.

Ambrose tried to reascend the sheer cliff face, but soon realised this was impossible. Since the path he had taken down was not renegotiable, he looked about for an alternative route up and saw, in seconds, that there was no other way out: he was trapped on the beach. He made a second, more urgent attempt to return the way he had come: an undignified, desperate scramble against the vertical rock that proved equally unsuccessful. His fingers tore at the layer of still-damp, slimy seaweed that coated the bottom two thirds of the wall. The topmost edge of this vegetation drew a line along the rock indicating the upper limit the water reached during high tide, two or three inches above his head. A swimmer could, perhaps, float, rise up with the incoming tide, reach the ledge and haul himself onto it, but Ambrose was not a swimmer.

Someone who was a very strong swimmer was now making their way towards him from the direction of the boat. Ambrose assumed their intentions were not good. The only thing he had that he could use to protect himself was Mel's camera, now hanging around his neck, which he could swing about on the end of the strap attached to its case: an ineffective weapon that was already almost in pieces. So badly damaged, it now occurred to him, that its condition could hardly be accounted for by being merely dropped or discarded onto the beach's soft, damp sand.

Then, with a burst of insight, he knew, without a shadow of doubt, that the camera had been thrown down, along with the plastic bag and bottle, from the top of the cliff.

Looking around he saw there were no other footprints among his own around the only point of access to the beach. Mel had never been down there. She had found something hidden away up in the house, or something hidden had found her, and she would stay with it now. She had an affinity with hidden things.

Somehow, in some way, a bargain had been struck. She had got what she had so desperately wanted, and probably a good deal more beside, but he, Ambrose, would pay the price.

Was the price.

The swimmer, having reached shallow water, was now forced to use some other means of progress. A stumpy, strongly-built, grey skinned, naked figure, she emerged, crouching, from the sea, and shook her long green hair out of her eyes with a flick of her head.

She stood for some time staring at Ambrose (or, gloating, as it seemed to him) then, moving unsteadily and taking her time, she lumbered towards him, dropping on all fours occasionally and floundering clumsily in the shallows, like a creature more at home in the sea than on land.

Her eyes were fixed on his, and his on hers, as she advanced. She seemed to approve of what she was looking at, as far as Ambrose could tell – her unconventional features made her expression unreadable – but he definitely did not like what he was seeing. Clutching the strap of the smashed camera in his fist, he pressed back against the solid rock behind him as though he hoped he might escape by slipping away into the forest of hanging skeins of weed that encrusted it. When she was close enough for him to smell her breath on his face, he opened his wounded mouth and tried to howl, but only managed smaller, sadder sounds as the tide continued its swift, inexorable rise and the last of the sand around his feet vanished beneath the advancing waves.

KIM NEWMAN

Just Like Eddy

THE EVER-BUSY KIM NEWMAN'S latest publications include his third *Anno Dracula* novel, *Dracula Cha Cha Cha* (aka *Judgment of Tears*) and the interactive novel *Life's Lottery*; the non-fiction film studies *Millennium Movies* (aka *Apocalypse Movies*) and *BFI Classics: Cat People*; plus three new collections, *Where the Bodies Are Buried*, *Seven Stars* and *Unforgivable Stories*. In the pipeline are three more novels, *An English Ghost Story*, *The Matter of Britain* (with Eugene Byrne) and *Johnny Alucard*.

"I wrote 'Just Like Eddy' for the 150th anniversary of Poe's death in October 1849," explains Newman, "and it duly appeared (very carefully proofread) in the issue of *Interzone* for that month. I keep being drawn back to Poe, who features as a viewpoint character in my hard-to-find 'Jack Yeovil' novel *Route 666* and, more extensively, as a vampire in *The Bloody Red Baron: Anno Dracula 1918*.

"Of the great many books on Eddy, the two I most consulted were biographies by Kenneth Silverman (*Edgar A. Poe: Mournful and Never-ending Remembrance*) and Jeffrey Myers (*Edgar Allan Poe: His Life & Legacy*). Poe remains the most consistently misspelled great author of all time."

L ET ME CALL MYSELF, FOR THE PRESENT, Edgar A. Poe. The fair screen now shining before me need not yet be sullied by my full appellation. This has been already too much an object for the scorn, for the horror, for the detestation of my soul. To the uttermost region of the globe have not the indignant winds bruited its unparalleled infamy? Oh, outcast of all outcasts most abandoned – to the earth art thou not for ever dead? to its honours, to its flowers, to its golden aspirations? – and a cloud, dense, dismal and limitless, does it not hang eternally between thy hopes and heaven?

Upon my writing-desk is a gruesome object in the form of a volume: cheaply-produced, ill-set, carelessly glued; issued not a year or two gone, but misdated through ignorance of the correct use of roman numerals. Less an edition than a falling from the presses, this book – for such we must call the damned thing, though so to do assaults our sensitive bibliophile vitals – is cast out to stalls and stores, for the penurious and the ignorant. It might be gawped over for an hour or two before its pages loosen like the leaves of October and are spilled in the streets. Upon its thin, ready-warped board cover is a rough, ugly woodcut: a grinning skull with eye-sockets too small, a downcast black bird with wings too large. And the title of this gathering of butcher's paper, as given on the ready-yellowed, coarse frontispiece, is:

TALES AND POEMS
by Edgar Allen Poe

Tales and Poems need not concern us. The texts are a mish-mash, lifted entire through ingenious photographic process from several other editions so the face and size of type changes from page to page, from story to poem. Of course, many errors and misprintings are carelessly scattered throughout the copy, like seed strewn for chickens.

And there, on the frontispiece, is the arch-error, the primal misprint, the eternal slip of the pen. Since I second ventured into the arena of print, dropping the dignified anonymity of "A Bostonian" – for so I signed my first published work, *Tamerlane and Other Poems* – to speak up for myself and proudly state my own, true name, to stand by my work and dare the world to take it and myself as they would, this has plagued me.

Edgar Allen Poe

Allen! Edgar Allen Poe! All-damned Allen! Always Allen, always. Allen! Allen! Allen! Though it is the work of a devil of the printer's variety, I cannot but think it also the product of the machinations of another of his breed, of more sulphurous and princely-yet-tenebrous mein.

Never am I rid of this phantom of my own making. The dreadful double has dogged me through the allotted span of my life and persisted even beyond the supposed release of widely-reported death. Edgar Allen Poe mocks my aspirations to Art and Science, unpicks the threads of my tapestry, gnaws ratlike at the foundations of my endeavour.

Allen is my imp of the perverse, my goblin damned, my ravening ghoul, my frightful fiend.

For the love of God, shall I never be rid of E. Allen Poe!

I concede that the Allen is my own fault, that he is my creation. All evil that he is comes from within me, and he is all that is base and degraded in my person. Yet he has a damnable life of his own, beyond my conscious influence, and directed entirely towards the destruction of my self, my reputation.

What is a man's name if not his reputation, his soul?

Each time *his* name appears in print, my own is devalued, trodden into charnel filth and forgotten.

The appearance of Allen is not confined to cheap, pirated editions that skim my most renowned works and pass them off as the ravings of a madman and a degenerate. Allen appears in learned commentaries, obituaries, scholarly histories, popular lectures, biographies and bibliographies, broadsheets and magaziness, the credits of motion pictures and television programmes, the collections of major universities, articles in every manner of publication, private letters that have strayed into the public purview, numberless schoolboy essays and compositions, plaques and honours and monuments. Immortalised a thousand thousand times, he is carried abroad through media undreamed-of at the time of his, and my, first fame. The thousand-and-third tale of Scheherezade is of his rise to prominence in this fabulous age of futurity.

Edgar Allen Poe "rules", as the graffito has it; and I, *le vraisemble* Edgar Poe, am lost, forgotten and impugned, cursed and doomed.

Like many of my sorrows, this has its beginning in the actions of the man who was never my father and acted, indeed, as no father to me.

I write, with distaste bitter still after more than a century and a half, of John Allan, of the trading house of Allan and Ellis. Upon the deaths of my true parents, David and Eliza Poe, I was taken as a babe into the house of Allan, a golden orphan, an ornament for the philistine businessman. With the death of his own wife, the devoted Frances, Allan began a programme of calculated torture by hope, dangling before me the prospect of wealth enough to support my literary endeavours but always snatching it away. My early failures, at university and West Point, can all be laid at the door of this Torquemada of the Modern Age, who mockingly refused either to cut me off and cast me out entirely or to properly finance my launch upon the literary world to which unasked-for poetical genius fit me.

When I was but two years of age, this creature prised apart my given name – Edgar Poe, honest and simple Edgar Poe of distinguished lineage – with prehensile fingers like those of a great orang-outan, and spat in his own patronymic, marking me for ever as a man with three names (one invariably misspelled).

This is the most hideous irony of the situation. I care not for the name Allan and wish it were not mine. Truly, he had no right to force it upon me. In railing against the malforming error of Allen-for-Allan, I defend not myself but the man who more than any other mortal sought to ruin me, to stand between me and my rightful position.

Allan! John Allan! I only ever signed myself Edgar Allan Poe when communicating with my *soi-disant* stepfather, usually in signing missives stating my desperate need for funds, in the hope of pricking his elephant-hide to awaken a conscience that was in him stillborn. Such letters were invariably unanswered, perhaps left in the rack for weeks on end as John Allan pursued his own mean pleasures. I understand that, in the writings composed during what is generally reckoned my lifetime, there survive only *two* minor instances of my use of the name Edgar Allan Poe, both from a period when I was unwisely tossing good emotional currency after bad by attempting reconciliation with a man beyond all decent feeling.

Many tales and poems and publications did I sign Edgar A. Poe. This, I admit, in mournful and never-ending remembrance.

This, even, was a grievous, a ruining error. I was born Edgar Poe. I am known as such to this day in that congenial country France – the only blessed dominion where American geniuses on the scale of myself and the estimable Mr Lewis are fully understood and appreciated.

I should never have succumbed to the temptation of a middle initial. It is a sheer puffery, whereby many authors of mediocre reputation and talents attempt to inflate their own by-line to something with cachet, with status.

He speaks a profound truth who warns you to beware authors – and especially *authoresses*, most especially my countrywomen – with three names. It seems these thrice-named ones are often afflicted with a peculiar and unwholesome compulsion to foist upon the public their maunderings in as many volumes as they have names, and indeed to pile upon such trilogies with additional instalments unpromised and unsought-for until the shelves of the book-sellers groan with heartfelt pain.

I should have abandoned even the token of Allan's name, that odious initial, that alien and alienating "A". I am and was proud of the Poes that came before me, the Revolutionary general and the great star of the stage. I found my only safe harbour amongst the circle of their relatives, my cousin-wife Virginia Clemm (my own darling Sissy) and her mother, Maria Clemm (my devoted Muddy). Yet – I curse my weakness and vanity, my shameful need for cash and the acute embarrassment of living always in a state of genteel beggary – the Poes were much reduced in circumstances, through no fault of theirs, and John Allan, was, through no endeavour of his own, colossally rich. A wealthy uncle died and left him a hoard of Croesus, a fabulous treasure beyond even that secreted by the pirate Captain Kidd. The gold tempted me, prevented me from breaking fully with this cruel man.

With money, what might I not have done? My cherished project, a true literary magazine for America, might have come to fruition and proved a very great success, much to the benefit of the culture of my homeland, which has – for the want of an influence such as *The Stylus* might have provided – descended into a barbarous, illiterate and nightmarish stew of ignorance and vulgarity beyond even the blackest of my black imaginings. *The Stylus* would have proved a forum for the highest of artistic and political debate: it could have presented reasoned, definitive

answer to those abolitionist fanatics who so dreadfully sundered
the country but a decade after I passed from public notice,
inflicting upon it a rapine from which it has never fully recovered
and elevating to wasteful mastery the brutish and barely human
blacks who were in my youth so properly and mercifully chained.
If we had been blessed with an income, my Sissy, rare and radiant
maiden whom the angels name Virginia, might have received
proper medical attention and survived beyond her tragically brief
lifespan, to bear me sons and daughters who would have carried
on my name and done me honour.

Allan denied me, denied *America*, these blessings.

Yet, each time I was on the point of abandoning entirely all
hope of aid from that quarter, some crumb, some trickle, would
come from John Allan. By keeping the ghost of his name within
mine, and with each appearance of my name in print above a tale
or a poem or an article or a work of criticism, I maintained the
limping, lagging last of our relations.

John Allan passed out of my life, married again and with fat,
bawling new heirs for his fortune. But, as he rode off in his gilded
carriage to undeseved bliss, another appeared and crept from the
shadows to torment me.

Edgar Allen Poe.

I cannot remember when he first appeared. It could not have
been in any periodical for which I laboured in an editorial
position: *The Southern Literary Messenger*, *Graham's Magazine*
or *The Broadway Journal*. I was a proofreader of unmatched
skill, as even those of my colleagues who became my bitterest foes
would have been forced to acknowledge. When the matter was
within my influence, I insisted upon the initial only, not the full
name. Edgar A. Poe was safe, but Edgar Allan Poe was a
dangerous venture which so often rebounded upon me.

No, Edgar Allen Poe must have been born in some other
connection. Scratched on an envelope by a barely-literate trades-
man, over one of the damnable reminders that elaborately bought
to my attention some debt as if it were possible that I could with
honour forget such a matter. Or perhaps it was printed above one
of the many, *many* – mostly anonymous with the full cowardice
such implies – attacks upon my work and character issued in
publications that were the despicable organs of that canting
gaggle of fools, knaves, toadies and dunderheads who then –

as now! – made American letters their own frogpond, croaking at each other and their pitifully few indentured readers; all the while contriving to do down and push under any truly original, important voice.

Was there initially malign intent? Surely, the first to have made the mistake – the *common* mistake, I have heard it called, though how such a lingering and deadly blight could ever be a commonality is beyond the confines even of my notoriously fevered brain – could not have known. No, it was *repetition* that had the power to bring into the world the fiend who built upon the foundations of John Allan and worked so devotedly towards my utter degradation and ruin.

At first, when grotesque tales reached me, I was indignant, certain that lies were being propagated by my so-called friends and acquaintances. Of course, none dared repeat such calumnies to my face, but I was always sensitive to whisperings, perhaps unnaturally so. His voice, Allen's, is always a whisper, a low-distinct and never-to-be-forgotten whisper which thrills to the very marrow of my bones, the whisper of a man dead yet unable to depart his mummifying corpse.

The world knows, or thinks it knows, my story. After my final break with Allan, I was forced to embark upon a perilous and rarely remunerative career in the employ of the periodicals of the day, all the while hoping in vain to combine pursuit of literary excellence with the plebeian necessity of earning a daily buck. Sole support of my sickly wife and her helpless mother, I took a succession of positions with a succession of publications, making fortunes for bloated and idle owners but not myself, and losing through my drunkenness or stubborn pride each employment, leaving behind only bad debts and tales and poems that have lasted to this day. It has been said, over and over, that I was a slave to the demon drink, that my condition was such that even a single glass of wine was enough to spin my brain into a frenzy, to send me on a binge that might last days and during which I was as one possessed, capable of any vice or insult, a terror to my friends and foes alike, yet so addicted to such stimulus that I would continue imbibing even to the point of physical collapse and, finally, death.

That, I maintain, was him.

Edgar Allen Poe.

Not I. Not Edgar Poe. Not, and it pains me to type the name to which I should never have laid claim, Edgar Allan Poe.

It was in Philadelphia, or perhaps New York, and after my Sissy had suffered the terrible onset of consumption, a vein in her throat exploding as her voice was raised in song, but before that dread disease took her away from me and robbed me of all hope for future happiness. I was writing so much and so fast that my fingers were permanently grooved by the pen and my hand was wrung with constant pain. Suddenly, without premonition, I was no longer welcome in the offices of publications with which I had hitherto enjoyed a cordial connection. The private homes of many were similarly closed to me, and the staff of certain hostelries or stores began to give me a wide berth in the street.

Had I somehow, unknown to myself, been transformed into a pariah?

I overheard stories of my exploits. I had assaulted this prominent novelist with a savage fury, importuned the wife of that noted editor with unbelievable license. More than once, I found Sissy in tears and had to coax from her the substance of some misdeed she had overheard ascribed to me. I found myself dunned by bills – yes, in that hated phantom name, but with my actual address – that I knew for certain I had never run up.

There was only one possible conclusion, the impossibility that I might unknowingly be the subject of these fantastic tales having been justly excluded.

My double was at large, wrecking my life.

My *doppelgänger*, as the Germans put it. Identical in every outward aspect, but inside a prodigy of evil, a warped mirror of my own self.

Many times, I was drive from home and position by Edgar Allen. He was a brawler and a drunkard, but possessed of the same canny intelligence that fired my own genius. I might be a pioneer among poets, but he was first among degenerates, as devoted to his calling as I to mine.

I set out to find him, and put an end to this sorry business between us. I knew he could be no more than a projection, a ghost before his time, escaped from my body but attached by a golden thread. If I were to snap him back, I would be free of him and he of me. We would be one mind, one soul. I was confident that I had the force of intellect and strength of character to deal with any ill influence he might have upon my thoughts.

It seemed that he was always just out of my sight. I might arrive at a place mere moments after his passing, which often put me in the position of answering for his misdeeds. My pursuit was dangerous, leading me to the receipt of many an unearned thrashing. Sissy and Muddy would tend my wounds, and worry over me, but my beautiful Sissy – her life leaking slowly, agonisingly away in a poetical tragedy of the first water – was in no condition to consider my poor health before her own. The walls appeared to be closing in on me and mine, and the scythe of death swished closer, ever closer, above the head of her whom I loved the most in all the world. It became paramount that I finish with this Allen, for only when he was a barely discernible heartbeat within the tomb of my mind would I be free to devote full energies to my husbandly duties and to the higher work of literature.

As dogged and perspicacious as any detective, I traced the impostor through reasoning. He led me from place to place, to other cities, and I apprehended that Allen was as intent on evading as Edgar was on ensnaring. In clues – the torn corner of a page scrawled with words in a caricature of my own hand, a button that upon examination I found missing from my own army greatcoat, lines of obscene verse scratched on the underside of a table in a low grog-shop – I found messages from him to me, from Edgar Allen to Edgar Poe. He could not bring himself to vanish into the mists, for he needed me at his heels to give his life purpose. Eventually, in dreadful and deathless despair, I realised he had almost won his final victory. In following him, I was compelled to venture into the dens of vice he frequented, and forced into many of the wretched habits that were his. Stories went back to Sissy and Muddy of me being seen in such-and-such a sinkhole of drunkenness and depravity; now, these tales were, in all particulars, sadly true.

The worst came when, after weeks in search of Edgar Allen, I decided finally to abandon the pursuit entirely. I purged myself of the obsession, and determined to let my rival go his own way. I would elevate my name so far above his that he could do me no harm. I returned to our poor home, bedraggled from my adventures and in a sorry state, to discover from Muddy that I was already in residence, closeted with Sissy, and that I had been so for some days.

Oh terror beyond imagining!

My home, shared with such tender and innocent souls, I had thought inviolate, off-limits as we said at West Point. Yet now it was transformed at a lightning-strike into a haunt of horrors, each familiar item of furniture or crockery become a mocking grotesque. My limbs would not serve me as I dashed for the stairs, and I seemed to plunge into a maelstrom of churning darkness. Our cat, a wise and humorous presence suddenly become a fire-eyed imp, was between my ankles, stretching out to undo my balance. Muddy, full as ever of concern for her Eddy, rushed to support me. At first bewildered by what she took to be my bilocation, that good woman became affrighted that I had fallen from an upstairs window and received ill-treatment, perhaps under the hooves of a horse, in the street. I found myself struggling with my wife's mother, a true mother to me, and terrifying her with my cries. The cat joined in with the sounding of ferocious mewls, rendering my already-taut nerves like the strings of a violin sawed at by the devil's fiddler.

Breaking free of Muddy, I ventured upstairs, dragging myself up by the banister, conscious of a growing terror that made my heart a bellows and caused the blood to pound in my temples like a pagan drumbeat.

The door of the room I shared with Sissy, my wife-daughter-lover-child-muse-sister, hung open. Within, a candle burned with sickly greenish flame.

I stepped across the threshold, and found Sissy sprawled atop the covers of our bed, night-clothes rent, scarlet blood discharging from her mouth. Other flowing wounds, open and intimate, marred the whiteness of her tiny form. She had been sorely abused. I am convinced that it was on that night she truly began the long, slow, heart-breaking business of dying. This was the worst the fiend Allen could do, the crime that was beyond all forgiveness.

Howling, I glimpsed my own two evil eyes as I smashed the mirror on the wall. That was the nearest I came to seeing him, until much later.

After that, I lost some days to hysteria.

Sissy, of course, died. I had opportunities after that and continued to write as ever, but my darker double had the upper hand. He grew bolder, taking advantage of my increasing reluctance to venture beyond my hearth, to perform ever more fantastic and appalling acts in my approximate name.

Edgar Allen Poe was busy in those years.

His name was everywhere. My own was quite eclipsed. I lost a deal of money and alienated a publisher who might have advanced my cause greatly by insisting a printer destroy an entire edition of my two-volume *Tales of the Folio Club* because the hated Edgar Allen Poe had signed the introduction to this collection of my greatest stories. With that abortion was lost an original tale of mystery, – in which the Chevalier Auguste Dupin penetrates the tangled puzzle of "The Suicides of Saint-Germain" – which would doubtless have been ranked among my finest pieces.

Allen even trespassed into print.

Now, I could not tell you which of my later works were his and which mine. Most of the famous pieces, the stories and the poems, are and remain mine. Too much of the journalism, the fillers and the canting reviews of unreadable books, are his. The worst tragedy is *Eureka*, an unwilling collaboration. The original manuscript of this essay was mine, a clear-sighted and visionary work which would have placed my name alongside not merely Milton and Shakespeare but Newton and Galileo. After a period of protracted study and insight, a single-theory-of-everything came to me and I was able to contrive no less than an explanation in a manner that could not be mistaken of the material and spiritual nature of the universe itself. When the work appeared in print, it had been tampered with by my rival. Whole passages were rewritten so that the meaning was horribly obscure, and the grand, beautiful design marred beyond repair by pernicious nonsense and stretches that crudely imitated my own style and manner as if composed by a trained ape with a nasty knack for mimicry. My critics, firmly in the Allen camp, were savage and merciless. It was a set-back I endeavoured to correct through lecturing and footnotes, but he had again lured me into evil ways and I could never reassemble my original version, could never recapture that moment of pure understanding that had prompted me to append such a thundercrack of a title to the book that should have been my finest but which became an embarrassment on a par with the poetry I tortured out of myself as a schoolboy.

The *Eureka* affair determined me to recommence my search for my enemy. Without a wife, I was less hampered by fear for my own safety. I was in my fortieth year, and the wrongs done me were stamped on my features. Implacable, purified by burning memory of the crimes against my soul, I turned about and looked for the trail.

It was late in the year of 1849 that I found him.

For months, I went from city to city, taking work as a lecturer and scribbler, capitalising on a fame which was now as much his as mine. I realised many who came to see me perform were hoping for a display of Edgar Allen-like madness and degeneracy rather than Edgar Poe-like sense and artistry. They were, for the most part, disappointed though, as before, the nearer I came to my quarry, the more like him I became.

I was unwelcome everywhere. Reports of my double came in from all quarters. He had engaged in fist-fights with editors and critics and common sots. He had approached literary ladies as if they were gutter drabs. He had declaimed his genius – my genius! – in such a manner as to alienate all who might have supported me. He had made fantastical claims of the wonders of the coming ages, misrepresenting as prophecy those fictions of mine presented as cautionary tales. He had delighted in the morbid and ghastly aspects of my work, but scorned the beauties and wonders I sought also to realise. He made bad jokes, undermining my once-prized reputation as a delightful wit; he even had the temerity to pass off as mine "X-ing the Paragrab", a leaden failure at humour on the subject, no less, of *misprints*.

Sometimes, I would lecture and *he* would take the money owed me, scattering it in the worst dives. He made a will that ensured the permanent blighting of my name, appointing my worst enemy – Rufus Griswold, Rough Rufus, Griswold the grisly – as my literary executor. For near a century, my works were always republished, ascribed as often as not to Edgar Allen, with a libellous biographical sketch by the ghastly Griswold which attributed to me all the misdeeds and imperfections of character of my foul persecutor.

We played tag throughout the cities of the eastern United States, Philadelphia, Boston, New York, Baltimore. I realised things had changed between us. He was hunting me, as I was him, and I feared he intended to do away with me, perhaps to wall me up living in a cellar, and take my place.

I contrived in small ways to thwart him. In New York, certain I was in danger of being murdered, I shaved off my moustache to make a difference between us, so *I* would no longer be blamed for *his* crimes. That was a mistake; it made me, Edgar Poe, less the real man, and he, Edgar Allen, more the original.

It was night in the lonesome October, in the worst year of the century, and Baltimore was in the throes of a corrupt and hard-fought election. Then and there, I caught up at long last with my nemesis. I came upon him, and knew him for who he was, in an alley-way between taverns, steaming with the discharges of chronic inebriates, caked with a filth of loathsome putrescence.

Edgar Allen Poe was in a sorry state, a grotesque caricature of myself, having accepted many bribes of drink for each of the many votes he had cast for either of the candidates. At last, he was collapsed, shortly before sunrise, a tiny slug of a man. His clothes were shoddy, more threadbare even than those to which I was reduced, and he was as he had always been, a living spectre with a broken mirror for a face.

"Thou art the man," I croaked.

It was but a moment's work to wring the life out of him. But as I choked, he uttered words.

It was Edgar Allen; but he spoke no longer in a whisper, and I could have fancied that I myself was speaking while he said:

"You have conquered and I yield. Yet, henceforward art thou also dead – dead to the World, to Heaven, and to Hope! In me didst thou exist – and, in my death, see by this image, which is thine own, how utterly thou hast murdered myself."

These were my own words, cast back to me like an echo in my skull. They shook me to the core, and I hurried away, unseen by those who gathered about the stinking body on the cobbles.

Or was I the one gasping his last? And the shadow fleeing, my enemy?

He is buried, under my name. My miserly cousin Neilson Poe had me interred without marker. Later, he raised a subscription for a tombstone which was smashed – by a derailing locomotive – before it could be erected.

What was carved on that stone? His name, or mine?

I am what I am called, am whichever of us is invoked, and I

shall be Edgar Allen as often as Edgar Poe. Each time the pernicious misspelling creeps into print the true Poe is beaked in the heart and the impostor reigns in illimitable triumph.

This is as it shall be, evermore.

CAITLÍN R. KIERNAN

The Long Hall on the Top Floor

TRAINED AS A PALAEONTOLOGIST, Caitlín R. Kiernan sold her first short story in 1993. Since then, her fiction has appeared in numerous anthologies and magazines, including *The Mammoth Book of Best New Horror Volume Nine* and *Ten*, *The Year's Best Fantasy and Horror Eleventh Annual Collection* and *Dark Terrors 2, 3* and *5*. Following the success of a "sampler", *Candles for Elizabeth*, her short stories have recently been collected in two volumes, *Tales of Pain and Wonder* and *From Weird and Distant Shores*. Kiernan's début novel, *Silk*, received both the International Horror Guild and Barnes & Noble Maiden Voyage awards for best first novel of 1998. She has recently completed her second novel, *Trilobite*. Aside from her prose work, the author also scripts *The Dreaming* and other projects for DC Comics/Vertigo.

About "The Long Hall on the Top Floor", Kiernan recalls: "The Harris Building of the story is real, a huge old warehouse on Birmingham, Alabama's, Southside, built in 1919 and surrounded now by a hodgepodge of much more recent (and inferior) architecture. The first time that I noticed it, the building gave me a bit of a shiver, though I could never say precisely why, and when looking for a suitable setting for this particular ghost story, I recalled my initial reaction to the place. That's often how my story's begin, the writing of them, after an encounter with a place that has left me feeling somewhat uncomfortable. Buildings and houses rarely actually frighten me, but they often leave a distinct sense of unease."

T HREE MONTHS SINCE DEACON SILVEY pulled up stakes and left Atlanta, what passed for pulling up stakes when all he had to begin with was a job in a laundromat in the afternoons and a job at a liquor store half the night, three hundred and twelve dollars and seventy-five cents hidden in the toe of one of his boots; and man, some motherfucker's gonna walk in off the street one night, some dusthead with a .35, and blow your brains out for a few bills from the register, and then it's the goddamn *laundromat* that gets held up, instead. Three Hispanic kids with baseball bats and a crowbar and he sat still and kept his mouth shut while they opened the coin boxes on every washer, every drier, watched them fill a pillow case almost to bursting with the bright and dull quarters that spilled like noisy, silver candy. And then they were gone, door cowbell ringing shut behind them, and Deke too goddamned astonished to do anything but sit and stare at the violated Maytags and Kenmores, at Herman and Lily Munster on the little black and white television behind the counter and the sound all the way down.

So a week later he was on the bus to Birmingham, everything he owned in one old blue suitcase and a cardboard box, Tanqueray box from behind the liquor store to hold his paperbacks and notebooks and all his ratty clothes stuffed into the suitcase. And some guy sitting next to him all the way, smoking Kools, black guy named Owen smoking Kools and watching the interstate night slip by outside, Georgia going to Alabama while he told Deacon Silvey about New Orleans, his brother's barber shop on Magazine Street where he was gonna work sweeping up hair and crap like that.

"Hell, man, it's worth a shit job to be down there," and Deacon thinking the man talked like he fell backwards off a Randy Newman song and landed on his head.

"How old you be, anyways?" and the man lit another Kool, mentholsmooth cloud from his lips and leaning across the aisle of the bus toward Deke. And "Thirty-two," Deacon answered. "Shit. Thirty-two? I'd give my left big toe to see thirty-two again.

Thirty-two, the womens still give a damn, you know?" And the bus rolled on and the man talked and smoked, until 3:45 a.m. when the Greyhound pulled up under the bugspecked yellow glare of the station and Deacon got off in downtown Birmingham.

So now Deacon works at the Highland Wash 'N' Fold every other night and a warehouse in the mornings, sleeps afternoons, not much different from Atlanta except mostly it's old drag queens and young slackers in the Wash 'N' Fold and no laundromat pirates so far. His new apartment a little bigger, two rooms and a bathroom, one corner for a kitchen, in a place that's built to look like a shoddy theme park excuse for a castle, QUINLAN CASTLE in big letters out front and four turrets to prove it. But the rent's something he can afford and the cockroaches stay off his bed if he sleeps with the light on so it could be worse, has been worse lots of times.

And tonight's Friday, so no laundromat until tomorrow and Deacon's sitting on a bench in a park down the hill from the castle, sipping a bottle of cheap gin, tightrope balancing act, staying drunk *and* making the quart last the night. July and here he is, sitting under the sodium arc glare on the edge of a basketball court, not even midnight yet, just sipping at his pine-scented booze and reading *The Martian Chronicles* by Ray Bradbury, "Mars is Heaven" and "Dark They Were and Golden-Eyed" and hoping he doesn't run out of gin before he runs out of night.

"Hey man," and Deke looks up, green eyes tracking drunkslow from the pages to Soda's face, hawknosed Soda and his twenty-something acne, battered skateboard tucked under one arm and he never smiles because he's lost too many teeth up front. "What's kickin'," and he's already parking his skinny ass on the bench next to Deacon like he's been invited; Deke slips the McCall's into the crook of one arm, knows that Soda's already seen the bottle but better late than never. "What?" and Soda doesn't answer, stares down at the raggedy cuffs of his jeans, at the place where the grass turns to concrete and Deacon's about to go back to his book when Soda says, "I heard you used to work for the cops, man. That true? You used to work for the cops, back in Atlanta?"

"Fuck off," Deke says and he's wondering what it feels like to be hit in the head with a skateboard when Soda shrugs and says,

"Look, I ain't tryin' to get in your shit, okay, it's just somethin' I heard."

And, "Then maybe you need to clean out your damn ears every now and then," Deke says and steals a sip from the bottle while Soda's still trying to figure out what he should say next.

"Yeah, well, that's what I heard, okay?"

"Soda, do I look like a goddamned cop to you?"

And Soda nervously rubs at a fat pimple on the end of his chin, rubs until it pops and the pus glistens wet under the street lights. "I didn't say you *were* a cop, asshole. I said, I heard you *worked* for them, that's all," and then the rest, quick, like he's afraid he's about to lose his courage so it's now or never. "I heard you could do that psychic shit, Deke. That they used to get you to find dead people by touching their clothes and find stolen cars and that sort of thing. I wasn't sayin' you were a cop."

And Deke wants to hit him, wants to knock the bony little weasel down and kick his last few front teeth straight down his throat. Because this isn't Atlanta and it's been four years since the last time he even talked to a cop. "Where the hell did you hear something like that, Soda? Huh? Who told you that?"

"Look, if I tell you that . . . Jesus, man, that just don't matter, okay? I'm tellin' you I heard this 'cause I gotta *ask* you somethin'. I'm about to ask you a favour and I don't need you freakin' out on me when I definitely did *not* say you were a cop, okay?" And now Deke's nodding his head, careful nod like a clock ticking, tocking, closing Ray Bradbury and his eyes fixed on Soda's chest, on his Beastie Boys T-shirt and a stain over one nipple that looks like strawberry jelly but probably isn't.

"What, Soda? What do you want?"

"It ain't even *for* me, Deke. It's this chick I know and she's kinda weird," and Soda draws little circles in the air, three quick orbits around his right ear, and, "But she's all right. And it ain't even really a favour, man, not exactly. Mostly we just need you to look at somethin' for us. *If* it's true, you workin' with the cops and all. You bein' psychic."

"How many *other* people have you told I was a 'psychic?'" and Deacon makes quotation marks with his fingers for emphasis.

"Nobody. Jesus, it ain't like I'm askin' you for money or dope or nothin'," and Deke snarls right back at him, "You don't have any idea *what* you're asking me, Soda. That's the problem." And

Soda's mouth open but Deke still talking or already talking again, not about to give him a chance.

"Whatever I did for the fucking cops, they *paid* me, Soda. Whatever I did, it wasn't for goddamn charity or out of the goodness of my heart."

And Soda makes an exasperated, whistling sound through the spaces where his missing front teeth should be, shakes his head and risks half a disgusted glance at Deacon. "What happens to make someone such a bitter motherfucker at your age, Deke? Fuckin' wino. I oughta have my head examined for believin' you ever done anything but suck down juice and watch people doin' their laundry." For a minute neither of them says anything, then, and there's only the cars and the crickets and what sounds like someone banging on the lid of a garbage can a long way off. Until Deacon sighs, takes a long pull from the bottle of gin and wipes his mouth on the back of his hand.

"Rule number one, Soda. If I do this, it's once and once only and you're never going to ask me for anything like this ever again."

Soda shrugs, shrug that'll have to pass for understanding, for agreement and "Yeah. So what's rule number two?" and Deke looks up at the sodium streetlight glare where the stars should be. "Rule number two, you tell anyone – no – if I find out you've *already* told anyone else about this, I'm going to find you, Soda, and stick the broken end of a Coke bottle so far up your ass your gums will bleed."

A little bit more than an understatement to say that Sadie Jasper is weird; three counties south of weird and straight on to creepy more like it. She's standing on the corner by Martin Flowers, staring in at the nightdark florist shop, real flowers and fake flowers and plaster angels behind the plate glass and when she turns and looks at Deacon Silvey and Soda her expression makes Deke think of a George Romero zombie on a really bad batch of crank, that blank, that tight, and her eyes so pale blue under all the tear and sleep-smeared eyeliner and mascara that they almost look white, boiled fish eyes squinting from that dead face.

"This is Deke," Soda says and Sadie holds her hand out like she's a duchess and expects Deacon to bow and kiss it. "He's the guy I was tellin' you about, okay?" Deacon shakes the girl's hand and she almost manages to look disappointed.

"So you're the skull monkey," she says and smiles like it's something she's been practicing for days and still can't get quite right. "The psychic criminologist," she says, draws the syllables out slow like refrigerated syrup, and tries to smile again. And, "Not exactly," Deacon says, wanting to be back on his bench in the park, reading about Martians, enjoying the way the gin makes his ears buzz, or all the way back in his apartment; anything but standing on a street corner with Soda and this cadaver in her black polyester pants suit and too-red lips and Scooby-Doo lunch box purse.

"Yeah, well, Soda told me you used to be a cop, but they fired you for being an alcoholic," she says and Deacon turns around and kicks Soda as hard as he can, rawscuffed toe of his size twelve Doc Marten connecting with Soda's shin like a leather sledge hammer and Soda screams like a girl and drops his skateboard. It rolls out into the street while Soda hops about on one foot, holding his kicked leg and cursing Deacon, fuck you, you asshole, fuck both of you, you broke my goddamn leg, and then a Budweiser delivery truck rumbles past and runs over his skateboard.

Deacon walks a hesitant few steps behind Sadie Jasper, all the way to the old Harris Transfer and Warehouse building over on Twenty-second. Just the two of them now, because when Soda finally stopped hopping around and cursing and saw what the Budweiser truck had done to his skateboard: flat, cracked fibreglass, three translucent yellow rubber wheels squashed out around the edges like the legs of a dead cartoon bug that's just been smacked with a cartoon fly-swatter, the fourth wheel rolling away down the street, spinning, frantic blur escaping any further demolition; when he saw it, took it all in, Soda made a strangled sound and sat down on the curb. Wouldn't talk to either of them or even go after what was left of his board, so they left him there, pitiful lump of patched denim and scabs and Deacon almost wished he hadn't kicked the son of a bitch, might actually have managed to feel sorry for him if not for Sadie, the fact that somehow his unfortunate promise to look at whatever it was they were going to look at had not been broken along with Soda's skateboard.

"I *wasn't* a cop," Deke says again and Sadie stops walking and looks back at him, waits for him to catch up and she's still squinting as if even the pissyellow street lights are too much for her smudgy, listless eyes. "But the psychic part, he wasn't lying about that, was he?" she asks and Deacon shrugs, instead of answering her says, "I don't think Soda meant to lie about anything. I think he's just stupid." And she smiles then, smiles for real this time instead of that forced and ugly expression from before and it makes her look a little bit less like a zombie.

"You really don't like to talk about this, do you?" she asks and Deke stops and stares up at the building, turn-of-the-century brick, rusted bars over broken windows and those jagged holes either swallowing the light or spitting it back out because it's blacker than midnight in a coffin in there, black like the second before the universe and Deke knows he needs another mouthful of gin before whatever's coming next.

"No," he says, unscrewing the cap on the bottle, "I don't," and Sadie nods while he tips the gin to his lips, while he closes his eyes and the alcohol burns its way into his belly and bloodstream and brain. "It hurts, doesn't it?" she whispers, and, Maybe I'm going to need two mouthfuls for this, Deke thinks and takes another drink.

"I knew a girl, when I lived down in Mobile," Sadie says, confession murmur like Deke's some kind of priest and she's about to give up some terrible sin. "She was a clairvoyant and it drove her crazy. She was always in and out of psych wards, you know, and finally, she overdosed on Valium." And "I'm not clairvoyant," Deacon says. "I get impressions, that's all. What I did for the cops, I helped them find lost things."

"Lost things," Sadie says, still talking like she's afraid someone will overhear. "Yeah, that's a good word for it." Deke looks at her, looks past her at the nightfilled building and, "A good word for what?" he asks.

"You'll see," she says and this time when Sadie Jasper smiles it makes him think of a hungry animal or the Grinch that stole Christmas.

They don't go in the door, of course, the locked and boarded door inside the marble arch and HARRIS chiseled deep into the pediment overhead. She leads him down the alley instead, to a place where someone's pried away the iron burglar bars and there are three or four wooden produce crates stacked under the window. Sadie scrambles up the makeshift steps and slips inside, slips smooth over the shattered glass like a raw oyster over sharp teeth, like she's done this a hundred times before and for all he knows she has, for all he knows she's living in the damn warehouse. Deacon looks both ways twice, up and down the alley, before he follows her.

And however dark it looks on the outside, it's twice that dark inside and the broken glass under Deke's boots makes a sound like he's walking on breakfast cereal. "Hold on a sec," Sadie says and then there's light, weak and narrow beam from a silver flashlight in her hand and he has no idea where she got it, maybe from her purse, maybe stashed somewhere in the gloom. White light across the concrete floor, chips and shards of window to phonydiamond twinkle, a few scraps of cardboard and what looks like a filthy, raveling sweater in one corner; nothing else, just this wide and dustdrowned room and Sadie motions toward a doorway with the beam of light.

"The stairs are over there," she says and leads the way. Deacon stays close, spooked, feeling foolish but not wanting to get too far away from the flashlight. The air in the warehouse smells like mildew and dust and cockroaches, rank, a closed away from the world odour that makes his nose itch, makes his eyes water a little.

"Oh, watch out for that spot there," Sadie says and the beam swings suddenly to her left and down and Deke sees the gaping hole in the floor, big enough to drop a truck through, that hole, big enough and black enough that Deke thinks maybe that's where all the dark inside the building's coming from, spilling up from the basement or sub-basement, maybe, and then the flashlight sweeps right again and he doesn't have to see the hole anymore. A flight of stairs instead, ascending into the nothing past the flashlight's reach, more concrete and a crooked steel handrail Deacon wouldn't trust for a minute.

"It's all the way at the top," Sadie says, and he notices that she isn't whispering anymore, something excited now in her cold and syrupy voice and Deke can't tell if it's fear or anticipation.

"What's all the way at the top, Sadie? What's waiting for us up there?"

"It's easier if I just show you, if you see it for yourself without me trying to explain," and she starts up the stairs, two at a time and taking the light away with her, leaving Deke alone next to the hole. So he hurries to catch up, chasing the bobbing flashlight beam and silently cursing Soda, wishing he'd taken the bottle straight back to his apartment instead of sitting down on that park bench to read. Up and up and up the stairwell, like Alice falling backwards and nothing to mark their progress past each floor but a closed door or a place where a door should be, nothing to mark the time but the dull echo of their feet against the cement. She's always three or four steps ahead of him and Deacon's out of breath, gasping the musty air and he yells at her to slow the fuck down, what's the goddamn hurry, but "We're almost there," she calls back and keeps going.

And finally there are no more stairs left to climb, a landing and a narrow window and at least it's not so dark up here. Deke leans against the wall, wheezing, trying to get his breath, his sides hurting, legs aching; he stares out through flyblown glass at the streets and rooftops below, a couple of cars and it all seems a thousand miles away, or a film of the world and if he broke this window there might be nothing on the other side at all.

"It's over here," Sadie says and the closeness of her voice does nothing about the hard, lonely feeling settling into Deacon Silvey. "This hallway here," she says, jabs the flashlight at the darkness like a knife as he turns away from the window. "First time I saw it, I was tripping and didn't think it was real. But I started dreaming about it and had to come back to see. For sure."

Deacon steps slowly away from the window, three slow steps and he's standing beside Sadie. She smells like sweat and tea rose perfume. Safe, familiar smells that make him feel no less alone, no less dread for whatever the fuck she's talking about. And, "There," she says and switches off the flashlight. "All the way at the other end of the hall."

For a moment Deacon can't see anything at all, a darting afterimage from the flashlight and nothing much else while his pupils swell, making room for light that isn't there.

"Do you feel it yet, Deacon?" she asks, whispering again, excited and he's getting tired of this, starts to say so, starts to say he doesn't feel a goddamn thing, but will she please turn the flashlight back on. But then he *does* feel something, cold air flowing thick and heavy around them now, open icebox air to fog their breath and send a painful rash of goosebumps across his arms. And it isn't *just* cold, it's indifference, the freezing temperature of an apathy so absolute, so perfect; Deacon takes a step backwards, one hand to his mouth but it's too late and the gin and his supper come up and splatter loud on the floor at his feet.

"You okay?" she asks and he opens his eyes, wants to slap her just for asking, but he nods his head, head filling with the cold and beginning to throb at the temples. "Do you want me to help you up?" she asks and he hadn't even realized he was on the floor, on his knees and she's bending over him. "Jesus," he croaks, throat raw, sore from bile and the frigid air. He blinks, tears in his eyes and it's a miracle they haven't frozen, he thinks, pictures himself crying ice cubes like Chilly Willy. His stomach rolls again and Deacon stares past the girl, down the hall, long stretch of nothing at all but closed doors and a tiny window at the other end.

No, not nothing, close but not exactly nothing, and he's trying to make his eyes focus, trying to ignore the pain in his head getting bigger and bigger, threatening to shut him down. Sadie's pulling him to his feet and Deke doesn't take his eyes off the window, the distant rectangle less inky by stingy degrees than the hall and "There," she says. "It's there."

And he knows this is only a dim shadow of the thing itself, this fluid stain rushing wild across the walls, washing watercolor thin across the window; shadow that could be the wings of a great bird or long, jointed legs moving fast through some deep and secret ocean. Neither of those things, no convenient, comprehensible nightmare, and he closes his eyes again. Sadie's holding his right hand, is squeezing so hard it hurts. "Don't look at it," he says, the floor beneath him getting soft now and he's slipping, afraid the floor's about to tilt and send them both sliding helplessly past the closed doors, toward the window, toward it.

"It doesn't want to be seen," he says, tasting blood and so he knows that he's bitten his tongue or his lip. "It wasn't *meant* to be seen."

"But it's beautiful," Sadie says, and there's awe in her voice and a sadness that hurts to hear.

There's a new smell, then, burning leaves and something sweet and rotten, something dead left by the side of the highway, left beneath the summer sun, and the last thing, before Deacon looses consciousness, slips mercifully from himself into a place where even the cold can't follow, the last thing, a sound like crying that isn't crying and wind that isn't blowing through the long hall.

Twenty minutes later and they're sitting together, each alone but one beside the other, on the curb outside the Harris Transfer and Warehouse building; Deacon still too sick to finish the gin, too sober, and Sadie quiet, waiting to see how this ends. A police car passes by, slows down and the cop gives them the hairy eyeball and for a second Deacon thinks maybe someone saw them climbing in or out of the window. But the cop keeps going, better trouble somewhere else tonight, and "I thought he was going to stop," Sadie says, trying to sound relieved.

"Why the fuck did you guys want me to see that?" Deke asks and no attempt to hide the anger swirling around inside his throbbing head, yellow hornets stinging the backs of his eyes. "Did you even have a reason, Sadie?" She kicks at the gravel and bits of trash in the gutter, doesn't look at him, draws a circle with the toe of one black tennis shoe.

"I guess I wanted to know it was real," she says, faint defiant edge in her voice, defiance or defense but nothing like repentance, nothing like sorry. "That's all. I figured you'd know, if it was. Real."

"And Soda, he never went up there with you, did he?" Sadie shakes her head, barks out a dry little excuse for a laugh. "Are you kidding? Soda gets scared walking past funeral parlors."

"Yeah," Deacon says, wishing he had a cigarette, wishing he'd kicked Soda a little harder. Sadie Jasper sighs loud and the rubber toe of her left shoe sends a spray of gravel onto the blacktop, little shower of limestone nuggets and sand and an old spark plug that clatters all the way to the broken yellow centre line.

"I know that you're sitting there thinking I'm a bitch," she says and kicks more grit after the spark plug. "Just some spooky bitch that's come along to fuck with your head, right?" Deacon doesn't deny it and anyway, she keeps talking.

"But Christ, Deacon. Don't you get sick of it? Day after motherfucking day, sunrise, sunset, getting drunk on that stuff so you don't have to think about how getting drunk is the only thing that makes your shabby excuse for a life bearable? Meanwhile, the whole shitty world's getting a little shittier, a little more hollow every goddamn day. And then, something like *that* comes along," and she turns and points toward the top floor of the warehouse. "Something that means *something*, you know? And maybe it's something horrible, so horrible you won't be able to sleep for a week, but at least when you're afraid you know you're fucking alive."

Deacon's looking at her now, and her whiteblue eyes glimmer wet, close to tears, crimson lips trembling and pressed together tight like a redink slash to underline everything that she's just said. No way he can tell her she's full of shit, because he knows better, has lived too long in the empty husk of his routine not to know better, but no way he can ever admit it, either. So he just stares at her until she blinks first, one tear past the eyeliner smear and down her cheek and she looks away.

"Jesus, you're an asshole," she says.

"Yeah? Well, maybe you wouldn't say that if you got to know me better," and he stands up, keeps the building and its ragged phantoms at his back. "Just promise me you'll stay away from this place, okay? Will you promise me that, Sadie?"

She nods and he guesses that's all he's gonna get for a promise, more than he expected. And then he leaves her sitting there by herself, walks away through the warm night, the air that stinks of car exhaust and cooling asphalt, and Deacon Silvey tries not to notice his long shadow, trailing along behind.

THOMAS TESSIER

Lulu

THOMAS TESSIER IS THE AUTHOR OF eight genre novels. His most recent, *Fog Heart*, received the International Horror Guild's Best Novel Award, was a Bram Stoker Award finalist, and was selected by *Publishers Weekly* as one of the Best Books of the Year. His short fiction has appeared in various anthologies, including *Dark Terrors 2* and *4*, *Best New Horror* and *The Year's Best Fantasy and Horror* series, and a collection, *Ghost Music and Other Tales*, was recently published by Cemetery Dance. His is currently still working on a new novel.

About the following story, the author reveals: "I love Lulu, a character made famous in the plays of Franz Wedekind, in the great silent film *Pandora's Box* by G.W. Pabst (starring Louise Brooks as Lulu), and in Alban Berg's powerful opera. Lulu is a kind of *femme fatale* and yet also an innocent, a dream lover, a womanchild and muse, benevolent but dangerous. She brings love, despair and death. Every writer knows a little of Lulu, though never as much as she knows about us. For a long time I wanted to place a small offering of my own at her feet, and this story is it."

> It seems to me that there can no longer be any choice
> between enduring the torment of reality, of false
> categories, soulless concepts, amorphous schemata,
> and the pleasure of living in a fully accepted unreality.
> – Joseph Roth, *Flight Without End*

I NEVER MET MY GRANDFATHER, LEO KUHN. He refused to come to America and live with us, despite repeated invitations from my father (his son), preferring to spend the last years of his life in the small Vienna apartment that had been his home since the end of World War II. Leo still had a few old friends there, and he lived with his memories. My father visited him twice, the second time accompanied by my mother. While they were there, late in January of 1961, my grandfather passed away quietly in his sleep one night. He had been in gradually declining health for some time. He was 66 years old.

Leo Kuhn, according to my father, was "a half-assed writer" who had published a lot of things back in the '20s and early '30s, but had never quite amounted to anything. He wrote short stories, articles, poems, topical essays and impressionistic sketches that appeared in the ephemeral press. What my father meant, I learned much later, was that Leo was impractical and never really earned a steady income. He was one of the many who, when young, manage to survive on the fringe of the literary world. You don't get paid much but you don't need much, and money doesn't seem to matter anyhow. Your writing does appear in print, and for a while at least, that's enough to sustain the hope that you will eventually mature into a writer of lasting significance.

Once you pass into your thirties, however, and have a wife and perhaps even a child or two, it becomes much more difficult to maintain this kind of life, even if history does not intervene. Leo knew important people and he was in fact well-connected, but he never managed to produce the great novel or stage play that would transform his career in a single stroke. Most likely he never had it in him, or perhaps the immediate demand for the next short piece and the next small payment kept getting in his way.

Vienna in those days, even with all the chaos and suffering that followed the Great War and the collapse of the Austro-Hungarian Empire, was still a lively city, fermenting with rich artistic and intellectual activity. My impression is that right up until the very last minute Leo spent most of his waking time at places like the Cafe Griensteidl and the Cafe Central, seated at a table in a corner, consuming endless cups of coffees, smoking one cigarette after another, and dashing off yet another *feuilleton* by day, then drinking wine or pilsener on into the night with friends and acquaintances from that floating world. Over the years he came to know, at least on a nodding basis, such figures as Schnitzler, Hofmannsthal, Musil, Werfel, Perutz, Zweig and Schoenberg – a stunning array of cultural titans.

Eventually, however, history did intervene. Karl Kraus once described Vienna, that City of Dreams, as "the proving ground for world destruction." The rise of Nazism in Germany and its rapid growth in Austria made it increasingly difficult for Leo to sell or publish his work. His wry humour and sarcasm had been displayed countless times in print, making serious enemies whose day would soon be at hand. And in any event, he was a Jew.

Several months ago, I came across some of Leo Kuhn's papers. A few diaries, notebooks and files of yellowed clippings that chipped off at the edges in my hands. They were in the attic. My father had just died and I was clearing out his house. I was annoyed but not entirely surprised that he had kept the existence of these papers secret from me for so long. I'm an associate professor of German Literature, I can speak, read and write the language fluently. My doctoral thesis was on the patterns of social unreality in von Doderer's *The Demons* and *The Waterfalls of Slunj*. My father certainly had to know that this material would be of tremendous interest to me, not only for any footnotes it might add to a particularly fascinating period of European literary history but also for whatever it could tell me about my own grandfather.

Over the years, however, I had come to understand that my father harboured a lot of anger and bitterness toward Leo. It had to do with their flight from Austria. Both Leo's family and that of his in-laws were reasonably well off. They had some relatives already in America, and apparently they had few illusions about the turn history was taking. Quietly, unobtrusively, they disposed of all their major assets and managed to transfer most of their funds out of the country. Family members made their way out of Austria in small groups over a period of time, usually on what were described as "holiday" or "business" trips from which, of course, they had no intention of returning.

No doubt some very substantial bribes were paid to facilitate all of this, but it was remarkably successful. By the early spring of 1938, when Austria became a province of the Reich in the *Anschluss*, most of my grandfather's and grandmother's families had already made it to the United States. Leo was not among them. He refused to believe that such drastic action was necessary. He thought that fascism was destined to fade quickly and that he was clever enough to weather the squall. He would somehow keep his contacts, he would write under pseudonyms, and he would emerge well-positioned in the aftermath of the storm. He did agree that his wife and their three-year-old son (my father) should leave with the others, and he promised to follow them if that truly became necessary.

Just a few months later, however, when he suddenly had to flee Austria in the aftermath of *Kristallnacht*, Leo went to Paris. The Nazis would subsequently chase him from that temporary haven, but then he found shelter in the south of France and remained in hiding there until the Liberation. He never did make any real attempt to reach his family, not even after the war, when Europe was in ruins and there was no point at all in trying to persuade them to return from America. In a sense, what Leo did was effectively to abandon his wife and son – or at least that is how my father apparently grew up seeing it.

All through my own childhood, no one spoke of these things. Not my father, not my mother, none of my cousins, my uncles or aunts. My grandmother died long before I was born – but even her cancer failed to bring Leo across the ocean. I'm sure my father regarded that as the final, unforgivable sin.

Years later, shortly before her own death, my mother did tell me that Leo was a black sheep figure in the family, an alcoholic, a foolish self-centered man who cared only for himself and for his writing, who would not change himself or his ways in order to reunite his family, even when he knew that his so-called "career" was marginal and his writing had no enduring value. He preferred to remain in postwar Vienna, clinging to his ghosts and tattered illusions.

That is probably not an inaccurate portrait of Leo, but it is incomplete.

Working only in my spare time, it took me months to decipher and read all of his surviving papers. The printed matter was occasionally interesting but did nothing to change the assessment that he was a minor writer, an adequate journalist who could not shake the notion that he was destined for higher things. Leo's handwriting was cramped and hasty, his words were long dark blots that reminded me of atonal note clusters and feverish, tortured music.

After the war, he wrote and published many short trivial things, but he kept coming back to one story, which he never finished. It was meant to be an account of his friendship with Joseph Roth in Paris, particularly in the weeks leading up to Roth's death there in 1939. Leo had known Roth in Vienna years before, but they did not become close until Leo arrived in Paris in 1938. Roth had been based there since 1933, having left Germany the day after Hitler took power.

Joseph Roth was very much the kind of writer that Leo Kuhn always wanted to be, and Leo adored him. Roth's haunting, elegiac novels, such as *The Radetzky March* and *Flight Without End*, captured both the fallen world of Austro-Hungary and the bleak estrangements of life in the Empire's wake. He was a major author, though his work has never found much of an audience in English, and, unlike Leo, Roth's extensive journalism never got in the way of his serious fiction. He wrote fifteen novels in the last fifteen years of his life, despite the fact that his personal circumstances grew increasingly nightmarish. His wife went mad, he was hounded by the Nazis, he was frequently destitute, and he was a determined alcoholic, right up until the day his heart finally gave out.

It seems to me that Leo could never make up his mind as to exactly what kind of piece he wanted to write about Joseph Roth. Some parts read like notes for a straightforward memoir, while other passages have the feel of fiction. Even with all that we do know about Roth, it is still impossible for me to be sure how much of what Leo wrote was true. At one point he cites Gautier's famous account of Gerard de Nerval as the literary model he would follow, but sometime later he appeared to change his mind, drawing black lines across whole paragraphs and scribbling brief, contradictory messages to himself.

- No, not an elegy
- This is a ghost story
- Inner story only
- Roth's ghosts were *real*
- Not right, be factual!
- Real love or mythic love

And so on. I often think of Leo Kuhn sitting alone in his small apartment, struggling through the whole drab decade of the 1950s with the numerous elements of his story, trying to force them together into a coherent whole. He failed, and I wonder why. If nothing else, Leo was a competent writer, he understood basic structure and he had a workable command of language. Furthermore, it gradually became clear to me that he had *all* of the story. Perhaps he simply could not bring himself to finish it, to let go of it. Perhaps he needed it as a continuing presence, to be worked on and lived with for the rest of his days. Or perhaps he was helpless, possessed by a story that was a kind of demon he could never exorcise.

Not surprisingly, I have the same kind of problem. This is not an essay or a memoir, nor is it fiction, though it undoubtedly contains some of all three – and I have no reliable idea which parts are which. A large part of it derives from Leo's own first-hand observations, but nearly as much of it draws on what Roth told him, and neither Leo Kuhn nor Joseph Roth were completely reliable.

I am attempting to put the pieces together now, both for Leo and for myself. I believe this is the story that ultimately cost my grandfather his family.

By the time Leo arrived in Paris in April 1938, Joseph Roth had long since fallen into the final pattern of his life: writing and drinking, furious bouts of the one followed by furious bouts of the other. He had spent some time in Brussels and Amsterdam, but he always returned to Paris, where the largest community of exiles from Germany and Austria had gathered. They subsisted in a dreamlike state of hope, waiting for reality somehow to annul itself so that they could resume their true lives. Roth saw them – and himself – as lost ghosts who linger on, incapable of accepting the fact that they had died and this world was no longer theirs.

Roth's circle of friends and acquaintances had shrunk practically to none, by his own choice. A woman named Sonja lived with him on and off. When she was there, Roth seemed to pull himself together. He ate better and would write a great deal in a short period of time. But sooner or later Sonja would disappear for a few days, and Roth immediately lost interest in anything. He

made the rounds of the cheap bars and taverns in the neighbourhood, drinking away the days and nights until Sonja came back to
rescue him again.

Leo had taken a single room in a house owned by an elderly
Russian, just around the corner from the Rue de la Vieille
Lanterne, where Roth lived in a small apartment. The first few
times they met, their conversations were brief and civil, but Roth
clearly intended to keep to himself. Gradually, however, Roth
began to accept Leo as more than just another neighbour, and to
feel comfortable with him. They shared a common past, in a way.
Leo was friendly but respectful, and made no demands or
judgements. In fact, he was always happy to accompany Roth
on his regular drinking excursions. They were the only times
when Roth really seemed to relax and would allow himself to
speak freely.

Their friendship was cemented on the night when the German
stranger came up to them on the street as they were making their
way from one tavern to another. The man wore a hat and
overcoat, and he was smoking a flat Turkish cigarette. He was
young, his skin was waxy smooth and his eyes were clear.

"Ah, the good Herr Nachtengel," Roth said sarcastically.

"Are you well, Herr Writer?" the German replied. "I hope
you're taking care of yourself. We don't want anything to happen
to you." A mirthless smile appeared on the man's face. "Someone
of your great – stature." It was obviously an insult, both personal
and literary. Roth was comparatively short, and he had no
international profile in the way that an author such as Thomas
Mann did.

Leo had barely taken in this brief exchange when the man
turned to him and smiled coldly. "How nice to meet you at last,
Herr Kuhn."

Roth grabbed Leo's arm and they brushed past the German.
Leo was quite startled that the man knew him by name. A few
minutes later, when they were alone in the back corner of a
basement bar, Roth explained patiently that there were scores of
German agents in Paris, each of them keeping track of numerous
exiles, waiting for the time when scores would be settled. There
would never be mercy for those who had committed political or
cultural offenses.

"You're on their list, same as me," Roth said with a faint smile, and then he laughed. "But cheer up. At least it's a sign that you did something right somewhere along the way."

Roth, who had never known his own father, was Jewish on his mother's side, but it was his writing that singled him out for special attention. His fiction was not at all directly political, nor did it espouse a certain cause. Instead, Roth chose to examine the effects of history on the lives of individual characters. His primary focus was always on the human. But as far back as 1923, in his very first novel, *The Spider Web*, he had written presciently about the extreme nationalist gangs and private militias forming throughout Germany, and in that serialized tale he had even made specific mention of Adolf Hitler, who was then still largely an unknown figure outside of the right-wing netherworld. The Munich Putsch, in which Hitler attempted to seize control of the Bavarian state government, did not take place until November of 1923 – ten long years before he finally became *führer* of all Germany. But Roth's early reference to him was the kind of thing that Hitler would neither forgive or forget.

That night was also the first time Leo spoke with Sonja. Roth got so drunk that Leo had to help him make it back to his apartment, and she was there when they arrived. It was obvious that she had just returned, and Roth was clearly very happy when he saw her. "My lover," he said again and again, as he held her in a clumsy embrace. "My muse." However, as soon as he sat down on the chaise, he leaned back, closed his eyes and passed out, his breathing loud but regular.

"Thank you," Sonja said to Leo as she led him to the door. "He will be all right, now that he's home."

She was short and no longer quite young, but still very attractive. Her hair was black, or a very dark brown, and it was cut short in a style that had gone out of fashion several years before. Her body was slim but pleasingly rounded. Her skin was very pale, yet as bright as alabaster. Her eyes had such a penetrating quality that Leo suddenly felt awkward and quickly turned away. He sensed some special power in her presence, a quality of strength and relentless honesty – although, the next day, he wondered if that wasn't just a wine-induced fantasy.

"I'll look in—"

"No, please don't," she told him. "He'll be writing."

"Of course."

"You're a writer, too, I can tell" she added, moving closer to Leo. "So, you understand. He needs to use his time."

"Yes." His throat was tight, he felt very warm, and he wanted to touch her, a thought – a sudden desire – that shocked him. "Of course."

"Time to do his work, to write."

Leo nodded, mumbled something, and left. The next day he woke up with his head full of dreamy, confused images of Sonja. It was difficult to understand why, since he had been with her for only a few moments. It had to be some implicit sexuality, the unspoken frankness in her eyes – the way she had looked at him. Certainly she was attractive, and he'd consumed a good deal of wine. Most likely he had gaped at her without even realizing it. Rather than act embarrassed or shy, or pretend that she hadn't noticed, her expression, her response, was to direct it right back to him – as if to say, Yes, and so? – forcing him to confront himself and his uncertain impulses.

It was disconcerting, all the more so the day after. Leo had no intentions toward the woman, and he would never want to disrupt Roth's personal life in the least way. He admired Roth so much that at times he even felt guilty about drinking excessively with him. Wouldn't it be better, after all, if Leo could persuade Roth to drink less and write more? But to do so would cost him Roth's friendship, that was quite clear. One time Roth told him, "I drink as atonement, otherwise I would not continue." Leo didn't fully understand exactly what Roth meant – that he would not continue to drink? write? live? When he asked, Roth frowned in irritation, gave a shrug and said, as if it were self-evident, "Continue."

In any event, Leo firmly believed that all serious writers sacrifice parts of their personal lives in order to accomplish what they do, and that the resulting work must justify the price paid.

That afternoon Leo made the first entry in his "Roth" notebook. But the first name that actually appears in it is Sonja.

Leo saw her again a few days later. It was growing dark at the end of the afternoon and he had just posted another pseudonymous article to Vienna. These harmless pieces on Parisian culture and social life still brought him a small return, but the market for them was vanishing quickly. Few in the Reich wanted to read or hear anything even vaguely positive about the French, no matter how non-political the topic might be. But Leo was not about to start writing the kind of anti-French nonsense that was now so much in demand in Germany. There were already plenty of literary whores working that dismal street, and it appalled him.

Leo saw Sonja emerge from the narrow Rue de la Vieille Lanterne, and he instinctively pursued her. A moment later, he caught up with her and they walked together for a while. Whether she spoke German or French, her pronunciation was exact but unaccented, almost characterless. She was at ease in both languages, so it was impossible to guess where she came from originally. But the pure sound of her voice was lovely to the ear, soft and rich. *Every time she spoke, I wanted to lean closer, to get as close as I could and let her voice wash over me,* Leo wrote.

The facts tumbled out hurriedly in his notebook. She told him that Roth had just fallen asleep after a long night and day of writing. Now he would be asleep for many hours, perhaps right through to the next morning. Roth's work was going well but it was very difficult and painful for him.

And when he slept like that, Sonja had to get out of the apartment – she had to live, breathe, relax. Roth knew, he understood her. All he wanted was for her to be there the next day, to come back to him when he had to start work again. Out of some peculiar need, he simply couldn't write without her nearby, and if she did not return after a while he would give up, go out and start drinking again.

Leo found all this fascinating, but it baffled him. Why did she leave and not come back for days on end? Their relationship appeared to have some mysterious aspect, but Leo would not dare ask either of them about it. He could only hope to learn more in time, for he was certain that it was a key element in any understanding of Roth and his great work. As for Sonja, she was quite intriguing in her own right, and Leo immediately enjoyed being in her presence. Nor did it escape his notice that she seemed quite happy to be with him.

After they had walked a short while it became apparent that Sonja had no particular destination in mind, so Leo took her to a brasserie he knew that served decent food and wine at working-class prices. It was as if he had taken her home. She relaxed at once, threw her wrap off her shoulders, and her face appeared to be lit up from within. He seldom needed to speak. She told him that she was a singer and had performed in numerous nightclubs in Germany and France, though not so much lately. She'd had a string of lovers, each of them worse than the one before. They were businessmen, schemers, criminals, and they had led her into trouble with the police at one point. She had used many different names, mostly to do with her stage act – Sonja, Kristen, Nelly, Mignon, among others. But all of that was in the past now, and she could only be interested in men who created, not destroyed. Men who wrote or painted or made music. Joseph Roth was small and unsightly, he had somewhat bulging eyes, his hair was disappearing, and his body was a wreck from years of heavy drinking. But he created, the fire in him was true and good, so Sonja would give him whatever he wanted and needed. After all the pain and trouble she had been through, she thought that love was an illusion, a fantasy – but one that was still, sometimes, worth the imaginative effort. Leo didn't know what to make of all this. She seemed both sophisticated and naive at the same time.

But it didn't matter. By then he was completely under her spell. The fire in her dark eyes, the way her hair moved as she spoke, her voice stirring him, seeming to speak right into his mind, the line of her throat, the way her breasts filled out her simple blouse, her small delicate hands – everything about her was so soothing and pleasing to him. He felt happily drowsy, from the food and wine and the heat of the nearby coal-fire, and he didn't want to move. It had been a long time since Leo had last enjoyed the company of a woman, much less one who made him feel thoroughly at ease, as Sonja did.

His wife – and this was the only direct comment I ever found by Leo about my grandmother – was a good woman, but she understood little of who he was and what internal forces drove him.

As the evening went on, Sonja even appeared to grow younger. There was more colour in her cheeks, her manner became more animated and girlish, but never loud or silly. It was delightful. *I realized that what I felt – in a genuine physical sense – was nothing less than the surging energy of life itself, radiating from her like heat and light from the sun,* Leo noted without irony the next day.

"Show me something you wrote," she said when they left the brasserie and were walking along the street. "Please?"

"All right," Leo replied after the briefest hesitation.

His room was small and chilly, but he lit a fire and poured some schnapps for both of them. She stood by the fire and quickly scanned a short tale of his that had been published the year before. When she put the magazine down on the table, she smiled at him – a smile that made him feel very good since it seemed to signal her approval of what he had written. They sat on the lumpy old chaise in front of the fireplace, the only suitable furniture, and almost at once Sonja raised one leg and swung herself around so that she was sitting on his lap, facing him, her legs on either side of his. Her hand stroked his cheek and teased his hair, she sipped her schnapps and then ran the tip of her tongue along his lips. She must have noticed the sudden conflict in Leo's expression, for her smile grew wider, and there was a measure of good-natured sympathy in it.

"Don't worry," she said. "He doesn't need me this way."

"He called you his lover."

"For him, love is only spiritual now. He's fighting death."

"Even so . . ."

"It's all right," Sonja assured him. "And you *do* need me this way. Don't you?" Her smile now naughty and complicitous. "No point in denying it."

"Already you know me too well."

"Leo, be bad with me."

She unhooked a couple of buttons on her blouse, took his hand and slid it inside, pressing it to her breast. She leaned closer, until their foreheads touched, and her mouth licked and nipped at his. Somehow, the glasses were quickly set aside, she had his pants open, and she pulled him into her. Their passion was as fierce as it was swift in its consummation.

"Give me a name," she whispered to him, after.

"What?"

"Give me a special name, so I'm yours alone."

"Oh, I don't know . . ."

"No one else will ever hear it," she insisted. "All those other names I've used were spoiled by other people. Except for Sonja, but that belongs to Joseph, you know."

"Lulu, that's who you are," he said, surprising himself.

"Ah, that's the first name I remember from childhood! I used to think it was so old-fashioned, but now you've rescued it for me." She kissed him.

"Where were you born?"

He felt her body shrug in his embrace. "Orphaned, I suppose."

Then desire intervened, slower this time but more powerful than before, a long, devastating yet beautiful expression of the lonely hunger and deep need within both of them.

Leo awoke cold and alone in the grey dawn. He crawled into bed and soon fell asleep again, waking late in the morning. He fretted through the rest of the day. He was too tired to work properly, but he jotted down brief notes to himself and worried about his friendship with Roth. Leo reminded himself again and again of what she had said: *He doesn't need me this way*. Nonetheless, it was imperative to keep this sudden liaison secret. There was no way of knowing how he might react. It would be bad enough if there were an angry break between Roth and Leo, but far worse if this interfered with Roth's work.

But Leo couldn't stay away, he wanted at least to see her again as soon as possible. That evening he knocked on the door of Roth's apartment, and a shouted voice invited him in. Roth was at his small rickety table, writing. Sonja sat on the rug at his feet, her head resting against his knee. Roth stood up and crossed the room to talk with Leo. He was working, quite busy, no time to spare just now, but perhaps in a few days he would meet Leo and they would go out for a drink. Leo understood, of course, and encouraged Roth to push ahead with his work. At one moment in the brief conversation, Leo's gaze drifted past Roth's shoulder to Sonja, who was still sitting on the rug. At once, her hands moved and touched her breasts, cupping them, and her face lit up with a large smile. She was so naughty! Leo had to look away immediately, and he was relieved that Roth apparently hadn't noticed anything unusual in his expression just then.

Two days later, in the early afternoon, his Lulu came to him and stayed for several hours. This soon became the new pattern in Leo's life. She would come to him whenever she could. Sometimes they went out to eat and drink, but time was so precious that they usually stayed in his room and made love, later resting in each other's arms before the fire, then making love again as often as they could before she eventually had to leave. She was a wild, imaginative lover, desperately needy but also infinitely giving. It was as if Leo had discovered true passion and desire for the first time in his life – and discovered, as well, that there is no end to it,

no logical conclusion, that it goes on and on as long as there is life
and imagination to illuminate its perpetual labyrinthine turns.

"Where did you go?" he asked her one day.

"When?"

"Those times when you used to leave Roth, and be gone for a
week or more. Where were you, what were you doing?"

A child-like pout. "It doesn't matter." Then she smiled. "That's
all over, finished. When I leave him now, it's only to come to
you."

"Yes, but—"

"Shhh," kissing him again and again. "Just fuck me."

Leo's need was as great as hers, and the more he had of his Lulu
the more he wanted. When she wasn't there with him, he soon
grew restless and he found it hard to concentrate on his work. He
constantly felt tired, or lazy, and could lie on the chaise for hours,
half-awake, recalling previous meetings with Lulu or trying to
imagine what delights the next one might include. At times he
scolded himself for acting like a lovesick boy, but then he would
think: *Yes, I am. So?*

Leo continued to see Roth fairly regularly, but there was a
distinct change in Roth's behaviour. Now that Sonja no longer
left him for very long, he was able to get more writing done. But
drink was still an essential part of his life, so he drank some as he
wrote, and once a week he went out for an extended binge with
Leo that would last from early in the evening until nearly dawn.
In spite of this, he did look a little healthier, or perhaps more at
peace in some way, and Leo later observed in his notebook that
his affair with Lulu was, ironically, secretly, having a beneficial
effect on Roth.

Like a man putting his affairs in order, Roth carefully began to
share more of his past life with Leo. After the Great War, he had
married – too soon, he later realized. His wife, Frieda, was a good
person, not unintelligent but a middle-class daughter who aspired
to a settled home life. She would make a good mother. She may
have fallen in love with the idea of marrying someone who would
eventually become a famous and successful writer. Roth was still
at a loss to explain why he had married her, except that perhaps
Frieda represented some image of stability he felt necessary in his
life at that time.

In practice, the reality was quite different for both of them. He soon found her uninteresting and complacent, even tiresome in her petty ways. But Roth could always escape, and did. Frieda was trapped in their apartment, left alone for days and nights at a time while Roth roamed the countryside on journalistic assignments or simply caroused in the cafes with his friends. Fear of how others would react, and perhaps a sense of her own failure as a wife, prevented Frieda from sharing her situation with anyone or doing anything about it. The powerful social constraints of her conventional upbringing and her own fragile nature only made matters worse, and Roth returned home one morning to find her curled up on the floor, peeling and eating wallpaper. She never completely recovered, and in time had to be placed in an institution. A couple of years later she contracted some illness, and died.

Roth never forgave himself. He found a new sense of urgency in his work, but writing was not an escape. He also took to drinking in a new way. It seemed to him that alcohol was a fitting, fine and ultimately final punishment. He would yield himself to it, and carry out the sentence. From that time on, his whole life became a kind of macabre race in which the goal was to write as much as he could and also to destroy himself in the process.

If Leo saw any parallels between Roth's personal life and his own, he did not enter them in his notes. I have to believe that he thought about them, was even haunted by them, for the rest of his life. It seems to me that Roth and Leo had both sacrificed their wives (and in Leo's case his son), probably without giving it much consideration at the time. They had chosen the artistic, literary life, and had lived it exactly as they saw fit, in a typically youthful and unfettered spirit – regardless of the consequences for those who were closest to them.

Roth subsequently had one romantic affair, with a young actress and writer named Irmgard Keun. They were together for a couple of years, drifting from one European city to another (outside of Germany). Their relationship was passionate and stormy, and ultimately doomed. She couldn't bear to sit by and observe Roth's self-destructive descent, nor could she save him from it. Finally, as much at his insistence, she pulled away and left him. Roth told Leo that he thought of Irmgard as his only "true" love, but that he accepted losing her – it was a necessary part of *his* sacrifice.

[Irmgard Keun was another of those whose names were on a

German list. She fled Holland when the Nazis invaded in 1940 and escaped to England, where she remained until her death in 1982. Her best novel was published in an English translation as *After Midnight*, Victor Gollancz Ltd, 1985.]

Sometime after that, Roth wandered into a dingy cellar bar in Montmartre, where he sat and drank, and watched and listened as a young woman "who was no longer quite so young" sang that most poignant and bitter song of abandoned love, *Surabaya-Johnny*. She told him later that he was the only one there who paid any attention, and that his eyes were "big and wet" when she finished. She wore a black slip. She said her name was Mimi. Before long, however, Roth began to call her Sonja.

He told Leo that without her he no longer had enough strength or will to write a single sentence.

Leo and his Lulu continued their affair, and it would seem that Roth never found out about it – or if he did, he never let on. By his own account, Leo was happier than he had ever been. She was a joy as well as a pleasure, child-like, almost innocent, but at the same time a profoundly erotic woman to whom nothing was new or forbidden. She was as much a fantasist as any storyteller, though her imagination expressed itself in who and how she was on any given day. Thus, her presence always had about it an air of anticipation and unpredictability that Leo found compulsive and addictive.

But there were certain worrying signs that he wondered about. She always came to him in a tired, pale condition. This was understandable, since she spent so much time sitting up with Roth as he wrote, and obviously there was nothing healthy about that way of life. They all were poor, ate badly and drank too much. All the same, he was shaken one time when, after making love, they were huddled beneath the blankets, luxuriating in their nakedness together, talking quietly about nothing in particular, and she suddenly murmured, "He's killing me, you know." But when he sat up in concern and asked her what she meant, she passed it off lightly. "Nothing, really. Not like that! It's just that at the end of each session, I feel like I've worked as hard as he has. I'm so exhausted I feel dead. That's all."

It pleased Leo to see how quickly she was transformed whenever she was with him. The colour would begin to resurface in her cheeks, her eyes grew brighter and her whole body brimmed with new energy. It was nothing less than the power of love and passion, visible to the naked eye, the two of them drawing new life and vigour from each other every time they met. And if their trysts generally left Leo in a similar state of exhaustion, so much so that even the following day he could barely do one hour's work, he was not bothered in the least. He willingly and completely surrendered himself to *the magic of Eros*. But Leo was still capable of giving the matter some practical consideration.

"You must live with me."

For once, she looked surprised. Then sad. "I can't. I belong to him, and I wouldn't do that to him. This is all you and I can have."

"He's going to die soon," Leo said. "You know it, too."

"Don't speak like that."

"And after the war, whenever it comes—"

"Please!" Now her expression was pained. "Don't write endings for us, not even imaginary ones. You have a wife and child somewhere, another life, and sooner or later you'll want it back. That is what the end of the war will mean to you, whenever it comes."

"No, no—"

"Don't," she cut him off. "It hurts too much."

"I'm sorry. My poor Lulu."

Then she showered his face with kisses, teasing his mouth. "Think of me as your dream lover. I only want to give you pleasure. Be happy with me."

He was. He even began to think that he would be happy to die with her, as life without her had become inconceivable to him. The day after a long encounter with Lulu, he would lie in bed or on the chaise for long hours on end in a kind of daze, his body weak, his mind adrift on a sea of images. It was hard to form clear thoughts. Much of this time was a blissful quietus, the aftermath. But one small part of his brain continued to ponder the internal dynamics of their situation, and Leo's notes reflect a deep-seated uncertainty.

Today she spoke to me of Courtly Love. It is deeply carnal, its whole point is consummation in body as well as spirit. For centuries the Church and society have worked strenuously to de-sexualize Courtly Love and turn it into some harmless, chivalrous claptrap. True Courtly Love is subversive, a threat to the

*existing order. Tristan went against the King. Women had the
power to pick and choose among men, to decide their own fate.*

Courtly Love is, by definition, adulterous.

Tristan possessed Isolde in the flesh – but could not keep her.

Leo asked Lulu what all of that had to do with the two of them.
She said that their love was like Courtly Love, freely given with no
expectation, and thus pure in and of itself. She wanted him to
know how much she cherished it.

Does she really understand? Leo asked himself later. *She has
her hand on the truth, but perhaps does not entirely grasp it. Any
good student of medieval history knows that the ultimate goal of
Courtly Love is not sexual, nor is it even spiritual. The true goal
of Courtly Love is death.*

Novalis: "Our love is not of this world."

Toward the end, Leo's notes were obsessive on the subject of
death. He believed that talk about Courtly Love was simply part
of the fantasy that Lulu spun for herself and for him, and as such
he enjoyed it. But death was the kernel of truth in the fantasy, and
Leo saw it differently, though in equally mythic terms. He began
to ruminate about the role of the Muse. Sonja was Roth's Muse.
Roth sucked the life and creative spirit out of her, which was why
he could write so much and so well when she was with him, and
could not when she was away. The Muse gave, but her giving was
also a real sacrifice of herself.

The other part of the dynamic (to stay with Leo's term) was his
relationship with Lulu. His dream lover. She was right about that,
there truly was a dream-like, unreal quality to the passion they
shared. It was a kind of mutual fantasy, in which he and Lulu
could escape the disappointing world outside for a little while,
and flee into the realm of pure desire. It was a fantasy he
cherished . . .

But Leo could also see the weak point in the equation. His life
force was being drained, and it was the only one that was not
being replenished adequately. The situation could not continue
this way indefinitely. The inexorable conclusion was death – his.
Whether Leo truly believed this is impossible to say, but he did
write this astonishing note: *If Roth were healthier I might have to
decide whether to kill him, but as it is I can at least hope to outlast
him.* Perhaps he was looking ahead to the prospect of Lulu
becoming his Muse. But then he would have to face the question

of where she would turn to draw strength in order to feed and inspire him in his work. There would have to be another "Leo," another lover. He had worked himself into an intellectual corner with heartbreaking implications. All of Leo's knowledge and understanding had turned poisonous, and he wanly noted: *If it proves necessary, I will submit. Roth is worth it. Lulu is worth it.*

All of this seemed quaint and amusing, the first time I read it. People take things so seriously, and years later it looks so different. Few of us can relate now to that time and place, that distant, dead culture. But these were very intelligent and gifted people, better-educated, thoughtful, questioning in a way that quite escapes us now – we have an answer for everything we ask, lucky as we are.

The more I stared at poor Leo's words, his clotted handwriting, the more I followed his tortured chain of thought – the more I sympathized with him and even came to believe him. Or at least to believe that he believed. If I could understand him, then I could forgive him for not being in my life. And the truth is, I wanted to forgive him, for Leo, like Joseph Roth, had chosen a remorseless faith in literature and its necessary way of life – which I secretly shared, but lacked the courage and foolishness to attempt.

Things played out his way, in a sense. On the last afternoon of what Leo called his "only genuine life," Lulu came to him and they passed a few hours in the most intense lovemaking, pressing the far edge of violence and unfathomable need, an experience that left them both in tears of joy, incapable of speaking until the time came when she had to leave. Roth would finish his book that night. He told her to ask Leo to join them the next evening to celebrate.

I understood: Roth had known all along.

The following afternoon, when he knocked on the door of Roth's apartment, there was no answer. Perhaps he had come too early. He tried the handle, and the door opened. Yes, there they were. Roth was asleep on the chaise, and Sonja was asleep in the narrow bed in the far corner of the room. Leo was about to back out quietly when Roth suddenly groaned and stirred. There was something vaguely alarming about the noise Roth made, so Leo carefully approached. Roth's eyes stared at him, and Leo had never seen such anguish. Roth's hand moved, barely. Leo interpreted it as a beckoning gesture, and he moved closer.

"I'm dead." Roth's voice was a feeble whisper.

"Lulu."

The word may not actually have escaped his lips, but Leo spoke it, and he turned immediately to the bed. He rushed across the room. She was there, he saw the blankets mounded up over her body. He recognized the beautiful curve of her hips, the correct length of her slender frame. He even saw, he was sure, the slight rise and fall of her shape as she breathed, deep in understandable sleep. When Leo put his hand on her shoulder, his memory-sensation was true, he knew exactly how her shoulder felt and recognized it again. But when he gently pulled back the layers of cheap fabric, they fell away from his hand. He uncovered nothing but the bottom sheet, which still bore the impress of a small body. Leo touched it, and he thought he could detect a fading warmth. But all the sheet held was dust and lint and bits of human grit. He pressed his face to the bed, and – oh God, yes – he could smell her in the most intimate way, as he had tasted and smelled her in love.

But she was gone, like a bed-ghost (*Bettgeist*).

Roth was still alive, and in agony. Leo hurried and performed the necessary function of getting help. Roth was taken to Saint-Jude, the nearest hospital for the poor. Strangely, Leo had no trouble sleeping that night. He left the door to his room unlocked, but he had no visitor. Lulu did not magically appear. Leo was allowed to see Roth the next morning. He was in a ward filled with dozens of patients, all from the bottom of French society. The conditions were mean and the pervasive smell was terrible. Roth had no strength left in him, almost no life at all. Only his lips and eyes moved a little. His large eyes were yellowish and his face appeared to have collapsed into itself. For several minutes he merely gazed at Leo, and his expression was impossible to decipher.

Finally, Leo found a few words. "Did you finish it?"

"Yes."

"Good. I'm so happy to hear that."

"Kuhn."

"Yes?"

"You're looking at the saddest man in Europe."

Then his eyes closed. Leo waited until he was sure that Roth's breathing continued. He smiled and patted Roth's hand. *No*, he thought as he turned away and started to leave. *Nobody so close to death can be that sad.*

Leo left his door unlocked again that night, probably still hoping somehow that Lulu would return to him. But she didn't. It was nearly noon when he awoke the following day. He felt rested, better physically now, though his heart was still sick with disappointment and sorrow.

As he was leaving to go to the hospital again, Leo almost walked right past a man lingering on the sidewalk. But there was something familiar – and then the man smiled and stepped closer.

"Herr Kuhn, how nice to see you again." The German agent.

Leo started to continue on his way. He had seen this man a number of times over the months. Leo refused to speak a word to him. But now the German reached out and took hold of Leo's arm.

"Just to save you the inconvenience," he said. "Your friend Herr Roth died this morning. No doubt you were expecting this, it's hardly a surprise, considering the foolish way he lived. One evening I saw him sitting alone in Bernier's – in the Rue de Faubourg, do you know it? – and I thought to myself, this is a man who died a long time ago but doesn't realize it. Nobody reads his sort of thing anymore now, do they? What do you think?"

Leo freed his arm and hurried away.

He remained in Montmartre, living in that room, until the following year, when he left for the south shortly before the Nazi occupation of Paris. He left just before dawn, successfully dodging Herr Nachtengel.

Joseph Roth's last novel, *The Legend of the Holy Drinker*, is now regarded as one of his finest works. It is a tale of atonement and redemption. Roth was forty-four years old when he died.

My grandfather, it seems, also drank heavily until the end of his life. But I don't think his drinking served the same purpose as Roth's. It seems more likely to me that Leo used alcohol as a consolation for the loss of Lulu, and perhaps also for the failings of his career as a writer – he was never the writer he wanted to be, and surely he understood that.

Yes, yes, I know she is gone, if indeed she was ever there. And I know she will never come back – I tell myself this everyday. But

*the rest of me is not convinced. So I light the fire every evening
and try again to put the words in order. Perhaps if I get the magic
pattern right, it will summon her back. My Muse, my lover – I
have no life without her.*

Romantic nonsense, the delusions of an old man – I suppose
they are. But I can understand his desire to believe now. Leo never
gave up on the only two things that really mattered to him after he
left Germany: his Lulu and his writing. Naturally, he couldn't
stop working on her story – their story. And he remained faithful
to her hopeless plea: "Don't write endings for us."

Every time I sit down to write an essay, a report, or even a
harmless little tale of my own (none of which has ever been
published), I think of my grandfather. His irrational faith in the
rightness of such work pleases me. I see it as a gift from him to me
– one that certainly skipped past my father. But it is a gift of very
mixed qualities. And, I remember my mother's warning to me.

Dawn is often at hand when I finish writing. I can make out
shapes in the thick grey light. I go to bed, and see once again the
shape of my lover beneath the blankets. I know so well the curve
of her hip, the length of her body. Sometimes the lingering
darkness fools me and for an awful moment I may not see her
hair on the pillow, and my heart races as my hand reaches to
touch her.

GRAHAM MASTERTON

The Ballyhooly Boy

GRAHAM MASTERTON AND HIS WIFE WIESCKA moved to Eire in the summer of 1999 and since then the view from his Gothic mansion overlooking Cork City has proved to be highly inspirational.

He has written a new volume in his series of horror novels for young adults, *Rook 4: Snowman*; a new novel for teenage readers, *Cut Dead*; as well as several short stories, a novella, and a full-length adult horror novel, *The DoorKeepers*. *The House That Jack Built* and *The Chosen Child* have both been recently reprinted in American editions, while his readership in France and Belgium has increased enormously. *The DoorKeepers* was published first in French before appearing in an English-language edition, and the following story first appeared in a Belgium magazine. He is also sponsoring the Prix Masterton, an annual literary award to the most creative horror writer working in the French language.

"I was inspired to write 'The Ballyhooly Boy' after a weekend drive through the countryside north of Cork," explains the author. "You can drive for miles and miles and there's nobody there. The signposts are highly erratic and it's easy to find yourself driving around in circles between high farm hedges, like a maze. We were almost beginning to panic when we found ourselves in Ballyhooly . . . but even that was like a village in a Lovecraft story, where the perspective of the buildings looked all wrong."

Rain came dredging down the street in misty grey curtains as we drew up outside the narrow terraced house in the middle of Ballyhooly. All of the houses in the row were painted different colours: sunflower yellows, crimsons, pinks and greens. In sullen contrast, Number 15 was painted as brown as peat.

Mr Fearon switched off the engine of his eight-year-old Rover and peered at the house through his circular James Joyce glasses. "I'll admit it doesn't look much. But prices have been very buoyant lately. You could get eighty-five thousand for it easy, if you put it on the market today."

I took in the peeling front door, the darkened and dusty front windows, the sagging net curtains in one of the upstairs rooms. I guessed that I *could* sell it straight away; but then it might be worth smartening it up a little. A coat of paint and a new bathroom suite from Hickey's could make all the difference between £85,000 and £125,000.

I climbed out of the car, tugging up my collar against the rain. A small brindled dog barked at me for invading its territory without asking. I shaded my eyes and looked in through the front window. It was too grimy to see much, but I could just make out a black fireplace and a tipped-over chair. The living-room was very small, but that didn't matter. I might redecorate Number 15, but I certainly wouldn't be living in it. Not here in Ballyhooly, which was little more than a crossroads ten miles north of Cork, with two pubs and a shop and a continuous supply of rain.

Mr Fearon made a fuss of finding the right key and unlocked the front door. He had to kick the weatherboard to open it; and it gave a convulsive shudder, like a donkey, when it's kicked. The doormat was heaped with letters and free newspapers and circulars. Inside the hallway, there was a strong smell of damp, and the brown wallpaper was peppered with black specks of mould.

"It'll need some airing-out, of course, but the roof's quite sound, and that's your main thing."

I stepped over the letters and looked around. Next to the front door stood a Victorian coat-and-umbrella-stand, with a blotchy, yellowed mirror, in which Mr Fearon and I looked as if we had both contracted leprosy. On the opposite wall hung a damp-faded print of a dark back street in some unidentifiable European city, with a cathedral in the background, and hooded figures concealed in its Gothic doorways. The green-and-brown diamond-patterned linoleum on the floor must have dated from the 1930s.

The sitting-room was empty of furniture except for that single overturned wheelback chair. A broken glass lampshade hung in the centre of the room.

"No water penetration," Mr Fearon remarked, pointing to the ceiling. But in one corner, there were six or seven deep scratchmarks close to the coving.

"What do you think caused those?" I asked him.

He stared at them for a long time and then shrugged.

We went through to the kitchen, which was cold as a mortuary. Which *felt* like a mortuary. Under the window there was a thick, old-fashioned sink, with rusty streaks in it. A gas cooker stood against the opposite wall. All of the glass in the cream-painted kitchen cabinets had been broken, and some of the frames had dark brown drips running down them, as if somebody had smashed the glass on purpose, in a rage, and cut their hands open.

Outside, I could see a small yard crowded with old sacks of cement and bricks and half a bicycle, and thistles that grew almost chest-high. And the rain, gushing from the clogged-up guttering, so that the wall below it was stained with green.

"I still can't imagine why your woman wanted to give me this place," I said, as we climbed the precipitous staircase. Halfway up, there was a stained-glass window, in amber, with a small picture in the centre of a winding river, and a dark castle, with rooks flying around its turrets.

"You'll be watching for the stair-carpet," Mr Fearon warned me. "It's ripped at the top."

Upstairs, there were two bedrooms, one of them overlooking the street and a smaller bedroom at the back. In the smaller bedroom, against the wall, stood a single bed with a plain oak bedhead. It was covered with a yellowing sheet. Above it hung a damp-rippled picture of the Cork hurling team, 1976. I went to the window and looked down into the yard. For some reason I didn't like this room. There was a sour, unpleasant smell in it, boiled vegetables and Dettol. It reminded me of nursing-homes, and old, pale people seen through rainy windows. It was the smell of hopelessness.

"Mrs Devlin wasn't a woman to explain herself," said Mr Fearon. "Her estate didn't amount to much, and she left most of it to her husband. But she insisted that this house should come to you. She said she was frightened of what would happen to her if it didn't."

I turned away from the window. "But she wouldn't explain why?"

Mr Fearon shook his head. "If I had any inkling, I'd tell you."

I still found it difficult to believe. Up until yesterday morning, when Mr Fearon had first called me, I had never heard of Mrs Margaret Devlin. Now I found myself to be one of the beneficiaries of her will, and the owner of a shabby terraced property in the rear end of nowhere in particular.

Not that I was looking a gift horse in the mouth. My Italian-style café in Academy Street in Cork hadn't been doing too well lately. Only three weeks ago I had lost my best chef Carlo, and I had always been badly under-financed. I had tried to recoup some of my losses by buying a £1,000 share in a promising-looking yearling called Satan's Pleasure, but it had fallen last weekend at Galway and broken its leg. No wonder Satan was pleased. He was probably laughing all the way back to Hell.

We left the house. Mr Fearon slammed the front door shut behind us – twice – and handed me the keys. "Well, I wish you joy of it," he said.

As I opened the car door, a white-haired priest came hurrying across the road in the rain. "Good morning to you!" he called out. He came up and offered me his hand. "Father Murphy, from St Bernadette's." He was a stocky man, with a large head, and glasses that enormously magnified his eyes. "You must be Jerry Flynn," he said. "You're very welcome to Ballyhooly, Jerry." I shook his hand. "Difficult place to keep a secret, Ballyhooly?"

"Oh, you'd be surprised. We have plenty of secrets here, believe me. But everybody knew who Margaret Devlin was going to give her house to."

"Everybody except me, apparently."

Father Murphy gave me an evasive smile. "Do you know what she said? She said it was destiny. I have to bequeath my house to Jerry Flynn. The wheel turning the full circle, so to speak."

"And what do you think she meant by that?"

"I believe that she was making her peace before God. The world is a strange place, Jerry. Doors may open, but they don't always lead us where we think they're going to."

"And this door?" I asked nodding toward Number 15.

"Well, who knows? But when you're back, don't forget to drop in to see me. My housekeeper makes the best tea brack in Munster. And we can talk. We really ought to talk."

I hadn't planned on going back to Ballyhooly for at least ten days. I was interviewing new chefs and I was also trying to borrow some more money from the bank so that I could keep the café afloat. I had already re-mortgaged my flat in Wellington Road, and even when I told my bank manager about my unexpected bequest he shook his head from side to side like a swimmer trying to dislodge water out of his ears.

But only two nights later the phone rang at half-past two in the morning. I sat up. The bedroom was completely dark, except for a diagonal line of sodium street-light crossing the ceiling. I scrabbled around my nightstand and knocked my glass of water onto the floor, the whole lot. The phone kept on ringing until I managed to pick it up. I don't like calls in the middle of the night: they're always bad news. Your father's dead. Your son's been killed in a car crash.

"Who is it?" I asked.

There was nothing on the other end of the line except for a thin, persistent crackling.

"Who is it? Is anybody there?"

The crackling went on for almost half a minute and then the caller hung up. *Click*. Silence.

I tried to get back to sleep, but I was wide awake now. I switched on the bedside light and climbed out of bed. My cat Charlie stared at me through slitted eyes as if I were mad. I went to the bathroom and refilled my glass of water. In the mirror over the washbasin I thought I looked strangely pale, as if a vampire had visited me when I was asleep. Even my lips were white.

The phone rang again. I went back into the bedroom and picked it up. I didn't say anything. Just listened. At first I heard nothing but that crackling noise again, but then a woman's voice said, "Is that Mr Jerry Flynn?"

"Who wants him?"

"Is that Mr Jerry Flynn who has the house in Ballyhooly?"

"Who wants him? Do you know what time it is?"

"Your have to go to your house, Jerry. You have to do what needs to be done."

"What are you talking about? What needs to be done?"

"It can't go on, Jerry. It has to be done."

"Look, who is this? It's two-thirty in the morning and I don't understand what the hell you're talking about."

"Go to your house, Jerry. Number Fifteen. It's the only way."

The woman hung up again. I stared at the receiver for a while, as if I expected it to say something else, and then I hung up, too.

For a change, it wasn't raining the next morning when I drove back to Ballyhooly, but the hills were covered with low grey clouds. The road took me over the Nagle mountains and across the stone bridge that spans the Blackwater river. I drove for almost twenty minutes and saw nobody, except for a farmhand driving a tractor heaped with sugar-beet. For some reason, they reminded me of rotting human heads.

When I reached Ballyhooly, I parked outside Number 15 and climbed out of my car. I hesitated for a few moments before I opened the front door, pretending to be searching for my keys. Then I turned around quickly to see if I could catch anybody curtain-twitching. But the street was empty, except for two young boys with runny noses and a dog that was trotting off on some self-appointed errand.

I pushed open the shuddering front door. The house was damp and silent. No new mail, only a circular advertising Dunne's Stores Irish bacon promotion. I walked through to the kitchen. It was so cold in there that my breath smoked. I opened one or two drawers. All I found was a rusty can-opener, a ball of twine and a half-empty packet of birthday-cake candles.

I went through to the living-room. Out on the street, an old man in a brown raincoat was standing on the opposite corner, watching the house and smoking. I picked up the fallen chair and set it straight.

The silence was uncanny. A truck drove past, then a motor-cycle, but I couldn't hear them at all. I felt as if I had gone completeley deaf.

I returned to the hallway and inspected myself in the blotchy Victorian mirror. I certainly didn't look well, although I couldn't think why. I felt tired, but that was only natural after an interrupted night. More than that, though, I felt unsettled, as if something were going to happen that I wasn't going to be able to control. Something unpleasant.

It was then that I glanced up the stairs. I said, "*Jesus!*" out loud, and my whole body tingled with fright.

Standing on the landing was a white-faced boy, staring at me intently. He appeared to be about eight or nine, with short brown hair that looked as if it had been cut with the kitchen scissors, and protruberant ears. He wore a grey sweater with darned elbows and long grey-flannel shorts. And he stared at me, in utter silence, without even blinking.

"What are you doing here?" I asked him. "You almost gave me a heart-attack."

He didn't say anything, but continued to stare at me, almost as if he were trying to stare me into non-existence.

"Come on," I said. "You can't stay here. This house belongs to me now. What have you been doing, playing? I used to do that, when I was your age. Play in this old derelict house. Ghosthunters."

Still the boy didn't speak. His fists were tightly clenched, and he breathed through his mouth, quite laboriously, as if he were suffering from asthma.

"Listen," I told him. "I'm supposed to be back in Cork by eleven. I don't know how you got in here, but you really have to leave."

The boy continued to stare at me in silence. I started to climb up the steep, narrow staircase toward him. As soon as I did so, he turned around and walked quite quickly across the landing, and disappeared into the smaller bedroom at the back of the house.

"Come on, son," I called to him. I was beginning to lose my patience. I climbed up the rest of the stairs and followed him through the bedroom door. "Breaking into other people's houses, that's trespass."

The bedroom was empty. There was nobody there. Only the bed with the yellowed sheet and the dull view down to the yard, with its weeds and its cement sacks.

I knelt down and looked under the bed. The boy wasn't there. I felt around the walls to see if there was a secret door, but all I felt was damp wallpaper. The sash window was jammed up with years of green paint; and the floor was covered in thin brown underlay, so the boy couldn't have lifted up any of the floor-boards. I even looked up the chimney, but that was ridiculous, and I felt ridiculous even when I was doing it. The flue was so narrow that even a hamster couldn't have climbed up it.

My irritation began to rearrange itself into a deeply disturbing sense of creepiness. If the boy hadn't hidden under the bed, and he hadn't climbed up the chimney, and he certainly hadn't escaped through the window, then where had he gone?

He couldn't have been a ghost. I refused to believe in ghosts. Besides, he had looked far too solid to be a ghost. Too normal, too real. What ghost has falling-down socks and darns in its sweater?

But he wasn't here. I had seen him standing at the top of the stairs. I had heard him breathing. But he wasn't here.

I went from room to room, searching them all. I didn't go up into the attic because I didn't have a ladder, but then the boy hadn't had a ladder, either, and there was a cobweb in the corner of the attic door which he would have had to have broken, even if he had found some miraculous way of getting up there. The house was empty. No boy, anywhere. I even opened up the gas oven.

I left the house much later than I had meant to, almost half an hour later. As I came out, and slammed the door shut, a woman approached me. She probably wasn't much older than thirty-five, but she looked forty at least. Her brown hair was tightly permed and she had the pinched face of a heavy smoker. She wore a cheap purple coat and a long black skirt with a fraying hem.

"Well, Jerry," she said, without any introduction, "you've seen what you have to do."

"Was it you who phoned me last night?"

"It doesn't matter who phoned you. You've seen what you have to do."

"I haven't the slightest idea what I have to do."

"You should be here at night then. When the screaming starts."

"Screaming? What screaming? What are you talking about?"

The woman took out a pack of Carroll's and lit one, and sucked it so hard that her cheeks were all drawn in. "We've been living next door to that for twenty-five years and what are *we* supposed to do? That house is all we've got. But my daughter's a nervous wreck and my husband tried to take his own life. And who can we tell? We'd never sell the property if everybody knew about it. Number seventeen they're the same. Nobody can stand it any more."

It started to rain again, but neither of us made any attempt to find shelter. "What's your name?" I asked her.

"Maureen," she said, blowing smoke.

"Well, tell me about this screaming, Maureen."

"It doesn't happen all the time. Sometimes we can go for weeks and we don't hear anything. But it's November now, and that's the anniversary, and then we hear it more and more, and sometimes it's unbearable, the screaming. You never heard such screaming in your whole life."

"The anniversary?" I asked her. "The anniversary of what?"

"The day the boy killed his whole family and then himself. In that house. Nobody found them till two days later. The *gardaí* thought the house was painted red, until they realized it was blood. I saw them carry the mother and the daughter out myself. I saw it myself. And you never saw such a frightful thing. He used his father's razor, and he almost took their heads off."

I looked away, down Ballyhooly's main road. I could see Father Murphy, not far away, white-haired, leaning against the rain, talking to a woman in a blue coat.

"Can't the priest help you?"

"Him? He's tried. But this is nothing to do with God, believe me."

"I don't see what I can do. I was bequeathed this house, by somebody I never even knew, and that's it. I run a café. I'm not an exorcist."

"You've seen the boy, though?"

I didn't say anything, but the woman tilted her head sideways and looked at me closely. "You've seen the boy. I can tell."

"I've seen – I don't know what I've seen."

"You've seen him. You've seen the boy. You can't deny it." She sucked at her cigarette again, more triumphantly this time.

"All right, yes. Is he a local boy?"

"He's the very same boy. The boy who killed his family, and then himself."

I didn't know what to say. I was beginning to suspect that Maureen had been drinking. But she kept on smoking and nodding as if she had proved her point beyond a shadow of a doubt, and that I was just being perverse to question the feasibility of a dead schoolboy walking around my newly-acquired house.

"I have to get back to Cork now," I told her. "I'm sorry."

"You've seen him and you're just going to leave? You don't think that you were given this house by accident? That your name was picked out with a pin?"

"Quite frankly I don't know *why* it was given to me."

"You were chosen, that's why. That's what Margaret – Mrs Devlin – always used to say to me. She was chosen and there was nothing she could do about it, except to pass it on."

I unlocked my car. Maureen started to become agitated, tossing her cigarette away and wiping her hands on the front of her coat, over and over, as if she couldn't get them clean.

"You mustn't go. Please."

"I'm sorry. I have a business to run."

But it was then that I saw one of the grubby upstairs curtains being drawn aside. Standing in the bedroom window, staring at me, was the white-faced boy. Somehow he must have hidden from me when I was searching the house, and here he was, mocking me.

I kicked open the front door and ran upstairs. I hurtled into the front bedroom but the boy was gone. He wasn't in the back bedroom, either. There was a tiny linen cupboard between the two rooms, but it was empty except for two folded sheets and a 60-watt lightbulb. I slapped the walls in both bedrooms, to see if they were hollow. I lifted up the mattress in the smaller bedroom, in case it was hollowed-out, and the boy had been concealing himself in there. It was stained, and damp, but it hadn't been tampered with.

Underneath it, however, lying on the bedsprings, I discovered a book. It was thin, like an exercise book, with a faded maroon cover, and it was disturbingly familiar. I picked it up and angled it toward the window, so that I could see what was printed on the front.

Bishop O'Rourke Memorial School, Winter 1976. The same junior school that I had attended, in Cork. I opened it up and leafed through it. I could even remember this particular yearbook. The sports reports. The opening of the new classroom extension.

The visit from the *Taoiseach*. And right at the back, the list of names of everybody in the school. Familiar names, all of them, but I couldn't remember many of their faces. And there was my name, too. Class III, Gerald Flynn, between Margaret Flaherty and Kevin Foley.

But what was it doing here, this book, hidden under the mattress in this run-down little house in Ballyhooly?

I looked around one more time. I still couldn't work out how the boy had managed to elude me, but I would make sure that he never got in here again. Tomorrow morning I would change the locks, front and back, and check that none of the windows could be opened from the outside.

As I left the house, Father Murphy came over.

"Everything in order?" he asked me, with that same evasive smile. A real priest's smile, always waiting for you to commit yourself.

"You said we ought to talk."

"We should," he said. "Come across and have a glass with me."

We crossed the street and went into a small pub called The Roundy House. Inside, there was a small bar, and a sitting-room with armchairs and a television, just like somebody's private home. Two young men sat at the bar, smoking, and they acknowledged Father Murphy with a nod of their heads.

We sat in the corner by the window. The afternoon light strained through the net curtains the colour of cold tea. Father Murphy clinked my half of Guinness, and then he said, "Maureen hasn't been upsetting you?"

"She told me that she could hear screaming."

"Well, yes. She's right. I've heard it myself."

"I've seen a boy, too. I saw him in the house, twice. I don't know how he got in there."

"He got in there because he's always in there."

"What are you trying to tell me, that he's a ghost?"

Father Murphy shook his head. "I don't believe in ghosts and I don't suppose that you do, either. But he's not alive in the way that you and I are alive. You can see him because he will occupy that house until he gets justice for what happened to him. That's my theory, anyway."

"You really think it's the same boy who killed his family?

That's not possible, is it? I mean, how can that be possible? He killed himself, too, and even if he hadn't, he'd be my age by now."

Father Murphy wiped foam from his upper lip. "What's been happening in that house isn't recognized by the teachings of the Church, Jerry. I've tried twice to exorcize it. The second time I brought down Father Griffin from Dublin. He said afterwards that no amount of prayer or holy water could cleanse that property, because it isn't possessed of any devil.

"It's possessed instead by the rage of a nine-year-old boy who was driven to utter despair. A child of God, not of Satan. His father was a drunk who regularly beat him. His mother neglected him and fed him on nothing but chips, if she fed him at all. His older sister had Down's Syndrome and he was expected to do everything for her, change her sheets when she wet the bed, everything. He lived in hell, that boy, and he had nobody to help him.

"My predecessor here did whatever he could, but it isn't easy when the parents are so aggressive. And he wasn't alone, this boy. He was only one of thousands of children all over the country whose parents abuse them, and who don't have anywhere to turn.

"Whatever it is in your house, Jerry – whatever kind of force it is – it's the force of revenge. A sense of rage and injustice so strong that it has taken on a physical shape."

"Even if that's true, father – what can *I* do about it?"

"You were chosen. I don't know why. Margaret Devlin said that *she* was chosen, too, when she inherited Number 15. And before her, Martin Donnolly. I never knew what became of him."

"So what happened to Margaret Devlin? How did she die?"

"Well, it was a tragedy. She took her own life. I believe she was separated from her husband or something of the kind. She took an overdose of paracetamol. Lay dead in the house for over a week."

On the drive back to Cork, under a late-afternoon sky as black as a crow's wing, I kept thinking about what Father Murphy had told me. *A sense of rage and injustice so strong that it has taken on a physical shape*. It didn't really make any scientific sense, or any theological sense, either, but in a way I could understand what he meant. We all get angry and frustrated from time to time, and when we do, we can all feel the uncontrollable beast that rises up inside us.

Katharine was waiting for me when I got back to my flat. She was a neat, pretty girl with a pale pre-Raphaelite face and long black hair. She helped me in the café from time to time, but her real job was making silver jewelry. We had nearly had an affair once, after a friend's party and too many bottles of Chilean sauvignon, but she was such a good friend that I was always glad that we had managed to resist each other. Mainly by falling asleep.

She wanted to know if I wanted to come to an Irish folk evening in McCurtain Street. She was dressed for it: with a blue silk scarf around her head and a long flowing dress with patterns of peacock feathers on it, and dozens of jangly silver bracelets. But I didn't feel in the mood for "Whiskey in the Jar" and "Goodbye Mrs Durkin". I poured us each a glass of wine and sat down on my big leather sofa, tossing Bishop O'Rourke's Memorial Junior School yearbook onto the coffee table.

"What's wrong?" asked Katharine. "The bank didn't turn you down, did they?"

"As a matter of fact they did, but that's not it."

She sat close beside me, and she had on some perfume like a pomander, cinnamon and cloves and orange-peel. "You've got something on your mind. I can tell."

I told her about Number 15 and the boy that I had seen on the landing. I told her about Maureen, too, and the screaming; and what Father Murphy had said about revenge.

"You don't believe any of it, do you? It sounds like a prime case of mass hysteria."

"I wasn't hysterical, but I saw the boy as clear as I can see you now. And I couldn't find how the hell he managed to get in and out of the house. There just wasn't any way."

She picked up the yearbook. "This is spooky, though, isn't it – finding your old junior school yearbook under the mattress?"

She read through the list of names in Class III. "Linda Ahern, remember her?"

"Fat. Freckles. The reddest hair you've ever seen. But when she turned fourteen, she was a cracker."

"Donal Coakley?"

"Thin. Weedy. We all used to chase him round the playground and pinch his biscuits."

"What a mean lot you were."

"Oh, you know what schoolkids are like."

"Ellen Collins?"

"Don't remember her."

"Martin Donnolly?"

I frowned at her. "Who did you say?"

"Martin Donnolly."

"I don't remember him, but that was the name of the man who owned Number 15 before Margaret Devlin."

"It's a common enough name, for goodness' sake."

"Yes, but who comes next? Margaret Flaherty. I wonder if she could have changed her name to Devlin when she married."

"Isn't there somebody you could ask?"

I called my old friend Tony O'Connell – the only former classmate from Bishop O'Rourke's who I still saw from time to time. He ran an auto repair business on the Patricks Mills Estate out at Douglas.

"Tony, you remember Margaret Flaherty?"

"How could I ever forget her? I was in love with her. I picked her a bunch of dandelions once and she threw them away and called me an idiot."

"Do you know if she married?"

"Oh, yes. She married some fellow much older than herself. A real waste of space. Estate agent, I think he was. Frank Devlin."

"And Martin Donnolly? Do you know what happened to him?"

"Martin? He moved to Fermoy or somewhere near there. They found him drowned in the Blackwater."

I put down the phone. "I may be making a wild assumption here," I told Katharine, "but it looks as if Number 15 is being passed from one old pupil of Bishop O'Rourke's to the next, alphabetically, down the class list. And everybody who owns it ends up dead."

"You'd better check some more," Katharine suggested. "See if you can find out what happened to Linda Ahern and Donal Coakley."

It took another hour. Outside, it had started to grow dark, that strange foggy disappearance of light that happens over Cork some evenings, because the River Lee brings in cold seawater from the Atlantic, the same reaches where the *Lusitania* was sunk, and the city turns chilly and quiet, as if it remembers the dead.

I found Ita Twomey, who was Linda Ahern's best friend when they were at school, by calling her mother. Ita was Mrs Desmond now, and lived in Bishopstown. "Linda was a single mother. But she inherited a house, I believe. But she was killed in a car accident on the N20 . . . both herself and her kiddie. They burned to death. The *gardaí* said that she drove her car deliberately into a bridge."

And Donal Coakley? I managed at last to find Vincent O'Brien, our class teacher at Bishop O'Rourke's. "You'll have to forgive me for sounding so hoarse. I was diagnosed with cancer of the larynx only two months ago. I'll be having a laryngectomy by Christmas, God willing."

"I'm trying to find out what happened to a classmate of mine called Donal Coakley."

"Donal? I remember Donal. Poor miserable kid. I don't know what happened to him. He was always very unhappy at school. All of the other kids used to bully him, every day. I don't suppose you did, Jerry, but you know how cruel children can be to each other, without even realising what they're doing. He was always playing truant, young Donal, because he didn't want to stay at home and he didn't want to go to school. Poor miserable kid. They were always stealing his lunch money and taking his sweeties and hitting him around. You never know why, do you? Just because his parents were poor and he always smelled a bit and had holes in his socks."

"But do you know what happened to him, after he left school?"

"I couldn't tell you. He never finished Bishop O'Rourke's. He left at mid-term. He couldn't take the bullying any longer. I think his parents moved. There was some trouble with the social services. I never heard where they went."

My mouth was as dry as if I had woken up from drinking red wine all night. "Donal was bullied that badly?"

"It happens in every school, doesn't it? It's kids, they have a sort of pack instinct. Anybody who doesn't fit in, they go for, and they never let up. Donal had second-hand shoes and jumpers with holes in them and of course that made him a prime target. I'm not talking about you, Jerry. I know you were very protective of the weaker kids. But it was a fact."

Protective? I thought of the time that I had snatched the Brennan's bread-wrapper in which Donal's mother had packed his jam sandwiches for him, and stamped on it. I thought of the time that five of us had cornered him by the boys' toilets and punched him and beaten him with sticks and rulers until he knelt down on the tarmac with his grubby hands held over his head to protect himself, not even crying, not even begging for mercy, though we kept on shouting and screaming at him.

Donal Coakley. My God. The shame of it made my cheeks burn, even after all these years. The day it was raining and we found out that he had lined his shoes with newspaper because they had holes in the soles. Wet pages from the *Evening Echo* folded beneath his socks.

"Is that all you wanted to know?" asked Vincent O'Brien.

I could hardly speak to him. "I'd forgotten Donal. I'd forgotten him. I don't think I wanted to remember."

I put down the phone and Katharine was staring at me in the strangest way. Or perhaps she wasn't. Perhaps I had suddenly realised what I had done, and everything was different.

"I – ah, I have to go back to Ballyhooly," I told her.

"You're not *crying*, are you?"

"Crying? What are you talking about? I have to go back to Ballyhooly, that's all."

"Tonight?"

"Yes, tonight. Now."

"Let me come with you. Something's happened, hasn't it? You'd be better off with somebody with you."

"Katharine – this is something I have to deal with on my own."

She took hold of my hands between hers. She stroked my fingers, trying to calm me down. "But you must tell me," she said. "It's something to do with Donal Coakley, isn't it?"

I nodded. I couldn't speak. She was right, damn it. She was right. I was crying. The boy on the landing was Donal Coakley. I had bullied him and tortured him and stolen his money and trodden on his lunch, and what had he ever had to go home to, except a drunken father who punched him and a mother who expected him to lay the fire and take care of his handicapped sister; and that damp bedroom in Ballyhooly.

I could have befriended him. I could have taken care of him.

But I was worse than any of the others. No wonder his father's razor had seemed like the only way out.

You don't know how dark it is in the Cork countryside at night, unless you've been there. Only a speckle of distant flickering lights as we drove over the Nagle mountains. It was cold but at least it was dry. We arrived in the middle of Ballyhooly at 11:37 and the Roundy House was emptying out, three or four locals laughing and swearing and a small brown-and-white dog barking at them disapprovingly.

"I don't know what you expect to find here," said Katharine.

"I don't know, either."

I helped her out of the car, but all the time I couldn't take my eyes off Number 15. Its windows looked blacker than ever; and in the orange light of Ballyhooly's main street, its paintwork looked even more scabrous and diseased.

"Is this it?" Katherine asked. "It looks derelict."

"It is." I unlocked the front door and kicked the weatherboard to open it. I switched on the light and, miraculously, it worked, even though it was only a single bare bulb. I had called the ESB only yesterday afternoon to have Number 15 reconnected. The damp smell seemed even stronger than ever, and I was sure that I could hear a dripping noise.

"This is a seriously creepy house," said Katharine, looking around. "How many people died here?"

"That night? All four of them. Donal's father and mother, Donal's sister, and Donal himself. And Margaret Flaherty died here, too."

"It smells like death."

"It smells more like dry rot to me," I said. But then I took two or three cautious steps into the hallway and sniffed again. "Dry rot, and something dead. Probably a bird, stuck down the chimney."

"What are you going to do?" asked Katharine.

"I don't know. But I have to do *something*."

We took a look in the living-room. The broken ceiling-light cast a diagonal shadow, which made the whole room appear to be sloping sideways, and distorted its perspective. The wind blew a soft lament down the chimney.

"What are those scratches?" asked Katharine, pointing up at the coving. "It looks like a lion's been loose."

"I asked the estate agent."

"And?"

"Either he didn't know or he didn't want to tell me."

I took Katharine into the kitchen. It was deadly cold, as always. I didn't really know what I was looking for. Just some sign of what was really happening here. Just some indication of what I could do to break the cycle of Donal Coakley's revenge.

If it *was* Donal Coakley, and not some madman playing games with us.

"Nothing here," said Katharine, opening the larder door and peering inside. Only an old bottle of Chef sauce, with a rusty, encrusted cap.

We went upstairs together. I hadn't realized how much the stairs creaked until now. Every one of them complained as if their nails were slowly being drawn out of them, like teeth. The landing was empty. The front bedroom was empty. The back bedroom was empty, too. The chill was intense: that damp, penetrating chill that characterizes bedrooms in old Irish houses.

"I think you should sell," said Katharine. "Get rid of the place as soon as you can. And make sure that you don't sell it to the next person on your class register."

"You may be right. And there was me, thinking this was going to solve all of my problems."

Katharine took a last look around the bedroom. "Come on," she said. "There's no point in staying here. There's nothing you can do."

But at that moment, we heard an appalling scream from downstairs. It was a woman's scream, but it was so shrill that it was almost like an animal's. Then it was joined by another scream – a man's. He sounded as if he were being fatally hurt, and he knew it.

"Oh my God," Katharine gasped. "Oh my God what is it?"

"Stay here," I told her.

"I'm coming with you. I just want to get out of here."

"*Stay here*! We don't know what the hell could be down there."

"Oh, God," she repeated; but her voice was drowned out by another agonized scream, and then another, and then another.

I started downstairs, ducking my head so that I could see through the banisters into the hallway. I was so frightened that I was making a thin pathetic whining noise, like a child.

The screams were coming from the living-room. The door was half-open, and the light was still on, but I couldn't see anything at all. No shadows, nothing. I reached the bottom of the stairs and edged my way along the hall until I was right beside the living-room door. The screams were hideous, and in between the screams I could hear a woman begging for her life.

I tried to peer in through the crack in the door, but I still couldn't see anything. I thought: there's only one thing for it. I've just got to crash into the room and surprise him, whoever he is, and hope that he isn't stronger and quicker and that he doesn't have a straight-razor.

I took a deep breath. Then I took a step back, lowered my shoulder and collided against the door. It slammed wide open, and juddered a little way back again. The screams abruptly stopped.

I was standing in a silent room – alone, with only a chair for company. Either we had imagined the screaming, or else it was some kind of trick.

I was still standing there, baffled, when I heard the bedroom door slamming upstairs, and more screaming. Only this time, I recognized who it was. Katharine, and she was shouting out, "*Jerry! Jerry! Jerry for God's sake help me Jerry for God's sake!*"

I vaulted back up the stairs, my vision jostling like a hand-held camera. The door to the smaller bedroom was shut – brown-painted wood, with a cheap plastic handle. I tried to open it but it was locked or bolted. And all the time Katharine was screaming and screaming.

"Katharine!" I yelled back. "Katharine, what's happening! I can't open the door!"

But all she could do was scream and weep and babble something incomprehensible, like "*no-no-no-you-can't-you-can't-be-you-can't—*"

I hurled myself against the door, shoulder-first, but all I did was bruise my arm. Katharine's screams reached a crescendo and I was mad with panic, panting and shaking. I propped my hands against the landing walls to balance myself, and I kicked at the door-lock – once, twice – and then the door-jamb splintered and the door shuddered open.

Katharine was lying on the bed. She was struggling and staring at me, her eyes wide open. She looked as if she were fastened onto the mattress with thick brown sticks – trapped, unable to move. But beside the bed stood a huge and complicated creature that I could hardly even begin to understand. It almost filled the room with arms and legs like an immense spider; and glossy brown sacs hung from its limbs like some kind of disgusting fruit. In the middle of it, and part of it, all mixed up in it, his head swollen out of proportion and his eyes as black as cellars stood Donal Coakley, in his grey flannel shorts and his patched-up jumper, his lips drawn back as if they had been nailed to his gums. He floated, almost, borne up above the threadbare carpet by the thicket of tentacles that sprouted out of his back.

The thick brown sticks that fastened Katharine to the bed were spider's legs – or the legs of the thing that Donal Coakley had created out of his need for revenge. This was revenge incarnate. This was what revenge looked like, when it reached such an intensity that it took on a life of its own.

In his right hand, Donal held a straight-razor, with a bloodied blade. It was only an inch above Katharine's neck. He had already cut her once, a very light cut, right across her throat, and blood was running into the collar of her green sweater.

I approached him as near as I dared. The whole room was a thicket of spider-like legs, and there was nothing on Donal's face to indicate that he could see me; or that he had any human emotions at all.

"What do you want me to do?" I asked him. "What do you want me to say? You want me to apologise, for bullying you? I bullied you, yes, and I'm sorry for it. I wish I'd never done it. But we were all young and ignorant in those days. We never guessed that you were so unhappy, and even if we'd known, I don't think that we would have cared.

"It's life, Donal. It's life. And you don't ease your own pain by inflicting it on others."

Donal raised his head a little. I didn't know whether he could see me or not. The criss-cross spider's legs that surrounded him twitched and trembled, as if they were eager to scuttle toward me.

"You don't know the meaning of pain," he said; and his voice sounded exactly as it had, all those years ago, in the playground of Bishop O'Rourke's. "You never suffered pain, any of you."

"Oh God," said Katharine, "please help me."

But without any hesitation at all, Donal swept the straight-razor from one side of her neck to the other. If you hadn't been paying any particular attention, you wouldn't have realized immediately what he had done. But he had sliced her neck through, almost to the vertebrae, and from that instant there was no chance at all of her survival. Blood suddenly sprayed everywhere, all over the bed, all up the walls, all over the carpet. No wonder the *gardaí* had broken into this house and thought that it was all decorated red.

Katharine twitched and shuddered. One hand tried to reach out for me. But I knew that Donal had killed her – and so, probably, did she. The blood was unbelievable: pints of it, pumped out everywhere. Donal's hands were smothered in it, and it was even splattered across his face.

I shall never know to this day exactly what happened next. But if you can accept that men and women become physically transformed, whenever they're truly vengeful, then you can understand it, even if you don't completely believe it. When Donal cut Katharine's throat, something happened to me. I'm not saying that it was similar to what happened to Donal. But my mind suddenly boiled over with the blackest of rages. I felt hatred, and aggression, but I also felt enormous power. I felt myself lifted up, surged forward, as if I had legs and arms that I had never had before, as if I had unimaginable power. I hurled myself at Donal, and the thicket of limbs that surrounded him, and grasped him around the waist.

He slashed at my face with his straight-razor. I knew he was cutting me. I could feel the blood flying. He struggled and screamed like a girl. But I forced him backward. I gripped his hair and clawed at his face. His spidery arms and legs were flailing at me, but I had spidery arms and legs that were more than the equal of his, and we fought for one desperate moment like two giant insects. My urge for revenge, though, was so much fiercer than his. I hurled him back against the bedroom window.

The glass cracked. The glazing-bars cracked. Then both of us smashed through the window and into the yard, falling fifteen feet onto bricks and bags of cement and window-frames. I lifted my head. I could feel the blood dripping from my lips. I felt bruised all over, as if I had been trampled by a horse. I could hear shouting in the street, and a woman screaming.

Donal Coakley was staring at me, only inches away, and his face was as white as the face of the moon.

"I've got you now, Jerry," he said; and he managed the faintest of smiles.

And that's my testimony; and that's all that I can tell you. You can talk to Father Murphy, for what it's worth. You can talk to Maureen. If she doesn't admit to the screaming, then it's only because she's worried about the value of her house. But it's all true; and I didn't touch Katharine, I swear.

If you can't find any trace of Donal, then I don't mind that, because it means that he's finally gone to his rest. But I'd be careful of who I bullied, if I were you; and I'd steer clear of white-faced boys in second-hand shoes. And I wouldn't have a vengeful thought in my head, not one. Not unless you want to find out what vengeance really is.

MICHAEL MARSHALL SMITH

Welcome

MICHAEL MARSHALL SMITH IS A NOVELIST AND SCREENWRITER. His first novel, *Only Forward*, won the August Derleth Award; his second, *Spares*, has been optioned by Steven Speilberg's DreamWorks SKG and translated in seventeen countries around the world, and his third, *One of Us*, is under option by Warner Brothers and Di Novi Pictures. His short stories have appeared in a wide number of anthologies and magazines, and a collection of his short fiction, *What You Make It*, was recently published by HarperCollins in the UK. He lives in London, with his wife Paula and two cats, where he is currently screenwriting and finishing his fourth novel, *The Straw Men*.

As Smith recalls: "The central event of 'Welcome' – a computer file suddenly showing a creation date which while calendrically feasible was technologically impossible – actually happened to me. I knew less about computers than I do now, and I remember the awed bafflement it caused me. I still have the file too: it was a short story of mine called 'Autumn', although transfers from computer to computer have rectified the dating error. This story is a telling of that event against a background of the recent hysteria about the Millennium bug – which as a long-term Mac user I felt quietly smug about – married with a hymn of hatred about dire day jobs . . ."

PAUL SWORE IMAGINATIVELY AND AT SOME LENGTH, glaring at the screen in front of him. His current sentence already boasted three "and's" and two "actually's", and was moreover set firmly on a course into the realms of pure nonsense. Its end dangled in space, peering nervously about for something to mean, but he despaired of even just getting it to the point where he could legitimately put a full stop after it.

He reached for the cigarettes on the window sill, glancing dully at the clock in the corner of the screen. 11:14 p.m. when he'd started work that evening, "Send in the Clones" had stood at eight hundred words. Three hours of effort had merely made it slightly shorter. The individual sentences were okay – he could usually come up with a trenchant observation or a fairly *bon mot* – but they were like a group of strangers trapped together on a bus, with no relationship to each other apart from the fact they appeared on the same page. Chances were that by the time Paul had massaged any coherence into the piece some bastard scientist would have invented a new technique and the whole subject would be out of date anyway. Again.

Enough, already. Paul command-clicked a Save and listened to the 1s and 0s on the hard disk feverishly playing musical chairs. Eventually the machine pinged at him and he quit out, yawning and slumping forward, noticing just how much his back hurt. And how tired he was. As ever: feeling shattered as a way of life. Haul yourself out of bed too tired to even focus. Drag your body around for the day, then go home. Work some more, then go to bed too late. Repeat until dead.

Suddenly the solution to the sentence he'd been working on popped into his head, a way of making it both say something intelligible and remain conventional English. The boys in the back room had evidently been beavering away at the problem, not noticing he'd given up for the night. He considered reloading the word-processor, found that he couldn't be bothered, and decided to jot it down in the document's information window instead.

Selecting "Clones" with a click on the document's icon, Paul hit the required key combination and typed the revised sentence into the little window which popped up. It didn't look quite as stirring on the screen, but it was going to have to do. He moved the cursor up towards the box which would close the window, his eyes straying over the information underneath.

Last Modified: Wednesday, December 15, 1999, 11:17 p.m.
Type: AllWrite Document. Document Size 7K. File Created . . .

Suddenly he stopped and leaned closer to the screen. Mouth open, he stared at the final line in the information window.

File Created: Mon, Sep 9, 1957, 5:02 p.m.

He shut the information window, then opened it again. It was still there. Obviously it was just a glitch of some kind, some binary dancer left standing when the music stopped, but in a funny sort of way he liked it. There was something appealingly odd about seeing "1957" up there, a year when the computer that was displaying it would have been a piece of science fiction.

Taking a gulp of cold tea, Paul started to apply some Scientific Method. The clock in the corner of the screen was showing the correct time, which proved that the motherboard battery was still functioning. He reloaded the word-processor and checked the story, which appeared fine. Then he created a test document, typing in a few words, saving it and quitting. Opening the new document's information window showed a file creation date of December 15, 1999. Pleased, Paul opened the "Clones" window again.

File Created: Mon, Sep 9, 1957, 5:02 p.m.

It was still just a glitch, a 5 and a 7 snatched out of the variable ether instead of two nines, but it was a weird and one-off glitch, and Paul felt vaguely cheered by it. He switched the computer off and rubbed his eyes. Time to give Jenny a ring.

In preparation he walked into the kitchen to make a fresh cup of tea, circling the phone as if it was an animal that had been recently and only partially tamed. Telephones are fine for conducting business, essential even. The whole edifice of commerce would come crashing down if people could see the chasm of boredom in the faces of those they dealt with. Over the phone it was possible to pretend things were important, when actually they were just jobs. Personal conversations were different, and Paul had come to dread them, even though the distance between him and Jenny meant that the phone mediated about eighty per cent of their relationship. Maybe if things were okay you could just breezily chat to each other, update on the unimportant things because the real things were okay. But things were not okay. They were not okay to the tune of two miserable years and a score line of Jenny: three affairs, Paul: nil. The last six months had been a

little better, and they had at least been together, but bridge-
building had in reality been limited to dropping a slim and fragile
plank between the two sides and spending occasional weekends
standing precariously in the middle. Unhappiness at not feeling
needed or wanted had become a part of Paul's life, his every
thought, like an interfaceless application running in the background of every moment. His mental soundtrack had become a
litany of miserable bitterness, and he hated himself for being that
way.

Settling back into the flat's one comfortable chair, Paul
propped the handset under his chin – the skill a legacy of long
hours at work spent listening to people whining at him over the
phone – and dialled the Cambridge number. A ringing tone
eventually emerged and Paul lit a cigarette in preparation. Five,
six rings. Christ, how long did it take to get from her room to the
hall – ten seconds? Nine, ten.

After twenty or so rings Paul quietly replaced the handset,
chewing the inside of his lip. He tried again, looking at his watch.
11:30 p.m. Another twenty rings. No reply. Breathing deeply he
put the phone down again.

What this time? Aerobics class go into overtime? *Another* drink
with the people from work? Why was she never bloody *in* when
he called?

"I went to the cinema with Val. I *told* you I was going to."

Till half eleven?

"We stopped off for a drink, alright? It's Christmas. God,
aren't I even allowed to . . ."

Been there, done that, seen it all before.

Of course that was all it was. Or one of a hundred variants. In a
way it was better than getting the engaged signal. That always
made him think she was curled up happily in her flat, chatting to
The Last One. She couldn't win either way. But then neither could
he.

Closing his eyes, Paul slowly calmed down. It wasn't fair to be
suspicious, to envy her friends and social life. But the Paul who
had been able to take things in his stride, to forgive and forget and
trust, was a Paul who'd never been lied to and never seen
infidelity, never sat at home knowing his girlfriend was at that
moment sleeping with someone else, someone older, taller and
more exciting than himself. He missed that Paul, mourned the

nicer man he thought he'd probably once been, but recognized the inevitability of his passing. He just hadn't been up to the job. Reality demanded psyches with crumple zones. He'd walked into the world with his head held high, and had the shit kicked out of him so many times that now he was hiding somewhere deep inside, waiting for a miracle without any hope at all.

It was time to go to bed. Looking like a hard drugs user might be part of what stopped him ever getting the small consolation of someone appearing to fancy him. That and being resolutely average looking, and not having a tan, and only being five feet, nine inches tall. Not that short, above average height, in fact, but ever since hearing Jenny's description of The Last One he'd gone round marvelling at how close the ground was to his head, feeling like a bloody dwarf.

But he didn't feel tired enough to trust himself to bed. It was there, and in this sort of mood, that he saw most clearly Jenny's kisses on someone else's neck and stomach, imagined scenarios that should have burned themselves out long ago, but which just got clearer every time. He tried the television, which offered two track-suited yobs talking about a group of musical track-suited yobs, and three conventionally-suited old twits gassing on about women in the church. Paul, who felt that the only priests who could be taken half-way seriously were Irish males in their fifties, turned it off again.

For want of anything better to do, he sat back down at his desk and turned the computer back on again, calling up "Clones" Information Window again. It was still there.

File Created: Mon, Sep 9, 1957, 5:02 p.m.

The strange thing was that it didn't look like a mistake. The "57" looked unremarkable; and solid. Paul reached for his diary and checked September 9th 1999. It had been a Thursday. So the day was wrong too.

Or was it? On a sudden whim he fired up his Organiser application, and asked it to Go To the relevant month in 1957, aware that he was feeling nervously excited.

And there it was. September 9th 1957 had been a Monday.

That was something else. Throwing up a couple of random numbers that happened to make a date was one thing, but getting the right *day* was, well it was something different again. Too intrigued to notice that for once neither Jenny nor work had a place in his mind, Paul sat back and smiled. He couldn't explain what he was seeing, and he was glad. He knew that basically it was still just a glitch, and that he ought to be worrying about system file corruption or I/O errors, but he didn't care. For some reason it was interesting, and exciting. It seemed to point to unusual territories, something intangible beyond the everyday. A glimpse of a land beyond the icy wastes of normality was worth having, even if it was just a code-generated mirage.

What it called for, of course, was a story. A little piece. Relaxing, blowing smoke up towards the ceiling, Paul worked around the idea, trying to see where it could lead. Man finds that a document he's created shows a creation date many years before his computer was invented, but which is still a genuine date. Computer time versus real time. Unreliability of binary truths. The Millennium bug. Something.

Nothing came, and he wasn't too concerned. He was beginning to feel sleepy, which meant that he could safely go to bed. It didn't matter if he couldn't get a story out of the glitch. It was still good that it had happened. And, of course, he had to go to work tomorrow.

He woke abruptly, hammered from sleep by his alarm. After turning it off by hitting it with his fist until it stopped, he hauled himself upright and lurched to the bathroom, still well over half asleep and feeling terrible. Sitting blankly in the bath, working up the energy to wash, he found that he was almost in tears.

As he shaved, he remembered the dream. He and Jenny had been at an event of some kind, a big party full of people in formal wear, and things between him and Jenny had been okay in a way they hadn't been for a while. As if there was a future to look forward to. Then she had been called away to the telephone. When she came back, she said that The Last One was coming to visit her, and that he'd be there for two weeks this time. Paul had been distracted by a sound of some kind, and before he'd had time to argue she'd disappeared into the crowd. He'd searched for her, and asked people if they'd seen where she went. All he got was smiles, and then the windows had burst inwards as an endless pack of wolves poured into the room.

More awake now, he knew he wouldn't cry, but also that he'd spend the day even more bitterly than normal. The thought of breakfast made him feel as nauseous as usual, and he smoked a few cigarettes instead, staring out the window with a cup of tea. He realized that Jenny and he still hadn't made any plans for what to do on December 31st. With less than two weeks to go, he was beginning to suspect it wasn't going to happen. What then? Arbitrary or not, surely it should herald a new beginning. Surely not just more of the same.

It rained as he walked to the station.

During the forty minute tube journey he climbed slowly towards the hard and brittle self he used these days, reading fitfully. The mornings were always the worst. Often he would find his mind working away at old hurts, and would have to force himself to read, to try to block them out. Sometimes he even found himself inventing things that might have happened, or could happen. Some part of him was locked away in a circle of hurt, and couldn't think about anything else. It couldn't hate her, so it hated him instead, punished him with make-believe and foreshadowing all possibilities – so that nothing would ever come as a surprise again. It was completely out of Paul's control, and all he could do was try to coat it with white noise. Reading wasn't working, so he looked around the carriage instead, trying to find something to look at, something to tether his attention to the outside world for a change.

In front of him stood a gaggle of girls in their late teens, gossiping in mock outraged terms about something some acquaintance of theirs had done. Paul silently bet that the girl's name was Laura. There seemed to be hundreds of Lauras out there, bad-mouthing their bosses, stealing other people's boyfriends, and never travelling on the tube. Just along from the girls was a man who looked like someone had found an enormous pear, painted it like a suit, and stuck a copy of the *Financial Times* in its mitts. Apart from that, the carriage looked as if it had been filled by extras from the "Random Commuters" department of Central Casting: pink eyes, clothes hastily de-crumpled, faces still half-asleep.

But two stops later, She got on.

Paul had no idea of her name, and no intention of trying to find out. She was in her late thirties, with dark brown hair, slim, tall. Unexceptional really, except that she looked nice, and friendly, and trustworthy, and seeing her gave him his customary pang of quiet desire and misery. A fat man in a brown suit oozed onto the train after her and blocked his sight line, and Paul turned back to his book, almost with relief. Better not to look.

After a while the words began to swim in front of his eyes and, to head his mind off from its accustomed paths, Paul worried at the problem of the story idea from the night before, feeling sure that something must be possible from a premise like that. Perhaps it could generate the kind of quirky piece which all the magazines seemed to be after. Maybe he might be able to sell something for once, start turning the dream of journalism into something approaching a reality. Nothing came, though. The idea seemed unwilling to be subsumed, and just sat there by itself.

In front of him Paul noticed a quiet couple holding hands, and knew immediately that they had just spent the night together for the first time, after an office party. A succession of images came into his mind: her hair, still wet from its morning wash, her normal routine disrupted; his face, smarting from using a razor found lying around in the bathroom, feeling oddly put together, wearing yesterday's shirt and smelling of someone else's deodorant. Neither of then quite sure what to say, how to be, struggling to deal with the suddenly widened perception of someone they saw every day at work. Confused memories of the night before, of the shock of so much skin.

The next stop was theirs and they stood up together, wavered, and then didn't hold hands as they got off the train.

Paul got off at Oxford Circus and trudged up Great Portland Street to the office. Everyone else was already at their desks. As always. One or two grunted at him as he went to the kitchen. He poured himself a cup of coffee and took it into his office, shutting the door behind him. Normally he left it open, to catch what stray gusts of camaraderie might come. This morning he needed ten minutes' peace, and wasn't in the mood for saying "Oh, really?". Then the phone rang and the first hassle of the day started. He opened the door.

He took his lunch at 2:00 p.m., as always. The shorter afternoon seemed to make the day go quicker, and he was generally so busy doing mindless things to unrealistic schedules that there wasn't a breathing space for time to drag in. Lunchtimes were often when he felt worse, in fact. He had time to resent the fact that the days went so quickly without him getting anything out of them, that he had no power in his job, only responsibility. And time to feel yet more fury at himself for apparently having nothing else to think about, for the constant black Mass in his head. He was terribly, terribly bored with himself. Perhaps it wasn't surprising if Jenny was too.

He walked out past the others, feeling their eyebrows raise. Taking your lunch break was deemed a sign of weakness, a lack of dedication. It made him feel as if he'd said something rude about the Queen Mother. The thing Paul found hardest to bear was having to pretend that he cared about the office, that it was his life. The others didn't seem to have to pretend. Egerton in particular appeared to *live* at the bloody place: virtually every day he'd proclaim with smug self-deprecation that he'd been there since 8:30 a.m. or even earlier. The required response seemed to be one of mingled awe and business-like respect. It made Paul want to grab him by the lapels and shake him vigorously, shouting "*Why*, you dull bastard?" loudly in his face.

A queue of people strung out of the snack bar, all waiting to take their sandwiches away so they could eat them at their desks with a telephone under each ear. Paul walked a further fifty yards to the Burger King. A blank-faced waitress sold him a hamburger and told him to enjoy his meal.

"I'll try," said Paul. She didn't smile, didn't look like she ever had, in fact.

Determined to relax, Paul lit a cigarette after his burger and tried to read. A middle-aged man nursing a coffee a few tables away asked for the time. Paul gave it to him. "Oh," the man said, and went back to staring at the table, nothing else to do, nothing to be on time for. Waiting the day away.

On the way out, Paul shoved his rubbish into a bin that said THANK YOU on it. A passing oriental table-clearer with cataclysmic acne thanked him too.

Adam was waiting for him when he got back to the office, sitting on his desk and using his phone, making no effort to cut the call short. "Here," he said, eventually, thrusting a sheaf of papers at him. "These have to be at the printers by four."

Paul stared at the bundle. The Association he worked for produced a stupendously boring magazine, which was nothing to do with him. He'd somehow ended up, however, with the responsibility of proof-reading the non-stories on non-issues – at some stage he must have made some ill-advised comment about being interested in journalism – and he was never given it until the last possible minute. In front of him was forty pages of galleys, the whole magazine.

"Adam, got rather a lot to do, actually . . ." he said, forcing himself to play his polite part in what was a monthly ritual.

"Got to go off today, alright?" Adam replied, looking past him, and then abruptly turned and walked away, dropping the proofs on Paul's desk.

An hour later, and less than a third of the way through, Paul paused to get a cup of coffee. As he passed Whitehead's office, the Director stepped out.

"Proofing done, is it?" he said, looking at the coffee in Paul's hand.

"Almost," Paul replied, trying to sound like a colleague, not a minion, "I'm about . . ."

"Got to go off today, you know." Whitehead said, and stepped back into his office, closing the door.

He finally finished at 6:10 p.m., having got none of his own work done. Adam took the proofs without a word. Through his door Paul saw he and Whitehead conferring over them. Adam looked at his watch and shook his head. Paul half-rose from his chair to go over and explain to Whitehead just why the proofs were late, then sat heavily down again. He could picture exactly what sort of reply he'd get. Brutally polite, like a genteel and immaculately-delivered punch in the mouth. Instead he tidied his desk until they had gone and then left the office, feeling the customary thread of weak relief at the end of something unpleasant and boring, amidst quiet despair in anticipation of the next.

The tube station was full of people, milling into a funnel struggling towards the one escalator out of three that was working. Paul let fluid hatred wash over him: surely it wasn't *that* difficult to keep escalators working? It was happening all over the Underground. Was the magic that kept them going really that arcane and impenetrable? For years they'd all worked fine, then suddenly it was apparently impossible to keep them running for more than ten minutes at a time. The week before, he'd noticed that one side of the steps leading out of the station had been roped off too. Not working either, presumably.

The platform was crowded, the destination board blank:

sightless eyes and sagging shoulders jostling in an ether of irritation. Someone had thrown themselves under a train, and Paul felt that he could see their point. How long would you have to stand, surrounded by desperate commuters, people angrily pacing in smaller and smaller circles until they were almost standing still, before you simply couldn't take it any more? Before you realized that there could be a new and unusual journey which you could start with a single step? He could almost see the bored fury seeping out of the rumpled and glowing bodies of the commuters around him, swirling like a hot mist around their feet. Perhaps when it reached head height they would all jump together, piling into the trench in front.

When a train finally arrived it was packed, and going somewhere he didn't want to go via somewhere he'd never heard of. The doors opened into a battle-zone of elbows and sweating flesh. Pressed from all sides, too close to faces, surrounded by dry red skin and sallow foreheads. Brutal stupidity and vapid waste hanging from straps, cheap suits and fat white calves. For a moment Paul experienced an alarming feeling of vertigo, unable to believe that there was anyone in the bodies around him, convinced that he was trapped in a humid abattoir and that what surrounded him were just carcasses, hung meat. Then a flick of greasy hair across his face and the unwelcome pressure of a man's hip brought him back, and it was a little better. But also worse. Too hemmed in to read his book, he succumbed to the thoughts that came, feeling nastier and more twisted with each one.

When the tube reached Leytonstone Paul had to fight his way off to avoid going down the wrong line. It was raining quite hard and he hunched into a corner of the open platform, lighting a cigarette with trembling hands. Of course it was illegal to smoke, but he was going to do it anyway. He forced a ten-minute train of thought concerning Jenny to stop by repeating a line over and over in his head until it was gone. Only then did he realize what the line actually was.

File Created: Mon, Sep 9, 1957, 5:02 p.m.

Gradually he calmed down, diffusing the hatred with a child-like fantasy about the woman on the morning train. Nothing sexual, nothing sordid, just thoughts of sitting with her, talking to her, and seeing her looking at him as if she loved him. It made him feel about four years old, which wasn't so bad. Except that he was standing alone on a platform in the rain, and when he got home his mother wouldn't be there, just a flat full of empty space and objects he couldn't remember buying.

Eventually another train meandered into the station, probably by accident, and Paul ducked through the nearest doors. The air was hot and rancid, and the carriage seemed deserted with its only five or six bedraggled survivors. As he sat down Paul looked at his watch. Nearly 8:00 p.m. Another half hour to get home. Have a shower, eat, try to wind down. Goodbye evening. And tomorrow's another day.

As the train pulled out, the girl sitting opposite went through a complex rigmarole of half-standing contortions as she tried to pull her skirt down. Not that it was riding up, as such: if you wear a skirt that ends about nine inches above the knee, Paul thought, then surely you must expect your legs to be a little bit visible. Presumably that was the point. So why the prim self-righteousness, the baleful stare?

Not wanting to read, but feeling compelled to make a show of not looking at the girl in the way she clearly thought he was going to, Paul stared at his book instead. She got off two stops later, leaving the carriage empty. Savouring the almost surreal feeling of space, he lounged back in the seat and relaxed, breathing deeply, looking around at the debris. Coke cans, tissues, burger wrappers and strewn pieces of newspaper. It looked like an urban back street painted by someone who wanted to live in the countryside.

Two minutes later the train was stationary again. Not at a station, of course, just stationary. Staring drowsily in front of him, Paul noticed an intact newspaper on one of the opposite seats and leaned forward to pick it up. In his current frame of mind he would be very unlikely to make any headway with either "Clones" or the new idea for a story. He might as well find out what was on television.

Before his hand was even close to it, he noticed something odd about the paper. At first he'd just taken it for a crumpled *Evening Standard*, but as he got nearer to it the stock seemed to get whiter, cleaner. He leaned back again, frowning. Slowly he moved his head, thankful that no one was in the carriage to witness what would have seemed like a very strange series of manoeuvres, and slightly worried that staring at computer screens might finally have damaged his eyes. At first the paper was a nasty grey, but as you got closer it became whiter, so white that the edges almost seemed blue. Then he realised that the paper was actually just white, but that there seemed to be an area of colour around it, a field of rich blue-purple. The paper wasn't crumpled and mauled as he'd first thought, but crisp, with edges that looked razor-sharp.

Tentatively he reached towards it again. The colours in the air about it grew stronger. He moved his head from side to side, but the field stayed where it was, proving that it wasn't his eyes at fault. The effect was hard to come to terms with, a pocket of super-intense hues which at the same time didn't interfere with the colour of the seat underneath it.

When his fingers touched the paper the riot of colour blinked out, leaving the carriage even more drab than before. Carefully, he picked it up. It felt very light. The paper was indeed very clean and new-looking, and the typeface seemed unfamiliar. Intrigued, Paul turned to the front page. At the top was just one word, the name of the paper. It was *Welcome*.

As the train started to move again, the driver presumably having finished whatever crossword he'd been working on, Paul looked more closely at the front page. He realized that the header typeface was in fact merely a standard Times or Plantin or whatever: it was the contents of the columns of type underneath it that were different. It was simply a list of names. Hundreds of them.

The next page was the same, and the next. Page after page, column after column, right down to the foot of the back page. Names. No headings, no photos, no adverts. Just names.

Paul scanned the edges of pages, looking for clues as to what the paper might be, but there was no publisher listed, or address. It was just a newspaper full of names, on crisp white paper. He looked down the columns, trying to pick out a pattern, but there was none. The names weren't in alphabetical order, were both men and women's. And that title. Still frowning, Paul turned back to the front page.

Welcome. Apart from being the nicest thing anyone had said to him all day, what did it mean? Welcome to what? Who were all these people, and what on earth was the point of printing all their names? Then his eyes caught something they'd only flicked over before. In the top right hand corner, the newspaper had a date. It was Monday, September 9th, 1957.

A grunt of surprize escaped as Paul's mouth dropped open, and his chest felt suddenly very cold. The sound of doors opening made him look up. It took him a moment to realize that the tube had reached his station. By that time they were closing again. Still clutching the paper in his hands, Paul leaped through the doors onto the empty platform. The train pulled off, and Paul stood and watched it go, dazed. He looked down, saw the paper in his hand, and tucked it inside his coat pocket to protect it from the rain. Then he put his head down and started walking quickly.

When he got to his front door he was tired and out of breath. Normally he took his time up the final hill, but tonight he had stalked up it rapidly and his heart was thudding painfully. He showered quickly and changed his clothes. Then with a cup of tea he sat next to the phone. He didn't think Jenny would actually be very interested, but she would have to do. Paul was as open to the idea of coincidence as the next man, but also aware of its limitations. This, he felt, was very beyond them. This erased the possibility of a computer glitch. What it opened up instead was far from clear. For the first time in what seemed like forever, he felt excited.

Hooking the phone under his chin and lighting a cigarette, he stabbed out the number. As it rung he reached out behind him and felt in the coat pocket for the paper, scrabbling it out just as the phone was picked up at the other end.

"Hi, it's me," he said.

There was a slight pause, and then Jenny said, "Oh, hello."

Paul felt his heart give its customary lurch at the tonelessness of her greeting, at the complete absence of any hint of interest or satisfaction at hearing his voice, and also felt a thread of anger. But he brushed it aside and launched into what had happened, spreading the paper out in front of him. He'd got as far as the title of the paper, speaking into a void, as far as he could tell for all of Jenny's exclamations of interest, when he looked down.

On his lap was a copy of the *Evening Standard*. It was very grubby and had a picture of Tony Blair on the front and a footballer on the back and was dated December 16th, 1999.

Feeling both foolish and betrayed, Paul rapidly leafed through the paper, blood rising to his face. Adverts for upcoming sales.

Share prices. Bollocks about the housing market. It was just the *Evening Standard*.

As was her custom, Jenny covered the silence by not saying anything.

Ten minutes later Paul put the phone down. Jenny had started saying she had work to do, and that anyway she was expecting a call from her mother. It had got bad long before that, though not because of what was said. They saved that up for the little time they had together. Just another duel of silences. Paul jollied along for as long as he could, as always, talking about his day, trying to get her to talk about hers, saying her name occasionally to check that she was still there. After a time he lost heart, and asked her what was wrong. She said that nothing was wrong. Why wasn't she saying anything then? She said that she was. Silence. Well she obviously *wasn't* saying anything, was she? How was she supposed to say anything when he was having a go at her for not saying anything. He wasn't having a go: something was obviously wrong, what was it? Nothing was wrong. Silence.

Glad that he hadn't done it in front of her again, Paul sat in the silent flat and cried. No mention had been made of how they were going to spend the Millennium.

After he was done he got up and switched the television on. There wasn't anything he wanted to watch. He had the *Evening Standard* now, didn't he, so he knew what was on. He just needed some background noise, something to link him to real time, the real world. Something also to dampen the constant noise of thought, the endless whirl of sentences with nowhere to go and nothing to absolve them. When he was honest with himself he could admit that he'd long ago given up all hope of getting anything he wrote published. All it was about now was trying to find some sticky lines to attach the thoughts to, to fasten them down and stop them tearing around his head like a flock of damaged birds, pecking viciously at him until the pain threatened to push him into a state of mind where he didn't feel safe with knives in the kitchen. One of the things the last two years had taught him was that you didn't have to have nothing to lose to sometimes want to lose it anyway.

He got some food together and ate it. Every now and then he looked at the newspaper, but it was still just an ordinary paper. His supper finished, he busied himself with washing up and making yet more tea. Tea and cigarettes, the pillars of his days. Until a couple of years ago, he had never cried. Now he seemed to be on the verge of tears all the time. He tried to ration himself, and never wanted to cry in front of Jenny again. He had used to feel strong, had used to feel her equal. Crying in front of her made him feel demeaned and weak, pathetic. It wasn't terribly manly, even for the post-modern neo-sensitives that women allegedly wanted these days. But sometimes he couldn't help it. What can you do if the only person you have to talk to is the person who makes you feel as bad as you do?

Sitting in his chair again, he stared belligerently at the paper on the floor. Obviously he'd just dozed off on the train and the date on his mind had woven a dream for him. When he'd jumped off at Loughton he'd felt disorientated and strange, and clearly that had been the result of being awakened by the opening doors and having to leap off the train still half asleep. It didn't really matter. He just felt very disappointed that it hadn't happened, that the glitch was still a glitch. For when he'd dreamed he'd seen that date on the paper he had been frightened at the thought that it was no longer just a mistake on the computer: but he had also been very happy.

By 10:30 p.m. the evening's viewing had got too boring to even just sit vacantly in front of. Paul thought about listening to a CD, but couldn't be bothered. He couldn't seem to really hear music any more. Going to bed would be a definite mistake. So by default he ended up in front of his computer, listening to the system load itself up. Maybe if he tacked yesterday night's sentence onto the end of "Clones" he would be able to see where to take it from there. Maybe he could actually get it finished. Maybe world peace would break out.

The machine pinged at him to signify readiness, and Paul called up "Clones" information window to copy down the sentence. After reading it twice he realized something he hadn't noticed the night before. It was crap.

He deleted it, all desire to work on the story gone, and sat with his head in his hands. The television burbled in the background, in excited transition from one late-night slot-filler to the next.

The File Creation date was still there, still just a glitch. Discredited though it was, it still made him smile wanly. His glazing eyes wandered down the screen as he absently moved the cursor in circles over it, watching it move over numbers and letters as if it was actually above them. As he tried to motivate himself into doing something constructive, the words he was circling over slowly came into focus. He read them, and the circle came to an abrupt halt. "Clones" information window said:

Document Size: 321K.

Three hundred and twenty one kilobytes? That couldn't be right: "Clones" was only two pages long, for God's sake. And the night before it had said 7K. He was sure it had. It must have done. Two pages was about 6 or 7K. 321K must be a few hundred pages, and "Clones" sure as hell wasn't that long. His Collected Works weren't that long.

That meant problems. That meant Problem City, in fact. Something bad must be happening to the Desktop File or Extents Tree, which meant not only that the file creation date *was* most likely just a glitch, but that if he wasn't careful everything on his hard disk would be crapped out of existence. Paul hurriedly loaded the word-processor. If it was just "Clones" that was affected, maybe it was okay. If not, then it was all hands to the floppy disks, with women and journalism off first.

The document took a long time to load, much longer than just two pages should. Then the machine pinged again, and a blank page filled the screen, surrounded by the word-processor's scroll bars and menus. That was as expected: he always left a blank page at the top of a document to fill the title and his address in when he'd finished, as a sort of completion ritual. He clicked on the scroll bar, bringing up the next portion of the page.

He saw that the first page was not blank as he'd left it, that the document now had a title. That title was *Welcome*.

Paul clicked the scroll bar once more, and again. The second page came up. It was divided into three neat columns, something his word-processor was not capable of doing. In each of those columns was a list of names.

It took Paul nearly ten minutes to click down through the document, one screen at a time. A few of the names he recognized, and he knew why. The list was similar to the one he'd seen on the train, but longer. One hundred and seventy pages of names. As he got towards the end of the document the scrolling seemed to get slower, more sluggish. At the bottom of the last page was a new line. It said "To all of you, Welcome."

Paul had just time to read this, and then the screen jittered and went blank.

He stared at it for some time, not smoking, not thinking. Just hearing names, seeing them in their orderly rows like some kind of roll call. Eventually he got up and turned the stalled computer off at the back. He could rebuild his Desktop file, and had a fairly recent backup of all his documents. None of it seemed very important. He noticed his cheeks were wet, and realized that he had been crying. But he didn't feel sad. He didn't really know what he felt. Something was there, but just out of reach.

He made a cup of tea, sat in his chair and waited. The time seemed to pass very quickly, easily, his mind an almost total and blessed blank. After a time he fell asleep, and did not dream.

As he smoked his breakfast the next morning the letter box clanged. Some post, for a change. The contents of a large manila envelope he knew before he opened it. Sure enough, it was another story rejection, with a form letter politely telling him to fuck off and die.

There was also a small light-blue envelope, with handwriting he recognized. A letter from Jenny, which could only mean bad news. He couldn't remember the last time she'd bothered to write. He opened it slowly, hands trembling.

The Last One, he read – although she of course used his real name, not realizing the vertiginous double-thump it always caused in Paul's heart – was coming to visit. Paul had known that it would happen sooner or later, but seeing his name again still made him feel dizzy. The Last One was an American. Every now and then he got a job as a courier and thus a free return flight to Britain. It was on one of these jaunts that Jenny had met him, and now he was coming over again, but with a difference. He had only been able to get a flight to Paris. And so Jenny was going to go over there for the weekend to see him.

There was a lot more, of course. A wealth of stuff about how it was reasonable of her to want to see someone that she'd had a relationship with; how it was important that she sorted out her feelings for him and that seeing him was the only way she could do that; how they would have different hotel rooms. But all of it was irrelevant. The fact was that he was coming, and she was going, and how Paul felt about it meant absolutely nothing to anyone.

Paul fought hard, his face reddening and neck spasming. However she dressed it up, it wasn't fair. And how like her not to mention it on the phone the night before, but wait for the letter to arrive, to give him time to lose his anger before they spoke of it. Time to become just a terribly hurt little boy, who could no more shout at her than he could leave her. She didn't realize that he couldn't hate her, that all he could do, whatever she did, was love her.

Putting his coat on, he left the house to go to work.

The train was late and he had to stand, clenching his fists tight to keep himself under control, the muscles in his face working. He'd been to Paris, knew where they'd go, the sights they'd see. And he knew that they would sleep together. They always did.

The woman got on as usual, but this morning all that her demure beauty did was push him closer to the edge. At the next stop a man got on and stood and talked to her. Paul could hear her laughing.

To one side another couple stood face to face with their arms around each other. She looked at his lips when he talked, her head tilted up, smiling. In the stillness of a tunnel, with the train stationary, Paul could hear the rustle of her hand on his coat.

He was late to work. Someone had been using his desk, and left a couple of pastry wrappers and a polystyrene cup amidst circular coffee marks on the surface. Paul shut the door and sat down. Over the course of ten minutes he calmed down a little, telling himself that perhaps this time things would sort themselves out. Even her leaving him would be something, a relief almost.

Eventually he opened his door and started the work he should have finished the day before. When his word-processor was loaded he ran his eyes down the list of documents, half-hoping that there would be one there called "Welcome". But there wasn't, and he felt confused and foolish for looking.

Fetching a cup of coffee mid-morning he ran into Adam, who stopped him. "Lot of mistakes in those galleys, you know," Adam said, "I had to go over them again myself."

Paul turned slowly and looked at him, feeling the skin stretch tightly over his face as he grinned. "Who gives a shit?" he asked. Walking back through the main office he regretted it, even

though the look on Adam's face had been worth seeing. Antag-
onizing the Assistant Director was a bad idea. He wished the
secretary, Susan, wasn't on holiday. She was the sole straightforward person in the office, and a chat with her might have brought
him down a bit, earthed him. The sleep he'd had the night before
didn't seem to have done him much good. His head felt cloudy
and distanced from what was going on. At 2:00 p.m. he decided
to skip lunch, but went out for a walk anyway to try to clear his
head.

He wandered without paying attention to where he was going,
and looked up suddenly to find himself in a deserted back street
that he'd never seen before. Which was odd, because he knew the
area quite well. The street could have been anywhere, in any
town. On a map it would have been just a straight little line, of no
relevance to anything around it. At the far end was a newspaper
kiosk. He walked up to it but there was nobody there, despite the
fact that it was evidently open for business. On the counter was a
single newspaper.

It was *Welcome*.

Looking up and down the street, Paul picked it up. It seemed to
be a different edition to the one he'd seen before, and a somewhat
strange one: the columns of names petered out halfway down the
second page. The rest of the pages were just blank. What on earth
was the point of a mostly blank newspaper? He looked at the
second page again, then with a yelp dropped the paper and
walked quickly away.

The columns on the second page had just grown longer.

By the time he got back to the office he regretted not keeping
the paper, though he knew it would probably just have been an
Evening Standard by then. He sat at his desk and tried to work,
but a date kept running through his mind over and over, blanking
out most other thoughts. Monday, September 9th, 1957. The
only thoughts it left room for were ones he didn't want. A hand
on Jenny's thigh, her arm around the waist of a man he'd never
seen, whose face he couldn't picture. A smile he never saw these
days, and crumpled sheets.

He kept looking up, expecting Whitehead to be standing
behind him. But there was only the wall, with a calender left
by the previous occupant. It showed scenes of European capitals
by night.

Lists of names marched through his head, and he typed to the pattern of their syllables. But they didn't fit the lines, and when he read what he'd typed nothing made sense except the rhythm. It sounded like the rhythm of a train. He deleted it all and stumbled out to get a coffee, past Whitehead's office – where he and Adam and Egerton stood in a huddle. They didn't look at him as he passed. He was invisible. He was fading. He was being left behind.

By 5:00 p.m. all he'd managed to do was put five pages of gibberish on the screen, green type on black with blue underlining that swirled into purple before his eyes. He saved it and turned the machine off. People looked up as he walked out of the office. This was early even for him. Emerging blinking into the light, he set off towards the tube. The winter afternoon was giving way to a storm and the dark clouds grew blue-black behind the buildings. Somewhere a child was crying, a hitching wail that spiralled up into the sky. Tell it like it is, Paul thought, tell it like it is.

On the platform deep in the earth he leaned against the wall and rubbed his forehead with the back of his hand. Despite the perspiration on his forehead he felt very cool, and everything he saw seemed very clear. A middle-aged black man walked past slowly, with a boxed computer under his arm, a Christmas present for his son, who was holding his other hand. Both were quiet and smiling at the end of a perfect day.

A train rocketed into the station and Paul ducked to look in the windows as they flashed past: a smear of yellow flickers smudged with torsos and arms. As the train slowed he moved towards it, ready to fight for a place. But no-one else seemed interested. They were all looking elsewhere.

Doors opened in front of him and he stepped into the warmth alone. The train pulled out of the light and into the waiting dark, and as he rocked to the rhythm of the names it came as no surprise to realize that the bodies hung around him were just that. Empty shells. The lights were no longer on, there was nobody home, and with that realization there came no fear at all.

Then he turned and saw the woman sitting there, looking straight at him. There was an empty seat beside her, just as there never was in the mornings. He knew that she'd been born on the 9th of September, and that she'd be there forever for him, and he knew that when he talked she'd listen, and she'd be looking at his lips.

The doors opened again, onto a deserted platform he'd never seen before, with a destination board that was blank. He let them close without a thought: it was a last chance he didn't want. The next thousand years could get along without him.

He threaded his way towards her, watching the dawning of her smile.

"Welcome," she said.

MICHAEL MARANO

Burden

MICHAEL MARANO'S WIDELY ACCLAIMED FIRST NOVEL *Dawn Song* – a story of AIDS, politics, succubi and a war in Hell between Belial and Leviathan – received both the International Horror Guild Award and the Bram Stoker Award. His short fiction has appeared in the anthologies *Peter S. Beagle's Immortal Unicorn*, *Chiaroscuro: A Treatment of Light and Shade in Words*, *The Bedlam Reports: Memoirs from Padded Cells*, and *Queer Fear*.

From 1990, under his own name and under his *nom de guerre* "Mad Professor Mike", Marano has reviewed horror movies in print and on the nationally syndicated Public Radio programme, *Movie Magazine* (produced at Western Public Radio in San Francisco and heard in 140 American markets). His punk/heavy metal style of criticism has been described as "combining the best of *Cahiers du Cinéma* with the spirit of pro-wrestling." He is now at work on his second novel.

Several incidents moved Marano to write "Burden", not the least of which was the death of his best friend, as he explains: "Back in the mid-1980s I was out with a group of gay friends who, over drinks, told incredibly grim and tasteless AIDS jokes that they explained away as just 'gallows humour'. I asked if they were all being careful, if they were practising safe sex, and they assured me they were. They're all dead now. While living in the San Francisco Bay Area in the early 1990s, I would go to the Castro district and find myself unable to breathe because of the heavy and all-pervasive *absence* of the newly dead. And just a while ago, I was watching a documentary about the early days of the AIDS epidemic when an interviewee said something to the effect of 'I'm sad my friends are gone, because no one is around to remember me if I die.' I wanted to ask him, 'What about *your* obligation to remember *them*?'"

W ITH NIGHT, COME THE SOUNDS.
       You hear them as you walk beneath halogen street-lamps that give light the colour of brandy, as October air touched with frost becomes warm, heavy as breath. Your step is muffled, as if you walk on a wool blanket. The sounds come, as they have come before, while dusk deepens and stars spread across the dull suburban sky, while lamplight and the flickering blue of TV screens fill the windows of the houses you pass.

Stiff leather creaks. Booted feet step. Chains hung from jackets clank. Keys dangling from out of pockets jangle.

You are alone, surrounded by sound.

Trying to walk away from it.

The summer-heat falls upon your back, your neck and your hands – which a moment before tingled with cold. You smell the scents of The City you left long ago. The humid, dirty air. The musk of leather and the skin of the men who wear it. Cigarettes and a blend of after-shaves sweetened by sweat. Under the brandy-light you feel, more than see, stars eclipsed by grey city sky.

Darkness huddles the street. Night folds upon night before you. The suburban street fades as the stars have faded – the brandy-light is gone. The shadows breathe. They mill and they whisper. You walk among them. They have no form.

Out of the ebony nothingness, from behind the curtain of night, Tony steps before you, as if he has stepped from around the corner of a building that is not there.

You stop, held by Tony's stare. You knew he would come. But not as he has.

Tony is shrunken and ashen. No longer able to fill his leather jacket as he had in life. The weight of chains on the jacket make it hang slackly. Tight jeans that had once glorified his manhood sag loosely, as if worn by a boy who has yet to grow into them. Above his black T-shirt, his neck is thin as an old woman's. Tendons show through the skin of his throat. His face is gaunt – skull-like as a death camp survivor.

You see in Tony's eyes an awful, lonely fear, a pleading that fixes your sight and settles in an icy pool near your heart.

He steps toward you. You feel the shadows behind you become heavier, many eyes on your back. The sounds of chains and keys and boots and heavy belt buckles grow louder, closer . . . more distinct. The shadows breathe. They mill and they whisper.

Tony reaches for you; his ill-fitting jacket falls from his shoulder. Part of you insists that this cannot be.

His hand is on your shoulder, cold through your wool coat in the midst of this invading heat. The cold of his hand walks through your flesh to the cold in your heart. The air is warm in your lungs. Tony's lips move as a child's move while reading. No words come. There is only the chorus of metal and leather as the shadows behind you shuffle.

You hear his distant voice as the lights of a passing car burn Tony out of the night.

The crunch of tyres smothers the sounds around you. The shadows at your back become wind. You feel living eyes upon you. Two children stare from the car's backseat window. As they pass, you realize you are cowering, your body hunched.

Stars fade into being. You feel them look down upon you, uncaring, as you straighten yourself.

Autumn wind comes, driving away the scents you have been breathing, replacing them with those of dead leaves, bitter smoke from fireplaces, the salt smell of the harbour.

Yet as you reach your apartment, you smell, just faintly, the scent of a leather jacket, of sweat tinged after-shave – as if you wear them yourself.

In darkness that is your own, sitting in a domicile that has never been a home to you, you think of Tony's eyes, how you would have longed for them to have held anger, accusation, the righteous fury of betrayal.

Not the awful desperation they did hold.

Dawn finds you awake, still sitting as birds begin to sing. You become aware, as you never have been before, of the beat of your heart and the flow of blood in your veins.

*　　　*　　　*

Veins bulge under the rubber tube around your arm.

The woman wears surgical gloves. She looks at your forearm, not your face, as she tells you, "You might want to look away if you're squeamish."

(*"Bashful?"*)

You don't look away as the needle goes in and blood arcs into the test tube. Someone once told you that blood is truly blue, and only turns red when exposed to air.

(*A clatter as jeans with a heavy belt buckle fall to the floor. "C'mon. Don't be shy."*)

The test tube fills. The blood looks black.

(*The Boy had been like Tony. A cocky, muscular, Italian kid who knew he was beautiful. You once knew the Boy's name, but you cannot, or choose not, to remember it now.*)

The woman whispers, "Okay," and pulls the needle out.

(*You had met The Boy in the park, which that night was so very much like the park in The City where men would walk together in pairs and threes to hidden places behind trees and bushes. Summer heat, summer sweat, summer air combining into an intoxicating liquor periodically spiked with amyl nitrate.*)

A warm red drop on your forearm, wiped away with cotton and cool alcohol. Rubber gloved hands apply a bandage.

(*You had felt a longing when you saw The Boy, beyond the sexual. You had wanted to be near The Boy so that you could say good-bye to Tony through him. For Tony had simply left . . . gone back to his family in Buffalo to die among people he could not stand to be near while in the prime of his life.*)

The woman labels the test tube with a number and puts it in a rack of others like it. She takes off her gloves and puts them in a red plastic container marked "BIOHAZARD".

(*At least you tell yourself that is why you let things go so fast with The Boy.*)

"We should have the results of your test in about six weeks," she says. A testimonial to the shittiness of this town, that all such blood work must be sent out-of-state in monthly batches.

(*Dangerously fast.*)

"And even if the initial results are positive, there is a possibility it could be a false positive."

(*Foolishly fast.*)

She hands you a slip of piss-yellow paper. It is a carbon copy of the label on your sample. "This is your test number. Call at the end of next month and give the receptionist the number. He'll tell you if the results are in, and you can come in for consultation."

(*Had you wanted this?*)

You walk the ugly green tiles of the Health Department toward the faint daylight at the end of the hall. You are nameless here, a number. It is for your own protection, to be nameless. Your anonymity is a shield. You leave the Health Department through a soot-covered glass door.

(*Had you wanted to be reckless? Had you wanted this worry gnawing inside you?*)

The river, such as it is, flows by in an eroding canal of poured concrete. It is only a few feet deep, and you think of the college kid last year who had tried to commit suicide by jumping off the bridge you are now passing. He had landed in silt up to his knees, trapped, his upper chest and head above the water.

You hate this small and ugly city full of small and ugly-minded people. You hate the shitty suburb where your cheap apartment is. You came here to live this life because you were afraid to live a life that would kill you. You fled The City when you crossed off your fifth friend in as many weeks from your address book . . . when you looked through that cheap booklet of grey vinyl and saw listing after listing that you had blotted out with marker . . . when you realized that an inky smear in someone else's address book could be your only epitaph.

You fled, because you knew the temptation to continue the life The City offered you would be too great if you had stayed.

(*Was The Boy an atonement? A punishment you inflicted upon yourself so you could make amends for the life and the people you abandoned?*)

Faceless pedestrians shuffle past.

Part of you is aroused by memories of The Boy. Even now, as your arm throbs where your blood has been drawn, you long for that moment when, for the first time in years, you had enjoyed sex free of the constraints of latex.

Part of you whispers that it is worth dying for such sex . . . that the enjoyment of such sex is part of your identity. You have a right to what you enjoy, no matter the consequences.

Later, in the indigo and umber of autumn twilight, you are frightened that you are capable of such thoughts.

With night, come the sounds.
Of chains, boots, keys and buckles.
You hear them in darkness.
You hear them in solitude.
Your radio, tuned to a banal talk show, fades to silence. Your drafty apartment becomes sweltering. Dusty air rising from the barely functional radiator is replaced by muggy summer air. You feel the calling of The City in your crotch. Just as long ago, in the life you abandoned, there had been the constant calling to the streets, to limbs and bodies, to thrusting hips and the taste of men.
Always, the calling.
You sit in darkness, trying to ignore the calling. Even as you remember, and as you feel again, what it had once done to you.
One late May, in your other life, you had worked in a bookstore near Columbia, taking second-hand text books from college brats eager to be rid of them. You felt the daylight fade, felt the coming of night like a rising fever. True summer had come early that year, announcing itself as an arousal spreading through you like the fire of brandy and the tingling thrill of poppers.
Working the late shift, which you had taken because it allowed you to sleep in, became intolerable.
A whiney Long Island girl, so much like your whiney sisters back home, demanded to know why she was not getting more money back for a book that was not on order for the next semester.
You stood from the counter and left, embracing the fever. Not caring that your fat and stupid boss saw you leave.
As you walked through the door, heat rose from your body to join the heat of the city. You felt yourself shimmer, felt the need to discharge the welcome fever with sex and the feel of hardmuscled flesh.
In the room you rented, you stripped off your ridiculous shirt with a collar, your narrow tie, your khakis. You clothed yourself in the identity you'd earned by coming to The City, pulling on the jeans and the black leather armor that kept at bay the life of snivelling mediocrity your parents had wanted you to embrace. Chains were your epaulets, a blue kerchief in your back pocket your standard.

You walked down the hall to Tony's room. You didn't knock – you never knocked.

Tony was lifting weights.

Sweat glistened on his body as he did military presses. He saw you in the mirror before him and smiled at your reflection, grunting as he pressed the barbell over his head.

He gave you that smart-assed Italian grin. Liking that you were watching, he did one more press, straining, the cords of his back and shoulders visible though his olive skin like cables.

He rested the barbell on his broad chest, then set it on the floor. He walked toward you, and pulled you close.

With the door still open, with Tony's sweat-stained cut-offs filling the room with the musk of his crotch, the two of you fucked, not caring who passed in the hallway.

Afterward, you both went to the streets, to Washington Square, your steps falling in with the chimes of chains and the bass of heavy boot steps, to cruise for more bodies, more satisfaction.

The night made you both drunk.

Now, in this night.

Now, in the alone.

The sounds come, calling you to a night fifteen years gone in a City hundreds of miles away.

You feel the fever again. It pulls you to the window.

You pull the frayed curtains aside.

And see dead men cruising each other.

Two lines of men in jeans and leather jackets make an alley of themselves. Other men mill and pace within this alley. They are emaciated. Desiccated. Yet they move with swaggers, with cocky masculinity. One among them is not sick, but flushed with health. Glowing with sexuality and strength.

It is The Boy.

You grip the curtains. Your breath hits the glass, which is cold in the midst of this summer heat. The glass fogs over. You see The Boy through the glass as if the fog is not there. He grabs one of the walking dead men.

They embrace and kiss. The dead man's leather jacket falls to the ground as they grope each other.

You wipe away the fog.

And wipe away the alley of dead men that has imposed itself

over the street outside your door. It vanishes behind the trail of your hand.

Where men walked, now leaves move in scuttling streams, driven by cold winds off the harbour.

You listen to your heart. Your pulse slows as you peer across the street to one of your neighbours' houses. Through the window of the other house, you see a flickering television screen that seems the size of a postage stamp from where you stand. Someone walks before the screen and stops. They turn and look at you, and with a start, you drop the curtain.

You turn and see Tony.

He is a deeper grey than the shadows of your bedroom. You see only yourself in the mirror behind Tony. He steps toward you and softly, lightly, grabs hold of your threadbare sweater.

"We needed you," he says in an intonation you feel as well as hear, fluttering upon your face and throat like moth wings.

Before you can think or speak or move, he steps around you to the curtains at your back. You turn as he walks. The curtains wave as he passes through them without parting them.

Banal talk radio fills the air, drafts displace the false summer, and you realize how alone you have been these last fifteen years.

"I'm okay."

You tell yourself this as the weeks to go by, as you wait for your test results.

You have been tested before, and you had been okay then.

You had been nervous then, while you waited for your blood to be shipped to some lab in the Midwest, waiting for your anonymous number to return to you with news of whether you would live through the next decade.

"I'm okay."

You say this out loud as you work your ridiculous job as the assistant administrator of a janitorial service, sending cleaning crews during the daylight hours to office buildings that have only a forty per cent rate of occupancy. Graft runs this shitty small city, and kickbacks are plentiful as construction companies continue to build-up what is grandiosely called "the downtown district".

You sit at your desk between making calls, as dust settles in unused rooms for which you are responsible, yet will never see. You wonder what the crews think as they enter these offices, to clean only the detritus these useless buildings shed.

"I'm okay."

You work alone.

No one hears you mutter to yourself. Even the old and rickety building in which you work in mostly empty. It is lunch hour. No one walks the halls.

You think of when you got the results of your first test, how you were so nervous you vomited in the alley behind the Health Department. The health care official smiled and said, "You're negative, you're fine. Nothing to worry about."

"*Nothing to worry about.*" She had no idea.

You thought of the number of men you'd been with, the men you'd been with who'd died, or were now dying, or who had disappeared, slinking away to die in home towns they had despised.

Since that day, you had practised safe sex.

Except for that night with The Boy.

"I'm okay."

And in daylight, the sounds come to you.

Your are alone in your office, hearing the clank of chains, the jangle of keys.

Your heart stops in your breast.

You tell yourself it is a janitor, a huge ring of keys to empty rooms in his hand. You tell yourself this, and you almost believe it.

Until Bobby steps into the doorway of your office.

He looks as he did in the beginning throes of his sickness, when you last saw him and pretended you did not know him. As you and Tony and your cruising buddies walked past him as he worked the corner of 53rd and 2nd, already a ghost of himself, already sick, one of the walking dead, peddling the poisoned fruit of his cock, ass, and mouth.

You walked past him, part of a living wall of leather, denim, and muscle as you and your buddies searched the city for one of the few bath houses not yet closed by the Health Department. You had all felt so lucky. So invincible. So immortal. Blissfully ignorant that some of those who were part of the living wall of denim and leather you moved within carried death inside them;

that their hearts were busy pumping a disease through their
bodies that would kill them, cell by cell.

Bobby worked his corner, skinny as a cur. You saw him, and
you knew each other. You saw him, and you saw the fear and the
shame in his eyes that he had been recognized.

Your friends all looked at him. These were the early days of the
plague, when one could still take comfort in the lie that only the
biggest sluts and the stupidest cruisers got infected. That only
junkies got infected. That some form of Calvinist election was
what doomed people on the scene. That only those stupid enough
to fuck the Angel of Death would be taken by the plague.

You, yourself, had fucked Bobby.

Just eight months before.

Someone, to this day, you do not know who, snorted as you
and the wall you were part of passed Bobby, going down to the
subway that would take you toward St Marks place. Then Tony
spoke loudly enough for Bobby to hear . . .

"*Kid should be wearing a fucking executioner's hood.*"

Now Bobby stands before you. Sick. Shivering. Desperate.
Junkie-pale in his leather and chains.

"I needed you, man," he says. He points to his sunken chest.
"Even like *this*, I fucking needed you."

You stand, yet say nothing. You have no words.

Bobby turns on his heel and looks at you as if you are shit he
has just stepped in. He walks down the hall, chains jangling
fainter and fainter . . .

You walk to the door and see him at the end of the hall.

The Boy is waiting for him there. They lock arms and go down
the rickety wooden stairway. As you enter the hall, the sounds of
their footfalls on the steps and of Bobby's chains are gone.

You stumble back into your office and see the lights of your
phone blinking, summoning you to send men to locked and
empty rooms that will never be occupied.

You think of the rooms of The City now empty of the life you
once led.

Weeks pass.

With the sounds and the visitations, the weeks pass.

Sick and dying men litter your home, incontinent in their denim
and leather. Each night, at three, you see Tony die. He quivers in

what looks like nightmare-laden sleep, quivers in a way that makes you think of a cat you saw die in the road when you were small.

"We needed you."

The words become a chant.

Echoing through your mind, your world. You do not escape the words. At work, you cannot function. The sounds of chains in the hall become a cacophony. You take sick leave. You do not know, do not care, who has replaced you at your desk.

You walk through leaves that crunch underfoot, over soil hardened with frost, surrounded by the step of boots on concrete. You sit watching a silent television as buckles and keys clatter around you with the constancy of waves breaking on a beach.

"We needed you."

The words become the fabric of night.

Lack of sleep makes you nearly mad. You think of killing The Boy. You think of tracking him down like some righteous movie hero and beating answers from him that will explain everything that is happening to you, that will provide you with a way to exorcise this torment. A few hours respite from the sounds restores enough balance for you to realize how absurd these thoughts are. No easy answers will come to you.

Yet you look for The Boy anyway, to find what answers you can.

In the grey of November daylight, when all this shitty town seems the colour of smoke, you go to the park where you met The Boy. No one is there. It is too cold and windy. You find nothing there but litter and whispering dead leaves. You go to a bar a few blocks away, a crappy little blue-collar place that specializes in serving the disowned faggot offspring of this dying industrial town.

A kid named Alan is at the bar, smoking expensive clove cigarettes. He is a watcher, not a cruiser. He has listened to you intently as you told him stories about The City back in the days when the idea of men fucking each other while wearing rubbers was the most absurd thing imaginable. Alan listened to you intently as you told him about the occasional bout of gonorrhea or syphilis you got when you were his age, and how a trip or two to the free clinic made these bouts less bothersome than a cold.

Alan is a sensitive kid, a poor-little-rich-boy romantic with big brown eyes like a deer. You do not like him. But you like how he listens to you very much. He broke up with his long-time lover in a series of annoyingly public incidents, and is now a barfly and a gossip, sitting here for days, watching other lives as he convinces himself of the tragic nature of his own.

You ask Alan about The Boy.

Alan thinks a moment, absently peeling the label off his bottle of beer with his thumb.

"Yeah. I know who you mean. He left town," he says with a shrug.

"When?"

"'Couple weeks ago."

"What's his name?"

Alan frowns, now looking intently at the work his thumb is doing.

"Frank, I think."

Frank. The name rings true.

"Where'd he go?"

"Back to Cranston."

"He's from there?"

"Yeah."

Alan, young enough to be your kid, does not know what this means. Alan, who had been five years old when you were seeing your friends crawl back to their home towns to die, cannot see that Frank went back to Cranston as the first step to his grave. Alan is from this city. He has never gone away to another place, never been more than fifteen miles from where you sit right now. He does not know what it means when a fag returns to his home town.

Now Alan looks at you.

"Why are you looking for him?"

He cocks his head slightly, fixing his big brown eyes on you, giving you what he must think passes for a meaningful look. He knows that you know he has been dumped. He thinks you are asking about someone you are stuck on. Now, in his stupid Pollyanna world view, two lonely people have the chance to not be lonely anymore.

In another life, you would have fucked the little brown-eyed dreamer and dumped him to teach him a lesson. For the sport of it.

You leave the bar, feeling his gaze on your back like fleas crawling on your skin.

In the grey daylight, you walk into a congregation of dead men. They have been waiting for you, expecting you after they have given you this respite. You realize they have left you alone long enough for you to discover what you have about The Boy. Now you must rejoin them, to take up your burden once again.

You stifle your sadness and your fear as they shuffle in a bank of fog-coloured bodies around you. They say nothing, but the sounds of their chains and keys is a layered chorus of heavy chimes around you. Tony is beside you, his mouth quivering, not trying to speak, not trying to whisper. His lips tremble out of some spastic disintegration of the nerves of his face.

Out of the corner of your eye, you see among the dead men a living face, keeping pace with you. You look to your left and see The Boy.

He smiles as you walk unthinking, within a bank of men made of fog. You know then that the young man named Frank was just a mask that this being has worn, just a mask that it wears now, for you. You know that you have seen him many times before, with many different faces. You have seen him walk away with your friends into shadowplaces, where he quietly slipped a drop of the shadows themselves into the streams of their blood. He is the darkness of the heavy ink you have used to blot out your friends' names from your address book, the hopelessness that called your friends back to their broken homes. He has walked behind you for fifteen years. Now he walks beside you, as you once again walk beside Tony.

"Hey, man!"

You turn to see Alan, trotting to catch up with you. The dead around you stop and huddle behind you like an army waiting at your command. The thing that wears Frank's face stands beside you, your lieutenant.

"What the fuck was that shit about?" he asks, now standing before you. "Giving me that fucking look and sticking me with paying for your beer? What's *up* with you?"

Alan is performing the classic role of the "don't-fuck-with-me" faggot. You have seen it many times before and performed it before much better, yourself. Though you had the bulk and the strength to back it up. Alan scowls at you. He is so young. So transparent. You know his type better than he knows himself.

He is doing this in the hope it will lead to a confession on your part about being hung up on Frank. That this bold and macho performance will lead to romance between you both. You hear dead voices murmur behind you, as you once heard voices murmur whenever a queen laid down a particularly vicious line of dish.

You look at Alan, and he steps back. There is a look in his eyes like that of an animal frozen before an oncoming car.

You feel the shadow that wears Frank's face slip its arm around your shoulder.

Alan walks back another step.

"Sorry, man."

He does not see them.

Of this, you are sure.

But he does feel them, as surely as he feels the bite of the November air around you.

He walks back to the bar as you walk within your own Purgatory.

With night, comes silence.

With night, you are no longer among the dead.

You no longer hear their words.

The silence fills everything.

You cannot sleep.

When the morning comes, you will know.

When the morning comes, the wait will be over.

In darkness, without the accusing company of phantoms, you have never felt more alone.

Monday morning, in late November.

The hallways of the Health Department are full.

People walk with brisk steps, carrying mugs of coffee, newspapers, clipboards, briefcases.

You wait outside the office where the woman drew your blood. There are at least fifteen men there with you. A batch of test results have come back over the weekend. No one makes eye contact. The fear of revealing an inner stigma through the gaze is too strong. The possibility of any man in the room being con-

demned is too great. The possibility of death knowing you
through the eyes of a man it has claimed is too great.

The men around you are called into the office one at a time by a
gesture.

The door opens. The woman summons you.

She is pleasant and reserved as she asks for your number, which
you provide by handing her the ugly slip of paper she handed you
six weeks ago.

She checks the computer readout before her, with its long
chains of numbers that you cannot fathom.

She looks at you. You see what is in her eyes, and you know she
has never gotten used to bestowing this news.

Even as she tells you of the possibility of a false positive and the
need of a further test, you know your life will be over, soon.

You walk past the river among the dead.

They have rejoined you.

They say nothing, yet you feel their anger.

You feel summer heat press around you as you shuffle past the
living. The first snow of the year falls around you.

It is summer.

It is The City.

But you feel neither the summer or The City, as you are clothed
in an eternal day of autumn grey.

Full of anger, full of need, you part the curtain of night to
accuse Alan of shirking his burden to remember you.

PAUL J. McAULEY

Naming the Dead

WHEN PAUL J. McAULEY WAS TWENTY, the first short story he ever finished writing was accepted by the American magazine *Worlds of if*, but the magazine went bankrupt before publishing it and he took this as a hint to concentrate on an academic career instead. He is now a full-time writer.

His first novel, *Four Hundred Billion Stars*, won the Philip K. Dick Memorial Award, while *Fairyland* was awarded the 1995 Arthur C. Clarke Award for best SF novel published in Britain and the John W. Campbell Award for best novel. In 1995 his short story "The Temptation of Dr. Stein" was presented with the British Fantasy Award, and in 1996 his novel *Pasquale's Angel* won the Sidewise Award for Best Long Form Alternate History fiction.

His acclaimed *The Book of Confluence* trilogy is actually a very long novel comprising *Child of the River*, *Ancients of Days* and *Shrine of Stars*, and his latest novel, *The History of Life*, was recently published by HarperCollins.

"Almost five years ago I moved to London," recalls McAuley. " 'Naming the Dead' is in part my belated response to that wonderful and terrible city. I began to write it for an anthology of psychic detective stories which Stephen Jones was editing, but I'd barely completed the first draft when I got sight of Kim Newman's novel-length set of framing stories and couldn't quite figure out how my story of a melancholic Victorian (based on someone I glimpsed through the window at a Spitafield's house) living in contemporary London would fit in. I set it aside, came back almost exactly a year later, and finished it in a steady burst of enthusiasm.

"Another story about Mr Carlyle appears in the second volume of Nicholas Royle's *Time Out Book of London Short Stories*, and some time this century I hope to include him in 'Dr. Pretorius and the Lost Temple'.

"I WANT YOU TO PROVE HE KILLED MY EMMA," the woman told me.

"You realize, madam,—"

"I only want to know."

"—that the police will not use anything I find as evidence."

"I have to know."

"Perhaps you should talk with someone else first."

"My husband divorced me. My mother and father are dead. My Emma is dead. I am alone, Mr Carlyle."

She was wrong, of course. None of us are alone. Neither the living nor the dead. Even in my sanctuary there were the feeble ghosts of the silkmaker and his wife. And there was the thing clinging to my would-be client's shoulder.

Her hands tightened on the straps of her handbag. She said, "I know what you are. I know what you can do. I want you to help me find my Emma."

I said, in my very best soothing voice, "Perhaps you would like some more tea, Mrs Stokes? And perhaps one of the delicious chocolate bourbon biscuits."

"I am quite calm, Mr Carlyle. I have no need of the sovereign remedy, and I think that you have eaten all the biscuits."

I had to admit that Mrs Stokes was a formidable woman. Although she was made uneasy by the steady hiss of the gas mantles, the green wallpaper, the heavy walnut furniture and the crowded ranks of books, she tried not to show it as she sat bolt upright in the wing armchair, clutching her quilted blue handbag to her lap as if it contained her life. It was four o'clock on a dreary wet November day, darkness already lying deep in the narrow streets outside, made more sepulchral by a distant glimpse of the bright neon of the curry houses and Bangladeshi video shops of Brick Lane. The coal fire gave out a withering heat, but Mrs

Stokes had kept on her gaberdine raincoat. She lived alone but she took trouble over her appearance out of habit, her lined face softened with pancake and blusher, her thin lips reddened with "Autumn Maple" lipstick, the white helmet of her hair stiffened by a new perm. When she leaned forward, she gave off an acrid little cloud compounded of the scent of face powder and Arpege. The thing at her shoulder glared at me with a mixture of spite and fear. It was her own ghost, but it had the heartshaped face of her dead daughter, whose photograph lay on the walnut table between us. She had spent much money and more energy finding me. I knew I was her last hope. I am the last hope of all who manage to find me.

Mrs Stokes – although she was divorced, she would never give up the Mrs – picked up the photograph. "He killed her, Mr Carlyle," she said. "I know that he did. He cut off her face. That was how she was found, naked, without a face. Like his other victims. But he wouldn't confess."

She said this quite dispassionately. Her eyes were hard and bright. She was long past crying. Years past. Emma had run away to London and been killed twelve years ago. Her body had been dumped in wasteland behind King's Cross. A year later, Robert Summers had been caught in a burnt-out lock-up close by, wearing the face of his victim and doing something so unspeakable to her body that two of the three policemen who made the arrest took early retirement after the trial. He was found sane, was sent down for the one murder. There was no evidence – blood, DNA, fingerprints, fibre – to tie him to the other six murders, nothing but the method of killing, the strangulation and partial flaying of the victims. His brief made a good case that he was a copycat killer. He had no previous criminal record, had held the same job, as an inventory clerk in one of the big Oxford Street department stores, for fifteen years. He got the usual tariff, reduced for good behaviour. He spent his last year in an open prison, had been on the streets for three weeks.

Emma Stoke's mother had started to look for someone like me as soon as she knew that Summers would be released. She had sold the house her husband had been forced to give her after the divorce. She had rented a room in Dalston, amongst the sound systems and Turkish restaurants. Money meant nothing to her.

She wanted nothing except to know. To know that he had done it. To purge any of Emma's ghosts, if they still remained.

I could cure her at once, of course, but I would not. I needed the money. Still, I felt sorry for her. I tried to explain again that anything I found could not be used in a court. There were still a few old-fashioned policemen who were sympathetic, but the system had changed.

"In any event," I said, "it is unlikely that any of Emma's ghosts will remember anything useful, something I can give the police so they can find some piece of tangible evidence. Ghosts rarely do remember what happened when they were cast off."

"That doesn't matter, Mr Carlyle. I have no faith in the police."

I knew a flat in one of the point blocks off Kingsland Road, not far from where she was renting a room, where you could hire a gun for fifty pounds an hour, no questions asked. But I doubted that she wanted revenge. And it was none of my business anyway. My business was with the dead.

I told her my terms. She had done her research. She had the money, and the other things. She handed over the money without a qualm, but it took a visible effort for her to give up the rest.

"You will find her," she said.

"I will get in contact with you when it is over."

She started to tell me the number of the pay telephone in the rooming house, but I said, "I do not use the telephone, Mrs Stokes. But be assured that I will be in contact with you when it is over. Not before. It might take some time."

"I have been waiting twelve years, Mr Carlyle."

On the way out, she asked the question most of my clients have not dared to ask. "Why do you live like this?"

She said it with a trace of her old prim, suburban judgmentalism. I said, "You will not need to come here again."

"I don't mind it. But it makes what you do seem like . . . an act. I hope it is not, Mr Carlyle. I have put my Emma in your hands."

I went to King's Cross first, but there was nothing of Emma Stokes there, nor of anything of the other victims. There were plenty of other ghosts, of course, mostly scraps of spent lust mingled with sparks of rage from the clients of the whores who still work the station, despite the security cameras and the extra police patrols. I dispatched them all, and afterwards became aware of an old woman watching me amongst the weeds on the far side of a tangle of rusting tracks. Her long black dress and shawl looked to be Victorian, and I made a note to investigate once the case was over. Long lived ghosts are rare, even in London. I thought that I knew them all, and I have a particular affinity for Victorian ghosts.

Later, when I asked the Librarian about her, he smiled faintly and said, "There are many of us you do not know about, Carlyle. The living cannot know all the names of the dead."

"But you know who she was?"

"As a matter of fact I do not. But I could make enquiries . . ."

"Not now."

"Because you wish me to observe this murderer of young girls. How poorly you must think of me, Carlyle, for you always force me to associate with these unsavoury characters."

"You don't have to do it." I had the things Mrs Stokes had given me in the pockets of my trenchcoat. The Librarian knew that they were there; his eyes, faint stars in his pale face, kept straying towards them.

"It is a living," he said. "Where is he?"

I told him, and he said, "Ah, the tea gardens, and the New River. I spent many a happy afternoon there in the bosky meadows."

There were no tea gardens there now. They had been built over long ago, and built over again with the interlocked decks of the Marquess Estate. Robert Summers had been given a one-bed-room flat there. I had watched him for most of the afternoon as he sat hunched on one of the benches in the triangular green in Islington, at the junction of Upper Street and Essex Road, had waited outside the nearby branch Sainsbury's while he spent an hour buying half a carrier bag's worth of groceries. A scrawny harmless man, unshaven, his iron-grey hair sticking up in a cowlick over a bland unlined face. He wore a new black suit and a dirty white shirt. People knew to give him a wide berth as he shuffled along.

But no ghosts clung to him. Perhaps he had lost them in prison to someone more powerful. Most ghosts are unfaithful, short-lived things.

The Librarian was one of the more persistent ghosts, the death shell of a man who had died in the mid-nineteenth century. He was, like many ghosts, vague about the person who had cast him off. He had not been a librarian, but something to do with the booktrade, perhaps a bookseller or a bookbinder or a printer. He had taken up semi-permanent residence in the reading room of the British Library, which was where I had come to consult with him, pretending to read a trade union history while conducting a whispered conversation. No one took any notice. A lot of the scholars and journalists who worked on the curved ranks of cubicles talked to themselves. It was raining, and the rain pattered on the high ceiling overhead.

I said, "What will you do, when this place is closed?"

"There are plenty of other accommodations. Or perhaps I will choose to pass over at last. The twentieth century is becoming tiresome, and I do not look forward to the millennium. Now, the stuff, if you please, and I will be gone as quickly as Puck or Ariel."

I took out the things Mrs Stokes had given me, and laid them on the reading desk. A square of blue nylon cut from one of Emma's old sheets. An old lipstick, dried out. A pair of plain white Marks and Spencer knickers. A photograph, formally posed.

The Librarian lowered his face to them, as greedy as an addict. He sighed, and said, "Yes, it is so strong, so good . . ." and then faded, the stars of his eyes going last of all. As I gathered up the material the electric bell rang. It was closing time.

Like the Librarian, I find the late twentieth century tiresome. Because of my dress and the furnishing of my house, most people assume that I affect a late Victorian style to express this distaste, but that is not the case. It is simply a style I have never outgrown. And it was the time in which my family first gained influence over the dead.

We had a long and honourable history as sin-eaters and scriers, but it was grandfather who began the trade in what is now known, inaccurately, as the paranormal. It was he who codified a systematic approach to the matter of the dead. I am the last of my line. My mother and father died when our house was destroyed by an ill-advised experiment, and when I had recovered I moved from Edinburgh to London, and bought a house in Spitalfields.

It was a Georgian house in poor repair, and I have done nothing since to modernize it, or, like some of my neighbours, to restore it to its original state. (I have several times resisted visits from well-meaning members of the self-styled historical society, who give conducted tours of their restored houses dressed in Georgian costume; but my black suit, paisley waistcoat, Homburg, walking stick and fob watch are not a costume.) There is no electricity, and no telephone, but those things are not necessary. As light attracts moths, so electricity attracts too many partial ghosts, and I do not need the distraction. I have gas mantles, and coal fires in the winter. And anyone who wants to find me will eventually do so, or they will discover in the process of trying to find me that they do not, after all, need my help.

But the most important thing is that it is a quiet house, a quiet place, and well protected. How difficult that is to find in any large city! All who died here died natural deaths; they led content and happy lives. When I found it, there were no ghosts thrown off by hate or fear, by ecstasy or enlightenment. Ghosts of the original owners, a Huguenot silkmaker and his wife, sometimes drift through the rooms, and the ghost of the cobbler who lived and worked in the basement for more than fifty years can sometimes be heard, but they are all weak and harmless fragments, no more of a nuisance than the mice which rustle behind the walnut panelling. A few imps of delirium left by the hippies who squatted there in the early seventies were easy to disperse, and other ghosts are kept at bay by soul catchers at doors and windows, and regular asperging with rosemary, moly, and rue.

Such places are increasingly rare as ghosts multiply. Fewer people seem inclined to a quiet death, and the jostle of the city's population fills its streets with malevolent ghosts cast off in moments of intense anger or fear. Traffic intersections are crowded with the remnants of motorists' frustrations; I am unable to visit hospitals, or to travel on the Underground, or pass near casinos (although they do not know it, gamblers are quite right to use fresh decks of cards with each session, for the ghosts which cling to used cards strongly affect the laws of chance). Many churches are still peaceful, as are certain graveyards. After all, very few die in either place, and those mourning the dead do not shed ghosts, for mourning is an emotional state akin to exhaustion, not a state of heightened awareness.

The long-dead, such as the Librarian, find the press of ghosts as tiresome as I. And of course for them certain ghosts are dangerous. There are lions and tigers and bears loose in the world. More of them, it seems, every year, as if the millennium on whose brink we tremble will after all be the threshold of the pit. London is crowded with ghosts, imps and other revenants, but the truly long-lived manifestations are dwindling. They are being eaten by those of their kind which require the energy of others to sustain them.

But that was not the immediate threat which manifested itself, as two men who materialized on either side of me as I was making my way through the crowded Spitalfield's market, the Sunday after Mrs Stokes had visited me. I had bought walnut bread at one stall, organic potatoes and cabbage at another, and a water-stained edition of Hick's *Death and Eternal Life*, which promised to be amusing. It was difficult to disengage as the two man took me by the elbows and steered me into a corner by one of the gates.

"We've been looking for you," the smaller one said. He was sweating despite the cold, a slight, sandy haired man with a narrow mustache, wearing an immaculate London Fog raincoat. There were imps clinging to his thinning hair, spiky black things that chittered like bats. He said, "You are a hard man to find."

"I am glad to hear it," I said. "My house is protected."

"But you aren't protected," the smaller man said, and told his companion, "Show him what I mean."

The larger man opened his leather jacket to show me the jointed metal truncheon tucked into the inside pocket.

"This is in the nature of a warning," the smaller man said.

"You have an infestation," I said. "Who is it that marked you?"

"Don't play games. I was warned about you and I don't believe in all that shit, all right?" The imps were whispering in his ears, and he said his piece defiantly, but his eyes glittered. He knew that he was trapped, although he did not understand how.

"Then you are in great danger, my friend."

"You be quiet! Roddy here has a lot of toys, and he likes using them. We could go back to your house and he'll give you a free trial."

"I do not think I could allow you to find my house. I expect that you have been looking for it all morning, and you have not found it. Nor will you. Give me the message, and leave."

The sandy-haired man handed me an envelope. "This will

explain everything. You are threatening the interests of a powerful man, Mr Carlyle."

"And who would he be?"

The imps chittered. The man said, "No names, no pack drill."

"Ah. One of those."

"You just stop. All right? Remember Edinburgh."

"What do you know about—"

But the little man was already walking away, head down, the
big man at his back, towards the black 500 series BMW parked
on the double yellow lines just outside the gate. I watched as they
got into the back of the car; someone was waiting inside, but I saw
only a shadow before the door closed and the car drove off.

There was a speck of an imp in the seal of the envelope, and I
crushed it by reflex. It was designed to do but one thing, squeal
that the envelope had been opened, and I gave it no chance to do
that. It could have told me nothing more than its existence already
told me, that the man who had sent the message knew something
about the matter of the dead.

Inside, the message was crude and shocking. I did not look at it
again, but called upon an old friend.

We met early the next morning near Smithfield Market, in one of
the public houses which are licensed to open at 6.30 am. Superintendent Rawles looked at the photograph that had been inside
the envelope and said that it was part of the crime scene doc-
umentation.

"I'll look into how it was leaked," he said. He was a tall,
slender, upright man, with close-cropped white hair and a military bearing, and one of the most honest men I have ever met. He
was working on his second pint of bitter while I ate the excellent
full English breakfast – the pinnacle of the cuisine of this wretched
country which I have adopted – which the public house served.

"It is not where the photograph came from which is important."

I described Mrs Stoke's commission, the two men who had
delivered the envelope, and my suspicion that this was the work
of a would-be necromancer who believed that he had some use for
the murderer, Robert Summers.

"There's an incident room already set up," Inspector Rawles
said. "Perhaps you can come in and look at the books, see if you

can spot these bad boys. But that's all I can let you do. It's out of my hands, Carlyle."

"You know that they will not be amongst your mugshots."

"No, I suppose not. She was your client. What was she doing there?"

"She had rented the room. I believe that she had sold her house."

"Keep away from Summers. We're watching him. Your client is dead; you don't have that job any more."

The Librarian was watching Summers. I said, "I do not need to go near him. Do you think he killed her?"

"You look pale," Rawles said. "Paler than usual, although I see that your appetite is as healthy as ever. You think this necromancer chap might actually be dangerous?"

"Only if he is more ignorant than usual. It is not the thought of him which makes me uncomfortable, despite this excellent repast, but the proximity of the market."

Rawles smiled. "The ghosts of cows?"

I used the last of the blood pudding – they served two kinds there, white and black – to wipe up the last of the egg yolk. "Animals leave no ghosts. It is not the meat market, but the public executions that were held here. Mary Tudor had two hundred martyrs burned; before that heretics and witches were roasted, burned or boiled alive. Traces remain, even after all these years. Effluvia from the crowd rather than the ghosts the poor tormented victims cast off at the death. Still, it is not as bad as the public transport system."

"You're too sensitive for this city, lad." Rawles looked at the polaroid again. "It has your artist's mark. But whoever did it didn't know much about skinning. Summers used a proper flensing knife, and he has had practise using it. Unfortunately he used a different knife each time, which is why the forensic boffins couldn't pin the full slate to him. But this wasn't done with a flensing knife. We think this was done with the same combat knife that the murderer used to cut her throat. We found the weapon, no prints of course, and it could have been bought in any one of a hundred shops. We're canvassing them, but I doubt if we'll get anywhere. This is a professional hit."

"It was meant as a message, to me. Summers is more than he seems."

"You stay away. We can handle it."

"He has no ghosts. He murdered at least fifteen girls and he has no ghosts at all."

"Is that strange? He was in prison a long time."

Rawles was a practical man; he had grasped many of the nuances of the matter of the dead instinctively.

"Not strange, but it is unusual, given the interest in him."

Rawles drained his pint. "Perhaps this chap who put the heavies on you took Summers' ghosts."

"Then why is Summers still of interest? You drink too much, Robert."

"And you have a healthy appetite. I have to see my chief in a couple of hours. A bloodless Ph.D in sociology who did about six hours on the beat before getting a desk job. He's fifteen years younger than me. He talks like a company executive: quotas and efficiency and targets. I'll retire next year. They'll probably put a computer in to replace me. This isn't like the old days, Carlyle."

"As I am all too unfortunately aware."

As we parted, he added, "I hope that's just a walking stick these days. If some eager young bobby thinks to take a look, he'll do you for carrying a concealed weapon."

It was not the last warning I was to receive that day.

My house is, as I have said, protected. There are not many streets at the heart of old Spitalfields, a brief grid with the market on one side and the exotic glamour of Brick Lane on the other, but for anyone searching for my house with malice in their hearts they can become impossibly tangled.

But my next warning did not knock upon my door. Instead, it came roaring and gurgling out of the slate sink in the kitchen which took up the basement where the cobbler had once worked. The noise shook the whole house, but I was already coming down the stairs with a candle; I had felt the wind of its approach.

The water spout had formed a thick column of water that shook and shivered as it spun around and around. It glowed with a faint, greenish light. It stank horribly.

A face formed on its shivering surface, the kind of face you might imagine seeing on the trunk of a tree where a branch has been torn away, or the kind of face which rises towards you out of the scintillae you make when you press your fingertips against your closed eyelids. An approximation of a face. It had no eyes but I knew it could see me as it whirled around. It made a horrid gargling sound when it spoke.

It spoke in Latin, and I knew at once what it was. The oldest of all the ghosts of London. At once, I made obeisance.

He had never been a person, and that made him more terrible and powerful than any ordinary ghost. He was something like the effluvia which had made me uncomfortable near Smithfield Market, the accumulated bloodlust of the tens of thousands of men and women who had come to watch the executions for sport. Like that, but far more powerful and focused, for he had been formed and reinforced by the sacrificial ceremonies of those who had worshipped at the Temple of Mithras, founded by Ulpius Silvanus, a veteran of the *II Legio Augusta* during the Roman occupation of Britain. Archaeologists found a relief sculpture of a god killing a bull, a sculpture of a river god and other remains in the middle of the Walbrook, the long-buried tributary around which the Romans had built their original settlement, but only I knew precisely where the temple had stood, and the nature of the rituals. There had been sacrifice of bulls, but also human sacrifice: the victims had been sealed in the belly of a brazen bull, and fires lit beneath it.

The thing which manifested itself through the drain of my kitchen sink was the remnant of the river god which worship and sacrifice had created. You might say that it was the echo of a collective mania so strong it had lasted for two thousand years. It spoke only in Latin, but because of my long apprenticeship to my father I was not only fluent in Latin but knew (unlike all living scholars of that dead language) how to pronounce it correctly. I even knew that Mithras had a Spanish accent; Ulpius Silvanus, like many of the legionaries who had occupied Britain, had come from the Mediterranean shore of Spain.

"You will not disturb the murderer," Mithras said. "You will leave all alone, and all will be well."

"Why is that? What is your interest?"

"I speak for all the dead."

"Then I am honoured that you should visit me." I took a steak from the meat safe and threw it into the whirling unstable column of water. It vanished at once, shredding into pulp and blood. It was to have been my supper, but I felt that propiation of the old god was more important. I had only ever seen Mithras once before, on an ill-advised expedition beneath London with the young engineer and Dr Pretorius, and that had been long ago, in my salad days.

Mithras said, "The sacrifice is acceptable. You may ask a question."

Once, dozens of bulls had been slaughtered in a single day in his honour. Men drunk on the thick red wine called Bull's Blood had run through the streets ahead of the animals before they had been sacrificed. The men who had fallen to the bulls had been as much sacrifices to Mithras as those roasted inside the brazen bull. Mithras had been very powerful. He had protected the Roman settlement from ancient indigenous ghosts of the wild lands outside the stockade walls. He survived only because he had once been so powerful. He was an echo, a revenant, but not without influence. I wondered how long it had been since someone had given him tribute.

"One question," he said again. "Ask!"

"Is Robert Summers owned by a living man?"

"There is no such person as Robert Summers."

"Then what is he?"

"You have asked your question. It is answered. Ask no more. Seek no more. You have some protection here, but I can remove it all if I wished."

"Where is the Librarian? Bring him here and I will speak with him."

The speed of the revolving column of water increased. Greasy droplets dashed against my face. The whirling water made a high wailing sound, and out of it Mithras said, "He no longer exists."

"Did Summers kill him? Or the man who has taken control of him?"

"Ask no more. Remember you live here upon my sufferance."

"Hmm. With respect that is not quite true. This place lies to the east of the walls of your city."

"Some of my dead lie nearby. It is enough."

I remembered then that a Roman cemetery had been discovered four hundred years ago, in the fields to the east of the priory of St Mary Spital. I opened my mouth to ask one more question, but the face dissolved or spread out across the glowing surface of the unstable column of water. The force which held the water together vanished.

I stepped back and dropped the candle as the flood spun out in an splattering arc across the kitchen. I was alone in darkness.

I could not let the mystery lie. Although my client was dead and the contract dissolved, it was clear that taking Mrs Stokes's money had put me in danger. Oh, not yet, but if I let it go then the amateur who was meddling with the ghosts of Robert Summers would do something stupid. Better to stop it now, whatever Mithras said, than wait until it got worse.

And besides, I had always liked the Librarian.

As I mopped the flood of stinking drain water from the old linoleum, I thought of a ghost who might be able to help me. I finished the work and carefully sprinkled dried rue and wild garlic on the last of the water before pouring it down the drain. It would not keep out the river god, of course, but it would stop imps and other sprites from following his path.

I made no other precautions. It would not do to attract attention.

I ate lunch at one of the fine Bangladeshi restaurants in Brick Lane, and then set off north. I could not ride in public transport because I needed to keep my mind clear (and taxis were worse repositories of shed moments of anger than buses). It was cold, a sharp dry cold, and the sky was clear except for a few high strands of cirrus, darkening in the east.

It took an hour to walk to the rooming house where Mrs Stokes had been murdered. I was happy to be alone with my thoughts. At one point I passed a mosque under construction, and wondered what ghosts it would add to the city, but for the most part I thought hard about what must be done.

Mrs Stokes had rented a room in one of the houses in the Victorian terraces behind Ridley Road Market. They had been poor things when they had been thrown up to help accommodate the increasing population of factory labourers, and they had not lasted well. There were three lidless dustbins and a broken pram amongst the dead weeds in the mean little garden, and a bored young constable stood in front of the door, which had been sealed with blue and white crime scene tape. The circus which accompanied any murder – and I do not mean the police, the forensic team, the ambulance and the crowd of morbid onlookers – had passed on.

But something lingered.

I had bought a slab of cheesecake in the twenty-four hour Jewish bakery, and I walked to the end of the road and ate it while I waited. The streetlights came on and the sky beyond them darkened. It was cold, and I wished that I had bought some coffee with the cheesecake.

But at last I caught a faint scent of face powder and Arpege, and without turning around I knew that she had come to me.

The ghost of Mrs Stokes was remarkably composed, but from my brief meeting with her when she had been alive I had expected nothing less. I had been counting on it, in fact. She knew that she was dead, although like all ghosts she did not remember dying. I remembered the photograph I had been given and thought that a mercy.

When the traffic had thinned out – she found the rushing cars a terrible distraction, as if each promised to bear her away to paradise – I walked along Balls Pond Road. She was at my back, talking about her Emma. I think that she had become fused or mixed with the thing which had been at her back when she had come to see me, or perhaps this was the same ghost, strengthened by the death of the woman who had thrown it off.

It would not matter soon. All that did matter was that it would do as I asked.

"I will see her again. My Emma, just as she was."

"Yes, you will see her again."

I could have removed the ghost at Mrs Stokes's back when she had first come to see me. She would have lost her obsession, and gone away. It was something I could have done with most of my clients, but I had needed the money. Now, I thought that it was fortunate that I had no scruples. For otherwise I would not have known what kind of creature Robert Summers was, and of the man who had an interest in him, until too late.

But I knew that it would still be difficult to stop them.

I tried to tell the ghost, but she babbled happily that it did not matter. "I know what I must do and I know I can do it. I can do it for my Emma. I know I can." And, "I will take her to the arms of

Jesus, Mr Carlyle. I will find the way." And, "How strange everything looks! Some things so bright, the rest so dark. I had a television once which showed pictures like this. The thing controlling its picture had broken. It was all light or all dark. I had to take it back to the shop and there was quite an argument over replacing it, although I was fully within my rights. Is this how it looks to you, Mr Carlyle?"

"Sometimes."

"No wonder you live the way you do. I know now why you have no electricity. I think I can see electricity now. Every car is a scrawled outline of electric wires, like the filaments in a light bulb."

No, she did not really understand. She seemed much younger. I think that she was assuming the form in which she remembered her daughter, but I did not dare look around to see.

The big, black BMW was parked on double yellow lines on Essex Road, by the stairs which led to the first floor deck of the block of flats. Its motor was idling – a white plume of exhaust waved in the air from its tailpipe – but I could not see who was inside because the windows were tinted.

Mrs Stokes knew that her Emma was not inside the car. I nearly lost her as she went gadding away towards Summers' flat, light and limber as a young girl. It was all I could do to restrain her as I went puffing up the stairs, but the swirling graffiti helped divert her attention.

At the top were the two men who had accosted me in Spitalfields Market. I had expected nothing less.

"You're not wanted here," the sandy haired one said sharply. "You clear off, granddad."

His boldness was a mask. I could smell his fear. His imps were a ruff of sharply angled black bodies tangled around his head, squeaking with fury.

"My business is with your master," I said. "I believe that he is in Robert Summer' flat. Stand aside, sir."

I was afraid, of course, but determined to see this through. It occurred to me that Mrs Stokes' obsession had transferred to me.

The sandy haired man raised a hand. He wore black leather gloves.

I unlatched my cane and whipped it up. The cover flew off, revealing the short, double-edged blade.

The sandy haired man barked a brief laugh and took a step backwards. "Who d'you think you are? Zorro? Put it away or you'll get hurt."

"Will you stand aside?"

"Get him," the sandy haired man said. His hand was inside his London Fog raincoat and I knew that he had a revolver. But he did not want to use it because it would immediately attract attention.

The big man stepped forward, his hands working, and I pointed the blade at his face so that he went cross-eyed as he tried to focus on it, then whipped it down and drew a line on the dirty rippled concrete of the walkway. The man's eyes followed and stayed there, and something in him relaxed. It was a small trick, but effective. He would stare at the line I had scratched into the concrete until I released him. He would not be able to move his eyes from it at all, even if all the women he most desired paraded naked in front of him. Already he was trying to break free – I could see sweat gathering on his forehead, and tears swelling in his unblinking eyes – but I knew that he could not.

The sandy haired man drew his revolver with a convulsive movement when I pointed my sword at him. "You stay there," he said. "Just keep still or you'll regret it."

I was tired of his threats. I dismissed his retinue of chattering imps and he batted wildly at the air around his head and looked at me as if for the first time. His mouth opened, but there was nothing to put words into it.

"Wait by the car," I suggested.

He nodded violently. "Yes. That's what I should do. He wants to see you. And I'll go and wait . . ."

"In the car."

After he had gone, I went past the big man – who strained and failed to lift his eyes – to the door of Robert Summers' flat. It had been painted pale blue a long time ago. Someone had sprayed a crude graffito of male genitalia on it in black touch-up paint. Someone else – or perhaps it had been the graffiti artist – had tried to kick in its lower panel, which was chipped and splintered around three smashed dents. It was ajar, and light spilled around it. As I raised my hand to push it open, a voice from inside said, "You are welcome to enter, ghost eater, but know that you do so of your own free will."

*   *   *

There was a short corridor with a kitchen on one side and a bathroom on the other. Both were unspeakably filthy. The light came from the room at the end, which was lit by the pitiless glare of an unshaded hundred watt bulb. There were no carpets, only stained and cracked chipboard. The wall paper, pink and silver stripes, had been sprayed with scribbled tags and obscenities. It smelt of urine and unwashed bodies, and mouldy dampness. It smelt of despair. It was the most evil place I had ever been in. If not for the ghost of Mrs Stokes clinging to my back I would have turned around and fled to the safety of my house, never to come out again.

Robert Summers stood in the middle of the room, his hands laced before his crotch. He did not acknowledge my entrance. He was as still as the man I had charmed. The harsh light shone off the bald patch on the crown of his head. He wore his expensive black suit. There was something wrong with his face. It was more wrinkled than I remembered, and seemed to have slipped, so that its bottom part rested on the collar of his stained white shirt.

Then I realized what it was. A mask. A mask made from the skinned face of Mrs Stokes.

Behind me, a man said, "You should not have come here, Mr Carlyle."

I turned. A man of medium height, his face masked by a trimmed beard and mirrored sunglasses, sat on a plastic chair of the kind sold as cheap patio furniture. He wore an impeccably tailored chalk stripe suit, a Turnball and Asser shirt, oxblood loafers. His shirt cuffs were fastened by onyx studs. There was a ten thousand pound oyster Rolex on his right wrist, and several heavy gold bracelets on his left. A circle had been drawn around him on the warped chipboard; even before I saw the black lamb dead in a corner I knew that the circle had been drawn with blood.

"Oh, I am well protected," the man said.

He had a cultivated voice, salted with an Eastern European accent. Lithuanian, perhaps, or Slovak. Although he was immaculately dressed and manicured, there was something indescribably filthy about him, as if an invisibly thin film of excrement covered him.

I held out my hand. "I am pleased to meet you, sir."

For a moment, I thought that he was about to stand up, but

then he flattened his palms on the flimsy arms of the plastic chair and relaxed and smiled. "You know that I will not leave the circle."

"I do not know you."

The man's smile broadened. He placed the tips of his fore-fingers to the end of his neat beard. "Ah, it is not so easy to learn my name."

"Yet I believe you know mine."

"Then I have the advantage. I see that you have a companion."

"Your creature did not eat all of her."

"Eat? Ah. I see. No, he does not do what you do. You have made a grave mistake, Mr Carlyle. You really should not have come here. *Why* did you come here?"

"Mrs Stokes is my client."

"The poor thing which clings to you is not your client. It is merely all that is left of her."

I thought it better to say nothing. I could have walked out of the room. Mrs Stokes would stay, of course. In a way, she would become united with her daughter again, and so I would have fulfilled the conditions of my contract. Even now she was yearn-ing towards Summers, as someone in the desert will stretch towards a handful of cool water. But if I let her go and left the room I knew that I could not stay in London. Perhaps there would be no place in the world which would be safe.

The man said, "I shall tell you why you are here. You came because you believe that you are the self-appointed spiritual guardian of the city. You believe that things must be always as they are, not as they should be. You hate change as much as the ghosts you fondly believe are your charges. You came here because you are a fool who believes his own boasts. You are nothing but a tricked-out ghost eater who makes a living duping the bereaved. I am here because it is long past time for change. There are new things loose in the world, wonderful things."

I said unwillingly, "Lions and tigers and bears."

"Yes. Fierce wild creatures created by the unique pressures at the end of this century. It is not your century, Mr Carlyle. You do not belong here."

I said, "Summers is your creature."

"I found him." The man could not resist boasting. It was his fatal flaw. It was the fatal flaw of all his kind. He said, "He was never really alive. A shell of a man, a bundle of habits. His work was trivial and meaningless. He had no personal life. On weekends he would sit on the edge of the sagging bed in his greasy bedsit staring at the patch of sky visible beyond the chimneypots and hoping for escape. That was his strongest desire, and at last it turned inward. He vanished into himself. He became as empty as his bedsit, and a new tenant arrived."

"It is lonely, is it not? That is why it kills."

"It has no human weakness, Mr Carlyle. It kills because that is what it is. That is its power."

He said this in such a gloating way that I felt physically ill. But I knew that he was wrong. If it killed only for the sake of killing, it did not need to wear the faces of its victims. And I knew then that the man did not fully understand his creature.

He said, "What will you do, Mr Carlyle? Run away? But where will you run to? Try and hide? But your hiding place will not last forever. Join me? But I do not need your help. Try and run me through with that pig sticker of yours. Go on. I know that you want to."

"I want to, but I will not. You are protected. But I will give you what you want."

And I released the ghost of Mrs Stokes.

She had been straining so hard to be released that it was a relief to let her go. She went with a joyful noise, as straight as an arrow.

I do not think that the man saw her – I do not think that he could see ghosts. He was sensitive to their presence, but that is not unusual. He was not interested in the matter of the dead, but only in power. The problem is not that the people do not believe, but that they believe in the wrong things, in numerology, spiritualism, tarot, crystals, and so on. As Lewis's devil remarked in *The Screwtape Letters*, the first step to damnation is to replace God with some other belief. The man's weakness was that he believed in his own power, but it is easy enough to find enough of the matter of the dead to dabble. The old necromancers were vain enough to write down their knowledge, and their encryption systems are no match for modern computers.

But knowledge and vain self-belief are not enough.

If the man did not see the poor woman's ghost, the Summers

creature did. Its head snapped up and it yawned, showing stained
false teeth, and gulped her down.

For a moment, nothing happened. The man clapped his clean
pink palms together in soft applause.

Then Summers tipped back his head and howled, and I knew
that Mrs Stokes had found her daughter.

It was all she wanted; all that she had left behind was a
single desire, hot and strong and vibrant. As sharp as a knife
through cloth, she had cut through the ghosts the Summers
creature had bound about itself, the ragged garment it had
woven as a disguise or an attempt to become human. Now it
burst apart.

It was as if a magnesium flare had been exploded in a cave full
of bats.

For a moment the room was full of ghosts and other revenants.
Behind me, the man screamed and screamed, but I hardly heard
him. The light bulb blew in a flurry of brief sparks. Ghosts flew
around me in the darkness. I like to think that I glimpsed Mrs
Stokes and her daughter, but I cannot be sure. There were so
many. And at the core of their whirling flight was the thing which
had bound them, shaggy and black. It was not something new but
something very old. I believe that it may have been prehistoric,
some remainder of a shamanistic dream or ritual. How badly it
wanted to be human! That is why it had killed, assembling a
persona from fragments of the dead. I dispatched it and the ghosts
fled in every direction.

There is not much left to tell. The man had buried his face in his
hands. Blood leaked between his fingers. I could smell the stench
of his voided bladder and bowels. I left him sitting within his
protective circle and walked home alone.

In the next few days I learned from the newspapers of an
increase in murders, suicides and other acts of violence. A man
threw himself amongst the lions in Regent's Park Zoo; a woman
set herself alight and jumped from Hungerford Bridge; another
woman was found chewing on the stringy corpse of one of the
ravens of the Tower of London.

It would pass, but I knew that things were changed. There were
new and terrible things awake in the world, and not all of them
belonged in the realm of the dead. For a very long time I had lived
as if things had not changed, as if this great and terrible century

was nothing more than a dream from which I would at last awake, free of the burden of my past, my own ghosts.

I knew now that no one could free me but myself. It was time to take up my own life, and walk freely in the city, amongst the living and the dead.

F. PAUL WILSON

Aftershock

F. PAUL WILSON IS THE AWARD-WINNING, bestselling author of more than twenty novels and dozens of short stories. Over six million copies of his books are in print in the US and his work has been translated into twenty-four foreign languages. He has also written for the stage, screen and interactive media. Most recently he brought back his popular Repairman Jack character in the novels *Legacies* and *Conspiracies*.

Currently he lives at the Jersey Shore with his wife Mary, where he is working on a new Repairman Jack novel and haunting eBay for weird clocks and Daddy Warbucks memorabilia.

As Wilson recalls about the following, Bram Stoker Award-winning novella: " 'Aftershock' owes its existence to Peter Crowther, who requested a ghost story (somewhere in the 5,000-word neighbourhood) for an anthology he was editing. While hunting up a way to put a different spin on such a hoary theme, I came across an article about a support group for survivors of lightning strikes. Survivors? Could there be that many? Turned out there are. Most of them along Florida's 'lightning alley'. Some who've been struck multiple times.

"Suddenly I had a story . . . 'Aftershock' tied up late and at nearly three times the word count Peter could handle, so I never sent it to him. Instead, Shawna McCarthy took it for *Realms of Fantasy*. But it will always be Peter's story."

"**P**LEASE, SIGNOR," THE CORPORAL SAYS in fairly decent English, shouting over the rising wind. "You are not permitted up there!"

I look down at him. "I'm well aware of that, but I'm all right. Really. Get back inside before you get hurt."

The patterned stone floor of the Piazza San Marco beckons three hundred feet below as he clings to one of the belfry columns and leans out just far enough to make eye contact with me up here on the uppermost ledge. His hat is off, but his black shirt identifies him as one of the local Carabinieri. Hopefully a couple of his fellows have a good grip on his belt. I can tell he's used up most of his courage getting this far. He's not ready to risk joining me up here. Can't say as I blame him. One little slip and he's a goner. I've developed a talent for reading faces, especially eyes, and his wide black pupils tell me how much he wants to go on living.

I envy that.

Less than an hour ago I was just another Venice tourist. I strolled through the crowded plaza, scattering the pigeon horde like ashes until I reached the campanile entrance. I stood on the line for the elevator like everyone else, and paid my eight thousand line for a ride to the top.

The Campanile di San Marco – by far the tallest structure in Venice, and one of the newest. The original collapsed shortly after the turn of the century but they replaced it almost immediately with this massive brick phallus the color of vodka sauce. Thoughtful of them to add an elevator to the new one. I would have hated climbing all those hundreds of steps to the top.

The belfry doubles as an observation deck: four column-bordered openings facing each point of the compass, screened with wire mesh to keep too-ardent photographers from tumbling out. The space was packed with tourists when I arrived – French, English, Swiss, Americans, even Italians. Briefly I treated myself to the view – the five scalloped cupolas of San Marco basilica almost directly below, the sienna mosaic of tiled roofs beyond, and the glittering, hungry Adriatic Sea encircling it all – but I didn't linger. I had work to do.

The north side was the least crowded so I chose that for my exit. I pulled out a set of heavy wire clippers and began making myself a doorway in the mesh. I knew I wouldn't get too far before somebody noticed, and sure enough, I soon heard cries of alarm behind me. A couple of guys tried to interfere but I bared my teeth and hissed at them in my best impression of a maniac until they backed off: let the police handle the madman with the wire cutter.

I worked frantically and squeezed through onto the first ledge, then used the mesh to climb to the second. That was hairy – I damn near slipped off. Once there, I edged my way around until I found a sturdy wire running vertically along one of the corners. I stopped and used the wire cutters to remove a three-foot section which I left on the ledge. Then I continued on until I reached a large marble sculpture of a griffin-like creature set into the brick on the south side. I climbed the sculpture to reach the third and highest ledge.

And so here I am, my back pressed against the green-tiled pinnacle as it angles to a point another thirty feet above me. The gold-plated statue of some cross-wielding saint – St Mark, probably – pirouettes on the apex. A lightning rod juts above him.

And in the piazza below I see the gathering gawkers. They look like pigeons, while the pigeons scurrying around them look like ants. Beyond them, in the Grand Canale, black gondolas rock at their moorings like hearses after a mass murder.

The young national policeman pleads with me. "Come down. We can talk. Please do not jump."

Almost sounds as if he really cares. "Don't worry," I say, tugging at the rope I've looped around the pinnacle and tied to my belt. "I've no intention of jumping."

"Look!" He points southwest to the black clouds charging up the coast of the mainland. "A storm is coming!"

"I see it." It's a beauty.

"But you will be strike by lightning!"

"I know," I tell him. "That's why I'm here."

The look in his eyes tells me he thought from the start I was crazy, but not this crazy. I don't blame him. He doesn't know what I've learned during the past few months.

The first lesson began thousands of miles away, on a stormy Tuesday evening in Memorial Hospital emergency room in Lakeland, Florida. I'd just arrived for the second shift and was idly listening to the staff chatter around me as I washed up.

"Oh, Christ!" said one of the nurses. "It's her again. I don't believe it."

"Hey, you're right!" said another. "Who says lightning doesn't strike twice?"

"Twice, hell!" said a third voice I recognized as Kelly Rand's, the department's head nurse. "It's this gal's third."

Curious, I dried off and stepped into the hallway. Lightning strike victims are no big deal around here, especially in the summer – but three times?

I saw Rand, apple shaped and middle aged, with hair a shade of red that does not exist in the human genome, and asked if I'd heard her right.

"Yessiree," she said. She held up a little metal box with a slim aerial wavering from one end. "And look what she had with her."

I took the box. *Strike Zone*^{TM} *Early Warning Lightning Alert* ran in red letters across its face.

"I'd say she deserves a refund," Rand said.

"How is she?"

"Been through x-ray and nothing's broken. Small third-degree burn on her left heel. Dr Ross took care of that. Still a little out of it, though."

"Where'd they put her?"

"Six."

Still holding the lightning detector, I stepped into cubicle six and found a slim blonde, her hair still damp and stringy from the rain, semi-conscious on the gurney, an IV running into her right arm. A nurse's aide was recording her vitals. I checked the chart when she was done.

Kim McCormick, age thirty-eight, found "disrobed and unconscious" under a tree bordering the ninth fairway at a local golf course. The personal info had been gleaned from a New Jersey driver license. No known local address.

A goateed EMS tech stuck his head into the cubicle. "She awake yet, Doc?"

I shook my head.

"All right, do me a favour, will you? When she comes to and asks about her golf clubs, tell her they was gone when we got there."

"What?"

"Her clubs. We never saw them. I mean, she was on a golf

course and sure as shit she's gonna be saying we stole them. People are always accusing us of robbing them or something."

"It says here she was naked when you found her."

"Not completely. She had on, like, sneakers, a bra, and you know, panties, but that was it." He winked and gave me a thumbs-up to let me know he'd liked what he'd seen.

"Where were her clothes?"

"Stuffed into some sort of gym bag beside her." He pointed to a vinyl bag under the gurney. "There it is. Her clothes was in there. Gotta run. Just tell her about the clubs, okay, Doc?"

"It's okay," said a soft voice behind me. I turned and saw the victim looking our way. "I didn't have any clubs."

"Super," the tech said. "You heard her." And he was gone.

"How do you feel?" I said, approaching the gurney.

Kim McCormick gazed at me through cerulean irises, dreamy and half obscured by her heavy eyelids. Her smile revealed white, slightly crooked teeth.

"Wonderful."

Clearly she was still not completely out of her post-strike daze.

"I hear this is the third time you've been struck by lightning. How in the—?"

She was shaking her head. "It's the eighth."

I grinned at the put-on. "Right."

"S'true."

My first thought was that she was either lying or crazy, but she didn't seem to care if I believed her. And in those half-glazed eyes I saw a secret pain, a deep remorse, a hauntingly familiar loss. The same look I saw in my bathroom mirror every morning.

"If that's true," I said, holding up her lightning detector, "you should find one of these that really works."

"Oh, that works just fine," she said.

"Then why—?"

"It's the only way I can be with my little boy."

I tried to speak but couldn't find a word to say. Stunned, I watched her roll over and go to sleep.

No way I could let her go without learning what she'd meant by that, so I kept looking in on her during my shift, waiting for her to wake up. After suturing the twenty-centimetre gash a kid from the local supermarket had opened in his thigh when his boxcutter slipped, I checked room six again and found it empty.

The desk told me she'd paid by credit card and taken off in a cab, lightning detector and all.

I spent the next week hunting her, starting with her Jersey address; I left messages on the answering machine there, but they were never returned. Finally, after badgering the various taxi companies in town, I tracked Kim McCormick to a TraveLodge out on 98.

I sat in my car in the motel parking lot one afternoon, gathering courage to knock on her door, and wondering at this bizarre urge. I'm not the obsessive type, but I knew her words would haunt me until I'd learned what they meant.

It's the only way I can be with my little boy.

Taking a deep breath, I made myself move. August heat and humidity gave me a wet slap as I stepped out and headed for her door. Nickel clouds hung low and a wind-driven Wal-Mart flyer wrapped itself around my leg like a horny mutt. I kicked it away.

She answered my knock almost immediately, but I could tell from her expression she didn't know me. To tell the truth, with her hair dried and combed, and colour in her cheeks, I barely recognized her. She wore dark blue shorts and a white LaCoste – sans bra, I noticed. I hadn't appreciated before how attractive she was.

"Yes?"

"Ms McCormick, I'm Dr Glyer. We met at the emergency room after you were—"

"Oh, yes! I remember you now." She gave me a crooked grin that I found utterly charming. "This a house call?"

"In a way." I felt awkward standing on the threshold. "I was wondering about your foot."

She stepped back into the room but didn't ask me in. "Still hurts," she said. I noticed the bandage on her left heel as she slipped her feet into a pair of backless shoes. "But I get around okay in clogs."

I scanned the room. A laptop sat on the night stand, screen-saver fish gliding across its screen. The bed was unmade, two Chinese food containers in the waste basket, a Wendy's bag next to the TV on the dresser. The Weather Channel was on, showing a map of Florida with a bright red rectangle superimposed on its midsection. The words "Severe Thunderstorm Warning" crawled along the bottom of the screen.

"Glad to hear it," I said. "Listen, I'd . . . I'd like to talk to you about what you said when you were in the ER."

"Sorry?" she said, cocking her head toward me. "I didn't catch that."

"I said I'd like to ask you about something you said when you were in the ER."

"What was that?" She said it absently as she hurried about the room, stuffing sundry items into her gym bag, one of which I recognized as her lightning detector.

"Something about being with your little boy."

That got her. She stopped and looked at me. "I said that?"

I nodded. " 'It's the only way I can be with my little boy,' to be exact."

She sighed. "I shouldn't have said that. I was still off my head from the shock, I guess. Forget it."

"I can't. It's haunted me."

She stepped closer, staring into my eyes. "Why should that haunt you?"

"Long story. That's why I was wondering if we might sit down somewhere and—"

"Maybe some other time," she said. "I'm just on my way out."

"Where? Maybe we can go together and talk on the way."

"You can't go where I'm going," she said, slipping past me and closing the door behind her. She flashed me a bright, excited smile as she turned away. "I'm off to see my little boy."

I watched her get into a white Mercedes Benz with Jersey plates. As she pulled away, I hurried to my car and followed. Her haste, the approaching storm, the lightning detector . . . I had a bad feeling about this.

I didn't bother hanging back – I doubted she knew what kind of car I was driving, or would be checking for anyone following her. She turned off 98 onto a two-lane blacktop that ran straight as the proverbial arrow toward the western horizon. A lot of Florida roads are like that. Why? Because they can be. The state is basically a giant sandbar, flat as a flounder's belly, and barely above sea level. Roads here don't have to wind around hills and valleys, so they're laid out as the shortest distance between two points.

Ahead the sky was growing rapidly more threatening, the grey clouds darkening; lightning flashed in their ecchymotic bellies.

The light had dimmed to late-dusk level by the time she turned off the blacktop and bounced northward along a sandy road. She stopped her car about fifty yards from a small rise where a majestic Nelson pine towered over the surrounding scrub. She got out with her gym bag in hand and hurried toward the tree in a limping trot. Wind whipped her shorts around her bare legs, twisted her hair across her face. A bolt of lightning cracked the sky far to my left, and thunder rumbled past a few seconds later. I gaped in disbelief as she pulled off her shirt and shorts, stuffed them into the bag, and seated herself on the far side of the trunk.

"She's crazy!" I said aloud as I gunned the engine.

I pulled past her car and stopped as close to the tree as the road would allow. Amid more lightning and thunder, I jumped out and dashed up the rise.

"Kim!" I shouted. "This is insane! Get away from there!"

She started at the sound of my voice, looked up, and threw her free arm across her breasts. Her other hand gripped the lightning detector, its red warning light blinking madly.

"Leave me alone! I know what I'm doing!"

"You'll be killed!" I picked up her gym bag and held it out to her. "Please! Get back in your car!"

Her face contorted with fury as she slapped the bag from my hand, then covered her breasts again. "Get out of here! You don't understand and you'll ruin everything!" Her voice rose to a scream. "Go *away!*"

I backed off, unsure of what to do. I debated grabbing her and wrestling her to safety, but did I have the right? As crazy as this seemed, Kim McCormick was a grown woman, and very determined to be here. A daylight-bright flash, followed instantaneously by a deafening crash of thunder and a torrent of cold rain, decided it. I ducked back toward my car.

"Keep your windows closed!" I heard Kim shout behind me. "And don't touch any metal!"

Drenched, I huddled on the front seat and did just that. The storm roared in with maniacal fury, lashing the car with gale-force winds and rain so heavy I felt as if I'd parked under a waterfall. I couldn't see Kim – couldn't even see the big Nelson pine. I hated the thought of her getting soaked and risking electrocution out there in the lightning-strobed darkness, but what could I do?

Mostly I resented feeling helpless. I fought the urge to throw the car into gear and leave Kim McCormick to her fate. I had to stay . . . *needed* to stay. I felt tenuously bound to this peculiar woman, by something unseen, unspoken.

The lightning and thunder finally abated as the storm chugged off to the east. When the rain had eased to a steady downpour, I lowered the window and squinted at the pine, afraid of what I'd see.

Kim was still huddled against the trunk, looking miserable: hair a rattail tangle, knees drawn up, head down, but seemingly none the worse for the terrible risk she'd taken.

I stepped out and tried not to stare at her glistening, pale skin as I approached. She glanced up at me. The bright excitement of an hour ago had fled her eyes, leaving a hollow look. I reached into her bag and pulled out her shirt. I held it out to her.

"*Now* can we talk?"

Kim pointed to a pink scar that puckered her right palm. "That's from the first time I was hit," she said.

I'd followed her back to her motel, waited while she took a quick shower, then brought her here to Cajun Heat, my favourite restaurant. She'd seemed pretty down when we were seated, but a couple of Red Stripes and an appetizer of steamed spiced shrimp had perked her up some.

"That one was an accident," she said. "I was visiting my sister in West Texas last year. She and her husband and I had been fishing on White River Lake when it started to get stormy. We came ashore and I was standing on the dock, helping unload the boat. It hadn't even started raining yet, but somehow I took a direct hit." She rubbed the scar. "I had a fishing rod in my hand, my palm against the reel. That's all I remember. Karen and Bill were knocked off their feet but they told me later they saw me fly twenty feet through the air. I broke my forearm when I landed. My heart had stopped. They had to give me CPR."

"You were lucky."

"Yeah, maybe." She stared at her palm with a rueful smile. Her wet hair was pulled back and fastened with an elastic band, making her look younger than her thirty-eight years. "Karen still jokes about how she thinks Bill was maybe a little too enthusiastic with the mouth-to-mouth."

I said, "So the first strike was accidental. After what I saw today, I gather the next seven were anything but. Dare I ask why?"

Kim continued staring at her palm. "You already think I'm nuts. I don't want you thinking I'm a complete psycho."

"Try me."

"Hmm?" She glanced up. "Sorry. I'm a little hard of hearing, especially when there's background noise."

"I said, Try me."

She looked me in the eye, then let out a deep sigh. "Immediately after that first strike, I saw my son Timmy. I could see the lake and the dock and the boat, but they were faint and ghostly. I was standing right where I'd been when I got hit, but I could see my body sprawled behind me. Karen and Bill were running toward it, but slowly, like they were swimming through molasses, and they too looked faint, translucent. Timmy, though – he looked perfectly real and solid, but he was far away, hovering over the water, waving to me. He looked healthy, like he'd never been sick, but he was so far away. He kept beckoning me closer but I couldn't move. Then he faded away."

The pieces fell into place, and there it was, staring me in the face. Somehow I'd sensed it. Now I knew.

"When did he die?"

She blinked in surprise, then looked away. "Almost three years ago." Her eyes brimmed with tears but none spilled over. "Two years, eleven months, two weeks, and three days, to be exact."

"You had a very vivid hallucin—"

"No," she said firmly, shaking her head. "He was *there*. You can't appreciate how real he was if you didn't see him. I'm a hard-headed realist, Dr Glyer, and—"

"Call me Joe."

"Okay. Fine. But let's get something straight, Dr Joe. I'm no New-Agey hollow-head into touchy-feely spirituality. I was an investment banker, and a damn good one – Wharton MBA, Salomon Brothers, the whole nine yards. I dealt with the reality of cold hard cash and down-and-dirty bottom lines every day. As far as the afterlife was concerned, I was right up there with the big-time skeptics. To me, life began when you were born, you lived out your years, then you died. That was it. Game over, no replay. But not anymore. This is real. I don't know what happened, or how it happened, but for an all-too-brief time after that lightning strike, I saw Timmy, and he saw me, and that changed everything." She closed her eyes. "I thought I was getting over losing him, but . . ."

No, I thought as her voice trailed off. You never get over it. But I said nothing.

"Anyway, at first I tried to duplicate the effect by shocking myself with my house current, but that didn't work. I concluded I'd need the millions of volts only lightning can provide to see Timmy again. So I went back to Texas and hung around that dock during half a dozen storms but I couldn't *buy* another hit."

"Are you trying to die?" I said. "Is that it?"

She tossed me a withering look. "I have a Ruger 9 mm automatic back at my motel room. When I want to die, I'll use that. I am *not* suicidal."

"Then what else do you call flirting with death like you did today? And you've been hit *eight* times? The fact that you're still alive is amazing – you've had a fantastic run of luck, but you've got to know that sooner or later it's going to run out."

The waitress arrived then and we dropped into silence as she set steaming plates of jambalaya before us.

"You don't know much about lightning, do you," Kim said when we were alone again.

"I've treated my share of—"

"But do you know that it's usually not fatal, that better than nine out of ten victims survive?"

Truthfully, I hadn't known the survival rate was that high. "Well, you're closing in on number ten."

She shrugged. "Just a number. The first shock on that dock in Texas should have killed me. The usual bolt carries a current of ten thousand amps at a hundred million volts. Makes the electric chair look like a triple-A battery. Of course the charge only lasts a tiny fraction of a second, but that first one was enough to put me into cardiac arrest. If Karen and Bill hadn't known CPR, we wouldn't be having this conversation."

She dug into her jambalaya and chewed for a few seconds.

"Good, isn't it," I said.

She nodded. "Delicious."

But she said it with no great conviction, and I got the feeling that eating was something Kim McCormick did simply to keep from feeling hungry.

"But where was I?" she said. "Oh, yes. After failing to get hit a second time in Texas, I started studying up on lightning. We still don't understand it completely, but what we do know is fascinating. Do realize that worldwide, every second of every minute of every day there are almost a thousand lightning flashes? Most are cloud to cloud or cloud to air. Only fifteen per cent hit the ground. Those are the ones I'm interested in."

This was the most animated I'd seen her. I leaned across the table, drawn by her enthusiasm.

"But tell me," I said. "You're from Jersey. You were first struck in Texas. What are you doing here?"

"It's where the lightning is. The National Weather Service keeps track of lighting – something called flash density ratings. According to their records, Central Florida is the lightning capital of the country, maybe the world. You've got this broad strip of hot, low-lying land between two huge, cooler bodies of water. Take atmospheric instability due to wide temperature gradients, add tons of moisture, and *voilà* – thunderstorm alley."

"Seems you've been pretty successful around here – if you can call getting hit by lightning success."

She smiled. "I do. I started up around the Orlando area because of all the lakes. Being out in a boat during a storm is the best way to get hit, but I started thinking it was too risky, too easy to get knocked overboard and drown. Or take a direct hit from a positive giant."

"A what?"

"A positive giant. They originate at the very top of the storm cell, maybe fifty thousand feet up, and they can strike thirty miles ahead of the storm. You've heard of people getting struck down by a so-called 'bolt from the blue'? That's a positive giant. I don't want to get hit by one of those because they're so much more powerful than a regular bolt. Almost always fatal." She pointed her fork at me. "See? Told you I'm not suicidal."

"I believe you, I believe you."

"Good. Anyway, I settled on golf courses as my best bet. The landscapers take down a lot of the little trees but tend to leave the really big ones between the fairways." She showed me a pink, half-dollar-size scar on her right elbow. "That's an exit burn from the strike at Ventura Country Club." She parted her hair to reveal a quarter-size scar on her right parietal scalp. "This one's an entry at Hunter's Creek Golf Club. I could show you more, but not in public. I've got other scars you can't see. Like a mild seizure disorder, for instance – I take Dilantin for that. And I've lost some of my hearing."

I was losing my appetite. This poor, deranged woman. "And did you see . . . ?"

"Timmy?" She smiled. Her eyes fairly glowed. "Yes. Every single time."

Kim McCormick was delusional. Had to be. And yet she was so convincing. But then that's the power of a delusion.

But what if it wasn't a delusion? What if she really . . . ?

I couldn't let myself go there.

"One of these times . . ." I said.

"You're right, I suppose. And I'm prepared for it. I've got a solid will: how I'm to be cremated, where my ashes will go, and a list of all the charities that'll share my assets. But I stack the deck in my favour when I go out. That's why I get under a tree. Odds are against taking a direct hit that way. You get a secondary jolt – a flash that jumps from the primary strike point – and so far that's worked just fine for my purposes. Plus I keep low to the ground to reduce my chance of being thrown too far."

"But why do you undress?"

"I figure wet skin attracts a charge better than wet fabric."

I shook my head. "How long are you going to keep this up?"

"Until I get closer to him. He seems nearer here than he was in Texas, but he's still too far away."

"Too far for what?"

"I need to see his eyes, hear his voice, read his lips."

"Why? What are you looking for?"

A lost look tinged with terrible sorrow fluttered across her features. Her voice was barely audible. "Forgiveness."

I stared at her.

"Don't ask," she whispered before I could speak. "Subject closed." She shook herself and gave me a forced smile. "Let's talk about something else. Anything but the weather."

*   *   *

I stand alone on a rotted wharf, engulfed in fog. The stagnant pond before me carries a vaguely septic stench. No sound, no movement. I wait. Soon I hear the creak of wood, the gentle lap of a polished hull gliding through still water. A dark shape appears, with the distinctive curved bow of a gondola. It noses toward me through the fog, but as it nears I notice something unusual about the hull. It's classic glossy black, like all gondolas, but the seating area is closed over. I realize with a start that the hull is a coffin . . . a child's coffin . . . and bright red blood is oozing from under the lid. I shout to the gondolier. He's gaunt, the traditional striped shirt hanging loose on his bony frame. His face is hidden by his broad straw hat until he lifts his head and stares at me. I scream when I see the scar running across his left eye. He grins and begins poling his floating sarcophagus away, back into the fog. I jump into the foul water and swim after him, stroking frantically as I try to catch up. But the gondola is too fast and the fog swallows it again, leaving me alone and lost in the water. I swim in circles, my arms growing weaker and weaker . . . finally they refuse to respond, dangling limply at my sides as I slip beneath the surface . . . water rushes into my nose and throat, choking me . . .

I awoke gagging and shaking, dangling half on, half off my bed. It took me a long time to shake off the after-effects of the nightmare. I hadn't had one like that in years. I knew why it had returned tonight: my afternoon with Kim McCormick.

Over the next few days I realized that Kim had invaded my life. I kept thinking of her alone in that motel room, eating fast food, her eyes glued to The Weather Channel as she tracked the next storm, planned her next brush with death. The image haunted me at night, followed me through the day. I found myself keeping The Weather Channel on at home, and ducking off to check it out on the doctors' lounge TV whenever I had a spare moment.

I guess my preoccupation became noticeable because Jay Ravener, head of the emergency department, pulled me aside and asked me if anything was wrong. Jay could never understand why a board-certified cardiologist like myself wanted to work as an emergency room doc. He was delighted to have access to someone with my training, but he was always telling me how much more money I could make as a staff cardiologist. Today, though, he was talking about enthusiasm, giving me a pep talk about how we were a team, and we all had to be players. He went on about how I hardly spoke to anyone on good days, and how lately I'd barely been there.

Probably true. No, undoubtedly true. I don't particularly care for anyone on the staff, or in the whole damn state, for that matter. I don't care to make chitchat. I come in, do my job – damn efficiently, too – and then I go home. I live alone. I read, watch TV, videos, go to the movies – all alone. I prefer it that way.

I know I'm depressed. But imagine what I'd be like without the forty milligrams of Prozac I take every day. I wasn't always this way, but it's my current reality, and that's how I choose to deal with it.

Fuck you, Jay.

I said none of this, however. I merely nodded and made concurring noises, then let Jay move on, satisfied that he'd done his duty.

But the episode made me realize that Kim McCormick had upset the delicate equilibrium I'd established, and I'd have to do something about her.

Just as she had researched lightning. I decided to research Kim McCormick.

Her driver license had listed a Princeton address. I began calling the New Jersey medical centers in her area, looking for a patient named Timothy McCormick. When I struck out there, I moved to Philadelphia. I hit pay dirt at CHOP – Children's Hospital of Philadelphia.

Being a doctor made it possible. Physicians and medical records departments are pretty tight-lipped about patient information when it comes to lawyers, insurance companies, even relatives. But when it's one doctor to another . . .

I asked Timothy McCormick's attending, to call me about him. After having me paged through the hospital switchboard, Richard Andrews, MD, pediatric oncologist, knew he was talking to a fellow physician, and was ready to open up. I told him I was treating Kim McCormick for depression that I knew stemmed from the death of her child, but she would give me no details. Could he help?

"I remember it like it was yesterday," he told me in a staccato rattle. "Sad case. Osteosarcoma, started in his right femur. Pretty well advanced, mets to the lung and beyond by the time it was diagnosed. He deteriorated rapidly but we managed to stabilize him. Even though he was on respiratory assist, his mother wanted him home, in his own room. She was loaded and equipped a mini-intensive care unit at home with around-the-clock skilled nursing. What could we say? We let her take him."

"And he died there, I gather?"

"Yeah. We thought we had all the bases covered. One thing we didn't foresee was a power failure. Hospitals have back-up generators, her house didn't."

I closed my eyes and suppressed a groan. I didn't have to imagine what awful moments those must have been, the horror of utter helplessness, of watching her child die before her eyes and not being able to do a thing about it. And the guilt afterwards . . . oh, lord, the crushing weight of self doubt and self damnation would be enough to make anyone delusional.

I thanked Dr Andrews, told him what a great help he'd been, and struggled through the rest of my shift. Usually I can grab a nap after 2:00 a.m. Not this time. I sat up, staring at The Weather Channel, watching with growing unease as the radar tracked a violent storm moving this way from Tampa.

I called Kim McCormick's motel room but she didn't answer. Did she guess it was me and knew I'd try to convince her to stay in? Or was she already out?

As the clock crawled toward 6:00 a.m. I stood with keys in hand inside the glass door to the doctor's parking lot and watched the western sky come alive with lightning, felt the door shiver in resonance with the growing thunder. So *much* lightning, and it was still miles off. If Kim was out there . . .

If? Who was I kidding? Of course she was out there. And I couldn't leave until my relief arrived. I prayed he'd show up early, but if anything, the storm would delay him.

Jerry Ross arrived up at 6:05, just ahead of a pair of ambulances, and I dashed for my car. The storm was hitting its stride as I raced along 98. I turned off onto what I thought was the right road, fishtailing as I gunned along, searching for that Nelson pine. I almost missed it in the downpour, and damn near ditched the car as I slammed on the brakes when I spotted it. I backed up to the access road and kicked up wet gravel as I headed for the tree.

The sight of her Mercedes offered some relief, and I let out a deep breath when I spotted the pale form huddled against the trunk. I barely knew this strange, troubled woman, and yet somehow she'd become very important to me.

I skidded to a stop and ran up the rise to where she sat, looking like a drowned rat. Halfway there the air around me flashed noon bright and the immediate crash of thunder nearly knocked me off my feet, but Kim remained unscathed.

"Not again!" she cried, not bothering to cover her breasts this time. She waved me off. "Get out of here!"

"You can't keep doing this!" I dropped to my knees beside her and tried not to stare. I couldn't help but notice that they were very nice breasts, not too big, not too little, just right, with deep brown nipples, jutting in the chill rain.

"I can do anything I damn well please! Now *go away!*"

'I'd been here only seconds but already my clothes were soaked through. I leaned closer, shouting over the deafening thunder.

"I know what happened – about Timmy, bringing him home, the power failure. But you can't go on punishing yourself."

She gave me a cold blue stare. "How do you—?"

"Doesn't matter. I just know. Tell me – was there a storm when the power went off?"

She nodded, still staring. The red blinker on her lightning detector was going berserk.

"Don't you see how it's all tied together?" I cried. "It's guilt and obsession. You need medication, Kim. I can help."

"I've *been* on medication," she snapped. "Prozac, Paxil, Zoloft, Effexor, Tofranil, you name it. Nothing worked. I'm not imagining this, *Doctor*. Timmy is there. I can feel him."

"Because you *want* him there!"

More lightning – so close I heard it sizzle.

"Damn you!" she gritted through clenched teeth during the ensuing thunderclap. I didn't hear those words, but I could read her lips. She closed her eyes a second, as if counting to ten, then looked at me again. "Do you have any children?"

I didn't hesitate. "No."

"Well, if you did, you'd understand when I say you *know* them. I *know* Timmy, and I know he's *there*. And since you've never had a child, then you can't understand what it's like to lose one." Her eyes were filling, her voice trembling. "How you'll do anything – risk everything – to have them back, even for an instant. So don't tell me I need medication. I need my little *boy!*"

"But I do understand," I said softly, feeling my own pain grow, wanting to stop myself before I went further but sensing it was already too late. "I—"

I stopped as my skin burst to life with a tingling, crawling sensation, and my body became a burning bee hive with all its panicked residents trying to flee at once through the top of my head. I had a flash of Kim with strands of her wet hair standing out from her head and undulating like live snakes, and then I was at ground zero at Hiroshima . . .

. . . an instant white-out and then the staticky blizzard wanes, leaving me kneeling by the tree, with Kim sprawled prone before me, flaming pine needles floating around me like lazy fireflies, and a man tumbling ever so slowly down the slope to my right. With a start I realize he's me, but the whole scene is translucent – I can see through the tree trunk – and pale, drained of colour, almost as if it's etched in glass, except . . .

. . . except for the tiny figure standing far across the marsh, a blotch of bright spring colour in this polar landscape. A little girl, her dark brown hair divided into two pony tails tied with bright green ribbon, and she's wearing a yellow dress, her favourite yellow dress . . .

. . . it's Beth . . . oh, Christ, it can only be Beth . . . but she's so far away.

A desperate cry of longing leaps to my lips as I reach for her, but I can make no sound, and the world fades to black, my Beth with it . . .

I sat up groggy and confused, my right shoulder alive with pain, and looked around. Lightning still flashed, thunder still bellowed, rain still gushed in torrents from above, but somehow the whole world seemed changed. What had happened just now? Could that have been my little Beth? Really Beth?

No. Not possible. And yet . . .

Kim's still white form caught my eye. She lay by the trunk. I tried to stand but my legs wouldn't go for it, so I crawled to her. She was still breathing. Thank God. Then she moaned and moved her legs. I tried to lift her but my muscles were jelly. So I cradled her in my arms, shielding her as best I could from the rain, and waited for my strength to return, my mind filled with wonder at what I had seen.

Could I believe it had been real? Did I dare?

Still somewhat dazed, I sat on Kim's motel bed, a towel around my waist, my clothes draped over the lampshades to dry. When she'd come to, we staggered to my car and I drove us here.

The room looked exactly as before, except a Hardy's bag had replaced the Wendy's. Kim emerged from the bathroom wearing a flowered sun dress, drying her hair with a towel. She was bouncing back faster than I was – practice, maybe. She looked pale but elated. I knew she must have seen her boy again.

I felt numb.

"Oh, God," she said and leaned closer. "Look at that burn!"

I glanced at the large blister atop my left shoulder. "It doesn't hurt as much as before."

"Oh, Joe, I'm so sorry you caught that flash too. I feel terrible."

"Don't," I said. "Not as if you didn't warn me."

"Still . . . let me get some of the cream they gave me for my heel. I'll make you—"

"I saw someone," I blurted.

She froze staring at me, her eyes bright and wide. "Did you? Did you really? You saw Timmy? Didn't I tell you!"

"It wasn't your son," I said.

She frowned. "Then who?"

"Remember by the tree, just before we got hit, when you asked me if I had any children? I said no, because . . . because I don't. At least not anymore. But I did."

"*Did*?" Kim said, staring at me.

"A beautiful, beautiful daughter, the most wonderful little girl in the world."

"Oh, dear God! You too?"

My throat had thickened to the point where I could only nod.

She stumbled to the bed and sat next to me. The thin mattress sagged deeply under our combined weight.

"You're sure it was her?"

Again I nodded.

"I didn't see her. And you didn't see Timmy?"

I shook my head, trying to remember. Finally I could speak. "Only Beth."

"How old was she?"

"Eight."

"Timmy was only five. Was it . . . ?" Her own throat seemed to clog as she placed her hand on my arm. "Did she have cancer too?"

"No," I said, and the memory began to hammer against the walls of the cell where I'd bricked it up. "She was murdered. Right in front of me." I held up my left arm to show her the seven-inch scar running up from the underside of my wrist. "This was all I got, but Beth died. And I couldn't save her."

Kim made a choking noise and I felt her fingers dig into my arm, her nails like claws. "No!" Her voice was muffled because she'd jammed the damp towel over her mouth. "Oh-no, oh-no, oh-no! You poor . . . oh, God, how . . . ?"

I heard a sound so full of pain it transfixed me for an instant until I realized it had come from me.

"No. I can't. Please don't ask. I can't, I can't, I can't."

How could I talk about what I couldn't even think about? I knew if I freed those memories, even for a single moment, I'd never cage them again. They'd rampage through my being as they'd done before, devouring me alive from the inside out.

I buried my face against Kim's neck. She cradled me in her arms and rocked me like a baby.

"What about Timmy's father?" I said, biting into my Egg McMuffin. "Does he know about all this?"

After clinging to Kim for I don't know how long, I'd finally pulled myself together. We were hungry, but my clothes were still wet. So she took my car and made a breakfast run to Mickey D's. I sat on the bed, Kim took the room's one upholstered chair. The coffee was warming my insides, the caffeine pulling me part way out of my funk, but I was still well below sea level.

"He doesn't know Timmy exists," she said. "Literally. We never married. He's a good man, very bright, but I dropped him when I learned I was pregnant."

"I don't follow."

"He'd have wanted to marry me, or have some part in my baby's life. I didn't want that." My expression must have registered how offensive I found that, because she quickly explained. "You've got to understand how I was then: a super career woman who could do it all, wanted it all, and strictly on her own terms. I went through the pregnancy by myself, took maternity leave at the last possible moment, figuring I'd deliver the child – I knew he was a boy by the third month – and set him up with a nanny while I jumped right back into the race. I saw myself spending a sufficient amount of quality time with him as I molded him to be a mover and a shaker, just like his mother." She shook her head. "What a jerk."

"And after the delivery?" I said, guessing the answer.

She beamed. "When they put that little bundle into my arms, everything changed. He was a miracle, by far the finest thing I'd ever done in my life. Once I got him home, I couldn't stop holding him. And when I'd finally put him into his bassinet, I'd pull up a chair and sit there looking at him . . . I'd put my pinkie against his palm and his little fingers would close around it, almost like a reflex, and that's how I'd stay, just sitting and staring, listening to him breathe as he held my finger."

I felt my throat tighten. I remembered watching Beth sleep when she was an infant, marvelling at her pudgy cheeks, counting the tiny veins on the surfaces of her closed eyelids.

"You sound like a wonderful mother."

"I was. That's no brag. It's just that it's simply not my nature to do things half way. Everything else in my life took a back seat to Timmy, I mean *way* back. It damn near killed me to end my maternity leave, but I arranged to do a lot of work from home. I wanted to be near him all the time." She blinked a few times and sniffed. "I'm so glad I made the effort. Because he didn't stay around very long." She rubbed a hand across her face and looked at me with reddened eyes. "How long since Beth . . . ?"

"Five years," I said. The longing welled up in me. "Sometimes I feel like I was talking to her just yesterday, other times it seems like she's been gone forever."

"But don't you see?" Kim said, leaning forward. "She's not gone. She's still here."

I shook my head. "I wish I could believe that."

The lightning episode was becoming less and less real with each passing minute. Despite what I'd seen, I found myself increasingly reluctant to buy into this.

"But you saw her, didn't you? You *knew* her, didn't you? Isn't seeing believing?"

"I don't know. Sometimes believing is seeing."

"But each of us saw our dead child. Can we *both* be crazy?"

"There's something called shared delusion. I could be—"

"Damn it!" she said, catapulting from the chair. "I'm not going to let you do this!" She yanked my pants from atop the lampshade and threw them at me. "You can't take this from me! I won't let you or anybody else tell me—"

I grabbed her wrist as she stormed past me. "Kim! I *want* to believe! Can't you see there's nothing in the world I want more? And that's what worries me. I may want it too much."

I pulled her into my arms and we stood there, clinging to each other in anguished silence. I could feel her hot breath on my bare shoulder. She lifted her face to me.

"Don't fight it, Joe," she said, her voice soft. "Go with it. Otherwise you'll be denying yourself—"

I kissed her on the lips.

She drew back. I didn't know where the impulse had come from, and it was a toss-up as to which of us was more surprised. We stared at each other for a few heartbeats, and then our lips were together again. We seemed to be trying to devour each other. She tugged at my towel, I pulled at her sun dress, she wore nothing beneath it, and we tumbled onto the unmade bed, skin to skin, rolling and climbing all over each other, frantic mouths and hands everywhere until we finally locked together, riding out a storm of our own making.

Afterwards, we clung to each other under the sheet. I stroked her back, feeling guilty because I knew it had been better for me than her.

"I'm sorry that was so quick," I said. "I'm out of practice."

"Don't be sorry," she murmured, kissing my shoulder. "Maybe it's all the shocks I've taken, but orgasms seem to be few and far between for me these days. I'm just glad to have someone I can feel close to. You don't know how lonely it's been, keeping this to myself, unable to share it. It's wonderful to be able to talk about it with someone who understands."

"I wish I did understand," I said. "Why is this happening?"

"Maybe all those volts alter the nervous system, change the brain's modes of perception."

"But I've never heard of anything like this. Why don't other lightning strike victims mention seeing a dead loved one?"

"Maybe they *have* seen them and never mentioned it. You're the only one I've told. But maybe it has to be someone who died during a storm. Did Beth—?"

"No," I said quickly, not allowing the scene to take shape in my mind. "Perfect weather."

"Then maybe it has to do with the fact that they both died as children, and they're still attached to their parents. They hadn't let go of us in life yet, and maybe that carries over into death."

"Almost sounds as if they're waiting for us," I said.

"Maybe they are."

The temperature in the room seemed to drop and Kim snuggled closer.

Later, when we went back to pick up Kim's car, we walked up to where the lightning had struck. The top of the Nelson pine was split and charred. As we stood under its branches, I relived the moment, seeing Beth again, reaching for her . . .

"I wish she'd been closer," I said.

"Yes." Kim turned to me. "Isn't it frustrating? When I took my second hit, up in Orlando, Timmy was closer than he'd been in Texas, and I thought he might move closer with each succeeding hit. But it hasn't worked that way. He stays about fifty yards away."

"Really? Beth seemed at least twice that." I pointed to the marshy field. "She was way over there."

Kim pointed north. "Timmy was that way."

I swiveled back and forth between where I'd seen Beth, and where Kim had seen Timmy, and an idea began to take shape.

"Tell me," I said. "Which way were you facing when you saw Timmy in Texas?"

She closed her eyes. "Let me think . . . the sun always rose over the end of the dock, so I guess I was facing east."

"Good." I took her shoulders and rotated her until she faced east. "Now, show me where Timmy was in relation to the end of the dock when he appeared in Texas."

She pointed northeast.

"I'll be damned," I said and trotted down the slope.

"Where're you going?"

I reached into my car and plucked the compass from my dashboard. Sometimes at night when I can't sleep I go out for long aimless drives and wind up God knows where. At those times it's handy to know which direction you're headed.

"All right," I said when I returned to Kim. "This morning Timmy was that way – the compass says that's a few degrees east of north. If you followed that line from here, it would run through New Jersey, wouldn't it?"

She nodded, her brow furrowing. "Yes."

"But in Texas – where in Texas?"

"White River Lake. West Texas."

"Okay. You saw him in a north-northeast direction. Follow that line from West Texas and I'll bet it takes you—"

"To Jersey!" She was squeezing my upper arm with both hands and jumping up and down like a little girl. "Oh, God—! That's where we lived! Timmy spent his whole life in Princeton!"

It's also where he died, I thought.

"I think a trip to Princeton is in order, don't you?"

"Oh, yes! Oh, God, yes!" Her voice cranked up to light speed. "Do you think that's where he is? Do you think he's still at the house? Oh, dear God! Why didn't I think of that?" She settled down and looked at me. "And what about Beth? You saw her . . . where?"

"East northeast," I said. I didn't need the compass to figure that.

"Where does that line go? Orlando? Kissimmee? Did you live around there?"

I shook my head. "No. We lived in Tampa."

"But that's the opposite direction. What's east northeast from here?"

I stared at the horizon. "Italy."

A week later we were sitting in the uppermost part of Kim's Princeton home waiting for an approaching storm to hit.

She had to have been earning *big* bucks as an investment banker to afford this place. A two-story Victorian – she said it was Second Empire style – with an octagonal tower set in the centre of its mansard roof. One look at that tower and I knew it could be put to good use.

I found a Home Depot and bought four eight-foot sections of

one-inch steel pipe, threaded at both ends, and three compatible couplers. I drilled a hole near the centre of the tower roof and ran a length through; I coupled the second length to its lower end, and ran that through, and so on until Kim had a steel lightning target jutting twenty-odd feet above her tower.

The tower loft was unfurnished, so I'd carried up a couple of cushions from one of her sofas. We huddled side by side on those. The lower end of the steel pipe sat in a large galvanized bucket of water a few feet in front of us – the bucket was to catch the rain that would certainly leak through my amateur caulking job at the roof line, the water to reduce the risk of fire.

I heard the first distant mutter of thunder and rubbed my hands together. Despite the intense dry heat up here, they felt cold and damp.

"Scared?" Kim said

"Terrified."

My first brush with lightning had been an accident. I hadn't known what was coming. Now I did. I was shaking inside.

Kim smiled and gave my arm a reassuring squeeze. "So was I, at first. Knowing I'm going to see Timmy helps, but still . . . it's the uncertainty that does it: *Is* it or *isn't* it going to hit?"

"How about I just say I don't believe in lightning? That'll make me feel better."

She laughed. "Hey, whatever works." She sidled closer. "But I think I know a better way to take your mind off your worries."

She began kissing me, on my eyes, my cheeks, my neck, my lips. And I began undoing the buttons on her blouse. We made love on the cushions in that hot stuffy tower, and were glazed with sweat when we finished.

A flash lit one of the eight slim windows that surrounded us, followed by a deep rumble.

"Almost here," I whispered.

Kim nodded absently. She seemed distant. I knew our love making had once again ended too quickly for her, and I felt bad. Over the past week I'd tried everything I knew to bring her through, but kept running into a wall I could not breach.

"I wish—" I began but she placed a finger against my lips.

"I have to tell you something. About Timmy. About the day he died."

I knew it had been tough on her coming back here. I'd seen his room – it lay directly below this little tower. Like so many parents who've lost a child, she'd kept it just as he'd left it, with toys on the counters and drawings on the wall. I would have done that with Beth's room, but my marriage fell apart soon after her death and the house was sold. Another child was living in Beth's room now.

"You don't—"

"Shush," she said. "Let me speak. I've got to tell you this. I've got to tell *someone* before . . ."

"Before what?"

"Before I explode. I brought Timmy home from the hospital to a room that was set up like the finest ICU. All his vital signs were monitored at the hospital by telemetry, he had round-the-clock skilled nursing to give him his chemotherapy, monitor his IVs, draw blood for tests, adjust his respirator."

"Why the respirator?" I couldn't help it – the doctor in me wanted to know.

"The tumour had spread to his lungs – he couldn't breathe without it. It'd also spread to many of his bones, even his skull. He was in terrible pain all the time. They radiated him, filled him with poisons that made him sicker, loaded him with dope to ease the pain, and kept telling me he had a fighting chance. He *didn't* have a chance. I knew it, and that was why I'd brought him home, so he could be in his own room, and so I could have every minute with him. But worse, Timmy knew it too. I could see it in his eyes when they weren't glazed with opiates. He was hanging by a thread but no one would let it break. He wanted to go."

I closed my eyes, thinking, Oh, no. Don't tell me this . . . I don't want to hear this . . .

"It was the hardest decision of my life. More than anything else in the universe, I wanted my little boy to live, because every second of his life seemed a precious gift to me. But why was I delaying the inevitable? For him, or for me? Certainly not for him, because he was simply existing. He couldn't read, couldn't even watch TV, because if he wasn't in agony, he was in the Demerol zone. That meant I was prolonging his agony for *me*, because I couldn't let him go. I *had* to let him go. As his mother, I had to do what was right for *him*, not for me."

"You don't have to go on," I said as she paused. "I can guess the rest."

Kim showed me a small, bitter smile. "No, I don't think you can." She let out a deep shuddering sigh and bit her upper lip. "So one day, as a thunderstorm came through, I dosed a glass of orange juice with some ipecac and gave it to Timmy's nurse. Ten minutes later, while she was in the bathroom heaving up her lunch, I sneaked down to the basement and threw the main breaker for the house. Then I rushed back up to the second floor to be with Timmy as he slipped away. But he wasn't slipping away. He was writhing in the bed, spasming, fighting for air. I . . . I was horrified, I felt as if my blood had turned to ice. I thought he'd go gently. It wasn't supposed to be like that. I couldn't bear it."

Tears began to stream down her face. The storm was growing around us but I was barely aware. I was focused on Kim.

"I remember screaming and running back down to the basement, almost killing myself on the way, and resetting the breaker. Then I raced back upstairs. But when I reached him, it was too late. My Timmy was gone, and I hadn't been there. He died alone. *Alone!* Because of me! I killed him!"

And now she was sobbing, deep wracking sounds from the pit of her soul. I took her in my arms and held her tight against me. She virtually radiated pain. At last I understood what was fueling the engine of this mad compulsion of hers. What an appalling burden to carry.

"It's all right, Kim," I whispered. "What you saw were muscle spasms, all involuntary. You did the right thing, a brave thing."

"*Was* it right?" she blurted through her sobs. "I know it wasn't brave – I mean, I lost my nerve and changed my mind – but was it *right*? Did Timmy really want to go, or was it me just thinking he did? Was his suffering too much for him to bear, or too much for me? That's what I've got to know. That's why I have to see him close up and hear what he's trying to say. If I can do that, just once, I swear I'll stop all this and run for a basement every time I hear a storm coming."

As if on cue, a blast of thunder shook the little tower and I became aware again of the storm. Rain slashed the windows and the darkened sky was alive with flashes. I stared at the steel pole a few feet before me and wanted to run. I could feel my heart hammering against my ribs. This was insane, truly insane. But I forced myself to sit tight and think about something else.

"It all makes sense now," I said.

"What?"

"Why we're seeing Beth and Timmy . . . they didn't *give up* their lives – life was *taken* from them."

Kim bunched a fist against her mouth. She closed her eyes and moaned softly.

"Through love in Timmy's case," I said quickly. I cupped my hand behind her neck and kissed her forehead. "But not in Beth's."

Kim opened her eyes. "Can't you tell me about it? Please?"

She'd shared her darkest secret with me, and yet I couldn't bring myself talk about it. I was about to refuse her when a deafening blast of thunder stopped me. I was dancing with death in this tower. What if I didn't survive? Kim should know. Suddenly I wanted her to know.

I closed my eyes and opened the gates, allowing the pent-up past to flow free. A melange of sights, smells, sounds eddied around me, carrying me back five years . . .

I steeled myself and began: "It was the first time in years I'd allowed myself more than a week away from my practice. Twelve whole days in Italy. We were all so excited . . ."

Angela was first generation Italian-American and the three of us trooped to the Old Country to visit her grandparents – Beth's great-grandparents. While Angela stayed in Positano, yakking in Italian to all her relatives, Beth and I dashed off for a quick, two-day jaunt to Venice. Yes, it's an overpriced tourist trap. Yes, it's the Italian equivalent of Disney World. But there's not another place in the world like it, and since the city is supposedly sinking at the rate of two-and-a-half inches per decade, I wanted Beth to experience it without a snorkel.

From the day she was born, Beth and I shared something special. I don't think I've ever loved anyone or anything more than that little baby. When I was home, I'd feed her; when I wasn't on call, I'd get up with her at night. Most parents love their kids, but Beth and I *bonded*. We were soulmates. She was only six, but I felt as if I'd known her all my life.

I wanted her to be rich in spirit and experience, so I never passed up a chance to show her the wonders of the world, the natural and the manmade. Venice was a little of both. We did all the touristy stuff – a gondola ride past Marco Polo's and Casanova's houses, shopping on the Rialto Bridge, eating gelato, crossing the Bridge of Sighs from the Doge's palace into the prison; we took boats to see the glassblowers on Murano and the lace makers on Burano, snagged a table at Harry's Bar where I treated her to a Shirley Temple while I tried a Bellinni. But no matter where we went or what we did, Beth kept dragging me back to Piazza San Marco so she could feed the pigeons. She was bonkers for those pigeons.

Vendors wheel little carts through the piazza, selling packets of birdseed, two thousand lire a pop. Beth must have gone through a dozen packets during our two-day stay. Pigeons have been called rats with feathers, and that may not be far off, but these have got to be the fattest, tamest feathered rats in the world. Sprinkle a little seed into your palm, hold it out, and they'll flutter up to perch on your hand and arm to eat it. Beth loved to stand with handfuls stretched out to both sides. The birds would bunch at her feet, engulf her arms, and even perch on her head, transforming her into a giggling mass of feathers.

I wasn't crazy about her being that close to so many birds – thoughts of the avian-born diseases like psittacosis that I'd studied in med school kept darting through my head – so I tried to limit her contact. But she got such a kick out of them, how many times could I say no? I even went so far as to let her talk me into doing her two-handed feeding trick. Soon I was inundated with feathers, holding my breath within a sea of fluttering wings. I couldn't see Beth but I could hear her distinctive belly laugh. When I finally shook off the pigeons, I found her red faced and doubled over with laughter.

What can be better than making a child laugh? The pigeons grossed me out, but so what? I eagerly grabbed more seed and did it again.

Finally it was time to leave Venice. The only flight we could book to Naples left Marco Polo at 6:30 a.m. the next morning, and the first public waterbus of the day would make a number of stops along the way and get us to the airport with only a few minutes to spare. Since I didn't want to risk missing the flight, I had the hotel concierge arrange for a private water taxi. It would pick us up at 5:00 a.m. at a little dock just a hundred feet from our hotel.

At 4:50 a.m., Beth and I were standing by our luggage at the end of Calle Larga San Marco. The tide was out and the canal smelled pretty rank. Even at this hour it was warm enough for short sleeves. I was taken with the silence of the city, the haunted emptiness of the dark streets: Venice on the cusp of a new day, when the last revelers had called it quits, and the earliest risers were just starting their morning coffee.

Beth was her usual bossy little self. As soon as she'd learned to string words together, she began giving directions like a sergeant major. She had no qualms about telling us what to wear, or what to buy in the supermarket or a department store, or setting up seating arrangements – "You sit there, Mommy, and Daddy, you sit there, and I'll sit right here in the middle." We called her "the Boss" in private. And here in Venice, without her mother around, Boss Beth took charge of me. I loved to humour her.

"Put the suitcases right there, Daddy. Yours on the inside and mine on the outside so that when the boat gets here we can put them right on. Now you stand right over here by me."

I did exactly as she told me. She wanted me close and I was glad to comply. Her voice trailed off after that and I could see her glancing around uneasily. I wasn't fully comfortable myself, but I talked about seeing Mommy in a few hours to take her mind off our isolation.

And then finally we heard it – the sputtering gurgle of an approaching *taxi acquei*. The driver, painfully thin, a cigarette drooping from his lips, pulled into the dock – little more than a concrete step-down – and asked in bad English if we were the ones going to the airport. We were, and as I handed him our two suitcases, I noticed the heavy droop of his left eyelid. My first thought was Bell's palsy, but then I noticed the scar that parted his eyebrow and ridged the lid below it.

I also noticed that he wasn't one to make contact with his good eye, and that his taxi didn't look to be in the best shape. A warning bell sounded in my head – not a full-scale alarm, just a troubled chime – but I knew if I went looking now for another taxi, we'd almost certainly miss the plane.

If only I'd heeded my instincts.

Beth and I sat together in the narrow, low-ceilinged cabin amidships as the driver wound his way into the wider, better-lit Grand Canal where we were the only craft moving. We followed that for awhile, then turned off into a narrower passage. After numerous twists and turns I was completely disoriented. Somewhere along the way the canal-front homes had been replaced by warehouses. My apprehension was rising, and when the engine began to sputter, it soared.

As the taxi bumped against the side of the canal, the driver stuck his head into the cabin and managed to convey that he was having motor trouble and needed us to come up front so he could open the engine hatch.

I emerged to find him standing in front of me with his arm raised. I saw something flash dimly in his hand as he swung it at me, and I managed to get my left arm up in time to deflect it. I felt a blade slice deep into my forearm and I cried out with the pain as I fell to the side. Beth started screaming, "Daddy! Daddy!" but that was all she managed before her voice died in a choking gurgle. I didn't know what he'd done to Beth, I just knew he'd hurt her and no way in hell was he going to hurt her again. Bloody, agonized arm and all, I launched myself at him with an animal roar. He was light and thin, and not in good shape. I took him by surprise and drove him back against the boat's console. Hard. He grunted and I swear I heard ribs crack. In blind fury I pinned him there and kept ramming my right forearm against his face and neck and kneeing him in the groin until he went limp, then I threw him to the deck and jumped on him a few times, driving my heels into his back to make sure he wouldn't be getting up.

Then I leaped to Beth and found her drenched in blood and just about gone. He'd slit her throat! Oh, Lord, oh, God, to keep her from screaming he'd cut my little girl open, severing one of her carotid arteries in the process. The wound gaped dark and wet, blood was everywhere. Whimpering like a lost, frightened child, I felt around in the wound and found the feebly pumping carotid stump, tried to squeeze it shut but it was too late, too late. Her mouth was slack, her eyes wide and staring. I was losing her, my Beth was dying and I couldn't do a thing to save her. I started shouting for help, I screamed until my throat was raw and my voice reduced to a ragged hiss, but the only replies were my own cries echoing off the warehouse walls.

And then the blood stopped pulsing against my fingers and I knew her little heart had stopped. CPR was no use because she had no blood left inside, it was all out here, soaking the deck and the two of us.

I held her and wept, rocking her back and forth, pleading with God to give her back to me. But instead of Beth stirring, the driver moved, groaning in pain from his broken bones. In a haze of rage as red as the sun just beginning to crawl over the horizon, I rose and began kicking and stomping on the driver, reveling in the wonderful crunch of his bones beneath my soles. I shattered his limbs and hands and feet, crushed his rib cage, pulped the back of his skull, and I relished every blow. When I was satisfied he was dead, I returned to Beth. I cradled her in my arms and sobbed until the first warehouse workers arrived and found us.

Kim clutched both my hands; tears streamed down her cheeks. Her mouth moved as she tried to speak, but she made no sound.

"The rest is something of a blur," I said. "An official inquiry into the incident – two people were dead, so I couldn't blame the Venice authorities for that – revealed that the killer had overheard the hotel arranging our water taxi ride. He borrowed a friend's boat and beat the scheduled taxi to the pick-up spot. The court determined that he was going to kill us, steal whatever valuables we'd bought or brought, and dump our bodies in the Adriatic. They suspected that Beth and I weren't his first victims.

"I was released, but then came the nightmare of red tape trying to return Beth's body to the States. Finally we brought her home and buried her, but my life was changed forever by then. The world was never the same without Beth. Neither was my marriage. Angela never said so, but I know she secretly blamed me for Beth's death. So did I. Angela and I split a year later. She couldn't live with me. Who could blame her? I could barely live with myself. Still can't."

"But you're *not* to blame," Kim said.

"I had a chance to save Beth before we stepped onto that water taxi, but I didn't take it. And Beth paid for it."

We sat in silence then, each mired in our pools of private guilt. Gradually I realized that the flashes outside were less frequent, the thunder not quite so loud.

"I think it's passed us by," I said.

Kim glanced around, frowning in disappointment. "Damn. We'll have to wait for another storm. That could be next week or next month around here." She pointed to the steel pole. "Oh, look. It's wet."

Fine rivulets of water were coursing down the surface of the steel.

"So much for my caulking skills. I'll see what I can do tomorrow."

Kim got on her knees and leaned forward to touch the wet surface and—

—the tower seemed to explode. I had an instant's impression of a deafening *buzz* accompanied by a rainbow shower of sparks within a wall of blazing light; boiling water exploded from the galvanized bucket as multiple arcs of blue-white energy converged from the pole onto Kim's outstretched arm. Her mouth opened wide in a silent scream while her body arched like a bow and shuddered violently, and then a searing bolt flashed from her opposite shoulder into me . . .

. . . the whiteout fades, as do the walls of the tower, leaving ghostly translucent afterimages, and I know which way to turn. I spot the tiny figure immediately, still in her yellow dress, standing so far away, suspended above the treetops. Beth! I call her name but there is no sound in this place. I try to move toward her but I'm frozen in space. I need to be closer, I need to see her throat . . . and then her hand goes to her mouth, and her eyes widen as she points to me. What? What's the matter?

I realize she's pointing behind me. I turn and see Kim's ghostly figure on the floor . . . so still . . . too still . . .

I came to and crawled to Kim. Her right arm was a smoking ruin, charred to the elbow, and she wasn't breathing. Panicked, I struggled upright and kneeled over her. I forced my rubbery arms to pound my fists on her chest to jolt her heart back to life – once, twice – then I started CPR, compressing her sternum and blowing into her mouth, five thrusts, one breath . . . five thrusts, one breath . . .

"Come on, Kim!" I shouted. I was so slick with sweat that my hands kept slipping off her chest. "Breathe! You can do it! Breathe, damn it!"

I saw her eyelids flutter. Her blue irises had lost their luster, but I sensed an exquisite joy in their depths as they fixed on me for a beseeching instant . . . the tiniest shake of her head, and then she was gone again.

I realized what she'd just tried to tell me: *Don't . . . please don't*.

But it wasn't in me to kneel here and watch the life seep out of her. I lurched again into CPR but she resisted my best efforts to bring her back. Finally, I stopped. Her skin was cooling beneath my palms. Kim was gone.

I stared at her pale, peaceful face. What was happening in that other place? Had she found her Timmy and the forgiveness she craved? Was she with him now and preferring to stay there?

I felt an explosive pressure building in my chest, mostly grief, but part envy. I let out an agonized groan and gathered her into my arms. I ached for her bright eyes, her crooked-toothed smile.

"Poor lost Kim," I whispered, stroking her limp hair. "I hope to God you found what you were looking for."

Just as with Beth, I held Kim until her body was cold and stiff.

Finally, I let her go. I dressed her as best I could, and stretched her out on the cushions. I called the emergency squad, then drove my car to the corner and waited until I saw them wheel her body out to the ambulance. Then I headed for the airport.

I hated abandoning Kim to the medical examiner, but I knew the police would want to question me. They'd want to know what the hell we were doing up in that tower during a storm. They might even take me into custody. I couldn't allow that.

I had someplace to go.

I arrived in Marco Polo Airport without luggage. The terminal snuggles up to the water, and the boats wait right outside the arrival terminal. I bought a ticket for the waterbus – I could barely look at the smaller, speedier water taxis – and spent the two-and-a-half mile trip across the Laguna Véneta fighting off the past.

I did pretty well leaving the dock and walking into the Piazza San Marco. I hurried through the teeming crowds, past the flooded basilica on the right, a Byzantine toad squatting in a tiny pond, and the campanile towering to my left. I almost lost it when I saw a little girl feeding the pigeons, but I managed to hold on.

I found a hotel in the San Polo district, bought a change of clothes, and holed up in my room, watching the TV, waiting for news of a storm.

*   *   *

And now the storm is here. From my perch atop the Campanile di San Marco I see it boiling across the Laguna Véneta, spearing the Lido with bolts of blue-white energy, and taking dead aim for my position. The piazza below is empty now, the gawkers chased by the thunder, rain, and lightning – especially the lightning. Even the brave young Carabinieri has discovered the proper relationship between discretion and valour and ducked back inside.

And me: I've cut the ground wire from the lightning rod above me. I'm roped to the tower to keep from falling. And I'm drenched with rain.

I'm ready.

Physically, at least. Mentally, I'm still not completely sure. I've seen Beth twice now. I *should* believe, I want to believe . . . but do I want it so desperately that I've tapped into Kim's delusion system and made it my own?

I'm hoping this will be my last time. If I can see Beth up close, see her throat, know that her wound has healed in this place where she waits, it will go a long way toward healing a wound of my own.

Suddenly I feel it – the tingle in my skin as the charge builds in the air around me – and then a deafening *zzzf!* as the bolt strikes the ungrounded rod above the statue of St Mark. Millions of volts slam into me, violently jerking my body . . .

. . . and then I'm in that other place, that other state . . . I look around frantically for a splotch of yellow and I almost cry out when I see Beth floating next to me. She's here, smiling, radiant, and so close I can almost touch her. I choke with relief as I see her throat – it's healed, the terrible grinning wound gone without a trace, as if it never happened.

I smile at her but she responds with a look of terror. She points down and I turn to see my body tumbling from the tower. The safety rope has broken and I'm drifting earthward like a feather.

I'm going to die.

Strangely, that doesn't bother me nearly as much as it should. Not in this place.

Then in the distance I see two other figures approaching, and as they near I recognize Kim, and she's leading a beaming tow-headed boy toward Beth and me.

A burst of unimaginable joy engulfs me. This is so wonderful . . . almost too wonderful to be real. And there lies my greatest

fear. Are they all – Beth, Kim, Timmy – really here? Or merely
manifestations of my consuming need for this to be real.

I look down and see my slowly falling body nearing the
pavement. Very soon I will know.

GENE WOLFE

A Fish Story

GENE WOLFE LIVES IN BARRINGTON, ILLINOIS. He fought in the Korean War and subsequently received a BSME from the University of Houston. His first book appeared in 1970, and he is the author of *Peace*, *The Book of the New Sun* and *The Book of the Long Sun*, amongst other works. His latest series, *The Book of the Short Sun*, comprises *On Blue's Waters*, *In Green's Jungles* and *Return to the Whorl*, while his most recent collection of short stories is entitled *Strange Travelers*.

It is a pleasure to once again welcome the author back to the pages of *Best New Horror* with this atmospheric short . . .

I AM ALWAYS EMBARRASSED BY THE TRUTH. For one thing, I am a writer of fiction, and know that coming from me it will not be believed; nor does it lend itself to neat conclusions in which the hero and heroine discover the lost silver mine. So bear with me, or read something else. This is true – and because it is, it is not quite satisfactory.

We three were on a fishing trip along a certain river in Minnesota. We had put Bruce's boat in the water that morning and made our way in a most dilatory fashion downstream, stopping for an hour or two at any spot we thought might have a muskie in it. That night we camped on shore. The next day we would make our way to the lake, where Bruce's wife and mine would meet us about six. Rab, who had never married, would ride as far as Madison with my wife and me. We had not caught much, as I remember; but we had enough to make a decent meal, and were eating it when we saw the UFO.

I do not mean that we saw a saucer-shaped mother ship from a far-off galaxy full of cute green people with feelers. When I say it was a UFO, I mean merely what those three letters indicate – something in the air (lights, in our case) we could not identify. They hovered over us for a half minute, drifted off to the north-east, then receded very fast and vanished. That was all there was to it; in my opinion, we witnessed a natural phenomenon of some sort, or had seen some type of aircraft.

But of course we started talking about them, and Roswell, and all that; and after a while Bruce suggested we tell ghost stories. "We've all had some supernatural experience," Bruce said.

And Rab said, "No."

"Oh, of course you have." Bruce winked at me.

"I didn't mean that nothing like this has ever happened to me," Rab said, "just that I don't want to talk about it."

I looked at him then. It was not easy to read his face in the firelight, but I thought he seemed frightened.

It took about half an hour to get the story out of him. Here it is. I make no comment because I have none to make; I do not know what it means, if it means anything.

"I've always hated ghosts and all that sort of thing," Rab began, "because I had an aunt who was a spiritualist. She used to read tea leaves, and bring her Ouija board when she came to dinner, and hold seances, and so on and so forth. When I was a little boy it scared me silly. I had nightmares, really terrible nightmares, and used to wake up screaming. All that ended when I was thirteen or fourteen, and since then I've despised the whole stupid business. Pretty soon one of you is going to ask if I've ever seen a ghost, so I'll answer that right now. No. Never.

"Well, you don't want my life history. Let's just say that I grew up, and after a while my mother and father weren't around any more, or married to each other either. My sister was living in England. She's moved to Greece, but I still hear from her at Christmas.

"One day I got home from work, and there was a message from Dane County Hospital on my machine. Aunt Elspeth was dying, and if I wanted to see her one last time, I had better get over there.

I didn't want to. I had disliked her all my life, and I was pretty sure the feeling was mutual. But I thought of her alone in one of those high, narrow beds, dying and knowing that nobody cared that she was dying. So I went.

It was the most miserable four or five hours I've ever spent. She looked like hell, and even though they had her in an oxygen tent, she couldn't breathe. She kept taking these great gasping breaths . . ."

Rab demonstrated.

"And in between breaths she talked. She talked about my grandparents' house, which I've never seen, and how it had been there when she and Mom were kids. Not just about them and my grandparents, but the neighbours, the dogs and cats they'd owned, and everything. The furniture. The linoleum on the kitchen floor. Everything. After a while I realized that she was still talking even when she wasn't talking. Do you know what I mean? She would be taking one of those horrible breaths, and I'd still hear her voice inside my head.

"It was getting pretty late, and I thought I'd better go. But there was something I wanted to say to her first – I told you how much I hate ghosts and all that kind of crazy talk. Anyway, I cut her off while she was telling about how she and my mother used to help my grandmother can tomatoes, and I said, 'Aunt Elspeth, I'd like you to promise me something. I want your word of honour on it. Will you do that? Will you give it to me?'

"She didn't say anything, but she nodded.

" 'I want you to promise me that when you're gone, if there's any possible way for you to speak to me, or send me a message – make any kind of signal of any sort – to say that there's another life after the life we know here, another existence on the other side of the grave, you won't do it. Will you give me your solemn promise about that, Aunt Elspeth? Please? And mean it?'

"She didn't say anything more after that, just lay there and glared at me. I wanted to go, and I tried to a couple of times, but I couldn't make myself do it. There she was, about the only person still left from my childhood, and she was dying – would probably die that night, they had said. So I sat there instead, and I wanted to take her hand but I couldn't because of the oxygen tent, and she kept on glaring at me and making those horrible sounds trying to breathe, and neither of us said anything. It must have been for about an hour.

"I guess I shut my eyes – I know I didn't want to look at her – and leaned back in the chair. And then, all of a sudden, the noises stopped. I leaned forward and turned on the little light at the head of her bed, and she wasn't trying to breathe any more. She was still glaring as if she wanted to run me through a grinder, but when I got up and took a step toward the door, her eyes didn't move. So I knew she was dead, and I ought to call the nurse or something, but I didn't."

Rab fell silent at that point, and Bruce said, "What did you do?"

"I just went out. Out of room, and out of the Intensive Care Wing, and out into the corridor. It was a pretty long corridor, and I had to walk, oh, maybe a hundred steps before I came to the waiting room. It was late by then, and there was only one person in it, and that one person was me."

Rab gave us a chance to say something, but neither of us did.

"I don't mean I went in. I didn't. I just stood out in the corridor and looked inside. And there I was, sitting in there. I had on a black turtleneck and a whiskey-colored suede sports jacket. I remember that, because I've never owned those clothes. It was my face behind my glasses, though. It was even my haircut. He – I – was reading *Reader's Digest* and didn't see me. But I saw myself, and I must have stood there for five minutes just staring at him.

"Then a nurse pushed past me and said, 'You can go in and see your aunt now, Mister Sammon.' He put down his magazine and stood up and said, 'Call me Rab.' And she smiled and said, 'You can see your Aunt Elspeth now, Rab.'

"I stepped out of the way and the nurse and I went past me and down the corridor toward the Intensive Care Wing. I watched till they had gone through the big double doors and I couldn't see them any more. Then I went into the waiting room and picked up that copy of the *Reader's Digest* that I had laid down and slipped it into my pocket, and went home and went to bed. I still have it, but I've never gotten up the nerve to read it."

Rab sighed. "That's my story. I don't imagine that yours will be true – I know both of you too well for that. But mine is."

"When you woke up in the morning, was your aunt still dead?" Bruce wanted to know.

Rab said, "Yes, of course. The hospital called me at work."

That bothered me, and I said, "When you started telling us about this, you said that there was a message from the hospital on your answering machine when you got home from the office. So the hospital didn't have your number there, presumably at least."

Rab nodded. "I suppose he gave it to them."

Nobody said much after that, and pretty soon we undressed and got into our sleeping bags. When we had been asleep for two or three hours, Rab screamed.

It brought me bolt upright, and Bruce, too. I sat up just in time to see Rab scream again. Then he blinked and looked around and said, "Somebody yelled. Did you hear it?"

Bruce was a great deal wiser than I. He said, "It was an animal, Rab. Maybe an owl. Go back to sleep."

Rab lay back down, and so did I; but I did not go back to sleep. I lay awake looking at the clouds, the moon, and the stars, and thinking about that midnight hospital waiting room in which the man who stood outside sat reading a magazine, wondering just how much power the recently dead may have to twist our reality, and their own.

There actually was something shrieking up on the bluff, but I cannot say with any confidence what it was. A wildcat, perhaps, or a cougar.

DAVID CASE

Jimmy

DAVID CASE'S FIRST COLLECTION, *The Cell: Three Tales of Horror*, appeared in 1969. It was followed by the novels *Fengriffen: A Chilling Tale*, *Wolf Tracks* and *The Third Grave*, which appeared from Arkham House. More recently, a new collection entitled *Brotherly Love and Other Tales of Faith and Knowledge* was published by Pumpkin Books. Outside the horror genre, Case has written more than three hundred books under at least seventeen pseudonyms, ranging from porn to Westerns. Two of his short stories. "Fengriffen" and the classic werewolf thriller "The Hunter", were filmed as —*And Now the Screaming Starts!* (1973) and *Scream of the Wolf* (1974), respectively. Meanwhile his first Western, *Plumb Drillin'*, which was originally set to be a movie starring the late Steve McQueen, has recently been re-optioned.

"I wrote an original, longer version of 'Jimmy' while living on a lake in Texas," reveals Case. "I had no particular idea about what to write and had always thought that by beginning with 'Once upon a time . . .' a story would follow. Sure enough, it did. I sent it to a useless agent who said it could not be published as the theme would offend the feminists. I put the manuscript away and forgot about it.

"Sometime later, back in London again, I recalled it, couldn't find the manuscript and wrote the shorter version from memory. Later, I found the original and discovered that the two versions are quite different."

I

O NCE UPON A TIME the last dinosaur came stomping through the primaeval mire, erect and alert and seeking its kind. It hooted forlornly and bellowed dismally, its tiny brain confused, for it could not know it was the very last in the whole wide world and its instinct cried out for a mate, the primal urge to reproduce in full control. It was a flesh-eater and there was plenty to eat, although the slow, clumsy plant-eaters had long since vanished, and from time to time the last dinosaur snatched up a small soft, scurrying animal and gulped it down, eating from fierce habit as the opportunity arose. Eating was subsidiary and incidental to its hopeless quest, nor did it know the furry creatures it devoured were largely responsible for its plight, having a taste for dinosaur eggs. The last dinosaur lived a long, long time, never knowing quite what he lusted for and never having bred. His corrupting body made a massive feast for the newly emerged, warm-blooded things and they survived and evolved through the aeons and, in time, came mankind, sprung from their loins and genes.

Now something else unique walked the land and it was the first of its kind . . .

II

Some millions of years later there was a town not far from where the last dinosaur had died, a small mountain village called Bleekerville with one main street which was also the highway running through. There was no home delivery of mail in Bleekerville and everyone got their mail at the post office which was on the main street and where Ben Marvin, as the only employee, was post master. Ben was bald and belligerent and hated being a civil servant. He seldom got a letter himself and never sent one, and he resented those who corresponded faithfully for causing him work. Ben would much rather have been on strike, like the Canadians and the Limeys always were or, even better, getting paid overtime to clear up the mess the strike had caused. But still, he functioned efficiently and the mail came in and went out. Two letters, both handwritten, had been despatched from that post office some fifteen years apart and both had reached their destination.

Dear Dr Franken,

I was reading in a magazine about how you can fix a woman who cannot bear children. Our own doctor give this magazine to me so I know it is genuine and not like things you read in newspapers on Sundays. I am wondering if you can cure me? Homer and me have tried very hard but there is no baby and we are both sad and want a child, a boy is better but a girl is all right and we would not complain. Our farm is prosperous and the bank says we can take out a second mortgage and if you can help us we will give anything. I am 42 and Homer is 45 but we are healthy and hope it is not too late. I will wait to hear from you if there is something you can do.

Yrs. truly,
Ethel Potter

Dear Daddy,

I hope you won't be terribly disappointed but I have decided to take a summer job instead of coming home when school gets out. I answered an ad in the paper and was asked to come for an interview and I was really surprised to be offered the position. I'll be working for a doctor in Bleekerville. You probably won't know where that is, but it's not too far from college and it's a lovely little town in the mountains, with a lake not far away and really brilliant colours in the trees at this time of year. I'm not quite sure what my duties will entail. Just a sort of Girl Friday, I guess – I'm sure not qualified for anything more. Maybe (boast, brag) the doctor just wants a pretty girl to glamorise his office. But he seems like a nice old guy and the pay is really good and I get room and board as well. It seems a shame to pass up such an opportunity and, also, to save enough from my wages so I won't be a financial burden on you, although I know you've never objected to that. I'm quite excited about starting work, whatever it turns out to be; it makes me feel real grown up to have a job. Don't be too awfully disappointed Daddy. I'll send you more details as soon as I'm settled in and in the meanwhile, you can write me at the post office box number above.

Any news from the globe-trotting artist, ha ha? All for now.
Love,
Rebecca.

What connection could these two letters sent from the same post office fifteen years apart possibly have?

III

Choice Lovelady pulled the patrol car up in front of the Wormwood house, under the trees, and sat behind the wheel for a while with the motor running, wondering if he should turn the car around and drive back to town without stopping.

He was feeling guilty.

Choice was the chief of police and figured he ought to know right from wrong. Well, he did, come to that, but it didn't signify if you did the wrong thing, anyhow. It sure made him feel like a hypocrite when he had to arrest some guy for a minor offence, though. The fact that Dick Wormwood was his friend and his deputy to boot made it worse. Choice could send Wormwood off on some police business at any time, knowing how long it would take and that the coast would be clear and it seemed an act of corruption as well as perfidy. Choice guessed it was always wrong to have an affair with a married woman, but it wasn't so bad with the wife of a stranger – although he didn't suppose the stranger would feel that way about it, when you came right down to it.

He almost drove off.

But then Hilda Wormwood came to the door, all smiling and happy to see him and it was too late. What Dick didn't know wouldn't hurt him, Choice reasoned, and it sure would as hell hurt Hilda if he didn't stop. He sighed and turned the ignition off and got out of the cruiser.

He was tall and lean and handsome, but he wore his pants low on his hips and his hat low on his brow and he walked with his torso arched just as if he was a redneck sheriff with a beer belly. He didn't know why he did that. Choice was an educated man but he just couldn't figure it out and guessed it was part of the image.

Hilda, auburn haired and buxom, offered him a cup of coffee but they both knew it was only a formality and when he declined she led him straight to the bedroom.

"How long do we have?" she asked breathlessly.

Sometimes his visits were slam bam.

"I sent Dick down to the county seat," Choice replied, with a twinge of shame.

"Oh, that's all right then," she said enthusiastically and, being shameless herself, she began to remove her clothing immediately. After a moment Choice followed suit and his reluctance and guilt began to recede under a surge of desire. But he knew it would be there, lurking just below the surface, ready to bubble up again when it was over.

Choice lay back in Wormwood's marital bed, satisfied and waiting patiently for a sense of shame to creep over him in the aftermath. Hilda snuggled against him in contentment. He wondered if she ever felt any guilt about it and had even asked her once, But she'd told him that her husband – his friend and deputy – never satisfied her and seemed to believe that justified adultery completely. Her auburn head was cuddled to his shoulder and he turned to whisper in her ear. But he couldn't find the words to tell her he intended to end their relationship and his lips moved soundlessly. Hilda thought it a nibble of affection and purred, making it all the harder.

Next time, he told himself.

He was looking towards the window, through a halo of her heavy hair. The window, shaded by overhanging boughs, was a pale oblong in the wall.

Choice blinked and frowned and stiffened.

For a terrible moment he had thought there was a face at that window, peering in intently – some rural voyeur or, worse, Dick Wormwood come home unexpectedly!

But when he looked again there was no one there and it hadn't looked much like a face, at that, just sort of face-shaped.

Choice guessed it had been a trick of the light and shadow. Then, for a fanciful moment, he wondered if it had been his conscience looking in?

The idea disturbed him and, although Hilda hinted about an encore, he left soon after that . . .

IV

Her name was Molly Carlyle but her father thought it was Ratbag for, in his indignation and being lumbered with a child, and drunk with it, he had written that name on her birth certificate form. Luckily, her mother, more kindly and sober, crossed it out and named her Molly. But she was a dutiful and obedient wife and never dared tell her husband what she had done, so Molly's father had always assumed that her legal name was Ratbag and that she only told people it was Molly for obvious reasons. When he was drunk he resented the fact that she had renounced the name by which she had been christened. Even the doctor who had delivered her called her Molly and it galled her father grievously. He often became abusive. That was one of the reasons why Molly had run away from home.

Now she used no name at all and had destroyed her identification documents, fearing she might be found out as a runaway minor and sent back home. She was sixteen and attractive and had been on the road for several weeks now, misbehaving when she got the chance.

Slim and lithe, if somewhat unwashed, she was walking down the dusty highway backwards, ready to hitchhike if a car came along but not much caring. It was a fine day and beautiful in the mountains and she was content to walk for a while.

When she saw a car approaching she started to hook her thumb up. Then she saw it was a police car and she thought, *Oh hell*, and stepped off the road into the trees, hoping she had not been seen. She moved back aways, ready to run if the car stopped. But it went on past. It was Choice Lovelady on his way back from Hilda Wormwood's and, intent on his own guilt, he hadn't seen the guilty little girl at all.

Not so very long ago, compared to the age of dinosaurs, this had been an untamed land and a mountain man named Joshua Crowe had set his traps and sold his pelts and lived in a shack with a squaw. One of his traps was meant for bear. There weren't many bear around in his day but he set the trap anyhow, not knowing what else to do with it. In due course, Crowe died of natural causes and his squaw moved away but the bear trap remained.

It was still there, heavily rusted and covered by moss and humus – and it was still coiled to spring, like some cold-blooded creature waiting with reptilian patience, jaws agape, for a passing meal. It wasn't far back from the highway, although there had been no highway when Crowe had placed it there.

Into this brutal and aging device stepped Molly Carlyle as she moved back to avoid the law.

The action was delayed, as if the springs, dormant through the years, had forgotten their function. The rust yielded with a grinding sound that caused the girl to look down in alarm. A layer of earth crumbled. Then the trap exploded with savage speed and the jaws snapped closed on Molly's slender ankle.

In awkward slow motion, she sat down, not knowing what had happened. She felt around, brushing loose earth away to discover the rusted clamp that held her. The pain climbed up her leg, but it wasn't as bad as she would have supposed; she guessed it would get worse. She could feel the bones shifting and knew that her ankle had been broken and the blood seeped out slowly. Her blood was exactly the same colour as the rust and, in shock, she found that remarkable.

She couldn't pry the trap open. She was twisted in an awkward position and couldn't get much leverage, nor was she very strong. She didn't panic and looked around for a broken branch or limb or an elongated stone she could use as a wedge, but all she found was a brittle stick that snapped immediately. She tugged at the trap but it was secure on a length of twisted chain and it hurt too much to try to pull it free. She started to panic a bit then. What if no one came along and found her? How long could a girl live without food and water and shelter? She began to shout, nor even caring if a cop should find her now. Even the comforts of her father's room and board were better than being in a bear trap. Her thoughts moved in strange patterns. She had always been kind to animals and protested against blood sports and the killing of baby seals; this was a strange reward. But she couldn't blame the bears. She even thought about suing whoever had set that trap and getting handsome compensation and she relished that revenge. But it didn't solve her problem. She struggled to free herself, paused to scream, struggled some more. She clenched her teeth and jerked back violently and the teeth just dug in deeper and the broken bones drew apart. Half her screams were deliberate cries for help and half were of pure agony.

When the bushes parted and a face looked out, Molly gave a cry of relief. Then she made a different sound, when she saw it was not someone come to rescue her – and that it wasn't quite human . . .

V

Unlike a man who thought he had named his daughter Ratbag, John Baltimore had always been a good father and he and Rebecca had grown even closer since her mother left. Baltimore had been a good husband, too, but that hadn't prevented his wife from going off to, as she put it, seek her own identity. John presumed it was some sort of mid-life crisis which he didn't understand. He hadn't even objected much. Jenny Baltimore had packed her bags and her art supplies and gone off to Europe to become a famous artist or a Bohemian or whatever. It had given him a bitter amusement, since he had paid for her classes at art school and knew full well she had no talent at all.

Jenny had been gone for two years now, her letters were infrequent and he couldn't say he missed her much. She never asked him for money and he supposed she was living in sin with some passionate patron of the arts. What, he wondered, would she find more glamourous – living in luxury with an Italian Count or in paupery in a Parisian garret? It was hard to say. Jenny was Jenny. She'd insisted the family car was a Volkswagen; now, at least, John drove a Cadillac.

But if he didn't miss Jenny noticeably, he missed Rebecca a great deal.

He hadn't heard from her in quite a while now and his last letter had been returned by the post office marked "Gone Away, No Forwarding Address".

John hoped she had not gone off to find herself.

He was getting worried.

At college, he had wrestled with some success and he was still fit and athletic, looking much sterner a man than he was. Abandoned by his spouse, he was supposed available and vulnerable and several of his wife's good friends, both married and not, had made investigative approaches. John had declined courteously and they thought him heartbroken. But in fact he was reasonably content with his bachelor life, although at times growing restless when he thought about Rebecca. John was a man who reacted rather than initiated and he was waiting for something to cause a reaction, although he didn't know it. Rebecca's framed photograph was beside the telephone, as if he wanted to make a connection. He looked at it often. She was slim and suntanned and golden. She would make some lucky man a good wife, he knew; she would make him a proud grandfather. But why had she stopped writing, why hadn't she phoned? Brooding over that, he would pace about the house as randomly as an Englishman looking for a queue to join.

Ethel Porter stood on the steps of the farm house and looked across the fields and trembled slightly. Her faded gingham dress fluttered in the breeze. Her old face was deeply lined and her eyes were haunted. She had not been quite right in the head for some time now, but she realized that so it couldn't be too serious. She wanted to call out. But she could hear the tractor in the north field and she was afraid that Homer would hear her if she called out aloud, so she only whispered it.

"Jimmy—"

She was going to have to confess to Homer when he came in and she wasn't looking forward to that, at all. He was a good husband and he never the once beat her, even though she felt she deserved it for failing him as a wife. He might beat her over this, though, and it would be justified. Homer had warned her so many times, stressing it as to a child. But it didn't seem natural to her to live the way they did and always to remember to lock the door of the special room. It hadn't always been necessary. They had always kept the tragedy a secret, but it was less than a year since all that caution and door locking had begun – since the last time he had been taken for treatment and it was might strange treatment that made things worse. How could she be expected to remember things like doors and locks? He had never run away before. Ethel had let him out without telling Homer and he'd come right back home. Well, he was a teenager; might be it was normal.

Jimmy—" she called, not loudly.

The blonde girl who could not remember who she was lay in bed and puzzled over it. She must be in a hospital room, she thought. She knew she was heavy with child. But she could not remember that having happened either, and she felt certain she had never been promiscuous. How strange it all was. How ironic, too. Her father had expected her to marry and have children and now she was soon to make him a grandfather. She recalled that clear as a bell. But she couldn't remember her father's name either. It was as if she suffered from some selective amnesia. Strangest of all, she felt rather contented. She would have expected to be panicky and distraught but she was calm and placid.

The doctor was a kindly man who came in frequently. Strange there were no nurses, though. She tried to search down through the flat calm of her mind and remember things. Sometimes, she almost did. But then the kindly doctor would stop by with his soothing medication and it would all fade away again.

She lay back, one hand on her rounded belly, perfectly comfortable. She was trying the remember the doctor's name and her own name and her father's name. She didn't think about her mother at all – and would have found that remarkable, had it occurred to her.

Molly Carlyle lay back too, but she wasn't at all comfortable with her foot locked in a bear trap and something very scary coming towards her.

It came slowly.

Molly screamed and screamed.

VI

As it happened, it was a lawman who heard Molly's cries, but it wasn't Choice Lovelady, it was Dick Wormwood on his way back from the county seat where he'd been sent on an errand he thought frivolous. It was pure chance he was there. He had pulled the patrol car to the side of the road so he would have both hands free to fill his battered briar pipe. But really he had stopped to consider something and the pipe and tobacco was only an excuse to stop.

Wormwood was wondering whether he should continue straight into town or stop at his house. There was no reason not to stop. Choice wouldn't know he was goofing off on duty and he would welcome a glass of beer at his own fireside.

The only thing was, Hilda might get to acting kittenish. He loved her and all, but she was always after him for sex, nagging and whining and complaining. He hadn't realized she was oversexed when he'd asked her to marry him. But then, maybe he had been more vigorous and venial in their courting days, as well. Now they had been man and wife so long it wasn't seemly to couple like crazed weasels day and night. Once a week suited him just fine, preferably on Saturday night. Still, Hilda hadn't been quite so demanding of late and he guessed he would risk it.

Then he heard the screams.

Lost in concentration and puffing on his pipe, the unexpected sounds didn't register at once. He was thinking that a man needed his breakfast cooked and a woman deserved a new bonnet two or three times a year and lawfully wedded folks hadn't ought to need all that hanky panky. Then he cocked his head and listened, frowning.

Wormwood often forgot he was a lawman.

But he remembered it now and figured it was his duty to investigate. He got out of the car, his pipe still clenched in his teeth, and moved into the trees. He called out. There was an answering scream and a scurrying in the bushes. A figure loomed up, twisting, vague in the shadows. There was something odd about the way it moved. Wormwood gaped and it never dawned on him to draw his gun. He stepped forward and the indistinct figure crashed through the undergrowth, all loose and lanky and spinning. Wormwood was more puzzled than alarmed. What in hell was going on? He moved after the fleeing figure but made no attempt to pursue it or command it to halt.

Looking after it, he had walked right up to the girl on the ground before he was aware of her. He looked down as she screamed yet again. Wormwood was a gentle man, although a lawman; when he saw the condition of the young girl in the trap, he turned ashen.

"Aw, jeez—" he said.

There was only one doctor in general practice in Bleekerville, although there was a clinic with a resident intern that the doctor considered a whippersnapper. Doc Tuttle was grey and ageing and had once been infamous for his moribund bedside manner. But that had been a decade ago and he was more considerate now. He had examined a lumberjack, those ten years past and had bluntly informed the man he had but six months to live. The lumberjack had gaped at him.

"Why would you tell a man a thing like that, Doc?" the man had said.

"Why because it's true," Tuttle replied.

"Yeah, but that ain't no cause to tell me, Doc; that is surely not right," the lumberjack protested. He was genuinely affronted.

Doc Tuttle, quite enjoying it, said, "Well, now that you know, you can get your affairs in order, you see." It seemed quite reasonable to him.

But not to the lumberjack, whose name was Bill Grimm and who said, "I got no affairs."

Doc Tuttle spread his hands out, not understanding Grimm's attitude. Grimm glared. It was like a chicken talking to sheep.

"I only got six months, huh?" Grimm muttered.

Then he said, "Well, happens that I might outlive you, come to that, Doc . . ."

He stood up, knocking his chair over and marched out of the consulting room and a few minutes later he marched right back in, without an appointment but with a double barrelled shotgun which he aimed with determination at Doc Tuttle's startled head.

"You got six minutes to live, Doc," the lumberjack diagnosed.

Doc Tuttle, too horrified to protest, stared into the big, smooth barrels and thought he was about to die.

"Best to see about getting your affairs in order, Doc," Grimm suggested. But Tuttle just sat there and looked back and forth between the shotgun and the clock on the wall and six minutes, seeming eternal, crept by. Then Grimm grunted and lowered the gun.

"Now you know how it feels, Doc, and might be you have learned a lesson," he said and left.

The event had a profound effect on Doc Tuttle and his bedside manner became far more mild and ambivalent.

That had been ten years ago and, as it happened, Bill Grimm was still alive, and so was the doctor, and it was to Tuttle's surgery that Dick Wormwood brought Molly Carlyle from her ordeal . . .

A tight-faced farmer stood in front of a big oak door and removed his frayed straw hat. Then he put it back on again, indecisively, as if not sure whether deference and respect was called for. With the hat on, he knocked on the door loudly and after a minute, a man in a white coat opened it.

"Ah, Homer . . . it will not be long now; soon you will be—"

the man in white began. Then he noticed the farmer's expression and frowned. He was an imposing figure and now, before he spoke, the farmer snatched his hat off again.

"You have not been a friend to us," he said.

The statement was evidently an exordium, but the farmer fell silent and, after a time and with a sigh, the other man spoke.

"There were miscalculations which I regret, as I have often told you," he said patiently. "My . . . our . . . hope is that the flaws will not be passed on to the next generation. Ahhh, Homer, pray it is so. Think, man! To time-warp evolution! To cause, with your genes, the creation of—"

He stopped abruptly as the farmer continued to stare balefully at him. It was obvious the man had something to say and didn't want to say it.

"Is it Ethel?" asked the man in white, softly, feeling responsible for her condition.

The farmer bowed his head.

"She has left the door open," he said.

Nothing more needed to be said. They looked at each other and the farmer looked worried; and the man in the white coat, who knew a lot more about it than did the farmer, looked a lot more worried . . .

John Baltimore was also worried.

He had not been happy when Rebecca wrote that she was taking a summer job and wouldn't be coming home for the school break, but he accepted it and had no wish to interfere in her life. When, later, she wrote that she had decided to suspend her education for a year, he accepted that as well, and even looked on the bright side, knowing she was working and living in a small town where the near occasion of sin would be slight, no problem with drugs or promiscuity such as plagued modern youth – not that he could imagine Rebecca ever being like that. She had always been a sweet, wholesome, old fashioned girl and never expressed the least desire to become a famous artist.

Her letters from Bleekerville had been frequent and cheerful. She was well satisfied with her job, if somewhat mystified at being paid so handsomely for doing so little. Yet they were vague too. She neglected to answer his casual questions and had never thought to send him a telephone number or the name of the doctor for whom she worked and her return address remained a post office box, that most neutral of things. But then her letters had arrived less often and became increasingly vague and disjointed and rambling and, now, he had had no word from her in months and his own letter had been returned and it was cause for concern.

John had phoned her college and it had confirmed that she had not returned, which he had expected – but he also learned that she had made no arrangements to suspend her education, she had simply not arrived when the new term began, which had annoyed the administrators and was not at all like Rebecca, a thoughtful girl who seldom acted on impulse.

John had been fretting and didn't know quite what to do about it. Possibilities sprang to mind: that she was living with a man out of wedlock and, ashamed, had fallen silent or that some adventurous trait inherited from her wandering mother had surfaced and that, too, she found too shameful to express. But in any event, it was so out of character for Rebecca to stay out of touch, knowing he would be worried and had no way to contact her, that he felt it must be something more, that there must be some logical reason for her lack of communication. Several times he had been on the point of driving to Bleekerville, but he had always resisted the urge, not wanting to show up like an "eat your peas" parent or a shotgun wedding organiser. So he waited and he read her letters over and over and he looked at her picture and at the telephone and he waited for something to which he could react.

VII

It was the first time that Dick Wormwood had ever drawn his gun in the course of his duty and then it was only to use the barrel to pry open the rusted bear trap, so it wasn't relevant. The girl was stunned and silent, sobbing without sound and staring at Wormwood in a sort of wary gratitude. Her clothing had been torn to shreds and her flesh showed through bloody. Wormwood thought it looked as if she'd been savaged by an animal, but he didn't look too closely, embarrassed by her exposure. A cop wasn't like a doctor, he figured, and had no mandate to peer at private parts.

He carried her to the patrol car and drove straight to Doc

Tuttle's without even using the radio, his pipe still clenched in his teeth, forgotten and cold, the stem chewed half through.

Wormwood left the girl in Tuttle's surgery and phoned the chief of police while Tuttle was examining her. Choice came in before the examination was over, looking a lot more official than he usually did. They stood in the doctor's office, amidst the book-lined walls, two tall men looking out of place in that setting. Wormwood gave him the details and Choice looked grim.

"What a thing! Lucky I happened along. Wasn't far from my house, matter of fact," Wormwood added, feeling guilty because he'd been going home for a beer and hoping Choice didn't think to ask why he'd been there. But Choice had his own guilt feelings about his deputy's house, although they were subdued now by outrage at such a criminal act. Things like that didn't happen in Bleekerville, within his jurisdiction; you didn't want to hear about them there in a doctor's office.

"What a thing," Wormwood said again. "There the poor kid was, her leg in a bear-trap, broken – and some guy comes along fixing to rape her!"

"Did he?"

Wormwood, uncomfortable with such subjects, blushed slightly. "Don't know. She didn't say, Choice. Didn't say nothing, come to that; guess she was in a state of shock and who can blame her?"

"You get a look at the bastard, Dick?"

"Just a glimpse. He must of heard me coming and hightailed it out of there. He was just ducking into the trees when I come upon it. Lanky fella, loose jointed, kind of herky jerky, you know?" He levered his elbows and forearms in demonstration.

Choice figured he should be writing these things down, but he didn't have his notebook.

"Didn't recognize him, then?" he said.

"Why, no. If I had . . ."

"No, no. It's just that I was thinking – what if it was some local fella? Jeez. How we gonna look at some guy we've known all our lives, we got to arrest him for a thing like this?"

"Yeah; well, he was unknown to me, glimpse that I got; likely a stranger passing through, huh? I'd wager on that, make it easier, we catch him."

"Um hum. Well. You happen to see what he was wearing,

Dick. What kind of clothing he had on? Like, maybe, he was
wearing a suit and tie, some city fella?

"Well, now, that is odd, Choice. Looked to me as he was
wearing . . . well . . . pyjamas," Wormwood mumbled. It
sounded daft to him and Choice blinked.

"I'll say it's odd. A guy bent on rape don't wear pyjamas like he
was going to a normal bed . . . Maybe we got some real loony
here . . ."

"Could be I was mistaken."

Choice peered at his friend and deputy and husband of his
mistress, knowing him well. "Don't suppose you had time to get
off a warning shot, huh?"

Wormwood, to whom it had not occurred, looked sheepish.
But he saw no castigation in Choice's gaze.

"Naw, no time for that," he muttered, and old Doc Tuttle came
in, wiping his hands . . .

Tuttle was looking puzzled and relieved and maybe a bit excited
at having been presented with such an egregious consultation.

"Well, she's going to be all right," he stated. "Her ankle is
broken but that was caused by the trap. She wasn't raped' – I'd
say that Dick arrived just in time to prevent it."

Wormwood, embarrassed about the gun, was pleased to hear
that.

"Her other wounds—" Doc started.

"There was plenty of blood," Wormwood put in.

"— were superficial," Tuttle continued. "It doesn't give me the
impression her attacker meant to savage her. It's more like he had
very long fingernails and just sort of scratched her incidentally in
the throes of passion and tearing at her clothing—"

Choice and Wormwood digested that fact – two men who often
had their own backs clawed painfully by the same enthusiastic
lady.

"Well, I've cleaned her up and dressed the wounds – just
scratches, really, as I said. I'd best phone the clinic and arrange
a room for her to recover . . ."

"Okay to talk to her, Doc?" Choice asked, not relishing the
prospect at all.

"I'd think so. She's disturbed, of course, and confused, but
lucid."

Choice went through to the surgery and Tuttle went to the telephone and Wormwood just stood where he was.

Now that it was over and she was safe, Molly Carlyle felt as if it had been a nightmare she'd awakened from, with a sense of total unreality. Even while the attack had been taking place, she had felt as much outraged as scared; now she felt more soiled than injured – abused, but she was used to that. She even felt scandalized. How could anyone do such a thing? And, come to that, what had that thing been? All she wanted now was a comfortable bed and some peace and she wasn't too happy when the chief of police came in and stood over her. He had his hat in his hand and looked friendly and concerned, just like any visitor at a hospital bed. When he asked her name she thought about it and decided not to tell him. Choice, who could not begin to imagine how a young lady must feel after such a hideous ordeal, didn't press it.

"I just couldn't believe it," she said. "I thought he had come to help me and he . . ." she grimaced. Choice saw she was pretty and had lilac eyes.

"Can you describe him, miss?"

"He was strange . . ."

"Well, I'd say so. But . . ."

"Never saw a thing like it . . . like he was wearing a Halloween mask, 'cept it wasn't a mask. I don't know. His face looked like it was forked out of a lump of sulphur . . . he had incandescent eyes . . ."

Choice was struck by the description, but didn't grasp it. He had an image of an Oriental with a bad case of acne.

"This man . . ." he began.

"Well, that's what was so strange," she said. "Maybe it wasn't a man . . ."

"Huh? Did an animal . . ."

"No, not an animal," she whispered. "But maybe not quite human, either . . ."

Choice guessed the girl was in deeper shock than she seemed and placed no credit in her statement. He figured to let her rest and then talk to her again, at the clinic. She wasn't making sense now. But then he suddenly remembered the face that may or may not have been looking into Hilda Wormwood's bedroom.

Very distinctly, vertebra by vertebra, Choice felt ice crawl up his spine . . .

VIII

There was a local newspaper, the *Bleekerville Eagle*, but it only came out once a week, on Fridays, so Art Slotnik, who was the only reporter, was thankful the girl had been attacked on Thursday. Slotnik was a scrawny, pale-eyed man with a big Adam's apple that went up and down his neck like a toy monkey on a stick. He wore a battered fedora pushed back on his brow and his necktie at half mast. Slotnik had proper newsman's instincts and when he heard about the girl it was like manna from Heaven. It was bizarre and it was horrific. A simple rape would not have been fascinating, but the gruesome details of this assault were just to his taste. The fact that she had been caught in a trap – and a bear trap, to boot – and that a man, hearing her cries for help, had attempted to rape her instead of freeing her, was the stuff of a reporter's dreams. The girl was even young and pretty as a bonus.

Of course, it would have been even better if he had succeeded in raping her, but a man couldn't have everything and Slotnik could hardly blame Dick Wormwood for interfering. The affair was cruel and callous and brutal, nectar and ambrosia to Slotnik. The fact that her description of her attacker was so weird didn't strike him as very meaningful, though, and he decided to play that angle down. It was only natural that such a man would be abnormal looking and, too, Slotnik was inclined to believe he had worn a mask. The *Eagle* was a tabloid in format but not in content, not sold at supermarket checkout counters and the details were lurid enough without sensationalism. Slotnik debated phoning the wire services but decided to wait and enjoy an exclusive scoop in the *Eagle*.

Molly lay in bed in a private room at the clinic with a cast on her leg and, all in all, she felt pretty good. The pain wasn't too bad and the wounds on her face and torso little more than scratches. They itched more than they hurt. It was the first time she'd had a bed and regular meals in weeks and she didn't even have to wash the dishes afterwards and she liked the fuss that was being made over her. She talked willingly to Slotnik and would have granted all the interviews asked of her, although she refused to give her name and was leery that her father might see her picture published. The mystery of remaining nameless charmed her; it was a revenge on her father, in a way. The attack in itself hadn't been any great trauma. She had lost her maidenhood long ago and, anyhow, the rape had not come to fulfilment. What did trouble her, though, was remembering what he had looked like and wondering what he had been. She thought of her assailant as he, for he obviously was male, but she wasn't at all sure he was a man. She recalled him in detail – most of all his enthusiasm.

Another girl lay in a similar bed and couldn't remember any details at all. Sometimes memory seemed about to rise to the surface but then the doctor, who seemed distracted and distressed today, gave her her relaxing medication and her memory submerged again and no longer seemed important.

There was never much crime in Bleekerville and Choice wasn't sure this had been much of a crime, either. The girl still refused to give him her name and if it hadn't been for the scratches and the fact that Wormwood had seen her attacker, Choice would have been inclined to think she was making it up or at least embellishing it. Some guy had found her and no doubt he was bent on rape, but it was only attempted rape, not so easy to prove, along with a case of assault. The man was probably not local, for rapists were not common in Bleekerville, and he had most likely moved on and if he tried it again, some other cop could deal with it. In fact, Choice was moralist enough to feel embarrassed by having such a thing as rape, even aborted rape, in his jurisdiction.

Choice and Wormwood had returned to the place before dark and poked around for clues, both feeling silly. They weren't Indian trackers; what did they hope to find? Actually, to his surprise, Choice did find a scrap of cotton on a thorn bush and it did look like pyjama material, at which both men shrugged and made no deductions. They took the rusted trap away but didn't consider dusting it for fingerprints, since the guy hadn't tried to free her. Wormwood went home and Choice returned to town, passing the Potter farm as it was growing dark – and on the porch of that farm an old woman kept her vigil and shivered as it got colder and worried that her son would catch a chill, wearing only his pyjamas.

*   *   *

Loose limbed, elastic, mute, flawed, a figure loped through the forest, head turning on a neck that twisted more than a neck was meant to. He was tired and hungry and knew where food and warmth were available, but its hunger was not yet compelling. It was less than human, but more, too, with senses and instincts not yet evolved in man and, in the gathering dusk, it came down from the hills behind the clinic, nostrils flaring, lips dragged back in a grimace, drawn to the mate that had been denied him. The clinic was a single-story building backing into the woods. He knew what window to go to.

Molly was mildly sedated and no sound alerted her. She just happened to turn towards the window as a face loomed up. Her mouth dropped open; his mouth was open; they seemed to be screaming silently at one another through the glass. Then Molly screamed aloud. The face at the window ducked away as the grey-haired nurse came in. She listened as Molly babbled, then went to the window and looked out, seeing no intruder.

"You were dreaming, child," she said.

Molly was half inclined to believe that as well. But the impression was solid enough. On later reflection, Molly thought he had looked just like a deprived child pressing his nose to the window of a candy store. She no longer felt so relaxed.

The *Bleekerville Eagle* had a small circulation, nearly all locals interested in church socials and what was playing at the cinema and who had been arrested for being drunk during the week. A few copies were mailed each week to people who had moved away and wanted to keep track of the dull news from home. One copy was sent, however, to a man who had never been in Bleekerville. He had written to the local chamber of commerce which was only a desk at the back of the hardware store, enclosing a blank cheque and asking for a subscription to be arranged. This was John Baltimore who, without much hope for it, thought there was always a chance that, in such a small community, his daughter might be mentioned, although he couldn't imagine why.

He had been receiving the *Eagle* for some weeks now and usually skimmed it casually. He was suitably shocked when he read Slotnik's account of the attack. John didn't connect it with

Rebecca right away, just thought such a vicious assault remarkable in a rural town she had told him was so dull and routine. He saw that the victim's name was not given, nor was there a picture. But that was understandable, protecting the identity of a young girl so brutally attacked. But Rebecca was a young girl and he hadn't heard from her in ages and he sat hard faced and thoughtful, crumbling the newspaper. It seemed most unlikely that it had been Rebecca but it wasn't an overlong journey to Bleekerville. Baltimore madeup his mind to drive there, and did so . . .

IX

The man in the white coat had lived nearby for fifteen years and had never taken the *Eagle*, nor any other newspaper, although he subscribed to a number of scientific journals. But when the farmer who was his nearest neighbour, and more, brought him a copy, he read Slotnik's report with a certain interest. He learned nothing from it. It was precisely the behaviour he would have predicted and it was a shame she had left the door unlocked. He was a disappointed man, but felt no guilt. Sacrifices had to be made in the cause of science, and nature itself was a history of failures and false starts and dead ends. Through all time, creatures had evolved, been found lacking and become extinct. A man would be vain, indeed, to believe he could get it right the first time, when nature seldom had.

And now nature had made its biggest blunder by experimenting with the big brain – a trial that threatened its own sovereignty. Man controlled the elements and held his own fate in human hands and evolution had ground to a halt as civilization spread. The strongest no longer bred more prolifically; a frail man was able to mate as easily as a healthy one; females were no longer dragged by their hair to a lair. With Cro-Magnon mankind had evolved as far as the race needed to progress and now survival of the fittest was no longer applicable. A catalyst was needed to spark a surge from stagnancy. To time-warp evolution, he had told the farmer, who dimly understood.

And having failed, like nature, he would try again.

There was a coffee-stained copy of the *Eagle* on the zinc counter of the Good News Cafe just west of town and Rocco Spetches looked at it as he sipped his beer from the bottle. He was a big, bearded man wearing a black leather jacket with buckskin thongs and he had a motorcycle parked outside. He found the report titillating and, on the whole, he approved of rape. Rocco was drinking slowly. He only had enough money for the one beer and he was hoping some wimp would come in and, intimidated, buy him another. When Rocco growled, wimps went for their wallets. When he heard a car pull into the lot he glanced out the grimy window and his hopes soared. The car was a Cadillac, which meant money, and the guy getting out was wearing a suit and tie, which indicated he was fair game. The man came in and sat at the counter and when he ordered a coffee instead of beer, Rocco grinned evilly and slid closer.

"Say, buddy—" he growled.

The man turned, all mild and polite and inoffensive. But when Rocco saw that his face was hard and his belly was flat and shoulders were wide, he thought better of it. He mumbled, "Nothin'—" and moved away.

John Baltimore drank his coffee and left.

X

There were only two cells at the Bleekerville jail and they had seldom housed more than weekend drunkards and the odd wife beater, and they had certainly never housed anything that wasn't human. Choice was reflecting on that as he returned from the clinic where he'd talked to the girl again, without enlightenment, and had been told by Rose, the nurse, about the face at the window, which was most likely just a nightmare. He figured the girl liked being the centre of attention and was playing up to it, or maybe she really had had a disturbing dream, which was understandable if there was any truth at all to her story. Choice passed the empty cells and went into his office. It looked like a jail in a cowboy film, with a locked gun rack on the wall and wanted posters as decor. But the gun rack only held hunting rifles and Choice wasn't a sheriff or a marshal. Dick Wormwood hadn't come in yet, but he wasn't late. Choice sat at his desk and a moment later there was a knock on the door, which wasn't closed, and a muscular, middle-aged man stepped in.

He was a stranger and Choice supposed he was a motorist

looking for directions or, broken down, in need of a mechanic. He didn't look at all like a rapist and he was quite human.

"I'm John Baltimore, chief," he said and looked to see if the name meant anything to Choice. It evidently didn't. The man looked sort of contrite, as if maybe he had run out of gas through inattention or run over a cat.

"Yeah?" Choice said.

"My daughter is, or was, working here in town but I haven't heard from her in a while and I –" he paused, not wanting to say he had come looking for her deliberately as if she were wayward or wanton. "I was in the area and thought I'd – well, hell, the truth is I read about this girl who was attacked and it worried me. Her name wouldn't be Rebecca?"

"Well, matter of fact, she won't give her name," Choice said. "Got a description?"

Baltimore wondered why he hadn't thought to bring her photograph. He said, "Blonde, nineteen, about five foot seven?"

Choice thought for a moment because girls changed the colour of their hair a lot. Then he said, "Naw. This kid can't be much more'n sixteen, got dark hair, runaway, I imagine."

Baltimore felt relieved, but not a lot since he hadn't thought it would be his daughter and he still didn't know where she was.

"I stopped by the clinic, actually, but the woman on the desk wouldn't let me see her without getting permission from you, chief. I believe she thought I was a reporter, which offended me a bit."

Choice smiled. He hadn't liked Slotnik's newspaper report and had told Rose not to admit any strangers and he was glad she hadn't, as a matter of authority, although it would have done no harm.

"Maybe you can help me, though," Baltimore said. "She was working for a doctor. Rebecca Baltimore, college student but she took a year off . . ."

"Name don't ring a bell. You sure you got the right town, mister? There's only the one doc here, Doc Tuttle, and there's been no girl working for him. There's the clinic, but she wasn't working there either." Choice shrugged. He figured the guy's daughter was avoiding him for some reason and had lied about her whereabouts, although the man looked all right to Choice. Baltimore stood there for a moment. He hadn't gotten permission to see the girl, but there was no point in it now. Why on earth had Rebecca made up such an elaborate deception? He doubted that was possible. But why would the chief of police lie? He thanked Choice and went out, passing Dick Wormwood who had arrived exactly on time and shared Choice's scepticism when told of the face at the clinic window – although not of that face at his own bedroom window, to be sure.

Baltimore stood at the counter for some time before Ben Marvin, who was not busy, took notice of him. But then Ben saw that this was a powerful-looking fellow and curbed his annoyance at being troubled.

"Yeah, I remember her, all right," Ben admitted. "But the rent on her box ran out. She didn't leave a forwarding address and she didn't cancel the box, neither. People ain't considerate that way. Fee runs out, I gotta plug up the keyhole, plenty of trouble . . ." On a whim, Baltimore rented a box for three months, which he never intended to use and would not cancel. On his way out, he looked in the phone book on the counter and got Doctor Tuttle's address. It was the longest of long shots, but what else did he have to go on? The cop could have been wrong; he was there and felt he should do something. He wasn't going to feel like just driving back home, either, and he booked a room at the Lumberman's Inn, which was just adequate and at the desk of which he got directions to Doc Tuttle's.

Doc Tuttle was in a grumpy mood, still quite pleased at having been the first to examine the poor, plundered girl but annoyed at Slotnik for not mentioning his name in the paper. You didn't often get a chance to practise in such unique circumstances and it was a shame Slotnik had not seen fit to accredit him. He guessed most of the locals would know, but still, a man liked to see his name in the newspaper and it would have been a good thing to have folks reminded he was still in practice. Lots of his former patients had abandoned him as he got older, going directly to the clinic or, if it wasn't an emergency, driving into the city. He didn't have a single appointment booked for the rest of the day and that added greatly to his grumpiness. When a stranger walked into his reception room, Tuttle was pleased, but then eyed the man warily, seeing he was big and stern looking and hoping he did not have to diagnose a terminal illness. But it developed the stranger was not ailing.

"Don't expect I've got the right doctor—"

"Only doctor you'll get here," Tuttle snapped, offended and misunderstanding, supposing he did not look professional enough or young enough to suit the well-dressed fellow who probably was suffering from an ingrown toenail and, maybe, gout.

"No, I meant – my daughter was employed by—"

"Not by me—"

"So I understand, Doctor. But – Rebecca Baltimore took a summer job in Bleekerville but stayed on, working for a local doctor—"

"Never worked for me; never had her for a patient, either. I treated a girl the other day, name of which I never learned, though—"

"The girl who was caught in a trap and attacked?"

"Why, yes, that is so," Tuttle said, pleased that a stranger should know about his involvement and looking more kindly on the man. He took out a cigarette case and lighted one. Doc Tuttle never smoked in solitude, but often did in company, to let folks know what he thought about the Surgeon General.

"Well, that's incidental; she wasn't my daughter. But –" John Baltimore hesitated, feeling he was becoming paranoid. Why should the chief of police lie? But he wanted to verify it. "What did this girl look like, by the way?"

"Oh, she was scratched up, broken – oh, I see. Small girl, maybe sixteen, dark hair—"

Baltimore gestured sideways. "Obviously, there has been a mix-up, some confusion. Isn't there another doctor in practice? Maybe not in town, but near enough to use the local post office?"

"Nope. I'm what you get in Bleekerville."

The man looked a bit disturbed and the doctor smoked ostentatiously, squinting. He was speculating on whether this talk of a girl might only be an ice-breaker, if the stranger was suffering from some embarrassing condition – a venereal disease or maybe piles – and was leading up to it in a round about way.

But, if so, he chickened out.

"Well, thank you for your time, Doctor," he said, and nodded and left. Tuttle was disappointed. In lieu of a patient to treat, he would just as soon have someone to talk to.

Doc Tuttle's surgery was in his home, a big, old white wooden house with a veranda, and John Baltimore stood on that veranda and wondered what to do now? He had come to a dead end. Although he'd always trusted Rebecca, he had to be suspicious now. Had she ever worked in Bleekerville at all? Her letters had been postmarked from there and his own letters, until the last one, had been received. Yet she had never responded immediately and his numerous questions had, for the most part, gone unanswered. Had she only been there long enough to rent the post office box and arranged for someone else to send her's on and reroute his own – some local girl she had met in college, perhaps? By why, for God's sake? Had she followed her mother to Europe? Well, she wasn't a liar, but a white lie was different. Knowing how much the truth would disturb him, Rebecca might have arranged the deception for the kindest of motives. Then whomsoever was handling her mail had left town, stopped for some reason, and the box rent had run out without Rebecca knowing it. It would explain it and he chewed over the logics.

Her own letters would have been returned to her in due course but she might be travelling around a great deal, unaware they had not reached her father and were following her through the labyrinth of the international post. He nodded a bit. It fell into place. He considered talking to the post master again to see if he recalled returning any mail from her box to Europe. Foreign transactions would no doubt be memorable in Bleekerville. But then he realized that Rebecca's letters to him would have been enclosed in an outer envelope addressed to whoever sent them on, person or agent.

Again it seemed a dead end but, on the whole, he quite liked the explanation. It proved her silence accidental and her deception for his own peace of mind. Eventually, she would find out that they had lost contact and no doubt write to him directly, confessing apologetically or weaving some new fabric of misdirection – also for his benefit. Baltimore wanted to believe this. If she had gone off in her mother's footsteps – well, maybe it was in her blood. And it was a hell of a lot better than other alternatives as to her whereabouts. Baltimore felt almost content and thought he might not even spend the night in town, but head back home and continue his vigil by the phone and the letter box.

Then Doc Tuttle came out of the house.

He had been looking out the front window in hopes of seeing approaching patients or maybe a traffic accident with casualties – not that he hoped for that, but if it happened someone had to tend to the injured and he was the only doctor in town – but when he saw John Baltimore standing on his veranda he suddenly remembered that, technically, he was not the only doctor.

He supposed it had no bearing but his waiting room was empty and he moved from the window to the screen door and stepped out. The door creaked and Baltimore turned, feeling silly for standing on another man's front porch as he patterned his personal thoughts.

"Saw you were still here," Tuttle said. "I don't know if it matters, and like I said I'm the only doctor here, leastwise – well, there is Dr Franken . . ."

Baltimore had been told by the chief of police and confirmed it in the phone book and then Tuttle had claimed the same singular status, and now he was changing his tune; was this some Byzantine conspiracy about to be revealed? Had Rebecca begged their silence? His face tightened, but Tuttle, in his innocence, didn't notice.

"But he isn't in practice, nor a real doctor, either, come to that. Not a GP or a surgeon, I mean to say. More of a research scientist, and likely retired now. Folks don't think of a man being a proper doctor if he don't treat their aches and pains and set their bones . . ." Tuttle seemed to approve of that attitude. "But, still, he has the label of Doctor, so it might be he is the man you want."

Baltimore felt guilty and paranoid again, for his instant assumption of conspiracy. He was not as interested in this new detail as he would have been a few minutes ago, for he had convinced himself that his theory was right and that Rebecca was in Europe – and safe. But still – he had only supposed she was employed by a medical practitioner and she had never claimed that. Rebecca had no qualifications in the field of medicine and it seemed possible she was, or had been, working for this Franken. Hadn't one of her earlier letters mentioned that he was an Austrian or German?

"Would he have need of a Girl Friday, would you know? Someone to handle his correspondence, maybe? Keep records or do odd jobs?"

"Doubt it," Tuttle said. "Can't say, though. I only met the man once and seen him half a dozen times in town and, like I say, he's probably retired – although it's funny he should settle in this area, knowing no one, unless he's a recluse. I've wondered about that and, fact is, I had something to do with him coming here, although not his staying on. Got no brief for the man, though, seeing as he once stole one of my patients."

Tuttle knew that sometimes he tended to talk too much and he paused now. But the man seemed willing to listen, even eager. "Old Ethel Potter, this would be near enough twenty years ago, fifteen at least, but she wasn't young then, either . . ." Tuttle paused again, considering the ethics of the matter. It wasn't correct to discuss a patient with a layman, certainly. But she'd not been his patient for a long time and, besides, they weren't talking in his consulting room. They were standing on his veranda, just like any two civilians in discourse.

"She couldn't get with child," he said, further soothing his conscience by avoiding professional terms. "I was unable to do anything for her, and told her straight out. But she kept nagging me, whining about how she had failed her husband by not bearing sons to work the farm. She'd come in twice a week, regular. I suggested she go to see a specialist, but she and Homer weren't much for travelling."

Baltimore leaned back on the railing, wondering where all this was leading, but waiting patiently enough. A breeze was ruffling the lawn as a background to the doctor's droning voice, moving just as slowly.

"Well, sir, as it happened, I was looking through some of the publications that the big drug companies are always clogging a doctor's post box up with and I found this report on a genetic breakthrough. Some article, I can't recall, don't imagine I understood it. But this Franken, Emile Franken, was reckoned to be a leading authority and I gave Ethel the magazine, more to get rid of her one day than anything else. I didn't see Ethel for a while. Then, damndest thing, who shows up but this Franken fella, asking how to get to the Potter farm. It seemed remarkable to Tuttle and he gave it a moment to sink in. "Might be it was an act of charity, might be it comes off his income tax, he needs a deduction, who knows? And sure enough. Old Ethel gets herself in the family way!" This was even more singular and Tuttle paused again, firing another defiant cigarette. His confidant looked suitably impressed, if not greatly so. He was half turned away, but, that could mean he was presenting his ear to hear every word.

"All smug and blooming, she has just got to let me know; she's bursting to rub it in and I guess she lost faith in me since I hadn't made her fertile.

"And for whatever reason, this Dr Franken buys the old Cleaver place and stays on, all to himself in that big old house. Still there, far as I know."

Tuttle could see that by this time his visitor was rapidly losing interest; although he was still polite enough, and he couldn't really blame him. All this had been a generation ago. Why am I rambling on like this? he wondered, but he continued anyway.

"My memory might not be so keen these days, but I can't recall that I ever did see that child; wasn't called to attend the birth. I'd remember that. Likely they took Ethel to some big hospital somewhere, research centre, maybe, but I didn't set eyes on her for some time and can't say about the offspring. She'd been real coy and smug when she first got pregnant, then she was gone and next time I saw her, it was in the street, she turned away. Avoided me ever since. I imagine there was a complication and it took the wind out of her sails, being as she was too old to bear and should of let nature take its course. Old Homer, that's her husband, never seemed friendly again, either – not unfriendly, you know, but preoccupied. I guess he wanted a child more'n she, there was trouble and he got to feeling guilty. Well, my guess is that the child was born not right. Could be it died, could be it was put in a home for the retarded. Never was told; never asked; I got no obligation to a child I never delivered."

By now Baltimore was paying scant attention and the doctor knew he'd jabbered away long enough and fell silent. But when Baltimore made no comment, Tuttle felt he had to conclude, if only to justify the build up.

"Never heard of anyone working for Franken . . ."

"Well, thank you again, Doctor. I . . ."

But Tuttle didn't stop, ". . . but you could check with him. He isn't in the phone book, might be an unlisted number, but his place is easy enough to find. I suppose you got a car? You drive out east, only the one road, first place you pass is the Worm-wood's, on the right; might not notice that, though, being set back in the trees. Dick Wormwood is the deputy and . . . but that don't matter . . . Past there you come to some dirt tracks leading up to the lake; there's some summer homes up there, pretty place; they are on the right, like Wormwood's. Next it's on your left, you'll come to the lane that leads up to the Potter's farm, she's the one I was going on about – and right past there—" he sounded triumphant – "is the Cleaver place, Franken's place, now."

He sighed down his cigarette and stopped.

Baltimore, innately courteous, waited for a moment, not long enough for Tuttle to get started again. Then he thanked the doctor once again, and went down the steps. His wide, sloping, wrestler's shoulders drooped and his head was lowered and, all in all, his attitude was not like that of a man departing a doctor's surgery following a favourable diagnosis. He was feeling depressed and didn't know why. He had another lead to follow now and, too, he had built up a theory more comforting than most, yet his mood was bleak. He had left his car at the Lumberman's Inn and walked to Tuttle's, and now he walked back along the main street, passing the post office but not stopping.

In the parking lot of the Inn, he stood beside his Cadillac and pondered. He could drive out east and call on Franken or drive out west and go home. He could go into the lounge and get drunk, too, but he wasn't much of a drinking man. His attention had been wavering when Tuttle gave him directions, but now he found that he remembered them and that seemed to decide the issue, his own memory being like an external fact to which he could react. He got in the car and drove off slowly, which was just as well.

As it was, he nearly ran over a red-headed girl on a bicycle . . .

XI

Lucy Marshall kept pushing Steve's hands away, but as soon as he sighed and stopped trying to touch her up, she snuggled up to him again. Her flirtation was frustrating the youth greatly and, inexperienced himself, he didn't know where it would lead. He didn't know Lucy very well, either. Her family had a rustic cabin by the lake but they lived in the city most of the time so he only met Lucy occasionally and hoped that, being a big city girl, she would prove promiscuous. She certainly looked the part in her tiny shorts and tight T-shirt, but her attitudes were ambiguous, both come-at-able and innocent at the same time.

Lucy wasn't really a tease, or at least did not mean to be nor realize that she was; a child on the threshold of becoming a young lady, her body bouncy and nubile but her emotions lagging somewhat behind, she was confused about such things, not sure what she felt or what she wanted. As soon as her parents had gone out, she had phoned young Steve to let him know she was alone at the cabin, hinting in a giggly fashion. Steve was a couple of years older and very much aware of his pubescence, although it had never been gratified. Quite naturally assuming her invitation implied some naughty fun and frolic, he had dashed straight over on his bicycle and had been more encouraged when he saw how immodestly she was garbed. Now they were sitting on the swing on the cabin porch, with the lake all pretty and placid before them and it seemed a perfect place for romance.

But Steve was alternatively being tantalized and turned down, tempted and then rebuked, and he was becoming as confused as she was. She wanted the boy to do exciting things to her, yet she didn't want to get carried away. Steve was only a casual boy-friend, if that, and she was worried about her reputation and her chastity. The cute little temptress was willing, then she was reluctant, innocently changing the pace and it was ruining the mood for the young man – who didn't understand such things, intuitively, as did the watcher in the woods.

He or it – something nearly human or someone not exactly human – stared at the courting couple, the girl's image imprinted in his yellow eyes like a cameo set in gold. One bare, horny foot pawed at the earth and he snorted silently, responding to the girl's arousal, more aware of it than she herself. His stringy sinews tensed; as he was ragingly rampant; his body urged him to advance, drawn to her magnetism, but he held back, for she was not alone and he was frightened of males. He lingered and lurked and seethed with need.

*　　*　　*

Steve was getting nowhere and it was getting unbearable and when, yet again, she brushed his desperate hands from her breasts, he abruptly stood up, rocking the swing. Embarrassed by his erection and not wanting to give her the satisfaction of knowing how much her teasing had affected him, he jammed his hands into his side pockets and hunched over to conceal his condition. Grumbling unhappily, he told her he had to leave – and to her surprise and dismay, he did so, mounting his bicycle awkwardly, thrown off balance by the weight in his groin. He called a curt goodbye and pedalled off down the dirt track towards the highway.

As soon as he was gone, Lucy regretted not having been more compliant and wished he would return. She had been enjoying herself enormously and what mild groping he had managed had excited her no end. But she was still half a child and, after a few minutes, bored with sitting there alone, she decided to take her own bicycle into town and get an ice cream cone and maybe find some other boy with whom to flirt. The bright red bike was leaning against the side of the cabin and, lithe and limber, she slid on to the seat. She started to pedal, presenting a delectable sight. Her plump boobs jiggled and her slim thighs flashed and the lower half moons of her trim bottom showed from her shorts as she pumped away. She had a glow of oestrum about her, more pronounced than she knew. But the lurker in the woods knew – and a gnarled and twisted figure stepped out into the path.

It startled Lucy so much that she made a comic book sound, "Eeeekkk—" and hit the pedals hard. A clawed hand snatched and brushed her hip. Then she was beyond him and pedalling for all she was worth. She was veering about crazily; she could hear footsteps pounding after her as the thing loped in pursuit. Her pony tail was streaming out behind her and one horny hand hooked at it like a commuter reaching for a strap. But then the distance between them increased. When she risked a glance back, she saw that terrible thing had come to a panting halt, but she kept on hurdling recklessly down the wooded track and when she came to the highway she careened out without pause, causing a driver in a Cadillac to hit the brakes hard. She hardly noticed the car. She pedalled down the road and into the town and she went straight to the police station.

XII

The heavy car skewed when John Baltimore hit the brakes and the girl furiously pedalling a red bicycle shot in front of him at an angle, tilted towards the car, momentum and gravity in fine balance. She flashed past without contact, but only by inches, and Baltimore fought against the skid, and controlling it, pulled over to the shoulder of the road. He was white faced and shaken. Baltimore was a man who liked kids and hoped one day to have grandchildren and he had damned near run the girl down. It had been her fault, certainly, pelting out of the side turning directly in front of the car. But still, if he hadn't been motoring down that road, heading east, it would not have nearly happened. It caused him to question his motives for being there and deepened his sense of depression. He almost turned around. But it wasn't much further to Franken's and when his nerves had calmed he proceeded on, finding the place easily enough and pulling into the front yard.

The house was large, built solidly of grey stone, at odds with local architecture. It struck Baltimore as a grim place and the huge oaken doors were damned near intimidating. Why would a man, with options, choose such a house unless he was a recluse – and, being a recluse, he would not offer room and board to an employee, even if he had need of one. It certainly wasn't a place Rebecca would be content with. The yard was muddy and untended, the windows shrouded by heavy curtains. The chimney looked functional but no smoke poured out on a fairly warm day.

Baltimore approached the front door, the soft mud sucking like gravity at his feet. He knocked and waited. No one came to the front door. He looked for a bell, found none and knocked again. If there was anyone home, they weren't receiving callers, but that didn't seem unlikely. He had arrived unannounced and could have been a salesman. He wandered around to the side of the house. There was a garage at the back, also built of stone, probably predating motorcars and of some previous function. The doors were open and there was no car within. Baltimore returned to the front door and knocked once again, then shrugged and was about to return to his car. As an afterthought, he searched his pockets and found the card he'd been given when he booked into the Lumberman's Inn. He scribbled his name on the back with a request that Franken phone him. There was a letter slot, for the house had been built in a more gracious age when mail was delivered with regularity, and Baltimore slid the card through that slot – where Franken, who was at home but was not receiving callers in Cadillacs, snatched it up at once – and frowned when he read the name.

John Baltimore was the last man on earth he wished to meet at the moment.

"Gargoyle."

She had thought for a few moments when they asked and, for want of a better word, said it. Choice and Wormwood regarded one another, then looked back at the little redhead who'd jumped from her red bicycle and rushed in so fast she'd left the bike to fall over in the road.

"Bogie man," she added. "Goblin."

Choice wondered if Lucy Marshall was jumping on the bandwagon? If she envied the attention the girl in the clinic had received. If so, she was a mighty fine actress, for she looked shaken to the core as she blurted her story out. Nor had there been any mention of gargoyles and goblins in Slotnik's newspaper reports. They had her repeat it a couple times and she began to calm down and, on the whole, they believed her. They didn't know what had chased her, but they believed it strange.

"You feel up to showing us where this happened?" Choice asked gently.

"No way! You ain't getting me anywhere near that thing!" she wailed.

"You'll be protected, miss," Wormwood put in, uncharacteristically patting his side arm.

"Yeah?" She cocked her head and gave the impression she was chewing gum, which she wasn't. "What makes you so sure guns would kill a thing like that?"

It gave them an eerie sensation.

"You have some place to stay in town, then, while we check it out?" Choice asked.

She didn't specifically, but she nodded.

She almost asked them to lock her up safely in a cell, but then thought better of it. Maybe that thing could bend bars and she knew it couldn't catch her on her bicycle.

"I'll be okay," she muttered. "But – you cops better be careful, you know?"

"We will. And Miss Marshall . . . I'd be obliged if you didn't tell anyone about this until we've had time to investigate, okay?" Choice requested.

"Sure," said Lucy, and she went out to blab it all over town, for it had sure been an adventure.

Wormwood looked with disapproval at the round rims of her ass showing under her shorts as she walked out and shook his head disparagingly.

"Young girl dresses like that—" he said.

"Yeah, well—" said Choice, who was something of a moralist himself, if a guilt-ridden one. "Still, how a girl dresses . . . ain't no mandate for a rapist."

"Why that is surely so," Wormwood agreed.

They started out the door and then Wormwood stopped, looking down and shifting the toe of his boot on the floor. Choice raised his eyebrows.

"I was thinking, Choice . . . maybe we had better take some rifles," Wormwood suggested sheepishly. It took Choice, who was well aware that Wormwood had never drawn his gun in the course of his duties, by surprise. But when he thought about it, and about what the girl had said, he figured it was a pretty good idea, at that.

XIII

John Baltimore was an infrequent and moderate drinker, but he wasn't in the mood to watch television in his room and he didn't have a book with him, nor the patience to read at the moment. He told the desk clerk he would be in the lounge in case of a phone call and went on in, sitting at the far end of a long, polished bar and ordering a bourbon. The lounge was decorated like a hunting lodge. Mounted deer heads gazed out with glass eyes and a stuffed fish was mounted in place of pride over the bar. There was a flagstone fireplace in need of dusting and, before it, a black bearskin rug. The trophies mildly disturbed Baltimore, who wondered why a man would want to shoot a deer? He had never hunted or fished, nor had he been to war, luckily being too young for Korea and to old and a family man at the time of Vietnam. He had never killed anything more than a fly or mosquito except once and that had only been a frog, but it still sometimes troubled his memory.

Once, as a child, he had been standing beside a trout stream watching the fish snatch at skimming insects and he had spotted a small green speckled frog in the reeds. He scooped it up curiously, feeling its heart beat, wishing it no harm. But then, not knowing why, he had tossed it into the pond. The frog was swimming even before it hit the water, back legs jerking like an experiment by Galvani. The frog splashed in and the pond instantly seemed to boil as the hungry fish swarmed up. But the frog was swimming so fast it barely brushed the surface and made it safely to the bank, where it lay quivering fearfully, its sides heaving in and out. John Baltimore picked it up again. He was proud of the little amphibian for having escaped the ravenous fish. Then he had tossed it in again.

The trout were ready this time.

The pond swirled in a miniature maelstrom and bits of white frog flesh bobbed on the roiling surface. John Baltimore had been horrified, filled with remorse and regret, never understanding why he had thrown it in twice. He had never killed anything more than an insect since that day – unlike the locals, hunters and all, who were starting to gather at the bar.

They wore plaid jackets like uniforms and, out of hunting season, still kept their deer tags pinned on like badges of rank. They paid no attention to the man at the end of the bar who wore a suit and a tie, and he heard their animated conversation only peripherally, as he waited for a phone call and thought about his daughter and about a small speckled frog.

He caught a phrase here and there.

"Bigfoot, maybe," he heard, and, "Yeti."

A burly man suggested getting up a hunting party, sounding more keen on the stalk than on any righteous duty to apprehend a danger; another opined that Choice would not look kindly on a bunch of armed men running around shooting each other out of season.

"Can't have this weirdo bothering our women."

"Not like they was local girls, though, the neither of them. I hear the first one was a runaway and that Marshall kid's family only comes once in a while."

"Yeah, that's so. And did you see how the Marshall kid was dressed? Jeez. Little tramp, you ask me, wearing them skimp shorts . . ."

"Enough to incite any man . . ."

"If it was a man . . ."

"A hush followed that statement and John Baltimore looked up. The hunters were exchanging speculative glances and they relished the idea that there might be something strange out there, some new species to shoot. Standing just inside the door, having entered and then halted, stood an ageing man in overalls and a straw hat. His head was cocked and he looked disturbed.

One of the hunters noticed him.

"Hey, Mr Potter – have a beer," he called.

Potter's head moved in an arc, as if he couldn't decide whether to nod or shake it in decline. His gnarled fists were clenched and he was agitated.

"What you think about this here monster, Homer?"

"Yeah, what's your opinion?"

"Has . . . What has happened?" Potter rasped.

"Ain't you heard? This guy, or whatever that Dick Wormwood scared off the gal in the trap . . . Chased the Marshall girl on her way to town . . ."

The blood drained from the farmer's lined face quite visibly.

"Was she hurt?" he croaked.

"Naw, didn't catch her."

"Ahhh," Potter sighed.

"Choice and Dick are out looking for it, or him, or whatever. We was thinking we might . . ."

But Homer Potter turned abruptly and walked out without another word. The hunters were surprised.

"What's eating him?"

"Never knowed old Homer to turn down a free beer."

"Maybe he's gone home to make sure the thing don't get Ethel," one said, and there was hearty laughter at such an idea. John Baltimore had recognized the name and had the farmer joined the group at the bar he might have asked him if Franken was still living down the road from Potter's farm. Then again, he might not have, for he was reticent about approaching strangers.

How should he know how firm was the bond between the ageing farmer and himself?

"If it is a man," one had said, and was it?

What is human, what not? Molly Carlyle was human and had had a birth certificate to prove it, before she had destroyed the document even though it was not the one her father thought she had been named by. But Ethel Potter's son had never had his birth registered, although he had a name which only Ethel ever used. If he thought as a human, and in English, he was thinking *What am I?* and *Who am I?* and *Why?* Who can say? But whether he reasoned or not, he had emotions akin to those of man, and one was fear. He feared the male of any species. He feared Homer who had never been cruel to him but could not keep the loathing from his face; he feared Franken in whose eyes failure lay as solidly as poured concrete; he feared the bull that bellowed in the barn when a cow was in season; and he feared the farm dog they had to get rid of after it bit him twice as a child.

He most certainly feared the two men he was watching from the trees as they walked up the path, carrying rifles and studying the ground and trying to puzzle things out . . .

"I don't believe in monsters," Dick Wormwood said, to Choice's surprise.

"Never supposed you did, Dick."

They were moving along the dirt track side by side, but Wormwood kept turning around and walking backwards at intervals, scanning the woods warily. He had thumbed the safety catch off his rifle – a thing he never did stalking a deer.

"What I mean is, just because a man don't believe in – 'em, don't mean they ain't scary. Monsters."

"This ain't no monster, Dick," Choice grunted.

"Well, I know that; that is what I'm saying."

They moved on. They could see where the tyres of Lucy's bicycle had rutted the track and they found other indentations and knelt to inspect them. But they didn't know what they were. They weren't the print of a deer's hooves nor the paw of a bear, nor had they been made by shoe or boot. But they weren't clearly demarcated and were crumbling at the edges. They followed on and soon came to the cabin, where they stood and looked all around and never saw the figure that blended into the trees at all. Choice went up on the porch and sat on the swing where Lucy Marshall had entertained young Steve so abortively. Wormwood came up and sat on the railing.

"What I mean about monsters," Wormwood began, then paused to order his thoughts. "When we were kids, we used to play a game, zombies and ghouls. Used to pay it with Vinny DiGiacomo. He was a year older than me, so he always got to be the monster. I'd hide and he'd pretend to be a zombie – sometimes it was a mummy or a wolfman, all the same thing. Usually I just hid behind a tree or something and it was only a little scary, tingly, like. I could run faster than Vinny, see, and knew I could get away. But one day I hid in the loft of his garage. I got down behind an old steamer trunk. It was kind of scary up there to begin with, dark and all. Then I heard Vinny coming up the steps. He's coming real slow. He always made a good monster, making himself all twisty and snarly and sort of hungry looking. He's up there in the loft with me. Maybe he knows right where I'm at. But he's playing the game, searching, coming closer. He's snorting and howling and stuff. I peek out over the trunk and he's moving all monstery. He gets closer. I can see he's getting carried away, drooling some. Well, I get so scared I think my heart is gonna stop. The closer he gets, the scareder I get. Now, I know it is only Vinny DiGiacomo, known him all my life, yet I ain't never been so scared as I was that day. That's what I meant about not having to believe in monsters to be scared of 'em, see?"

Choice said he saw, and did.

Neither speculated that monsters get scared too.

XIV

Home from town and horrified, Homer Potter tried in his gruff way to comfort his good wife.

"'Twas not your fault, Ethel, nor that of my seed. Was what was done to us, our acids changed . . ." Ethel looked blank. Homer had never understood it, either, and had turned his frayed hat in his hands whenever Franken tried to explain about chromosomes and heredity and evolution. The words meant nothing, he only knew it had failed and, blaming Franken, he also blamed himself. It made him feel unwholesome.

"Try to understand . . . might be better if he don't come home."

"Jimmy?" she said.

"Homer nodded grimly.

"Not come home? Jimmy?"

Homer was glad when the phone rang, knowing her mind would wander and they needn't return to this talk. He lifted the receiver with his back to her. Looking out the window, she paid no attention.

It was Franken on the phone.

"Has he returned?"

"No, and worse. I just been to town. Another girl has been . . . no, not that. She got away, but . . ." He lowered his voice. "Choice and Dick are out hunting him and there was talk in town of forming a posse. They don't know. How in hell could they? We got to find him first. He'll be frightened. He won't know what a gun is . . . and they won't know what . . . who . . . he is. We better look . . ."

"I have been occupied," Franken said, and there was something dismal in his voice.

Homer stiffened, glancing towards Ethel.

"The child? It has arrived?"

"Yes."

"And—"

"You'd better come, Homer," Franken sighed. "It is a thing we must decide together.

Homer put the phone down. He was ashen and shaken. There had been no hope in Franken's tone and the farmer was thinking of his wife. It would be the last straw for her sanity, he knew. If she found out. It was clear what must be decided.

Unlike her lover, Hilda Wormwood was at peace with herself. She knew that adultery was sinful, but that only added spice to it and she had rationalized the affair quite nicely. If Dick had satisfied her as was her wifely right and entitlement, she wouldn't have taken a lover and it was as simple as that.

But today she was feeling sorry for herself. Dick had rejected her that morning and Choice had not stopped by, and it just wasn't fair that a good-looking woman with a husband and a lover should be deprived. Restless and morose, she had been pacing around the house ever since she'd washed the breakfast dishes, indignant and neglected. After a while, she went out in the yard. Dick had cautioned her to stay in the house and keep the door locked, but she paid scant attention and forgot it now.

She strolled down the path that threaded through the trees and came to the swift-flowing stream bordering their property. There was a crude wooden bench there and she sat there on the bank of the stream. There was a cool breeze that emphasised the warmth of her body. The stream ran fast but, where she sat, a crescent tidal pool was cut into the bank, nudged into the soft earth. Looking down, Hilda could see the reflection of her solid white thighs in the pool. She moved her legs apart. The vee of her panties showed in the water. On a sudden whim, more through boredom than need or arousal, she decided to caress herself right there in the open. It was naughty for a married woman to practise self-abuse, and Hilda was always intrigued by naughtiness. Sometimes she wished she had taken to the streets instead of the bridal bed.

Smiling sheepishly, she hiked her haunches up and tugged her panties down, kicking one foot free and leaving them hobbled around the other ankle. She arched and tilted her belly up and, still staring down at the reflection, she began to rub herself slowly with both hands. She was taking her time, enjoying the slow build-up of a leisurely and lingering self-indulgence.

As she began to simmer, she extended her legs and her arched feet slid through the still pool and out into the current. Her panties slipped from her foot and drifted away, spinning in the stream like gossamer flotsam. They were her best panties and Hilda knew she should retrieve them, but it was starting to feel really good now and she began to massage herself faster and stare after the panties at the same time, her concentration divided.

Then she blushed deeply.

Her panties had wrapped round the ankle of a man who had just stepped out into the centre of the stream from the opposite bank, clinging like bunting. Someone was watching her! She was mortified. It wasn't so much that she had been caught with her hands in the cookie jar as it was embarrassing to have anyone know she was reduced to self-caress, like some ageing spinster unable to find a man. She looked up slowly, flushed with shame. Her eyes trailed up that tense, vibrant body.

When she saw the thing that was watching her, she felt more than shame.

Hilda sat, frozen by fear, and it came up through the stream with her panties still wrapped round one ankle, crouched low, knuckles skimming the water, nostrils flaring as it breathed in her self-induced arousal. A scream caught in her throat. She leaped up and slipped on the slick bank. As she turned she lost her footing and fell face down in the stream. She got her knees under her, but then it was clawing at her from behind, hauling her haunches up as it hammered in blind passion. She kicked and her ankles were seized. Her face was down in the stream and she was screaming under water. She tried to hold her breath but she could not restrain the screams. Even as she drowned, she knew it was by accident. When finally it was finished with a silent sigh, her killer did not know she was dead.

John Baltimore had had three drinks and that was more than enough and there had been no phone call for him. He went up to his room and stood just inside the door, turning from side to side. He didn't feel like lying on the bed and he didn't feel like sitting in the chair. He felt certain that a letter from Rebecca was waiting for him at home – or that his telephone was ringing unanswered. What was the point in staying here? He decided to drive out to Franken's once again and then, whether he contacted the man or not, to head back home. He went back downstairs, wondering if he was fit to drive but driving regardless.

He had already passed the lane leading up to the Potter place when, on a sudden impulse, he braked and reversed. There was a connection, or had once been, between the farmer and Franken, unlikely as it seemed, and it was quite possible that the Potters would know if Franken had had a girl working for him and staying with him. Baltimore wanted to get that resolved. He drove slowly up the furrowed lane and stopped in the farmyard. Ethel Potter was standing on the porch, all grey and faded and she showed no curiosity at all when Baltimore got out of his car and approached her.

"Mrs Potter?"

She made no reply, looking beyond him.

"I'm trying to contact Dr Franken . . ."

That registered and she regarded him. "Have you come for the blessed event?" she asked. "I had hoped he would summon a proper doctor this time." Baltimore looked puzzled but she failed to notice. "He will be at home. Her time is near and he cannot leave her alone." She pointed in the direction of Franken's.

"You mistake me, I'm afraid."

"You aren't a doctor? Oh, dear. My son's child is due, you know. My grandchild. Oh, I will be so proud . . . if only . . . the birth is normal and the child is not flawed. Jimmy was such a dear child but . . ."

Baltimore could not make head nor tail of this. It was related somehow to Tuttle's rambling tale, but he'd paid little attention to that and it had nothing to do with his own interests. He waited until her voice trailed off, then asked if there had been a young lady staying at Franken's recently.

"Why, the mother to be, of course. No one else," the old woman replied.

Baltimore frowned. Had his daughter gotten pregnant? By this woman's son – the son that Dr Tuttle had not delivered and never seen and supposed abnormal? Was that the reason for Rebecca's silence, that she was ashamed to bear a child out of wedlock?

"Who . . . is the mother?" he asked carefully.

"I can't recall her name," Ethel Potter said. "Isn't that silly of me? I must have known it but . . . I can't even remember the wedding, for shame. My memory is no longer sound. I recall her, though. Perfectly well. A healthy girl, young and fair and sturdy. She will, she must, bear a hale and healthy child. You see, Jimmy was odd because of my age. But his own child, bred with a normal girl . . . a college student, as I recall . . ."

Baltimore felt his spine tingle. Dark draughts of premonition nagged at his mind. This old woman was barely lucid and he could get no answers, no proper replies. She was scanning the distance again, as if she had forgotten he was standing there. He saw a tear well up in her eye and she began to sob, mumbling meaninglessly. "Where can he be?" she asked. "Jimmy," she said. Baltimore quite suddenly became exasperated. She was swaying on the steps above him and he took her by the shoulders, shaking her quite gently, wanting to jar her back to reality.

"Mrs Potter!" he said and she clicked her teeth and said, "Jimmy—"

Then Jimmy was there.

*   *   *

The primal urge was satisfied now. The first of his kind had mated again – and had no concept that his seed was spilled into lifeless loins, as wasted as Onanism. He came running home to his mother, to food and shelter and warmth and he would have been smiling, had those strange lips been able to smile. He bounded from the trees without caution, for this was his home and here he had nothing to fear – and saw his mother shaking in the hands of a stranger. He feared the man, but she was his mother and instinct overwhelmed his terror. Driven by emotions not so far removed from humanity, he surged forwards and would have been howling had he been able.

John Baltimore stepped back and looked with horror on the thing that was rushing towards him, fingers clawed, mouth foaming, limbs festooned in shreds and rags. He was too terrified to flee as he faced this nightmare. He took another backwards step and then it was upon him, splayed hands locked on his throat. Baltimore fell and it crouched over him. He struggled to throw it off, to gain a hold. There seemed no substance to grasp. The thing's arms revolved fully in their sockets, its spine snaked sigmoidally. There was no resistance in its form – and little strength. The fingers on Baltimore's muscular neck were like putty.

They rolled in this strange embrace and in silence. Baltimore heaved atop the creature and took that sulphurous head between his hard hands. He twisted. The thing's neck wound around like an elastic band, turning as no neck should turn, no spinal column rotate. Its head went around, reversing in Baltimore's hands. Turning completely, the face looked up at the old woman on the porch. Baltimore had the strength of desperation, half-mad in his terror; and it was young, and weak, and flawed.

The face spun up again and, at the last moment, Baltimore saw pleading in the creature's eyes.

And then its neck was broken.

Baltimore dragged himself away, panting, supported by one elbow on the ground and gazing in horror as the thing flopped and jerked in its death throes. The movements were like a small speckled frog's in his memory, arms and legs flailing from the broken body. Baltimore heard a scream, but it was not from the dying thing, it came from Ethel Potter as she staggered from the steps and dropped to her knees beside her mortally shattered son. She held the wobbling head to her breast and stroked the waxen hair and moaned, "Jimmy – oh, my Jimmy—" Then it was no longer jerking and Ethel Potter looked with loathing upon John Baltimore, that gentle man who had killed her child.

"Why?" she whispered pitiably. "Why would you harm him. He was only a boy . . ."

XV

Homer Potter, usually deferential, walked right in so briskly that Franken stepped back without closing the door. They stood in the hallway. The heavy oak door swung back and forth as if in the grip of an unseen hand.

"Well?" Homer said.

"You may curse me," Franken said.

"And I damned well have—"

Franken shrugged. "I had hoped that in the second generation the disorders would not be dominant, but he has bred true; the child, too, is flawed. And yet . . . who can say? Perhaps I have not failed; perhaps it is the form nature would have chosen, in the fullness of time, merely hastened by my methods."

Homer wondered if the man was trying to justify himself. He didn't seem unhappy and Homer, thinking more of his wife than anything else, resented it.

"We must consider euthanasia and decide between us. It is a dead end; it would be a mercy . . ."

"It will be murder," Homer said. Yet he had Ethel to consider; it would kill her to know.

Franken saw this. "Ethel can be told the child was still born and need never see it."

"And the mother?"

"There are drugs to selectively erase memory. It will be a mercy to her, as well. If you agree . . ."

"I don't know," Homer mumbled. He looked down the long corridor. He didn't know whether he wanted to go back there; it would be easier to leave it in Franken's hands. But still . . .

"You must not regret this too greatly," Franken was saying. "It was not all in vain. I have learned a great deal and the next time . . ."

Homer stiffened and his face darkened.

"You would do it again?" he rasped.

"Of course. With suitable subjects. Nature herself fails and starts anew . . ."

Homer was trembling with rage.

"You will still play God?" he growled.

It was spoken in fury but, to Franken, it seemed right. He felt Godlike, in a modest way. He was a creator, moulding a new species from common clay, breathing life into a super race. The conceit caused him to smile slightly and, at that smile, Homer raised his knotted farmer's fist and shook it in Franken's face. Franken stepped back, lifting a hand defensively. He stepped towards the door. The oak door was still swinging and in that open doorway, haggard and grim, stood John Baltimore.

He had heard.

Where is my daughter?" he asked, his voice hollow.

Franken backed away from Baltimore but Homer was behind him, his first still raised in rage and Franken felt trapped between these two men who, so very different, had one thing in common.

"What? There is no one here—" Franken squealed.

"I have killed," John Baltimore said. It was not a threat; it was a statement of fact, more a confession than a challenge. His deep voice sounded through the house – and jogged the clouded memory of a young blonde girl who lay in bed, her newborn baby cradled to her breast.

"Daddy?" called Rebecca.

When he heard her voice, Baltimore started, wondering if his mind had run amok. Yet, with a sickening certainty, he had known. He moved past Franken, who cringed, but Baltimore ignored him. Rebecca called again and he followed the sound and walked in.

She looked up and now she could remember some things.

"Daddy, you've come," she said, and smiled, as relaxed and glowing as any new mother in a maternity ward, knowing he had always wanted grandchildren. Baltimore stood over the bed and looked down in icy horror. "I'm so glad you're here, Daddy," she said. And he looked.

Rebecca's smile became uncertain and she asked, "What's wrong, Daddy?"

But John Baltimore could not speak.

After a few moments Homer Potter walked in and stood beside Baltimore. Their shoulders touched. Side by side, like any proud grandparents, they looked down and their grandchild gurgled and opened his sulphurous eyes . . .

TIM LEBBON

White

TIM LEBBON HAS HAD OVER EIGHTY SHORT STORIES published in magazines and anthologies since 1995. His first novel, *Mesmer*, appeared from Tanjen in 1997 and was shortlisted for a British Fantasy Award the following year. His second book *Faith in the Flesh*, a volume of two novellas from RazorBlade Press, was runner-up in the Best Collection category.

His novella *Naming of Parts* is available from PS Publishing, while *Hush*, a novel written in collaboration with Gavin Williams, is also out from RazorBlade. His latest novel, *The Nature of Balance*, will be published by Leisure Books in the USA, and he also has short stories forthcoming in anthologies such as *Outside the Cage*, *Judas Street*, *Beneath the Ground*, *The Mammoth Book of Sword and Honour* and *Last Days*.

"White" was published by MOT Press in 1999 and has subsequently been nominated for an International Horror Guild Award, as well as being selected by Ellen Datlow for *The Year's Best Fantasy and Horror: Thirteenth Annual Collection*.

As the author explains: "When Andy Fairclough invited me to write a novella for the launch title of his MOT Press, it seemed the perfect opportunity to try something I'd been keen to do for quite some time: a siege story. But I wanted it to be a little more than simply a group of people stuck in a house, threatened by something outside; I wanted the siege mentality to be much more claustrophobic and powerful. With this is mind, and setting it all against a blinding white landscape, it turned into a pretty dark novella."

I: The Colour of Blood

WE FOUND THE FIRST BODY TWO DAYS BEFORE CHRISTMAS.

Charley had been out gathering sticks to dry for tinder. She had worked her way through the wild garden and down toward the cliffs, scooping snow from beneath and around bushes and bagging whatever dead twigs she found there. There were no signs, she said. No disturbances in the virgin surface of the snow; no tracks; no warning. Nothing to prepare her for the scene of bloody devastation she stumbled across.

She had rounded a big boulder and seen the red splash in the snow which was all that remained of a human being. The shock froze her comprehension. The reality of the scene struggled to imprint itself on her mind. Then, slowly, what she was looking at finally registered.

She ran back screaming. She'd only recognized her boyfriend by what was left of his shoes.

We were in the dining room trying to make sense of the last few weeks when Charley came bursting in. We spent a lot of time doing that: talking together in the big living rooms of the manor; in pairs, crying and sharing warmth; or alone, staring into darkening skies and struggling to discern a meaning in the infinite. I was one of those more usually alone. I'd been an only child and contrary to popular belief, my upbringing had been a nightmare. I always thought my parents blamed me for the fact that they could not have any more children, and instead of enjoying and revelling in my own childhood, I spent those years watching my mother and father mourn the ghosts of unborn offspring. It would have been funny if it were not so sad.

Charley opened the door by falling into it. She slumped to the floor, hair plastered across her forehead, her eyes two bright sparks peering between the knotted strands. Caked snow fell from her boots and speckled the timber floor, dirtied into slush. The first thing I noticed was its pinkish tinge.

The second thing I saw was the blood covering Charley's hands.

"Charley!" Hayden jumped to his feet and almost caught the frantic woman before she hit the deck. He went down with her, sprawling in a sudden puddle of dirt and tears. He saw the blood then and backed away automatically. "Charley?"

"Get some towels," Ellie said, always the pragmatist, "and a fucking gun."

I'd seen people screaming – all my life I'd never forgotten Jayne's final hours – but I had never seen someone actually *beyond* the point of screaming. Charley gasped and clawed at her throat, trying to open it up and let out the pain and the shock trapped within. It was not exertion that had stolen her breath; it was whatever she had seen.

She told us what that was.

I went with Ellie and Brand: Ellie had a shotgun cradled in the crook of her arm, a bobble hat hiding her severely short hair, her face all hard. There was no room in her life for compliments, but right now she was the one person in the manor I'd choose to be with. She'd been all for trying to make it out alone on foot; I was so glad that she eventually decided to stay.

Brand muttered all the way. "Oh fuck, oh shit, what are we doing coming out here? Like those crazy girls in slasher movies, you know? Always chasing the bad guys instead of running from them? Asking to get their throats cut? Oh man . . ."

In many ways I agreed with him. According to Charley there was little left of Boris to recover, but she could have been wrong. We owed it to him to find out. However harsh the conditions, whatever the likelihood of his murderer – animal or human – still being out here, we could not leave Boris lying dead in the snow. Apply whatever levels of civilization, foolish custom or superiority complex you like, it just wasn't done.

Ellie led the way across the manor's front garden and out onto the coastal road. The whole landscape was hidden beneath snow, like old sheet-covered furniture awaiting the homecoming of long-gone owners. I wondered who would ever make use of this land again – who would be left to bother when the snow did finally melt – but that train of thought led only to depression.

We crossed the flat area of the road, following Charley's earlier footprints in the deep snow; even and distinct on the way out, chaotic on the return journey. As if she'd had something following her.

She had. We all saw what had been chasing her when we slid and clambered down toward the cliffs, veering behind the big rock that signified the beginning of the coastal path. The sight of Boris opened up and spread across the snow had pursued her all the way, and was probably still snapping at her heels now. The smell of his insides slowly cooling under an indifferent sky. The sound of his frozen blood crackling under foot.

Ellie hefted the gun, holding it waist-high, ready to fire in an instant. Her breath condensed in the air before her, coming slightly faster than moments before. She glanced at the torn-up Boris, then surveyed our surroundings, looking for whoever had done this. East and west along the coast, down toward the cliff edge, up to the lip of rock above us, east and west again; Ellie never looked back down at Boris.

I did. I couldn't keep my eyes off what was left of him. It looked as though something big and powerful had held him up to the rock, scraped and twisted him there for a while, and then calmly taken him apart across the snow-covered path. Spray patterns of blood stood out brighter than their surroundings. Every speck was visible and there were many specks, thousands of them spread across a ten metre area. I tried to find a recognizable part of him, but all that was even vaguely identifiable as human was a hand, stuck to the rock in a mess of frosty blood, fingers curled in like the legs of a dead spider. The wrist was tattered, the bone splintered. It had been snapped, not cut.

Brand pointed out a shoe on its side in the snow. "Fuck, Charley was right. Just his shoes left. Miserable bastard always wore the same shoes."

I'd already seen the shoe. It was still mostly full. Boris had not been a miserable bastard. He was introspective, thoughtful, sensitive, sincere, qualities which Brand would never recognize as anything other than sourness. Brand was as thick as shit and twice as unpleasant.

The silence seemed to press in around me. Silence, and cold, and a raw smell of meat, and the sea chanting from below. I was surrounded by everything.

"Let's get back," I said. Ellie glanced at me and nodded.

"But what about—" Brand started, but Ellie cut in without even looking at him.

"You want to make bloody snowballs, go ahead. There's not much to take back. We'll maybe come again later. Maybe."

"What did this?" I said, feeling reality start to shimmy past the shock I'd been gripped by for the last couple of minutes. "Just what the hell?"

Ellie backed up to me and glanced at the rock, then both ways along the path "I don't want to find out just yet," she said.

Later, alone in my room, I would think about exactly what Ellie had meant. *I don't want to find out just yet*, she had said, implying that the perpetrator of Boris's demise would be revealed to us soon. I'd hardly known Boris, quiet guy that he was, and his fate was just another line in the strange composition of death that had overcome the whole country during the last few weeks.

Charley and I were here in the employment of the Department of the Environment. Our brief was to keep a check on the radiation levels in the Atlantic Drift, since things had gone to shit in South America and the dirty reactors had begun to melt down in Brazil. It was a bad job with hardly any pay, but it gave us somewhere to live. The others had tagged along for differing reasons; friends and lovers of friends, all taking the opportunity to get away from things for a while and chill out in the wilds of Cornwall.

But then things went to shit here as well. On TV, minutes before it had ceased broadcasting for good, someone called it the ruin.

Then it had started to snow.

Hayden had taken Charley upstairs, still trying to quell her hysteria. We had no medicines other than aspirin and cough mixtures, but there were a hundred bottles of wine in the cellar. It seemed that Hayden had already poured most of a bottle down Charley's throat by the time the three of us arrived back at the manor. Not a good idea, I thought – I could hardly imagine what ghosts a drunken Charley would see, what terrors her alcohol-induced dreams held in store for her once she was finally left on her own – but it was not my place to say.

Brand stormed in and with his usual subtlety painted a picture of what we'd seen. "Boris's guts were just everywhere, hanging on the rock, spread over the snow. Melted in, like they were still hot when he was being cut up. What the fuck would do that? Eh? Just what the fuck?"

"Who did it?" Rosalie, our resident paranoid, asked.

I shrugged. "Can't say."

"Why not?"

"Not won't," I said, "can't. Can't tell. There's not too much left to tell by, as Brand has so eloquently revealed."

Ellie stood before the open fire and held out her hands, palms up, as if asking for something. A touch of emotion, I mused, but then my thoughts were often cruel.

"Ellie?" Rosalie demanded an answer.

Ellie shrugged. "We can rule out suicide." Nobody responded.

I went through to the kitchen and opened the back door. We were keeping our beers on a shelf in the rear conservatory now that the electricity had gone off. There was a generator, but not enough fuel to run it for more than an hour every day. We agreed that hot water was a priority for that meagre time, so the fridge was now extinct.

I surveyed my choice: Stella; a few final cans of Caffreys; Boddingtons. That had been Jayne's favourite. She'd drunk it in pints, inevitably doing a bad impression of some moustachioed actor after the first creamy sip. I could still see her sparkling eyes as she tried to think of someone new . . . I grabbed a Caffreys and shut the back door, and it was as the latch clicked home that I started to shake.

I'd seen a dead man five minutes ago, a man I'd been talking to the previous evening, drinking with, chatting about what the hell had happened to the world, making inebriated plans of escape, knowing all the time that the snow had us trapped here like chickens surrounded by a fiery moat. Boris had been quiet but thoughtful, the most intelligent person with us at the manor. It had been his idea to lock the doors to many of the rooms because we never used them, and any heat we managed to generate should be kept in the rooms we did use. He had suggested a long walk as the snow had begun in earnest and it had been our prevarication and, I admit, our arguing that had kept us here long enough for it to matter. By the time Boris had persuaded us to make a go of it, the snow was three feet deep. Five miles and we'd be dead. Maximum. The nearest village was ten miles away.

He was dead. Something had taken him apart, torn him up, ripped him to pieces. I was certain that there had been no cutting involved as Brand had suggested. And yes, his bits did look melted into the snow. Still hot when they struck the surface, blooding it in death. Still alive and beating as they were taken out.

I sat at the kitchen table and held my head in my hands. Jayne had said that this would hold all the good thoughts in and let the bad ones seep through your fingers, and sometimes it seemed to work. Now it was just a comfort, like the hands of a lover kneading hope into flaccid muscles, or fear from tense ones.

It could not work this time. I had seen a dead man. And there was nothing we could do about it. We should be telling someone, but over the past few months any sense of "relevant authorities" had fast faded away, just as Jayne had two years before; faded away to agony, then confusion, and then to nothing. Nobody knew what had killed her. Growths on her chest and stomach. Bad blood. Life.

I tried to open the can but my fingers were too cold to slip under the ring-pull. I became frustrated, then angry, and eventually my temper threw the can to the floor. It struck the flagstones and one edge split, sending a fine yellowish spray of beer across the old kitchen cupboards. I cried out at the waste. It was a feeling I was becoming more than used to.

"Hey," Ellie said. She put one hand on my shoulder and removed it before I could shrug her away. "They're saying we should tell someone."

"Who?" I turned to look at her, unashamed of my tears. Ellie was a hard bitch. Maybe they made me more of a person than she.

She raised one eyebrow and pursed her lips. "Brand thinks the army. Rosalie thinks the Fairy Underground."

I scoffed. "Fairy-fucking-Underground. Stupid cow."

"She can't help being like that. You ask me, it makes her more suited to how it's all turning out."

"And how's that; exactly?" I hated Ellie sometimes, all her stronger-than-thou talk and steely eyes. But she was also the person I respected the most in our pathetic little group. Now that Boris had gone.

"Well," she said, "for a start, take a look at how we're all reacting to this. Shocked, maybe. Horrified. But it's almost like it was expected."

"It's all been going to shit . . ." I said, but I did not need to continue. We had all known that we were not immune to the rot settling across society, nature, the world. Eventually it would find us. We just had not known when.

"There is the question of who did it," she said quietly.

"Or what."

She nodded. "Or what."

For now, we left it at that.

"How's Charley?"

"I was just going to see," Ellie said. "Coming?"

I nodded and followed her from the room. The beer had stopped spraying and now fizzled into sticky rivulets where the flags joined. I was still thirsty.

Charley looked bad. She was drunk, that was obvious, and she had been sick down herself, and she had wet herself. Hayden was in the process of trying to mop up the mess when we knocked and entered.

"How is she?" Ellie asked pointlessly.

"How do you think?" He did not even glance at us as he tried to hold onto the babbling, crying, laughing and puking Charley.

"Maybe you shouldn't have given her so much to drink," Ellie said. Hayden sent her daggers but did not reply.

Charley struggled suddenly in his arms, ranting and shouting at the shaded candles in the corners of the room.

"What's that?" I said. "What's she saying?" For some reason it sounded important, like a solution to a problem encoded by grief.

"She's been saying some stuff," Hayden said loudly, so we could hear above Charley's slurred cries. "Stuff about Boris. Seeing angels in the snow. She says his angels came to get him."

"Some angels," Ellie muttered.

"You go down," Hayden said, "I'll stay here with her." He wanted us gone, that much was obvious, so we did not disappoint him.

Downstairs, Brand and Rosalie were hanging around the mobile phone. It had sat on the mantelpiece for the last three weeks like a gun without bullets, ugly and useless. Every now and then someone would try it, receiving only a crackling nothing in response. Random numbers, recalled numbers, numbers held in the 'phone's memory, all came to naught. Gradually it was tried less – every unsuccessful attempt had been more depressing.

"What?" I said.

"Trying to call someone," Brand said. "Police. Someone."

"So they can come to take fingerprints?" Ellie flopped into one of the old armchairs and began picking at its upholstery, widening a hole she'd been plucking at for days. "Any replies?"

Brand shook his head.

"We've got to do something," Rosalie said, "we can't just sit here while Boris is lying dead out there."

Ellie said nothing. The telephone hissed its amusement. Rosalie looked to me. "There's nothing we can do," I said. "Really, there's not much to collect up. If we did bring his . . . bits . . . back here, what would we do?"

"Bury . . ." Rosalie began.

"Three feet of snow? Frozen ground?"

"And the things," Brand said. The phone cackled again and he turned it off.

"What things?"

Brand looked around our small group. "The things Boris said he'd seen."

Boris had mentioned nothing to me. In our long, drunken talks, he had never talked of any angels in the snow. Upstairs, I'd thought that it was simply Charley drunk and mad with grief, but now Brand had said it too I had the distinct feeling I was missing out on something. I was irked, and upset at feeling irked.

"Things?" Rosalie said, and I closed my eyes. *Oh fuck, don't tell her*, I willed at Brand. She'd regale us with stories of secret societies and messages in the clouds, disease-makers who were wiping out the inept and the crippled, the barren and the intellectually inadequate. Jayne had been sterile, so we'd never had kids. The last thing I needed was another one of Rosalie's mad ravings about how my wife had died, why she'd died, who had killed her.

Luckily, Brand seemed of like mind. Maybe the joint he'd lit up had stewed him into silence at last. He turned to the fire and stared into its dying depths, sitting on the edge of the seat as if wondering whether or not to feed it some more. The stack of logs was running low.

"Things?" Rosalie said again, nothing if not persistent.

"No things," I said. "Nothing." I left the room before it all flared up.

In the kitchen I opened another can, carefully this time, and poured it into a tall glass. I stared into creamy depths as bubbles passed up and down. It took a couple of minutes for the drink to settle, and in that time I had recalled Jayne's face, her body, the best times we'd had together. At my first sip, a tear replenished the glass.

That night I heard doors opening and closing as someone wandered between beds. I was too tired to care who.

*   *   *

The next morning I half expected it to be all better. I had the bitter taste of dread in my mouth when I woke up, but also a vague idea that all the bad stuff could only have happened in nightmares. As I dressed – two shirts, a heavy pullover, a jacket – I wondered what awaited me beyond my bedroom door.

In the kitchen Charley was swigging from a fat mug of tea. It steamed so much, it seemed liable to burn whatever it touched. Her lips were red-raw, as were her eyes. She clutched the cup tightly, knuckles white, thumbs twisted into the handle. She looked as though she wanted to never let it go.

I had a sinking feeling in my stomach when I saw her. I glanced out of the window and saw the landscape of snow, added to yet again the previous night, bloated flakes still fluttering down to reinforce the barricade against our escape. Somewhere out there, Boris's parts were frozen memories hidden under a new layer.

"Okay?" I said quietly.

Charley looked up at me as if I'd farted at her mother's funeral. "Of course I'm not okay," she said, enunciating each word carefully. "And what do you care?"

I sat at the table opposite her, yawning, rubbing hands through my greasy hair, generally trying to disperse the remnants of sleep. There was a pot of tea on the table and I took a spare mug and poured a steaming brew. Charley watched my every move. I was aware of her eyes upon me, but I tried not to let it show. The cup shook, I could barely grab a spoon. I'd seen her boyfriend splashed across the snow, I felt terrible about it, but then I realized that she'd seen the same scene. How bad must she be feeling?

"We have to do something," she said.

"Charley—"

"We can't just sit here. We have to go. Boris needs a funeral. We have to go and find someone, get out of this God-forsaken place. There must be someone near, able to help, someone to look after us? I need someone to look after me."

The statement was phrased as a question, but I ventured no answer.

"Look," she said, "we have to get out. Don't you see?" She let go of her mug and clasped my hands; hers were hot and sweaty. "The village, we can get there, I know we can."

"No, Charley," I said, but I did not have a chance to finish my

sentence (*there's no way out, we tried, and didn't you see the
television reports weeks ago?*) before Ellie marched into the room.
She paused when she saw Charley, then went to the cupboard and
poured herself a bowl of cereal. She used water. We'd run out of
milk a week ago.

"There's no telephone," she said, spooning some soggy corn
flakes into her mouth. "No television, save some flickering
pictures most of us don't want to see. Or believe. There's no
radio, other than the occasional foreign channel. Rosie says she
speaks French. She's heard them talking of 'the doom'. That's
how she translates it, though I think it sounds more like 'the ruin'.
The nearest village is ten miles away. We have no motorized
transport that will even get out of the garage. To walk it would be
suicide." She crunched her limp breakfast, mixing in more sugar
to give some taste.

Charley did not reply. She knew what Ellie was saying, but
tears were her only answer.

"So we're here until the snow melts," I said. Ellie really was a
straight bitch. Not a glimmer of concern for Charley, not a word
of comfort.

Ellie looked at me and stopped chewing for a moment. "I think
until it does melt, we're protected." She had a way of coming out
with ideas that both enraged me, and scared the living shit out of
me at the same time.

Charley could only cry.

Later, three of us decided to try to get out. In moments of stress,
panic and mourning, logic holds no sway.

I said I'd go with Brand and Charley. It was one of the most
foolish decisions I've ever made, but seeing Charley's eyes as she
sat in the kitchen on her own, thinking about her slaughtered
boyfriend, listening to Ellie go on about how hopeless it all was
. . . I could not say no. And in truth, I was as desperate to leave as
anyone.

It was almost ten in the morning when we set out.

Ellie was right, I knew that even then. Her face as she watched
us struggle across the garden should have brought me back
straight away: she thought I was a fool. She was the last person
in the world I wanted to appear foolish in front of, but still there

was that nagging feeling in my heart that pushed me on – a mixture of desire to help Charley and a hopeless feeling that by staying here, we were simply waiting for death to catch us up.

It seemed to have laid its shroud over the rest of the world already. Weeks ago the television had shown some dreadful sights: people falling ill and dying in their thousands; food riots in London; a nuclear exchange between Greece and Turkey. More, lots more, all of it bad. We'd known something was coming – things had been falling apart for years – but once it began it was a cumulative effect, speeding from a steady trickle toward decline, to a raging torrent. *We're better off where we are*, Boris had said to me. It was ironic that because of him, we were leaving.

I carried the shotgun. Brand had an air pistol, though I'd barely trust him with a sharpened stick. As well as being loud and brash, he spent most of his time doped to the eyeballs. If there was any trouble, I'd be watching out for him as much as anything else.

Something had killed Boris and whatever it was, animal or human, it was still out there in the snow. Moved on, hopefully, now it had fed. But then again perhaps not. It did not dissuade us from trying.

The snow in the manor garden was almost a metre deep. The three of us had botched together snow shoes of varying effectiveness. Brand wore two snapped-off lengths of picture frame on each foot, which seemed to act more as knives to slice down through the snow than anything else. He was tenaciously pompous; he struggled with his mistake rather than admitting it. Charley had used two frying pans with their handles snapped off, and she seemed to be making good headway. My own creations consisted of circles of mounted canvas cut from the redundant artwork in the manor. Old owners of the estate stared up at me through the snow as I repeatedly stepped on their faces.

By the time we reached the end of the driveway and turned to see Ellie and Hayden watching us, I was sweating and exhausted. We had travelled about fifty metres.

Across the road lay the cliff path leading to Boris's dismembered corpse. Charley glanced that way, perhaps wishing to look down upon her boyfriend one more time.

"Come on," I said, clasping her elbow and heading away. She offered no resistance.

The road was apparent as a slightly lower, smoother plain of snow between the two hedged banks on either side. Everything was glaring white, and we were all wearing sunglasses to prevent snow-blindness. We could see far along the coast from here as the bay swept around toward the east, the craggy cliffs spotted white where snow had drifted onto ledges, an occasional lonely seabird diving to the sea and returning empty-beaked to sing a mournful song for company. In places the snow was cantilevered out over the edge of the cliff, a deadly trap should any of us stray that way. The sea itself surged against the rocks below, but it broke no spray. The usual roar of the waters crashing into the earth, slowly eroding it away and reclaiming it, had changed. It was now more of a grind as tonnes of slushy ice replaced the usual white horses, not yet forming a solid barrier over the water but still thick enough to temper the waves. In a way it was sad; a huge beast winding down in old age.

I watched as a cormorant plunged down through the chunky ice and failed to break surface again. It was as if it were committing suicide. Who was I to say it was not?

"How far?" Brand asked yet again.

"Ten miles," I said.

"I'm knackered." He had already lit up a joint and he took long, hard pulls on it. I could hear its tip sizzling in the crisp morning air.

"We've come about three hundred metres," I said, and Brand shut up.

It was difficult to talk; we needed all our breath for the effort of walking. Sometimes the snow shoes worked, especially where the surface of the snow had frozen the previous night. Other times we plunged straight in up to our thighs and we had to hold our arms out for balance as we hauled our leg out, just to let it sink in again a step along. The rucksacks did not help. We each carried food, water and dry clothing, and Brand especially seemed to be having trouble with his.

The sky was a clear blue. The sun rose ahead of us as if mocking the frozen landscape. Some days it started like this, but the snow never seemed to melt. I had almost forgotten what the ground below it looked like; it seemed that the snow had been here forever. When it began our spirits had soared, like a bunch of school-kids waking to find the landscape had changed overnight.

Charley and I had still gone down to the sea to take our readings, and when we returned there was a snowman in the garden wearing one of her bras and a pair of my briefs. A snowball fight had ensued, during which Brand became a little too aggressive for his own good. We'd ganged up on him and pelted him with snow compacted to ice until he shouted and yelped. We were cold and wet and bruised, but we did not stop laughing for hours.

We'd all dried out in front of the open fire in the huge living room. Rosalie had stripped to her knickers and danced to music on the radio. She was a bit of a sixties throwback, Rosalie, and she didn't seem to realize what her little display did to cosseted people like me. I watched happily enough.

Later, we sat around the fire and told ghost stories. Boris was still with us then, of course, and he came up with the best one which had us all cowering behind casual expressions. He told us of a man who could not see, hear or speak, but who knew of the ghosts around him. His life was silent and senseless save for the day his mother died. Then he cried and shouted and raged at the darkness, before curling up and dying himself. His world opened up then, and he no longer felt alone, but whoever he tried to speak to could only fear or loath him. The living could never make friends with the dead. And death had made him more silent than ever.

None of us would admit it, but we were all scared shitless as we went to bed that night. As usual, doors opened and footsteps padded along corridors. And, as usual, my door remained shut and I slept alone.

Days later the snow was too thick to be enjoyable. It became risky to go outside, and as the woodpile started to dwindle and the radio and television broadcasts turned more grim, we realized that we were becoming trapped. A few of us had tried to get to the village, but it was a half-hearted attempt and we'd returned once we were tired. We figured we'd travelled about two miles along the coast. We had seen no one.

As the days passed and the snow thickened, the atmosphere did likewise with a palpable sense of panic. A week ago, Boris had pointed out that there were no 'plane trails anymore.

This, our second attempt to reach the village, felt more like life and death. Before Boris had been killed we'd felt confined, but it also gave a sense of protection from the things going on in the world. Now there was a feeling that if we could not get out, worse things would happen to us where we were.

I remembered Jayne as she lay dying from the unknown disease. I had been useless, helpless, hopeless, praying to a God I had long ignored to grant us a kind fate. I refused to sit back and go the same way. I would not go gently. Fuck fate.

"What was that?"

Brand stopped and tugged the little pistol from his belt. It was stark black against the pure white snow.

"What?"

He nodded. "Over there." I followed his gaze and looked up the sloping hillside. To our right the sea sighed against the base of the cliffs. To our left – the direction Brand was now facing – snowfields led up a gentle slope towards the moors several miles inland. It was a rocky, craggy landscape, and some rocks had managed to hold off the drifts. They peered out darkly here and there, like the faces of drowning men going under for the final time.

"What?" I said again, exasperated. I'd slipped the shotgun off my shoulder and held it waist-high. My finger twitched on the trigger guard. Images of Boris's remains sharpened my senses. I did not want to end up like that.

"I saw something moving. Something white."

"Some snow, perhaps?" Charley said bitterly.

"Something running across the snow," he said, frowning as he concentrated on the middle-distance. The smoke from his joint mingled with his condensing breath.

We stood that way for a minute or two, steaming sweat like smoke signals of exhaustion. I tried taking off my glasses to look, but the glare was too much. I glanced sideways at Charley. She'd pulled a big old revolver from her rucksack and held it with both hands. Her lips were pulled back from her teeth in a feral grimace. She really wanted to use that gun.

I saw nothing. "Could have been a cat. Or a seagull flying low."

"Could have been." Brand shoved the pistol back into his belt and reached around for his water canteen. He tipped it to his lips and cursed. "Frozen!"

"Give it a shake," I said. I knew it would do no good but it may shut him up for a while. "Charley, what's the time?" I had a watch but I wanted to talk to Charley, keep her involved with the present, keep her here. I had started to realize not only what a stupid idea this was, but what an even more idiotic step it had been letting Charley come along. If she wasn't here for revenge, she was blind with grief. I could not see her eyes behind her sunglasses.

"Nearly midday." She was hoisting her rucksack back onto her shoulders, never taking her eyes from the snowscape sloping slowly up and away from us. "What do you think it was?"

I shrugged. "Brand seeing things. Too much wacky baccy."

We set off again. Charley was in the lead, I followed close behind and Brand stumbled along at the rear. It was eerily silent around us, the snow muffling our gasps and puffs, the constant grumble of the sea soon blending into the background as much as it ever did. There was a sort of white noise in my ears: blood pumping; breath ebbing and flowing; snow crunching underfoot. They merged into one whisper, eschewing all outside noise, almost soporific in rhythm. I coughed to break the spell.

"What the hell do we do when we get to the village?" Brand said.

"Send back help," Charley stated slowly, enunciating each word as if to a naïve young child.

"But what if the village is like everywhere else we've seen or heard about on TV?"

Charley was silent for a while. So was I. A collage of images tumbled through my mind, hateful and hurtful and sharper because of that. Hazy scenes from the last day of television broadcasts we had watched: loaded ships leaving docks and sailing off to some nebulous sanctuary abroad; shootings in the streets, bodies in the gutters, dogs sniffing at open wounds; an airship, drifting over the hills in some vague attempt to offer hope.

"Don't be stupid," I said.

"Even if it is, there will be help there," Charley said quietly.

"Like hell." Brand lit up another joint. It was cold, we were risking our lives; there may very well be something in the snow itching to attack us . . . but at that moment I wanted nothing more than to take a long haul on Brand's pot, and let casual oblivion anaesthetize my fears.

*   *   *

An hour later we found the car.

By my figuring we had come about three miles. We were all but exhausted. My legs ached, knee joints stiff and hot as if on fire.

The road had started a slow curve to the left, heading inland from the coast toward the distant village. Its path had become less distinct, the hedges having sunk slowly into the ground until there was really nothing to distinguish it from the fields of snow on either side. We had been walking the last half-hour on memory alone.

The car was almost completely buried by snow, only one side of the windscreen and the iced-up aerial still visible. There was no sign of the route it had taken; whatever tracks it had made were long-since obliterated by the blizzards. As we approached the snow started again, fat flakes drifting lazily down and landing on the icy surface of last night's fall.

"Do not drive unless absolutely necessary," Brand said. Charley and I ignored him. We unslung our rucksacks and approached the buried shape, all of us keeping hold of our weapons. I meant to ask Charley where she'd got hold of the revolver – whether she'd had it with her when we both came here to test the sea and write environmental reports which would never be read – but now did not seem the time. I had no wish to seem judgmental or patronizing.

As I reached out to knock some of the frozen snow from the windscreen a flight of seagulls cawed and took off from nearby. They had been all but invisible against the snow, but there were at least thirty of them lifting as one, calling loudly as they twirled over our heads and then headed out to sea.

We all shouted out in shock. Charley stumbled sideways as she tried to bring her gun to bear and fell on her back. Brand screeched like a kid, then let off a pop with his air pistol to hide his embarrassment. The pellet found no target. The birds ignored us after the initial fly-past, and they slowly merged with the hazy distance. The new snow shower brought the horizon in close.

"Shit," Charley muttered.

"Yeah." Brand reloaded his pistol without looking at either of us, then rooted around for the joint he'd dropped when he screamed.

Charley and I went back to knocking the snow away, using our gloved hands to make tracks down the windscreen and across the bonnet. "I think it's a Ford," I said uselessly. "Maybe an old Mondeo." Jayne and I had owned a Mondeo when we'd been courting. Many was the time we had parked in some shaded woodland or beside units on the local industrial estate, wound down the windows and made love as the cool night air looked on. We'd broken down once while I was driving her home; it had made us two hours late and her father had come close to beating me senseless. It was only the oil on my hands that had convinced him of our story.

I closed my eyes.

"Can't see anything," Charley said, jerking me back to cold reality. "Windscreen's frozen up on the inside."

"Take us ages to clear the doors."

"What do you want to do that for?" Brand said. "Dead car, probably full of dead people."

"Dead people may have guns and food and fuel," I said. "Going to give us a hand?"

Brand glanced at the dark windshield, the contents of the car hidden by ice and shadowed by the weight of snow surrounding it. He sat gently on his rucksack, and when he saw it would take his weight without sinking in the snow, he re-lit his joint and stared out to sea. I wondered whether he'd even notice if we left him there.

"We could uncover the passenger door," Charley said. "Driver's side is stuck fast in the drift, take us hours."

We both-set about trying to shift snow away from the car. "Keep your eyes open," I said to Brand. He just nodded and watched the sea lift and drop its thickening ice-floes. I used the shotgun as a crutch to lift myself onto the bonnet, and from there to the covered roof.

"What?" Charley said. I ignored her, turning a slow circle, trying to pick out any movement against the fields of white. To the west lay the manor, a couple of miles away and long since hidden by creases in the landscape. To the north the ground still rose steadily away from the sea, rocks protruding here and there along with an occasional clump of trees hardy enough to survive Atlantic storms. Nothing moved. The shower was turning quickly into a storm and I felt suddenly afraid. The manor was at least three miles behind us; the village seven miles ahead. We were in the middle, three weak humans slowly freezing as nature freaked out and threw weeks of snow and ice at us. And here we were, convinced we could defeat it, certain in our own puny minds that we were the rulers here, we called the shots. However much we polluted and contaminated, I knew, we would never call the shots. Nature may let us live within it, but in the end it would purge and cleanse itself. And whether there would be room for us in the new world . . .

Perhaps this was the first stage of that cleansing. While civilization slaughtered itself, disease and extremes of weather took advantage of our distraction to pick off the weak.

"We should get back," I said.

"But the village—"

"Charley, it's almost two. It'll start getting dark in two hours, maximum. We can't travel in the dark; we might walk right by the village, or stumble onto one of those ice overhangs at the cliff edge. Brand here may get so doped he thinks we're ghosts and shoot us with his pop-gun."

"Hey!"

"But Boris . . ." Charley said. "He's . . . we need help. To bury him. We need to tell someone."

I climbed carefully down from the car roof and landed in the snow beside her. "We'll take a look in the car. Then we should get back. It'll help no one if we freeze to death out here."

"I'm not cold," she said defiantly.

"That's because you're moving, you're working. When you walk you sweat and you'll stay warm. When we have to stop – and eventually we will – you'll stop moving. Your sweat will freeze, and so will you. We'll all freeze. They'll find us in the thaw, you and me huddled up for warmth, Brand with a frozen reefer still in his gob."

Charley smiled, Brand scowled. Both expressions pleased me.

"The door's frozen shut," she said.

"I'll use my key." I punched at the glass with the butt of the shotgun. After three attempts the glass shattered and I used my gloved hands to clear it all away. I caught a waft of something foul and stale. Charley stepped back with a slight groan. Brand was oblivious.

We peered inside the car, leaning forward so that the weak light could filter in around us.

There was a dead man in the driver's seat. He was frozen solid, hunched up under several blankets, only his eyes and nose visible. Icicles hung from both. His eyelids were still open. On the dashboard a candle had burnt down to nothing more than a puddle of wax, imitating the ice as it dripped forever toward the floor. The scene was so still it was eerie, like a painting so life-like that textures and shapes could be felt. I noticed the driver's door handle was jammed open, though the door had not budged against the snowdrift burying that side of the car. At the end he had obviously attempted to get out. I shuddered as I tried to imagine this man's lonely death. It was the second body I'd seen in two days.

"Well?" Brand called from behind us.

"Your drug supplier," Charley said. "Car's full of snow."

I snorted, pleased to hear the humour, but when I looked at her she seemed as sad and forlorn as ever. "Maybe we should see if he brought us anything useful," she said, and I nodded.

Charley was smaller than me so she said she'd go. I went to protest but she was already wriggling through the shattered window, and a minute later she'd thrown out everything loose she could find. She came back out without looking at me.

There was a rucksack half full of canned foods; a petrol can with a swill of fuel in the bottom; a novel frozen at page ninety; some plastic bottles filled with piss and split by the ice; a rifle, but no ammunition; a smaller rucksack with wallet, some papers, an electronic credit card; a photo wallet frozen shut; a plastic bag full of shit; a screwed-up newspaper as hard as wood.

Everything was frozen.

"Let's go," I said. Brand and Charley took a couple of items each and shouldered their rucksacks. I picked up the rifle. We took everything except the shit and piss.

It took us four hours to get back to the manor. Three times on the way Brand said he'd seen something bounding through the snow – a stag, he said, big and white with sparkling antlers – and we dropped everything and went into a defensive huddle. But nothing ever materialized from the worsening storm, even though our imaginations painted all sorts of horrors behind and beyond the snowflakes. If there were anything out there, it kept itself well hidden.

The light was fast fading as we arrived back. Our tracks had been all but covered, and it was only later that I realized how

staggeringly lucky we'd been to even find our way home. Perhaps
something was on our side, guiding us, steering us back to the
manor. Perhaps it was the change in nature taking us home,
preparing us for what was to come next.

It was the last favour we were granted.

Hayden cooked us some soup as the others huddled around the
fire, listening to our story and trying so hard not to show their
disappointment. Brand kept chiming in about the things he'd seen
in the snow. Even Ellie's face held the taint of fading hope.

"Boris's angels?" Rosalie suggested. "He *may* have seen angels,
you know. They're not averse to steering things their way, when it
suits them." Nobody answered.

Charley was crying again, shivering by the fire. Rosalie had
wrapped her in blankets and now hugged her close.

"The gun looks okay." Ellie said. She'd sat at the table and
stripped and oiled the rifle, listening to us all as we talked. She
illustrated the fact by pointing it at the wall and squeezing the
trigger a few times. *Click click click*. There was no ammunition
for it.

"What about the body?" Rosalie asked. "Did you see who it
was?"

I frowned. "What do you mean?"

"Well, if it was someone coming along the road toward the
manor, maybe one of us knew him." We were all motionless save
for Ellie, who still rooted through the contents of the car. She'd
already put the newspaper on the floor so that it could dry out, in
the hope of being able to read at least some of it. We'd made out
the date: one week ago. The television had stopped showing
pictures two weeks ago. There was a week of history in there, if
only we could save it.

"He was frozen stiff," I said. "We didn't get a good look . . .
and anyway, who'd be coming here? And why? Maybe it was a
good job—"

Ellie gasped. There was a tearing sound as she peeled apart
more pages of the photo wallet and gasped again, this time
struggling to draw in a breath afterwards.

"Ellie?"

She did not answer. The others had turned to her but she
seemed not to notice. She saw nothing, other than the photo-

graphs in her hand. She stared at them for an endless few seconds, eyes moist yet unreadable in the glittering fire light. Then she scraped the chair back across the polished floor, crumpled the photo's into her back pocket and walked quickly from the room.

I followed, glancing at the others to indicate that they should stay where they were. None of them argued. Ellie was already half-way up the long staircase by the time I entered the hallway, but it was not until the final stair that she stopped, turned and answered my soft calling.

"My husband," she said, "Jack. I haven't seen him for two years." A tear ran icily down her cheek. "We never really made it, you know?" She looked at the wall beside her, as though she could stare straight through and discern logic and truth in the blanked-out landscape beyond. "He was coming here. For me. To find me."

There was nothing I could say. Ellie seemed to forget I was there and she mumbled the next few words to herself. Then she turned and disappeared from view along the upstairs corridor, shadow dancing in the light of disturbed candles.

Back in the living room I told the others that Ellie was all right, she had gone to bed, she was tired and cold and as human as the rest of us. I did not let on about her dead husband, I figured it was really none of their business. Charley glared at me with bloodshot eyes, and I was sure she'd figured it out. Brand flicked bits of carrot from his soup into the fire and watched them sizzle to nothing.

We went to bed soon after. Alone in my room I sat at the window for a long time, huddled in clothes and blankets, staring out at the moonlit brightness of the snow drifts and the fat flakes still falling. I tried to imagine Ellie's estranged husband struggling to steer the car through deepening snow, the radiator clogging in the drift it had buried its nose in, splitting, gushing boiling water and steaming instantly into an ice-trap. Sitting there, perhaps not knowing just how near he was, thinking of his wife and how much he needed to see her. And I tried to imagine what desperate events must have driven him to do such a thing, though I did not think too hard.

A door opened and closed quietly, footsteps, another door slipped open to allow a guest entry. I wondered who was sharing a bed tonight.

I saw Jayne, naked and beautiful in the snow, bearing no sign of the illness that had killed her. She beckoned me, drawing me nearer, and at last a door was opening for me as well, a shape coming into the room, white material floating around its hips, or perhaps they were limbs, membranous and thin . . .

My eyes snapped open and I sat up on the bed. I was still dressed from the night before. Dawn streamed in the window and my candle had burnt down to nothing.

Ellie stood next to the bed. Her eyes were red-rimmed and swollen. I tried to pretend I had not noticed.

"Happy Christmas," she said. "Come on. Brand's dead."

Brand was lying just beyond the smashed conservatory doors behind the kitchen. There was a small courtyard area here, protected somewhat by an overhanging roof so that the snow was only about knee-deep. Most of it was red. A drift had already edged its way into the conservatory, and the beer cans on the shelf had frozen and split. No more beer.

He had been punctured by countless holes, each the width of a thumb, all of them clogged with hardened blood. One eye stared hopefully out to the hidden horizon, the other was absent. His hair was also missing; it looked like he'd been scalped. There were bits of him all around – a finger here, a splash of brain there – but he was less mutilated than Boris had been. At least we could see that this smudge in the snow had once been Brand.

Hayden was standing next to him, posing daintily in an effort to avoid stepping in the blood. It was a lost cause. "What the hell was he doing out here?" he asked in disgust.

"I heard doors opening last night," I said. "Maybe he came for a walk. Or a smoke."

"The door was mine," Rosalie said softly. She had appeared behind us and nudged in between Ellie and me. She wore a long, creased shirt. Brand's shirt, I noticed. "Brand was with me until three o'clock this morning. Then he left to go back to his own room, said he was feeling ill. We thought perhaps you shouldn't know about us." Her eyes were wide in an effort not to cry. "We thought everyone would laugh.

Nobody answered. Nobody laughed. Rosalie looked at Brand with more shock than sadness, and I wondered just how often he'd opened her door in the night. The insane, unfair notion that she may even be relieved flashed across my mind, one of those awful thoughts you try to expunge but which hangs around like a guilty secret.

"Maybe we should go inside," I said to Rosalie, but she gave me such an icy glare that I turned away, looking at Brand's shattered body rather than her piercing eyes.

"I'm a big girl now," she said. I could hear her rapid breathing as she tried to contain the disgust and shock at what she saw. I wondered if she'd ever seen a dead body. Most people had, nowadays.

Charley was nowhere to be seen. "I didn't wake her," Ellie said when I queried. "She had enough to handle yesterday. I thought she shouldn't really see this. No need."

And you? I thought, noticing Ellie's puffy eyes, the gauntness of her face, her hands fisting open and closed at her sides. *Are you all right? Did you have enough to handle yesterday?*

"What the hell do we do with him?" Hayden asked. He was still standing closer to Brand than the rest of us, hugging himself to try to preserve some of the warmth from sleep. "I mean, Boris was all over the place, from what I hear. But Brand . . . we have to do something. Bury him, or something. It's Christmas, for God's sake."

"The ground's like iron," I protested.

"So we take it in turns digging," Rosalie said quietly.

"It'll take us—"

"Then I'll do it myself." She walked out into the blooded snow and shattered glass in bare feet, bent over Brand's body and grabbed under each armpit as if to lift him. She was naked beneath the shirt. Hayden stared in frank fascination. I turned away, embarrassed for myself more than for Rosalie.

"Wait," Ellie sighed. "Rosalie, wait. Let's all dress properly, then we'll come and bury him. Rosalie." The girl stood and smoothed Brand's shirt down over her thighs, perhaps realizing what she had put on display. She looked up at the sky and caught the morning's first snowflake on her nose.

"Snowing," she said. "Just for a fucking change."

We went inside. Hayden remained in the kitchen with the outside door shut and bolted while the rest of us went upstairs to dress, wake Charley and tell her the grim Yule tidings. Once Rosalie's door had closed I followed Ellie along to her room. She opened her door for me and invited me in, obviously knowing I needed to talk.

Her place was a mess. Perhaps, I thought, she was so busy being strong and mysterious that she had no time for tidying up. Clothes were strewn across the floor, a false covering like the snow outside. Used plates were piled next to her bed, those at the bottom already blurred with mould, the uppermost still showing the remains of the meal we'd had before Boris had been killed. Spaghetti bolognaise, I recalled, to Hayden's own recipe, rich and tangy with tinned tomatoes, strong with garlic, the helpings massive. Somewhere out there Boris's last meal lay frozen in the snow, half digested, torn from his guts—

I snorted and closed my eyes. Another terrible thought that wouldn't go away.

"Brand really saw things in the snow, didn't he?" Ellie asked.

"Yes, he was pretty sure. At least, *a* thing. He said it was like a stag, except white. It was bounding along next to us, he said. We stopped a few times but I'm certain I never saw anything. Don't think Charley did, either." I made space on Ellie's bed and sat down. "Why?"

Ellie walked to the window and opened the curtains. The snowstorm had started in earnest, and although her window faced the Atlantic all we could see was a sea of white. She rested her forehead on the cold glass, her breath misting, fading, misting again. "I've seen something too," she said.

Ellie. Seeing things in the snow. Ellie was the nearest we had to a leader, though none of us had ever wanted one. She was strong, if distant. Intelligent, if a little straight with it. She'd never been much of a laugh, even before things had turned to shit, and her dogged conservatism in someone so young annoyed me no end.

Ellie, seeing things in the snow.

I could not bring myself to believe it. I did not want to. If I did accept it then there really were things out there, because Ellie did not lie, and she was not prone to fanciful journeys of the imagination.

"What something?" I asked at last, fearing it a question I would never wish to be answered. But I could not simply ignore it. I could not sit here and listen to Ellie opening up, then stand and walk away. Not with Boris frozen out there, not with Brand still cooling into the landscape.

She rocked her head against the glass. "Don't know. Something white. So how did I see it?" She turned from the window, stared at me, crossed her arms. "From this window," she said. "Two days ago. Just before Charley found Boris. Something flitting across the snow like a bird, except it left faint tracks. As big as a fox, perhaps, but it had more legs. Certainly not a deer."

"Or one of Boris's angels?"

She shook her head and smiled, but there was no humour there. There rarely was. "Don't tell anyone," she said. "I don't want anyone to know. But! We will have to be careful. Take the guns when we try to bury Brand. A couple of us keep a look-out while the others dig. Though I doubt we'll even get through the snow."

"You and guns," I said perplexed. I didn't know how to word what I was trying to ask.

Ellie smiled wryly. "Me and guns. I hate guns."

I stared at her, saying nothing, using silence to pose the next question.

"I have a history," she said. And that was all.

Later, downstairs in the kitchen, Charley told us what she'd managed to read in the paper from the frozen car. In the week since we'd picked up the last TV signal and the paper was printed, things had gone from bad to worse. The illness that had killed my Jayne was claiming millions across the globe. The USA blamed Iraq. Russia blamed China. Blame continued to waste lives. There was civil unrest and shootings in the streets, mass-burials at sea, martial law, air strikes, food shortages . . . the words melded into one another as Rosalie recited the reports.

Hayden was trying to cook mince pies without the mince. He was using stewed apples instead, and the kitchen stank sickeningly sweet. None of us felt particularly festive.

Outside, in the heavy snow that even now was attempting to drift in and cover Brand, we were all twitchy. Whoever or – now more likely – whatever had done this could still be around. Guns were held at the ready.

We wrapped him in an old sheet and enclosed this in torn black plastic bags until there was no white or red showing. Ellie and I dragged him around the corner of the house to where there were some old flowers beds. We started to dig where we remembered them to be, but when we got through the snow the ground was too hard. In the end we left him on the surface of the frozen earth and covered the hole back in with snow, mumbling about burying him when the thaw came. The whole process had an unsettling sense of permanence.

As if the snow would never melt.

Later, staring from the dining room window as Hayden brought in a platter of old vegetables as our Christmas feast, I saw something big and white skimming across the surface of the snow. It moved too quickly for me to make it out properly, but I was certain I saw wings.

I turned away from the window, glanced at Ellie and said nothing.

II: The Colour of Fear

During the final few days of Jayne's life I had felt completely hemmed in. Not only physically trapped within our home – and more often the bedroom where she lay – but also mentally hindered. It was a feeling I hated, felt guilty about and tried desperately to relieve, but it was always there.

I stayed, holding her hand for hour after terrible hour, our palms fused by sweat, her face pasty and contorted by agonies I could barely imagine. Sometimes she would be conscious and alert, sitting up in bed and listening as I read to her, smiling at the humourous parts, trying to ignore the sad ones. She would ask me questions about how things were in the outside world, and I would lie and tell her they were getting better. There was no need to add to her misery. Other times she would be a shadow of her old self, a grey stain on the bed with liquid limbs and weak bowels, a screaming thing with bloody growths sprouting across her skin and pumping their venom inward with uncontrollable, unstoppable tenacity. At these times I would talk truthfully and tell her the reality of things, that the world was going to shit and she would be much better off when she left it.

Even then I did not tell her the complete truth: that I wished I were going with her. Just in case she could still hear.

Wherever I went during those final few days I was under assault, besieged by images of Jayne, thoughts of her impending death, vague ideas of what would happen after she had gone. I tried to fill the landscape of time laid out before me, but Jayne never figured and so the landscape was bare. She was my whole world; without her I could picture nothing to live for. My mind was never free although sometimes, when a doctor found time to visit our house and *tut* and sigh over Jayne's wasting body, I would go for a walk. Mostly she barely knew the doctor was there, for which I was grateful. There was nothing he could do. I would not be able to bear even the faintest glimmer of hope in her eyes.

I strolled through the park opposite our house, staying to the paths so that I did not risk stepping on discarded needles or stumbling across suicides decaying slowly back to nature. The trees were as beautiful as ever, huge emeralds against the grimly polluted sky. Somehow they bled the taint of humanity from their systems. They adapted, changed, and our arrival had really done little to halt their progress. A few years of poisons and disease, perhaps. A shaping of the landscape upon which we projected an idea of control. But when we were all dead and gone our industrial disease on the planet would be little more than a few twisted, corrupted rings in the lifetime of the oldest trees. I wished we could adapt so well.

When Jayne died there was no sense of release. My grief was as great as if she'd been killed at the height of health, her slow decline doing nothing to prepare me for the dread that enveloped me at the moment of her last strangled sigh. Still I was under siege, this time by death. The certainty of its black fingers rested on my shoulders day and night, long past the hour of Jayne's hurried burial in a local football ground alongside a thousand others. I would turn around sometimes and try to see past it, make out some ray of hope in a stranger's gaze. But there was always the blackness bearing down on me, clouding my vision and the gaze of others, promising doom soon.

It's ironic that it was not death that truly scared me, but living. Without Jayne the world was nothing but an empty, dying place.

Then I had come here, an old manor on the rugged South West coast. I'd thought that solitude – a distance between me and the terrible place the world was slowly becoming – would be a balm to my suffering. In reality it was little more than a placebo and realizing that negated it. I felt more trapped than ever.

The morning after Brand's death and botched burial – Boxing Day – I sat at my bedroom window and watched nature laying siege. The snow hugged the landscape like a funeral shroud in negative. The coast was hidden by the cliffs, but I could see the sea further out. There was something that I thought at first to be an iceberg and it took me a few minutes to figure out what it really was; the upturned hull of a big boat. A ferry, perhaps, or one of the huge cruise liners being used to ship people south, away from blighted Britain to the false promise of Australia. I was glad I could not see any more detail. I wondered what we would find washed up in the rock pools that morning, were Charley and I to venture down to the sea.

If I stared hard at the snowbanks, the fields of virgin white, the humped shadows that were our ruined and hidden cars, I could see no sign of movement. An occasional shadow passed across the snow, though it could have been from a bird flying in front of the sun. But if I relaxed my gaze, tried not to concentrate too hard, lowered my eyelids, then I could see them. Sometimes they skimmed low and fast over the snow, twisting like sea-serpents or Chinese dragons and throwing up a fine mist of flakes behind them. At other times they lay still and watchful, fading into the background if I looked directly at them until one shadow looked much like the next, but could be so different.

I wanted to talk about them. I wanted to ask Ellie just what the hell they were, because I knew that she had seen them too. I wanted to know what was happening and why it was happening to us. But I had some mad idea that to mention them would make them real, like ghosts in the cupboard and slithering wet things beneath the bed. Best ignore them and they would go away.

I counted a dozen white shapes that morning.

"Anyone dead today?" Rosalie asked.

The statement shocked me, made me wonder just what sort of relationship she and Brand had had, but we all ignored her. No need to aggravate an argument.

Charley sat close to Rosalie, as if a sharing of grief would halve it. Hayden was cooking up bacon and bagels long past their sell-by date. Ellie had not yet come downstairs. She'd been stalking the manor all night, and now we were up she was washing and changing.

"What do we do today?" Charley asked. "Are we going to try to get away again? Get to the village for help?"

I sighed and went to say something, but the thought of those things out in the snow kept me quiet. Nobody else spoke, and the silence was the only answer required.

We ate our stale breakfast, drank tea clotted with powdered milk, listened to the silence outside. It had snowed again in the night and our tracks from the day before had been obliterated. Standing at the sink to wash up I stared through the window, and it was like looking upon the same day as yesterday, the day before, and the day before that; no signs of our presence existed. All footprints had vanished, all echoes of voices swallowed by the snow, shadows covered with another six inches and frozen like corpses in a glacier. I wondered what patterns and traces the snow would hold this evening, when darkness closed in to wipe us away once more.

"We have to tell someone," Charley said. "Something's happening, we should tell someone. We have to do something, we can't just . . ." She trailed off, staring into a cooling cup of tea, perhaps remembering a time before all this had begun, or imagining she could remember. "This is crazy."

"It's God," Rosalie said.

"Huh?" Hayden was already peeling wrinkled old vegetables ready for lunch, constantly busy, always doing something to keep his mind off everything else. I wondered how much really went on behind his fringed brow, how much theorizing he did while he was boiling, how much nostalgia he wallowed in as familiar cooking smells settled into his clothes.

"It's God, fucking us over one more time. Crazy, as Charley says. God and crazy are synonymous."

"Rosie," I said, knowing she hated the shortened name, "if it's not constructive, don't bother. None of this will bring—"

"Anything is more constructive than sod-all, which is what you lot have got to say this morning. We wake up one morning without one of us dead, and you're all tongue-tied. Bored? Is that it?"

"Rosalie, why—"

"Shut it, Charley. You more than anyone should be thinking about all this. Wondering why the hell we came here a few weeks ago to escape all the shit, and now we've landed right in the middle of it. Right up to our armpits. Drowning in it. Maybe one of us is a Jonah and it's followed—"

"And you think it's God?" I said. I knew that asking the question would give her open opportunity to rant, but in a way I felt she was right, we did need to talk. Sitting here stewing in our own thoughts could not help anyone.

"Oh yes, it's His Holiness," she nodded, "sitting on his pedestal of lost souls, playing around one day and deciding, hmm, maybe I'll have some fun today, been a year since a decent earthquake, a few months since the last big volcano eruption. Soooo, what can I do?"

Ellie appeared then, sat at the table and poured a cup of cold tea that looked like sewer water. Her appearance did nothing to mar Rosalie's flow.

"I know, he says, I'll nudge things to one side, turn them slightly askew, give the world a gasp before I've cleaned my teeth. Just a little, not so that anyone will notice for a while. Get them paranoid. Get them looking over their shoulders at each other. See how the wrinkly pink bastards deal with that one!"

"Why would He do that?" Hayden said.

Rosalie stood and put on a deep voice. "Forget me, will they? I'll show them. Turn over and open your legs, humanity, for I shall root you up the arse."

"Just shut up!" Charley screeched. The kitchen went ringingly quiet, even Rosalie sitting slowly down. "You're full of this sort of shit, Rosie. Always telling us how we're being controlled, manipulated. Who by? Ever seen anyone? There's a hidden agenda behind everything for you, isn't there? If there's no toilet paper after you've had a crap you'd blame it on the global dirty-arse conspiracy!"

Hysteria hung silently in the room. The urge to cry grabbed me, but also a yearning to laugh out loud. The air was heavy with held breaths and barely restrained comments, thick with the potential for violence.

"So," Ellie said at last, her voice little more than a whisper, "let's hear some truths."

"What?" Rosalie obviously expected an extension of her foolish monologue. Ellie, however, cut her down.

"Well, for starters has anyone else seen things in the snow?" Heads shook. My own shook as well. I wondered who else was lying with me. "Anyone seen anything strange out there at all?" she continued. "Maybe not the things Brand and Boris saw, but something else?" Again, shaken heads. An uncomfortable shuffling from Hayden as he stirred something on the gas cooker.

"I saw God looking down on us," Rosalie said quietly, "with blood in his eyes." She did not continue or elaborate, did not go off on one of her rants. I think that's why her strange comment stayed with me.

"Right," said Ellie, "then may I make a suggestion. Firstly, there's no point trying to get to the village. The snow's even deeper than it was yesterday, it's colder, and freezing to death for the sake of it will achieve nothing. If we did manage to find help, Boris and Brand are long past it." She paused, waiting for assent.

"Fair enough," Charley said quietly. "Yeah, you're right."

"Secondly, we need to make sure the manor is secure. We need to protect ourselves from whatever got at Brand and Boris. There are a dozen rooms on the ground floor, we only use two or three of them. Check the others. Make sure windows are locked and storm shutters are bolted. Make sure French doors aren't loose or liable to break open at the slightest . . . breeze, or whatever."

"What do you think the things out there are?" Hayden asked. "Lock pickers?"

Ellie glanced at his back, looked at me, shrugged. "No," she said, "I don't think so. But there's no use being complacent. We can't try to make it out, so we should do the most we can here. The snow can't last forever, and when it finally melts we'll go to the village then. Agreed?"

Heads nodded.

"If the village is still there," Rosalie cut in. "If everyone isn't dead. If the disease hasn't wiped out most of the country. If a war doesn't start somewhere in the meantime."

"Yes," Ellie sighed impatiently, "if all those things don't happen." She nodded at me. "We'll do the two rooms at the back. The rest of you check the others. There are some tools in the big cupboard under the stairs, some nails and hammers if you need them, a crowbar too. And if you think you need timber to nail across windows . . . if it'll make you feel any better . . . tear up some floorboards in the dining room. They're hardwood, they're strong."

"Oh, let battle commence!" Rosalie cried. She stood quickly, her chair falling onto its back, and stalked from the room with a swish of her long skirts. Charley followed.

Ellie and I went to the rear of the manor. In the first of the large rooms the snow had drifted up against the windows to cut out any view or light from outside. For an instant it seemed as if nothing existed beyond the glass and I wondered if that was the case, then why were we trying to protect ourselves?

Against nothing.

"What do you think is out there?" I asked.

"Have you seen anything?"

I paused. There was something, but nothing I could easily identify or put a name to. What I had seen had been way beyond my ken, white shadows apparent against whiteness. "No," I said, "nothing."

Ellie turned from the window and looked at me in the half-light, and it was obvious that she knew I was lying. "Well, if you do see something, don't tell."

"Why?"

"Boris and Brand told," she said. She did not say any more. They'd seen angels and stags in the snow and they'd talked about it, and now they were dead.

She pushed at one of the window frames. Although the damp timber fragmented at her touch, the snow drift behind it was as effective as a vault door. We moved on to the next window. The room was noisy with unspoken thoughts, and it was only a matter of time before they made themselves heard.

"You think someone in here has something to do with Brand and Boris," I said.

Ellie sat on one of the wide window sills and sighed deeply. She ran a hand through her spiky hair and rubbed at her neck. I wondered whether she'd had any sleep at all last night. I wondered whose door had been opening and closing; the prickle of jealousy was crazy under the circumstances. I realized all of a sudden how much Ellie reminded me of Jayne, and I swayed under the sudden barrage of memory.

"Who?" she said. "Rosie? Hayden? Don't be soft."

"But you do, don't you?" I said again.

She nodded. Then shook her head. Shrugged. "I don't bloody know, I'm not Sherlock Holmes. It's just strange that Brand and Boris . . ." She trailed off, avoiding my eyes.

"I have seen something out there," I said to break the awkward silence. "Something in the snow. Can't say what. Shadows.

Fleeting glimpses. Like everything I see is from the corner of my eye."

Ellie stared at me for so long that I thought she'd died there on the window sill, a victim of my admission, another dead person to throw outside and let freeze until the thaw came and we could do our burying.

"You've seen what I've seen," she said eventually, verbalizing the trust between us. It felt good, but it also felt a little dangerous. A trust like that could alienate the others, not consciously but in our mind's eye. By working and thinking closer together, perhaps we would drive them further away.

We moved to the next window.

"I've known there was something since you found Jack in his car," Ellie said. "He'd never have just sat there and waited to die. He'd have tried to get out, to get here, no matter how dangerous. He wouldn't have sat watching the candle burn down, listening to the wind, feeling his eyes freeze over. It's just not like him to give in."

"So why did he? Why didn't he get out?"

"There was something waiting for him outside the car. Something he was trying to keep away from." She rattled a window, stared at the snow pressed up against the glass. "Something that would make him rather freeze to death than face it."

We moved on to the last window, Ellie reached out to touch the rusted clasp and there was a loud crash. Glass broke, wood struck wood, someone screamed, all from a distance.

We spun around and ran from the room, listening to the shrieks. Two voices now, a man and a woman, the woman's muffled. Somewhere in the manor, someone else was dying.

The reaction to death is sometimes as violent as death itself. Shock throws a cautious coolness over the senses, but your stomach still knots, your skin stings as if the Reaper is glaring at you as well. For a second you live that death, and then shameful relief floods in when you see it's someone else.

Such were my thoughts as we turned a corner into the main hallway of the manor. Hayden was hammering at the library door, crashing his fists into the wood hard enough to draw blood. "Charley!" he shouted, again and again. "Charley!" The door shook under his assault but it did not budge. Tears streaked his face, dribble strung from chin to chest. The dark old wood of the door sucked up the blood from his split knuckles. "Charley!"

Ellie and I arrived just ahead of Rosalie.

"Hayden!" Rosalie shouted.

"Charley! In there! She went in and locked the door, and there was a crash and she was screaming!"

"Why did she—" Rosalie began, but Ellie shushed us all with one wave of her hand.

Silence. "No screaming now," she said.

Then we heard other noises through the door, faint and tremulous as if picked up from a distance along a bad telephone line. They sounded like chewing; bone snapping; flesh ripping. I could not believe what I was hearing, but at the same time I remembered the bodies of Boris and Brand. Suddenly I did not want to open the door. I wanted to defy whatever it was laying siege to us here by ignoring the results of its actions. Forget Charley, continue checking the windows and doors, deny who-ever or whatever it was the satisfaction—

"Charley," I said quietly. She was a small woman, fragile, strong but sensitive. She'd told me once, sitting at the base of the cliffs before it had begun to snow, how she loved to sit and watch the sea. It made her feel safe. It made her feel a part of nature. She'd never hurt anyone. "Charley."

Hayden kicked at the door again and I added my weight, shouldering into the tough old wood, jarring my body painfully with each impact. Ellie did the same and soon we were taking it in turns. The noises continued between each impact – increased in volume if anything – and our assault became more frantic to cover them up.

If the manor had not been so old and decrepit we would never have broken in. The door was probably as old as all of us put together, but its surround had been replaced some time in the past. Softwood painted as hardwood had slowly crumbled in the damp atmosphere and after a minute the door burst in, frame splintering into the coldness of the library.

One of the three big windows had been smashed. Shattered glass and snapped mullions hung crazily from the frame. The cold had already made the room its home, laying a fine sheen of frost across the thousands of books, hiding some of their titles from view as if to conceal whatever tumultuous history they contained.

Snow flurried in, hung around for a while then chose somewhere to settle. It did not melt. Once on the inside, this room was now a part of the outside.

As was Charley.

The area around the broken window was red and Charley had spread. Bits of her hung on the glass like hellish party streamers. Other parts had melted into the snow outside and turned it pink. Some of her was recognizable – her hair splayed out across the soft whiteness, a hand fisted around a melting clump of ice – other parts had never been seen before, because they'd always been inside.

I leaned over and puked. My vomit cleared a space of frost on the floor so I did it again, moving into the room. My stomach was in agonized spasms but I enjoyed seeing the white sheen vanish, as if I were claiming the room back for a time. Then I went to my knees and tried to forget what I'd seen, shake it from my head, pound it from my temples. I felt hands close around my wrists to stop me from punching myself, but I fell forward and struck my forehead on the cold timber floor. If I could forget, if I could drive the image away, perhaps it would no longer be true.

But there was the smell. And the steam, rising from the open body and misting what glass remained. Charley's last breath.

"Shut the door!" I shouted. "Nail it shut! Quickly!"

Ellie had helped me from the room, and now Hayden was pulling on the broken-in door to try to close it again. Rosalie came back from the dining room with a few splintered floorboards, her face pale, eyes staring somewhere no one else could see.

"Hurry!" I shouted. I felt a distance pressing in around me; the walls receding; the ceiling rising. Voices turned slow and deep, movement became stilted. My stomach heaved again but there was nothing left to bring up. I was the centre of everything but it was all leaving me, all sight and sound and scent fleeing my faint. And then, clear and bright, Jayne's laugh broke through. Only once, but I knew it was her.

Something brushed my cheek and gave warmth to my face. My jaw clicked and my head turned to one side, slowly but inexorably. Something white blurred across my vision and my other cheek burst into warmth, and I was glad, the cold was the enemy, the cold brought the snow, which brought the fleeting things I had seen outside, things without a name or, perhaps, things with a million names. Or things with a name I already knew.

The warmth was good.

Ellie's mouth moved slowly and watery rumbles tumbled forth. Her words took shape in my mind, hauling themselves together just as events took on their own speed once more.

"Snap out of it," Ellie said, and slapped me across the face again.

Another sound dragged itself together. I could not identify it, but I knew where it was coming from. The others were staring fearfully at the door, Hayden was still leaning back with both hands around the handle, straining to get as far away as possible without letting go.

Scratching. Sniffing. Something rifling through books, snuffling in longforgotten corners at dust from long-dead people. A slow regular beat, which could have been footfalls or a heartbeat. I realized it was my own and another sound took its place.

"What . . .?"

Ellie grabbed the tops of my arms and shook me harshly. "You with us? You back with us now?"

I nodded, closing my eyes at the swimming sensation in my head. Vertical fought with horizontal and won out this time. "Yeah."

"Rosalie," Ellie whispered. "Get more boards. Hayden, keep hold of that handle. Just keep hold." She looked at me. "Hand me the nails as I hold my hand out. Now listen. Once I start banging, it may attract—"

"What are you doing?" I said.

"Nailing the bastards in."

I thought of the shapes I had watched from my bedroom window, the shadows flowing through other shadows, the ease with which they moved, the strength and beauty they exuded as they passed from drift to drift without leaving any trace behind. I laughed. "You think you can keep them in?"

Rosalie turned a fearful face my way. Her eyes were wide, her mouth hanging open as if readying for a scream.

"You think a few nails will stop them—"

"Just shut up," Ellie hissed, and she slapped me around the face once more. This time I was all there, and the slap was a burning sting rather than a warm caress. My head whipped around and by the time I looked up again Ellie was heaving a board against the doors, steadying it with one elbow and weighing a hammer in the other hand.

Only Rosalie looked at me. What I'd said was still plain on her face – the chance that whatever had done these foul things would find their way in, take us apart as it had done to Boris, to Brand and now to Charley. And I could say nothing to comfort her. I shook my head, though I had no idea what message I was trying to convey.

Ellie held out her hand and clicked her fingers. Rosalie passed her a nail.

I stepped forward and pressed the board across the door. We had to tilt it so that each end rested across the frame. There were still secretive sounds from inside, like a fox rummaging through a bin late at night. I tried to imagine the scene in the room now but I could not. My mind would not place what I had seen outside into the library, could not stretch to that feat of imagination. I was glad.

For one terrible second I wanted to see. It would only take a kick at the door, a single heave and the whole room would be open to view, and then I would know whatever was in there for the second before it hit me. Jayne perhaps, a white Jayne from elsewhere, holding out her hands so that I could join her once more, just as she had promised on her death bed. *I'll be with you again*, she had said, and the words had terrified me and comforted me and kept me going ever since. Sometimes I thought they were all that kept me alive. *I'll be with you again*.

"Jayne . . ."

Ellie brought the hammer down. The sound was explosive and I felt the impact transmitted through the wood and into my arms. I expected another impact a second later from the opposite way, but instead we heard the sound of something scampering through the already shattered window.

Ellie kept hammering until the board held firm, then she started another, and another. She did not stop until most of the door was covered, nails protruding at crazy angles, splinters under her fingernails, sweat running across her face and staining her armpits.

"Has it gone?" Rosalie asked. "Is it still in there?"

"Is what still in there, precisely?" I muttered.

We all stood that way for a while, panting with exertion, adrenaline priming us for the chase.

"I think," Ellie said after a while, "we should make some plans."

"What about Charley?" I asked. They all knew what I meant: *we can't just leave her there; we have to do something; she'd do the same for us*:

"Charley's dead," Ellie said, without looking at anyone. "Come on." She headed for the kitchen.

"What happened?" Ellie asked.

Hayden was shaking. "I told you. We were checking the rooms, Charley ran in before me and locked the door, I heard glass breaking and . . ." He trailed off.

"And?"

"Screams. I heard her screaming. I heard her dying."

The kitchen fell silent as we all recalled the cries, as if they were still echoing around the manor. They meant different things to each of us. For me death always meant Jayne.

"Okay, this is how I see things," Ellie said. "There's a wild animal, or wild animals, out there now."

"What wild animals!" Rosalie scoffed. "Mutant badgers come to eat us up? Hedgehogs gone bad?"

"I don't know, but pray it is animals. If a person has done all this, then they'll be able to get in to us. However fucking goofy crazy, they'll have the intelligence to get in. No way to stop them. Nothing we could do." She patted the shotgun resting across her thighs as if to reassure herself of its presence.

"But what animals—"

"Do you know what's happening everywhere?" Ellie shouted, not just at doubting Rosie but at us all. "Do you realize that the world's changing? Every day we wake up there's a new world facing us. And every day there're fewer of us left. I mean the big us, the world-wide us, us humans." Her voice became quieter. "How long before one morning, no one wakes up?"

"What has what's happening elsewhere got to do with all this?" I asked, although inside I already had an idea of what Ellie meant. I think maybe I'd known for a while, but now my mind was opening up, my beliefs stretching, levering fantastic truths into place. They fitted; that terrified me.

"I mean, it's all changing. A disease is wiping out millions and no one knows where it came from. Unrest everywhere, shootings, bombings. Nuclear bombs in the Med, for Christ's sake. You've heard what people have called it; it's the Ruin. Capital R, people. The world's gone bad. Maybe what's happening here is just not that unusual any more."

"That doesn't tell us what they are," Rosalie said. "Doesn't explain why they're here, or where they come from. Doesn't tell us why Charley did what she did."

"Maybe she wanted to be with Boris again," Hayden said.

I simply stared at him. "I've seen them," I said, and Ellie sighed. "I saw them outside last night."

The others looked at me, Rosalie's eyes still full of the fear I had planted there and was even now propagating.

"So what were they?" Rosalie asked. "Ninja seabirds?"

"I don't know." I ignored her sarcasm. "They were white, but they hid in shadows. Animals, they must have been. There are no people like that. But they were canny. They moved only when I wasn't looking straight at them, otherwise they stayed still and . . . blended in with the snow." Rosalie, I could see, was terrified. The sarcasm was a front. Everything I said scared her more.

"Camouflaged," Hayden said.

"No. They blended in. As if they melted in, but they didn't. I can't really . . ."

"In China," Rosalie said, "white is the colour of death. It's the colour of happiness and joy. They wear white at funerals."

Ellie spoke quickly, trying to grab back the conversation. "Right. Let's think of what we're going to do. First, no use trying to get out. Agreed? Good. Second, we limit ourselves to a couple of rooms downstairs, the hallway and staircase area and upstairs. Third, do what we can to block up, nail up, glue up the doors to the other rooms and corridors."

"And then?" Rosalie asked quietly. "Charades?"

Ellie shrugged and smiled. "Why not? It is Christmas time."

I'd never dreamt of a white Christmas. I was cursing Bing fucking Crosby with every gasped breath I could spare.

The air sang with echoing hammer blows, dropped boards and groans as hammers crunched fingernails. I was working with Ellie to board up the rest of the downstairs rooms while Hayden and

Rosalie tried to lever up the remaining boards in the dining room. We did the windows first, Ellie standing to one side with the shotgun aiming out while I hammered. It was snowing again and I could see vague shapes hiding behind flakes, dipping in and out of the snow like larking dolphins. I think we all saw them, but none of us ventured to say for sure that they were there. Our imagination was pumped up on what had happened and it had started to paint its own pictures.

We finished one of the living rooms and locked the door behind us. There was an awful sense of finality in the heavy thunk of the tumblers clicking in, a feeling that perhaps we would never go into that room again. I'd lived the last few years telling myself that there was no such thing as never – Jayne was dead and I would certainly see her again, after all – but there was nothing in these rooms that I could ever imagine us needing again. They were mostly designed for luxury, and luxury was a conceit of the contented mind. Over the past few weeks, I had seen contentment vanish forever under the grey cloud of humankind's fall from grace.

None of this seemed to matter now as we closed it all in. I thought I should feel sad, for the symbolism of what we were doing if not for the loss itself. Jayne had told me we would be together again, and then she had died and I had felt trapped ever since by her death and the promise of her final words. If nailing up doors would take me closer to her, then so be it.

In the next room I looked out of the window and saw Jayne striding naked towards me through the snow. Fat flakes landed on her shoulders and did not melt, and by the time she was near enough for me to see the look in her eyes she had collapsed down into a drift, leaving a memory there in her place. Something flitted past the window, sending flakes flying against the wind, bristly fur-spiking dead white leaves.

I blinked hard and the snow was just snow once more. I turned and looked at Ellie, but she was concentrating too hard to return my stare. For the first time I could see how scared she was – how her hand clasped so tightly around the shotgun barrel that her knuckles were pearly white, her nails a shiny pink – and I wondered exactly what *she* was seeing out there in the white storm.

By midday we had done what we could. The kitchen, one of the living rooms and the hall and staircase were left open; every other room downstairs was boarded up from the outside in. We'd also covered the windows in those rooms left open, but we left thin viewing ports like horizontal arrow slits in the walls of an old castle. And like the weary defenders of those ancient citadels, we were under siege.

"So what did you all see?" I said as we sat in the kitchen. Nobody denied anything.

"Badgers," Rosalie said. "Big, white, fast. Sliding over the snow like they were on skis. Demon badgers from hell!" She joked, but it was obvious that she was terrified.

"Not badgers," Ellie cut in. "Deer. But wrong. Deer with scales. Or something. All wrong."

"Hayden, what did you see?"

He remained hunched over the cooker, stirring a weak stew of old vegetables and stringy beef. "I didn't see anything."

I went to argue with him but realized he was probably telling the truth. We had all seen something different, why not see nothing at all? It was just as unlikely.

"You know," said Ellie, standing at a viewing slot with the snow reflecting sunlight in a band across her face, "we're all seeing white animals. White animals in the snow. So maybe we're seeing nothing at all. Maybe it's our imaginations. Perhaps Hayden is nearer the truth than all of us."

"Boris and the others had pretty strong imaginations, then," said Rosalie, bitter tears animating her eyes.

We were silent once again, stirring our weak milk-less tea, all thinking our own thoughts about what was out in the snow. Nobody had asked me what I had seen and I was glad. Last night they were fleeting white shadows, but today I had seen Jayne as well. A Jayne I had known was not really there, even as I watched her coming at me through the snow. *I'll be with you again.*

"In China, white is the colour of death," Ellie said. She spoke at the boarded window, never for an instant glancing away. Her hands held onto the shotgun as if it had become one with her body. I wondered what she had been in the past: *I have a history,* she'd said. "White. Happiness and joy."

"It was also the colour of mourning for the Victorians," I added.

"And we're in a Victorian manor." Hayden did not turn

around as he spoke, but his words sent our imaginations scurrying.

"We're all seeing white animals," Ellie said quietly. "Like white noise. All tones, all frequencies. We're all seeing different things as one."

"Oh," Rosalie whispered, "well that explains a lot."

I thought I could see where Ellie was coming from, at least, I was looking in the right direction. "White noise is used to mask other sounds," I said.

Ellie only nodded.

"There's something else going on here." I sat back in my chair and stared up, trying to divine the truth in the patchwork mould on the kitchen ceiling. "We're not seeing it all."

Ellie glanced away from the window, just for a second. "I don't think we're seeing anything."

Later we found out some more of what was happening. We went to bed, doors opened in the night, footsteps creaked old floorboards. And through the dark the sound of lovemaking drew us all to another, more terrible death.

III: The Colour of Mourning

I had not made love to anyone since Jayne's death. It was months before she died that we last indulged, a bitter, tearful experience when she held a sheet of polythene between our chests and stomachs to prevent her diseased skin touching my own. It did not make for the most romantic of occasions, and afterward she cried herself to sleep as I sat holding her hand and staring into the dark.

After her death I came to the manor, the others came along to find something or escape from something else, and there were secretive noises in the night. The manor was large enough for us to have a room each, but in the darkness doors would open and close again, and every morning the atmosphere at breakfast was different.

My door had never opened and I had opened no doors. There was a lingering guilt over Jayne's death, a sense that I would be betraying her love if I went with someone else. A greater cause of my loneliness was my inherent lack of confidence, a certainty that no one here would be interested in me: I was quiet, introspective, and uninteresting, a fledgling bird devoid of any hope of taking wing with any particular talent. No one would want me.

But none of this could prevent the sense of isolation, subtle jealousy and yearning I felt each time I heard footsteps in the dark. I never heard anything else – the walls were too thick for that, the building too solid – but my imagination filled in the missing parts. Usually, Ellie was the star. And there lay another problem – lusting after a woman I did not even like very much.

The night it all changed for us was the first time I heard someone making love in the manor. The voice was androgynous in its ecstasy, a high keening, dropping off into a prolonged sigh before rising again. I sat up in bed, trying to shake off the remnants of dreams that clung like seaweed to a drowned corpse. Jayne had been there, of course, and something in the snow, and another something which was Jayne and the snow combined. I recalled wallowing in the sharp whiteness and feeling my skin sliced by ice edges, watching the snow grow pink around me, then white again as Jayne came and spread her cleansing touch across the devastation.

The cry came once more, wanton and unhindered by any sense of decorum.

Who? I thought. *Obviously Hayden but who was he with? Rosalie? Cynical paranoid, terrified Rosalie?*

Or Ellie?

I hoped Rosalie.

I sat back against the headboard, unable to lie down and ignore the sound. The curtains hung open – I had no reason to close them – and the moonlight revealed that it was snowing once again. I wondered what was out there watching the sleeping manor, listening to the crazy sounds of lust emanating from a building still spattered with the blood and memory of those who had died so recently. I wondered whether the things out there had any understanding of human emotion – the highs, the lows, the tenacious spirit that could sometimes survive even the most downhearting, devastating events – and what they made of the sound they could hear now. Perhaps they thought they were screams of pain. Ecstasy and thoughtless agony often sounded the same.

The sound continued, rising and falling. Added to it now the noise of something thumping rhythmically against a wall.

I thought of the times before Jayne had been ill, before the great decline had really begun, when most of the population still thought humankind could clean up what it had dirtied and repair what it had torn asunder. We'd been married for several years, our love as deep as ever, our lust still refreshing and invigorating. Car seats, cinemas, woodland, even a telephone box, all had been visited by us at some stage, laughing like adolescents, moaning and sighing together, content in familiarity.

And as I sat there remembering my dead wife, something strange happened. I could not identify exactly when the realization hit me, but I was suddenly sure of one thing: the voice I was listening to was Jayne's. She was moaning as someone else in the house made love to her. She had come in from outside, that cold unreal Jayne I had seen so recently, and she had gone to Hayden's room, and now I was being betrayed by someone I had never betrayed, ever.

I shook my head, knowing it was nonsense but certain also that the voice was hers. I was so sure that I stood, dressed and opened my bedroom door without considering the impossibility of what was happening. Reality was controlled by the darkness, not by whatever light I could attempt to throw upon it. I may as well have had my eyes closed.

The landing was lit by several shaded candles in wall brackets, their soft light barely reaching the floor, flickering as breezes came from nowhere. Where the light did touch it showed old carpet, worn by time and faded by countless unknown footfalls. The walls hung with shredded paper, damp and torn like dead skin, the lath and plaster beneath pitted and crumbled. The air was thick with age, heavy with must, redolent with faint hints of hauntings. Where my feet fell I could sense the floor dipping slightly beneath me, though whether this was actuality or a runover from my dream I was unsure.

I could have been walking on snow.

I moved toward Hayden's room and the volume of the sighing and crying increased. I paused one door away, my heart thumping not with exertion but with the thought that Jayne was a dozen steps from me, making love with Hayden, a man I hardly really knew.

Jayne's dead, I told myself, and she cried out once, loud, as she came. Another voice then, sighing and straining, and this one was Jayne as well.

Someone touched my elbow. I gasped and spun around, too shocked to scream. Ellie was there in her night-shirt, bare legs hidden in shadow. She had a strange look in her eye. It may have been the subdued lighting. I went to ask her what she was doing here, but then I realized it was probably the same as me. She'd stayed downstairs last night, unwilling to share a watch duty, insistent that we should all sleep.

I went to tell her that Jayne was in there with Hayden, then I realized how stupid this would sound, how foolish it actually *was*.

At least, I thought, *it's not Ellie in there. Rosalie it must be. At least not Ellie. Certainly not Jayne.*

And Jayne cried out again.

Goosebumps speckled my skin and brought it to life. The hairs on my neck stood to attention, my spine tingled.

"Hayden having a nice time?" someone whispered, and Rosalie stepped up behind Ellie.

I closed my eyes, listening to Jayne's cries. She had once screamed like that in a park, and the keeper had chased us out with his waving torch and throaty shout, the light splaying across our nakedness as we laughed and struggled to gather our clothes around us as we ran.

"Doesn't sound like Hayden to me," Ellie said.

The three of us stood outside Hayden's door for a while, listening to the sounds of lovemaking from within – the cries, the moving bed, the thud of wood against the wall. I felt like an intruder, however much I realized something was very wrong with all of this. Hayden was on his own in there. As we each tried to figure out what we were really hearing, the sounds from within changed. There was not one cry, not two, but many, overlying each other, increasing and expanding until the voice became that of a crowd. The light in the corridor seemed to dim as the crying increased, though it may have been my imagination.

I struggled to make out Jayne's voice and there was a hint of something familiar, a whisper in the cacophony that was so slight as to be little more than an echo of a memory. But still, to me, it was real.

Ellie knelt and peered through the keyhole, and I noticed for the first time that she was carrying her shotgun. She stood quickly and backed away from the door, her mouth opening, eyes widening. "It's Hayden," she said aghast, and then she fired at the door handle and lock.

The explosion tore through the sounds of ecstasy and left them in shreds. They echoed away like streamers in the wind, to be replaced by the lonely moan of a man's voice, pleading not to stop, it was so wonderful so pure so alive . . .

The door swung open. None of us entered the room. We could not move.

Hayden was on his back on the bed, surrounded by the whites from outside. I had seen them as shadows against the snow, little more than pale phantoms, but here in the room they stood out bright and definite. There were several of them; I could not make out an exact number because they squirmed and twisted against each other, and against Hayden. Diaphanous limbs stretched out and wavered in the air, arms or wings or tentacles, tapping at the bed and the wall and the ceiling, leaving spots of ice like ink on blotting paper wherever they touched.

I could see no real faces but I knew that the things were looking at me.

Their crying and sighing had ceased, but Hayden's continued. He moved quickly and violently, thrusting into the malleable shape that still straddled him, not yet noticing our intrusion even though the shotgun blast still rang in my ears. He continued his penetration, but slowly the white lifted itself away until Hayden's cock flopped back wetly onto his stomach.

He raised his head and looked straight at us between his knees, looked *through* one of the things where it flipped itself easily across the bed. The air stank of sex and something else, something cold and old and rotten, frozen forever and only now experiencing a hint of thaw.

"Oh please . . ." he said, though whether he spoke to us or the constantly shifting shapes I could not tell.

I tried to focus but the whites were minutely out of phase with my vision, shifting to and fro too quickly for me to concentrate. I thought I saw a face, but it may have been a false splay of shadows thrown as a shape turned and sprang to the floor. I searched for something I knew – an arm kinked slightly from an old break; a breast with a mole near the nipple; a smile turned wryly down at the edges – and I realized I was looking for Jayne.

Even in all this mess, I thought she may be here. *I'll be with you again*, she had said.

I almost called her name, but Ellie lifted the shotgun and shattered the moment once more. It barked out once, loud, and everything happened so quickly. One instant the white things were there, smothering Hayden and touching him with their fluid limbs. The next, the room was empty of all but us humans, moth-eaten curtains fluttering slightly, window invitingly open. And Hayden's face had disappeared into a red mist.

After the shotgun blast there was only the wet sound of Hayden's brains and skull fragments pattering down onto the bedding. His hard-on still glinted in the weak candlelight. His hands each clasped a fistful of blanket. One leg tipped and rested on the sheets clumped around him. His skin was pale, almost white.

Almost.

Rosalie leaned against the wall, dry heaving. Her dress was wet and heavy with puke and the stink of it had found a home in my nostrils. Ellie was busy reloading the shotgun, mumbling and cursing, trying to look anywhere but at the carnage of Hayden's body.

I could not tear my eyes away. I'd never seen anything like this. Brand and Boris and Charley, yes, their torn and tattered corpses had been terrible to behold, but here . . . I had seen the instant a rounded, functional person had turned into a shattered lump of meat. I'd seen the red splash of Hayden's head as it came apart and hit the wall, big bits ricocheting, the smaller, wetter pieces sticking to the old wallpaper and drawing their dreadful art for all to see. Every detail stood out and demanded my attention, as if the shot had cleared the air and brought light. It seemed red-tinged, the atmosphere itself stained with violence.

Hayden's right hand clasped onto the blanket, opening and closing very slightly, very slowly.

Doesn't feel so cold. Maybe there's a thaw on the way, I thought distractedly, trying perhaps to withdraw somewhere banal and comfortable and familiar . . .

There was a splash of sperm across his stomach. Blood from his ruined head was running down his neck and chest and mixing with it, dribbling soft and pink onto the bed.

Ten seconds ago he was alive. Now he was dead. Extinguished, just like that.

Where is he? I thought. *Where has he gone?*

"Hayden?" I said.

"He's dead!" Ellie hissed, a little too harshly.

"I can see that." But his hand still moved. Slowly. Slightly.

Something was happening at the window. The curtains were still now, but there was a definite sense of movement in the darkness beyond. I caught it from the corner of my eye as I stared at Hayden.

"Rosalie, go get some boards," Ellie whispered.

"You killed Hayden!" Rosalie spat. She coughed up the remnants of her last meal, and they hung on her chin like wet boils. "You blew his head off! You shot him! What the hell, what's going on, what's happening here. I don't know, I don't know . . ."

"The things are coming back in," Ellie said. She shouldered the gun, leaned through the door and fired at the window. Stray shot plucked at the curtains. There was a cessation of noise from outside, then a rustling, slipping, sliding. It sounded like something flopping around in snow. "Go and get the boards, you two."

Rosalie stumbled noisily along the corridor toward the staircase.

"You killed him," I said lamely.

"He was fucking them," Ellie shouted. Then, quieter: "I didn't mean to . . ." She looked at the body on the bed, only briefly but long enough for me to see her eyes narrow and her lips squeeze tight. "He was fucking them. His fault."

"What were they? What the hell, I've never seen any animals like them."

Ellie grabbed my biceps and squeezed hard, eliciting an unconscious yelp. She had fingers like steel nails. "They aren't animals," she said. "They aren't people. Help me with the door."

Her tone invited no response. She aimed the gun at the open window for as long as she could while I pulled the door shut. The shotgun blast had blown the handle away, and I could not see how we would be able to keep it shut should the whites return. We stood that way for a while, me hunkered down with two fingers through a jagged hole in the door to try to keep it closed,

Ellie standing slightly back, aiming the gun at the pocked wood. I wondered whether I'd end up getting shot if the whites chose this moment to climb back into the room and launch themselves at the door . . .

Banging and cursing marked Rosalie's return. She carried several snapped floor boards, the hammer and nails. I held the boards up, Rosalie nailed, both of us now in Ellie's line of fire. Again I wondered about Ellie and guns, about her history. I was glad when the job was done.

We stepped back from the door and stood there silently, three relative strangers trying to understand and come to terms with what we had seen. But without understanding, coming to terms was impossible. I felt a tear run down my cheek, then another. A sense of breathless panic settled around me, clasping me in cool hands and sending my heart racing.

"What do we do?" I said. "How do we keep those things out?"

"They won't get through the boarded windows," Rosalie said confidently, doubt so evident in her voice.

I remembered how quickly they had moved, how lithe and alert they had been to virtually dodge the blast from Ellie's shotgun . . .

I held my breath; the others were doing the same.

Noises. Clambering and a soft whistling at first, then light thuds as something ran around the walls of the room, across the ceiling, bounding from the floor and the furniture. Then tearing, slurping, cracking, as the whites fed on what was left of Hayden.

"Let's go down," Ellie suggested. We were already backing away.

Jayne may be in danger, I thought, recalling her waving to me as she walked naked through the snow. If she was out there, and these things were out there as well, she would be at risk. She may not know, she may be too trusting, she may let them take advantage of her, abuse and molest her—

Hayden had been enjoying it. He was not being raped; if anything, he was doing the raping. Even as he died he'd been spurting ignorant bliss across his stomach.

And Jayne was dead. I repeated this over and over, whispering it, not caring if the others heard, certain that they would take no notice. Jayne was dead. Jayne was dead.

I suddenly knew for certain that the whites could smash in at any time, dodge Ellie's clumsy shooting and tear us to shreds in seconds. They could do it, but they did not. They scratched and tapped at windows, clambered around the house, but they did not break in. Not yet.

They were playing with us. Whether they needed us for food, fun, or revenge, it was nothing but a game. Ellie was smashing up the kitchen.

She kicked open cupboard doors, swept the contents of shelves onto the floor with the barrel of the shotgun, sifted through them with her feet, then did the same to the next cupboard. At first I thought it was blind rage, fear, dread; then I saw that she was searching for something.

"What?" I asked. "What are you doing?"

"Just a hunch."

"What sort of hunch? Ellie, we should be watching out—"

"There's something moving out there," Rosalie said. She was looking through the slit in the boarded window. There was a band of moonlight across her eyes.

"Here!" Ellie said triumphantly. She knelt and rooted around in the mess on the floor, shoving jars and cans aside, delving into a splash of spilled rice to find a small bottle. "Bastard. The bastard. Oh God, the bastard's been doing it all along."

"There's something out there in the snow," Rosalie said again, louder this time. "It's coming to the manor. It's . . ." Her voice trailed off and I saw her stiffen, her mouth slightly open.

"Rosalie?" I moved towards her, but she glanced at me and waved me away.

"It's okay," she said. "It's nothing."

"Look." Ellie slammed a bottle down on the table and stood back for us to see.

"A bottle."

Ellie nodded. She looked at me and tilted her head. Waiting for me to see, expecting me to realize what she was trying to say.

"A bottle from Hayden's food cupboard," I said.

She nodded again.

I looked at Rosalie. She was still frozen at the window, hands pressed flat to her thighs, eyes wide and full of the moon. "Rosie?" She only shook her head. Nothing wrong, the gesture said, but it did not look like that. It looked like everything was wrong but she was too afraid to tell us. I went to move her out of the way, look for myself, see what had stolen her tongue.

"Poison," Ellie revealed. I paused, glanced at the bottle on the table. Ellie picked it up and held it in front of a candle, shook it, turned it this way and that. "Poison. Hayden's been cooking for us ever since we've been here. And he's always had this bottle. And a couple of times lately, he's added a little extra to certain meals."

"Brand," I nodded, aghast. "And Boris. But why? They were outside, they were killed by those things—"

"Torn up by those things," Ellie corrected. "Killed in here. Then dragged out."

"By Hayden?"

She shrugged. "Why not? He was fucking the whites."

"But why would he want to . . . Why did he have something against Boris and Brand? And Charley? An accident, like he said?"

"I guess he gave her a helping hand," Ellie mused, sitting at the table and rubbing her temples. "They both saw something outside. Boris and Brand, they'd both seen things in the snow. They made it known, they told us all about it, and Hayden heard as well. Maybe he felt threatened. Maybe he thought we'd steal his little sex mates." She stared down at the table, at the rings burnt there over the years by hot mugs, the scratches made by endless cutlery. "Maybe they told him to do it."

"Oh, come on!" I felt my eyes go wide like those of a rabbit caught in car headlights.

Ellie shrugged, stood and rested the gun on her shoulder. "Whatever, we've got to protect ourselves. They may be in soon, you saw them up there. They're intelligent. They're—"

"Animals!" I shouted. "They're animals! How could they tell Hayden anything? How could they get in?"

Ellie looked at me, weighing her reply.

"They're white animals, like you said!"

Ellie shook her head. "They're new. They're unique. They're a part of the change."

New. Unique. The words instilled very little hope in me, and Ellie's next comment did more to scare me than anything that had happened up to now.

"They were using Hayden to get rid of us. Now he's gone . . . well, they've no reason not to do it themselves."

As if on cue, something started to brush up against the outside wall of the house.

"Rosalie!" I shouted. "Step back!"

"It's alright," she said dreamily, "it's only the wind. Nothing there. Nothing to worry about." The sound continued, like soap on sandpaper. It came from beyond the boarded windows but it also seemed to filter through from elsewhere, surrounding us like an audio enemy.

"Ellie," I said, "what can we do?" She seemed to have taken charge so easily that I deferred to her without thinking, assuming she would have a plan with a certainty which was painfully cut down.

"I have no idea." She nursed the shotgun in the crook of her elbow like a baby substitute, and I realized I didn't know her half as well as I thought. Did she have children? I wondered. Where were her family? Where had this level of self-control come from?

"Rosalie," I said carefully, "what are you looking at?" Rosalie was staring through the slit at a moonlit scene none of us could see. Her expression had dropped from scared to melancholy, and I saw a tear trickle down her cheek. She was no longer her old cynical, bitter self. It was as if all her fears had come true and she was content with the fact. "Rosie!" I called again, quietly but firmly.

Rosalie turned to look at us. Reality hit her, but it could not hide the tears. "But he's dead," she said, half question, half statement. Before I could ask whom she was talking about, something hit the house.

The sound of smashing glass came from everywhere: behind the boards across the kitchen windows; out in the corridor; muffled crashes from elsewhere in the dark manor. Rosalie stepped back from the slit just as a long, shimmering white limb came in, glassy nails scratching for her face but ripping the air instead.

Ellie stepped forward, thrust the shotgun through the slit and pulled the trigger. There was no cry of pain, no scream, but the limb withdrew.

Something began to batter against the ruined kitchen window, the vibration travelling through the hastily nailed boards, nail heads emerging slowly from the gouged wood after each impact. Ellie fired again, though I could not see what she was shooting at. As she turned to reload she avoided my questioning glance.

"They're coming in!" I shouted.

"Can it!" Ellie said bitterly. She stepped back as a sliver of timber broke away from the edge of one of the boards, clattering to the floor stained with frost. She shouldered the gun and fired twice through the widening gap. White things began to worm their way between the boards, fingers perhaps, but long and thin and more flexible than any I had ever seen. They twisted and felt blindly across the wood . . . and then wrapped themselves around the exposed nails.

They began to pull.

The nails squealed as they were withdrawn from the wood, one by one.

I hefted the hammer and went at the nails, hitting each of them only once, aiming for those surrounded by cool white digits. As each nail went back in the things around them drew back and squirmed out of sight behind the boards, only to reappear elsewhere. I hammered until my arm ached, resting my left hand against the vibrating timber. Not once did I catch a white digit beneath the hammer, even when I aimed for them specifically. I began to giggle and the sound frightened me. It was the voice of a madman, the utterance of someone looking for his lost mind, and I found that funnier than ever. Every time I hit another nail it reminded me more and more of an old fairground game. Pop the gophers on the head. I wondered what the prize would be tonight.

"What the hell do we do?" I shouted.

Rosalie had stepped away from the windows and now leaned against the kitchen worktop, eyes wide, mouth working slowly in some unknown mantra. I glanced at her between hammer blows and saw her chest rising and falling at an almost impossible speed. She was slipping into shock.

"Where?" I shouted to Ellie over my shoulder.

"The hallway."

"Why?"

"Why not?"

I had no real answer, so I nodded and indicated with a jerk of my head that the other two should go first. Ellie shoved Rosalie ahead of her and stood waiting for me.

I continued bashing with the hammer, but now I had fresh targets. Not only were the slim white limbs nudging aside the boards and working at the nails, but they were also coming through the ventilation bricks at skirting level in the kitchen. They would gain no hold there, I knew; they could never pull their whole body through there. But still I found their presence abhorrent and terrifying, and every third hammer strike was directed at these white monstrosities trying to twist around my ankles.

And at the third missed strike, I knew what they were doing. It was then, also, that I had some true inkling of their intelligence and wiliness. Two digits trapped my leg between them – they were cold and hard, even through my jeans – and they jerked so hard that I felt my skin tearing in their grasp.

I went down and the hammer skittered across the kitchen floor. At the same instant a twisting forest of the things appeared between the boards above me, and in seconds the timber had started to snap and splinter as the onslaught intensified, the attackers now seemingly aware of my predicament. Shards of wood and glass and ice showered down on me, all of them sharp and cutting. And then, looking up, I saw one of the whites appear in the gap above me, framed by broken wood, its own limbs joined by others in their efforts to widen the gap and come in to tear me apart.

Jayne stared down at me. Her face was there but the thing was not her; it was as if her image were projected there, cast onto the pure whiteness of my attacker by memory or circumstance, put there because it knew what the sight would do to me.

I went weak, not because I thought Jayne was there – I knew that I was being fooled – but because her false visage inspired a flood of warm memories through my stunned bones, hitting cold muscles and sending me into a white-hot agony of paused circulation, blood pooling at my extremities, consciousness retreating into the warmer parts of my brain, all thought of escape and salvation and the other two survivors erased by the plain whiteness that invaded from outside, sweeping in through the rent in the wall and promising me a quick, painful death, but only if I no longer struggled, only if I submitted—

The explosion blew away everything but the pain. The thing above me had been so intent upon its imminent kill that it must have missed Ellie, leaning in the kitchen door and shouldering the shotgun.

The thing blew apart. I closed my eyes as I saw it fold up before me, and when I opened them again there was nothing there, not even a shower of dust in the air, no sprinkle of blood, no splash of insides. Whatever it had been it left nothing behind in death.

"Come on!" Ellie hissed, grabbing me under one arm and hauling me across the kitchen floor. I kicked with my feet to help her then finally managed to stand, albeit shakily.

There was now a gaping hole in the boards across the kitchen windows. Weak candlelight bled out and illuminated the falling snow and the shadows behind it. I expected the hole to be filled again in seconds and this time they would pour in, each of them a mimic of Jayne in some terrifying fashion.

"Shut the door," Ellie said calmly. I did so and Rosalie was there with a hammer and nails. We'd run out of broken floor boards, so we simply nailed the door into the frame. It was clumsy and would no doubt prove ineffectual, but it may give us a few more seconds.

But for what? What good would time do us now, other than to extend our agony?

"Now where?" I asked hopelessly. "Now what?" There were sounds all around us; soft thuds from behind the kitchen door, and louder noises from further away. Breaking glass; cracking wood; a gentle rustling, more horrible because they could not be identified. As far as I could see, we really had nowhere to go.

"Upstairs," Ellie said. "The attic. The hatch is outside my room, its got a loft ladder, as far as I know it's the only way up. Maybe we could hold them off until . . ."

"Until they go home for tea," Rosalie whispered. I said nothing. There was no use in verbalizing the hopelessness we felt at the moment, because we could see it in each other's eyes. The snow had been here for weeks and maybe now it would be here forever. Along with whatever strangeness it contained.

Ellie checked the bag of cartridges and handed them to me. "Hand these to me," she said. "Six shots left. Then we have to beat them up."

It was dark inside the manor, even though dawn must now be breaking outside. I thanked God that at least we had some candles left . . . but that got me thinking about God and how He would let this happen, launch these things against us, torture us with the promise of certain death and yet give us these false splashes of hope. I'd spent most of my life thinking that God was indifferent, a passive force holding the big picture together while we acted out our own foolish little plays within it. Now, if He did exist, He could only be a cruel God indeed. And I'd rather there be nothing than a God who found pleasure or entertainment in the discomfort of His creations.

Maybe Rosalie had been right. She had seen God staring down with blood in his eyes.

As we stumbled out into the main hallway I began to cry, gasping out my fears and my grief, and Ellie held me up and whispered into my ear. "Prove Him wrong if you have to. Prove Him wrong. Help me to survive, and prove Him wrong."

I heard Jayne beyond the main front doors, calling my name into the snowbanks, her voice muffled and bland. I paused, confused, and then I even smelled her; apple-blossom shampoo; the sweet scent of her breath. For a few seconds Jayne was there with me and I could all but hold her hand. None of the last few weeks had happened. We were here on a holiday, but there was something wrong and she was in danger outside. I went to open the doors to her, ask her in and help her, assuage whatever fears she had.

I would have reached the doors and opened them if it were not for Ellie striking me on the shoulder with the stock of the shotgun.

"There's nothing out there but those things!" she shouted. I blinked rapidly as reality settled down around me but it was like wrapping paper, only disguising the truth I thought I knew, not dismissing it completely.

The onslaught increased.

Ellie ran up the stairs, shotgun held out before her. I glanced around once, listening to the sounds coming from near and far, all of them noises of siege, each of them promising pain at any second. Rosalie stood at the foot of the stairs doing likewise. Her face was pale and drawn and corpse-like.

"I can't believe Hayden," she said. "He was doing it with them. I can't believe . . . does Ellie really think he . . .?"

"I can't believe a second of any of this," I said. "I hear my dead wife." As if ashamed of the admission I lowered my eyes as I walked by Rosalie. "Come on," I said. "We can hold out in the attic."

"I don't think so." Her voice was so sure, so full of conviction, that I thought she was all right. Ironic that a statement of doom should inspire such a feeling, but it was as close to the truth as anything.

I thought Rosalie was all right.

It was only as I reached the top of the stairs that I realized she had not followed me.

I looked out over the ornate old banister, down into the hallway where shadows played and cast false impressions on eyes I could barely trust anyway. At first I thought I was seeing things because Rosalie was not stupid; Rosalie was cynical and bitter, but never stupid. She would not do such a thing.

She stood by the open front doors. How I had not heard her unbolting and opening them I do not know, but there she was, a stark shadow against white fluttering snow, dim daylight parting around her and pouring in. Other things came in too, the whites, slinking across the floor and leaving paw prints of frost wherever they came. Rosalie stood with arms held wide in a welcoming embrace.

She said something as the whites launched at her. I could not hear the individual words but I sensed the tone; she was happy. As if she were greeting someone she had not seen for a very long time.

And then they hit her and took her apart in seconds.

"Run!" I shouted, sprinting along the corridor, chasing Ellie's shadow. In seconds I was right behind her, pushing at her shoulders as if this would make her move faster. "Run! Run! Run!"

She glanced back as she ran. "Where's Rosalie?"

"She opened the door." It was all I needed to say. Ellie turned away and concentrated on negotiating a corner in the corridor.

From behind me I heard the things bursting in all around. Those that had slunk past Rosalie must had broken into rooms from the inside even as others came in from outside, helping each other, crashing through our pathetic barricades by force of cooperation.

I noticed how cold it had become. Frost clung to the walls and the old carpet beneath our feet crunched with each footfall. Candles threw erratic shadows at icicle-encrusted ceilings. I felt ice under my fingernails.

Jayne's voice called out behind me and I slowed, but then I ran on once more, desperate to fight what I so wanted to believe. She'd said we would be together again and now she was calling me . . . but she was dead, she was dead. Still she called. Still I ran. And then she started to cry because I was not going to her, and I imagined her naked out there in the snow with white things everywhere. I stopped and turned around.

Ellie grabbed my shoulder, spun me and slapped me across the face. It brought tears to my eyes, but it also brought me back to shady reality. "We're here," she said. "Stay with us." Then she looked over my shoulder. Her eyes widened. She brought the gun up so quickly that it smacked into my ribs, and the explosion in the confined corridor felt like a hammer pummelling my ears.

I turned and saw what she had seen. It was like a drift of snow moving down the corridor towards us, rolling across the walls and ceiling, pouring along the floor. Ellie's shot had blown a hole through it, but the whites quickly regrouped and moved forward once more. Long, fine tendrils felt out before them, freezing the corridor seconds before the things passed by. There were no faces or eyes or mouths, but if I looked long enough I could see Jayne rolling naked in there with them, her mouth wide, arms holding whites to her, into her. If I really listened I was sure I would hear her sighs as she fucked them. They had passed from luring to mocking now that we were trapped, but still . . .

They stopped. The silence was a withheld chuckle.

"Why don't they rush us?" I whispered. Ellie had already pulled down the loft ladder and was waiting to climb up. She reached out and pulled me back, indicating with a nod of her head that I should go first. I reached out for the gun, wanting to give her a chance, but she elbowed me away without taking her eyes off the advancing white mass. "Why don't they . . .?"

She fired again. The shot tore a hole, but another thing soon filled that hole and stretched out toward us. "I'll shoot you if you stand in my way any more," she said.

I believed her. I handed her two cartridges and scurried up the ladder, trying not to see Jayne where she rolled and writhed, trying not to hear her sighs of ecstasy as the whites did things to her that only I knew she liked.

The instant I made it through the hatch the sounds changed. I heard Ellie squeal as the things rushed, the metallic clack as she slammed the gun shut again, two explosions in quick succession, a wet sound as whites ripped apart. Their charge sounded like a steam train: wood cracked and split; the floorboards were smashed up beneath icy feet; ceiling collapsed. I could not see, but I felt the corridor shattering as they came at Ellie, as if it were suddenly too small to house them all and they were ploughing their own way through the manor.

Ellie came up the ladder fast, throwing the shotgun through before hauling herself up after it. I saw a flash of white before she slammed the hatch down and locked it behind her.

"There's no way they can't get up here," I said. "They'll be here in seconds."

Ellie struck a match and lit a pathetic stub of candle. "Last one." She was panting. In the weak light she looked pale and worn out. "Let's see what they decide," she said.

We were in one of four attics in the manor roof. This one was boarded but bare, empty of everything except spiders and dust. Ellie shivered and cried, mumbling about her dead husband Jack frozen in the car. Maybe she heard him. Maybe she'd seen him down there. I found with a twinge of guilt that I could not care less.

"They herded us, didn't they?" I said. I was breathless and aching, but it was similar to the feeling after a good workout; enlivened, not exhausted.

Ellie shrugged, then nodded. She moved over to me and took the last couple of cartridges from the bag on my belt. As she broke the gun and removed the spent shells her shoulders hitched. She gasped and dropped the gun.

"What? Ellie?" But she was not hearing me. She stared into old shadows which had not been bathed in light for years, seeing some unknown truths there, her mouth falling open into an expression so unfamiliar on her face that it took me some seconds to place it – a smile. Whatever she saw, whatever she heard, it was something she was happy with.

I almost let her go. In the space of a second, all possibilities flashed across my mind. We were going to die, there was no escape, they would take us singly or all in one go, they would starve us out, the snow would never melt, the whites would change and grow and evolve beneath us, we could do nothing, whatever they were they had won already, they had won when Humankind brought the ruin down upon itself . . .

Then I leaned over and slapped Ellie across the face. Her head snapped around and she lost her balance, falling onto all fours over the gun.

I heard Jayne's footsteps as she prowled the corridors searching for me, calling my name with increasing exasperation. Her voice was changing from sing-song, to monotone, to panicked. The whites were down there with her, the white animals, all animals, searching and stalking her tender naked body through the freezing manor. I had to help her. I knew what it would mean but at least then we would be together, at least then her last promise to me would have been fulfilled.

Ellie's moan brought me back and for a second I hated her for that. I had been with Jayne and now I was here in some dark, filthy attic with a hundred creatures below trying to find a way to tear me apart. I hated her and I could not help it one little bit.

I moved to one of the sloping rooflights and stared out. I looked for Jayne across the snowscape, but the whites now had other things on their mind. Fooling me was not a priority.

"What do we do?" I asked Ellie, sure even now that she would have an idea, a plan. "How many shots have you got left?"

She looked at me. The candle was too weak to light up her eyes. "Enough." Before I even realized what she was doing she had flipped the shotgun over, wrapped her mouth around the twin barrels, reached down, curved her thumb through the trigger guard and blasted her brains into the air.

It's been over an hour since Ellie killed herself and left me on my own.

In that time snow has been blown into the attic to cover her body from view. Elsewhere it's merely a sprinkling, but Ellie is little more than a white hump on the floor now, the mess of her head a pink splash across the ever-whitening boards.

At first the noise from downstairs was terrific. The whites raged and ran and screamed, and I curled into a ball and tried to prepare myself for them to smash through the hatch and take me apart. I even considered the shotgun . . . there's one shot left . . . but Ellie was brave, Ellie was strong. I don't have that strength.

Besides, there's Jayne to think of. She's down there now, I know, because I have not heard a sound for ten minutes. Outside it is snowing heavier than I've ever seen, it must be ten feet deep, and there is no movement whatsoever. Inside, below the hatch and throughout the manor, in rooms sealed and broken open, the whites must be waiting. Here and there, Jayne will be waiting with them. For me. So that I can be with her again.

Soon I will open the hatch, make my way downstairs and out through the front doors. I hope, Jayne, that you will meet me there.

PETER STRAUB

Pork Pie Hat

PETER STRAUB'S LATEST NOVEL, *Mr. X*, recently won the Bram Stoker Award (his third). His other acclaimed books include *Ghost Story*, *Shadowland*, *The Talisman* (with Stephen King), *Koko*, *Mystery*, *The Throat* and *The Hellfire Club*. A second collection of his shorter fiction, *Magic Terror*, was recently published by Random House.

Straub has also won two World Fantasy Awards, the British Fantasy Award and an International Horror Guild Award. In 1998, he was named Grand Master at the World Horror Convention.

"One Sunday afternoon in 1957," recalls the author, "the American television network CBS broadcast a stunning hour-long live programme consisting entirely of performances by significant jazz musicians who had been assembled specifically for the occasion. The programme was called *The Sound of Jazz*, and fortunately it was taped. Nothing like it will ever be seen again. Count Basie, Coleman Hawkins, Thelonious Monk, Roy Eldridge, Ben Webster, Pee Wee Rusell, Red Allen, and other great musicians – Jimmy Rushing! Vic Dickenson! – simply raised their instruments, or, in the cases of Basie and Monk, sat down before them, and played while the cameras took everything in.

"One of the most moving performances was Billie Holiday's 'Fine and Mellow', in which instrumentalists soloed for one chorus apiece between each of her choruses. One of these soloists was the great tenor saxophone player Lester Young, then near the end of his life. Young's chorus is simple, profound, heartbreak-

ing. It makes me cry almost every time I see it. A man barely
capable of playing anything at all summons a kind of other-
worldly majesty and embodies it in a perfect statement. At first, I
wondered how Young could have reached such a moment in his
art; mainly, though, I wanted to represent as well as I could what
it must have been like to walk into some club, sit down at a table,
and see him play."

I

IF YOU KNOW JAZZ, YOU KNOW ABOUT HIM, and the title of this
memoir tells you who he is. If you don't know the music, his
name doesn't matter. I'll call him Hat. What does matter is what he
meant. I don't mean what he meant to people who were touched by
what he said through his horn. (His horn was an old Selmer
Balanced Action tenor saxophone, most of its lacquer worn off.)
I'm talking about the whole long curve of his life, and the way that
what appeared to be a long slide from joyous mastery to outright
exhaustion can be seen in another way altogether.

Hat did slide into alcoholism and depression. The last ten years
of his life amounted to suicide by malnutrition, and he was almost
transparent by the time he died in the hotel room where I met him.
Yet he was able to play until nearly the end. When he was
working, he would wake up around seven in the evening, listen
to Frank Sinatra or Billie Holiday records while he dressed, get to
the club by nine, play three sets, come back to his room sometime
after three, drink and listen to more records (he was on a lot of
those records), and finally go back to bed around the time day
people begin thinking about lunch. When he wasn't working, he
got into bed about an hour earlier, woke up about five or six, and
listened to records and drank through his long upside-down day.

It sounds like a miserable life, but it was just an unhappy one.
The unhappiness came from a deep, irreversible sadness. Sadness
is different from misery, at least Hat's was. His sadness seemed
impersonal – it did not disfigure him, as misery can do. Hat's
sadness seemed to be for the universe, or to be a larger than usual
personal share of a sadness already existing in the universe. Inside
it, Hat was unfailingly gentle, kind, even funny. His sadness

seemed merely the opposite face of the equally impersonal happiness that shone through his earlier work.

In Hat's later years, his music thickened, and sorrow spoke through the phrases. In his last years, what he played often sounded like heartbreak itself. He was like someone who had passed through a great mystery, who *was passing* through a great mystery, and had to speak of what he had seen, what he was seeing.

II

I brought two boxes of records with me when I first came to New York from Evanston, Illinois, where I'd earned a BA in English at Northwestern, and the first thing I set up in my shoebox at the top of John Jay Hall in Columbia University was my portable record player. I did everything to music in those days, and I supplied the rest of my unpacking with a soundtrack provided by Hat's disciples. The kind of music I most liked when I was twenty-one was called "cool" jazz, but my respect for Hat, the progenitor of this movement, was almost entirely abstract. I didn't know his earliest records, and all I'd heard of his later style was one track on a Verve sampler album. I thought he must almost certainly be dead, and I imagined that if by some miracle he was still alive, he would have been in his early seventies, like Louis Armstrong. In fact, the man who seemed a virtual ancient to me was a few months short of his fiftieth birthday.

In my first weeks at Columbia I almost never left the campus. I was taking five courses, also a seminar that was intended to lead me to a Master's thesis, and when I was not in lecture halls or my room, I was in the library. But by the end of September, feeling less overwhelmed, I began to go downtown to Greenwich Village. The IRT, the only subway line I actually understood, described a straight north-south axis which allowed you to get on at 116th Street and get off at Sheridan Square. From Sheridan Square radiated out an unimaginable wealth (unimaginable if you'd spent the previous four years in Evanston, Illinois) of cafes, bars, restaurants, record shops, bookstores, and jazz clubs. I'd come to New York to get a MA in English, but I'd also come for this.

I learned that Hat was still alive about seven o'clock in the evening on the first Saturday in October, when I saw a poster bearing his name on the window of a storefront jazz club near St

Mark's Place. My conviction that Hat was dead was so strong
that I first saw the poster as an advertisement of past glory. I
stopped to gaze longer at this relic of a historical period. Hat had
been playing with a quartet including a bassist and drummer of
his own era, musicians long associated with him. But the piano
player had been John Hawes, one of *my* musicians – John Hawes
was on half a dozen of the records back in John Jay Hall. He must
have been about twenty at the time, I thought, convinced that the
poster had been preserved as memorabilia. Maybe Hawes' first
job had been with Hat – anyhow, Hat's quartet must have been
one of Hawes' first stops on the way to fame. John Hawes was a
great figure to me, and the thought of him playing with a back
number like Hat was a disturbance in the texture of reality. I
looked down at the date on the poster, and my snobbish and rule-
bound version of reality shuddered under another assault of the
unthinkable. Hat's engagement had begun on the Tuesday of this
week – the first Tuesday in October – and its last night took place
on the Sunday after next – the Sunday before Halloween. Hat was
still alive, and John Hawes was playing with him. I couldn't have
told you which half of this proposition was the more surprising.

To make sure, I went inside and asked the short, impassive man
behind the bar if John Hawes were really playing there tonight.
"He'd better be, if he wants to get paid," the man said.

"So Hat is still alive," I said.

"Put it this way," he said. "If it was you, you probably
wouldn't be."

III

Two hours and twenty minutes later, Hat came through the front
door, and I saw what he meant. Maybe a third of the tables
between the door and the bandstand were filled with people
listening to the piano trio. This was what I'd come for, and I
thought that the evening was perfect. I hoped that Hat would stay
away. All he could accomplish by showing up would be to steal
soloing time from Hawes, who, apart from seeming a bit disengaged, was playing wonderfully. Maybe Hawes always seemed a
bit disengaged. That was fine with me. Hawes was *supposed* to be
cool. Then the bass player looked toward the door and smiled,
and the drummer grinned and knocked one stick against the side

of his snare drum in a rhythmic figure that managed both to suit what the trio was playing and serve as a half-comic, half-respectful greeting. I turned away from the trio and looked back toward the door. The bent figure of a light-skinned black man in a long, drooping, dark coat was carrying a tenor saxophone case into the club. Layers of airline stickers covered the case, and a black porkpie hat concealed most of the man's face. As soon as he got past the door, he fell into a chair next to an empty table – really fell, as if he would need a wheelchair to get any farther.

Most of the people who had watched him enter turned back to John Hawes and the trio, who were beginning the last few choruses of "Love Walked In". The old man laboriously unbuttoned his coat and let it fall off his shoulders, onto the back of the chair. Then, with the same painful slowness, he lifted the hat off his head and lowered it to the table beside him. A brimming shotglass had appeared between himself and the hat, though I hadn't noticed any of the waiters or waitresses put it there. Hat picked up the glass and poured its entire contents into his mouth. Before he swallowed, he let himself take in the room, moving his eyes without changing the position of his head. He was wearing a dark grey suit, a blue shirt with a tight tab collar, and a black knit tie. His face looked soft and worn with drink, and his eyes were of no real colour at all, as if not merely washed out but washed clean. He bent over, unlocked the case, and began assembling his horn. As soon as "Love Walked In" ended, he was on his feet, clipping the horn to his strap and walking toward the bandstand. There was some quiet applause.

Hat stepped neatly up onto the bandstand, acknowledged us with a nod, and whispered something to John Hawes, who raised his hands to the keyboard. The drummer was still grinning, and the bassist had closed his eyes. Hat tilted his horn to one side, examined the mouthpiece, and slid it a tiny distance down the cork. He licked the reed, tapped his foot twice, and put his lips around the mouthpiece.

What happened next changed my life – changed me, anyhow. It was like discovering that some vital, even necessary substance had all along been missing from my life. Anyone who hears a great musician for the first time knows the feeling that the universe has just expanded. In fact, all that happened was that Hat had started playing "Too Marvelous For Words" one of the twenty-odd songs that were his entire repertoire at the time. Actually, he was playing some oblique, one-time-only melody of his own that floated above "Too Marvelous For Words", and this spontaneous melody seemed to me to comment affectionately on the song while utterly transcending it – to turn a nice little song into something profound. I forgot to breathe for a little while, and goosebumps came up on my arms. Half-way through Hat's solo, I saw John Hawes watching him and realized that Hawes, whom I all but revered, revered *him*. But by that time, I did, too.

I stayed for all three sets, and after my seminar the next day, I went down to Sam Goody's and bought five of Hat's records, all I could afford. That night, I went back to the club and took a table right in front of the bandstand. For the next two weeks, I occupied the same table every night I could persuade myself that I did not have to study – eight or nine, out of the twelve nights Hat worked. Every night was like the first: the same things, in the same order, happened. Half-way through the first set, Hat turned up and collapsed into the nearest chair. Unobtrusively, a waiter put a drink beside him. Off went the pork-pie and the long coat, and out from its case came the horn. The waiter carried the case, pork-pie, and coat into a back room while Hat drifted toward the bandstand, often still fitting the pieces of his saxophone together. He stood straighter, seemed almost to grow taller, as he got on the stand. A nod to his audience, an inaudible word to John Hawes. And then that sense of passing over the border between very good, even excellent music and majestic, mysterious art. Between songs, Hat sipped from a glass placed beside his left foot. Three forty-five minute sets. Two half-hour breaks, during which Hat disappeared through a door behind the bandstand. The same twenty or so songs, recycled again and again. Ecstasy, as if I were hearing *Mozart* play Mozart.

One afternoon toward the end of the second week, I stood up from a library book I was trying to stuff whole into my brain – *Modern Approaches to Milton* – and walked out of my carrel to find whatever I could that had been written about Hat. I'd been hearing the sound of Hat's tenor in my head ever since I'd gotten out of bed. And in those days, I was a sort of apprentice scholar: I thought that real answers in the form of interpretations could be found in the pages of scholarly journals. If there were at least a thousand, maybe two thousand, articles concerning John Milton in Low Library, shouldn't there be at least a hundred about Hat? And out of the hundred shouldn't a dozen or so at least begin to explain what happened to me when I heard him play? I was looking for *close readings* of his solos, for analyses that would explain Hat's effects in terms of subdivided rhythms, alternate chords, and note choices, in the way that poetry critics parsed diction levels, inversions of metre, and permutations of imagery.

Of course I did not find a dozen articles that applied a musicological version of the New Criticism to Hat's recorded solos. I found six old concert write-ups in the *New York Times*, maybe as many record reviews in jazz magazines, and a couple of chapters in jazz histories. Hat had been born in Mississippi, played in his family band, left after a mysterious disagreement at the time they were becoming a successful "territory" band, then joined a famous jazz band in its infancy and quit, again mysteriously, just after its breakthrough into nationwide success. After that, he went out on his own. It seemed that if you wanted to know about him, you had to go straight to the music: there was virtually nowhere else to go.

I wandered back from the catalogues to my carrel, closed the door on the outer world, and went back to stuffing *Modern Approaches to Milton* into my brain. Around six o'clock, I opened the carrel door and realized that *I* could write about Hat. Given the paucity of criticism of his work – given the virtual absence of information about the man himself – I virtually had to write something. The only drawback to this inspiration was that I knew nothing about music. I could not write the sort of article I had wished to read. What I could do, however, would be to interview the man. Potentially, an interview would be more valuable than analysis. I could fill in the dark places, answer the unanswered questions – why had he left both bands just as they began to do well? I wondered if he'd had problems with his father, and then transferred these problems to his next bandleader. There had to be some kind of story. Any band within smelling distance of its first success would be more than reluctant to lose its star soloist – wouldn't they beg him, bribe him, to stay? I could think of other questions no one had ever asked: who had influenced him? What did he think of all those tenor players whom he had influenced? Was he friendly with any of his artistic children? Did they come to his house and talk about music?

Above all, I was curious about the texture of his life – I wondered what his life, the life of a genius, tasted like. If I could have put my half-formed fantasies into words, I would have described my naive, uninformed conceptions of Leonard Bernstein's surroundings. Mentally, I equipped Hat with a big apartment, handsome furniture, advanced stereo equipment, a good but not flashy car, paintings . . . the surroundings of a famous American artist, at least by the standards of John Jay Hall and Evanston, Illinois. The difference between Bernstein and Hat was that the conductor probably lived on Fifth Avenue, and the tenor player in the Village.

I walked out of the library humming "Love Walked in".

IV

The dictionary-sized Manhattan telephone directory chained to the shelf beneath the pay telephone on the ground floor of John Jay Hall failed to provide Hat's number. Moments later, I met similar failure back in the library after having consulted the equally impressive directories for Brooklyn, Queens, and the Bronx, as well as the much smaller volume for Staten Island. But of course Hat lived in New York: where else would he live? Like other celebrities, he avoided the unwelcome intrusions of strangers by going unlisted. I could not explain his absence from the city's five telephone books in any other way. Of course Hat lived in the Village – that was what the Village was *for*.

Yet even then, remembering the unhealthy-looking man who each night entered the club to drop into the nearest chair, I experienced a wobble of doubt. Maybe the great man's life was nothing like my imaginings. Hat wore decent clothes, but did not seem rich – he seemed to exist at the same oblique angle to worldly success that his nightly variations on "Too Marvelous For Words" bore to the original melody. For a moment, I pictured my genius in a slum apartment where roaches scuttled across a bare floor and water dripped from a rip in the ceiling. I had no idea of how jazz musicians actually lived. Hollywood, unafraid of cliché, surrounded them with squalor. On the rare moments when literature stooped to consider jazz people, it, too, served up an ambiance of broken bedsprings and peeling walls. And literature's bohemians – Rimbaud, Jack London, Kerouac, Harte

Crane, William Burroughs – had often inhabited mean, unhappy rooms. It was possible that the great man was not listed in the city's directories because he could not afford a telephone.

This notion was unacceptable. There was another explanation – Hat could not live in a tenement room without a telephone. The man still possessed the elegance of his generation of jazz musicians, the generation that wore good suits and highly polished shoes, played in big bands, and lived on buses and in hotel rooms.

And there, I thought, was my answer. It was a comedown from the apartment in the Village with which I had supplied him, but a room in some "artistic" hotel like the Chelsea would suit him just as well, and probably cost a lot less in rent. Feeling inspired, I looked up the Chelsea's number on the spot, dialled, and asked for Hat's room. The clerk told me that he wasn't registered in the hotel. "But you know who he is," I said. "Sure," said the clerk. "Guitar, right? I know he was in one of those San Francisco bands, but I can't remember which one."

I hung up without replying, realizing that the only way I was going to discover Hat's telephone number, short of calling every hotel in New York, was by asking him for it.

V

This was on a Monday, and the jazz clubs were closed. On Tuesday, Professor Marcus told us to read all of *Vanity Fair* by Friday; on Wednesday, after I'd spent a nearly sleepless night with Thackeray, my seminar leader asked me to prepare a paper on James Joyce's "Two Gallants" for the Friday class. Wednesday and Thursday nights I spent in the library. On Friday I listened to Professor Marcus being brilliant about *Vanity Fair* and read my laborious and dimwitted Joyce paper, on each of the five pages of which the word "epiphany" appeared at least twice, to my fellow-scholars. The seminar leader smiled and nodded throughout my performance and when I sat down metaphorically picked up my little paper between thumb and forefinger and slit its throat. "Some of you students are so *certain* about things," he said. The rest of his remarks disappeared into a vast, horrifying sense of shame. I returned to my room, intending to lie down for an hour or two, and woke up ravenous ten hours later, when even the West End bar, even the local Chock Full O' Nuts, were shut for the night.

On Saturday night, I took my usual table in front of the bandstand and sat expectantly through the piano trio's usual three numbers. In the middle of "Love Walked In" I looked around with an insider's foreknowledge to enjoy Hat's dramatic entrance, but he did not appear, and the number ended without him. John Hawes and the other two musicians seemed untroubled by this break in the routine, and went on to play "Too Marvelous For Words" without their leader. During the next three songs, I kept turning around to look for Hat, but the set ended without him. Hawes announced a short break, and the musicians stood up and moved toward the bar. I fidgeted at my table, nursing my second beer of the night and anxiously checking the door. The minutes trudged by. I feared he would never show up. He had passed out in his room. He'd been hit by a cab, he'd had a stroke, he was already lying dead in a hospital room – just when I was going to write the article that would finally do him justice!

Half an hour later, still without their leader, John Hawes and other sidemen went back on the stand. No one but me seemed to have noticed that Hat was not present. The other customers talked and smoked – this was in the days when people still smoked – and gave the music the intermittent and sometimes ostentatious attention they allowed it even when Hat was on the stand. By now, Hat was an hour and a half late, and I could see the gangsterish man behind the bar, the owner of the club, scowling as he checked his wristwatch. Hawes played two originals I particularly liked, favourites of mine from his Contemporary records, but in my mingled anxiety and irritation I scarcely heard them.

Toward the end of the second of these songs, Hat entered the club and fell into his customary seat a little more heavily than usual. The owner motioned away the waiter, who had begun moving toward him with the customary shot glass. Hat dropped the porkpie on the table and struggled with his coat buttons. When he heard what Hawes was playing, he sat listening with his hands still on a coat button, and I listened, too – the music had a tighter, harder, more modern feel, like Hawes' records. Hat nodded to himself, got his coat off, and struggled with the snaps on his saxophone case. The audience gave Hawes unusually appreciative applause. It took Hat longer than usual to fit the horn together, and by the time he was up on his feet, Hawes and the other two musicians had turned around to watch his progress as if they feared he would not make it all the way to the bandstand. Hat wound through the tables with his head tilted back, smiling to himself. When he got close to the stand, I saw that he was walking on his toes like a small child. The owner crossed his arms over his chest and glared. Hat seemed almost to float onto the stand. He licked his reed. Then he lowered his horn and, with his mouth open, stared out at us for a moment. "Ladies, ladies," he said in a soft, high voice. These were the first words I had ever heard him speak. "Thank you for your appreciation of our pianist, Mr Hawes. And now I must explain my absence during the first set. My son passed away this afternoon, and I have been . . . busy . . . with details. Thank you."

With that, he spoke a single word to Hawes, put his horn back in his mouth, and began to play a blues called "Hat Jumped Up", one of his twenty songs. The audience sat motionless with shock. Hawes, the bassist, and the drummer played on as if nothing unusual had happened – they must have known about his son, I thought. Or maybe they knew that he had no son, and had invented a grotesque excuse for turning up ninety minutes late. The club owner bit his lower lip and looked unusually introspective. Hat played one familiar, uncomplicated figure after another, his tone rough, almost coarse. At the end of his solo, he repeated one note for an entire chorus, fingering the key while staring out toward the back of the club. Maybe he was watching the customers leave – three couples and a couple of single people walked out while he was playing. But I don't think he saw anything at all. When the song was over, Hat leaned over to whisper to Hawes, and the piano player announced a short break. The second set was over.

Hat put his tenor on top of the piano and stepped down off the bandstand, pursing his mouth with concentration. The owner had come out from behind the bar and moved up in front of him as Hat tip-toed around the stand. The owner spoke a few quiet words. Hat answered. From behind, he looked slumped and tired, and his hair curled far over the back of his collar. Whatever he had said only partially satisfied the owner, who spoke again before leaving him. Hat stood in place for a moment, perhaps not noticing that the owner had gone, and resumed his tip-toe glide toward the door. Looking at his back, I think I took in for the first time how genuinely *strange* he was. Floating through the door in his grey flannel suit, hair dangling in ringlet-like strands past his collar, leaving in the air behind him the announcement about a dead son, he seemed absolutely separate from the rest of humankind, a species of one.

I turned as if for guidance to the musicians at the bar. Talking, smiling, greeting a few fans and friends, they behaved just as they did on every other night. Could Hat really have lost a son earlier today? Maybe this was the jazz way of facing grief – to come back to work, to carry on. Still it seemed the worst of all times to approach Hat with my offer. His playing was a drunken parody of itself. He would forget anything he said to me; I was wasting my time.

On that thought, I stood up and walked past the bandstand and opened the door – if I was wasting my time, it didn't matter what I did.

He was leaning against a brick wall about ten feet up the alleyway from the club's back door. The door clicked shut behind me, but Hat did not open his eyes. His face tilted up, and a sweetness that might have been sleep lay over his features. He looked exhausted and insubstantial, too frail to move. I would have gone back inside the club if he had not produced a cigarette from a pack in his shirt pocket, lit it with a match, and then flicked the match away, all without opening his eyes. At least he was awake. I stepped toward him, and his eyes opened. He glanced at me and blew out white smoke. "Taste?" he said.

I had no idea what he meant. "Can I talk to you for a minute, sir?" I asked.

He put his hand into one of his jacket pockets and pulled out a half pint bottle. "Have a taste." Hat broke the seal on the cap, tilted it into his mouth, and drank. Then he held the bottle out toward me.

I took it. "I've been coming here as often as I can."

"Me, too," he said. "Go on, do it."

I took a sip from the bottle – gin. "I'm sorry about your son."

"Son?" He looked upward, as if trying to work out my meaning. "I got a son – out on Long Island. With his momma.' He drank again and checked the level of the bottle.

"He's not dead, then."

He spoke the next words slowly, almost wonderingly. "No-body-told-me-if-he-is." He shook his head and drank another mouthful of gin. "Damn. Wouldn't that be something, boy dies and nobody tells me? I'd have to think about that, you know, have to really *think* about that one."

"I'm just talking about what you said on stage."

He cocked his head and seemed to examine an empty place in the dark air about three feet from his face. "Uh huh. That's right. I did say that. Son of mine passed."

It was like dealing with a sphinx. All I could do was plunge in. "Well, sir, actually there's a reason I came out here," I said. "I'd like to interview you. Do you think that might be possible? You're a great artist, and there's very little about you in print. Do you think we could set up a time when I could talk to you?"

He looked at me with his bleary, colourless eyes, and I wondered if he could see me at all. And then I felt that, despite his drunkenness, he saw everything – that he saw things about me that I couldn't see.

"You a jazz writer?" he asked.

"No, I'm a graduate student. I'd just like to do it. I think it would be important."

"Important." He took another swallow from the half pint and slid the bottle back into his pocket. "Be nice, doing an *important* interview."

He stood leaning against the wall, moving further into outer space with every word. Only because I had started, I pressed on: I was already losing faith in this project. The reason Hat had never been interviewed was that ordinary American English was a foreign language to him. "Could we do the interview after you finish up at this club? I could meet you anywhere you like." Even as I said these words, I despaired. Hat was in no shape to know what he had to do after this engagement finished. I was surprised he could make it back to Long Island every night.

Hat rubbed his face, sighed, and restored my faith in him. "It'll have to wait a little while. Night after I finish here, I go to Toronto for two nights. Then I got something in Hartford on the thirtieth. You come see me after that."

"On the thirty-first?" I asked.

"Around nine, ten, something like that. Be nice if you brought some refreshments."

"Fine, great," I said, wondering if I would be able to take a late train back from wherever he lived. "But where on Long Island should I go?"

His eyes widened in mock-horror. "Don't go nowhere on Long Island. You come see me. In the Albert Hotel, Forty-Ninth and Eighth. Room 821."

I smiled at him – I had guessed right about one thing, anyhow. Hat did not live in the Village, but he did live in a Manhattan hotel. I asked him for his phone number, and wrote it down, along with the other information, on a napkin from the club. After I folded the napkin into my jacket pocket, I thanked him and turned toward the door.

"Important as a mother-fucker," he said in his high, soft, slurry voice.

I turned around in alarm, but he had tilted his head toward the sky again, and his eyes were closed.

"Indiana," he said. His voice made the word seem sung. "Moonlight in Vermont. I Thought About You. Flamingo."

He was deciding what to play during his next set. I went back inside, where twenty or thirty new arrivals, more people than I had ever seen in the club, waited for the music to start. Hat soon reappeared through the door, the other musicians left the bar, and the third set began. Hat played all four of the songs he had named, interspersing them through his standard repertoire during the course of an unusually long set. He was playing as well as I'd ever heard him, maybe better than I'd heard on all the other nights I had come to the club. The Saturday night crowd applauded explosively after every solo. I didn't know if what I was seeing was genius or desperation.

An obituary in the Sunday *New York Times*, which I read over breakfast the next morning in the John Jay cafeteria, explained some of what had happened. Early Saturday morning, a thirty-eight year old tenor saxophone player named Grant Kilbert had been killed in an automobile accident. One of the most successful jazz musicians in the world, one of the few jazz musicians, known outside of the immediate circle of fans, Kilbert had probably been Hat's most prominent disciple. He had certainly been one of my favourite musicians. More importantly, from his first record, *Cool Breeze*, Kilbert had excited respect and admiration. I looked at the photograph of the handsome young man beaming out over the neck of his saxophone and realized that the first four songs on *Cool Breeze* were "Indiana", "Moonlight in Vermont", "I Thought About You", and "Flamingo". Sometime late Saturday afternoon, someone had called up Hat to tell him about Kilbert. What I had seen had not merely been alcoholic eccentricity, it had been grief for a lost son. And when I thought about it, I was sure that the lost son, not himself, had been the important mother-fucker he'd apothesized. What I had taken for spaciness and disconnection had all along been irony.

Part Two

I

On the 31st of October, after calling to make sure he remembered our appointment, I did go to the Albert Hotel, room 821, and interview Hat. That is, I asked him questions and listened to the long, rambling, often obscene responses he gave them. During the long night I spent in his room, he drank the fifth of Gordon's gin, the "refreshments" I brought with me – all of it, an entire bottle of gin, without tonic, ice, or other dilutants. He just poured it into a tumbler and drank, as if it were water. (I refused his single offer of a "taste".) I frequently checked to make sure that the tape recorder I'd borrowed from a business student down the hall from me was still working, I changed tapes until they ran out, I made detailed back-up notes with a ballpoint pen in a stenographic notebook. A couple of times, he played me sections of records that he wanted me to hear, and now and then he sang a couple of bars to make sure that I understood what he was telling me. He sat me in his only chair, and during the entire night stationed himself, dressed in his pork-pie hat, a dark blue chalk-stripe suit, and white button-down shirt with a black knit tie, on the edge of his bed. This was a formal occasion. When I arrived at nine o'clock, he addressed me as "Mr Leonard Feather" (the name of a well-known jazz critic), and when he opened his door at six-thirty the next morning, he called me "Miss Rosemary". By then, I knew that this was an allusion to Rosemary Clooney, whose singing I had learned that he liked, and that the nickname meant he liked me, too. It was not at all certain, however, that he remembered my actual name.

I had three sixty-minute tapes and a notebook filled with handwriting that gradually degenerated from my usual scrawl into loops and wiggles that resembled Arabic more than English. Over the next month, I spent whatever spare time I had transcribing the tapes and trying to decipher my own handwriting. I wasn't sure that what I had was an interview. My carefully-prepared questions had been met either with evasions or blank, silent refusals to answer – he had simply started talking about something else. After about an hour, I realized that this was his interview, not mine, and let him roll.

After my notes had been typed up and the tapes transcribed, I put everything in a drawer and went back to work on my MA. What I had was even more puzzling than I'd thought, and straightening it out would have taken more time than I could afford. So the rest of that academic year was a long grind of studying for the comprehensive exam and getting a thesis ready. Until I picked up an old *Time* magazine in the John Jay lounge and saw his name in the "Milestones" columns, I didn't even know that Hat had died.

Two months after I'd interviewed him, he had begun to haemorrhage on a flight back from France; an ambulance had taken him directly from the airport to a hospital. Five days after his release from the hospital, he had died in his bed at the Albert.

After I earned my degree, I was determined to wrestle something useable from my long night with Hat – I owed it to him. During the first weeks of that summer, I wrote out a version of what Hat had said to me and sent it to the only publication I thought would be interested in it. *Downbeat* accepted the interview, and it appeared there about six months later. Eventually, it acquired some fame as the last of his rare public statements. I still see lines from the interview quoted in the sort of pieces about Hat never printed during his life. Sometimes they are lines he really did say to me; sometimes they are stitched together from remarks he made at different times; sometimes, they are quotations I invented in order to be able to use other things he did say.

But one section of that interview has never been quoted, because it was never printed. I never figured out what to make of it. Certainly I could not believe all he had said. He had been putting me on, silently laughing at my credulity, for he could not possibly believe that what he was telling me was literal truth. I was a white boy with a tape recorder, it was Halloween, and Hat was having fun with me. He was *jiving* me.

Now I feel different about his story and about him, too. He was a great man, and I was an unwordly kid. He was drunk, and I was priggishly sober, but in every important way, he was functioning far above my level. Hat had lived forty-nine years as a black man in America, and I'd spent all of my twenty-one years in white suburbs. He was an immensely talented musician, a man who virtually thought in music, and I can't even hum in tune. That I expected to understand anything at all about him staggers me now. Back then, I didn't know anything about grief, and Hat wore grief about him daily, like a cloak. Now that I am the age he was then, I see that most of what is called information is interpretation, and interpretation is always partial.

Probably Hat was putting me on, jiving me, though not maliciously. He certainly was not telling me the literal truth, though I have never been able to learn what the literal truth of this case was. It's possible that even Hat never knew what was the literal truth behind the story he told me – possible, I mean, that he was still trying to work out what the truth was, nearly forty years after the fact.

II

He started telling me the story after we heard what I thought were gunshots from the street. I jumped from the chair and rushed to the windows, which looked out onto Eighth Avenue. "Kids," Hat said. In the hard yellow light of the streetlamps, four or five teenage boys trotted up the Avenue. Three of them carried paper bags. "Kids shooting?" I asked. My amazement tells you how long ago this was.

"Fireworks," Hat said. "Every Halloween in New York, fool kids run around with bags full of fireworks, trying to blow their hands off."

Here and in what follows, I am not going to try to represent the way Hat actually spoke. I cannot represent the way his voice glided over certain words and turned others into mushy growls, though he expressed more than half of his meaning by sound; and I don't want to reproduce his constant, reflexive obscenity. Hat couldn't utter four words in a row without throwing in a "motherfucker." Mostly, I have replaced his obscenities with other words, and the reader can imagine what was really said. Also, if I tried to imitate his grammar, I'd sound racist and he would sound stupid. Hat left school in the fourth grade, and his language, though precise, was casual. To add to these difficulties, Hat employed a private language of his own, a code to ensure that he would be understood only by the people he wished to understand him. I have replaced most of his code words with their equivalents.

It must have been around one in the morning, which means that I had been in his room about four hours. Until Hat explained the "gunshots," I had forgotten that it was Halloween night, and I told him this as I turned away from the window.

"I never forget about Halloween," Hat said. "If I can, I stay home on Halloween. Don't want to be out on the street, that night."

He had already given me proof that he was superstitious, and as he spoke he glanced almost nervously around the room, as if looking for sinister presences.

"You'd feel in danger?" I asked.

He rolled gin around in his mouth and looked at me as he had in the alley behind the club, taking note of qualities I myself did not yet perceive. This did not feel at all judgmental. The nervousness I thought I had seen had disappeared, and his manner seemed marginally more concentrated than earlier in the evening. He swallowed the gin and for a couple of seconds looked at me without speaking.

"No," he finally said. "Not exactly. But I wouldn't feel safe, either."

I sat with my pen half an inch from the page of my notebook, uncertain whether or not to write this down.

"I'm from Mississippi, you know."

I nodded.

"Funny things happen down there. Back when I was a little kid, it was a whole different world. Know what I mean?"

"I can guess," I said.

He nodded. "Sometimes people disappeared. They'd be *gone*. All kinds of stuff used to happen, stuff you wouldn't even believe in now. I met a witch-lady once who could put curses on you, make you go blind and crazy. Another time, I saw a mean, murdering son of a bitch named Eddie Grimes die and come back to life – he got shot to death at a dance we were playing, he was *dead*, and a woman went down and whispered to him, and Eddie Grimes stood right back up on his feet. The man who shot him took off double-quick and he must have kept on going, because we never saw him after that."

"Did you start playing again?" I asked, taking notes as fast as I could.

"We never stopped," Hat said. "You let the people deal with what's going on, but you gotta keep on playing."

"Did you live in the country?" I asked, thinking that all of this sounded like Dogpatch – witches and walking dead men.

He shook his head. "I was brought up in town, Woodland, Mississippi. On the river. Where we lived was called Darktown, you know, but most of Woodland was white, with nice houses and all. Lots of our people did the cooking and washing in the big houses on Miller's Hill, that kind of work. In fact, we lived in a pretty nice house, for Darktown – the band always did well, and my father had a couple of other jobs on top of that. He was a good piano player, mainly, but he could play any kind of instrument. And he was a big, strong guy, nice-looking, real light-complected, so he was called Red, which was what that meant in those days. People respected him."

Another long, rattling burst of explosions came from Eighth Avenue. I wanted to ask him again about leaving his father's band, but Hat once more gave his little room a quick inspection, swallowed another mouthful of gin, and went on talking.

"We even went out trick or treating on Halloween, you know, like the white kids. I guess our people didn't do that everywhere, but we did. Naturally, we stuck to our neighborhood, and probably we got a lot less than the kids from Miller's Hill, but they didn't have anything up there that tasted as good as the apples and candy we brought home in our bags. Around us, people made instead of bought, and that's the difference." He smiled at either the memory or the unexpected sentimentality he had just revealed – for a moment, he looked both lost in time and uneasy with himself for having said too much. "Or maybe I just remember it that way, you know? Anyhow, we used to raise some hell, too. You were *supposed* to raise hell, on Halloween."

"You went out with your brothers?" I asked.

"No, no, they were—" He flipped his hand in the air, dismissing whatever it was that his brothers had been. "I was always apart, you dig? Me, I was always into my own little things. I was that way right from the beginning. I play like that – never play like anyone else, don't even play like myself. You gotta find new places for yourself, or else nothing's happening, isn't that right? Don't want to be a repeater pencil." He saluted this declaration with another swallow of gin. "Back in those days, I used to go out with a boy named Rodney Sparks – we called him Dee, short for Demon, 'cause Dee Sparks would do anything that came into his head. That boy was the bravest little bastard I ever knew. He'd wrassle a mad dog. And the reason was, Dee was the preacher's boy. If you happen to be the preacher's boy, seems like you gotta prove every way you can that you're no Buster Brown, you know? So I hung with Dee, because I wasn't any Buster Brown, either. This is when we were eleven, around then – the time when you talk about girls, you know, but you still aren't too sure what that's about. You don't know what *anything's* about, to tell the truth. You along for the ride, you trying to pack in as much fun as possible. So Dee was my right hand, and when I went out on Halloween in Woodland, I went out with *him*."

He rolled his eyes toward the window and said, "Yeah." An expression I could not read at all took over his face. By the standards of ordinary people, Hat almost always looked detached, even impassive, tuned to some private wavelength, and this sense of detachment had intensified. I thought he was changing mental gears, dismissing his childhood, and opened my mouth to ask him about Grant Kilbert. But he raised his glass to his mouth again and rolled his eyes back to me, and the quality of his gaze told me to keep quiet.

"I didn't know it," he said, "but I was getting ready to stop being a little boy. To stop believing in little boy things and start seeing like a grown-up. I guess that's part of what I liked about Dee Sparks – he seemed like he was a lot more grown-up than I was, shows you what my head was like. The age we were, this would have been the last time we went out on Halloween to get apples and candy. From then on, we would have gone out mainly to raise hell. Scare the shit out of the little kids. But the way it turned out, it was the last time we ever went out on Halloween."

He finished off the gin in his glass and reached down to pick the bottle off the floor and pour another few inches into the tumbler. "Here I am, sitting in this room. There's my horn over there. Here's this bottle. You know what I'm saying?"

I didn't. I had no idea what he was saying. The hint of fatality clung to his earlier statement, and for a second I thought he was going to say that he was here but Dee Sparks was nowhere because Dee Sparks had died in Woodland, Mississippi, at the age of eleven on Halloween night. Hat was looking at me with a steady curiosity which compelled a response. "What happened?" I asked.

Now I know that he was saying *It has come down to just this, my room, my horn, my bottle*. My question was as good as any other response.

"If I was to tell you everything that happened, we'd have to stay in this room for a month." He smiled and straightened up on the bed. His ankles were crossed, and for the first time I noticed that his feet, shod in dark suede shoes with crepe soles, did not quite touch the floor. "And, you know, I never tell anybody everything, I always have to keep something back for myself. Things turned out all right. Only thing I mind is, I should have earned more money. Grant Kilbert, he earned a lot of money, and some of that was mine, you know."

"Were you friends?" I asked.

"I knew the man." He tilted his head and stared at the ceiling for so long that eventually I looked up at it, too. It was not a remarkable ceiling. A circular section near the center had been replastered not long before.

"No matter where you live, there are places you're not supposed to go," he said, still gazing up. "And sooner or later, you're gonna wind up there." He smiled at me again. "Where we lived, the place you weren't supposed to go was called The Backs. Out of town, stuck in the woods on one little path. In Darktown, we had all kinds from preachers on down. We had washerwomen and blacksmiths and carpenters, and we had some no-good thieving trash, too, like Eddie Grimes, that man who came back from being dead. In The Backs, they started with trash like Eddie Grimes, and went down from there. Sometimes, our people went out there to buy a jug, and sometimes they went there to get a woman, but they never talked about it. The Backs was *rough*. What they had was *rough*." He rolled his eyes at me and said,

"That witch-lady I told you about, she lived in The Backs." He snickered. "Man, they were a mean bunch of people. They'd cut you, you looked at 'em bad. But one thing funny about the place, white and coloured lived there just the same – it was *integrated*. Backs people were so evil, colour didn't make no difference to them. They hated everybody anyhow, on principle." Hat pointed his glass at me, tilted his head, and narrowed his eyes. "At least, that was what everybody *said*. So this particular Halloween, Dee Sparks says to me after we finish with Darktown, we ought to head out to The Backs and see what the place is really like. Maybe we can have some fun.

"The idea of going out to The Backs kind of scared me, but being scared was part of the fun – Halloween, right? And if anyplace in Woodland was perfect for all that Halloween shit, you know, someplace where you might really see a ghost or a goblin, The Backs was better than the graveyard." Hat shook his head, holding the glass out at a right angle to his body. A silvery amusement momentarily transformed him, and it struck me that his native elegance, the product of his character and bearing much more than of the handsome suit and the suede shoes, had in effect been paid for by the surviving of a thousand unimaginable difficulties, each painful to a varying degree. Then I realized that what I meant by elegance was really dignity, that for the first time I had recognized actual dignity in another human being, and that dignity was nothing like the self-congratulatory superiority people usually mistook for it.

"We were just little babies, and we wanted some of those good old Halloween scares. Like those dumbbells out on the street, tossing firecrackers at each other." Hat wiped his free hand down over his face and made sure that I was prepared to write down everything he said. (The tapes had already been used up.) "When I'm done, tell me if we found it, okay?"

"Okay," I said.

III

"Dee showed up at my house just after dinner, dressed in an old sheet with two eyeholes cut in it and carrying a paper bag. His big old shoes stuck out underneath the sheet. I had the same costume, but it was the one my brother used the year before, and it dragged along the ground and my feet got caught in it. The eyeholes kept sliding away from my eyes. My mother gave me a bag and told me to behave myself and get home before eight. It didn't take but half an hour to cover all the likely houses in Darktown, but she knew I'd want to fool around with Dee for an hour or so afterwards.

"Then up and down the streets we go, knocking on the doors where they'd give us stuff and making a little mischief where we knew they wouldn't. Nothing real bad, just banging on the door and running like hell, throwing rocks on the roof, little stuff. A few places, we plain and simple stayed away from – the places where people like Eddie Grimes lived. I always thought that was funny. We knew enough to steer clear of those houses, but we were still crazy to get out to The Backs.

"Only way I can figure it is, The Backs was *forbidden*. Nobody had to tell us to stay away from Eddie Grimes' house at night. You wouldn't even go there in the daylight, 'cause Eddie Grimes would get you and that would be that.

"Anyhow, Dee kept us moving along real quick, and when folks asked us questions or said they wouldn't give us stuff unless we sang a song, he moaned like a ghost and shook his bag in their faces, so we could get away faster. He was so excited, I think he was almost shaking.

"Me, I was excited, too. Not like Dee – sort of sick-excited, the way people must feel the first time they use a parachute. Scared-excited.

"As soon as we got away from the last house, Dee crossed the street and started running down the side of the little general store we all used. I knew where he was going. Out behind the store was a field, and on the other side of the field was Meridian Road, which took you out into the woods and to the path up to The Backs. When he realized that I wasn't next to him, he turned around and yelled at me to hurry up. *No*, I said inside myself, *I ain't gonna jump outta of this here airplane, I'm not dumb enough to do that*. And then I pulled up my sheet and scrunched up my eye to look through the one hole close enough to see through, and I took off after him.

"It was beginning to get dark when Dee and I left my house, and now it was dark. The Backs was about a mile and a half away, or at least the path was. We didn't know how far along that path you had to go before you got there. Hell, we didn't even know what it was – I was still thinking the place was a collection of little houses, like a sort of shadow-Woodland. And then, while we were crossing the field, I stepped on my costume and fell down flat on my face. Enough of this stuff, I said, and yanked the damned thing off. Dee started cussing me out, I wasn't doing this stuff the right way, we had to keep our costumes on in case anybody saw us, did I forget that this is Halloween, on Halloween a costume *protected* you. So I told I him I'd put it back on when we got there. If I kept on falling down, it'd take us twice as long. That shut him up.

"As soon as I got that blasted sheet over my head, I discovered that I could see at least a little ways ahead of me. The moon was up, and a lot of stars were out. Under his sheet, Dee Sparks looked a little bit like a real ghost. It kind of glimmered. You couldn't really make out its edges, so the darn thing like *floated*. But I could see his legs and those big old shoes sticking out.

"We got out of the field and started up Meridian Road, and pretty soon the trees came up right to the ditches alongside the road, and I couldn't see too well any more. The road seemed like it went smack into the woods and disappeared. The trees looked taller and thicker than in the daytime, and now and then something right at the edge of the woods shone round and white, like an eye – reflecting the moonlight, I guess. Spooked me. I didn't think we'd ever be able to find the path up to The Backs, and that was fine with me. I thought we might go along the road another ten-fifteen minutes, and then turn around and go home. Dee was swooping around up in front of me, flapping his sheet and acting bughouse. *He* sure wasn't trying too hard to find that path.

"After we walked about a mile down Meridian Road, I saw headlights like yellow dots coming towards us fast – Dee didn't see anything at all, running around in circles the way he was. I shouted at him to get off the road, and he took off like a rabbit – disappeared into the woods before I did. I jumped the ditch and hunkered down behind a pine about ten feet off the road to see who was coming. There weren't many cars in Woodland in those days, and I knew every one of them. When the car came by, it was Dr Garland's old red Cord – Dr Garland was a white man, but he had two waiting rooms and took coloured patients, so coloured patients was mostly what he had. And the man was a heavy drinker, *heavy* drinker. He zipped by, goin' at least fifty, which was mighty fast for those days, probably as fast as that old Cord would go. For about a second, I saw Dr Garland's face under his white hair, and his mouth was wide open, stretched like he was screaming. After he passed, I waited a long time before I came out of the woods. Turning around and going home would have been fine with me. Dr Garland changed everything. Normally, he was kind of slow and quiet, you know, and I could still see that black screaming hole opened up in his face – he looked like he was being tortured, like he was in Hell. I sure as hell didn't want to see whatever *he* had seen.

"I could hear the Cord's engine after the tail lights disappeared. I turned around and saw that I was all alone on the road. Dee Sparks was nowhere in sight. A couple of times, real soft, I called out his name. Then I called his name a little louder. Away off in the woods, I heard Dee giggle. I said he could run around all night if he liked but I was going home, and then I saw that pale silver sheet moving through the trees, and I started back down Meridian Road. After about twenty paces, I looked back, and there he was, standing in the middle of the road in that silly sheet, watching me go. Come on, I said, let's get back. He paid me no mind. Wasn't that Dr Garland? Where was he going, as fast as that? What was happening? When I said the doctor was probably out on some emergency, Dee said the man was going *home* – he lived in Woodland, didn't he?

"Then I thought maybe Dr Garland had been up in The Backs. And Dee thought the same thing, which made him want to go there all the more. Now he was determined. Maybe we'd see some dead guy. We stood there until I understood that he was going to go by himself if I didn't go with him. That meant that I *had* to go. Wild as he was, Dee'd get himself into some kind of mess for sure if I wasn't there to hold him down. So I said okay, I was coming along, and Dee started swooping along like before, saying crazy stuff. There was no way we were going to be able to find some little old path that went up into the woods. It was so dark, you couldn't see the separate trees, only giant black walls on both sides of the road.

"We went so far along Meridian Road I was sure we must have passed it. Dee was running around in circles about ten feet ahead of me. I told him that we missed the path, and now it was time to get back home. He laughed at me and ran across to the right side of the road and disappeared into the darkness.

"I told him to get back, damn it, and he laughed some more and said I should come to *him*. Why? I said, and he said, Because this here is the path, dummy. I didn't believe him – came right up to where he disappeared. All I could see was a black wall that could have been trees or just plain night. Moron, Dee said, look down. And I did. Sure enough, one of those white things like an eye shone up from where the ditch should have been. I bent down and touched cold little stones, and the shining dot of white went off like a light – a pebble that caught the moonlight just right. Bending down like that, I could see the hump of grass growing up between the tire tracks that led out onto Meridian Road. He'd found the path, all right.

"At night, Dee Sparks could see one hell of a lot better than me. He spotted the break in the ditch from across the road. He was already walking up the path in those big old shoes, turning around every other step to look back at me, make sure I was coming along behind him. When I started following him, Dee told me to get my sheet back on, and I pulled the thing over my head even though I'd rather have sucked the water out of a hollow stump. But I knew he was right – on Halloween, especially in a place like where we were, you were safer in a costume.

"From then on in, we were in No Man's Land. Neither one of us had any idea how far we had to go to get to The Backs, or what it would look like once we got there. Once I set foot on that wagontrack I knew for sure The Backs wasn't anything like the way I thought. It was a lot more primitive than a bunch of houses in the woods. Maybe they didn't even have houses! Maybe they lived in caves!

"Naturally, after I got that blamed costume over my head, I couldn't see for a while. Dee kept hissing at me to hurry up, and I kept cussing him out. Finally I bunched up a couple handfuls of the sheet right under my chin and held it against my neck, and that way I could see pretty well and walk without tripping all over myself. All I had to do was follow Dee, and that was easy. He was only a couple of inches in front of me, and even through one eye-hole, I could see that silvery sheet moving along.

"Things moved in the woods, and once in a while an owl hooted. To tell you the truth, I never did like being out in the woods at night. Even back then, give me a nice warm bar-room instead, and I'd be happy. Only animal I ever liked was a cat, because a cat is soft to the touch, and it'll fall asleep on your lap. But this was even worse than usual, because of Halloween, and even before we got to The Backs, I wasn't sure if what I heard moving around in the woods was just a possum or a fox or something a lot worse, something with funny eyes and long teeth that liked the taste of little boys. Maybe Eddie Grimes was out there, looking for whatever kind of treat Eddie Grimes liked on Halloween night. Once I thought of that, I got so close to Deep Sparks I could smell him right through his sheet.

"You know what Dee Sparks smelled like? Like sweat, and a little bit like the soap the preacher made him use on his hands and face before dinner, but really like a fire in a junction box. A sharp, kind of bitter smell. That's how excited he was.

"After a while we were going uphill, and then we got to the top of the rise, and a breeze pressed my sheet against my legs. We started going downhill, and over Dee's electrical fire, I could smell wood smoke. And something else I couldn't name. Dee stopped moving so sudden, I bumped into him. I asked him what he could see. Nothing but the woods, he said, but we're getting there. People are up ahead somewhere. And they got a still. We got to be real quiet from here on out, he told me, as if he had to, and to let him know I understood I pulled him off the path into the woods.

"Well, I thought, at least I know what Dr Garland was after.

"Dee and I went snaking through the trees – me holding that blamed sheet under my chin so I could see out of one eye, at least, and walk without falling down. I was glad for that big fat pad of pine needles on the ground. An elephant could have walked over that stuff as quiet as a beetle. We went along a little further, and it got so I could smell all kinds of stuff – burned sugar, crushed juniper berries, tobacco juice, grease. And after Dee and I moved a little bit along, I heard voices, and that was enough for me. Those voices sounded angry.

"I yanked at Dee's sheet and squatted down – I wasn't going any farther without taking a good look. He slipped down beside me. I pushed the wad of material under my chin up over my face, grabbed another handful, and yanked that up, too, to look out under the bottom of the sheet. Once I could actually *see* where we were, I almost passed out. Twenty feet away through the trees, a

kerosene lantern lit up the grease-paper window cut into the back
of a little wooden shack, and a big raggedly guy carrying another
kerosene lantern came stepping out of a door we couldn't see and
stumbled toward a shed. On the other side of the building I could
see the yellow square of a window in another shack, and past
that, another one, a sliver of yellow shining out through the trees.
Dee was crouched next to me, and when I turned to look at him, I
could see another chink of yellow light from some way off in the
woods over that way. Whether he knew it not, he'd just about
walked us straight into the middle of The Backs.

"He whispered for me to cover my face. I shook my head. Both
of us watched the big guy stagger toward the shed. Somewhere in
front of us, a woman screeched, and I almost dumped a load in
my pants. Dee stuck his hand out from under his sheet and held it
out, as if I needed *him* to tell me to be quiet. The woman screeched
again, and the big guy sort of swayed back and forth. The light
from the lantern swung around in big circles. I saw that the woods
were full of little paths that ran between the shacks. The light hit
the shack, and it wasn't even wood, but tar paper. The woman
laughed or maybe sobbed. Whoever was inside the shack
shouted, and the raggedy guy wobbled toward the shed again.
He was so drunk he couldn't even walk straight. When he got to
the shed, he set down the lantern and bent to get in.

"Dee put his mouth up to my ear and whispered, Cover up –
you don't want these people, to see who you are. Rip the eyeholes,
if you can't see good enough.

"I didn't want anyone in The Backs to see my face. I let the
costume drop down over me again, and stuck my fingers in the
nearest eyehole and pulled. Every living thing for about a mile
around must have heard that cloth ripping. The big guy came out
of the shed like someone pulled him out on a string, yanked the
lantern up off the ground, and held it in our direction. Then we
could see his face, and it was Eddie Grimes. You wouldn't want to
run into Eddie Grimes anywhere, but The Backs was the last place
you'd want to come across him. I was afraid he was going to start
looking for us, but that woman started making stuck pig noises,
and the man in the shack yelled something, and Grimes ducked
back into the shed and came out with a jug. He lumbered back
toward the shack and disappeared around the front of it. Dee and
I could hear him arguing with the man inside.

"I jerked my thumb toward Meridian Road, but Dee shook his head. I whispered, Didn't you already see Eddie Grimes, and isn't that enough for you? He shook his head again. His eyes were gleaming behind that sheet. So what do you want, I asked, and he said, I want to see that girl. We don't even know where she is, I whispered, and Dee said, All we got to do is follow her sound.

"Dee and I sat and listened for a while. Every now and then, she let out a sort of whoop, and then she'd sort of cry, and after that she might say a word or two that sounded almost ordinary before she got going again on crying or laughing, the two all mixed up together. Sometimes we could hear other noises coming from the shacks, and none of them sounded happy. People were grumbling and arguing or just plain talking to themselves, but at least they sounded normal. That lady, she sounded like *Halloween* – like something that came up out of a grave.

"Probably you're thinking what I was hearing was sex – that I was too young to know how much noise ladies make when they're having fun. Well, maybe I was only eleven, but I grew up in Darktown, not Miller's Hill, and our walls were none too thick. What was going on with this lady didn't have anything to do with fun. The strange thing is, Dee didn't know that – he thought just what you were thinking. He wanted to see this lady getting humped. Maybe he even thought he could sneak in and get some for himself, I don't know. The main thing is, he thought he was listening to some wild sex, and he wanted to get close enough to see it. Well, I thought, his daddy was a preacher, and maybe preachers didn't do it once they got kids. And Dee didn't have an older brother like mine, who sneaked girls into the house whenever he thought he wouldn't get caught.

"He started sliding sideways through the woods, and I had to follow him. I'd seen enough of The Backs to last me the rest of my life, but I couldn't run off and leave Dee behind. And at least he was going at it the right way, circling around the shacks sideways, instead of trying to sneak straight through them. I started off after him. At least I could see a little better ever since I ripped at my eyehole, but I still had to hold my blasted costume bunched up under my chin, and if I moved my head or my hand the wrong way, the hole moved away from my eye and I couldn't see anything at all.

"So naturally, the first thing that happened was that I lost sight of Dee Sparks. My foot came down in a hole and I stumbled ahead for a few steps, completely blind, and then I hit a tree. I just came to a halt, sure that Eddie Grimes and a few other murderers were about to jump on me. For a couple of seconds I stood as still as a wooden Indian, too scared to move. When I didn't hear anything, I hauled at my costume until I could see out of it. No murderers were coming toward me from the shack beside the still. Eddie Grimes was saying *You don't understand* over and over, like he was so drunk that one phrase got stuck in his head, and he couldn't say or hear anything else. That woman yipped, like an animal noise, not a human one – like a fox barking. I sidled up next to the tree I'd run into and looked around for Dee. All I could see was dark trees and that one yellow window I'd seen before. To hell with Dee Sparks, I said to myself, and pulled the costume off over my head. I could see better, but there wasn't any glimmer of white over that way. He'd gone so far ahead of me I couldn't even see him.

"So I had to catch up with him, didn't I? I knew where he was going – the woman's noises were coming from the shack way up there in the woods – and I knew he was going to sneak around the outside of the shacks. In a couple of seconds, after he noticed I wasn't there, he was going to stop and wait for me. Makes sense, doesn't it? All I had to do was keep going toward that shack off to the side until I ran into him. I shoved my costume inside my shirt, and then I did something else – set my bag of candy down next to the tree. I'd clean forgotten about it ever since I saw Eddie Grimes' face, and if I had to run, I'd go faster without holding onto a lot of apples and chunks of taffy.

"About a minute later, I came out into the open between two big old chinaberry trees. There was a patch of grass between me and the next stand of trees. The woman made a gargling sound that ended in one of those fox-yips, and I looked up in that direction and saw that the clearing extended in a straight line up and down, like a path. Stars shone out of the patch of darkness between the two parts of the woods. And when I started to walk across it, I felt a grassy hump between two beaten tracks. The path into The Backs off Meridian Road curved around somewhere up ahead and wound back down through the shacks before it came to a dead end. It had to come to a dead end, because it sure didn't join back up with Meridian Road.

"And this was how I'd managed to lose sight of Dee Sparks. Instead of avoiding the path and working his way north through the woods, he'd just taken the easiest way toward the woman's shack. Hell, I'd had to pull him off the path in the first place! By the time I got out of my sheet, he was probably way up there, out in the open for anyone to see and too excited to notice that he was all by himself. What I had to do was what I'd been trying to do all along, save his ass from anybody who might see him.

"As soon as I started going as soft as I could up the path, I saw that saving Dee Sparks' ass might be a tougher job than I thought – maybe I couldn't even save my own. When I first took off my costume, I'd seen lights from three or four shacks. I thought that's what The Backs was – three or four shacks. But after I started up the path, I saw a low square shape standing between two trees at the edge of the woods and realized that it was another shack. Whoever was inside had extinguished his kerosene lamp, or maybe wasn't home. About twenty – thirty feet on, there was another shack, all dark, and the only reason I noticed that one was, I heard voices coming from it, a man and a woman, both of them sounding drunk and slowed-down. Deeper in the woods past that one, another grease-paper window gleamed through the trees like a firefly. There were shacks all over the woods. As soon as I realized that Dee and I might not be the only people walking through the Backs on Halloween night, I bent down low to the ground and damn near slowed to a standstill. The only thing Dee had going for him, I thought, was good night vision – at least he might spot someone before they spotted him.

"A noise came from one of those shacks, and I stopped cold, with my heart pounding away like a bass drum. Then a big voice yelled out, *Who's that?*, and I just lay down in the track and tried to disappear. *Who's there?* Here I was calling Dee a fool, and I was making more noise than he did. I heard that man walk outside his door, and my heart pretty near exploded. Then the woman moaned up ahead, and the man who'd heard me swore to himself and went back inside. I just lay there in the dirt for a while. The woman moaned again, and this time it sounded scarier than ever, because it had a kind of a chuckle in it. She was crazy. Or she was a witch, and if she was having sex, it was with the Devil. That was enough to make me start crawling along, and I kept on crawling until I was long past the shack where the man had heard me. Finally I got up on my feet again, thinking that if I didn't see Dee Sparks real soon, I was going to sneak back to Meridian Road by myself. If Dee Sparks wanted to see a witch in bed with the Devil, he could do it without me.

"And then I thought I was a fool not to ditch Dee, because hadn't he ditched me? After all this time, he must have noticed that I wasn't with him any more. Did he come back and look for me? The hell he did.

"And right then I would have gone back home, but for two things. The first was that I heard that woman make another sound – a sound that was hardly human, but wasn't made by any animal. It wasn't even loud. And it sure as hell wasn't any witch in bed with the Devil. It made me want to throw up. That woman was being *hurt*. She wasn't just getting beat up – I knew what that sounded like – she was being hurt bad enough to drive her crazy, bad enough to kill her. Because you couldn't live through being hurt bad enough to make that sound. I was in The Backs, sure enough, and the place was even worse than it was supposed to be. Someone was killing a woman, everybody could hear it, and all that happened was that Eddie Grimes fetched another jug back from the still. I froze. When I could move, I pulled my ghost costume out from inside my shirt, because Dee was right, and for certain I didn't want anybody seeing my face out there on *this* night. And then the second thing happened. While I was pulling the sheet over my head, I saw something pale lying in the grass a couple of feet back toward the woods I'd come out of, and when I looked at it, it turned into Dee Sparks' Halloween bag.

"I went up to the bag and touched it to make sure about what it was. I'd found Dee's bag, all right. And it was empty. Flat. He had stuffed the content into his pockets and left the bag behind. What that meant was, I couldn't turn around and leave him – because he hadn't left me after all. He waited for me until he couldn't stand it any more, and then he emptied his bag and left it behind as a sign. He was counting on me to see in the dark as well as he could. But I wouldn't have seen it at all if that woman hadn't stopped me cold.

"The top of the bag was pointing north, so Dee was still heading toward the woman's shack. I looked up that way, and all I could see was a solid wall of darkness underneath a lighter darkness filled with stars. For about a second, I realized, I had felt pure relief. Dee had ditched me, so I could ditch him and go home. Now I was stuck with Dee all over again.

"About twenty feet ahead, another surprise jumped up at me out of darkness. Something that looked like a little tiny shack began to take shape, and I got down on my hands and knees to crawl toward the path when I saw a long silver gleam along the top of the thing. That meant it had to be metal – tar paper might have a lot of uses, but it never yet reflected starlight. Once I realized that the thing in front of me was metal, I remembered its shape and realized it was a car. You wouldn't think you'd come across a car in a down-and-out rathole like The Backs, would you? People like that, they don't even own two shirts, so how do they come by cars? Then I remembered Dr Garland driving away speeding down Meridian Road, and I thought *You don't have to live in The Backs to drive there*. Someone could turn up onto the path, drive around the loop, pull his car off onto the grass, and no one would ever see it or know that he was there.

"And this made me feel funny. The car probably belonged to someone I knew. Our band played dances and parties all over the county and everywhere in Woodland, and I'd probably seen every single person in town, and they'd seen me, too, and knew me by name. I walked closer to the car to see if I recognized it, but it was just an old black Model T. There must have been twenty cars just like it in Woodland. Whites and coloureds, the few coloureds that owned cars, both had them. And when I got right up beside the Model T, I saw what Dee had left for me on the hood – an apple.

"About twenty feet further along, there was an apple on top of a big old stone. He was putting those apples where I couldn't help but see them. The third one was on top of a post at the edge of the woods, and it was so pale it looked almost white. Next to the post one of those paths running all through The Backs led back into the woods. If it hadn't been for that apple, I would have gone right past it.

"At least I didn't have to worry so much about being making noise once I got back into the woods. Must have been six inches of pine needles and fallen leaves underfoot, and I walked so quiet I could have been floating – I've worn crepe soles ever since then, and for the same reason. You walk *soft*. But I was still plenty scared – back in the woods there was a lot less light, and I'd have to step on an apple to see it. All I wanted was to find Dee and persuade him to leave with me.

"For a while, all I did was keep moving between the trees and try to make sure I wasn't coming up on a shack. Every now and then, a faint, slurry voice came from somewhere off in the woods, but I didn't let it spook me. Then, way up ahead, I saw Dee Sparks. The path didn't go in a straight line, it kind of angled back and forth, so I didn't have a good clear look at him, but I got a flash of that silvery-looking sheet way off through the trees. If I sped up I could get to him before he did anything stupid. I pulled my costume up a little further toward my neck and started to jog.

"The path started dipping *downhill*. I couldn't figure it out. Dee was in a straight line ahead of me, and as soon as I followed the path downhill a little bit, I lost sight of him. After a couple more steps, I stopped. The path got a lot steeper. If I kept running, I'd go ass over teakettle. The woman made another terrible sound, and it seemed to come from everywhere at once. Like everything around me had been *hurt*. I damn near came unglued. Seemed like everything was *dying*. That Halloween stuff about horrible creatures wasn't any story, man, it was the way things really were – you couldn't know anything, you couldn't trust anything, and you were surrounded by *death*. I almost fell down and cried like a baby boy. I was lost. I didn't think I'd ever get back home.

"Then the worst thing of all happened.

"I heard her die. It was just a little noise, more like a sigh than anything, but that sigh came from everywhere and went straight into my ear. A soft sound can be loud, too, you know, be the loudest thing you ever heard. That sigh about lifted me up off the ground, about blew my head apart.

"I stumbled down the path, trying to wipe my eyes with my costume, and all of a sudden I heard men's voices from off to my left. Someone was saying a word I couldn't understand over and over, and someone else was telling him to shut up. Then, behind me, I heard running – heavy running, a man. I took off, and right away my feet got tangled up in the sheet and I was rolling downhill, hitting my head on rocks and bouncing off trees and smashing into stuff I didn't have any idea what it was. *Biff bop bang slam smash clang crash ding dong*. I hit something big and solid and wound up half-covered in water. Took me a long time to get upright, twisted up in the sheet the way I was. My ears buzzed, and I saw starts – yellow and blue and red stars, not real ones. When I tried to sit up, the blasted sheet pulled me back down, so I got a faceful of cold water. I scrambled around like a fox in a trap, and when I finally got so I was at least sitting up, I saw a slash of real sky out the corner of one eye, and I got my hands free and ripped that hole in the sheet wide enough for my whole head to fit through it.

"I was sitting in a little stream next to a fallen tree. The tree was what had stopped me. My whole body hurt like the dickens. No idea where I was. Wasn't even sure I could stand up. Got my hands on the top of the fallen tree and pushed myself up with my legs – blasted sheet ripped in half, and my knees almost bent back the wrong way, but I got up on my feet. And there was Dee Sparks, coming toward me through the woods on the other side of the stream.

"He looked like he didn't feel any better than I did, like he couldn't move in a straight line. His silvery sheet was smearing through the trees. *Dee got hurt, too*, I thought – he looked like he was in some total panic. The next time I saw the white smear between the trees it was twisting about ten feet off the ground. *No*, I said to myself, and closed my eyes. Whatever that thing was, it wasn't Dee. An unbearable feeling, an absolute despair, flowed out from it. I fought against this wave of despair with every weapon I had. I didn't want to know that feeling. I couldn't know that feeling – I was eleven years old. If that feeling reached me when I was eleven years old, my entire life would be changed, I'd be in a different universe altogether.

"But it did reach me, didn't it? I could say *no* all I liked, but I couldn't change what had happened. I opened my eyes, and the white smear was gone.

"That was almost worse – I wanted it to be Dee after all, doing something crazy and reckless, climbing trees, running around like a wild man, trying to give me a big whopping scare. But it wasn't Dee Sparks, and it meant that the worst things I'd ever imagined were true. Everything was dying. You couldn't know anything, you couldn't trust anything, we were all lost in the midst of the death that surrounded us.

"Most people will tell you growing up means you stop believing in Halloween things – I'm telling you the reverse. You start to grow up when you understand that the stuff that scares you is part of the air you breathe.

"I stared at the spot where I'd seen that twist of whiteness, I guess trying to go back in time to before I saw Dr Garland fleeing down Meridian Road. My face looked like his, I thought – because now I knew that you really *could* see a ghost. The heavy footsteps I'd heard before suddenly cut through the buzzing in my head, and after I turned around and saw who was coming at me down the hill, I thought it was probably my own ghost I'd seen.

"Eddie Grimes looked as big as an oak tree, and he had a long knife in one hand. His feet slipped out from under him, and he skidded the last few yards down to the creek, but I didn't even try to run away. Drunk as he was, I'd never get away from him. All I did was back up alongside the fallen tree and watch him slide downhill toward the water. I was so scared I couldn't even talk. Eddie Grimes' shirt was flapping open, and big long scars ran all across his chest and belly. He'd been raised from the dead at least a couple of times since I'd seen him get killed at the dance. He jumped back up on his feet and started coming for me. I opened my mouth, but nothing came out.

"Eddie Grimes took another step toward me, and then he stopped and looked straight at my face. He lowered the knife. A sour stink of sweat and alcohol came off him. All he could do was stare at me. Eddie Grimes knew my face all right, he knew my name, he knew my whole family – even at night, he couldn't mistake me for anyone else. I finally saw that Eddie was actually afraid, like he was the one who'd seen a ghost. The two of us just stood there in the shallow water for a couple more seconds, and then Eddie Grimes pointed his knife at the other side of the creek.

"That was all I needed, baby. My legs unfroze, and I forgot all my aches and pains. Eddie watched me roll over the fallen tree and lowered his knife. I splashed through the water and started moving up the hill, grabbing at weeds and branches to pull me along. My feet were frozen, and my clothes were soaked and muddy, and I was trembling all over. About half way up the hill, I looked back over my shoulder, but Eddie Grimes was gone. It was like he'd never been there at all, like he was nothing but the product of a couple of good raps to the noggin.

"Finally, I pulled myself shaking up over the top of the rise, and what did I see about ten feet away through a lot of skinny birch trees but a kid in a sheet facing away from me into the woods, and hopping from foot to foot in a pair of big clumsy shoes? And what was in front of him but a path I could make out from even ten feet away? Obviously, this was where I was supposed to turn up, only in the dark and all I must have missed an apple stuck onto a branch or some blasted thing, and I took that little side trip downhill on my head and wound up throwing a spook into Eddie Grimes.

"As soon as I saw him, I realized I hated Dee Sparks. I wouldn't have tossed him a rope if he was drowning. Without even thinking about it, I bent down and picked up a stone and flung it at him. The stone bounced off a tree, so I bent down and got another one. Dee turned around to find out what made the noise, and the second stone hit him right in the chest, even though it was his head I was aiming at.

"He pulled his sheet up over his face like an Arab and stared at me with his mouth wide open. Then he looked back over his shoulder at the path, as if the real me might come along at any second. I felt like pegging another rock at his stupid face, but instead I marched up to him. He was shaking his head from side to side. *Jim Dawg*, he whispered, *what happened to you?* By way of answer, I hit him a good hard knock on the breastbone. *What's the matter?* he wanted to know. *After you left me*, I say, *I fell down a hill and ran into Eddie Grimes*.

"That gave him something to think about, all right. Was Grimes coming after me, he wanted to know? Did he see which way I went? Did Grimes see who I was? He was pulling me into the woods while he asked me these dumb-ass questions, and I shoved him away. His sheet flopped back down over his front, and he looked like a little boy. He couldn't figure out why I was mad at him. From his point of view, he'd been pretty clever, and if I got lost, it was my fault. But I wasn't mad at him because I got lost. I wasn't even mad at him because I'd run into Eddie Grimes. It was everything else. Maybe it wasn't even him I was mad at.

"*I want to get home without getting killed*, I whispered. *Eddie ain't gonna let me go twice*. Then I pretended he wasn't there any more and tried to figure out how to get back to Meridian Road. It seemed to me that I was still going north when I took that tumble downhill, so when I climbed up the hill on the other side of the creek I was still going north. The wagon-track that Dee and I took into The Backs had to be off to my right. I turned away from Dee and started moving through the woods. I didn't care if he followed me or not. He had nothing to do with me any more, he was on his own. When I heard him coming along after me, I was sorry. I wanted to get away from Dee Sparks. I wanted to get away from everybody.

"I didn't want to be around anybody who was supposed to be my friend. I'd rather have had Eddie Grimes following me than Dee Sparks.

"Then I stopped moving, because through the trees I could see one of those grease-paper windows glowing up ahead of me. That yellow light looked evil as the Devil's eye – everything in The Backs was evil, poisoned, even the trees, even the air. The terrible expression on Dr Garland's face and the white smudge in the air seemed like the same thing – they were what I didn't, want to know.

"Dee shoved me from behind, and if I hadn't felt so sick inside I would have turned around and punched him. Instead, I looked over my shoulder and saw him nodding toward where the side of the shack would be. He wanted to get closer! For a second, he seemed as crazy as everything else out there, and then I got it: I was all turned around, and instead of heading back to the main path, I'd been taking us toward the woman's shack. That was why Dee was following me.

"I shook my head. No, I wasn't going to sneak up to that place. Whatever was inside there was something I didn't have to know about. It had too much power – it turned Eddie Grimes around, and that was enough for me. Dee knew I wasn't fooling. He went around me and started creeping toward the shack.

"And damndest thing, I watched him slipping through the trees for a second, and started following him. If he could go up there, so could I. If I didn't exactly look at whatever was in there myself, I could watch Dee look at it. That would tell me most of what I had to know. And anyways, probably Dee wouldn't see anything anyhow, unless the front door was hanging open, and that didn't seem too likely to me. He wouldn't see anything, and I wouldn't either, and we could both go home.

"The door of the shack opened up, and a man walked outside. Dee and I freeze, and I mean *freeze*. We're about twenty feet away, on the side of this shack, and if the man looked sideways, he'd see our sheets. There were a lot of trees between us and him, and I couldn't get a very good look at him, but one thing about him made the whole situation a lot more serious. This man was white, and he was wearing good clothes – I couldn't see his face, but I could see his rolled up sleeves, and his suit jacket slung over one arm, and some kind of wrapped-up bundle he was holding in his hands. All this took about a second. The white man started carrying his bundle straight through the woods, and in another two seconds he was out of sight.

"Dee was a little closer than I was, and I think his sight line was a little clearer than mine. On top of that, he saw better at night than I did. Dee didn't get around like me, but he might have recognized the man we'd seen, and that would be pure trouble. Some rich white man, killing a girl out in The Backs? And us two boys close enough to see him? Do you know what would have happened to us? There wouldn't be enough left of either one of us to make a decent smudge.

"Dee turned around to face me, and I could see his eyes behind his costume, but I couldn't tell what he was thinking. He just stood there, looking at me. In a little bit, just when I was about to explode, we heard a car starting up off to our left. I whispered at Dee if he saw who that was. *Nobody*, Dee said. Now, what the hell did that mean? Nobody? You could say Santa Claus, you could say J. Edgar *Hoover*, it'd be a better answer than Nobody. The Model T's headlights shone through the trees when the car swung around the top of the path and started going toward Meridian Road. *Nobody I ever saw before*, Dee said. When the headlights cut through the trees, both of us ducked out of sight. Actually, we were so far from the path, we had nothing to worry about. I could barely see the car when it went past, and I couldn't see the driver at all.

"We stood up. Over Dee's shoulder I could see the side of the shack where the white man had been. Lamplight flickered on the ground in front of the open door. The last thing in the world I wanted to do was to go inside that place – I didn't even want to walk around to the front and look in the door. Dee stepped back from me and jerked his head toward the shack. I knew it was going to be just like before. I'd say no, he'd say yes, and then I'd follow him wherever he thought he had to go. I felt the same way I did when I saw that white smear in the woods – hopeless, lost in the midst of death. *You go, if you have to*, I whispered to him, *it's what you wanted to do all along*. He didn't move, and I saw that he wasn't too sure about what he wanted any more.

"Everything was different now, because the white man made it different. Once a white man walked out that door, it was like raising the stakes in a poker game. But Dee had been working toward that one shack ever since we got into The Backs, and he was still curious as a cat about it. He turned away from me and started moving sideways in a straight line, so he'd be able to peek inside the door from a safe distance.

"After he got about half way to the front, he looked back and waved me on, like this was still some great adventure he wanted me to share. He was afraid to be on his own, that was all. When he realized I was going to stay put, he bent down and moved real slow past the side. He still couldn't see more than a sliver of the inside of the shack, and he moved ahead another little ways. By then, I figured, he should have been able to see about half of the inside of the shack. He hunkered down inside his sheet, staring in the direction of the open door. And there he stayed.

"I took it for about half a minute, and then I couldn't any more. I was sick enough to die and angry enough to explode, both at the same time. How long could Dee Sparks look at a dead whore? Wouldn't a couple of seconds be enough? Dee was acting like he was watching a goddamn Hopalong Cassidy movie. An owl screeched, and some man in another shack said *Now that's over*, and someone else shushed him. If Dee heard, he paid it no mind. I started along toward him, and I don't think he noticed me, either. He didn't look up until I was past the front of the shack, and had already seen the door hanging open, and the lamplight spilling over the plank floor and onto the grass outside.

"I took another step, and Dee's head snapped around. He tried to stop me by holding out his hand. All that did was make me mad. Who was Dee Sparks to tell me what I couldn't see? All he did was leave me alone in the woods with a trail of apples, and he didn't even do that right. When I kept on coming, Dee started waving both hands at me, looking back and forth between me and the inside of the shack. Like something was happening in there that I couldn't be allowed to see. I didn't stop, and Dee got up on his feet and skittered toward me.

"*We gotta get out of here*, he whispered. He was close enough so I could smell that electrical stink. I stepped to his side, and he grabbed my arm. I yanked my arm out of his grip and went forward a little ways and looked through the door of the shack.

"A bed was shoved up against the far wall, and a woman lay naked on the bed. There was blood all over her legs, and blood all over the sheets, and big puddles of blood on the floor. A woman in a raggedy robe, hair stuck out all over her head, squatted beside the bed, holding the other woman's hand. She was a coloured woman – a Backs woman – but the other one, the one on the bed, was white. Probably she was pretty, when she was alive. All I could see was white skin and blood, and I near fainted.

"This wasn't some white-trash woman who lived out in The Backs – she was brought there, and the man who brought her had killed her. More trouble was coming down than I could imagine, trouble enough to kill lots of our people. And if Dee and I said a word about the white man we'd seen, the trouble would come right straight down on us.

"I must have made some kind of noise, because the woman next to the bed turned halfways around and looked at me. There wasn't any doubt about it – she saw me. All she saw of Dee was a dirty white sheet, but she saw my face, and she knew who I was. I knew her, too, and she wasn't any Backs woman. She lived down the street from us. Her name was Mary Randolph, and she was the one who came up to Eddie Grimes after he got shot to death and brought him back to life. Mary Randolph followed my Dad's band, and when we played roadhouses or coloured dance halls, she'd be likely to turn up. A couple of times she told me I played good drums – I was a drummer back then, you know, switched to saxophone when I turned twelve. Mary Randolph just looked at me, her hair stuck out straight all over her head like she was already inside a whirlwind of trouble. No expression on her face except that look you get when your mind is going a mile a minute and your body can't move at all. She didn't even look surprised. She almost looked like she *wasn't* surprised, like she was expecting to see me. As bad as I'd felt that night, this was the worst of all. I liked to have died. I'd have disappeared down an anthill, if I could. I didn't know what I had done – just be there, I guess – but I'd never be able to undo it.

"I pulled at Dee's sheet, and he tore off down the side of the shack like he'd been waiting for a signal. Mary Randolph stared into my eyes, and it felt like I had to pull myself away – I couldn't just turn my head, I had to *disconnect*. And when I did, I could still feel her staring at me. Somehow I made myself go down past the side of the shack, but I could still see Mary Randolph inside there, looking out at the place where I'd been.

"If Dee said anything at all when I caught up with him, I'd have knocked his teeth down his throat, but he just moved fast and quiet through the trees, seeing the best way to go, and I followed after. I felt like I'd been kicked by a horse. When we got on the path, we didn't bother trying to sneak down through the woods on the other side, we lit out and ran as hard as we could – like wild dogs were after us. And after we got onto Meridian Road, we ran toward town until we couldn't run any more.

"Dee clamped his hand over his side and staggered forward a little bit. Then he stopped and ripped off his costume and lay down by the side of the road, breathing hard. I was leaning forward with hands on my knees, as winded as he was. When I could breathe again, I started walking down the road. Dee picked himself up and got next to me and walked along, looking at my face and then looking away, and then looking back at my face again.

"*So?* I said.

"*I know that lady*, Dee said.

"Hell, that was no news. Of course he knew Mary Randolph – she was his neighbour, too. I didn't bother to answer, I just grunted at him. Then I reminded him that Mary hadn't seen his face, only mine.

"*Not Mary*, he said. *The other one.*

"He knew the dead white woman's name? That made everything worse. A lady like that shouldn't be in Dee Sparks' world, especially if she's going to wind up dead in The Backs. I wondered who was going to get lynched, and how many.

"Then Dee said that I knew her, too. I stopped walking and looked him straight in the face.

"*Miss Abbey Montgomery*, he said. *She brings clothes and food down to our church, Thanksgiving and Christmas.*

"He was right – I wasn't sure if I'd ever heard her name, but I'd seen her once or twice, bringing baskets of ham and chicken and boxes of clothes to Dee's father's church. She was about twenty years old, I guess, so pretty she made you smile just to look at.

From a rich family in a big house right at the top of Miller's Hill. Some man didn't think a girl like that should have any associations with coloured people, I guess, and decided to express his opinion about as strong as possible. Which meant that we were going to take the blame for what happened to her, and the next time we saw white sheets, they wouldn't be Halloween costumes.

"*He sure took a long time to kill her*, I said.

"And Dee said, *She ain't dead*.

"So I asked him, What the hell did he mean by that? I saw the girl. I saw the blood. Did he think she was going to get up and walk around? Or maybe Mary Randolph was going to tell her that magic word and bring her back to life?

"*You can think that if you want to*, Dee said. *But Abbey Montgomery ain't dead.*

"I almost told him I'd seen her ghost, but he didn't deserve to hear about it. The fool couldn't even see what was right in front of his eyes. I couldn't expect him to understand what happened to me when I saw that miserable . . . that *thing*. He was rushing on ahead of me anyhow, like I'd suddenly embarrased him or something. That was fine with me. I felt the exact same way. I said, *I guess you know neither one of us can ever talk about this*, and he said, *I guess you know it, too*, and that was the last thing we said to each other that night. All the way down Meridian Road Dee Sparks kept his eyes straight ahead and his mouth shut. When we got to the field, he turned toward me like he had something to say, and I waited for it, but he faced forward again and ran away. Just ran. I watched him disappear past the general store, and then I walked home by myself.

"My mom gave me hell for getting my clothes all wet and dirty, and my brothers laughed at me and wanted to know who beat me up and stole my candy. As soon as I could, I went to bed, pulled the covers up over my head, and closed my eyes. A little while later, my mom came in and asked if I was all right. Did I get into a fight with that Dee Sparks? Dee Sparks was born to hang, that was what she thought, and I ought to have a better class of friends. *I'm tired of playing those drums, Momma*, I said, *I want to play the saxophone instead.* She looked at me surprised, but said she'd talk about with Daddy, and that it might work out.

"For the next couple days, I waited for the bomb to go off. On the Friday, I went to school, but couldn't concentrate for beans.

Dee Sparks and I didn't even nod at each other in the hallways –
just walked by like the other guy was invisible. On the weekend I
said I felt sick and stayed in bed, wondering when that whirlwind
of trouble would come down. I wondered if Eddie Grimes would
talk about seeing me – once they found the body, they'd get
around to Eddie Grimes real quick.

"But nothing happened that weekend, and nothing happened
all the next week. I thought Mary Randolph must have hid the
white girl in a grave out in The Backs. But how long could a girl
from one of those rich families go missing without investigations
and search parties? And, on top of that, what was Mary Randolph doing there in the first place? She liked to have a good time,
but she wasn't one of those wild girls with a razor under her skirt
– she went to church every Sunday, was good to people, nice to
kids. Maybe she went out to comfort that poor girl, but how did
she know she'd be there in the first place? Misses Abbey Mont-
gomerys from the hill didn't share their plans with Mary Ran-
dolphs from Darktown. I couldn't forget the way she looked at
me, but I couldn't understand it, either. The more I thought about
that look, the more it was like Mary Randolph was saying
something to me, but what? *Are you ready for this? Do you
understand this? Do you know how careful you must be?*

"My father said I could start learning the C-melody sax, and
when I was ready to play it in public, my little brother wanted to
take over the drums. Seems he always wanted to play drums, and
in fact, he's been a drummer ever since, a good one. So I worked
out how to play my little sax, I went to school and came straight
home after, and everything went on like normal, except Dee
Sparks and I weren't friends any more. If the police were searching for a missing rich girl, I didn't hear anything about it.

"Then one Saturday I was walking down our street to go the
general store, and Mary Randolph came through her front door
just as I got to her house. When she saw me, she stopped moving
real sudden, with one hand still on the side of the door. I was so
surprised to see her that I was in a kind of slow-motion, and I
must have stared at her. She gave me a look like an X-ray, a look
that searched around down inside me. I don't know what I
saw, but her face relaxed, and she took her hand off the door and
let it close behind her, and she wasn't looking inside me any more.
Miss Randolph, I said, and she told me she was looking forward

to hearing our band play at a Beergarden dance in a couple of weeks. I told her I was going to be playing the saxophone at that dance, and she said something about that, and all the time it was like we were having two conversations, the top one about me and the band, and the one underneath about her and the murdered white girl in The Backs. It made me so nervous, my words got all mixed up. Finally she said *You make sure you say hello to your Daddy from me, now*, and I got away.

"After I passed her house, Mary Randolph started walking down the street behind me. I could feel her watching me, and I started to sweat. Mary Randolph was a total mystery to me. She was a nice lady, but probably she buried that girl's body. I didn't know but that she was going to come and kill *me*, one day. And then I remembered her kneeling down beside Eddie Grimes at the roadhouse. She had been *dancing* with Eddie Grimes, who was in jail more often than he was out. I wondered if you could be a respectable lady and still know Eddie Grimes well enough to dance with him. And how did she bring him back to life? Or was that what happened at all? Hearing that lady walk along behind me made me so uptight, I crossed to the other side of the street.

"A couple days after that, when I was beginning to think that the trouble was never going to happen after all, it came down. We heard police cars coming down the street right when we were finishing dinner. I thought they were coming for me, and I almost lost my chicken and rice. The sirens went right past our house, and then more sirens came toward us from other directions – the old klaxons they had in those days. It sounded like every cop in the state was rushing into Darktown. This was bad, bad news. Someone was going to wind up dead, that was certain. No way all those police were going to come into our part of town, make all that commotion, and leave without killing at least one man. That's the truth. You just had to pray that the man they killed wasn't you or anyone in your family. My Daddy turned off the lamps, and we went to the window to watch the cars go by. Two of them were state police. When it was safe, Daddy went outside to see where all the trouble was headed. After he came back in, he said it looked like the police were going toward Eddie Grimes' place. We wanted to go out and look, but they wouldn't let us, so we went to the back windows that faced toward Grimes' house. Couldn't see anything but a lot of cars and police standing all over the road back there. Sounded like they were knocking down Grimes' house with sledge hammers. Then a whole bunch of cops took off running, and all I could see was the cars spread out across the road. About ten minutes later, we heard lots of gunfire coming from a couple of streets further back. It like to have lasted forever. Like hearing the Battle of the Bulge. My momma started to cry, and so did my little brother. The shooting stopped. The police shouted to each other, and then they came back and got in their cars and went away.

"On the radio the next morning, they said that a known criminal, a Negro man named Edward Grimes, had been killed while trying to escape arrest for the murder of a white woman. The body of Eleanore Monday, missing for three days, had been found in a shallow grave by Woodland police searching near an illegal distillery in the region called The Backs. Miss Monday, the daughter of grocer Albert Monday, had been in poor mental and physical health, and Grimes had apparently taken advantage of her weakness to either abduct or lure her to The Backs, where she had been savagely murdered. That's what it said on the radio – I still remember the words. *In poor mental and physical health. Savagely murdered.*

"When the paper finally came, there on the front page was a picture of Eleanore Monday, a girl with dark hair and a big nose. She didn't look anything like the dead woman in the shack. She hadn't even disappeared on the right day. Eddie Grimes was never going to be able to explain things, because the police had finally cornered him in the old jute warehouse just off Meridian Road next to the general store. I don't suppose they even bothered trying to arrest him – they weren't interested in *arresting* him. He killed a white girl. They wanted revenge, and they got it.

"After I looked at the paper, I got out of the house and ran between the houses to get a look at the jute warehouse. Turned out a lot of folks had the same idea. A big crowd strung out in a long line in front of the warehouse, and cars were parked all along Meridian Road. Right up in front of the warehouse door was a police car, and a big cop stood in the middle of the big doorway, watching people file by. They were walking past the doorway one by one, acting like they were at some kind of exhibit. Nobody was talking. It was a sight I never saw before in that town, whites and coloured all lined up together. On the other side of the warehouse, two groups of men stood alongside the road, one colored and one white, talking so quietly you couldn't hear a word.

"Now I was never one who liked standing in lines, so I figured I'd just dart up there, peek in, and save myself some time. I came around the end of the line and ambled toward the two bunches of men, like I'd already had my look and was just hanging around to enjoy the scene. After I got a little past the warehouse door, I sort of drifted up alongside it. I looked down the row of people, and there was Dee Sparks, just a few yards away from being able to see in. Dee was leaning forward, and when he saw me he almost jumped out of his skin. He looked away as fast as he could. His eyes turned as dead as stones. The cop at the door yelled at me to go to the end of the line. He never would have noticed me at all if Dee hadn't jumped like someone just shot off a firecracker behind him.

"About half way down the line, Mary Randolph was standing behind some of the ladies from the neighbourhood. She looked terrible. Her hair stuck out in raggedy clumps, and her skin was ashy, like she hadn't slept in a long time. I sped up a little, hoping she wouldn't notice me, but after I took one more step, Mary Randolph looked down and her eyes hooked into mine. I swear, what was in her eyes almost knocked me down. I couldn't even tell what it was, unless it was pure hate. Hate and pain. With her eyes hooked into mine like that, I couldn't look away. It was like I was seeing that miserable, terrible white smear twisting up between the trees on that night in The Backs. Mary let me go, and I almost fell down all over again.

"I got to the end of the line and started moving along regular and slow with everybody else. Mary Randolph stayed in my mind and blanked out everything else. When I got up to the door, I barely took in what was inside the warehouse – a wall full of bulletholes and bloodstains all over the place, big slick ones and little drizzly ones. All I could think of was the shack and Mary Randolph sitting next to the dead girl, and I was back there all over again.

"Mary Randolph didn't show up at the Beergarden dance, so she didn't hear me play saxophone in public for the first time. I didn't expect her, either, not after the way she looked out at the warehouse. There'd been a lot of news about Eddie Grimes, who they made out to be less civilized than a gorilla, a crazy man who'd murder anyone as long as he could kill all the white women first. The paper had a picture of what they called Grimes' 'lair', with busted furniture all over the place and holes in the walls, but they never explained that it was the police tore it up and made it look that way.

"The other thing people got suddenly all hot about was The Backs. Seems the place was even worse than everybody thought. Seems white girls besides Eleanore Monday had been taken out there – according to some, there was even white girls living out there, along with a lot of bad coloureds. The place was a nest of vice, Sodom and Gomorrah. Two days before the town council was supposed to discuss the problem, a gang of white men went out there with guns and clubs and torches and burned every shack in The Backs clear down to the ground. While they were there, they didn't see a single soul, white, coloured, male, female, damned or saved. Everybody who lived in The Backs had skedaddled. And the funny thing was, long as The Backs had existed right outside of Woodland, no one in Woodland could recollect the name of anyone who had ever lived there. They couldn't even recall the name of anyone who had ever gone there, except for Eddie Grimes. In fact, after the place got burned down, it appeared that it must have been a sin just to say its name, because no one ever mentioned it. You'd think men so fine and moral as to burn down The Backs would be willing to take the credit, but none ever did.

"You could think they must have wanted to get rid of some things out there. Or wanted real bad to forget about things out there. One thing I thought, Dr Garland and the man I saw leaving that shack had been out there with torches.

"But maybe I didn't know anything at all. Two weeks later, a couple things happened that shook me good.

"The first one happened three nights before Thanksgiving. I was hurrying home, a little bit late. Nobody else on the street, everybody inside either sitting down to dinner or getting ready for it. When I got to Mary Randolph's house, some kind of noise coming from inside stopped me. What I thought was, it sounded exactly like somebody trying to scream while someone else was holding a hand over their mouth. Well, that was plain foolish, wasn't it? How did I know what that would sound like? I moved along a step or two, and then I heard it again. Could be anything,

I told myself. Mary Randolph didn't like me too much, anyway. She wouldn't be partial to my knocking on her door. Best thing I could do was get out. Which was what I did. Just went home to supper and forgot about it.

"Until the next day, anyhow, when a friend of Mary's walked in her front door and found her lying dead with her throat cut and a knife in her hand. A cut of fatback, we heard, had boiled away to cinders on her stove. I didn't tell anybody about what I heard the night before. Too scared. I couldn't do anything but wait to see what the police did.

"To the police, it was all real clear. Mary killed herself, plain and simple.

"When our minister went across town to ask why a lady who intended to commit suicide had bothered to start cooking her supper, the Chief told him that a female bent on killing herself probably didn't care *what* happened to the food on her stove. Then I suppose Mary Randolph nearly managed to cut her own head off, said the minister. A female in despair possesses a godawful strength, said the Chief. And asked, wouldn't she have screamed if she'd been attacked? And added, couldn't it be that maybe this female here had secrets in her life connected to the late savage murderer named Eddie Grimes? We might all be better off if these secrets get buried with your Mary Randolph, said the Chief. I'm sure you understand me, Reverend. And yes, the Reverend did understand, he surely did. So Mary Randolph got laid away in the cemetery, and nobody ever said her name again. She was put away out of mind, like The Backs.

"The second thing that shook me up and proved to me that I didn't know anything, that I was no better than a blind dog, happened on Thanksgiving day. My daddy played piano in church, and on special days, we played our instruments along with the gospel songs. I got to church early with the rest of my family, and we practised with the choir. Afterwards, I went to fooling around outside until the people came, and saw a big car come up into the church parking lot. Must have been the biggest, fanciest car I'd ever seen. Miller's Hill was written all over that vehicle. I couldn't have told you why, but the sight of it made my heart stop. The front door opened, and out stepped a coloured man in a fancy grey uniform with a smart cap. He didn't so much as dirty his eyes by looking at me, or at the church, or at anything around him. He stepped around the front of the car and opened the rear door on my side. A young woman was in the passenger seat, and when she got out of the car, the sun fell on her blonde hair and the little fur jacket she was wearing. I couldn't see more than the top of her head, her shoulders under the jacket, and her legs. Then she straightened up, and her eyes lighted right on me. She smiled, but I couldn't smile back. I couldn't even begin to move.

"It was Abbey Montgomery, delivering baskets of food to our church, the way she did every Thanksgiving and Christmas. She looked older and thinner than the last time I'd seen her alive – older and thinner, but more than that, like there was no fun at all in her life anymore. She walked to the trunk of the car, and the driver opened it up, leaned in, and brought out a great big basket of food. He took into the church by the back way and came back for another one. Abbey Montgomery just stood still and watched him carry the baskets. She looked – she looked like she was just going through the motions, like going through the motions was all she was ever going to do from now on, and she knew it. Once she smiled at the driver, but the smile was so sad that the driver didn't even try to smile back. When he was done, he closed the trunk and let her into the passenger seat, got behind the wheel, and drove away.

"I was thinking, *Dee Sparks was right, she was alive all the time.* Then I thought, *No, Mary Randolph brought her back, too, like she did Eddie Grimes. But it didn't work right, and only part of her came back.*

"And that's the whole thing, except that Abbey Montgomery didn't deliver food to our church, that Christmas – she was travelling out of the country, with her aunt. And she didn't bring food the next Thanksgiving, either, just sent her driver with the baskets. By that time, we didn't expect her, because we'd already heard that, soon as she got back to town, Abbey Montgomery stopped leaving her house. That girl shut herself up and never came out. I heard from somebody who probably didn't know any more than I did that she eventually got so she wouldn't even leave her room. Five years later, she passed away. Twenty-six years old, and they said she looked to be at least fifty."

IV

Hat fell silent, and I sat with my pen ready over the notebook, waiting for more. When I realized that he had finished, I asked, "What did she die of?"

"Nobody ever told me."

"And nobody ever found who had killed Mary Randolph."

The limpid, colourless eyes momentarily rested on me. "Was she killed?"

"Did you ever become friends with Dee Sparks again? Did you at least talk about it with him?"

"Surely did not. Nothing to talk about."

This was a remarkable statement, considering that for an hour he had done nothing but talk about what had happened to the two of them, but I let it go. Hat was still looking at me with his unreadable eyes. His face had become particularly bland, almost immobile. It was not possible to imagine this man as an active eleven year old boy. "Now you heard me out, answer my question," he said.

I couldn't remember the question.

"Did we find what we were looking for?"

Scares – that was what they had been looking for. "I think you found a lot more than that," I said.

He nodded slowly. "That's right. It was more."

Then I asked him some question about his family's band, he lubricated himself with another swallow of gin, and the interview returned to more typical matters. But the experience of listening to him had changed. After I had heard the long, unresolved tale of his Halloween night, everything Hat said seemed to have two separate meanings, the daylight meaning created by sequences of ordinary English words, and another, nightime meaning, far less determined and knowable. He was like a man discoursing with eerie rationality in the midst of a surreal dream – like a man carrying on an ordinary conversation with one foot placed on solid ground and the other suspended above a bottomless abyss. I focused on the rationality, on the foot placed in the context I understood; the rest was unsettling to the point of being frightening. By six-thirty, when he kindly called me "Miss Rosemary" and opened his door, I felt as if I'd spent several weeks, if not whole months, in his room.

Part Three

I

Although I did get my MA at Columbia, I didn't have enough money to stay on for a PhD., so I never became a college professor. I never became a jazz critic, either, or anything else very interesting. For a couple of years after Columbia, I taught English in a high school, until I quit to take the job I have now, which involves a lot of travelling and pays a little bit better than teaching. Maybe even quite a bit better, but that's not saying much, especially when you consider my expenses. I own a nice little house in the Chicago suburbs, my marriage held up against everything life did to it, and my twenty-two year old son, a young man who never once in his life for the purpose of pleasure read a novel, looked at a painting, visited a museum, or listened to anything but the most readily available music, recently announced to his mother and myself that he has decided to become an artist, actual type of art to be determined later, but probably to include aspects of photography, video tape, and the creation of "installations". I take this as proof that he was raised in a manner that left his self-esteem intact.

I no longer provide my life with a perpetual sound track (though my son, who has moved back in with us, does), in part because my income does not permit the purchase of a great many compact discs. (A friend presented me with a CD player on my forty-fifth birthday.) And these days, I'm as interested in classical music as in jazz. Of course, I never go to jazz clubs when I am home. Are there still people, apart from New Yorkers, who patronize jazz nightclubs in their own home towns? The concept seems faintly retrograde, even somehow illicit. But when I am out on the road, living in airplanes and hotel rooms, I often check the jazz listings in the local papers to see if I can find some way to fill my evenings. Many of the legends of my youth are still out there, in most cases playing at least as well as before. Some months ago, while I was San Francisco, I came across John Hawes' name in this fashion. He was working in a club so close to my hotel that I could walk to it.

His appearance in any club at all was surprising. Hawes had ceased performing jazz in public years before. He had earned a great deal of fame (and undoubtedly, a great deal of money) writing film scores, and in the past decade, he had begun to appear in swallow-tail coat and white tie as a conductor of the standard classical repertoire. I believe he had a permanent post in some city like Seattle, or perhaps Salt Lake City. If he was spending a week playing jazz with a trio in San Francisco, it must have been for the sheer pleasure of it.

I turned up just before the beginning of the first set, and got a table toward the back of the club. Most of the tables were filled – Hawes' celebrity had guaranteed him a good house. Only a few minutes after the announced time of the first set, Hawes emerged through a door at the front of the club and moved toward the piano, followed by his bassist and drummer. He looked like a more successful version of the younger man I had seen in New York, and the only indications of the extra years were his silvergrey hair, still abundant, and a little paunch. His playing, too, seemed essentially unchanged, but I could not hear it in the way I once had. He was still a good pianist – no doubt about that – but he seemed to be skating over the surface of the songs he played, using his wonderful technique and good time merely to decorate their melodies. It was the sort of playing that becomes less impressive the more attention you give it – if you were listening with half an ear, it probably sounded like Art Tatum. I wondered if John Hawes had always had this superficial streak in him, or if he had lost a certain necessary passion during his years away from jazz. Certainly he had not sounded superficial when I had heard him with Hat.

Hawes, too, might have been thinking about his old employer, because in the first set he played "Love Walked In", "Too Marvelous For Words", and "Up Jumped Hat". In the last of these, inner gears seemed to mesh, the rhythm simultaneously relaxed and intensified, and the music turned into real, not imitation, jazz. Hawes looked pleased with himself when he stood up from the piano bench, and half a dozen fans moved to greet him as he stepped off the bandstand. Most of them were carrying old records they wished him to sign.

A few minutes later, I saw Hawes standing by himself at the end of the bar, drinking what appeared to be club soda, in proximity to his musicians but not actually speaking with them. Wondering if his allusions to Hat had been deliberate, I left my table and walked toward the bar. Hawes watched me approach out of the side of his eye, neither encouraging nor discouraging me. When I introduced myself, he smiled nicely and shook my hand and waited for whatever I wanted to say to him.

At first, I made some inane comment about the difference between playing in clubs and conducting in concert halls, and he replied with the noncommital and equally banal agreement that yes, the two experiences were very different.

Then I told him that I had seen him play with Hat all those years ago in New York, and he turned to me with genuine pleasure in his face. "Did you? At that little club on St Mark's Place? That sure was fun. I guess I must have been thinking about it, because I played some of those songs we used to do."

"That was why I came over," I said. "I guess that was one of the best musical experiences I ever had."

"You and me both." Hawes smiled to himself. "Sometimes, I just couldn't believe what he was doing."

"It showed," I said.

"Well." His eyes slid away from mine. "Great character. Completely otherwordly."

"I saw some of that," I said. "I did that interview with him that turns up now and then, the one in *Downbeat*."

"Oh!" Hawes gave me his first genuinely interested look so far. "Well, that was him, all right."

"Most of it was, anyhow."

"You cheated?" Now he was looking even more interested.

"I had to make it understandable."

"Oh, sure. You couldn't put in all those ding-dings and bells and Bob Crosbys." These had been elements of Hat's private code. Hawes laughed at the memory. "When he wanted to play a blues in G, he'd lean over and say, 'Gs, please.'"

"Did you get to know him at all well, personally?" I asked, thinking that the answer must be that he had not – I didn't think that anyone had ever really known Hat very well.

"Pretty well," Hawes said. "A couple of times, around '54 and '55, he invited me home with him, to his parents' house, I mean. We got to be friends on a Jazz at the Phil tour, and twice when we were in the South, he asked me if I wanted to eat some good home cooking."

"You went to his home town?"

He nodded. "His parents put me up. They were interesting people. Hat's father, Red, was about the lightest black man I ever saw, and he could have passed for white anywhere, but I don't suppose the thought ever occurred to him."

"Was the family band still going?"

"No, to tell you the truth, I don't think they were getting much work up toward the end of the forties. At the end, they were using a tenor player and a drummer from the high school band. And the church work got more and more demanding for Hat's father."

"His father was a deacon, or something like that?"

He raised his eyebrows. "No, Red was the Baptist minister. The reverend. He ran that church. I think he even started it."

"Hat told me his father played piano in church, but . . ."

"The reverend would have made a hell of a blues piano player, if he'd ever left his day job."

"There must have been another Baptist church in the neigh-bourhood," I said, thinking this the only explanation for the presence of two Baptist ministers. But why had Hat not men-tioned that his own father, like Dee Sparks's, had been a clergy-man?

"Are you kidding? There was barely enough money in that place to keep one of them going." He looked at his watch, nodded at me, and began to move closer to his sidemen.

"Could I ask you one more question?"

"I suppose so," he said, almost impatiently.

"Did Hat strike you as superstitious?"

Hawes grinned. "Oh, he was superstitious, all right. He told me he never worked on Halloween – he didn't even want to go out of his room on Halloween. That's why he left the big band, you know. They were starting a tour on Halloween, and Hat refused to do it. He just quit." He leaned toward me. "I'll tell you another funny thing. I always had the feeling that Hat was terrified of his father – I thought he invited me to Hatchville with him so I could be some kind of buffer between him and his father. Never made any sense to me. Red was a big strong old guy, and I'm pretty sure a long time ago he used to mess around with the ladies, reverend or not, but I couldn't ever figure out why Hat should be afraid of him. But whenever Red came into the room, Hat shut up. Funny, isn't it?"

I must have looked very perplexed. "Hatchville?"

"Where they lived. Hatchville, Mississippi – not too far from Biloxi."

"But he told me—"

"Hat never gave too many straight answers," Hawes said. "And he didn't let the facts get in the way of a good story. When you come to think of it, why should he? He was *Hat*."

After the next set, I walked back uphill to my hotel, wondering again about the long story Hat had told me. Had there been any truth in it at all?

II

Three weeks later I found myself released from a meeting at our Midwestern headquarters in downtown Chicago earlier than I had expected, and instead of going to a bar with the other wandering corporate ghosts like myself, made up a story about having to get home for dinner with visiting relatives. I didn't want to admit to my fellow employees, committed like all male business people to aggressive endeavours such as raquetball, drinking, and the pursuit of women, that I intended to visit the library. Short of a trip to Mississippi, a good periodical room offered the most likely means of finding out once and for all how much truth had been in what Hat had told me.

I hadn't forgotten everything I had learned at Columbia – I still knew how to look things up.

In the main library, a boy set me up with a monitor and spools of microfilm representing the complete contents of the daily newspapers from Biloxi and Hatchville, Mississippi, for Hat's tenth and eleventh years. That made three papers, two for Biloxi and one for Hatchville, but all I had to examine were the issues dating from the end of October through the middle of November – I was looking for references to Eddie Grimes, Eleanore Monday, Mary Randolph, Abbey Montgomery, Hat's family, The Backs, and anyone named Sparks.

The Hatchville *Blade*, a gossipy daily printed on each-coloured paper, offered plenty of references to each of these names and places, and the papers from Biloxi contained nearly as many – Biloxi could not conceal the delight, disguised as horror, aroused in its collective soul by the unimaginable events taking place in the smaller, supposedly respectable town ten miles west. Biloxi was riveted, Biloxi was superior, Biloxi was virtually intoxicated with dread and outrage. In Hatchville, the press maintained a persistent optimistic dignity: when wickedness had appeared, justice official and unofficial had dealt with it. Hatchville was shocked but proud (or at least pretended to be proud), and Biloxi all but preened. The *Blade* printed detailed news stories, but the Biloxi papers suggested implications not allowed by Hatchville's version of events. I needed Hatchville to confirm or question Hat's story, but Biloxi gave me at least the beginning of a way to understand it.

A black ex-convict named Edward Grimes had in some fashion persuaded or coerced Eleanore Monday, a retarded young white woman, to accompany him to an area variously described as "a longstanding local disgrace" (the *Blade*) and "a haunt of deepest vice" (Biloxi) and after "the perpetration of the most offensive and brutal deeds upon her person" (the *Blade*) or "acts which the judicious commentator must decline to imagine, much less describe" (Biloxi) murdered her, presumably to ensure her silence, and then buried the body near the "squalid dwelling" where he made and sold illegal liquor. State and local police departments acting in concert had located the body, identified Grimes as the fiend, and, after a search of his house, had tracked him to a warehouse where the murderer was killed in a gun battle. The *Blade* covered half its front page with a photograph of a gaping double door and a bloodstained wall. All Mississippi, both Hatchville and Biloxi declared, now could breathe more easily.

The *Blade* gave the death of Mary Randolph a single paragraph on its back page, the Biloxi papers nothing.

In Hatchville, the raid on The Backs was described as an heroic assault on a dangerous criminal encampment which had somehow come to flourish in a little-noticed section of the countryside. At great risk to themselves, anonymous citizens of Hatchville had descended like the army of the righteous and driven forth the hidden sinners from their dens. Troublemakers, beware! The Biloxi papers, while seeming to endorse the action in Hatchville, actually took another tone altogether. Can it be, they asked, that the Hatchville police had never before noticed the existence of a Sodom and Gomorrah so close to the town line? Did it take the savage murder of a helpless woman to bring it to their attention? Of course Biloxi celebrated the destruction of The Backs – such vileness must be eradicated – but it wondered what else had been destroyed along with the stills and the mean buildings where loose women had plied their trade. Men ever are men, and those who have succumbed to temptation may wish to remove from the face of the earth any evidence of their lapses. Had not the police of Hatchville ever heard the rumor, vague and doubtless baseless, that operations of an illegal nature had been performed in the selfsame Backs? That in an atmosphere of drugs, intoxication, and gambling, the races had mingled there, and that "fast" young women had risked life and honour in search of illicit thrills? Hatchville may have rid itself of a few buildings, but Biloxi was willing to suggest that the problems of its smaller neighbour might not have disappeared with them.

As this campaign of innuendo went on in Biloxi, the *Blade* blandly reported the ongoing events of any smaller American city. Miss Abigail Montgomery sailed with her aunt, Miss Lucinda Bright, from New Orleans to France for an eight-week tour of the continent. The Reverend Jasper Sparks of the Miller's Hill Presbyterian Church delivered a sermon on the subject "Christian Forgiveness." (Just after Thanksgiving, the Reverend Sparks' son, Rodney, was sent off with the blessings and congratulations of all Hatchville to a private academy in Charleston, South Carolina.) There were bake sales, church socials, and costume parties. A saxophone virtuoso named Albert Woodland demonstrated his astonishing wizardy at a well-attended recital presented in Temperance Hall.

Well, I knew the name of at least one person who had attended the recital. If Hat had chosen to disguise the name of his home town, he had done so by substituting for it a name that represented another sort of home.

But, although I had more ideas about this than before, I still did not know exactly what Hat had seen or done on Halloween night in The Backs. It seemed possible that he had gone there with a white boy of his age, a preacher's son like himself, and had the wits scared out of him by whatever had happened to Abbey Montgomery – and after that night, Abbey herself had been sent out of town, as had Dee Sparks. I couldn't think that a man had murdered the young woman, leaving Mary Randolph to bring her back to life. Surely whatever had happened to Abbey Montgomery had brought Dr Garland out to The Backs, and what he had witnessed or done there had sent him away screaming. And this event – what had befallen a rich young white woman in the shadiest, most criminal section of a Mississippi county – had led to the slaying of Eddie Grimes and the murder of Mary Randolph. Because they knew what had happened, they had to die.

I understood all this, and Hat had understood it, too. Yet he had introduced needless puzzles, as if embedded in the midst of this unresolved story were something he either wished to conceal or not to know. And concealed it would remain; if Hat did not know it, I never would. He had deliberately obscured even basic but meaningless facts: first Mary Randolph was a witch-woman from The Backs, then she was a respectable church-goer who lived down the street from his family. Whatever had really happened in The Backs on Halloween night was lost for good.

On the *Blade's* entertainment page for a Saturday in the middle of November I had come across a photograph of Hat's family's band, and when I had reached this hopeless point in my thinking, I spooled back across the pages to look at it again. Hat, his two brothers, his sister, and his parents stood in a straight line, tallest to smallest, in front of what must have been the family car. Hat held a C-melody saxophone, his brothers a trumpet and drumsticks, his sister a clarinet. As the piano player, the reverend carried nothing at all – nothing except for what came through even a grainy, sixty-year old photograph as a powerful sense of self. Hat's father had been a tall, impressive man, and in the photograph he looked as white as I did. But what was impressive was not the lightness of his skin, or even his striking handsomeness: what impressed was the sense of authority implicit in his posture, his straightforward gaze, even the dictatorial set of his chin. In retrospect, I was not surprised by what John Hawes had told me, for this man could easily be frightening. You would not wish to oppose him, you would not elect to get in his way. Beside him, Hat's mother seemed vague and distracted, as if her husband had robbed her of all certainty. Then I noticed the car, and for the first time realized why it had been included in the photograph. It was a sign of their prosperity, the respectable status they had achieved – the car was as much an advertisement as the photograph. It was, I thought, an old Model T Ford, but I didn't waste any time speculating that it might have been the Model T Hat had seen in The Backs.

And that would be that – the hint of an absurd supposition – except for something I read a few days ago in a book called *Cool Breeze: The Life of Grant Kilbert*.

There are few biographies of any jazz musicians apart from Louis Armstrong and Duke Ellington (though one does now exist of Hat, the title of which was drawn from my interview with him), and I was surprised to see *Cool Breeze* at the B. Dalton in our local mall. Biographies have not yet been written of Art Blakey, Clifford Brown, Ben Webster, Art Tatum, and many others of more musical and historical importance than Kilbert. Yet I should not have been surprised. Kilbert was one of those musicians who attract and maintain a large personal following, and twenty years after his death, almost all of his records have been released on CD, many of them in multi-disc boxed sets. He had been a great, great player, the closest to Hat of all his disciples. Because Kilbert had been one of my early heroes, I bought the book (for thirty-five dollars!) and brought it home.

Like the lives of many jazz musicians, I suppose of artists in general, Kilbert's had been an odd mixture of public fame and private misery. He had committed burglaries, even armed rob-beries, to feed his persistent heroin addiction; he had spent years in jail; his two marriages had ended in outright hatred; he had managed to betray most of his friends. That this weak, narcissistic louse had found it in himself to create music of real tenderness and beauty was one of art's enigmas, but not actually a surprise. I'd heard and read enough stories about Grant Kilbert to know what kind of man he'd been.

But what I had not known was that Kilbert, to all appearances an American of conventional northern European, perhaps Scan-dinavian or Anglo-Saxon, stock, had occasionally claimed to be black. (This claim had always been dismissed, apparently, as another indication of Kilbert's mental aberrancy.) At other times, being Kilbert, he had denied ever making this claim.

Neither had I known that the received versions of his birth and upbringing were in question. Unlike Hat, Kilbert had been interviewed dozens of times both in *Downbeat* and in mass-market weekly news magazines, invariably to offer the same story of having been born in Hattiesburg, Mississippi, to an unmusical, working-class family (a plumber's family), of knowing virtually from infancy that he was born to make music, of begging for and finally being given a saxophone, of early mastery and the dazzled admiration of his teachers, then of dropping out of school at sixteen and joining the Woody Herman band. After that, almost immediate fame.

Most of this, the Grant Kilbert myth, was undisputed. He had been raised in Hattiesburg by a plumber named Kilbert, he had been a prodigy and high-school dropout, he'd become famous with Woody Herman before he was twenty. Yet he told a few friends, not necessarily those to whom he said he was black, that he'd been adopted by the Kilberts, and that once or twice, in great anger, either the plumber or his wife had told him that he had been born into poverty and disgrace and that he'd better by God be grateful for the opportunities he'd been given. The source of this story was John Hawes, who'd met Kilbert on another long JATP tour, the last he made before leaving the road for film scoring.

"Grant didn't have a lot of friends on that tour," Hawes told the biographer. "Even though he was such a great player, you never knew what he was going to say, and if he was in a bad mood, he was liable to put down some of the older players. He was always respectful around Hat, his whole style was based on Hat's, but Hat could go days without saying anything, and by those days he certainly wasn't making any new friends. Still, he'd let Grant sit next to him on the bus, and nod his head while Grant talked to him, so he must have felt some affection for him. Anyhow, eventually I was about the only guy on the tour that was willing to have a conversation with Grant, and we'd sit up in the bar late at night after the concerts. The way he played, I could forgive him a lot of failings. One of those nights, he said that he'd been adopted, and that not knowing who his real parents were was driving him crazy. He didn't even have a birth certificate. From a hint his mother once gave him, he thought one of his birth parents was black, but when he asked them directly, they always denied it. These were white Mississippians, after all, and if they had wanted a baby so bad that they taken in a child who looked completely white but maybe had a drop or two of black blood in his veins, they weren't going to admit it, even to themselves."

In the midst of so much supposition, here is a fact. Grant Kilbert was exactly eleven years younger than Hat. The jazz encyclopedias give his birth date as November first, which instead of his actual birthday may have been the day he was delivered to the couple in Hattiesburg.

I wonder if Hat saw more than he admitted to me of the man leaving the shack where Abbey Montgomery lay on bloody sheets; I wonder if he had reason to fear his father. I don't know if what I am thinking is correct – I'll never know that – but now, finally, I think I know why Hat never wanted to go out of his room on Halloween nights. The story he told me never left him, but it must have been most fully present on those nights. I think he heard the screams, saw the bleeding girl, and saw Mary Randolph staring at him with displaced pain and rage. I think that in some small closed corner deep within himself, he knew who had been the real object of these feelings, and therefore had to lock himself inside his hotel room and gulp gin until he obliterated the horror of his own thoughts.

STEVE RASNIC TEM

Tricks & Treats
One Night on
Halloween Street

FOR THE SECOND TIME IN THIS VOLUME, we return to Steve Rasnic Tem's haunted Halloween Street – a place where dark and dangerous things hide behind the masks of childhood.

"I love writing these shorter-than-short pieces," says Tem, "and in particular tales like 'Tricks & Treats', which are mini-anthologies of such writings. In part because they embody so well that favoured sensation of having created something from nothing."

The author has also compiled two new short fiction collections: *City Fishing*, which recently appeared from Silver Salamander Press, contains thirty-four stories and is the largest collection produced by the Seattle-based publisher to date, while Ash-Tree Press will be releasing a collection of Tem's more ghostly stories early in 2001.

Meanwhile, a chapbook entitled *The Man on the Ceiling*, written with his wife Melanie, was published by Bob Garcia/ American Fantasy and premiered at The 10th Annual World Horror Convention in Denver, where the writers were amongst the guests of honour.

TRICKS

I**T WAS SUPPOSED TO BE THE LAST TIME** they'd all go trick or treating together, but it didn't seem right that the gang go out now that Tommy was dead.

Every year all the gang had gone trick or treating together: Allison and Robbie, Maryanne and John, Sandra and Willona and Felix and Randall. And Tommy. They'd been doing it since fourth grade. Now they were teenagers, and they figured this was the last time. The last chance to do it up right.

Not that they'd ever done anything particularly malicious on Halloween. A few soaped windows. A few mailboxes full of cow shit. Not much more than that.

But Tommy had said this particular Halloween needed to be special. "For chrissakes, it's the last *time!*"

But then Tommy had died in that big pile-up on the interstate. They'd all gone to the funeral. They'd seen the casket lowered into the ground, the earth dark as chocolate. It wasn't like in the movies. This movie, Tommy's movie, would last forever. Sandra kept saying that word, "forever," like it was the first time she'd ever heard it.

The dead liked playing tricks. She figured that out quick. Dying was a great trick. It was great because people just couldn't believe it. You'd play the trick right in front of their eyes and they still just couldn't believe it.

He'd only been dead a week when Sandra wondered if Tommy's life itself had been a trick. She couldn't remember his face anymore. Even when she looked at pictures of him something felt wrong. Tommy had this trick: he was never going to change, and because he didn't change she couldn't remember what he looked like.

Sandra and Willona had both had crushes on Tommy. And now he was going to be their boyfriend forever. He used to take them both to the horror shows, even the ones they were too young for. He knew places he could get them in. Sandra thought about those shows a lot – she figured Willona did, too. Tommy loved the horror shows. Now he was the star of his own horror show that played in their heads every night. He'd always be with them, because they just couldn't stop thinking about him.

Sometimes it felt so great just to be alive, now that somebody you knew was dead. Sandra thought that must be the ugliest feeling in the world, but it was real. That was what Halloween was all about, wasn't it? Remembering the dead and celebrating hard because you weren't one of them.

Tommy had liked Halloween the best of all of them – he'd been the one who'd organized all their parties, the one who'd come up with the tricks they would play. So this last night as they went door to door they thought of him when they called out "Trick or treat!" They thought of him while they munched on the candy on their way to the next house, like they were eating his memory a piece at a time.

Halloween Street was always the last place to go. It was traditional. You could play the best tricks on Halloween Street, too, since none of the neighbours ever came out to bother you. You could just do whatever you pleased.

Sandra led the way to the first house on the street: a tall thing missing most of its roof and leaning toward the rest of the block like it was drunk. She knocked on the door and knocked on the door until finally they gave up and started to go away. But as they turned away the door opened and oranges came rolling out for all of them. They put them into their sacks and walked on down the street.

At the next house, a wide place with fire damage on the outside walls, Willona did the knocking. An old man with no teeth gave each of them a peanut butter log and then they left and walked on down the street.

The middle two houses looked even emptier than the others, twins that seemed to be looking at each other all the time with small window eyes. Maryanne and John knocked at both houses and at each house one of the old twin brothers who lived there gave them a box of raisins.

By the time they all got to the end of the street the sacks were getting heavy, unbelievably heavy and Sandra insisted that they sit down to rest. The gang sat in a circle and reached into their sacks for the goodies.

When Sandra looked into her sack her orange had turned into Tommy's head, bleeding from a gash that crossed the crown of his head.

When Willona reached into her sack for the peanut butter log she found a slippery finger instead, Tommy's ring wedged on it so tightly she couldn't get it off no matter how hard she tried.

What John and Maryanne found in their sacks when they went looking for the raisins was a mass of black insects, each one carrying a small pale bit of Tommy's broken flesh.

But the gang never said a word to each other about what they had found, nor did they show any alarm on their faces. They went on munching and smacking their lips, giggling to themselves because it was so good to be alive on this the final Halloween of their childhoods.

And thinking about how this was Tommy's last trick on them – and what a grand trick it was! – and how this was their last trick on Tommy.

THE INVISIBLE BOY

J.P. was acting stupid again. Susan was sorry she'd brought him along, as usual, but she never had any choice anyway. J.P. always went where he wanted to go, and unfortunately the places he wanted to go always seemed to be the places she wanted to go.

She tried to walk as far away from him as possible so that maybe people wouldn't know that he was her brother. But people always knew anyway. Like she had a big sign: J.P.'S SISTER, painted on her forehead.

He looked so stupid in his regular streetclothes on Halloween night. That yellow shirt and those brown corduroy pants he always wore. Always. He never took them off, and she didn't think he ever washed them. It made her mad that Mom let him get away with stuff like that.

J.P. was so ignorant. *I'll be the invisible boy*, he said, and laughed that stupid horse laugh of his. *I'll wear my same old clothes but I'll be the invisible boy so that no one can see me!*

"J.P., you're so ignorant!" she'd said but he'd just laughed at her. That stupid laugh. Here she'd worked forever on her fairy princess costume – it had wings and everything – and her brother thought he could be the invisible boy just by saying he was the invisible boy.

You can't see me! he'd said.

"J.P., that's dumb! Of course I can see you! You're wearing

that stupid yellow shirt and those stupid brown pants and no way are you an invisible boy!"

He'd looked worried then. *Don't tell anybody you can see me, then . . . don't tell or you'll ruin everything!*

It made her mad when he asked her that because he knew she could never tell him no. He always took advantage of her. It made her feel stupid, too.

"OK OK . . . let's just go."

So they started across the street just as a car was coming across the bridge onto Halloween Street when J.P. turned to her and started making faces just like he always did. And Susan started screaming just like she always did.

And the car passed through J.P., the headlights trapped inside him for a second like he was burning smoke, just like it always did.

J.P., the Invisible Boy, turned around and looked at her and laughed that stupid horse laugh of his before jumping backwards onto the sidewalk and then walking backwards like that all the way up Halloween Street.

J.P. was so ignorant.

PAINTED FACES

She always thought that the costumes which were just painted faces were the best.

You could make almost any kind of face with the paint. You could tear the skin in red or bruise it in blue. You could dirty it with brown or you could make it shine with the heat of the sun. If anybody said you were ugly you could make yourself beautiful.

And if anybody said you were beautiful you could make yourself ugly, too.

On Halloween Street the painted faces were always the best. Somebody would always paint themselves up to look like your mother or to look like your father, your brother or your sister. Faces you knew so well but which you were afraid you really didn't know at all.

Because faces were painted and you could always wash them off. Because faces were painted and you could always change them.

Every once in awhile she would reach up to her mom or her dad's face and rub and rub as hard as she could.

And sometimes, after a long time of rubbing and crying about the rubbing, the paint would come off.

SACK LUNCH

He was just a little boy but he carried the biggest treat sack any of the kids had ever seen. It grew out of his hands like a big dark hole and it reached to the ground and even dragged behind him for several feet.

Some of the big boys thought it was silly – he looked crazy dragging that big sack around, almost tripping over it every second and stepping on it all the time. But what if he got more candy because he was such a little boy carrying such a great big sack? Adults were funny that way – they might think it was cute.

So they stopped him, and they took the big sack away from him, and just for a moment they considered dropping it and running away because the sack was so light, and felt so strange in their hands – like an oily cloud as it rose and drifted and hummed as the October wind wrapped it around them.

But they just had to look inside.

Later, when the little boy picked the big sack up out of the street it felt just a little heavier, and there were harsh whispers inside.

But they didn't last for long.

SWEET & SOUR

The boy loved the taste of sweet and sour. Sweet, then sour. Sour, then sweet. Ice cream, then pickles. Lemons, then peaches.

"That's the way of things," his daddy used to tell him. "You wouldn't know the good without the bad to compare it to." His daddy used to say that over and over to him, like some kind of preacher with his sermon. But his daddy just had no idea. Why was one thing good and the other thing bad? Sweet and sour. It was just another flavour, another kind of taste.

Grapefruit and strawberries. Kisses and slaps. Silk and razor blades. Living and dying.

The boy was too old to be out trick or treating. He knew that but he liked the candy too much. He had a sweet tooth. He had a sour tooth.

That night on Halloween Street he was having the best time. Hardly anyone seemed to be home in those houses but he didn't care. There were lots of little kids running up and down that street with their silly store-bought costumes and their grocery sacks full of treats.

He helped one little kid pick up all his spilled candy. He took another kid's mask off and threw it in the creek. He cut a little girl's arm with the penknife he carried and tried to comfort her when she cried. He pulled her arm up to his lips and teeth and tasted her frightened skin: he couldn't figure out if it tasted sweet or if it tasted sour, and finally decided it was both.

He ate as much of his favourite candy as he could steal, until he was almost sick with it. Almost, but not quite. Sweet and sour. Sour and sweet.

Rhubarb and honey. Sugar and alum.

He liked being the biggest one out on Halloween Street, using just his sweetest smile and his most twisted snarl for a costume. But that didn't mean he wanted to be an adult. Adults didn't know a thing, for all they acted like they knew everything. They didn't know that clover stems were sweet, or that dandelion stems were as sour as can be. They never tasted them like kids did.

Adults had the power, but they were just a few trick or treats away from dying. Sweet and sour. Sour and sweet. The boy didn't want to die, although sometimes he didn't much like living. Limes and strawberries. Hugs and teeth.

He ran up onto each house on Halloween Street, knocking on doors and ringing bells. Sometimes the curtains moved, but no one came to the door. Sometimes someone came to the door, but you couldn't see their face.

A little goblin came around the corner, an ugly mask on the beautiful little body. The boy smiled and frowned, took out his knife and went to give the goblin a little kiss.

The goblin reached up its arms to hug the big boy, but the goblin's little fingers were too sharp, and the big boy's skin too thin.

The boy smiled and frowned, and turned upside down.

He lay there until morning came up and his eyelids went down, smelling the fruit trees and tasting his own blood.

Was it Delicious? Or was it Granny Smith? The boy couldn't decide.

BUTCHER PAPER

Jean had spent weeks arranging the outing. The terminal kids got out all too rarely, although most of them were still ambulatory. Just bureaucratic hospital regs that made no sense. Anxieties over law suits. But she'd gotten to the right people and worn them down. And they put her in charge.

The kids were given any materials they wanted so that they might construct their own costumes. The first few days they'd just stared at the materials – picking up glue and markers and glitter and putting them right back down again, touching the giant roll of butcher's paper again and again as if it were silk – as if these were alien artifacts that they were handling, objects which might have been contaminated with some rare disease.

She wasn't prepared for what the kids finally came up with.

Each kid had wrapped his or her body in the stiff brown butcher's paper. Wide rolls of tape were used to fasten the pieces together securely. When they were all done they looked like a walking line of packages. Packages of meat.

And that was the way they went out on Halloween Street. And that was the way they went out.

CLOWNS

The only ones that really scared her were the clowns. Clown masks always smiled, but that made it even harder to guess at the faces underneath.

Sometimes you could tell from the eyes inside the holes: they'd be red or dark above the impossible ugly smile. But sometimes you couldn't see the eyes.

Sometimes all you could see were the spaces where the eyes were missing. Sometimes all you could see was the space where the mouth was missing.

She thought it must be terrible pretending to smile all the time. She thought it must be terrible to be a smile.

But the clowns filled the streets during Halloween every year, more and more of them every year, and the most hideous of all the clowns seemed to be on Halloween Street this year. She saw clowns with large scars across their faces and big ball noses chewed by something worse than a rat. She saw clowns with vampire teeth sticking out from their messy red lips and clowns with mouths and ears sewn shut by bright blue shoe-laces. There were mad clowns and suicidal clowns, crazed and sick and dead clowns. And half of them didn't carry treat sacks. And half of those were much too large to be children in disguise.

Laugh, child! said a voice behind her. She turned and there was the fattest clown she had ever seen, with rolls of brightly painted fat spilling out of his baggy white pants.

Be happy! said another voice, and suddenly there was the thinnest clown she had ever seen, his shirt torn away to show the white flesh like tissue covering the narrow rib cage.

Smile . . . said a crawling clown with a head like a snake. *Sing a merry tune . . .* said a leaping clown with red axes for hands.

And she felt so scared she did begin to laugh, laughing so hard until she peed her pants and then laughing some more. Laughing so hard that when a clown no more than six inches tall and with an orange rat's tail hanging out of the back of his pants handed her a tube of black grease paint she took it, and drew her own smile around her shrieking lips.

So that ever after that she could smile, no matter how she felt inside.

MASKS OF ME

Ronald went to the door and was surprised to see a little boy standing there wearing a mask that looked just like Ronald's own face.

"Where'd you get that mask of me?" Ronald asked, but the little boy just turned and ran away. Ronald went out on the front porch and yelled as loudly as he could, "WHERE'D YOU GET THAT MASK OF ME?" But the little boy just kept on running, and never looked back.

Ronald jumped off the porch and ran after the little boy. Behind him, he could hear his mother and father calling after him in panic, but Ronald kept running, just knowing that he *had* to catch that little boy and find out about the mask of his own face.

"I WON'T HURT YOU! I JUST WANT TO KNOW ABOUT THAT MASK OF ME!" he called, but the little boy just kept getting further and further away, like he had leopard legs or something. Leopard legs and Ronald's own face.

He chased that little boy with the mask of himself up Fredericks Lane and down Lincoln Avenue. He spun into Jangle Road so fast he almost fell down. The wind was blowing hard and the trees were moving like they were getting ready to dance and the whole thing made Ronald feel like he was flying, soaring after that little boy wearing his mask of Ronald.

". . . where'd you get that mask of me . . ." Ronald tried to say but the wind caught his words and blew them away so hard he could hardly hear them himself.

". . . where'd you . . . where'd you . . ." the wind spat back at him.

Then finally the little boy turned onto Halloween Street and Ronald felt pretty good about that because he knew Halloween Street was a dead end. But he wasn't ready for all the kids trick or treating there, hundreds of them of all sizes, and all of them wearing these masks with Ronald's own face.

"Where'd you get those masks of me?" Ronald cried out in confusion.

"Where'd you get that mask of me?" they all chorused back in panic and fatigue.

". . . where'd you . . . where'd you . . ." the wind gently crooned.

And then there was nothing else to say. All the children with Ronald's face sat down on Halloween Street and said nothing. Ronald wondered if maybe they were all waiting for the real Ronald to stand up, for the real Ronald to make it perfectly clear exactly who was who.

So the real Ronald stood up and tried to take his face off, just to show all the others that it wasn't a mask. And all the other real Ronalds stood up and tried to take their faces off, to finally put an end to the crowded masquerade.

And all of Ronald's faces did come off. And there were the Willies and the Anns and the Bobbies and the Janes. And there was no one named Ronald there at all.

And no one could remember ever knowing any kid with such a strange name.

PLAY PARTY

Ellen left the party early because she didn't belong.
  Freddie left the party early because he didn't belong.
  Willa left the party early because she didn't belong.
  Johnny left the party early because he didn't belong.
  They wandered their separate ways toward Halloween Street, empty and waiting sacks clutched desperately in their hands.
  Behind them faded the community sounds, the get-together songs of corn-husking, apple-paring, rock and roll dancing, bobbing for apples and stealing a kiss.

> *Come, all ye young people that's wending your way,*
> *And sow your wild oats in your youthful day . . .*

But there would always be a place where the loners could go.

> *So choose your partner and be marching along . . .*

Halloween Street was always open to the Ellens, the Willas, the Freddies and Johnnys.

> *For daylight is past, the night's coming on . . .*

Where the doors to the empty houses would open only to their special knocks.
  And close them up safe. And close them up tight.

JACK

Marsha cut her thumb real bad last year carving pumpkins, so this year her dad said she couldn't carve pumpkins at all. He said she was too careless. She didn't understand how he could remember things that far back – sometimes she had trouble just remembering what happened last week – but he did. And she had made him mad the last couple of days and sometimes that made him remember more. She had let the soup boil over on the stove and she had borrowed her mother's ring and lost it and she had let the baby crawl away when she was supposed to be watching him.
  Sometimes it was hard for her to remember things especially

when she was excited about something like Halloween. But Dad didn't seem to understand that at all. That's why she'd taken the knife out of the kitchen and hid it in her treat sack. There was a big pumpkin patch behind Halloween Street and she'd find herself one there to carve.

All up and down Halloween Street the jack o'lanterns were wonderful this year. She didn't know any of the people who lived on this street, and she didn't know anyone else who did either, and that made her wonder all the more what kind of people would carve such great pumpkins.

On the pumpkins there were faces with great moustaches and faces with huge noses. Enormous, deep-set eyes and mouths that stretched ear-to-ear. Some of the pumpkins had other vegetables attached – carrots and onions and potatoes and turnips – to make features that stood out on the pumpkin's head. There were pumpkin cats and pumpkin dogs, bats, walruses, spiders, and fish.

There was every kind of face on those pumpkins a person could imagine: faces Marsha had seen lots of times and faces Marsha had never seen once in her entire life.

But there wasn't a single pumpkin that matched anyone in her head she might have called a "Jack." As far as Marsha was concerned there wasn't a "Jack o' lantern" in the bunch. So she'd just have to make herself one.

She slipped down a well-worn pathway that ran between two dilapidated houses, crept along a waist-high fence whose paint had peeled and furred to the point where it gave her the creeps just to touch it, until finally she stepped out into the pumpkin patch: yards and yards of green foliage studded with the big orange pumpkins.

She couldn't see the ends of the patch – it stretched out as far as she could see on this side of the river. But for all the pumpkins to choose from, finding the right one for "Jack" was easy.

It was a squat, warped-looking thing just beginning to rot. But she could already see Jack's face in the bulgy softness of its sides. She cleared off the dirt from its surface, pulled out the knife, and stuck it in as deep as she could make it go. The patch sighed and shook as she wiggled the knife back and forth. It felt icky, like she was carving up a baby or something.

Finally Jack's face started coming out of all that softness: a wide mouth with teeth as big as knife blades, a nose like a hog's nose, or maybe some other animal that liked to stick its face down in the mud, and two deep deep little eye holes, like the eyeballs had sunk way down so that you couldn't look at them, so that you could never know exactly what old Jack was feeling.

That was the other thing – somehow Marsha just knew that Jack's face was old, as old a face as Marsha had ever seen. So old it was, like Jack could have nothing in common with Marsha, or even care.

So that after she'd made Jack, Marsha decided she really didn't like him very much. The fact was, she hated him. So she dropped him on his big ugly face and ran out of there. She ran out of the patch and back down the path that led between the dark houses and out into the shadowy lane that was Halloween Street itself. Then she remembered she had forgotten the kitchen knife.

It wasn't an ordinary knife – it was part of a set her parents got for their wedding and it had a different sort of handle and once her dad found it gone then he would know who had taken it.

Marsha went back up the pathway slowly, but when she reached the pumpkin patch she saw that a man was standing there, right in the middle of the Halloween Street pumpkin patch, just staring at her.

He wore a big black coat and a big black hat and his hands had been swallowed up by big orange gloves.

And Marsha could see that he was standing right where she had dropped Jack. So her parents' kitchen knife had to be some place near his feet.

"Excuse me, sir?" she said and the man took a step toward he. "Did you see . . ." And the man took another step. ". . . a knife?" And the man stepped closer still.

When the man took several more fast steps Marsha turned and ran. She ran back down the path and she ran out in the street but when she turned her head the man was right there.

So she ran to the end of the street and beat on a door there but she could hear the man coming up the steps and so she ran to the edge of the porch and jumped off and ran to the next empty house with a pumpkin on the porch and then the next and then the next but nobody ever answered even though all the jack o'lanterns were lit and she could hear the man behind her with every terrified step.

Finally she was stuck in one corner of a dark yard and there was no place to turn and the man was coming right up to her he was so tall she couldn't see the top of him and he had one orange hand held up high.

"Your knife, I've got your knife, little girl," the man said in a friendly voice and she felt all better again.

Until he took off his hat with that big orange glove of his and his head was that pumpkin she carved, that big old ugly Jack with the knife blade teeth and her parents' kitchen knife was stuck in all the way to the handle right beside his nose but he didn't seem to mind.

OWLS

All night long the owls gathered in the trees up and down Halloween Street.

All night long they rustled their feathers and stared with their eyes of glass.

All night long they wept while the children played.

For owls know that some days the sacks are empty. For owls know a sack can't be filled with wishes.

And owls know the children eventually go home, lock their doors, and never come out again.

The children hooted and screeched their way from house to house, the tears of the owls glistening on their shoes.

TREATS

Almost midnight, when the last of the children should have been home, but were not, their bags too full of treats to carry, and Halloween Street full of the sounds of rustling costumes and laughter, candles were seen to light up all over the lane and both sides of the creek.

The children, if they hadn't been so excited by the bizarre and exciting shapes of each other, by the heady scent of coloured sugars in their bags, might have been a little frightened by this, but for the moment it seemed like a great deal of fun. The world was full of treats for them, and each new event offered them more. They all laughed out loud.

Some of them cheered.

But then the individual flames began to drift away from their individual candletops, rising swiftly to join one another in the sky above, where they paused as if sad and reluctant before floating up into the dark night.

As quickly as that. As quickly as a hungry child emptying his bag of its bright and shiny, but ultimately unsatisfying, treats.

Only one child cried, but all the others recognized what he felt. For a brief moment they thought of the ends of things, of how alone they were in this dark and treatless night.

One by one the children drifted away to home and their separate dreams, even the youngest among them trying to pretend he was younger still, a baby, some unknowing sprite who might last this night forever.

STEPHEN JONES & KIM NEWMAN

Necrology: 1999

IN THE FINAL YEAR OF THE TWENTIETH CENTURY, we remember those writers, artists, performers and technicians who, during their lifetimes, made significant contributions to the horror, science fiction and fantasy genres (or left their mark on popular culture in other ways) . . .

AUTHORS/ARTISTS

Hollywood screenwriter **Harvey Miller**, whose credits include *Jekyll and Hyde. . .Together Again*, died of heart failure on January 8th, aged 63.

Outspoken writer and feminist **Naomi Mitchison** (Naomi Margaret Haldane) died on January 11th at her home on the Mull of Kintyre in Scotland, aged 101. A member of the Fabian Society and an unsuccessful candidate for Parliament in 1935, she had more than 100 books published, including the historical fantasy *The Corn King and the Spring Queen* (aka *The Barbarians*, 1931), *We Have Been Warned*, *The Big House*, *Travel Light*, *Memoirs of a Spacewoman*, *Solution Three* and *Not by Bread Alone*.

Belfast-born novelist and screenwriter **Brian Moore** died of pulmonary fibrosis after a short illness at his home in Malibu, California, on January 10th, aged 77. Best known for his first novel, *The Lonely Passion of Judith Hearne* (1955), his scripts included Alfred Hitchcock's *Torn Curtain* and the near-future CBS-TV movie *Catholics*.

Science fiction scholar and mystery novelist **Frank McConnell** (Frances DeMay McConnell) died on January 15th of liver failure after a bad fall the month before. He was 59, and his books include *The Time Machine and The War of the Worlds: A Critical Edition* and *The Science Fiction of H.G. Wells*. McConnell was working on a book about Frankenstein at the time of his death.

Robert L. Duncan who, with his wife Wanda, scripted numerous episodes of such 1960s Irwin Allen TV shows as *Lost in Space*, *Land of the Giants* and *Time Tunnel*, died on January 28th, aged 71.

SF critic and writer **Robert "Buck" [Stratton] Coulson** died of internal haemorrhaging on February 19th, aged 70. He had been ill for many years with diabetes, asthma and heart disease. Co-editor (with his wife Juanita) of the Hugo Award-winning SF fanzine *Yandro* (1953–86), he wrote several books, including two *Man from U.N.C.L.E.* novelizations in collaboration with Gene DeWeese under the name "Thomas Stratton".

British author **Pansy Pakenham [Lamb]** died on the same day, aged 94. Her ghost story "The Cook's Room" appeared in *The Evening Standard Second Book of Strange Stories* (1937).

Depressive British playwright **Sarah Kane** apparently committed suicide by hanging herself on February 20th. She was 28. All her acclaimed plays, which include *Blasted*, *Phaedra's Love*, *Cleansed* and *Crave*, are about atrocities and collapsing societies.

American movie critic **Gene Siskel** died the same day from a brain tumour, aged 53.

Prolific pulp writer **Michael [Angelo] Avallone [Jr]**, who made his début in *Weird Tales* in 1953, died of heart failure on February 26th, aged 74. The author of nearly 250 books, he wrote genre fiction under various names, including *The Craghold Legacy* and its sequels (as "Edwina Noone"), *The Vampire Cameo* (as "Dorothea Nile"), *Warlock's Woman* (as "Jean-Anne de Pre") and *The Hoodoo Horror* (as "Stuart Jason"). Among his other novels are *The Voodoo Murders*, *Shoot It Again Sam*, *The Haunted Hall* and *Fallen Angel* plus other titles featuring "Satan Sleuth", including *The Werewolf Walks Tonight*. Avallone also novelized *Shock Corridor* (as "Steve Michaels"), Robert Bloch's

The Night Walker (as "Sidney Stuart"), *One More Time*, *Beneath the Planet of the Apes*, *Carquake*, *Charlie Chan and the Curse of the Dragon Queen*, *Friday the 13th Part 3 3-D*, Boris Karloff's *Tales of the Frightened*, and TV's *The Man from U.N.C.L.E.*, *The Girl from U.N.C.L.E.* and *The Partridge Family* (as "Vance Stanton").

Archie Comics creator/publisher **John L. Goldwater** died of a heart attack at his home in New York City on February 26th, aged 83. In 1954 he helped found the repressive Comics Code Authority and was its president for twenty-five years.

The 19th Lord Dunsany, **Randal Arthur Plunkett**, the only son of the noted fantasy author and poet, died in Ireland in February, aged 92. His 86-year-old wife, The Dowager Lady Dunsany, died at the beginning of August.

Argentinean writer and editor **Adolfo Bioy Casares**, who frequently collaborated with his life-long friend Jorge Luis Borges, died in Buenos Aires on March 8th, aged 84. He wrote a number of "magic realism" stories (often with his wife) and edited *The Book of Fantasy*, first published in 1940.

Lee Falk (Leon Falk), the creator of 1930s comic strip heroes Mandrake the Magician and The Phantom, died of congestive heart failure in New York on March 13th, aged 87. After the Second World War he became a playwright and theatrical producer, directing Dame May Whitty in a production of *Night Must Fall* and Charlton Heston in *Bell, Book and Candle*. Both Mandrake and The Phantom have been widely adapted into movies, serials, TV and other media, and Falk even scripted the stage musical *Mandrake the Magician and the Enchantress*.

Oscar-winning screenwriter and director **Garson Kanin**, whose credits include the Academy Award-nominated *A Double Life*, plus *Adam's Rib*, *Pat and Mike* and *The Girl Can't Help It*, died of heart failure the same day, aged 86. He was married to actress Ruth Gordon (who died in 1985).

Legendary Los Angeles crime reporter **Nieson Himmel** also died on March 13th of pneumonia-related complications, aged 77. He covered the Black Dahlia and Bugsy Siegel murders and during the 1940s briefly roomed with L. Ron Hubbard.

85-year-old comics writer **John Broome**, the creator of 1940s comic strip heroes Green Lantern and The Flash, died of a heart attack in a hotel swimming pool in Thailand while on vacation with his wife Peggy. He also wrote scripts for such DC titles as *The Atomic Knights*, *The Justice League of America*, *Detective Chimp* and *Captain Comet* until his retirement in 1970, and during the 1940s he sold science fiction stories to the pulps.

Horror writer **Ray Russell** died of complications from a series of strokes at a nursing home in Los Angeles on March 15th, aged 74. His 1961 novella "Sardonicus" (filmed by William Castle from a screenplay by the author) was described by Stephen King as "perhaps the finest example of the modern Gothic ever written." Russell was an editor at *Playboy* from 1954–60, and remained a contributing editor at the magazine until the mid-1970s (he anonymously edited the 1960s anthologies, *The Playboy Book of Science Fiction and Fantasy* and *The Playboy Book of Horror and the Supernatural*). His own books include *The Case Against Satan* (1962), *Unholy Trinity: Three Short Novels of Gothic Terror*, *Prince of Darkness*, *Sagittarius*, *Incubus*, *The Book of Hell*, *The Devil's Mirror* and *Absolute Power*, and he scripted the movies *The Premature Burial*, *Zotz!*, *The Man With X-Ray Eyes*, *The Horror of it All* and *Chamber of Horrors*. Russell won the 1991 World Fantasy Award and the 1993 Bram Stoker Award for Life Achievement.

Viennese-American film composer **Ernest Gold** died from complications following a stroke on March 17th, aged 77. His memorable scores include *On the Beach*, *It's a Mad Mad Mad Mad World* and the Academy Award-winning *Exodus*, plus *The Falcon's Alibi*, *Unknown World*, *U.F.O.*, *The Screaming Skull* and *Tarzan's Fight for Life*.

American editor and publisher **James** [Allen] **Turner** died of liver and colon cancer on March 28th, aged 54. From 1973 he was the editor of Arkham House publishers, controversially moving the imprint away from its Lovecraftian horrors and into commercial SF and fantasy publishing. Dismissed by co-owner April Derleth in 1996, who wanted Arkham to return to its more traditional roots, he started his own imprint, Golden Gryphon Books, publishing collections by James Patrick Kelly, R. Garcia y Robertson and Robert Reed, plus a Lovecraft-inspired anthology. Previously-announced collections by Tony Daniel and Neal Barrett, Jr. remained unpublished at the time of Turner's death.

80-year-old British artist **Gerald A. Facey**, who painted the covers for *Tarzan Adventures* and such early Spencer magazines as *Futuristic Science Stories* and *Wonders of the Spaceways*, died during the Spring. 87-year-old TV scriptwriter **Gilbert Ralston**, whose credits include *Star Trek* and *Wild Wild West*, died of congestive heart failure around the same time.

Helen Aberson [Mayer], who wrote the story about a flying elephant that formed the basis of Walt Disney's 1941 cartoon *Dumbo*, died in New York City on April 3rd, aged 91. When the story was published as a Roll-a-Book in 1939 it was co-credited to illustrator Harold Pearl. Although she continued to write children's stories into the 1960s, no other titles were apparently published.

British lyricist and composer **Lionel Bart** (Lionel Begleiter), whose film credits include *From Russia With Love* and *Oliver!*, died of cancer the same day, aged 68. He wrote a musical called *Quasimodo*, and lost all his money and rights on a flop Robin Hood show entitled *Twang!*

Dr Frederick Albert Thorpe OBE, who invented and promoted large-print books, died on April 8th, aged 85.

Jack Schiff, who was managing editor at DC Comics and worked on such titles as *Superman* and *Batman*, died on April 30th, aged 89.

Donald Stewart, who scripted *Deathsport* and *The Hunt for Red October*, also died in April.

Cartoonist and author **Shel Silverstein** (aka "Uncle Selby") died of a heart attack at his home in Florida on May 9th, aged 66. His humorous books for children include *The Giving Tree*, *The Missing Piece*, *Where the Sidewalk Ends*, *A Light in the Attic* and *Falling Up*. His song "A Boy Named Sue" became a hit for Johnny Cash in 1969.

Austrian-born literary agent and former pulp writer **Larry Sternig** died of cancer on May 15th, aged 90. A contributor to such titles as *Thrilling Wonder Stories*, *Planet Stories* and *Fantastic Adventures*, he became a literary agent on the suggestion of Robert Bloch, and his clients included Andre Norton.

Beverly Lewis; 51-year-old vice president and senior editor at Bantam, died on May 24th after collapsing in a Manhattan street. Her authors included Dean Koontz.

Comic book writer **Paul S. Newman**, who worked on such titles as *Star Trek*, *Twilight Zone* and the *Space Cadets* newspaper strip, died of a heart attack on May 30th, aged 75.

Fashion photographer **David Seidner**, who wrote *Eiko and Coppola on Dracula*, died of AIDS in Miami Beach on June 6th, aged 42.

Christina Foyle, who began working in her father's London bookshop and never left, died on June 8th, aged 88. The store, which was started in 1904, grew to thirty miles of shelves under her management. Miss Foyle, as she liked to be called, was famous for her Literary Luncheons, whose guests included Kingsley Amis, D.H. Lawrence, J.B. Priestley, George Bernard Shaw, H.G. Wells and James Herbert. She was worth £59 million. Her thirteen cats went to her former housekeeper and she left her handyman £100,000 in her will, with the proviso that he look after her pet dog Bobby and six tortoises.

Marie [Antoinette] **Landis**, who collaborated with her long-lost second cousin Brian Herbert (son of Frank Herbert) on five short stories and the novels *Memorymakers* and *Blood on the Sun*, died of cancer on June 19th, aged 78.

Film historian and special effects illustrator **George E. Turner** died on June 20th, aged 73. A former editor of *American Cinematographer* magazine, he co-wrote *The Making of King Kong* with Dr Orville Goldner, *Human Monsters (The Bizarre Psychology of Movie Villains)* and three volumes of *The Forgotten Horrors* with Michael Price, plus *The Cinema of Adventure, Romance and Terror*. His film credits include *Creature* and *The Shape of Things to Come*.

73-year-old rare bookdealer **John D. Roles** was strangled to death in his Liverpool home on June 24th. Although the house was set on fire by his killer, fireman managed to save most of his stock of 40,000 volumes. Social worker and book and postcard collector Andrew John Swift was subsequently charged with the crime. During the 1950s Roles was the first editor of the SF magazine *Morph*, and he was a member of the Liverpool Science Fiction Society.

Blacklisted Hollywood screenwriter **Frank Tarloff** died of lung cancer on June 25th, aged 83. He wrote *School for Scoundrels*, *Father Goose*, *The Double Man* and *The Secret War of Harry Frigg*, amongst other movies.

Scottish author and publisher **Chris** (Joseph Christopher) **Boyce** died of a heart attack on June 29th, aged 55. His prizewinning SF novel *Catchworld* was published in 1975 as co-winner of the Gollancz/*Sunday Times* SF Novel Award, and in 1990 he founded publishers Dog and Bone Press with his wife Angela Mullane and Alasdair Gray.

He's sleeping with the fishes now. Best known for his 1969 bestseller about the Mafia, *The Godfather*, novelist and Oscar-winning screenwriter **Mario Puzo** died from apparent heart failure on July 2nd, aged 78. Along with the 1972 adaptation of his novel and its two sequels, he also contributed to the scripts of *Earthquake*, *Superman* (1978) and *Superman II*.

Screenwriter **Ronny Graham**, whose credits include Mel Brooks' *History of the World Part 1* and *Spaceballs*, died on July 4th, aged 79.

John F. Kennedy Jr., publisher of *George* magazine and the son of the assassinated American president, was killed along with his wife Carolyn and her sister Lauren Bessette when the light plane he was piloting crashed into the sea off Martha's Vineyard on July 16th. He was aged 38 and worth an estimated fortune of $200 million.

Fanzine editor **George "Lan" Laskowski**, who twice won the Hugo Award for *Lan's Lantern*, died after a long battle with pancreatic cancer on July 20th, aged 50.

American editor, publisher and bookseller **William Targ** died after a long illness on July 22nd, aged 92. In 1942 he joined World Publishing, where he issued *Best Supernatural Stories of H.P. Lovecraft* (1945) and several first editions of Raymond Chandler. Later, as editor-in-chief at Putnam, he bought Mario Puzo's *The Godfather*. In his 1975 autobiography *Indecent Pleasures* he noted: "The trouble with the publishing business is that too many people who have half a mind to write a book do so."

Michael Ressner, who created the *Rocky Jones, Space Ranger* TV and comic book series, died on August 4th.

A day after suffering a severe stroke, 71-year-old Irish fan and SF author **James White** died on August 23rd without regaining consciousness. He had lived with diabetes for more than fifty years. He began his fiction career in *New Worlds* in 1953 and is best known for his "Sector General" novels set on a xenobiological space hospital. These include such titles as *Hospital Station*, *Star Surgeon*, *Ambulance Ship* and *Star Healer*.

Author and screenwriter **David Karp** died of emphysema on

September 11th, aged 77. His novel *One* (aka *Escape to No-where*) was SF and he scripted the TV movies *The Brotherhood of the Bell* and *Merlin and the Sword*.

89-year-old Australian-born screenwriter **Ivan Goff**, who usually worked in collaboration with Ben Roberts, died on September 23rd. His credits include the 1957 biopic of Lon Chaney, Sr., *Man of a Thousand Faces*, and the TV series *Charlie's Angels* and *Time Express* (starring Vincent Price).

Fantasy author and creator of the popular "Darkover" series **Marion [Eleanor] Zimmer Bradley** died on September 25th, three days after suffering a major heart attack from which she never regained consciousness. She was 69. Bradley began publishing professionally in 1953, and her books include the 1983 Arthurian bestseller *The Mists of Avalon* (which has never been out of print) and the *Sword and Sorceress* anthology series. She also created her own eponymous fiction magazine in 1988. The "Darkover" series, a mixture of fantasy and SF, started in 1958 and now includes more than a dozen novels, collections and anthologies. Bradley was cremated, with her ashes to be scattered on Glastonbury Tor in England.

Swedish science fiction author and the father of Swedish fandom, **Sture L'nnerstrand** died on September 30th, aged 80.

65-year-old **Judith Exner** (Judith Katherine Inmoor) who claimed to be a former mistress of American President John F. Kennedy and, simultaneously, Chicago Mafia boss Sam Giancana, died in September. She married actor William Campbell in 1952, but following her divorce two years later she also had affairs with singer Frank Sinatra and Giancana's henchman Johnny Rosselli. In 1975 she was subpoenaed to testify before a Senate committee investigating the CIA's involvement in a plot to overthrow Fidel Castro.

Chicago-born scriptwriter **Stuart E. McGowan**, aged 95, who wrote more than fifty Westerns plus *Jeepers Creepers* (1939) and *Valley of the Zombies*, also died in September. He directed numerous episodes of the 1953–54 Saturday morning TV series *Sky King*.

Bestselling Australian author **Morris L. West**, whose novels include *The Shoes of the Fisherman* (filmed in 1968), *The Devil's Advocate* and *Children of the Sun*, died while in the middle of a sentence, at his desk in Sydney on October 9th, aged 83.

British author, publisher and editor **John** [Charles Heywood] **Hadfield**, whose many anthologies included *A Chamber of Horrors* (1965), died on October 10th, aged 92.

Charles D. (Derwin) **Hornig**, who took over the editorship of Hugo Gernsback's SF pulp *Wonder Stories* in 1933 at the age of 17, died of the effects of heart disease on October 11th, aged 83. He later edited *Science Fiction*, *Future Fiction* and *Science Fiction Quarterly*. A life-long pacifist, he was imprisoned by his own country during the Second World War.

64-year-old British SF artist **Eddie** (Edward John) **Jones** died in hospital during a blood transfusion on October 15th, several weeks after suffering a stroke. A popular and prolific artist from the mid-1950s until the early 1980s, his first book cover was for Badger Books in 1959. In Germany, Jones produced the covers for around 850 issues of *Terra Astra* magazine and in recent years he painted military figures for a model shop in Liverpool. With no known relatives or funds to cover the funeral expenses, they were payed for by his German agent.

American songwriter **Hamilton Gilkyson**, who wrote the classic "Memories Are Made of This", died the same day, aged 83. He also worked on Disney's *The Jungle Book* ("The Bare Necessities") and *The Aristocats*.

79-year-old Irish fan writer **Walt** (Walter Alexander) **Willis** died of a heart attack on October 20th after spending more than a year in hospital. He produced the fanzines *Slant* (1948–53) with James White, the Hugo-nominated *Hyphen* (1952–65) with Chuck Harris and others, and *The Enchanted Duplicator* (1954) with Bob Shaw. Most of his writing was collected by Richard Bergeron in the 614-page hardcover *Warhoon 28*, and Willis was Fan Guest of Honour at MagiCon, the 1992 World Science Fiction Convention.

Screenwriter **William Goodhart**, whose credits included *Exorcist II The Heretic*, died of heart disease the same day, aged 74.

Composer **Frank DeVol** died on October 27th, aged 88. His fourty-seven film scores include *What Ever Happened to Baby Jane?*, *Hush. . .Hush Sweet Charlotte*, *Cat Ballou*, *The Dirty Dozen*, *Doc Savage* and *Pillow Talk*. On radio he was a musical director for Rudy Vallee and others, and he also created the theme song for TV's *The Brady Bunch*.

American mystery novelist and editor **Howard V. Browne** died on October 28th, aged 91. During the 1940s he was associate editor of the SF pulp magazines *Amazing Stories* and *Fantastic Adventures* and edited the mystery magazine *Mammoth Detective* from 1942–47. He launched the digest magazine *Fantastic* in 1952 before moving on to Hollywood, where he wrote scripts for TV and movies.

Novelist and screenwriter (*Bunny Lake is Missing*) **Penelope Mortimer** also died in October, as did 71-year-old British SF author **Geoffrey John Barrett**, who wrote twenty-four novels (also published under the pseudonyms "Edward Leighton", "Dennis Summers" and "James Wallace") for Robert Hale between 1973–78.

Former literary agent **Clarissa Luard**, who was once married to author Salman Rushdie, died of cancer on November 4th, aged 50. While working at A.P. Watt she agented several SF authors and more recently was responsible as Senior Literature Officer for the Arts Council's dealings with *Interzone*.

Crime and thriller novelist **George V. Higgins**, whose books include his début novel *The Friends of Eddie Coyle* (filmed in 1973), died on November 6th, aged 59.

Expatriate American author **Paul [Frederick] Bowles** died of a heart attack in Tangiers, Morocco, on November 18th, aged 88. Influenced by Edgar Allan Poe and *Doctor Dolittle* author Hugh Lofting, Bowles is best known for his 1947 existentialist novel *The Sheltering Sky* (filmed by Bernardo Bertolucci in 1990), while his collection of horror stories, *The Delicate Prey*, appeared in 1951. His friends included Jean Cocteau, Ezra Pound, Truman Capote, William Burroughs, Gertrude Stein, Alice B. Toklas, Jack Kerouac and other literary figures. Bowles also composed scores for theatrical productions by Joseph Losey, Orson Welles (*Doctor Faustus*) and Tennessee Williams, and he wrote the music for several films, including *Cyrano de Bergerac* (1950). His omnibus of prose and photographs, *Too Far from Home*, was published in 1995.

TV writer **Andrew Russell** died the same day, aged 84. His credits include *The Honeymooners*, *The Phil Silvers Show*, *Art Carney Meets Peter and the Wolf*, and such movies as *Stiletto* and *The Borgia Stick*.

Anthology editor and former president of First Fandom and the New York Science Fiction Society ("The Lunarians"), **Art** (Arthur

William) **Saha** died of cancer on November 19th, aged 76. He had first been diagnosed with the disease in 1972 and donated his body to medical science. With Donald Wollheim he co-edited *The World's Best SF* series (1972–90) and took over editing *The Year's Best Fantasy Stories* from Lin Carter (1981–88), both for DAW Books. He is also credited with coining the term "Trekkies" in an early 1970s issue of *TV Guide*.

Novelist and screenwriter **Joseph DiMona**, whose credits include the 1964 fantasy *The Incredible Mr. Limpet*, also died of cancer in November.

80-year-old Czechoslovakian author and astronomical artist **Ludek Pesek** died of a heart attack in Zurich, Switzerland, on December 4th.

Japanese composer **Masaru Sato** died on December 5th, aged 71. His more than 300 movie scores include *Gigantis the Fire Monster*, *Half Human*, *The H-Man*, *Lost World of Sinbad*, *Ebirah Horror of the Deep*, *Son of Godzilla*, *Tidal Wave*, *Godzilla vs. the Bionic Monster*, *Throne of Blood*, *Yojimbo* and *Sanjuro*.

Former Pocket Books SF editor and agent **Adele Leone** died from the effects of auto-immune disease scleroderma on December 7th, aged 48.

British publisher **Sir Rupert Hart-Davis**, whose eponymous imprint published many books by Ray Bradbury and E.C. Tubb during the 1950s and '60s, died on December 8th, aged 92.

American author **Joseph Heller**, whose 1961 début novel *Catch-22* (filmed in 1970) sold more than ten million copies in the US alone, died of a heart attack on December 12th, aged 76. He wrote five other novels plus the screenplays for *Sex and the Single Girl*, *Casino Royale* and *Dirty Dingus Magee*.

British historical novelist **Mary Brown**, whose fantasy books include *The Unlikely Ones* (1986), *Pigs Don't Fly*, *Master of Many Treasures*, *Strange Deliverance* and *Dragonne's Eg*, died in Spain on December 20th, aged 70.

Composer and songwriter **Curtis Mayfield** died in Atlanta on December 26th, aged 57. He had been left paralyzed from a stage accident in 1990. Best known for such hits as "People Get Ready", "Talking About My Baby" and "Keep on Pushing", he also produced the score for *Superfly* (1972), which he reworked with rap music eighteen years later for *The Return of Superfly*.

49-year-old author and screenwriter **Michael** [McEachern] **McDowell** died of AIDS-related complications on December 27th in Boston. He entered the horror field in the late 1970s with a string of superior novels, including *The Amulet, Cold Moon Over Babylon, The Elementals, Toplin* and the six-part *Blackwater* series. Under the pseudonym "Nathan Aldyne", he teamed up with Dennis Schuetz to write four gay detective novels, and as "Axel Young" the pair wrote the dark fantasies *Blood Rubies* and *Wicked Stepmother*. Following scripts for such TV series as *Tales from the Darkside, Amazing Stories* and *Monsters*, he wrote the movies *Beetle Juice* (with Warren Skaaren), *High Spirits, Tales from the Darkside The Movie, The Nightmare Before Christmas* and *Thinner*. After being diagnosed with the disease in 1994, McDowell began teaching screenwriting at Boston University and Tufts University. He was working on a *Beetle Juice* sequel and a new version of *The Nutcracker* at the time of his death.

American author and screenwriter **David Duncan** died the same day, aged 86. His thirteen novels included such SF and fantasy titles as *The Shade of Time* (1946), *Dark Dominion, Beyond Eden, Occam's Razor* and *The Madrone Tree*, and he scripted *The Leech Woman* and George Pal's 1960 film version of *The Time Machine*.

ACTORS/ACTRESSES

Veteran Native American character actor **Iron Eyes Cody**, whose first name was either Oscar or Oakie, died on January 4th. He was aged around 94, and he appeared in wild west shows and circuses before making his film début in 1919 as an extra. His credits include such classic serials as *The Return of Chandu* (with Bela Lugosi), *Hawk of the Wilderness* and *Perils of Nyoka*, along with *Riders of the Whistling Skull, Monster in the Closet* and numerous other movies. In the 1970s he was known for the Keep America Beautiful anti-littering campaign.

89-year-old British-born actor/TV director **Robert Douglas** (Robert Douglas Finlayson), whose credits include *Adventures of Don Juan, Mystery Submarine, The Questor Tapes, Alfred Hitchcock Presents, One Step Beyond, Thriller, The Invisible Man, Twilight Zone, Lost in Space, The Invaders* and the 1959 movie *Tarzan the Ape Man*, died on January 11th.

Actress and voice artist **Betty Lou Gerson** died of a massive stroke on January 12th, aged 84. She appeared in *The Fly* (1958) with Vincent Price and contributed characterizations to Disney's *Cinderella* (1949), *Mary Poppins* and *One Hundred & One Dalmatians* (1961, as the evil Cruella de Vil).

British character actor **Robin Bailey** died on January 14th, aged 79. Best known for the TV series *I Didn't Know You Cared* and *Sorry I'm a Stranger Here Myself*, he appeared in such films as *Blind Terror* and *Screamtime*.

The 7 foot 4 inch actor **John Bloom**, who played the cut-price Frankenstein Monster in Al Adamson's *Dracula vs. Frankenstein* (1970), died of heart failure on January 15th, aged 54. His other credits include *The Incredible 2-Headed Transplant*, *Brain of Blood*, *The Dark*, *The Hills Have Eyes Part II*, *Harry and the Hendersons* and *Star Trek VI The Undiscovered Country*.

American actress and author **Susan Strasberg**, the daughter of drama teacher Lee Strasberg (who died in 1982), died of breast cancer in New York on January 21st, aged 61. She appeared in Hammer's *Taste of Fear* (with Christopher Lee), AIP's *The Trip* and *Psych-Out*, *Hauser's Memory*, *Psycho Sisters*, *The Legend of Hillbilly John* (based on stories by Manly Wade Wellman), *Frankenstein* (1973), the 1977 adaptation of Graham Masterton's *The Manitou*, *Bloody Birthday*, *Sweet Sixteen*, *Hollywood Ghost Stories* and *The Returning*. She was briefly married in 1965 to actor Christopher Jones.

Former child star and Our Gang member, actress **Jonni Paris**, died of cancer on January 26th, aged 66.

The dumbest member of the Dead End Kids, East Side Kids and Bowery Boys, 78-year-old **Huntz Hall** (Henry Hall), died of heart failure on January 30th. Along with Leo Gorcey and the rest of the gang he appeared in *Dead End* (1937), *Angels with Dirty Faces*, *Junior G-Men*, *Spooks Run Wild* (with Bela Lugosi), *Sea Raiders*, *Junior G-Men of the Air*, *Ghosts on the Loose* (again with Lugosi), *Spook Busters*, *Mr. Hex*, *Master Minds* (with Glenn Strange), *Ghost Chasers*, *The Bowery Boys Meet the Monsters*, *Bowery to Bagdad*, *Hold That Hypnotist*, *Spook Chasers* and *Up in Smoke*. His other film credits include *The Return of Dr X*, *Wonder Man*, *Cyclone*, *Auntie Lee's Meat Pies* and Disney's *Herbie Rides Again*. Hall, who credited Shemp Howard with teaching him comedy, was sent to trial for possessing marijuana in 1948 and arrested for drunkenness and disturbing the peace on several occasions during the 1950s.

Radio announcer **Ed Herlihy**, whose film credits include *Zelig*, *King of Comedy*, *Pee Wee's Big Adventure* and *Who Framed Roger Rabbit?*, died the same day, aged 89.

Stripper **Lili St. Cyr**, who appeared in such 1950s burlesque films as *Varietease* and *Striporama* alongside Bettie/Betty Page, also died in January.

Overweight American character actress **Shirley Stoler**, who portrayed homicidal nurse Martha Beck in *The Honeymoon Killers* (1970), died of heart failure on February 17th, aged 70. Her other credits include *The Deer Hunter*, *The Attic* and *Frankenhooker*. There is apparently a possibility that Stoler may also have been known as "Shirley Kilpatrick", the star of *The Astounding She-Monster* (1958).

British TV comedians **Robin Nedwell**, whose co-starred in various *Doctor. . .* series, and **Derek Nimmo**, who appeared in *The Liquidator*, *Casino Royale* and *One of Our Dinosaurs is Missing*, also died in late February.

59-year-old British pop singer **Dusty Springfield** (Mary Isobel Catherine Bernadette O'Brien) died of breast cancer on March 2nd, the day she should have collected her OBE from the Queen. Her version of Burt Bacharach's wonderful "Look of Love" is in the James Bond spoof *Casino Royale*, and "Son of a Preacher Man" turned up in *Pulp Fiction*. A gay icon in later years, she was inducted into the Rock and Roll Hall of Fame in New York two weeks after her death.

1950s American leading man **Lee Philips** died on March 3rd from a parkinson's-like illness, aged 72. He appeared in such shows as *The Twilight Zone* and *Alfred Hitchcock Presents* before becoming a TV director with *The Stranger Within*, *The Spell* and such series as *Kung Fu*, *The Ghost and Mrs. Muir* and *Space*.

Del Close, who was the resident director of Chicago's Second City improv comedy group from 1973–82, died of emphysema and related health problems on March 4th, aged 64. As a theatrical director and teacher he worked with John Belushi, Gilda Radner, Bill Murray, John Candy, Chris Farley, Dennis Miller, Harold Ramis and many others. He appeared in such films as *Beware: The Blob* and the 1988 remake of *The Blob*, and co-scripted with John Ostrander the DC Comics horror anthology *Wasteland* (1987–89). A life-long fan of fantastic and macabre literature, his last request was for his skull to be cleaned and then bequeathed to Chicago's Goodman Theater, where it will be used for the part of Yorick in future performances of *Hamlet*.

American actor and Broadway musical star **Richard Kiley** died on March 5th, aged 76. His credits include *The Little Prince* and *Phenomenon* (1996) plus, on TV, the 1969 *Night Gallery* pilot, *Angel on My Shoulder* (as the Devil), *The Bad Seed*, *Tales of Tomorrow*, *Alfred Hitchcock Presents*, *Alfred Hitchcock Hour*, *Suspense*, *The New People*, *The Twilight Zone* and *Ray Bradbury Theater*. His voice was also heard in *Howard the Duck* and *Jurassic Park*.

Character actor **Graham Armitage**, whose credits include *The Devils*, *The Private Life of Sherlock Holmes*, *The Boy Friend* and TV's *The Avengers*, *The Saint* and *Doctor Who*, died on March 6th, aged 63. He played Sherlock Holmes for five years on radio in South Africa.

Often cast as a Soviet villain, German-born character actor **Stefan Schnabel** died on March 11th, aged 87. He appeared in *Journey Into Fear* (1942) *The 27th Day*, *Blood Bath* (1975), *Firefox*, *Dracula's Widow* (as Van Helsing) and TV's *Lights Out*, *Inner Sanctum*, *Captain Video* and *Alfred Hitchcock Presents*. His other credits include *The Passion of Dracula* on stage and *War of the Worlds* on radio.

The first actor to portray Superman on screen, former dancer **Kirk Alyn** (John Feggo, Jr.), died of Alzheimer's disease in a Texas hospital on March 14th, aged 88. He played the Man of Steel in the eponymous 1948 serial and its 1950 sequel, *Atom Man vs. Superman*, before turning up uncredited as Lois Lane's father in the 1978 version. "Playing Superman ruined my career and I'm bitter about the whole thing," the actor later remarked. "I couldn't get another job in Hollywood." His other credits include *A Guy Named Joe*, *The Time of Their Lives*, *The Three Musketeers* (1948), *When Worlds Collide*, *Scalps* and the serials *Daughter of Don Q*, *Radar Patrol vs. Spy King*, *Federal Agents vs. Underworld Inc.* and *Blackhawk*.

63-year-old British entertainer **Rod Hull**, best known for his act with his aggressive puppet Emu, died after falling off the roof of his home while adjusting a TV aerial on March 18th. A spokesperson from The Royal Society for the Prevention of Accidents said "This is a tragic reminder to us all of the dangers of doing home repairs."

73-year-old British TV comedian **Ernie Wise** (Ernest Wiseman) died on March 21st, following triple heart bypass surgery. Along with his partner Eric Morecambe (who died in 1984), he starred in the 1983 old dark house TV movie *Night Train to Murder* and they will no doubt still be turning up in endless re-runs of their popular variety show on BBC-TV well into the twenty-first century.

29-year-old TV actor **David Strickland**, one of the stars of the American TV sitcom *Suddenly Susan*, was found hanged in a Las Vegas motel room on March 22nd. His final film, *Forces of Nature*, had opened in the number one slot at the US box office only days before.

Australian-born stuntman/bit player/stunt arranger **Gil** (Gilbert) **Perkins** who, along with Eddie Parker, stunt doubled a frail Bela Lugosi as the Frankenstein monster in *Frankenstein Meets the Wolf Man*, died on March 28th, aged 91. The swimming champion's numerous other credits include *The Most Dangerous Game*, *King Kong* (1933), *The Invisible Man*, *She* (1935), *Whistling in the Dark*, *The Adventures of Robin Hood*, *Dr. Jekyll and Mr. Hyde* (1941), *Spy Smasher*, *G-Men vs. the Black Dragons*, *Captain America* (1944), *The Black Widow*, *Abbott and Costello Meet Dr. Jekyll and Mr. Hyde*, *Teenage Monster*, *Valley of the Dragons* and *Batman* (1966). In 1960 he co-founded the Stuntmen's Association of Motion Pictures.

Singing cowboy **Eddie Dean** (Edgar D. Glossup) who starred in a number of "B" Westerns in the 1940s and '50s, also died in March, aged 92.

Sultry Hollywood leading lady **Faith Domergue**, a protégée of Howard Hughes, who starred in *This Island Earth*, *It Came from Beneath the Sea*, *Cult of the Cobra*, *The Atomic Man*, *Voyage to the Prehistoric Planet*, *Legacy of Blood*, *The House of Seven Corpses* and *Psycho Sisters*, died of cancer on April 4th, aged 74.

Dependable British actor **Bob Peck**, best known for his role as game warden Robert Muldoon in *Jurassic Park*, also died of cancer the same day, aged 53. His other credits include the 1990 remake of *Lord of the Flies*, *Slipstream*, *Fairytale: A True Story* and the 1986 TV mini-series *Edge of Darkness*.

Stella Zucco, the widow of veteran horror star George Zucco (who died in 1960), died on April 5th, aged 99.

Former radio actress and voice artist **Jean Vander Pyl,** whose most famous creation was Wilma Flintstone in the long-running Hanna-Barbera series *The Flintstones,* died of lung cancer on April 10th, aged 79. She also worked on such other cartoon TV series as *Quick Draw McGraw, Huckleberry Hound, Top Cat* and *Yogi Bear,* plus the features *A Man Called Flintstone* and *Jetsons The Movie.* In 1995 she told an interviewer that she was paid $250 an episode for *The Flintstones* and, when the series ended in 1966, she quickly agreed to accept $15,000 in lieu of residual payments from syndication. Today it is estimated that not a minute goes by in which the show is not being watched somewhere in the world.

British actor, director, composer, singer and former child star **Anthony [George] Newley** died of cancer in Florida on April 14th, aged 67. He appeared in *Vice Versa* (1947), *Oliver Twist,* Hammer's *X The Unknown, Dr. Dolittle* and *Can Hieronymous Merkin Ever Forget Mercy Humpe and Find True Happiness?,* while as a lyricist he contributed to *Goldfinger, Willy Wonka & the Chocolate Factory* and *Vampira.* As a pop singer Newley appeared in the British charts seven times, including two number ones. He lost his virginity to Diana Dors, allegedly had an affair with Barbara Steisand, and one of his three ex-wives was actress Joan Collins. Douglas E. Winter was a big fan.

TV's Grandma Walton, American character actress **Ellen Corby** (Ellen Hansen), died the same day after a long illness, aged 87. Her many credits include *The Spiral Staircase* (1946), *It's a Wonderful Life, The Fabulous Joe, Mighty Joe Young* (1949), *Angels in the Outfield* (1951), *The Bowery Boys Meet the Monsters,* Hitchcock's *Vertigo, Macabre, Visit to a Small Planet, The Strangler, Hush. . .Hush Sweet Charlotte, The Ghost and Mr. Chicken, The Gnome-Mobile, The Legend of Lylah Claire* and the pilot for TV's *The Invaders.*

Spanish-born ventriloquist **Señor Wences** (Wenceslao Moreno), whose act with Pedro the head in a box and Johnny the squeaky-voiced hand puppet was a huge hit on TV's *Ed Sullivan Show* in the 1950s and '60s, died on April 20th, aged 103. With his catchphrases "S'ok" and "S'alright", Wences also toured with

Dean Martin and Jerry Lewis, appeared in a Broadway show with Danny Kaye and apparently played every casino in Las Vegas.

American band leader, singer and leading man of the 1920s and '30s **Charles "Buddy" Rogers**, died on April 21st, aged 94. He appeared in *Wings* (1927), *Paramount on Parade* and *The Mexican Spitfire Sees a Ghost*, amongst many other movies, and was married to silent screen star Mary Pickford (who died in 1979).

British childrens' radio presenter **Eileen Browne** (Eileen Mitchell), who for nearly fifteen years began each episode of the BBC's *Listen With Mother* with the words "Are you sitting comfortably? Then I'll begin," died after a long battle against cancer in April, aged 76. During the 1950s she was also the voice of Jenny on BBC-TV's *The Woodentops*.

Bushy-eyebrowed character actor **Bert Remsen** died on April 22nd, aged 74. His credits include *Moon Pilot, Dead Ringer, Brewster McCloud, Tarantulas the Deadly Cargo, Space, TerrorVision, Sundown the Vampire in Retreat, Dick Tracy* (1990), *Peacemaker, Evil Spirits, Independence Day*, plus numerous TV appearances. He received the Purple Heart for wounds received in Okinawa during the Second World War.

Popular BBC-TV presenter **Jill Dando** was murdered on her doorstep in London's Fulham on April 26th by a single shot to the head. She was 37. Thirteen months afterwards, police charged an unemployed musician with her murder.

American leading man **Rory Calhoun** (Francis Timothy Durgin) died from complications of emphysema and diabetes on April 28th, aged 76. Although his finest moment was probably *Motel Hell*, his other movies include *The Red House, The Colossus of Rhodes, Night of the Lepus, Angel, Avenging Angel, Hell Comes to Frogtown* and *Roller Blade Warriors Taken By Force*. In the late 1950s he produced and starred in *The Texan* TV series. In 1969 he was divorced by his long-time wife Lita Baron, who claimed that he had affairs with seventy-nine women (including Betty Grable and Lana Turner).

37-year-old **Zoe Tamerlis** (Zoe Tamerlund) died of heart failure in Paris in April. She starred as a mute homicidal nun in Abel Ferrera's *Ms.45* and also scripted and appeared in Ferrara's *Bad Lieutenant*.

Hellraising British leading man **Oliver Reed**, the nephew of director Sir Carol Reed, died of a heart attack while drinking with his wife Josephine and a group of friends in Malta on May 2nd. He was 61. Reed began his film career at Hammer and was later cast as unruly rebels, subsequently living out his life as one. He was reputedly fired from the set of *Cutthroat Island* for flashing star Geena Davis. His many credits include *The Curse of the Werewolf*, *The Two Faces of Dr. Jekyll*, *The Damned*, *Captain Clegg*, *Paranoiac*, *The Shuttered Room*, *The Devils*, *Z.P.G.*, *Blue Blood*, *And Then There Were None*, *Tommy*, *Burnt Offerings*, *Condorman*, *The Brood*, *Dr. Heckyl & Mr. Hype*, *Two of a Kind* (as the Devil), *Spasms*, *Gor*, *The House of Usher* (1989), *The Adventures of Baron Munchausen*, *The Pit and the Pendulum* (1991), *Severed Ties* and *Funny Bones*. The actor's head was digitally composited on to a body double to complete his role in Ridley Scott's *The Gladiator*.

British children's TV presenter **Johnny Morris**, who for years supplied the irritating voices of the animals in the *Animal Magic* series, died on May 6th, aged 82. The BBC dropped the show in 1983 after twenty-one years, and at the time of his death Morris was about to make a comeback in a similar series for ITV.

British leading man and novelist **Sir Dirk Bogarde** (Derek Julius Gaspard Ulric Niven Van Den Bogaerde) died of a heart attack on May 8th, aged 78. Best remembered for his light comedies in the 1950s and '60s (notably Rank's *Doctor* series), he also appeared in *Victim*, *The Mind Benders*, *The Servant*, *Modesty Blaise*, *Our Mother's House*, *Oh What a Lovely War*, *Death in Venice*, *The Night Porter*, *Providence* and *The Vision*. He played author Roald Dahl in the 1981 TV movie *The Patricia Neal Story: An Act of Love*. Bogarde, who was knighted in 1992, wrote seven volumes of autobiography and celebrated selling a million books in 1996.

67-year-old voice actor **Edmund Gilbert** also died the same day of lung cancer. His numerous credits include *The Jetsons*, *Captain Planet and the Planeteers*, *The Toxic Crusaders*, *The Tick*, *Freakazoid!*, *Batman Mask of the Phantasm* and *The Pagemaster*.

34-year-old former child actress **Dana Plato**, co-star of the 1980s NBC-TV series *Diff'rent Strokes*, was found dead from an apparent drug overdose on May 8th in her Oklahoma motor home, the day after appearing on Howard Stern's radio show. She had small parts in *Beyond the Bermuda Triangle*, *Exorcist II*

The Heretic and *Return to Boggy Creek* before playing Kimberly on *Diff'rent Strokes* (from which she was fired in 1984 for being pregnant). She subsequently posed nude for *Playboy* in 1989, was found guilty of the armed robbery of a Las Vegas video store in 1991, went to jail for a month the following year after forging prescriptions for nearly 1,000 Valium tablets, appeared in the violent CD-ROM *Night Trap* in 1993 and had breast implants before playing a lesbian in the softcore *Different Strokes* (1996).

American character actor **Albert Popwell**, who appeared in *Dirty Harry* and all four sequels, died while undergoing open heart surgery on May 9th, aged 72. His other credits include the two *Cleopatra Jones* movies, *Probe*, *Scissors* and numerous TV shows.

Veteran American character actor **Henry Jones**, aged 86, died on May 17th from injuries suffered in a fall. Often cast as meek victims or scheming villains, he appeared in *The Bad Seed* (1956), *The Girl Can't Help It*, Hitchcock's *Vertigo*, *Project X*, *Deathtrap*, *Arachnophobia* and *Dick Tracy* (1990), as well as numerous TV shows.

British character actor **Norman Rossington** died of cancer on May 21st, aged 70. He appeared in more than forty films, including three *Carry On* movies, *A Night to Remember*, *Lawrence of Arabia*, *Saturday Night and Sunday Morning*, *A Hard Day's Night* (with the Beatles), *Double Trouble* (with Elvis Presley), *Deathline* (with Christopher Lee) and *Go For a Take*. On TV he was in *I Claudius* and played the gravedigger in a production of *Hamlet* starring Richard Chamberlain. More recently, Rossington was featured in the London stage production of Disney's *Beauty and the Beast*.

Viennese-born American actress **Vanessa Brown** (Smylla Brind), who originated the role on Broadway that Marilyn Monroe played in the film version of *The Seven Year Itch*, died of cancer the same day, aged 71. Her film credits include *Youth Runs Wild* (as Tessa Brind), *Tarzan and the Slave Girl* (as Jane), *The Ghost and Mrs. Muir* and *The Witch Who Came from the Sea*. She apparently had an I.Q. of 165 and in later years turned to politics and writing.

34-year-old Canadian WWF wrestler **Owen Hart** (aka the masked "Blue Blazer"), the brother of Bret "The Hitman" Hart, was killed in Kansas City on May 24th after he fell ninety feet into the ring when a stunt went wrong. He was reportedly planning to give up the sport the following year.

American leading lady of the 1940s **Hillary Brooke** (Beatrice Peterson) died on May 25th, aged 84. She appeared in *Dr. Jekyll and Mr. Hyde* (1941), *Sherlock Holmes and the Voice of Terror, Jane Eyre* (1943), *Sherlock Holmes Faces Death, Ministry of Fear, The Enchanted Cottage, Crime Doctor's Courage, The Woman in Green, Road to Utopia, Strange Impersonation, Let's Live Again, Africa Screams, The Lost Continent* (1951), *Abbott and Costello Meet Captain Kidd, The Maze, Invaders from Mars* (1953) and *The Man Who Knew Too Much* (1956). On TV she was a regular on *The Abbott and Costello Show* (1953–54).

German character actor **Horst Frank**, who starred as mad genius Dr Ood in *The Head* (1959), died of heart failure on May 25th, aged 69. He also appeared in *The Vengeance of Fu Manchu* and *Albino* (both with Christopher Lee), Dario Argento's *The Cat O'Nine Tails* and *The Elixirs of the Devil*.

Spanish-born Mexican wrestler **Fernando Osés** died of a heart attack in May, aged 77. He appeared in numerous *Santo* and *Blue Demon* movies, several of which he also scripted.

1950s radio ventriloquist **Peter Brough**, the voice of dummy Archie Andrews on the BBC's *Educating Archie*, died on June 3rd, aged 83. The show often attracted an audience of more than fifteen million listeners and Julie Andrews regularly featured as Archie's girlfriend. When the show failed on TV in 1956, Brough returned to running the family's clothing business.

Following the stroke he suffered in 1996, 73-year-old American singer and songwriter **Mel Tormé** died on June 5th after falling into a coma. Best known for such ballads as "The Christmas Song" (aka "Chestnuts Roasting on an Open Fire"), Tormé appeared in several films (including the 1944 *Ghost Catchers*), was married in the 1960s to actress Janette Scott, and his son Tracy created the TV series *Sliders*.

He's dead, Jim. 79-year-old American character actor **DeForest Kelley**, *Star Trek*'s Dr Leonard "Bones" McCoy, died of stomach cancer on June 11th in the Motion Picture and Television Fund Hospital in Los Angeles. His other credits include *Fear in the Night* (1947) and the infamous *Night of the Lepus*. He retired from acting in 1991.

British-born character actor **Douglas Seale** died in a New York hospital on June 13th, aged 85. He portrayed Santa Claus in *Ernest Saves Christmas* and also appeared in *Ghostbusters II*, *Almost an Angel* and *Mr. Destiny*, and voiced the Sultan in Disney's *Aladdin*.

Eccentric British pop singer and founder and leader of the Official Monster Raving Loony Party, **Screaming Lord Sutch** (David Sutch), was found hanged on June 16th. Aged 58, he had been suffering from long-term depression and had apparently been upset that his party could not afford to field any candidates in recent Euro elections. His minor hits include "She's Fallen in Love With a Monster Man", "Jack the Ripper", "Murder in the Graveyard", a cover of "Flying Purple People Eater", "Dracula's Daughter" and "Monster in Black Tights". He held the records for being the country's longest-serving political leader and the candidate who stood the most times in parliamentary elections.

American child actor **Bobs Watson**, whose credits include *On Borrowed Time* (as the boy who traps Death up a magical apple tree) and *What Ever Happened to Baby Jane?* before he became a Methodist minister, died on June 27th, aged 68.

German character actor **Siegfried Lowitz**, who appeared in *The Invisible Dr. Mabuse*, *The Brain* and *The Sinister Monk*, died in Munich on the same day, aged 84.

Irish-born clairvoyant and ghost-hunter **Tom Corbett** also died on June 27th, aged 81. He was employed as a special advisor on the 1973 film *The Legend of Hell House*.

Carlos Rogers, the 47-year-old grandson of 1930s Hollywood star Will Rogers, was found on June 29th slumped over a toilet, having died from a drinking binge in a $200-a-month room in a boarding house in Ohio. It was subsequently discovered that the adopted son of Will Rogers, Jr. (who himself apparently committed suicide in 1993) had assets worth more than $500,000.

1930s leading lady **Dorothy Lee**, who appeared in various Wheeler and Wolsey films, also died in June, aged 88.

American leading lady of the 1930s, **Sylvia Sidney** (Sophia Kosow), whose career spanned seventy years, died of throat cancer on July 1st, aged 88. She appeared in Hitchcock's *Sabotage*, *You Only Live Once*, *Dead End*, *Do Not Fold Spindle or Mutilate*, *Death at Love House*, *God Told Me To*, *Snowbeast*, *Damien Omen II*, *Hammett*, *Beetle Juice* and *Mars Attacks*. She was also a regular on the brief 1998 revival of TV's *Fantasy Island*.

78-year-old British music hall comedian turned tough guy actor **Jack Watson** died of a stroke on July 4th. He began his career playing Biggles on radio in the 1930s, and his many film credits include *Konga*, Hammer's *The Gorgon*, *The Night Caller*, *Every Home Should Have One*, *Tower of Evil*, *From Beyond the Grave* and *Schizo*.

Irish character actor **Donal McCann**, who appeared in the 1986 adaptation of Clive Barker's *Rawhead Rex* and *High Spirits*, died of pancreatic cancer on July 17th, aged 56.

American character actress **Sandra Gould**, who played the nosy neighbour Gladys Kravitz in TV's *Bewitched*, died on July 20th, aged 73. After surviving open-heart surgery, Gould died from a blood clot which caused a massive stroke. Her other credits include *The Ghost and Mr. Chicken*, *Chatterbox*, and the voice of Betty Rubble on TV's *The Flintstones*.

American actress and publisher of the childrens' book *Tubby the Tuba* (written by her husband), **Ruth Enders Tripp** died on July 28th after a long illness. She was 79, and her credits included *The Christmas That Almost Wasn't* and TV's *Mr. I. Magination*.

American singer **Guy Mitchell** (Al Cernick), who appeared in a number of movies and the TV series *Whispering Smith* in the 1950s, also died in July, aged 74. So, too, did character actor **Bill Owen MBE**, who for twenty-seven years appeared in BBC-TV's *Last of the Summer Wine*. In 1956 he starred in the London stage premier of *The Threepenny Opera*, and wrote the lyrics for a number of hit songs for Sacha Distel, Engelbert Humperdinck and Cliff Richard. Other July fatalities were Mexican wrestler [Rodolfo] **Cavernario Galindo** [Ramirez], who appeared in *Samson vs. the Vampire Women*, *Samson in the Wax Museum* and *Santo y Blue Demon vs. Los Monstruos*; French-born **Yoko Tani**, aged 67, who appeared in *Ali Baba and the Forty Thieves* (1954), *First Spaceship on Venus*, *The Secret of Dr. Mabuse* and *Invasion*; and American actor **Ray Young**, who played Bigfoot in the 1977 TV series *Bigfoot and Wildboy* and also appeared in *Blood of Dracula's Castle*, *Five Bloody Graves*, *Genesis II*, *Blue Sunshine* and *The Return of the Beverly Hillbillies* (as Jethro).

Brawny American leading man **Victor Mature**, once known as "The Hunk", died of cancer on August 4th, aged 86. His films include *One Million B.C.* (with Lon Chaney, Jr.), *I Wake Up Screaming*, John Ford's *My Darling Clementine* (as Doc Holliday), *Moss Rose* (with Vincent Price and George Zucco), *Kiss of Death*, *Samson and Delilah* (1949 and 1984 versions) and The Monkees' *Head*. Mature had a reputation for being so cheap that he insisted on keeping his wardrobe from each film.

Prolific American character actor **Brion James** died of a heart attack in Malibu on August 7th, aged 54. His more than 100 action and exploitation credits (many of them direct to video) include *Blade Runner* (as Leon the replicant), *Southern Comfort*, *48 Hours*, *Crimewave*, *Enemy Mine*, *Steel Dawn*, *Flesh & Blood*, *Cherry 2000*, *Red Scorpion*, *Street Asylum*, *Mutator*, *The Horror Show*, *Mom*, *Black Magic*, *Time Runner*, *Wishman*, *Future Shock*, *Scanner Cop*, *Frogtown II*, *The Player*, *The Fifth Element*, *Virtual Assassin*, *The Killing Jar*, *Evil Obsession* and *Pterodactyl Woman from Beverly Hills*.

40-year-old **Nerine Kidd**, the reportedly alcoholic wife of actor William Shatner, was found by her husband drowned in their North Hollywood swimming pool on August 11th. The couple would have celebrated their second wedding anniversary in November.

American leading man **Ross Elliott**, who appeared in *The Beast from 20,000 Fathoms*, *Tarantula*, *The Indestructible Man*, *Monster on the Campus*, *The Crawling Hand* and numerous other movies, died of cancer on August 12th, aged 82.

72-year-old American character actor **Charles Macaulay**, who portrayed Count Dracula in *Blacula* and also appeared in *Head*, *The Twilight People*, *The House of Seven Corpses* and TV's *Night Gallery*, died of cancer on August 13th.

American leading lady of the 1940s and '50s **Marguerite Chapman** died on August 31st, aged 81. Her films include *Charlie Chan at the Wax Museum*, *The Body Disappears*, *Spy Smasher*, *Flight to Mars*, *The Seven Year Itch* and *The Amazing Transparent Man*.

American leading lady **Nancy Guild**, whose credits include *Black Magic* and (Abbott and Costello). . .*Meet the Invisible Man*, also died in August, aged 74.

Hawaiian-born actress **Laurette Luez**, who appeared in *Prehistoric Women*, *Bomba and the African Treasure*, *Siren of Bagdad*, *Jungle Gents* and played the exotic Karamaneh on the 1956 TV series *The Adventures of Fu Manchu*, died on September 12th, aged 71.

85-year-old British leading lady **Joan Gardner** (Joan Korda), who was married to director Zoltan Korda and appeared in *The Scarlet Pimpernel* and *The Man Who Could Work Miracles*, died of cancer in Beverly Hills on September 17th.

71-year-old British crooner **Frankie Vaughan** (Frank Abelsohn) died of a heart condition the same day, following emergency surgery. Although he appeared in such movies as *These Dangerous Years*, *Heart of a Man* and *Let's Make Love* (with Marilyn Monroe), his career in Hollywood never really took off. 1999 marked the 50th anniversary of Vaughan's entry into showbusiness.

George C. (Campbell) **Scott**, the first actor to ever refuse an Academy Award (in 1970 for *Patton*), died of a ruptured abdominal aortic aneurysm at his California home on September 22nd, aged 71. The star of such films as *The List of Adrian Messenger*, *Dr. Strangelove*, *The Bible*, *They Might Be Giants*, *The Day of the Dolphin*, *The Changeling*, *The Formula*, Stephen King's *Firestarter* and *The Exorcist III*, plus TV versions of *Jane Eyre* (1972), *Beauty and the Beast* (1977), *A Christmas Carol* (1984) and *The Murders in the Rue Morgue* (1986), reportedly drank himself to death after the failure of his five marriages to actresses Carolyn Hughes, Patricia Reed, Colleen Dewhurst (who he married twice, and who died in 1992) and Trish Van Devere. His nose was broken four times in bar brawls.

91-year-old Canadian **Murray Wood**, who played several different Munchkins in *The Wizard of Oz* (1939), died on September 25th.

73-year-old British actress and wife of scriptwriter Frank Launder **Bernadette O'Farrell**, who played Maid Marion in TV's *The Adventures of Robin Hood* (1955–59), died in Monaco on September 26th. She also appeared in the 1952 movie *The Genie*.

Veteran British leading lady **Chili Bouchier** (Dorothy Irene Bouchier), who began her long career in silent films and was known as "the brunette bombshell", also died in September, aged 90. Her credits include *The Ghost Goes West* (1936), *Mr. Satan* and *The Mind of Mr. Reeder*. The same month saw the death of 75-year-old American actress **Ruth Roman**, whose credits include *Jungle Queen*, *Casablanca*, Hitchcock's *Strangers On a Train*, *Joe Macbeth*, *The Baby* and *Day of the Animals*.

British actor **Noel Johnson**, who played the title roles in the radio serials *Dick Barton Special Agent* and *Dan Dare Pilot of the Future*, died on October 1st. He also appeared in *Frightmare*, Hitchcock's *Frenzy*, *For Your Eyes Only* and on TV in *A for Andromeda*, *The Andromeda Breakthrough*, *Doctor Who* and *Doomwatch*.

Former child singing star **Lena Zavaroni** died of bronchial pneumonia the same day after undergoing a neurosurgery three weeks earlier to treat her depression after suffering from anorexia for more than twenty years. The 35-year-old Scots-born performer, who found fame in the 1970s on the TV talent show *Opportunity Knocks*, had taken a drugs overdose shortly before the operation and weighed less than four stones at the time of her death.

73-year-old American actor **Lee Richardson**, who appeared in *Network*, *The Believers*, *The Fly 2* and *The Exorcist III*, died on October 2nd from complications following a perforated ulcer.

British character actress **Megs** (Mauguette Mary) **Jenkins** died on October 5th, aged 81. She played the troubled housekeeper, Mrs. Grose, in *The Innocents* (1961) and also appeared in the 1974 TV remake, *The Turn of the Screw*. Her other credits include the 1948 version of *The Monkey's Paw* (she repeated her role in the 1974 TV adaptation for *Orson Welles' Great Mysteries*), *Green for Danger*, *Bunny Lake is Missing* and *Asylum*.

Blonde American actress **Maris** (Mary Alice) **Wrixon**, who appeared in *Jeepers Creepers*, *The Ape* and *British Intelligence* (both with Boris Karloff), *White Pongo*, *Face of Marble* and the serial *The Master Key*, died on October 6th, aged 81.

92-year-old British-born Hollywood leading lady **Helen Vinson** (Helen Rulfs), whose credits include 1935's *The Tunnel* (aka *Transatlantic Tunnel*), *I Am a Fugitive from a Chain Gang* and *The Lady and the Monster*, died in Chapel Hill, North Carolina, on October 7th.

62-year-old **Robert "Gino" Morella**, better known as former WWF world heavyweight champion "Gorilla Monsoon", died the same day of complications arising from a heart attack. He was the longtime announcing partner of Jesse "The Body" Ventura and the only person to have fought Andre the Giant, Antonio Inoki and Muhammed Ali.

The 7 foot 1 inch-tall basketball star **Wilt Chamberlain**, who played with the Philadelphia Warriors, the Harlem Globe Trotters and the Los Angeles Lakers, died on October 12th of a heart attack following dental surgery. He was aged 63 and claimed to have slept with 20,000 women. He made his film début as the untrustworthy Bombaata in *Conan the Destroyer*.

American character actor **Richard B. Shull** died of a heart attack on October 13th, aged 70. He co-starred with John Schuck in the 1976 TV series *Holmes and Yoyo*, and also appeared in *The Anderson Tapes*, *Klute*, *Ssssssss*, *The Big Bus*, *The Pack*, *Heartbeeps*, and *Splash*.

American actress and voice artist **Paddi Edwards** died of respiratory failure on October 18th, aged 67. Her voice was heard in *Ghostbusters* and she appeared in *Halloween III Season of the Witch*, *It Came Upon a Midnight Clear* and TV's *Star Trek The Next Generation*.

61-year-old American singer and character actor **Hoyt Axton** died on October 26th after suffering two heart attacks. He had been in failing health for a few years following a stroke. A member of the 1960s group Three Dog Night, his songs include "Joy to the World" (used on TV's *The X Files*) and "The Pusher" (performed by Steppenwolf in *Easy Rider*), and he appeared in such films as *Gremlins*, *Endangered Species*, *Retribution*, *Buried Alive*, *Alien Invasion* and *King Cobra*. His mother, Mae Boren Axton (who died in 1997) wrote the music for "Heartbreak Hotel".

American actor **Steve** (Stephen) **Roberts** died of cancer on October 26th, aged 82. His credits include *Song of Bernadette*, *Miracle on 34th Street* (1947), *The Twonky*, *Gog*, *Terrified*, *Diary of a Madman*, *Brainstorm* (1965) and *Escape from the Planet of the Apes*.

81-year-old American singer, dancer and actress **Grace McDonald** died of double pneumonia on October 30th. She appeared in *Destiny*, *Flesh and Fantasy*, *Crazy House* and *Murder in the Blue Room*.

British TV and radio comedian **Deryck Guyler**, a regular on the *Please Sir!* series (1968–72) who also had roles in *A Hard Day's Night*, *Help!*, *Barry McKenzie Holds His Own*. . . and *One of Our Dinosaurs is Missing*, also died in October. So, too, did British actor **Eric Lander**, who co-starred in the long-running Scotland Yard series *No Hiding Place* (1959–67), and 75-year-old singer **Ella Mae Morse**, who joined Jimmy Dorsey's band in 1939 when she was only fourteen and appeared in such films as *Ghost Catchers* (1944).

Japanese actor **Minoru Chiaki** died on November 2nd, aged 82. He played the last of the eponymous *Seven Samurai* to die and also appeared in Kurosawa's other classics, *Rashomon*, *Throne of Blood* and *The Hidden Fortress*, plus the first Godzilla sequel *Gigantis the Fire Monster*.

71-year-old British actor **Ian Bannen** was killed in a car crash near Loch Ness while holidaying in Scotland on November 3rd. His film credits include *Macbeth* (1959), *Jane Eyre* (1970), *Fright*, *Doomwatch*, *From Beyond the Grave*, *The Watcher in the Woods*, *Gorky Park*, *Witch Story*, *Ghost Dad* and the 1980 BBC-TV version of *Dr. Jekyll and Mr. Hyde*.

Black actress **Mabel King**, who appeared in *Ganja and Hess*, *The Wiz* (as Evillene the Wicked Witch), *Scrooged* and *Dead Men Don't Die*, died of diabetes on November 9th, aged 66.

American voice artist **Mary Kay Bergman**, Disney's "official" voice of Snow White, committed suicide by shooting herself on November 11th, aged 38. She portrayed both Batgirl and Barbara Gordon in the *Batman & Mr. Freeze: Subzero* animated movie, played Daphne Blake in *Scooby-Doo on Zombie Island* and *Scooby-Doo and the Witch's Ghost*, as "Shannen Cassidy" was all but one of the female voices on TV's *South Park* (and the 1999 movie), and voiced various characters in *Hercules*, *Star Wars Episode I: The Phantom Menace* and *The Iron Giant*.

Donald Mills, the last of the original dancing Mills Brothers, died of complications from pneumonia on November 13th. His film credits include *The Big Broadcast* (1932) and *Operator 13*.

90-year-old flamboyant gay campaigner, raconteur and author **Quentin Crisp** (Denis Pratt) died in Manchester on November 21st, the day before he was due to start a new run of his one-man show. Best known for his 1968 autobiography *The Naked Civil Servant* (filmed for TV in 1975 with John Hurt playing Crisp), the former male prostitute also published the Gothic fantasy *Chog* in 1979 and appeared in such films as *The Bride* (as Baron Frankenstein's assistant Dr. Zahlus) and *Orlando* (as Queen Elizabeth I). Disillusioned with England, Crisp moved permanently to America in 1978 and he was the inspiration for Sting's song "An Englishman in New York".

Former Bowery Boy "Whitey", **Billy** (William) **Benedict**, who appeared in *The Adventures of Captain Marvel*, *The Mad Doctor*, *Dressed to Kill*, *Ghosts on the Loose*, *The Lady and the Monster*, *Spook Busters*, *Mr. Hex*, *Master Minds*, *Ghost Chasers*, *The Magnetic Monster*, Ed Wood Jr's *Bride of the Monster*, *Sherlock Holmes in New York*, *Computercide* and many others, died of complications from heart surgery on November 25th, aged 82.

Latvian-born **Wolf Ruviskis**, who grew up in Argentina and moved to Mexico in the 1940s to become a professional wrestler, died the same day. He appeared in more than 100 films and played the masked hero Neutron in six movies. He later opened a chain of restaurants and became a stage magician and mentalist.

American actress and comedienne **Madeline Kahn** died of ovarian cancer in New York on December 3rd, aged 57. She was twice nominated for an Academy Award, and her film credits include such Mel Brooks productions as *Blazing Saddles*, *Young Frankenstein* and *High Anxiety*, plus *The Adventures of Sherlock Holmes' Smarter Brother*, *Simon*, *Wholly Moses*, *Slapstick of Another Kind*, *An American Tail* and *A Bug's Life* (as the voice of Gypsy).

American leading man **John Archer** (Ralph Bowman), who will be best remembered for his opening narration of *The Shadow* radio show in the 1940s ("Who knows what evil lurks in the hearts of men?"), died of lung cancer on December 5th, aged 84. The father of actress Anne Archer, his film credits include *Dick Tracy Returns*, *King of the Zombies*, *Bowery at Midnight*, *Sherlock Holmes in Washington*, *Destination Moon*, *She Devil* (1957) and *I Saw What You Did* (1965).

The last of the singing cowboy stars, **Rex Allen** [Sr], who made more than thirty films for Republic Studios in the 1950s and starred in the TV series *Frontier Doctor* (1958–59), died on December 17th in Tucson, Arizona, when a woman friend in a Cadillac accidently ran over him in his driveway. He was 77, and narrated more than eighty Disney True-Life Adventures and the cartoon film *Charlotte's Web*. His seven country music hits included "Crying in the Chapel", which reached No. 4 in the charts in 1953 and later became a hit for Elvis Presley.

85-year-old British actor **Desmond Llewelyn**, who portrayed gadget creator Q in seventeen James Bond films, died of massive internal injuries after being involved in a head-on car crash while returning from a book signing in East Sussex on December 19th. The actor had made his final appearance in the film series in *The World is Not Enough*, released only a few weeks earlier. His uncredited screen début was in the Will Hay comedy *Ask a Policeman* (1938), and his other credits include Hammer's *Curse of the Werewolf*, *Cleopatra* (1963), *Chitty Chitty Bang Bang*, and TV's *The Invisible Man*, *Danger Man* and *Doom Watch*.

British stage and screen actor **Peter Jeffrey**, best remembered for his role as Scotland Yard's Inspector Trout in both *The Abominable Dr. Phibes* and *Dr. Phibes Rises Again*, died of prostate cancer on Christmas Day, aged 70. His other credits include *Goodbye Gemini*, Hammer's *Countess Dracula*, *If. . .O Lucky Man!*, *Britannia Hospital*, *The Adventures of Baron Munchausen* (1989) and the TV movies *Hands of a Murderer* (as Mycroft Holmes), *Rasputin*, *The Tale of Sweeny Todd* and *The Moonstone*.

TV's Lone Ranger (1949–57), **Clayton** (Jack Carlton) **Moore**, died of a heart attack on December 28th, aged 85. After appearing in Monogram's *Black Dragons* with Bela Lugosi, he became a leading man at Republic during the 1940s, starring in such serials as *Perils of Nyoka*, *The Crimson Ghost*, *Jesse James Rides Again*, *Adventures of Frank and Jesse James*, *G-Men Never Forget*, *Ghost of Zorro*, *Jungle Drums of Africa* and *Radar Men from the Moon*. He also starred in *The Lone Ranger* and *The Lone Ranger and the Lost City of Gold*, but in the early 1980s he was prohibited by a studio law suit from making any more public appearances wearing his Lone Ranger mask.

Actress **April Kent** died the same day of a heart attack in Paris. She appeared in *The Incredible Shrinking Man*.

British TV and film actor **John Arnatt** also died in December, aged 83. Best remembered as the villain in the series *The Adventures of Robin Hood* (1955–59), he also appeared in Hammer's *Dick Barton at Bay*, *Dr. Crippen*, *Licensed to Kill* (1966) and *Crucible of Terror*.

FILM/TV TECHNICIANS

76-year-old American TV director **Buzz Kulik** (Seymour Kulik) died of heart failure on January 13th. His credits include *The*

Twilight Zone, Vanished, Matt Helm and the 1989 version of *Around the World in 80 Days*.

One of Britain's most successful film producers from the late 1940s until the mid-1970s, **Betty E.** (Evelyn) **Box** died on January 15th, aged 83. Her films include *Miranda, Helter Skelter* (1949), *The Thirty-Nine Steps* (1959), *Deadlier Than the Male, Some Girls Do, Quest for Love, Percy, Percy's Progress* and Rank's popular *Doctor* series. She was married to *Carry On* producer Peter Rogers and was appointed OBE in 1958.

American TV writer, producer and director **Nicholas J. Corea**, whose credits include *The Incredible Hulk, Airwolf, Outlaws* and the TV movie *Archer: Fugitive from the Empire*, died of cancer on January 17th, aged 56.

Prolific Italian producer, director, cinematographer and writer **Aristide Massaccesi** died of a heart attack on January 23rd, aged 63. His many pseudonyms include "Joe D'Amato", "David Hills", "Kevin Mancuso", "Peter Newton" and "Chana Lee Sun", amongst others. Perhaps best known for the 1970s *Black Emanuelle* films with Laura Gemser, his horror titles include *Death Smiles on a Murderer, Buried Alive, Emanuelle and the Last Cannibals, The Anthropophagous Beast, Absurd, Porno Holocaust, Witchery* and *Frankenstein 2000*. His output slowed in the mid-1980s as he turned to sword & sorcery (*Ator the Fighting Eagle*) and science fiction (*2020 Texas Gladiators*), as well as hard– and softcore pornography.

Hollywood production designer **Michael White**, whose credits include *Armageddon* and *Crimson Tide*, also died in January.

Pioneer animation director **Herb** (Herbert) **Klynn**, whose numerous credits include TV's *Gerald McBoing-Boing, Mr. Magoo* and the animated titles for *I Spy*, died on February 3rd after a lengthy illness. He was 83.

British special effects supervisor **Dennis Hall** died on February 12th, aged 72. Among the films he worked on are *2001: A Space Odyssey, Blade Runner, Alien* and *A Clockwork Orange*, and he supervised such animated productions as *Watership Down* and much of *Yellow Submarine*.

TV director and former actor **Noam Pitlik**, whose credits include *Bewitched* and *I Dream of Jeannie*, died of lung cancer on February 18th, aged 66. He also appeared in *Hogan's Heroes* and the movie *The Greatest Story Ever Told*.

Italian film director **Vittorio Cottafavi** also died at the beginning of February, aged 84. His films include *Revolt of the Gladiators* and *Hercules Conquers Atlantis*.

British puppeteer **Christine Glanville**, who designed and operated many of the characters for TV's *Thunderbirds*, died on March 1st, aged 75. She began her collaboration with producer Gerry Anderson in 1956 on the *Twizzle* and *Torchy* TV series, and continued with *Four Feather Falls*, *Fireball XL5*, *Supercar*, *Stingray* and *Space Precinct*.

Reclusive American writer, producer and director **Stanley Kubrick** died at his estate in Hertfordshire, England, on March 7th, aged 70. His family would not release details of the cause of death. Although Kubrick's thirteen films won a total of eight Academy Awards, none were for Best Director. His 1962 movie *Lolita* features a clip from Hammer's *The Curse of Frankenstein*, and his other credits include such flawed masterpieces as *Dr. Strangelove, or How I Learned to Stop Worrying and Love the Bomb*, *2001: A Space Odyssey*, *A Clockwork Orange*, Stephen King's *The Shining*, *Full Metal Jacket* and *Eyes Wide Shut*, which he had just completed editing. An extreme perfectionist, former *Look* photographer Kubrick insisted on having control over every aspect of his later films, and he was known to shoot up to 100 takes of a scene. *AI*, a science fiction project Kubrick had been developing for years from a story by Brian Aldiss, was subsequently acquired by Steven Spielberg.

Terry Hodel, who produced Los Angeles SF radio show *Hour 25* after her husband Mike's death in 1986, died of cancer on March 17th, aged 61.

Set decorator **Mickey S. Michaels**, whose credits include *Psycho III*, *Star Trek VI The Undiscovered Country*, *Crimson Tide* and TV's Emmy-nominated *Battlestar Galactica* and the pilot for *Star Trek: Deep Space Nine*, died on March 20th, aged 67.

Producer/actor **Gary Morton**, the former husband of Lucille Ball (who died in 1989), also died in March.

American screenwriter and director **Howard R. Cohen**, whose films for Roger Corman include *Saturday the 14th*, *Saturday the 14th Strikes Back* and *Space Raiders*, died of a heart attack on April 3rd, aged 57. His other credits include *Vampire Hookers*, *Stryker*, *Lords of the Deep*, *Deathstalker III* and *IV*, and *Bar-*

barian Queen and *Barbarian Queen II: The Empress Strikes Back*.

American producer **Aubrey Schenck** whose films include *Shock* (with Vincent Price), *The Black Sleep* (with Bela Lugosi), *Pharaoh's Curse*, *Voodoo Island* and *Frankenstein 1970* (both with Boris Karloff), *Robinson Crusoe on Mars*, *Daughters of Satan* and *Superbeast*, died on April 14th, aged 90.

German-American film editor **Rudi Fehr** died of a heart attack on April 16th, aged 88. His credits include *Between Two Worlds*, *Possessed*, *Key Largo*, *House of Wax*, *Dial M for Murder* and *One from the Heart*.

Writer/director **Gordon Hughes**, whose credits include the classic radio series *Lights Out*, died of heart failure on April 19th, aged 89. He later worked in TV.

Still photographer and producer **Sam Shaw**, best remembered for his photo of Marilyn Monroe standing over a subway grating, and veteran Warner Bros. animator **Charles McKimson**, also both died in April.

American set decorator **Jerry Wunderlich**, whose credits include the Oscar-nominated *The Exorcist*, *Audrey Rose*, *War-Games* and *My Science Project*, died of a heart attack on May 14th, aged 74.

American TV producer **Buck Houghton** died the same day, aged 84. From 1959–62 he worked on Rod Serling's *The Twilight Zone*.

Percussionist **James Blades OBE**, who was responsible for the sound of the J. Arthur Rank film gong, died at his home in Surrey on May 19th, aged 97.

Waldo Semon, the man who created bubble gum during his 37-year career with B.F. Goodrich Co., died on May 26th, aged 100. For the same company Semon also invented vinyl, which has since become the second most-used plastic in the world. He was awarded 116 patents before he retired in 1963.

70-year-old special effects designer **Marv Ystrom**, who created the effects for such films as *The Exorcist*, *Star Trek The Motion Picture*, *The Final Countdown* and *All of Me*, plus the TV series *I Dream of Jeannie*, died on June 4th of a ruptured aneurysm.

British special effects designer **John Stears**, who won Academy Awards for his work on *Star Wars* and the James Bond film *Thunderball*, died of a stroke on June 28th, aged 64. He was responsible for creating Bond's Aston Martin DB5 in *Goldfinger*; R2-D2, C3PO and the light sabres in *Star Wars*, the special effects in *FX Murder by Illusion*, and the flying car in *Chitty Chitty Bang Bang*. His other credits include *Theatre of Blood*, *Outland*, *Haunted Honeymoon*, *Escape 2000*, the TV mini-series of *The Martian Chronicles* and the pilot for *Babylon 5*.

British producer **Sir John Woolf**, who founded Romulus Films in 1949 with his brother James (who died in 1966), died of a heart attack on June 28th, aged 86. Together they produced *Pandora and the Flying Dutchman*, *The African Queen*, *Beat the Devil*, *Richard III* (1955) and *Moulin Rouge*, amongst other titles. Individually, John went on to produce *Oliver!*, *Day of the Jackal* (1973), plus *Orson Welles' Great Mysteries* and *Roald Dahl's Tales of the Unexpected* on Anglia TV.

American music impresario and film and theatre producer **Allan Carr** died of cancer on June 29th, aged 62. After distributing the cannibal movie *Survive!* in America and turning it into a big hit, he was also involved with *Grease* and its sequel, *La Cage aux Folles* and *Can't Stop the Music*. He is credited with discovering stars Michelle Pfeiffer and Steve Guttenberg, and once had his jaw wired shut to stop himself overeating.

American director **Edward Dmytryk**, who went to jail and spent several years in exile as one of "The Hollywood Ten" because of McCarthy's communist witch-hunt, died of heart and kidney failure on July 1st, aged 90. His many films include *The Devil Commands* (with Boris Karloff), *Captive Wild Woman*, *Hitler's Children*, *Murder My Sweet*, *Crossfire*, *The Caine Mutiny*, *Warlock*, *Mirage* and *Bluebeard* (1972).

Television executive and vice-president of the Children's Television Workshop, **Edward L. Palmer**, died on August 1st of prostate cancer, aged 66. His shows included *Sesame St.* and *Ghostwriter*.

Japanese cinematographer **Kazuo Miyagawa**, best known for his work with such directors as Akira Kurosawa (*Rashomon*) and Kenji Mizoguchi (*Ugestu Monogatari*), died of kidney failure on August 7th, aged 91.

British music manager **Bob Herbert**, who discovered the Spice Girls and also managed boy band Five, was killed in a car crash in Windsor Great Park on August 9th. He was 57, and in the 1980s had launched the careers of brothers Luke and Matt Goss as Bros.

Stop-motion animator, special effects supervisor and director **David Allen**, who received an Academy Award nomination for his work on *Young Sherlock Holmes*, died of cancer on August 26th, aged 54. Among his many other credits are *When Dinosaurs Ruled the Earth*, *The Crater Lake Monster*, *The Howling*, *Caveman*, *Honey I Shrunk the Kids*, **Batteries Not Included* and numerous titles for producer Charles Band, including *Laserblast*, *Ragewar*, *Robot Jox*, *Crash and Burn*, *Doctor Mordrid* and the *Subspecies* and *Puppet Master* series. His long-cherished project *The Primevals* was still in development after more than twenty years.

Stage designer **Carl Toms**, whose early career involved creating the costumes for such Hammer epics as *She* and *One Million Years B.C.*, also died in August. As did pioneer American TV director **George Gould**. He worked on many episodes of *Tom Corbett, Space Cadet* and invented an early electronic matte system.

Writer/director **Joseph Green**, whose credits include the legendary *The Brain That Wouldn't Die*, died of liver failure in New York City on September 1st, aged 71.

89-year-old British film director and former editor **Charles Crichton**, whose credits include such Ealing Studios classics as *Dead of Night* (the golfing ghost story), *Hue and Cry*, *The Lavender Hill Mob* and *The Titfield Thunderbolt*, plus the SF TV movie *Into Infinity* and episodes of *The Avengers* and *Space: 1999*, died after a short illness on September 14th. In 1987 he came out of retirement after twenty-three years to direct *A Fish Called Wanda*, for which he received an Academy Award nomination.

86-year-old Academy Award-winning editor and occasional director **Howard F. Kress**, who worked on *Dr. Jekyll and Mr. Hyde* (1941), *The Poseidon Adventure*, *The Towering Inferno* and *The Swarm*, died on September 18th.

Australia's chief film censor **Kathryn Paterson** died of cancer on September 20th. She was 36.

American producer/director **Carl K. Hittleman**, who scripted *Jesse James Meets Frankenstein's Daughter* and *Billy the Kid vs. Dracula*, died on September 22nd, aged 92.

Allen Funt, who created TV's *Candid Camera* and produced and starred in the 1970 film version, *What Do You Say to a Naked Lady?*, also died in September, aged 85.

67-year-old **Dean O'Brien**, who produced the TV series *V*, died after a lung transplant in Los Angeles on October 2nd.

Hollywood agent **Meyer Mishkin**, whose clients included Tyrone Power, Gregory Peck, Lee Marvin, Charles Bronson, Kirk Douglas, James Coburn, Richard Dreyfuss, Tom Skerritt, Gary Busey and Claude Akins, died on October 9th, aged 87.

British producer, sound recordist, editor and writer **Dallas Bower** died on October 18th, aged 82. A former director of BBC-TV (1936–39), his varied credits include Hitchcock's *Blackmail* (sound), *Henry V* (associate producer), the 1950 French *Alice in Wonderland* (director) and the TV series *Sir Lancelot* (producer).

Veteran publicist **Jim Moran** died the same day, aged 91. Famous for actually selling iceboxes to Eskimos, looking for needles in a haystack, changing horses in midstream and sitting on an ostrich egg (for *The Egg and I*), he was also the publicist on *The Third Man*.

Amanda Schofield, who was publicity manager for the James Bond films, died on October 24th, aged 39.

Writer/director **Abraham Polonsky**, who was blacklisted by the communist witch-hunt from 1948 until the late 1960s, died of an apparent heart attack on October 26th, aged 88. He directed *Force of Evil*, *Tell Them Willie Boy is Here* and *Avalanche Express*, anonymously scripted *Odds Against Tomorrow* and *Madigan*, and in later years drafted a version of *Battlefield Earth*.

84-year-old British-born visual effects supervisor and matte artist **Albert J. Whitlock** died the same day after a lengthy illness. He won Academy Awards for his work on *Earthquake* and *The Hindenburg*, and his many other credits (often for Universal) include Hitchcock's *The Birds*, *Marnie*, *Torn Curtain*, *Frenzy* and *Family Plot*, *Greystoke*, *Dune*, *History of the World Part 1*, *Diamonds Are Forever*, *The Sentinel*, *Exorcist II The Heretic*, *High Anxiety*, *The Car*, *Dracula* (1979), *The Wiz*, *Ghost Story*, *Heartbeeps*, *Cat People* (1982), *The Thing*, *Psycho 2* and *The Neverending Story 2*.

TV producer **Hugh Benson**, whose credits include *The Brotherhood of the Bell*, *The Eyes of Charles Sand*, *A Fire in the Sky* and *Goliath Awaits*, died of cancer on October 28th, aged 82.

American film and TV director **James Goldstone** died of cancer on November 5th, aged 68. His many credits include *Brother*

John, They Only Kill Their Masters, Rollercoaster, When Time Ran Out, the pilot for *Ironside*, the second pilot for *Star Trek* ("Where No Man Has Gone Before") and episodes of *The Outer Limits* (the two-part "The Inheritors"), *The Fugitive, The Man from U.N.C.L.E.* and *Voyage to the Bottom of the Sea*.

American TV writer, producer and director **Gene Levitt** died of prostate cancer on November 15th, aged 79. He created and scripted the 1977 pilot TV movie for *Fantasy Island* and directed *The Phantom of Hollywood* and episodes of *Night Gallery* and *Kolchak: The Night Stalker*.

Hollywood costume designer **Adele Balkan** died of cancer on November 20th, aged 92. Her many credits include DeMille's *Cleopatra* (1934), Hitchcock's *Notorious* (1946), *Mighty Joe Young* (1949), and *The Ten Commandments* (1956).

American editor **Robert F. Shugrue**, whose credits include *Star Trek III The Search for Spock* plus such TV movies as Ray Bradbury's *The Screaming Woman, A Howling in the Woods, I Love a Mystery* (1973), *The Dark Secret of Harvest Home, The Invisible Man* (1975) and *Gemini Man*, died of heart failure on November 27th, aged 62.

Blacklisted director **John Berry** died of pleurisy on November 29th, aged 82. He worked in Europe during the 1950s and '60s before returning to American films in the late 1970s. His credits include the TV movie remake of *Angel on My Shoulder* (1980).

Showbusiness lawyer **Milton "Mickey" Rudin** died of pneumonia on December 13th, aged 79. His client list included Frank Sinatra, Marilyn Monroe, Elizabeth Taylor and The Jackson Five. He also appeared in bit parts in a number of "Rat Pack" films.

French writer-director **Robert Bresson** died on December 18th, aged 98. His films include *Lancelot du Lac* and *Le Diable Probablement*.

London-born Hollywood director **Irving Rapper** died on December 20th, aged 101. Long associated with Warner Bros., his many film credits include the classic *Now Voyager, The Adventures of Mark Twain* (1944), *Rhapsody in Blue, Strange Intruder, The Christine Jorgenson Story* and *Born Again*.

90-year-old Egyptian-born Italian director **Riccardo Freda** died on December 22nd after a long illness. Widely regarded as the father of the Italian horror film, second only to Mario Bava, he revived that country's moribund horror genre in 1956 with *The Devil's Commandment*, starring his wife Gianna Maria Canale and ultimately completed by Bava. Under the pseudonyms "Robert Hampton" and "Richard Freda", Freda went on to make such films as *Caltiki the Immortal Monster*, *The Witch's Curse*, *The Horrible Dr. Hichcock*, *The Ghost*, *Double Face* and *Murder Obsession*.

USEFUL ADDRESSES

THE FOLLOWING LISTING OF ORGANIZATIONS, publications, dealers and individuals is designed to present readers with further avenues to explore. Although I can personally recommend all those listed on the following pages, neither myself nor the publisher can take any responsibility for the services they offer. Please also note that all the information below is subject to change without notice.

ORGANIZATIONS

The British Fantasy Society (http://www.herebedragons.co.uk/bfs) began in 1971 and publishers the bi-monthly *Prism UK: The British Fantasy Newsletter*, produces other special booklets, and organizes the annual British FantasyCon and semi-regular meetings in London. Yearly membership is £20.00 (UK), £25.00 (Europe) and £30.00 (America and the rest of the world) made payable in sterling to "The British Fantasy Society" and sent to The BFS Secretary, c/o 201 Reddish Road, South Reddish, Stockport SK5 7HR, UK. E-mail: syrinx.2112@btinternet.com

Horror Writers Association (http://www.horror.org/) was formed in the 1980s and is open to anyone seeking Active, Affiliate or Associate membership. The HWA publishes a regular *Newsletter* and organizes the annual Bram Stoker Awards ceremony. Standard membership is $55.00 (USA), £38.00/$65.00 (overseas); Corporate membership is $100.00 (USA), £74.00/$120.00 (overseas), and Family Membership is $75.00 (USA), £52.00/$85.00 (overseas). Send to "HWA", PO Box 50577 Palo Alto, CA 94303, USA. If paying by sterling cheque send to "HWA", c/o 24 Pearl Road, London E17 4QZ.

World Fantasy Convention (http://www.farrsite.com/wfc/) is an annual convention held in a different (usually American) city each year.

MAGAZINES

Cinefantastique (http://www.cfq.com) is a bi-monthly SF/fantasy/ horror movie magazine with a "Sense of Wonder". Cover price is $5.95/Cdn$9.50/£4.30 and a 12-issue subscription is $48.00 (USA) or $55.00 (Canada and overseas) to PO Box 270, Oak Park, IL 60303, USA. E-mail: mail@cfq.com

Interzone is Britain's leading magazine of science fiction and fantasy. Single copies are available for £3.00 (UK) or £3.50/$6.00 (overseas) or a 12-issue subscription is £34.00 (UK), $60.00 (USA) or £40.00 (overseas) payable by cheque or International Money Order. Payments can also be made by MasterCard, Visa or Eurocard to "Interzone", 217 Preston Drove, Brighton, BN1 6FL, UK.

Locus (http://www.Locusmag.com) is the monthly newspaper of the SF/fantasy/horror field. $4.95 a copy, a 12-issue subscription is $46.00 (USA), $50.00 (Canada), $75.00 (Europe), $85.00 (Australia, Asia and Africa) to "Locus Publications", PO Box 13305, Oakland, CA 94661, USA or "Locus Subscription", Fantast (Medway) Ltd, PO Box 23, Upwell Wisbech, Cambs PE14 9BU, UK. E-mail: Locus@Locusmag.com

The Magazine of Fantasy & Science Fiction (http:// www.fsfmag.com) has been publishing some of the best imaginative fiction for more than fifty years, now under the capable editorship of Gordon Van Gelder. Single copies are $3.50 (US) or $3.95 (Canada) and an annual subscription (which includes the double October/November anniversary issue) is $29.97 (US) and $37.97 (rest of the world). US cheques or credit card information to "Fantasy & Science Fiction", 143 Cream Hill Road, West Cornwall, CT 06796, USA, or subscribe online.

Science Fiction Chronicle is a bi-monthly news and reviews magazine that covers the SF/fantasy/horror field. It was recently sold to DNA Publications, who plan to ultimately increase the frequency back to monthly. A one-year subscription is $20.00 (USA), $26.75 (Canada, including GST) and $30.00 (rest of the world). Make cheques payable to "DNA Publications" and send to PO Box 2988, Radford, VA 24143–2988, USA. E-mail: dnapublications@iname.com

SFX is a monthly multi-media magazine of science fiction, fantasy and horror. Single copies are £3.25 or a 12-issue subscription via sterling cheque or credit card is £32.50 (UK), £35.00 (Europe), £39.00 (USA) or £55.00 (rest of the world) to "Future Publishing Ltd", SFX, FREEPOST BS4900, Somerton, Somerset TA11 6BR, UK, or overseas subscribers to "Future Publishing Ltd", SFX, Cary Court, Somerton, Somerset TA11 6TB, UK. E-mail: subs@futurenet.co.uk

Starburst (http://www.visimag.com) is a monthly magazine of sci-fi entertainment. Cover price is £3.25 (UK)/$5.99 (USA)/ Cdn$8.95 (Canada). Yearly subscriptions comprise 12 regular issues ("budget") or 12 regular issues and four quarterly Specials ("full") at £49.00 full/£35.00 budget (UK), $93.00 full/$64.00 budget (USA), £60.00 full/£42.00 budget (Europe airmail and rest of the world surface) or £76.00 full/£53.00 budget (rest of the world airmail) to "Visual Imagination Limited", Starburst Subscription, PO Box 371, London SW14 8JL, UK, or PMB#469, PO Box 6061, Sherman Oaks, CA 91413, USA. E-mail: mailorder@-visimag.com

The Third Alternative (http://www.tta-press.freewire.co.uk) is a quarterly magazine of new "slipstream" fiction, interviews and articles. Cover price is £3.25/$7.00, and a six-issue subscription is £18.00 (UK), £21.00 (Europe), $36.00 (America) or £24.00 (rest of the world) to "TTA Press", 5 Martins Lane, Witcham, Ely, Cambs CB6 2LB, UK. You can also subscribe by credit card via the secure website. E-mail: ttapress@aol.com

Video Watchdog (http://www.cinemaweb.com/videowd) is a monthly magazine described as "the Perfectionist's Guide to Fantastic Video". $6.50 a copy, an annual 12-issue subscription is $48.00 bulk/$70.00 first class (USA), $66.00 surface/$88.00 airmail (overseas). US funds only or Visa/MasterCard to "Video Watchdog", PO Box 5283, Cincinnati, OH 45205–0283, USA. E-mail: Videowd@aol.com

BOOK DEALERS

Cold Tonnage Books offers excellent mail order new and used SF/ fantasy/horror, art, reference, limited editions etc. with regular catalogues. Write to Andy & Angela Richards, 22 Kings Lane, Windlesham, Surrey GU20 6JQ, UK. Credit cards accepted. Tel: +44 (0) 1276–475388. E-mail: andy@coldtonnage.demon.co.uk

Don Cannon – Books has a shop at 406 E. Commonwealth Ave., Suite 3, Fullerton, CA 92836, USA (call first) selling recently published and out-of-print horror/suspense/fantasy/SF books. The mail order address is PO Box 918, Fullerton, CA 92836, USA with occasional catalogues. Credit cards accepted. Tel: (714) 449–0810. E-mail: doncannonbks@earthlink.net

Ken Cowley offers mostly used SF/fantasy/horror/crime/ supernatural, collectibles, pulps, videos etc. by mail order with 2–3 catalogues per year. Write to Trinity Cottage, 153 Old Church Road, Clevedon, North Somerset, BS21 7TU, UK. Tel: +44 (0) 1275–872247.

Richard Dalby issues semi-regular mail order lists of used ghost and supernatural volumes at very reasonable prices. Write to 4 Westbourne Park, Scarborough, North Yorkshire YO12 4AT, UK. Tel: +44 (0) 1723 377049.

Dark Delicacies is a friendly Burbank, California, store specializing in horror books, vampire merchandize and signings. They also do mail order and run money-saving book club and membership discount deals. 4213 West Burbank Blvd., Burbank, CA 91505, USA. Tel: (818) 556–6660. Credit cards accepted. E-mail: darkdel@darkdel.com

DreamHaven Books & Comics (http://www.visi.com/dreamhvn/) store and mail order offers new and used SF/fantasy/horror/art and illustrated etc. with regular catalogues. Write to 912 West Lake Street, Minneapolis, MN 55408, USA. Credit cards accepted. Tel: (612) 823-6070. E-mail: dreamhvn@visi.com

Fantastic Literature (http://www.netcomuk.co.uk/sgosden) mail order offers new and used SF/fantasy/horror etc. with regular catalogues. Write to Simon G. Gosden, 35 The Ramparts, Rayleigh, Essex SS6 8PY, UK. Credit cards accepted. Tel: +44 (0) 1268–747564. E-mail: sgosden@netcomuk.co.uk

Fantasy Centre shop and mail order has mostly used SF/ fantasy/horror, art, reference, pulps etc. at reasonable prices with regular bi-monthly catalogues. Write to 157 Holloway Road, London N7 8LX, UK. Credit cards accepted. Tel/Fax: +44 (0)20-7607 9433. E-mail: books@fantasycentre.demon.co.uk

House of Monsters (http://www.visionvortex/houseofmonsters) is a small treasure-trove of a store only open at weekends from noon that specializes in horror movie memorabilia, toys, posters, videos, books and magazines. 1579 N. Milwaukee Avenue, Gallery 218, Chicago, IL 60614, USA. Credit cards accepted. Tel: (773) 292-0980. E-mail: Homonsters@aol.com

Mythos Books (http://www.abebooks.com/home/mythos-books/) mail order presents books and curiosities for the Love-craftian scholar and collectors of horror, weird and supernatural fiction with regular catalogues and e-mail updates. Write to 218 Hickory Meadow Lane, Poplar Bluff, MO 63901-2160, USA. Credit cards accepted. Tel: (573) 785–7710. E-mail: dwynn @Idd.net

Porcupine Books offers extensive mail order lists of used fantasy/horror/SF titles via e-mail (brian@porcupine.demon. co.uk) or write to 37 Coventry Road, Ilford, Essex IG1 4QR, UK. Tel: +44 (0)20 8554-3799.

Kirk Ruebotham sells out of print and used horror/SF/fantasy/ crime and related non-fiction, with regular catalogues. Write to 16 Beaconsfield Road, Runcorn, Cheshire WA7 4BX, UK. Tel: +44 (0) 1928 560540. E-mail: kirk@ruebotham.freeserve.co.uk

Zardoz Books (http://www.zardozbooks.co.uk) are mail order dealers in used vintage and collectable paperbacks, especially movie tie-ins, with regular catalogues. Write to 20 Whitecroft, Dilton Marsh, Westbury, Wilts BA13 4DJ, UK. Credit cards accepted. Tel: +44 (0) 1373 865371. E-mail: 100124.262@com-puserve.com

MARKET INFORMATION AND NEWS

DarkEcho is an excellent free service offering news, views and information of the horror field every week through e-mail. To subscribe, e-mail editor Paula Guran at darkecho@aol.com with "Subscribe" as your subject or see http://www.darkecho.com for more information.

The Gila Queen's Guide to Markets (http://www.gilaqueen. com/) is a regular publication detailing markets for SF/fantasy/ horror plus other genres, along with publishing news, contests, dead markets, anthologies, updates, etc. A sample copy is $6.00 and subscriptions are $45.00 (USA), $49.00 (Canada) and $60.00 (overseas). Back issues are also available. Cheques or money orders should be in US dollars and sent to "The Gila Queen's Guide to Markets", PO Box 97, Newton, NJ 07860-0097, USA. E-mail: Kathryn@gilaqueen.com or GilaQueen@worldnet.att.net. In the UK *The Gila Queen* is distributed by: BBB Distribution (http://www.bbr-online.com). Contact Chris Reed, PO Box 625, Sheffield, S1 3GY UK. E-mail: c.s.reed @bbr-online.com

Hellnotes (http://www.hellnotes.com) is described as "Your Insider's Guide to the Horror Field". This weekly Newsletter is available on e-mail for $15.00 per year or hardcopy subscriptions are available for $40 per year. To subscribe by credit card, go to: http://www.hellnotes.com/subscribe.htm To subscribe by mail, send US check or money order (made out to "David B. Silva") to: Hellnotes, 27780 Donkey Mine Road, Oak Run, CA 96069, USA. Tel/Fax: (916) 472-1050. E-mail: dbsilva@hellnotes .com or pfolson@bresnanlink.net The Hellnotes Bookstore can be found at http://www.hellnotes.com/book_store

Horroronline.com (http://www.horroronline.com) describes itself as "the horror fan's number one resource for news and information about dark entertainment" on the Internet. It includes reviews, articles, interviews and features on current film, video, comics, games and literature, including more than 1,200 horror movie reviews.

Scavenger's Newsletter (http://www.cza.com/scav/index.html) is a monthly newsletter for SF/fantasy/horror writers with an interest in the small press. News of markets, along with articles, letters and reviews. A sample copy is $2.50 (USA/Canada) and £2.40/$3.00 (overseas). An annual subscription is $22.00 by first class mail (USA), $21.00 (Canada) and £22.80/$27.00 (overseas). *Scavenger's Scrapbook* is a twice yearly round-up, available for $4.00 (USA/Canada) and $5.00 (overseas). A year's subscription to the *Scrapbook* is $7.00 (USA/Canada) and $8.00 (overseas), payable to "Janet Fox" and send to 833 Main, Osage City, KS 66523-1241, USA. Canadian/foreign orders sent to the US address should be in a bank draft on a US bank in US funds. E-mail: foxscav1@jc.net Website: http://www.jlgiftsshop.com/scav/index .html In the UK contact Chris Reed, BBR Distribution, PO Box 625, Sheffield S1 3GY, UK. (http://www.bbr-online.com). E-mail: c.s.reed@bbr-online.com

Zene (http://www.tta-press.freewire.co.uk) is described as "The

Definitive Guide to the World's Independent Press". Six-issue subscriptions are £12.00 (UK), £15.00 (Europe), $24.00 (USA/Canada) and £18.00 (rest of the world). Payable to "TTA Press", 5 Martins Lane, Witcham, Ely, Cambs CB6 2LB, UK. E-mail: tta-press@aol.com

Other titles available from Robinson Publishing

The Mammoth Book of Haunted House Stories
Ed. Peter Haining   £6.99 [ ]
The first major anthology of the best tales about haunted houses. All are fictional, but many are based on real-life hauntings.

The Mammoth Book of Unsolved Crimes
Ed. Roger Wilkes   £6.99 [ ]
Thirty unsolved criminal cases from around the world, told by leading authors and journalists in the field of crime writing, including Eric Ambler, Brian Masters and Colin Wilson. Nearly all are murder cases, and all end in a mystery who did it?

Sleep of Death   Phillip Gooden   £6.99 [ ]
An Elizabethan murder mystery featuring Shakespearean player Nick Revill.

The Mammoth Book of Murder   Colin Wilson   £7.99 [ ]
A companion volume to the best-selling *The Mammoth Book of True Crime* by the same author.

Robinson books are available from all good bookshops or direct from the publishers. Just tick the titles you want and fill in the form below.

TBS Direct
Colchester Road, Frating Green, Colchester, Essex CO7 7DW
Tel: +44 (0) 1206 255777
Fax: +44 (0) 1206 255914
Email: sales@tbs-ltd.co.uk

UK/BFPO customers please allow £1.00 for p&p for the first book, plus 50p for the second, plus 30p for each additional book up to a maximum charge of £3.00

Overseas customers (inc. Ireland), please allow £2.00 for the first book, plus £1.00 for the second, plus 50p for each additional book.

Please send me the titles ticked.

NAME (Block letters) . . . .

ADDRESS . . . .

. . . .

POSTCODE. . . . .

I enclose a cheque/PO (payable to TBS Direct) for . . . .

I wish to pay by Switch/Credit card

Number . . . .

Card Expiry Date . . . .

Switch Issue Number . . . .